More Praise for John Irving and...

...Setting Free The Bears

"The most nourishing, satisfying comedy I have read in years. I admire the hell out of it."

—Kurt Vonnegut, Jr.

"When the great zoo bust finally comes through and some of the beasts run free, the drama encompasses the longings and agonies of youth.... A complex and moving novel."

—*Time*

...The Water–Method Man

"Three or four times as funny as most novels."

—*The New Yorker*

"The novel flows with an undercurrent of whimsy that keeps a silly grin on the reader's face, and is punctuated by madcap twists that turn the grin into chair–shaking laughter."

—*Newsday*

...The 158–Pound Marriage

"Deft, hard–hitting.... What he demonstrates beautifully is that a one–to–one relationship is more demanding than a free–for–all."

—*The New York Times Book Review*

"Irving looks cunningly beyond the eye–catching gyrations of the mating dance to the morning–after implications."

—*The Washington Post*

JOHN IRVING

THREE COMPLETE NOVELS

JOHN IRVING

THREE COMPLETE NOVELS

SETTING FREE THE BEARS

•

THE WATER–METHOD MAN

•

THE 158–POUND MARRIAGE

WINGS BOOKS
New York

This 1995 edition is published by Wings Books,
distributed by Random House Value Publishing, Inc.,
201 East 50th Street, New York, New York 10022,
http://www.randomhouse.com/
by arrangement with Random House, Inc.

Random House
New York • Toronto • London • Sydney • Auckland

Printed and bound in the United States of America

Library of Congress Cataloging–in–Publication Data

Irving, John, 1942–
[3 by Irving]
John Irving : three complete novels.
p.   cm.
Contents : Setting free the bears — The water–method man
— The 158–pound marriage.
ISBN 0–517–14654–1 (Hardcover)
1. Humorous stories, American.   I. Title.
PS3559.R8A6   1995

813'.54—dc20   95–6300
                                                                CIP

8 7 6 5 4 3 2

CONTENTS

INTRODUCTION
IV

SETTING FREE THE BEARS
1

THE WATER–METHOD MAN
285

THE 158–POUND MARRIAGE
561

Introduction

Superior fiction asks three things of the novelist: Vigorous feeling for life as we live it. Then imaginative force, strong enough to subvert and rebuild unhindered. And then—but this is rare and so essential that we might call it the "reality principle" of fiction—shrewd sense to keep the first two locked in stubborn love with each other.

The three in combination are a priceless gift, and to say that John Irving is vastly gifted is to say precisely that he possesses the proven talents which make for major fiction. He has published four novels in ten years, and with the appearance, in 1978, of *The World According to Garp,* he has taken his place in the front rank of American fiction. Other novelists of his generation (Irving was born in 1942) may be equally prolific; but there is something singular, something uncommonly thorough about Irving's work to this point—as if his books were the working out of a design, a *télos,* a fierce implicit vision now realized and fully set forth. In retrospect this is easily seen. Rising directly out of the three novels in this volume, *Garp* marks a clear culmination, a first phase complete in itself, a proof of promise that becomes, in turn, the signal and certification of a mature, commanding career.

Irving's grasp on fact is firm, yet not so cramped as to dampen his delight in wild fabulation. To manage this balance with compassion and comic liberty is chief among his strengths. Not fact but fact perceived is fiction's rightful domain, and Irving has been quick to take this special license to its limit. Rampant invention is central to his art, and one of the finest pleasures to be got from reading his novels resides in the multiplicity of styles, the range of forms and abrupt imaginative turns to be found in each book. Irving's multiple manner, if I may call it such, his will to come at the world from different directions, is one of the outstanding traits of *Garp*; but this remarkable flair for confluence—stories inside stories, genres circumventing genres—is already handled with mastery in Irving's first novel, *Setting Free the Bears,* published in 1968, and with a freedom almost wanton in *The Water-Method Man,* which appeared in 1972. Only *The 158-Pound Marriage* departs from mixed form; published in 1974, it is as lean and concentrated as a mine shaft. But in every case Irving's habit of originality provokes surprise and enjoyment. And there is, finally, a further pleasure when we read these novels in sequence: each is wholly distinct, in conception and style, from its companions.

The novels in this volume are so unlike that we might almost think of them as books by different authors. But only at first glance. For what informs all three, inspiring each with intense consistency, is John Irving's peculiar vision, his odd way of seeing the world. Friendship, marriage and family are his primary themes, but at that blundering level of life where mishap and folly—something close to joyful malice—perpetually intrude and disrupt, often fatally. Life, in Irving's fiction, is always under siege. Harm and disarray are daily fare, as if the course of love could *not* run true. As if existence were governed by caprice and mockery, by the perverse power of some yet-to-be-charted tenth planet; and if a sign or emblem were wanted for this new ruler of the zodiac, there is no doubt, in Irving's universe, what name and shape it would take.

In *The World According to Garp* there is a summer scene by the ocean, an episode wherein little Walt, so very young and vulnerable, is repeatedly warned by his parents to beware of the undertow along a stretch of dangerous shore. The undertow, they remind him, is very wicked today. Look out for the undertow. One morning they spot their small son alone on the beach, staring intently at the incoming waves. When asked what he's doing, he says, "I'm trying to see the Under Toad." All along he had mistaken the correct word and mythicized the fear it signaled into a creature of invisible but monstrous being. And Walt is right. Arising as if from the sea, the Under Toad squats upon the world's rim, bloated and watchful, the sign of a new star under whose baleful dispensation life must henceforth proceed.

Novel by novel, Irving has moved steadily toward more intimate knowledge of this sinister energy. His relish for German words, together with the way Vienna—a city symbolizing death—haunts everything he has written, gives an almost historical tremor to the pun on *Tod,* while the corresponding pun on *Unter* suggests a depth of being which in theology has been called "the demonic," by which is meant life perversely pitted against itself, a will to mockery and mutilation, eruptions of exuberant spite. These are the forces to which Irving has adjusted his vision; and therefore his insistence on bizarre events and sad outcomes, on stories "rich with lunacy and sorrow," as he says in *Garp*.

Irving's intent as a novelist has been to fix the perception of life's demonic undertow at exactly those points where, any day, any one of us might slip and be sucked down. He aims, that is, to confront the habits of the Under Toad directly. Irving takes for granted that the world is mucked up beyond even provisional redemption; that personal destiny is again and again derailed by impersonal forces; that no leader, faith or ideology will arrive to save us from the mess in which we founder. It is perhaps even the case that some secret region of the soul takes pride in destruction, seeking collusion with that which will bring it to ruin. How, then, do we make a defense? There is no solution, of course, but if Irving has done much to reveal our predicament, his temper as an artist suggests that to which we too may look for support. To a courage which stares the Under Toad straight in the eye. To a compassion which allows respect for suffering without self-pity or loss of detachment. And finally to laughter, to the boisterous, even ruthless thrust of comedy.

This is admittedly hard medicine. But that life is a string of clumsy catastrophes and idiot accidents can hardly be denied. At the same time, the whole business appears so melodramatic and silly as hardly to matter at all. Mastery of this situation comes through a vision which can manage both sides equally: hence Irving's manner of mixing disaster and farce, his blend of gravity and humor, his bent for revealing an element of self-parody in the most pitiful moments. Most extraordinary—this irks some readers, but for most of us has been a source of keen exhilaration—is Irving's capacity for bounce and resilience and something akin to hard-minded glee, his determination to face that which *laughs at* and, mindful of all pain, all pathos, *laugh back.*

A world at war is the worst world possible, and this is where, in *Setting Free the Bears,* Irving starts. There are plenty of horrendous moments in this novel, yet from such unhappy material Irving produces nonstop laughter. The impact of war upon civilians, its chaos and rapidity of event, its deadly whirling force—all this comes across with convincing power. So does the maniacal behavior of ordinary people trapped in a world of seismic upset. How does Irving make this funny? How, without the aid of tragic resolution —for in an age so warped and bedraggled there is no hope of high closure —can crass, undignified suffering be turned to catharsis? The answer is in good part the secret of his art. Sorrow divested of terror and pity becomes lunatic, and lunacy on its own ground is comic. Irving knows that under grotesque pressure and robbed of choice, men and women respond to their fate in ways which are brave but also ridiculous, jerked this way and that by shifting circumstance and an acceleration of coincidence that render attempts at sane action ludicrous. If this is indeed the case, and if no one is exempt, then the determination to laugh *at* becomes likewise the duty to laugh *with,* the sole mode of compassion, of human communion, available in a world whose overseer is the Under Toad.

But if war's concussion is its center, *Setting Free the Bears* is not, properly speaking, a "war novel" at all. The book's main line of action, which culminates in animal apocalypse when the Vienna zoo is "liberated," takes place in the sixties, which is to say in the far-reaching shadow of World War II. And here Irving's love of stories within stories becomes especially effective. *Setting Free the Bears* is composed of three separate layers, each story bearing strongly upon the others, but each distinct in content and stylistic presentation. The "Pre-History" covers wartime Vienna and partisan scrambles in Yugoslavia. The "Zoo Watch" contains some of the most original writing in modern fiction and celebrates Irving's strange fellow-feeling for animals, as if in his view our humanity is not complete without acknowledgment of the animal dimension of being. Finally, there is the picaresque tale of the two young men who ramble about the Austrian countryside, planning their "zoo bust," heading for hilarious ruin.

The picaresque mode is freewheeling, open-ended, unpredictable. In its explosive brutality, so is war. And so too, in its certain uncontrollability, must be the release of a zoo full of animals, the fierce and the timid alike, some to eat, most to be eaten. But to see things this way is also, indeed inevitably, to behold life as foredoomed, in which case the novelist becomes, as T. S. Garp will say of himself, "a doctor who sees only terminal cases." The tendency in Irving's fiction is toward epilogue, and one of the most remarkable things about his first three novels, viewed from the vantage of *Garp,* is that they can be read as one extended fictional enterprise. Together they track our spiritual passage from its origins in reaction to the inhuman revelations of World War II, through the anomie of the fifties, the radical rampage and self-destructive experiments of the sixties, toward the struggle for adulthood and survival which characterized the seventies.

To argue that Irving planned this *Bildungsroman* of our time would be excessive. Nonetheless, his deep sense of demonic turbulence, his comic reception of life as "a ludicrous and doomed effort at reclassification," and his steady sympathy for those who sustain damage and maimed hope and still fight to be normal—to love, raise children, stay sane—combine to make Irving especially suited to record the havoc and madness we everywhere witness during these last-gasp days of our century. Thus while those who screw up in *Setting Free the Bears* pay with their lives, the screwed-up hero of *The Water-Method Man* persists through his folly and earns a second chance. The bitter outcome of *The 158-Pound Marriage,* however, suggests that a second chance is only, after all, a chance, and that the perversity of the human heart is sufficient to ensure that the Under Toad will more than likely have its way, leaving its victims to laugh or curse as they can.

The Water-Method Man takes its young protagonist through two wives and a side trip to Vienna on his precarious approach to adulthood. The zany freedom of male companionship ends in a ghost tank at the bottom of the Danube, making way for the beginning of serious male-female relations as the hero, nicknamed Bogus, gets his penis back to normal working order. Children and the responsibilities of parenthood begin to figure importantly, and perhaps because these are fundamentally hopeful themes, Irving's second novel is also his most relaxed piece of writing. It is likewise—apart from *Garp*—his most intricate, a virtuoso performance in juxtapositions. Script and scenes from a *cinéma vérité* film replay the story in parody; and against these, like the backdrop of night, Irving unwinds the blood-and-guts saga of *Akthelt and Gunnel,* an epic poem in "Old Low Norse," in which, as in cartoonlike dream, the Under Toad rules.

For its dextrous comedy, for its energetic play with form, *The Water-Method Man* provides happy relief. It also serves as a bridge from the kind of world determined by impersonal forces to the closer, more self-inflicted world of private relationships. But if history is a field of ruin, so too is the shut sphere of marriage—marriage, that is, as an experiment and a test which some survive and others do not. In this latter sense, *The 158-Pound Marriage* is surely a black and ruthless book. The title refers to a middleweight wrestling match, where falls are fast and expected, where expertise in tactics counts more than brute force, where consequences may be dire but scarcely the substance of champions. Starting with the commonplace of adultery, Irving traces the soul's unrest, its stupid preference for pain and complication, through two couples who switch partners and pursue their odd indulgences to the point of no return. There is no overt violence, but the outcome can only be buffoonery and hate, with the hint that this particular "match" was fixed from the onset—that one of the couples may have played this game before.

Roped off from connection with the larger world, Irving's *ménage à quatre* is strictly a collision of personalities. And whereas sex in the earlier novels was an easy-going gift, in *The 158-Pound Marriage* sex becomes the source of subtle disruptive powers, the occasion for setting free something a good deal more brutal than bears. Which is to say that Irving's humor, as strong as ever, has moved closer to the tears which such sad and twisted goings-on must, if released from comic check, draw forth from the unhappy heart.

That a serious novel like *The World According to Garp* should become genuinely popular confirms the good sense of common readers generally.

It is evident, however, that Irving's celebrated fourth novel owes much to the three earlier novels, and I do not think the popularity of *Garp* rests entirely with the obvious benefits of a good story and the accessibility of wonderfully straightforward prose. John Irving belongs to a small group of contemporary writers, chief among whom must be included Kurt Vonnegut, Joseph Heller and Thomas Pynchon, novelists whose work has inspired respect for the plainest of reasons—these people write a kind of fiction useful, as genuine art must always be useful, to spiritual need. Fiction speaks to us, touches our deepest fears and wishes, insofar as it articulates our embattled sense of being *in* the world, thereby confirming the self in its struggle to face and endure (and perhaps pull free from) the besetting difficulties of a time and condition. One prominent critic has suggested that the key to Irving's kind of novelist is the mobilization of paranoia as a mode of universal insight. Given the threat of terminal wreckage—the proliferation of war, famine and genocide, helpless governments and collapsing economies, nuclear befoulment and the possibility of a Final Solution that would be truly final—little wonder that those who take their stand vis-à-vis the Under Toad have gained our special regard.

Facing prospects so oppressive, Irving's kind of novelist has worked out a number of strategies. Vonnegut combines a so-it-goes stoicism with the cosmic perspective of science fiction. Heller penetrates infernal darkness through the hysterical drain-off of a central insidious event. Pynchon seems openly to side with destructive energy, celebrating its negative splendor, reveling in its promise of doom. But whereas Vonnegut and Heller accept our condition of victimhood as final, and Pynchon identifies with existence-as-aggressor, Irving has stubbornly refused to capitulate. Rebellion, defiance, even derision, inform his art. He confronts threat with jeers, perceives pain in terms of farce, stays afloat in a sea of destruction by direct immersion (the equivalent of compassion), and rebukes fate by playing with the ways the Under Toad plays with us.

Reading Irving's novels, we are so engaged by their exuberance, their humor and what appears to be sheer delight in mischief that the world seems almost jolly, a slaughterhouse fitted up with fun-house mirrors, a hell of an entertaining place. And this, it seems to me, is Irving's victory: the whole damned human lot is funny, our "ludicrous and doomed effort at reclassification" is a stale bleak joke, but a joke all the same, our general plight an occasion for having the next-to-last laugh, no matter if it dies in mid-burst. As an artist of utmost earnestness, Irving tells the hardest kind of truth, but in the telling insists upon the freedom to have fun. Critics have sometimes missed the horror at the heart of Irving's vision. They have observed his high-spirited frolic and presumed, mistakenly, that Irving's whole point as a writer is play. Maybe, but with one decisive difference: this kind of play, defiant, boisterous, recklessly brave, is Irving's hard-minded prescription for survival.

John Irving's fiction comes down to this: it serves our need for spiritual defense. Is this no more than a bag of brilliant tricks? Possibly, but against an adversary like the Under Toad the tactics of the trickster—prominent in myths of every culture—are indispensable. Without them the enormous pressures of dread and savagery would surely grind us down to nothingness. All comic artists are tricksters. They skate on thin ice, they make us laugh, they help us to hang on. And the survival value of laughter, in times like ours, cannot be too highly prized. For sanity, for endurance, for necessary pleasure, no other stance works half so well.

Terrence Des Pres

Setting Free
The Bears

This book is for
VIOLETTE and CO
in memory of
GEORGE

Siggy

A Steady Diet in Vienna

I could find him every noon, sitting on a bench in the Rathaus Park with a small, fat bag of hothouse radishes in his lap and a bottle of beer in one hand. He always brought his own saltshaker; he must have had a great number of them, because I can't recall a particular one from the lot. They were never very fancy saltshakers, though, and once he even threw one away; he just wrapped it up in the empty radishbag and tossed it in one of the park's trashcans.

Every noon, and always the same bench—the least splintery one, on the edge of the park nearest the university. Occasionally he had a notebook with him, but always the corduroy duckhunter's jacket with its side slash-pockets, and the great vent-pocket at the back. The radishes, the bottle of beer, a saltshaker, and sometimes the notebook—all of them from the long, bulging vent-pocket. He carried nothing in his hands when he walked. His tobacco and pipes went in the side slash-pockets of the jacket; he had at least three different pipes.

Although I assumed he was a student like myself, I hadn't seen him in any of the university buildings. Only in the Rathaus Park, every noon of the new spring days. Often I sat on the bench opposite him while he ate. I'd have my newspaper, and it was a fine spot to watch the girls come along the walk; you could peek at their pale, winter knees—the hardboned, blousy girls in their diaphanous silks. But he didn't watch them; he just perched as alertly as a squirrel over the bag of radishes. Through the bench slats, the sun zebra-striped his lap.

I'd had more than a week of such contact with him before I noticed another of his habits. He scribbled things on the radishbag, and he was always stashing little pieces of bag in his pockets, but more often he wrote in the notebook.

One day he did this: I saw him pocket a little note on a bag piece, walk away from the bench, and a bit down the path decide to have another look. He pulled out the bag piece and read it. Then he threw it away, and this is what I read:

The fanatical maintenance of good habits is necessary.

It was later, when I read his famous notebook—his Poetry, as he spoke of it—that I realized this note hadn't been entirely thrown away. He'd simply cleaned it a little.

Good habits are worth being fanatical about.

But back in the Rathaus Park, with the little scrap from the radishbag, I couldn't tell he was a poet and a maxim-maker; I only thought he'd be an interesting fellow to know.

Hard Times

There's a place on Josefsgasse, behind the Parliament Building, known for its fast, suspicious turnover of secondhand motorcycles. I've Doktor Ficht to thank for my discovery of the place. It was Doktor Ficht's exam I'd just flunked, which put me in a mood to vary my usual noon habit in the Rathaus Park.

I went off through a number of little arches with boggy smells, past cellar stores with mildewy clothes and into a section of garages—tire shops and auto-parts places, where smudged men in overalls were clanking and rolling things out on the sidewalk. I came on it suddenly, a dirty showcase window with the cardboard sign FABER'S in a corner of glass; nothing more in the way of advertising, except the noise spuming from an open doorway. Fumes dark as thunderclouds, an upstarting series of blatting echo-shots, and through the showcase window I could make out the two mechanics racing the throttles of two motorcycles; there were more motorcycles on the platform nearest the window, but these were shiny and still. Scattered about on the cement floor by the doorway, and blurred in exhaust, were various tools and gas-tank caps—pieces of spoke and wheel rim, fender and cable—and these two intent mechanics bent over their cycles; playing the throttles up and down, they looked as serious and ear-ready as any musicians tuning up for a show. I inhaled from the doorway.

Watching me, just inside, was a gray man with wide, oily lapels; the buttons were the dullest part of his suit. A great sprocket leaned against the doorway beside him—a fallen, sawtoothed moon, so heavy with grease it absorbed light and glowed at me.

"Herr Faber himself," the man said, prodding his chest with his thumb. And he ushered me out the doorway and back down the street. When we were away from the din, he studied me with a tiny, gold-capped smile.

"Ah!" he said. "The university?"

"God willing," I said, "but it's unlikely."

"Fallen in hard times?" said Herr Faber. "What sort of a motorcycle did you have in mind?"

"I don't have anything in mind," I told him.

"Oh," said Faber, "it's never easy to decide."

"It's staggering," I said.

"Oh, don't I know?" he said. "Some bikes are such animals beneath you, *really*—veritable beasts! And that's exactly what some have in mind. Just what they're looking for!"

"It's makes you giddy to think of it," I said.

"I agree, I agree," said Herr Faber. "I know just what you mean. You should talk with Herr Javotnik. He's a student—like yourself! And he'll be back from lunch presently. Herr Javotnik is a wonder at helping people make up their minds. A *virtuoso* with decisions!"

"Amazing," I said.

"And a joy and a comfort to me," he said. "You'll see." Herr Faber cocked his slippery head to one side and listened lovingly to the *burt, burt, burt* of the motorcycles within.

The Beast Beneath Me

I recognized Herr Javotnik by his corduroy duckhunter's jacket with the pipes protruding from the side slash-pockets. He looked like a young man coming from a lunch that had left his mouth salty and stinging.

"Ah!" said Herr Faber, and he took two little side steps as if he would do a dance for us. "Herr Javotnik," he said, "this young man has a decision to make."

"So that's it," said Javotnik, "—why you weren't in the park?"

"Ah! Ah?" Herr Faber squealed. "You know each other?"

"Very well," Javotnik said. "I should say, very well. This will be a most personal decision, I'm sure, Herr Faber. If you'd leave us."

"Well, yes," said Faber. "Very well, very well"—and he sidled away from us, returning to the exhaust in his doorway.

"A lout, of course," said Javotnik. "You've no mind to buy a thing, have you?"

"No," I said. "I just happened along."

"Strange not to see you in the park."

"I've fallen in hard times," I told him.

"Whose exam?" he asked.

"Ficht's."

"Well, Ficht. I can tell you a bit about him. He's got rotten gums, uses a little brush between his classes—swabs his gums with some gunk from a brown jar. His breath could wilt a weed. He's fallen in hard times himself."

"It's good to know," I said.

"But you've no interest in motorcycles?" he asked. "I've an interest myself, just to hop on one and leave this city. Vienna's no spot for the spring, really. But of course, I couldn't go more than half toward any bike in there."

"I couldn't either," I said.

"That so?" he said. "What's your name?"

"Graff," I told him. "Hannes Graff."

"Well, Graff, there's one especially nice motorcycle in there, if you've any thoughts toward a trip."

"Well," I said, "I couldn't go more than half, you know, and it seems you're tied up with a job."

"I'm never tied up," said Javotnik.

"But perhaps you've gotten in the habit," I told him. "Habits aren't to be scoffed at, you know." And he braced back on his heels a moment, brought up a pipe from his jacket and clacked it against his teeth.

"I'm all for a good whim too," he said. "My name's Siggy. Siegfried Javotnik."

And although he made no note of it at the time, he would later add this idea to his notebook, under the revised line concerning habit and fanaticism —this new maxim also rephrased.

Be blissfully guided by the veritable urge!

But that afternoon on the sidewalk he was perhaps without his notebook or a scrap of radishbag, and he must have felt the prompting of Herr Faber, who peered so anxiously at us, his head darting like a snake's tongue out of the smoggy garage.

"Come with me, Graff," said Siggy. "I'm going to sit you on a beast."

So we crossed the slick floor of the garage to a door against the back wall, a door with a dartboard on it; both the door and the dartboard hung askew. The dartboard was all chewed up, the bull's-eye indistinguishable from the matted clots of cork all over—as if it had been attacked with wrenches instead of darts, or by mad mechanics with tearing mouths.

We went out into an alley behind the garage.

"Oh now, Herr Javotnik," said Faber. "Do you really think so?"

"Absolutely," said Siegfried Javotnik.

It was covered with a glossy black tarp and leaned against the wall of the garage. The rear fender was as thick as my finger, a heavy chunk of chrome, gray on the rim where it took some of the color from the mudcleats, deep-grooved on the rear tire—tire and fender and the perfect gap between. Siggy pulled the tarp off.

It was an old, cruel-looking motorcycle, missing the gentle lines and the filled-in places; it had spaces in between its parts, a gap where some clutterer might have tried to put a toolbox, a little open triangle between the engine and the gas tank too—the tank, a sleek teardrop of black, sat like a too small head on a bulky body; it was lovely like a gun is sometimes lovely—for the obvious, ugly function showing in its most prominent parts. It weighed, all right, and seemed to suck its belly in, like a lean, hunched dog in the tall grass.

"A virtuoso, this boy!" Herr Faber said. "A joy and a comfort."

"It's British," said Siggy. "Royal Enfield, some years ago when they made the pieces look like the way they worked. Seven hundred cubic centimeters. New tires and chains, and the clutch has been rebuilt. Like new."

"This boy, he loves this old one!" said Faber. "He worked on it all on his own time. It's like *new!*"

"It's new, all right," Siggy whispered. "I ordered from London—new clutch and sprocket, new pistons and rings—and he thought it was for his other bikes. The old thief doesn't know what it's worth."

"Sit on it!" Herr Faber said. "Oh, just sit, and feel the beast beneath you!"

"Half and half," whispered Siggy. "You pay it all now, and I'll pay you back with my wages."

"Start it up for me," I said.

"Ah well," said Faber. "Herr Javotnik, it's not quite ready to start up now, is it? Maybe it needs gas."

"Oh no," said Siggy. "It should start right up." And he came alongside me and pumped on the kick starter; there was very little fiddling—a tickle to the carburetor, the spark retard out and back. Then he rose up beside me and dropped his weight on the kicker. The engine sucked and gasped, and the stick flew back against him; but he tromped it again, and quickly again, and this time it caught—not with the *burt*ing of the motorcycles inside: with a lower, steadier *borp, borp, borp,* as rich as a tractor.

"Hear that?" cried Herr Faber, who suddenly listened himself—his head tilting a bit, and his hand slicking over his mouth—as if he'd expected to hear a valve tapping, but didn't; expected to hear a certain roughness in the idle, but couldn't—at least, not quite. And his head tilted more.

"A virtuoso," said Faber, who was beginning to sound as if he believed it.

Herr Faber's Beast

Herr Faber's office was on the second floor of the garage, which looked as if it couldn't have a second floor.

"A grim urinal of a place," said Siggy, whose manners were making Herr Faber nervous.

"Have we set a price on that one?" Faber asked.

"Oh yes, we have," said Siggy. "Twenty-one hundred schillings, it was, Herr Faber."

"Oh, a very good price," said Faber in an unwell voice.

I paid.

"And might I trouble you further, Herr Faber?" said Siggy.

"Oh?" Faber moaned.

"Might you give me my wages up to today?" said Siggy.

"Oh, Herr Javotnik!" Faber said.

"Oh, Herr Faber," said Siggy. "Could you manage it?"

"You're a cruel schemer after an old man's money," Faber said.

"Now, I've made some rare deals for you," said Siggy.

"You're a dirty young cheating scheming bastard," Herr Faber said.

"Do you see, Graff?" said Siggy. "Oh, Herr Faber," he said, "I believe there's a veritable beast at home in your gentle heart."

"Frotters!" Herr Faber shouted. "Thieving frotters everywhere I turn!"

"If you could manage my wages," said Siggy. "If you could just do that, I'd be off with Graff here. We've got some fine tuning to do."

"Ah!" Faber cried. "That motorcycle doesn't need a bath!"

Fine Tuning

So we sat in the evening at the Volksgarten Café and looked over the rock garden to the trees, and looked down in the pools of red and green water, reflecting the green and red lights strung over the terrace. The girls were all out; through the trees their voices came suddenly and thrillingly to us; like birds, girls in the city are always preceded by the noises they make— their heels on the walk, and their cock-sure voices confiding to each other.

"Well, Graff," said Siggy, "it's a blossom of a night."

"It is," I agreed—the first heavy night of the spring, with a damp, hard-to-remember heat in the air, and the girls with their arms bare again.

"We'll make it a *zounds!* of a trip," said Siggy. "I've thought about this for a long time, Graff, and I've got the way not to spoil it. No planning, Graff—that's the first thing. No mapping it out, no dates to get anywhere, no dates to get back. Just think of things! Think of mountains, say, or think of beaches. Think of rich widows and farm girls! Then just point to where you feel they'll be, and pick the roads the same way too—pick them for the curves and hills. That's the second thing—to pick roads that the beast will love.

"How do you like the motorcycle, Graff?" he asked.

"I love it," I said, although he'd driven me on it no more than a few blocks, from Faber's round the Schmerlingplatz and over to the Volksgarten. It was a fine, loud, throbbing thing under you—sprang off from the stops like a great wary cat; even when it idled, the loathsome pedestrians never took their eyes off it.

"You'll love it more," said Siggy. "Up in mountains. We'll go to Italy! We'll travel light—that's third, traveling light. I'll take my big rucksack, all our stuff in one pack and sleeping bags rolled on top. Nothing else. Just some fishing rods. We'll fish through the mountains to Italy!

"Frot Doktor Ficht!" he cried.

"Frot him," I said.

"May his teeth all fall out!"

"In the opera."

"Frot him good!" said Siggy. And then he said, "Graff? You're not sorry you flunked, are you? I mean, it doesn't matter so much."

"It couldn't matter," I said, and it really didn't—with the night air smelling like a young girl's hair. The tendrils of the heavy trees stooped and swooshed over the rock garden, and hushed the sounds of waterlap in the pools.

"Early in the morning," said Siggy, "we'll load up and slip away. You can just hear us! We'll be rumbling past the university before old Ficht has swabbed his gums! We'll be out of Vienna before he's uncorked his gunky jar.

"We'll go by the palace. We'll wake up everyone! They'll think it's a runaway *Strassenbahn*—or a hippopotamus!"

"A farting hippopotamus," I said.

"A whole army of them farting!" said Siggy. "And then we'll be out on the curvy roads. We'll have trees overhead and crickets smacking off our helmets."

"I don't have a helmet," I said.

"I've got one for you," said Siggy, who'd been getting ready for this trip.

"What else do I need?" I asked.

"Goggles," he said. "I've got them too. A World War One pilot's goggles —frog eyes, with yellow lenses. They're terrifying! And boots," said Siggy. "I've got real trompers for you."

"We should go pack," I said.

"Well, we should finish our beers."

"And then go."

"Go off in a roar!" said Siggy. "And tomorrow night we'll have a sip from a river in the mountains, or a drink of a lake. Sleep in the grass, let the sun wake us."

"With dew on our lips."

"With country girls beside us!" said Siggy. "Barring acts of God."

So we drank up. There was a murmur of voices on the terrace, faces from the tables round us swam and bobbed in our beers.

Then the pumping of the kick starter, and the faraway sucking sound of the pistons that seemed to be rising from miles beneath the engine. The grunt of it catching, and the slow, untroubled drumming of its even idle. Siggy let it warm, and I looked over the hedgerows to the tables on the terrace. The onlookers weren't irritated, but they stopped their murmuring and cocked their heads to us; the slow beat of our engine was in rhythm with the first buffs of the spring-heavy air.

And there was a new lump in the back vent-pocket of Siggy's duck-hunter's jacket; when I looked again at our table, I saw that the saltshaker was gone.

The First Act of God

Siggy drove. We came through an arch into the Plaza of Heroes; I tipped back my head and watched the pigeons cross the tops of the buildings; the pudgy Baroque cupids peered at me from the government houses. The morning seemed more golden than it was, through the famous yellow tint of my World War One pilot's goggles.

A cheek-chewing old woman wheeled a pushcart full of flowers along the Mariahilferstrasse, and we pulled to the curb beside her to buy some saffron crocuses; we stuck them in the air holes of our crash helmets. "Boys up to no good," said the floppy-gummed hag.

We drove on, tossing our flowers to the girls who waited for buses. The girls had their scarves off their heads; the scarves flapped about their throats, and most of the girls had flowers already.

We were early; we met the horsecarts coming to the Naschmarkt with their vegetables and fruits, and more flowers. Once we passed a horse who'd been shell-shocked by the traffic, and who pranced at our motorcycle. The drivers were cheerful and shouting from their squealing wagonseats; some of the drivers had their wives and children with them, it was such a glorious day.

Schönbrunn Palace looked lonely; no tourist buses, no crowds with cameras. A cool mist hung over the palace grounds; a thin haze crept close to the trimmed hedgerows, stole turtlelike across the green, green lawns. We watched the country roll in and be pushed back.

In the suburb of Hietzing, on the country edge of the palace grounds, we smelled the first zoo whiffs from the Hietzinger Zoo.

We stopped for a traffic light, and an elephant trumpeted over our idle.

"We've time enough, haven't we?" said Siggy. "I mean, we've all the time in the world, as I see it."

"We shouldn't leave Vienna," I said, "without seeing how spring has struck the zoo."

Well, yes—the Hietzinger Zoo, gated by stone, admission granted by a jowled toad of a man with a gambler's green eyeshade. Siggy parked the motorcycle out of the sap drip, out from under the trees and flush to the gambler's booth—the ticket taker's domish stall—over which we saw the giraffe's head tottering on its neckpole. The shambly heap of the giraffe followed its neck; bucket-hooved, its legs tried to keep up. There was a raw, hairless spot on its thin chin where it had scraped the high storm fence.

The giraffe looked down the fence line to the greenhouses of the botanical gardens; the plates of glass were still frosty with dew. It was too early for much sun, and there was no one else to watch the giraffe. Down the long cobbly alley, between the buildings and cages, there was no one but a cage-cleaner, who sagged with his mop.

Heitzinger Zoo hadn't been there long, but the buildings were as old as Schönbrunn; a part of the palace grounds, the buildings were all rubbled now—unroofed, three-walled, with the open spaces filled in by bars or screens. The animals had inherited the ruins.

The zoo was waking up and making public sounds. The walrus belched in his murky pool; we saw his old fish stiff on the pool curb, where he'd nudged them out of his water and left their scales on his mustache. The duck pond was talking breakfast, and down the alley some animal hammered in its cage.

The Rare Birds Building made a din for us—little and large ladies in costume hats with broken, choir voices; and overlording the dull-clothed condors sat hugely on the toppled columns, perched on the fallen bust of some Habsburg great. They took the statues' pedestals for their own, and glared at the meshing pulled over the ruin above them. A split carcass of sheep lay in the weeds of the building's floor, and some South American with a terrifying wing-span had old meat in his breast feathers; the flies zipped from sheep side to bird, and the condor snapped his nicked, bone-colored beak at them.

"Our feathered friends," said Siggy, and we went on to see what was thumping in its cage.

It was the Famous Asiatic Black Bear, crouched in a back corner of his cage and rocking himself sideways to slam his buttocks into the bars. There was a little printed history of the bear, fixed to a map of the world, with the species' roaming area shaded black and a red star to mark the spot where he was taken—in the Himalayas—by a man named Hinley Gouch. The Asiatic Black Bear, the history explained, had his cage facing away from the other bears because he was "enraged" when he saw them; he was a particularly ferocious bear, the history said, and iron bars enclosed him in his own three-sided ruin because he was capable of digging through concrete.

"I wonder how old Gouch got him?" said Siggy.

"Nets, perhaps," I said.

"Or maybe he just talked him into coming to Vienna," said Siggy. But we didn't think Hinley Gouch was a Viennese. More likely he'd been one of those misplaced Britishers, in league with a hundred brawny Sherpas who'd routed the bear into a ready-dug pit.

"It would be fun getting him and Gouch together again," said Siggy, and we didn't look at the other bears.

There were people coming down the alley behind us now, and a group watched the giraffe scrape its chin. The building in front of us was for small mammals; it was a restored ruin, with four more or less original walls, a roof and boarded windows. Inside, a sign told us, were the nocturnal beasts —"who are always asleep and anonymous in other zoos." But here they had infrared light in the thick-glassed cages, and the animals behaved as if it were night. We could see them in a purplish glow, but the world outside their glass was black for them; they went unsuspiciously about their nocturnal habits, never knowing they were watched.

There was an aardvark, or earth pig, sluffing off old bristles on a rough board hung over him for that purpose. There were giant anteaters licking bugs off the glass, and the arboreal rat of Mexico. There was a bat-eared fox and a ring-tailed lemur; and a two-toed sloth who seemed, upsidedown, to catch our movements on the other side of the glass—whose dark little eyes, not so big as his nostrils, seemed to follow us dimly in the outside world, which wasn't quite dark for him. But for the others there was nothing; not for the flying phalanger, and not for the slow loris, was there anything beyond the infrared under glass. And maybe not for the sloth, either; maybe it was only dizziness from hanging upsidedown that made his eyes roam after us.

In the aisles between the cages it was dark, but our hands were tinted purple and our lips were green. There was a special sign on the giant anteaters' glasshouse; an arrow indicated a little trough on the bottom corner of the glass, leading into the anteaters' lair. When you put your fingers there, an anteater came to lick. The long tongue came through the maze that kept the world from getting in; there was a new look in the anteater's eye, upon finding a finger in the dark. But it licked like any tongue does, and made us feel a little closer to the nocturnal habits of the beasts.

"Oh, God!" said Siggy.

And people had found the Small Mammal House now. Children squealed through the infrared aisles; their mauve hair and bright pink eyes—their green tongues waggling.

So we took a dirt path off the alley; we'd had quite enough of ruins. And we came to an open area where the Miscellaneous Range Animals were— including the Assorted Antelopes. Now this was better. There were zebras nuzzling along the fence line, hipping up to each other and blowing in each other's ears; their stripes ran cross-pattern to the hexagons of the fence, and it made us giddy to see them move.

Outside the fence and coming toward us was a wild-haired little boy who wheezed and held his crotch as he ran. The boy ran past us and stopped, bent over as if he'd been kicked. He dropped his cupped palm down between his knees. "Lord! Balls!" he hooted. Then he grabbed himself up again, and rabbited down the dirt path away from us.

There was no question that he'd seen the oryx with the rapierlike horns, very long and nearly straight, spiraled on the basal half and sloped backward on the same plane with the wrinkly forehead and the sleek black nose;

no question he'd seen the old oryx under his thin shade tree, brindled by the sun- and shade-spots dappling his back—a soft, lowing look in his large black eyes. A bull oryx too, by his low, heavy chest and his thick-wrinkled neck. The slope of his back ran downhill off the hump of his neck to the base of his tail. And a bull from just under his buttocks, he was, all the way to the knots on his lean knees.

"God, Siggy," I said. "How big, do you think?"

"The biggest ever, Graff," said Siggy. They had to dangle cock-eyed, just to fit in the oryx's narrow hind stance.

So we read the history of the oryx from East Africa, "best-armed of all antelopes."

"Hinley Gouch," said Siggy, "never had the balls to be responsible for this."

And quite true, so we read—this oryx had been born in the Hietzinger Zoo, and that certainly made us glum.

So down the dirt path, back to the gate; we passed all the signs for the pachyderms, and only gave a glance to the little wallaroo—"the famous hill-living and very agile kangaroo." It lolled on its side, propped on an elbow and scratching its hip with a curled fist. It gave us a short look with its long, bored face.

Then we were passing the sign for the Big Cats, and passing the glint off the gambler's green eyeshade—his ticket booth surrounded by an eager human covey—passing heads turned toward the groggy, waking caterwaul of a lion; heads were turned upward to greet the giraffe.

Outside the zoo, there were two girls admiring our motorcycle. One of them admired it so much that she sat on it, hugging the gas tank between her knees; she was a thick, busty girl whose black sweater had ridden up over her paunch. And her hips jiggled taut each time she clamped that lovely teardrop of a tank.

The other girl stood in front of the bike, fingering the cables for the clutch and front brake; she was a very thin girl, with more ribs to show than breast. With a yellow hue to her face, she had a sad, wide mouth. Her eyes were as gentle as the oryx's.

"Well, Siggy," I said, "it's surely an act of God."

And it wasn't even ten in the morning.

God Works in Strange Ways

"Graff," said Siggy, "that fat one's surely not for me."

But when we came closer, we saw how the thin girl's lips had a bluish tint, as if she'd been long immersed in water and had taken some chill.

And Siggy said, "That thin one's not too healthy-looking. Perhaps, Graff, you can set her straight."

When we were up to them, the fat girl said to her companion, "See now? I told you it was two boys taking a trip." She jounced on the seat of the motorcycle, flapping the gas tank between her thighs.

"Well," said Siggy. "Thinking of driving off with it, were you?"

"Was not," the fat girl said. "But I could drive this thing if I wanted to."

"Bet you could," said Siggy. He patted the gas tank and drummed his fingers over her knee.

"Watch out for him," the thin girl said. She had a strange spasm in her chin, and she wouldn't stop playing with the cables; looped under the handlebars, the cables were all atangle from her twisting them.

"Say, Graff," Siggy whispered. "Do you think that thin one's contagious? I don't mind if you want her. I'll just make do with the old fatty here."

And the fat one said, "Say, you boys. Would you buy us a beer?"

"There's a place for beer in the zoo," said the thin one.

"We've just been in the zoo," I said.

And Siggy whispered, "It's rabies, Graff. She's got rabies."

"You've not been in the zoo with a girl on your arm!" the fat one said. "And you've not gone through the Tiroler Garten, I'll bet. There's a mile of moss and ferns, and you can take off your shoes."

"Well, Graff," said Siggy. "What do you say?"

"He's wild for it!" the fat girl shouted.

"Graff?" said Siggy.

"Well, sure," I said. "We're in no hurry."

"Fate shapes our course," said Siggy.

So we went to the *Biergarten,* surrounded by bears—and all of them watched us, except the Famous Asiatic Black Bear, whose cage didn't allow him to face the *Biergarten,* or other bears.

The polar bears sat and panted in their swimming pool; now and then they took a slow, loud lap. The brown bears paced, brushing their thick coats against the bars; their heads swayed low to the ground, in rhythm with some ritual of stealth they were born knowing and pointlessly never forgot —no matter how out of place wariness was to them here.

Downwind from our table and Cinzano umbrella, squat and hot in their shared cage, was a reeking pair of Rare Spectacled Bears from the Andes —"the bears with the cartoon countenance." They looked like they'd been laughed right out of Ecuador.

And Siggy was unnerved to find no radishes in the *Biergarten*. The dark, fat girl was named Karlotta, and she had a pastry with her beer; but the thin one was Wanga, and she would have nothing but syrupy bock. Siggy touched his fat Karlotta under the table; my Wanga's hand was dry and cool.

"Oh, they should have more ice for the polar bears," said Wanga. And no more for you, I thought.

"Siggy," said Karlotta, "could use a little ice himself." And her arms went under the table, groping for him. She had dark little ringlets for bangs, glossy and damp on her forehead.

The Spectacled Bears had a blotch of white running forehead-to-nose and over their throats. Their squint-eyes were bandit-masked in shaggy black mats like the rest of their fur; their coats looked oddly slept on, like a series of cowlicks. They rapped their long claws on the cement.

Poor Wanga ran her tongue lightly over her lips, as if she were feeling out where she was chapped and hurt.

"Is this your first trip?" she asked.

"Oh, I've been all over," I said.

"To the Orient?" she asked.

"All over the Orient."

"In Japan?"

"Bangkok," I said.

"Where's Bangkok?" said Wanga, so softly I leaned near to her.

"India," I said. "Bangkok, India."

"Oh, India," she said. "The people are very poor there."

"Yes, very," I agreed, and watched her touch gently her broad mouth— hide her thin lips with her pale hand.

"You there!" said Karlotta to me. "Don't you hurt her. Wanga, tell me if he hurts you."

"We're talking," Wanga said.

"Oh, he's a nice boy," said Karlotta, and from under the table she gave me a slight goose with her wedging toe.

The Spectacled Bears slumped against each other, shoulder to shoulder; one dropped its head on the other's chest.

"Graff," said Siggy, "don't you think Karlotta would enjoy the oryx?"

"I want to see the hippo," Karlotta said. "The hippo and the rhino."

"Karlotta wants everything big," said Siggy. "Well, Karlotta, it's the oryx for you."

"We'll meet you behind the hippohouse," I said. Because I didn't want frail Wanga to see the oryx. Thus Siggy has it in his notebook:

You have to draw the line somewhere.

"Karlotta," said Siggy, "this oryx will give you some jolt." And Karlotta rubbed her paunch with the palm of her hand.

"Ha!" she said.

The Rare Spectacled Bears sat upright and stared.

The Hippohouse

There was a moat around the rhino's field, and a fence on the outside of the moat. If the rhino tried to ram the fence, he'd break his legs falling into the moat; the kneepieces of the rhino's armor were cracked and open, like sun-splits in baked clay.

The field he jogged in was flat, and the grass was beaten to scruff. The field was somewhat elevated too—a hard, dry plateau surrounded by the hippohouse and the high, iron gates to the Tiroler Garten. If you lay flat on the ground just inside the Tiroler Garten, you could see under the boughs of the trees, through the gardens all the way to Maxing Park. If you sat up out of the ferns, you could see the rhino's back—the top of his driftwood head and the tip of his horn. The ground shook when the rhino ran.

Wanga and I lay in the ferns, peeking for Siggy and fat Karlotta.

"Where are you traveling now?" she asked.

"To the Arctic Circle," I said.

"Oh!" she said. "I'd love to come. I mean, if you were traveling alone, I'd ask to come with you."

"And I'd let you," I said. But when I nuzzled the down on her arm, she sat up and looked again for Siggy and Karlotta.

We heard Siggy trumpeting at the rhino; for a while I couldn't see him, but I knew Siggy's poetry voice. He bellowed somewhere along the rhino's field, and we could hear Karlotta tittering. When we saw them, they were arm in arm behind the hippohouse and coming for the gate of the Tiroler Garten.

From the wild eyes of Karlotta, it was easy to see that she would be one of us—marked for life; to remember always having seen the oryx.

"Let's hide from them," I said, and I tugged Wanga down in the ferns.

But her eyes were startled and she lay on her back, hugging herself. "Karlotta!" she called.

"You! Boy!" Karlotta shouted. "Are you hurting her?"

"We're talking," said Wanga, "but we're over here."

And they came along the fence line to us; Siggy slapped through the deep ferns, one hand up under Karlotta's sweater and cupped round her lumpy side.

"Well, Graff," said Siggy, "my Karlotta was properly impressed with the oryx."

"Who could fail to be?" I said.

"What?" asked Wanga. "With what?"

"Not for you, dear," Karlotta said. "You're a dear boy, you," she told me. "That was nothing for Wanga to see."

"It's for the world to see!" said Siggy.

"Stuff you," Karlotta said, and she went tugging him off to another fern patch.

When we were all lying down, we couldn't see each other. Close to the ground was an air trap, and the rich scent of some animal's dung settled over us.

"I believe that's rhino stuff!" Siggy called.

"Or hippo," I said.

"Something large and prolific," said Siggy.

"Hippos never leave the water," Karlotta said.

"Oh, they must!" said Siggy. "It's hard to imagine . . ."

And Wanga curled in the crook of my arm, knees up tight and a cool hand on my chest. We could hear the stirrings of Siggy and Karlotta; twice Siggy hooted like a wild bird.

Well, as the notebook wisely imparts:

Time passes, praise God.

And then we were hearing Karlotta. "You're not so funny *all* the time," she was saying. And when I looked, I saw Siggy's upstretched arm—waving above the ferns a mighty pair of black lace bloomers.

"You're just too much of a stuffing clown," said Karlotta, and I saw her bare, thick foot thrash upward through the ferns. "You can't ever be serious, you frotter!" she said. "Oh, there's something definitely wrong with you."

Then Siggy sat up and grinned toward our fern patch; he wore the thigh-wide bloomers for a hat. Karlotta swatted him with a clod of weeds, and Siggy danced over to us.

When Karlotta stalked after him, she swung at her side a black lace bra with a pink bow—one cup loaded with sod. It dangled from her wrist like a battler's sling.

"Here comes the giant-killer," said Siggy.

Karlotta's breasts sagged to her movable paunch. When her sweater rode up, I caught a peek of dark nipple-bit.

Then Wanga was out of my arms and running down the fence line to the gate; she ran in a buffeted way, like a leaf blown along by varying gusts—through the gate and back into the zoo.

"Hey!" I said. "Hey, Wanga!"

"Mine! Mine, Graff," said Siggy. "I'll get her." He flipped the bloomers to Karlotta and was off running himself.

"No!" I yelled. "Siggy, I'll go!" But Karlotta had moved alongside me; when I tried to stand, she threw her hip into me and knocked me down in the ferns.

"Oh, let *him* be the clown," she said, and she knelt beside me. "Dear boy," said Karlotta, "You've some *morality* about you. You're not a bit like him." And when I tried to sit up, she smothered my face in her bloomers and held me down. Then she peeked under the glorious panties and kissed me with her peach-sweet lips. "Hush, hush," she said, and she pressed me into the damp ground.

We rolled in the hidden and airless, dung-smelling patch; the sounds of the zoo merged and were lost in the lashing of ferns, and the rhino shook the ground.

And when we heard the birds again, their voices were raucous and demanding. The great cats were snarling for meat and revolution.

"Feeding time," said Karlotta. "And I've not yet seen the hippo."

So I tried walking, and she followed me, steering me into the hippohouse, a great vat sunk in the middle of a greenhouse, with a rail around the water so the children wouldn't fall in. At first, there was nothing but murk in the vat.

"Oh, he'll be coming up now, any time," said Karlotta. She scratched herself and showed me a leer. "My left boob's itchy," she whispered. "There's a truckload of ground in my bra." She squirmed and goosed me where I stood, and I watched the bilious pool with the fruit floating in it—and big, bobbing thatches of celery. Suddenly there were bubbles.

First we saw nostrils—two gaping holes, quite bottomless—and then came the thick-lidded eyes. Its head kept rising and rising, and its long pink mouth kept opening and opening; I saw the stump of an impossible epiglottis; I smelled from its dank, empty mouth a whole windowbox of rotted geraniums. The children threw food to it, and it rested its chin on the pool curb; the children threw peanuts, marshmallows and caramel corn—they threw paper bags and souvenirs of the zoo, an old man's newspaper and a tiny pink sneaker. When the hippo had enough, he just rolled his head off the curb and made the pool a sea. He sprayed us and sank in his vat.

"He'll be up again now," said Karlotta. "God, he could swallow me whole!"

On the back of Karlotta's sturdy leg was the imprint of a fern—an accurate fossil on her dark, flexing calf. I slipped away from the vat rim unnoticed, and left Karlotta in the hippohouse.

Drawing the Line

"I don't know how you could have done it," said Siggy. "You've such bad taste."

"Where did Wanga go?" I said.

"I lost her somewhere, Graff. I was just trying to get away from that fatty there."

"We went to the hippohouse," I said. "In a few hours it's going to be dark."

"Thank yourself for that, Graff. Honestly, I don't know how you could have! There's a point, you know, where a fellow should stop and think."

"If we left now," I said, "we'd be in the country before dark."

"Karlotta!" said Siggy. "I just can't imagine! Rich as mud, was it? I should think you'd feel contaminated."

"You're a crude oaf!" I said. "Wearing her bloomers for a hat, dancing around like a jester."

"But I draw the line somewhere, Graff. Oh yes." And he began to fiddle with the motorcycle.

"Well, how frotting grand of you that is!" I said. "It might interest you to know that it wasn't so bad. Not at all bad!"

"I've no doubt of that, Graff," he said. "Skill is more common than beauty." Well, stuffed and officious, that line reappears in his jottings:

Finesse is no substitute for love.

And at the zoo gate he was ignoring me, rising up on the kick starter and throwing down all his weight.

"You're a doctrinaire forker, Siggy," I said.

But the engine caught and he throttled it up and down, nodding his head to the music. I swung up behind him, and we buckled on our crash helmets. Then on with my World War One pilot's goggles, to tint my world yellow —to pinch and addle my mind.

"Siggy?" I said. But he didn't hear.

He turned us out of the Platz at the Hietzinger Zoo, while behind us the lions were roaring for freedom and food, and Karlotta, I could easily imagine, was in the process, both awkward and admiring, of feeding herself to the hippo.

Night Riders

For several towns now, we hadn't seen a gasthaus lighted. There were farms with one tiny light still burning, most likely an attic light left burning always —a beacon to say: There's someone still up, if you've any plans to sneak about. There'd be a dog, too, who really was awake.

But the towns were all dark, and we roared through them, seeing no one; just once, we saw a man peeing in a fountain. We caught him suddenly in our headlight and in the clamor of our engine, and he dove to the ground, still fumbling himself, as if we'd been so many megatons dropped out of the night. That was in a place called Krumnussbaum; just before Blindenmarkt, Siggy stopped. He killed the engine and headlight, and the quiet of the woods sealed up the road.

"Did you see that man back there?" he said. "Have you looked at these towns? It must have been like this during the blackout." And we thought about that a minute, while the woods went cautiously about their night noises again, and *things* came out to watch.

When he turned on the headlight, the trees seemed to leap back out of the road; centuries of night-watchers scurried back in hiding—ferrets and owls, and the ghosts of Charlemagne's lookouts.

"Once," said Siggy, "I found a very old helmet in the woods. It had a spike and visor on it." And his voice hushed the night noises; we heard the river for the first time.

"Is that ahead of us?" I said.

So he worked the kick starter and got us moving slowly. We crossed the Ybbs just out of Blindenmarkt, and Siggy swung the bike sideways on the bridge. Just out of the headlight's beam the river was a black, rumpled sheet in the wind, but the spot where the light struck seemed waterless; the river was shallow and clear, and we saw the pebbles on the bottom as if there'd been no water to cover them.

A logger's road ran beside the river, and snow was still in the cool woods; patches of it were yellowed in our headlight and laced with dark needles from the firs. There were smudges of bright chalk-colors on the trees marked for lumber, and the road wound with the river.

When the river made a bend away from us, the bank widened; we jounced off the center crown and slithered over the wet grass to a flat place on the bank. There were frogs and mice in the grass.

I listened for dogs. If there'd been a farm very near, we'd surely have heard a dog. But instead there was only the river and the wind creaking the bridge out on the main road, the wind brushing through the tight forest—like silent city men creeping through coat closets; not the noises soldiers would make, with their iron parts clanking between the trees.

The Ybbs had a muted rattle and a thousand separate trickles. We unloaded the motorcycle in whispers, not missing a word of the night. When we laid the groundcloth down, we had to pinch the mice out from under it. We were still in sight of the bridge on the main road, but in all the time we stayed awake, there was nothing passing by. The bridge line across the sky made the only geometry above the riverbed; the only other shapes were the jagged ripples in the water and the black, uneven tree line against the brighter night. There were rock pools near the bridge pilings, and the waterlap tossed its phosphorescence to the moon.

Siggy was sitting up in his bag.

"What do you see?" I said.

"Giraffes, ducking under the bridge."

"That would be nice," I said.

"*How* nice!" said Siggy. "And the oryx! Can't you see him wading across the river, dipping those fantastic balls?"

"Freeze them off," I said.

"No!" said Siggy. "*Nothing* could damage that oryx!"

Living Off the Land

There was a boulder under the bridge, and it made a tiny waterfall to clean our trout in; we let the water spill into their slit, flapping bellies, sluice about their lovely ribs and fill them up to their high, springy breastbones. You could clamp up their belly slits and pinch on the bulge; the water came out of their gills, first pink and then clear.

We took twelve trout between us and plunked down their innards on the bouldertop. Then we sat by the motorcycle and watched the crows swoop under the bridge, diving for the fish guts until the rock was picked bare. When the sun came off the water and hung level with the bridge, we thought we'd find a farm and make our deal for breakfast.

The road was soft and we slipped off the high crown into the ruts; Siggy drove slowly and we both leaned back to catch all the air smells, of pine pitch in the woods, and of clover and sweet hay beyond. The woods were thinning, fields swelled behind and beside them; the river was white-capped, running deeper and faster, and nudging a fine froth out to the cutaway banks.

Then the road climbed a little and the river ran down and away from us; we could see a village now—a squat church with an onion-shaped spire, and some solid buildings close together in a one-street town. But before the village was a farm, and Siggy turned in.

The driveway was a slough of mud, as plastic as dough, and our rear wheel sunk to the drive chain; we wallowed, caught in a sponge. There was a goat on the bank of the driveway and we aimed at it, posting on the foot pedals. The goat bolted when we made the bank; we thrummed past a pigpen, the little pigs springing like cats, and the big pigs running like fat ladies in spike heels. The mudcleats whacked themselves clean of the driveway slop; the mudsplatter pelted behind us. The bolting goat had roused the farmer and his wife.

A most jovial Herr Gippel and his Frau Freina looked quite eager to make the exchange—coffee and potatoes for half our trout, and the coffee was black-bean roast.

Frau Freina tried to say, with her pale, winking eyes: Oh, come see how pretty my kitchen is! She had a proud, motherly, grouselike swell to her breast.

And this Gippel appeared an expert in feeding.

"You're a fine fish eater," Siggy told him.

"Oh, we eat a lot of trout," he said. He'd pinch them up at the tails and coax the meat off neat. He kept a tidy stack of skeletons to one side of his plate.

"But so *many* trout!" Freina said.

"And we're just starting out at this business," said Siggy. "Living off the land, Graff! Back to the simple laws of nature."

"Oh, now," Gippel said, "you would have to go and remind me of *laws.*"

"And we've had such a lovely meal," Frau Freina said.

"But the question of *laws* came up, dear," said Gippel. "And it was *twelve* trout they had between them."

"Oh, I know," Freina said. "But we wouldn't have had the same breakfast if there'd been just *ten.*"

"Just five apiece," said Gippel. "What you're *allowed,* of course. But my Freina's right. It wouldn't have been the same breakfast at all."

"I think this is terrible," Freina said, and she went out on the porch.

"Herr Siggy," Gippel said, "I just wish you hadn't brought it up."

"What did I bring up?" said Siggy.

"Laws!" said Gippel. "You went and reminded me." And Freina came back in the screen door and gave Siggy a green piece of paper, face down.

"What's that?" I said.

"It's our fine!" said Siggy.

"Oh!" Gippel cried. "What manner of man am I?"

"Who in hell are you?" said Siggy.

"The fish-and-game warden," Gippel said.

"This is just terrible," said Freina, and she went out again.

"It's nice," said Siggy. "I always say it's nice to make a friend of the local gamekeeper."

"Oh, that's something to be thankful for," said Gippel. "That's why it's only fifty schillings."

"Fifty schillings?" I said.

"It was the least I could do," said Gippel, who moved to the screen door himself now. "If you'll excuse me a moment," he said. "I'm just so ashamed." And he went very sadly out on the porch.

"The frotting thief!" I said. "How close is the bike parked?"

"Well, Graff," said Siggy. "It's parked about a foot from where Gippel's sitting, giving comfort to his gentle wife."

"Fifty schillings, Sig!" I said.

But Siggy took the right note from his duckjacket. "You go give them this comfort, Graff," he said. "I'll be just a minute inside."

So I went to cheer up the kindly people; we all sat on the porch and watched the witless goat squaring off with the motorcycle, trying to get up the nerve for the initial ram.

Then Siggy came out, quite choked up himself, and that was enough to set off poor Freina again. "Oh, they're sure lovely boys!" she wept.

"Oh, sweet, sweet," said Gippel. "The laws are just vile!" he roared. "Allowances should be made for boys like these."

But Siggy said, "Now, now"—with a forearm bolstering up his belly. "It was such a feed we had, it was worth fifty schillings." And that *did* surprise all of us—brought Freina back to her senses and her alert, pale, winking eyes. Poor Gippel was agog, with nothing more to say.

So they watched us climb on the motorcycle. We stood off the goat and were careful this time to avoid the driveway. The pigs began their insane running.

"It's amazing," I said to Siggy, "the deals one can make for breakfast." But I felt something hard against his belly, under his duckjacket. "What have you got there?" I said.

"Frau Freina Gippel's fryingpan," said Siggy, "and one flint, one bottleo-pener, one corkscrew and a saltshaker."

Well, we were pinched by the fence rows when we came near the road, and we were forced into the driveway for a moment. But this time we had the speed behind us and we slurred out on the road. We could see Gippel waving both his arms like a madman; Frau Freina was swelling her breast and waving, kissing her fingers goodbye to us. The tires skidded us into the ruts, and again beat themselves clean of the driveway. The old mud flung madly after us; *thot, thot, thot* it went on the downhill road.

"There are certain investments required," said Siggy, "if one is to live off the land." And the fryingpan was still warm under his jacket.

Where the Walruses Are

As the notebook has it:

> There are certain investments required.

And so. It was lunchtime when we rode into Ulmerfeld and bought two bottles of beer. We were nearly out of the village when Siggy saw the windowbox hung to a second-story window of a gasthaus.

"Radishes!" said Siggy. "I saw their little greens peeking over!"

We drove up under the window, and I steadied the motorcycle while Siggy stood on the gas tank; on his toes, he would just get his hands over the rim of the box.

"I can feel them," he said. "They were just watered—sweet snappy baby ones!"

He stuffed them in his duckjacket, and we drove through Ulmerfeld, still following the Ybbs. A mile or so out of the village, we cut through a meadowbank to the river.

"After all, Graff," said Siggy. "This day still owes us a piece of our fifty schillings."

And with that for grace, we opened our beers with Frau Freina's opener, and salted our radishes from Freina's shaker. Freina had a wondrously unclogged shaker. The radishes were crunchy and moist, and Siggy planted the greens.

"Do you think they'll grow?" he said.

"Well, anything's possible, Siggy."

"Yes, anything is," he said, and we flicked our close-nibbled stumps to the river, watching them bob under and spin to the crest of the current again, like hats with pinwheels on the heads of drowning boys.

"Upstream," I said, "there's got to be a dam."

"Oh, a great falls in the mountains," said Siggy. "And think of the fishing above the dam!"

"I'll bet there's grayling, Sig."

"And walruses, Graff."

We lay back in the meadow and tooted the bottlenecks of our beers. Crows again, downstream, were circling the radish stumps.

"Is there anything a crow won't eat, Sig?"

"Walruses," he said. "Couldn't possibly eat a walrus."

"Well, that's amazing," I said.

The spring-damp was still on the ground, but the thick grass seemed to trap the sun and hold it against me; I was warmed into closing my eyes. I could hear the crows telling off the river, and the crickets were sawing in the fields. Siggy was chinking the bottleneck on his teeth.

"Graff," he said.

"Hm."

"Graff?"

"Here," I said.

"It was a terrible scene in that zoo," he said. "I think it would be better if we had them out here."

"Those girls?" I said.

"Not the girls!" he cried. "I meant the animals! Wouldn't they have a time out here?"

And I could see it with my eyes closed. The giraffes were nipping the buds off the treetops; the anteaters gobbled waterbugs from the fine lace of foam on the shore.

"Those *girls!*" said Siggy. "God, Graff—what a frotting ninny you can be."

So the sun and the beer settled our sleep; the Rare Spectacled Bears were kissing in whispers, and the oryx chased all the frotting ninnies out of the meadow. On the bruise-purple Ybbs the walrus was rowing a boat with his flippers, sunning his tusks and bleaching his mustache, and he didn't see the hippo who lurked in the deep pool by the bank—the disguised hippo in a veil of froth, mouth agape for the walrus, rowboat and all.

I woke up to warn the walrus; the giraffes had munched the meadow until they'd reached the sun and dragged it down. The down sun glinted through the grass, caught the motorcycle and stretched the shadow of wheels and engine over the river; the river raced under the motorcycle like a fast, bruised road.

"Siggy," I said. "It's time we moved."

"Gently, Graff," he said. "I'm watching them. They're stepping out of their cages, free as us."

So I let him watch awhile, and I watched the sun flattening the meadow out red, and the river running out of sun. I had a look upstream, but there was no peeking the mountains yet.

Going Nowhere

Out of the valley and the night bugs, the road turned to tar, then back to dirt, and always now the river was hidden from us in the thick tunnel of firs. The heavy gargle of the motorcycle beat against the forest, and our echo crashed alongside—as if other riders paced themselves to us and moved unseen through the woods.

Then we climbed out of the firs too, and the night was sharp enough to breathe in careful bits. We were aware of space again, and the sudden, looming things to fill it—a rocking black barn with great wind-swung doors, and triangular pieces of window casting a severed headlight back to us; something shuffling off the road, throwing its fierce eyes over its shoulder, hunched like a bear—or a bush; a farmhouse shuddering in its sleep, and a yapping dog who sprinted alongside us—over my shoulder, its eyes getting smaller and blinking out of the dancing-red taillight. And on the valley side, dropping below us, the little peaks of treetops were pitched like tents along the road.

"I think we've lost the river," said Siggy. He was shifting down to the upgrade; he went third to second and gave us a full throttle. We tossed a wake of soft dark dirt behind, and I leaned forward with my chest up on his back; I could feel him begin to lean before the bike would lay over, and I could lean through the corners—as perfectly with him as a rucksack on his back.

Then the road dropped out from under us, and our headlight darted straight out into the night, with the momentum of the motorcycle bearing us levelly into the sky; when the front wheel touched the road again, we were carried madly downhill to a wooden bridge. Siggy hit first gear, but he still had to brake, and the rear wheel moved up beside us; we skipped across the bridge planks like a crab.

"It's the river," said Siggy, and we went back to peek.

He wrenched down the headlight and slanted the beam to the river, but there wasn't any river. He pressed the kill button on the engine, and we *heard* a river—we heard the wind making the bridge planks groan—and we felt how the bridge rails were damp from a rising spray. But in the light's beam there was only a gorge falling into darkness; and the tilted firs, holding to the gorge walls, reached for help and didn't dare look down.

The river had taken a shortcut; it sawed the mountain in two. We peered into the blank awhile. There'd be no fish in the morning unless we dared some horrible pendency before breakfast.

So we found a spot flat enough for the groundcloth, and set back enough from the edge of the great gorge. It was so cold we made a rumpus of undressing in our bags.

"Graff," said Siggy. "If you get up to pee, don't walk the wrong way."

And later, our bladders must have remembered what he said—or else, must have been listening too long to the river-gush. Because we both had to get up. And oh, it was cold, stepping naked and fearful across the field.

"How does the oryx keep his warm?" said Siggy.

"I've been thinking," I said. "Don't you think all of that might have been a disease?"

"Oh, Graff!" said Siggy. "It's surely a case of over-health."

"He must feel quite vulnerable," I said.

And we did a clutching, vulnerable dance back to our bags. The bags had stayed warm for us; we curled, and felt the mouseful field scurry. The night was so chilly I think the mice crept up and slept warm against us.

"Graff," said Siggy. "I've been thinking too."

"Very good, Sig."

"No, really thinking, Graff."

"What, then?" I said.

"Do you think there's a nightwatchman at the Hietzinger Zoo—inside the grounds all night? Just peeking around?"

"Communing with the oryx?" I said. "Asking him his secret?"

"No, just in there," said Siggy. "Do you think someone's in there at night?"

"Sure," I said.

"I think so too," he said.

I saw the guard muttering to the bears, waking up the oryx to ask the potent question; by the early dawn hours the guard walked hunched like an ape, swung from cage to cage, baiting the animals in their own languages.

"Graff?" said Siggy. "Do you remember any closed doors in the Small Mammal House? Was there anything that looked like a closet?"

"A closet in infrared?"

"A guard's got to have someplace to go, Graff. Someplace for sitting and having his coffee, and a spot to hang the keys."

"Why, Siggy!" I said. "Are you scheming a zoo bust?"

"Oh, wouldn't that be something, Graff? Wouldn't that be something rare? Just to let them go!"

"The rarest of fun!" I said.

And a veritable gaggle of bears went waddling out the main gate, carrying with them the ticket taker's booth, in which the man with the gambler's green eyeshade was crying for mercy.

But I said, "Except, of course, it wouldn't be any fun going back to Vienna. That's at the very *bottom* of things I'd like to do."

I opened my eyes and saw the lovely pale stars above me; the stunted, desperate firs were climbing out of the gorge. Siggy was sitting up.

"What's at the very *top* of things you'd like to do, Graff?"

"Have you ever seen the sea?" I said.

"Only in movies."

"Did you see *From Here to Eternity?*" I said. "It was an American film, with Deborah Kerr and Burt Lancaster. Burt was rolling Deborah in the surf."

"It wasn't the sea you were interested in, Graff."

"Wouldn't that be something, though?" I said. "Camped down on a beach somewhere—in Italy, maybe."

"I saw that movie too," said Siggy. "I felt that their crotches must have been sandy."

"Well, I'd like to see the sea," I said. "And fish some more, up in the mountains."

"And roll Deborah Kerr in the surf, Graff?"

"Why not?"

"And frot a whole herd of country girls, Graff?"

"Not a whole herd," I said.

"But one fine piece of a girl, Graff? Just one to make a world out of you awhile?"

"Suits me," I said.

"Suits you, indeed, Graff," he said. "You dreaming romantic ninny-ass bastard."

"Well, what do *you* want to do, then?" I said.

"Well, you can frot all you want," said Siggy, and he lay back down, his arms crossed outside the bag; his arms were all the bare, pale colors of the stars in the stinging night. "That zoo won't be going anywhere," he said.

I gave a glance to the firs in the gorge, but they hadn't climbed out yet. Siggy didn't move; his hair fell over his pillow of duckjacket and touched the shiny grass. I was sure that he slept, but before I slept myself, he mumbled me a groggy little bedtime song:

> Frau Freina Gippel's lost her pan.
> And never will she find it.
> The Frau has teeth on her behind,
> But Gippel doesn't mind it.

Going Somewhere

There was a frost in the morning, and the grass reflected a thousand different prism-shapes of sun; the meadowbank to the river gorge was like a ballroom floor, catching the patterns of an intricate chandelier. I lay on my side and squinted through the frost-furry grass to the gorge wall. The groundcloth was cool on my cheek, and the grass spears seemed bigger than the trees; the frost-melt lay in bright pools between the spears. There was a cricket coming along, using the grass for stilts to span the droplets—lake-sized, for a cricket; its joints were frosty, and it seemed to be thawing as it walked.

When you're level with it, a cricket can be fierce—a giant anthropod come bending down the jungle, stepping over oceans. I growled at it, and it stopped.

Then I heard bells, not far away.

"Cowbells!" said Siggy. "We're going to be trampled! Oh, pushed down the gorge!"

"Church bells," I said. "We must be near a village."

"Well, frot me," said Siggy, and he peeked out of his bag.

But my cricket was gone.

"What are you looking for, Graff?"

"A cricket."

"A cricket's quite harmless."

"This was an especially big one," I said. But it wasn't under the ground-cloth, so I got out of my bag and stepped on the frost-stiff grass.

Well, the dew made me dance, and with that giddy gorge close by, I got much more interested in dancing than finding my cricket. But Siggy watched me coldly, and not for long; he huffed himself out of his bag and began stomping around the groundcloth—not at all the same sort of dance I was doing.

"You don't have to get up yet," I said.

"Well, I don't recommend watching you in the nude," he said.

"Well, be careful with your stamping," I said. "You'll get my cricket." But I stood oddly embarrassed in front of him.

"Let's have some coffee and find a more fishable part of this river," he said, like a frotting scoutmaster. And I forgot about my probable trodden cricket—watching him load the motorcycle, like a frotting sergeant.

Se we left for the next town.

Hiesbach was less than a mile up the road; it was a town piled against a hillside—old, rounded, gray-stone buildings heaped like egg boxes, with the usual, outstanding, squat and onion-headed church that hunched beside the road like an old, toothless lion who wouldn't attack any more.

When we got there, Mass was over; stiff, crinkly families milled on the church steps, creaking their once-a-week shoes. The smaller boys bolted for a *Gasthof* opposite the Holy Onion Head: FRAU ERTL'S OLD GASTHOF.

Siggy rapped the sign as we went in. "Graff," he whispered, "Beware of the Ertl." So we came in agiggle.

"Well," said fat Frau Ertl, "you're very welcome."

"Oh, thank you," Siggy said.

"Coffee?" I asked the Ertl. "Is it hot?"

"And a place to wash our hands?" said Siggy.

"Oh, of course," she said, pointing us out the back door. "But the light bulb's burnt out, it seems."

If there ever could have been a light bulb. Because the *pissoir* was a dirt-floor stall in back of the *Gasthof* and next to a long, narrow pen for goats. The goats watched us work the pump. Siggy pumped the water over the back of his head; when he shook his head, the goats bleated and butted against the gate of the pen.

"My poor goats," said Siggy, and he went over to the pen to tug their chins. Oh, they loved him, it was easy to see. "Graff," he said, "step inside and see if anyone's coming."

Inside it was filling up—the families together with their coffees and sausages, the lone men together at a long table with their beers.

"Ah," said the Ertl. "I've your coffees by the window."

So when Siggy came in, we went to our table—next to a family with a cantankerous-looking grandfather for a leader. The family's youngest, a boy, watched us over his long sausage and roll, and his chin drooped in what he was gnawing.

"Gross little boy," Siggy whispered, and he made a face at him. The boy stopped eating and stared, so Siggy made a threatening gesture with his fork —stabbing air—and the boy pulled his grandfather's ear. When the old man looked at us, Siggy and I were just sipping our coffees; we saluted, and the grandfather pinched the boy under the table.

"Just eat, boy," the grandfather said.

So the boy looked out the window, and was the first to see the goats.

"Goats out!" he shouted, and the grandfather gave him another pinch. "Boys who keep seeing things should hold their tongues!" he said.

But others were looking now; the grandfather saw them too.

"I shut the gate," said Frau Ertl. "I shut them up before Mass."

Some older boys swaggered and shoved each other out of the *Gasthof;* the goats shyly herded by the church. And the pinching grandfather leaned over us. "Frau Ertl's a widow," he said. "She needs someone to keep her goat pen shut." Then he choked on whatever he was eating and had a little spasm over it.

The goats were nodding to each other, clattering off balance, up and down the church steps. The boys had herded them against the door, but no one dared to go up the steps after them, and mess one's Sunday clothes.

We went outside and watched, listening to the bells from another village —striking Sunday morning with insistent, hurry-up echo-shots that muted the end of each note.

"That's St. Leonhard's bells," said a woman. "We've got our own bells, and I'd like to know why they're not ringing on Sunday." And the issue was seized, taken up by other voices:

"But our bell ringer's eating his breakfast."

"Drinking his breakfast, you mean."

"The old swiller."

"And the children don't miss a thing."

"We've our own church and our own bells, and why should we have to listen to somebody else's?"

"Religious fanatics," Siggy whispered—but he was interested in the goats. The mob was trying to scare them off the steps.

"Go get that bell ringer," the woman said, but the bell ringer had been warned of the plot already; he stood on the steps of the *Gasthof,* a beer in his hand, wrinkling the veins on his nose to the sun.

"Now, ladies," he said. "Kindly ladies, I could never hope to attain"— and he swallowed a belch that made his eyes water—"to achieve," he said, "the mastery of bell-ringing that my competitor in St. Leonhard has"—and he let it come: a sharp, ringing belch. "Has attained," he said, and went back inside.

"Someone else," the woman said, "should learn how to ring the bells."

"Oh," said the pinching grandfather, "there's not much to it."

"Too much for you," the woman said, "or you'd be doing it, all right. You're just dying for something to do."

And a hardfaced girl flicked her saucy, hard butt at the grandfather; stepping in front of him, she brushed his chin with the down of her arm; she stretched herself away from him, almost leaving her leg behind—toe down, her skirt tugged to mid-thigh. Her little calf leapt high above her ankle and knotted like a fist.

"Too much for you," she said, and skipped away from him, out into the street.

"Look at those goats, there!" said Siggy. "Why don't they bolt? They should bolt right by those brats. Bolt!" he hooted.

And the grandfather looked at us; he eased himself down a step or two and sat on the stairs by us. "What did you say, there?" the grandfather said.

"It's a goat call," said Siggy. "It works for some."

But the grandfather was staring too hard; he clicked his teeth. "You're a queer rascal," he said, and he picked up Siggy's hand. "I saw you," he whispered, and Siggy jerked his hand away.

"Where's St. Leonhard and its famous bells?" I said.

"Over the mountain," said the grandfather. "And not much of a mountain, either, but to hear this town talk, you'd think it was Alps. Not much of a church, either, and nobody who's much of anything living here—but to hear this town talk. And there's nothing to ringing their damn bells!"

"Go do it, then," said Siggy.

"I could!" the grandfather said.

"Do it, then," said Siggy. "Ring the piss out of them! Get the whole town rolling in the street, holding their ears!"

"I can't climb all those stairs," said the grandfather. "I'd get winded halfway up."

"We'll *carry* you up," said Siggy.

"Who are you anyway?" the grandfather said. And he whispered to me, "I saw him. He took the saltshaker off the table—Frau Ertl's shaker—and he stuffed it in that funny pocket."

"Oh, why don't they bolt, Graff?" said Siggy. And a brat had the leg of one now; it bleated and kicked, but it was slipping down the steps.

"You think you know so much about goats," said the grandfather. "You let them out, didn't you? You're just that sort of madman."

Then they had the one goat down.

"Let's go, Graff," said Siggy.

"I'm going to tell," the grandfather said, and he blushed. "Widow Ertl thinks I'm just an old duffer who doesn't know anything."

"She'll think he's more of a duffer if he tells—won't she, Graff?"

"Oh," said the grandfather, "I'll let you get away before I tell."

"Ah, Graff," said Siggy, "the terrible chances old duffers will take!"

And when we were started, they had a second goat down. The first goat was on its feet, but a fat girl had it in a headlock and its beard was ratily plucked.

Its pink mouth was open for bleating, but we couldn't hear it calling us over the motorcycle.

As the notebook has it:

> Goats won't bolt! But they aren't *wild* animals.
> Take heart, you *wild* animals!

Fairies All Around

When we came into St. Leonhard, the bell ringer was still at it; he was trembling the church.

"What a racket!" said Siggy. "Bong! Bong! Bong!" he shouted at the belfry.

And a thin little girl with a licorice stick saw him shout. She looked up to the church as if she expected the clapper to break loose from the bell and fly at us.

"Bong!" Siggy said to her, and we went into a *Gasthof.*

Mass had been over some time, and the *Gasthof* was almost empty. A natty, quick-moving man stood staring out the window at our motorcycle. Every time he raised his beer he looked like he was going to toss it over his shoulder; he stood with one foot on top of the other, suddenly losing his balance and regaining it with a hop and two-step.

The tired bartender, the *Wirt,* was reading a newspaper spread on the counter. We bought two bottles of cold beer, a loaf of bread and a two-schilling butter pat.

And the tired *Wirt* asked, "All in one bag?"

"Oh, sure," I said.

"I'll have to give you two bags," he said. "I haven't a bag big enough for the whole works."

And the frisky man at the window turned round so suddenly he made us jump.

"Put the bottles up your asses!" he shouted. "Put the bread in another bag!"

"God!" said Siggy. "Frot you!"

"Eh?" the man cried, and he did his hop and two-step at us. "Frot me, eh? *Eh!*" he shrieked, as if something were caught in his throat.

"Better watch out for him," the *Wirt* said.

"I certainly will," said Siggy.

"Because he'll sue you," the *Wirt* said.

"Sue us?" I said.

"It's a profession with him," said the *Wirt.*

And the man who was going to sue said, "Put your asses in one bag."

"Now look out, you," said Siggy.

But the *Wirt* caught his arm. "Better for you to look out," he said. "He'll let you hit him and then he'll sue you. He'll say he can't breathe because of his jaw, he'll say he gets headaches when he eats. Oh, we don't get many strangers here, but he goes after every one."

"I'll give you the scrap of your life!" the suer yelled. He gave us the two-step again, cupping his beerglass in his palm and slopping his beer.

"I warn you, he won't fight," said the *Wirt.* "He just sues."

"I can't imagine," I said.

"It's amazing, I know," said the tired *Wirt,* as if he were falling asleep over it. "And he even gets away with it," he said.

"How can he get away with it?" said Siggy.

We three stood together and watched him, standing one foot on the other, tottering and squirming his knees like a child trying hard not to wet his pants. But there wasn't anything childish in the man's face. He opened his fly and poured his beer inside his pants.

"He's a bit queer too," said the *Wirt.*

And he gave us the two-step, but he was losing his nattiness fast; he flapped his pants fly open and closed, and the beer foam spit down his leg. He winked at Siggy. "You-you," he slobbered, "you-you!"

"He'll sue!" the *Wirt* cried, but he missed stopping Siggy's arm.

Because Siggy already had his helmet off the counter, and he swung it twice-round by the chin strap, full circles of his arm, and swung it up under the surprised frisky man—caught him in the open crotch and tumbled his one-footed stance. The man howled over hind-end, his knees flinging up to his chest.

"Really," the *Wirt* said, "he'll sue you, I know it."

"You're an utter dope," said Siggy. "And you can tell him we went the other way."

"Well, sure I can," said the moping *Wirt.* "I don't mind at all, boys."

And we walked quickly out of there, with no bags at all for what we'd bought; we left the dullest *Wirt* I'd ever met—with his *Gasthof,* and with the other's singed-mouse howl.

At the motorcycle, I stuffed the things into Siggy's vent-pocket.

"Christ, Sig," I said. "Letting goats loose, bashing queers!"

"Well, frot me, then," said Siggy.

"Oh, we're quite a pair," I said, meaning nothing by it, and he turned on the seat; he stared at me.

His voice, then, came up so shrill it seemed to startle the motorcycle. "Are we now, Graff? Well, there's a butter pat for the pan, and bread for crumbs to roll the trout in. And there's beer for me to pour in my fly! And maybe I'll choke on a fish bone and let you botch the rest of the day by yourself!"

"Oh, frot," I said. "Oh, Jesus, Sig."

And just as he chunked the bike in gear, the thin little girl came up to us from nowhere and touched Siggy's hand with her licorice stick—touched

him lightly and magically, as if her licorice were the Good Fairy's wand.
The notebook records it in poetry:

> Oh, the things you want
> Are very private—
> Private, private,
> Very private.
> Oh, the only ways there are
> To get them
> Are very public—
> Public, public,
> Very ugly-public.
> So God help us, Graff.
> Great Bear, Big Dipper,
> Help us both.

Which must be one of his worst poems.

The Second Sweet
Act of God

From St. Leonhard the road turned steeply downhill, cutting high-banked
and gravelly switchbacks to where the Ybbs would spill out of the mountain
at Waidhofen. The gravel was soft and loose in the banks, and we tried to
stay near the middle of the road; our rear wheel moved us all aslither, and
we rode with our weight off the seat, pushed forward on the foot pedals.

The first of the orchards began less than a mile below St. Leonhard—
apple orchards, the tree rows stretching on both sides of the road, the young
trees snappy in the wind and the old twisties squatting immovable; the grass
between the tree rows was mown and lumped, smelling sickish-sweet in the
sun. The apple buds were coming to blossom.

Now we posted on the foot pedals and let the bike scatter under us like
a horse; it was some road, all right, the way it dropped and bent, giving us
a flash of trees on one side and then the other; the raspy grasshoppers
snapping out of the ditches, and the blackbirds swooping to near-collision.

Then the girl's braid seemed to whip out at us as she flung her head round
to our noise and skipped herself out of the road. It was a thick auburn braid,
waist-length, with the end of it flicking her high, swinging rump, and there

was more wind filling her skirt than hips. The gravel was too loose for braking, so we had just this flash of her—her long brown legs, and her long fingers flicking down to her knees, pinching her skirt safe around her. Then I was looking over my shoulder, and she was turning her face away—tossing her braid out beside her; it did a snake dance in the sun while the wind held it up. I could almost have reached it, but the wind dropped it on her shoulder and she tugged it roughly to her cheek; that was all I saw of her, except for a laundry bag adangle from one of her arms. She straightened her brown leather jacket with a tug as rough as she gave to her braid. Then we lost her in a switchback.

"Did you see her face, Sig?"

"You weren't looking at her face, either."

"When I turned around, I was. She hid it from me."

"Ah," said Siggy. "She feels guilty about it. An ill omen, Graff."

But I looked for more of her along the road, as if girls with braids so auburn and rich were as prolific as apple buds and grasshoppers.

Great Bear, Big Dipper, Thy Ways Are Strange Indeed

Well, under the apple trees there was deadfall and winter pruning that the firewood men had missed. The low boughs with blossoms and buds; the bee boxes propped on apple crates, the bee abodes painted white and set high up so the tractors and horsecarts wouldn't bump them over and spill the hives. It was all bees' work in the orchards now; the bees were out opening the apple buds, from blossom to blossom—oh, the friend of the flower and fertilization, the polliniferous bee!

"Isn't fertilization grand?" said Siggy.

And the deadwood under the tree was easy to snap up small—was making a quick-hot coal bed for us; we sprinkled the coals with water to put the flame down. Then we set the pan on the fired rocks and popped our butter into the pan. Siggy crumbed the crust of the bread loaf, and we rolled the wet trout until they were furry with crumbs.

The slim trickle of a trout stream crossed the road and the orchards and leaned down the mountain—to where we would go and see Waidhofen, after our lunch.

The stream was so tiny we'd almost missed it; the bridge was so thin we'd almost been sifted through the slats. But the trout here hadn't been shy about rising; now they spattered in the pan and tuned their music to the bee drone in the orchards.

And a bee flew a blossom over the stream; the air current dropped from under him, and the bee got his wings wet, paddling an apple petal now. But he was better off floating air than water; the giant trout pulled out from the bank, rose and nosed bee and blossom down its throat—left barely a ripple mark in its descent.

"There's one we missed," I said.

"There's one who'd have eaten your whole rod," said Siggy.

We ate a bit messily ourselves, picking with jackknives until the trout were cool enough for our hands. And of course we had the beer cooling in the stream, waiting to go with an after-lunch pipe.

Belly-up to the sun, then, with the bee drone all around us; I couldn't see the road from the orchard, just the bridge rail underlining the treetops, the green-blotched bouquets of blossom and bud. This world is kind to itself, I thought. Well, the bees make honey for the beekeeper, the bees multiply the orchardman's apples; no one's hurt by that. And if oily Herr Faber were a beekeeper, and Gippel an orchardman, wouldn't they be all right too?

So I said, "Well, Sig, I could never tire of this."

"One day it rains," he said. "One day it snows."

And the notebook turns everything to poetry:

> Fate waits.
> While you hurry
> Or while you wait,
> It's all the same to Fate.

Then I saw her head moving gently above the bridge rail; she had one hand on the rail, and I think she was tippytoeing so she wouldn't rouse us. The red braid was pulled over her shoulder and tucked in the collar of her leather jacket; she tugged a thick knot of hair to her throat like a scarf, and her long face came down over it. The rail cut her off at the waist, so it was only a bit more than a bust of her that was sneaking by us.

I kept my eyes half closed, and I whispered, "Look there, Sig, but be easy —don't open your eyes. On the bridge, look."

"Frotting Graff!" said Siggy, and he bolted upright. "Look *where* without opening my eyes? Look *how?*"

And the girl gave a little cry; she nearly bobbed out of my sight. I had to sit up to see her skip off the bridge and cross to the far side of the road. She was protecting her legs with her laundry bag.

"It's the girl, Siggy."

"Oh, dandy," he said.

But the girl was still walking away.

"Here!" I called. "Can we give you a ride?"

"A ride with us?" said Siggy. "Three on our bike?"

"Where are you going?" I shouted. Now I had to stand up to see her.

"She's running away from home, Graff. We won't be a party to that."

"I'm not," said the girl, not looking back at us. But she stopped.

"I didn't know she could hear, Graff. And anyway," he whispered, "I know she's running away."

The girl turned a bit more to us, still keeping her legs behind the laundry bag.

"Where are you going?" I asked.

"I've a new job in Waidhofen," she said, "and I'm going to it."

"What was your old job?" said Siggy.

"I took care of an aunt," she said, "in St. Leonhard. But I've another aunt in Waidhofen, and she owns a *Gasthof*. She's giving me wages and a room of my own."

"Did the other aunt die?" said Siggy.

"We were just leaving for Waidhofen," I said.

"We were just having a nap, Graff," said Siggy.

But the girl came back a little. She came kneeing her laundry bag in front of her, keeping her face down—her eyes under lashes and under the shadow of her hair. Her face seemed to catch a blush-color from her braid. She looked at the motorcycle.

"There's no room for me on that," she said. "Where would I be?"

"Between us," I told her.

"Who drives?" she asked.

"I do," said Siggy. "And Graff would lovingly hold you on."

"You could wear my helmet," I told her.

"Could I?" she said. "You wouldn't mind?"

"You'd have to leave your braid out," said Siggy. "Wouldn't she, Graff?"

But I scurried him back to pick up the fishing stuff; we cooled off the pan in the stream. The girl was tying the laundry bag drawstrings round her waist, letting the bag hang down in front of her.

"Can I just sit this on my lap?" she asked.

"Oh yes, yes," I said. And Siggy gouged the panhandle into my belly.

"She's just a skinny baby one, Graff. She can't possibly give you much of a ride."

"Oh, turn it off, Sig," I whispered. "Just turn it off a bit."

"Fate waits," he mumbled. "Great Bear, Big Dipper, how you can wait!"

What All of Us
Were Waiting For

"Never done this before," she said.

And when she was on behind Siggy, I squeezed up behind her—sliding our rucksack back on the fender so I could hang a bit of my rear over the seat.

"I don't need to be held," she said. "I'm in here tight enough."

Then Siggy bucked the ditch up out of the orchard; he raised the front wheel off the ground and brought it down again so gently that it seemed to kiss the road. The rear wheel went mushing out of the soft.

"Hold," said the girl; she was tossed back against me a moment, and her braid hung to my lap. I caught her between my knees and pinched her to the seat. "Better," she said. "That's enough." And we came down the pitch into the switchbacks; the road was so worn and such a leathery color, it looked like a razor strop. The trees seemed bent by the sky, but we were the crooked ones—leaned-over through the switchbacks, and barely out of one before we were leaning into another.

"Hold," the girl said. "More." But I had no place to put my feet; the girl hooked her sandal heels over my foot pedals, and I held my feet up so they wouldn't be burned on the exhaust pipes. I put my hands on her hips and touched my thumbs together at her spine. "That's better," she said. "That's enough."

The wind took the tassel end of her braid and lashed it upward at my chin, but the weight of her hair hung against my chest in a wine-colored goblet-shape—coming down loose and full from the helmet to her first braid knot. I leaned a bit forward and pressed her braid against my chest; and she pressed forward to Siggy.

Oh, girl, I thought, what lovely taut tendons hold your ankle to your calf!

It was her laundry bag keeping her skirt in her lap, and her elbows pinched her skirt to her thighs; she had her hands tucked in the famous vent-pocket of Siggy's duckjacket, as if she were using it as a muff against the wind.

Her hair was sweeter then the mow-smells, richer than the honeydrip hung from the bee boxes' little screen doors.

We were taking the switchbacks in slithers, plowing the gravel-mush out to the bank.

"Frot me," said Siggy. "There's some load pushing us along."

"You've got the helmet on wrong," I said to her ear, so soft it tickled my nose.

"Never mind now," she said. "Just hold."

I could peek how the helmet nearly covered her eyes and rode high up on the back of her head; she gripped the chin strap in her mouth, and it cut off the ends of her words.

"It's the Ybbs, there," she said—and through the long-falling orchard I had a glimpse of wide water, black as oil in the shade firs at the meadow bottom.

At the next switchback we saw it again, only now it was hammering over a falls. A mudstone town with rust-colored roofs began where the black of the river fell to foam—fell to a broth, bone-colored and bubbly. And there were towers flying the canton flags, peep sights and gun slits in the water-front castles, and arching bridges of stone, and little, swinging wood walks spanning the offshoots of the river that ran through the streets. And garden plots too, with the fading, fake colors of the city flower markets.

But Siggy had taken too much of a look; he'd gone too high up on the bank of the switchback, and the crown of the road was turned against us. Siggy was fighting the gravel-mush on the fat lip of the bank. "Oh, frot!" he said. "Oh, frot frot frot!"

One cheek of my rump wobbled down on the fender; I was tipped, and there was no place for my poor feet.

So my thumbs slipped apart at the girl's spine; I plunged my hands under her laundry bag and into her lap.

"Don't, you!" she said. And her elbows flew up under my arms, like the startled winging of a grouse; her skirt fluttered up to her thigh. I at least had a glimpse of that hard, round leg before my other rump cheek sat on the fender too; I was pushed between the seat and rucksack, with no place for my poor feet, and with no way to steady my slipping. My weight pushed the fender down; I was warmed by the wheel rub. And I was slipping more. It was my left leg that touched the pipe first, at mid-calf, and I had no choice but to scissor the bike to stay on.

So the pipes received my calves like the griddle grabs the bacon.

"Oh, he's burning!" the girl said.

"Is it Graff?" said Siggy. "God, I thought it was my brakes!"

But there was no stopping quick in the gravel-mush at a downhill pitch; of course he had to ride the bank out. Siggy wedged us upright in an orchard ditch, and he lifted me off—over the rucksack—though I was glued to the pipes and needed yanking.

"Oh, we'll have to soak your pants off," he said.

"*Ai!*" I said. "Oh *ai, ai!*"

"Shut your mouth, Graff," he said, "or you'll lose all dignity."

So I clamped on the hoots that were pelting up and down my throat—
I wouldn't let them out—and they sank down to my poor calves: my sticky,
gravel-spattered calves, looking more melted than burnt.

"Oh, don't touch them!" said the girl. "Oh, look at you!"

But I looked at her, with her cock-eyed helmet, and I thought: How I'd
like to bash you up good and hang you by your frotting hair!

"Oh, you," she said. "When you grabbed, I didn't know you were falling!"

"God," said Siggy, "doesn't he stink?"

"Oh, frot you!" I said.

"We'll need a bath to soak him in," said Siggy.

"There's my aunt's," the girl said. "Oh, her *Gasthof* has baths and
baths."

"That you could stand, Graff—baths and baths."

"So get him back on," said the girl. "I'll show you the way."

And, oh, did the wind sting me—ice on my scorches. I hugged the girl;
she reached back one arm and wrapped me around her. But the terrible
hoots were rising within me—I was going to be gagged, so I closed my
mouth on her neck, for the sake of my silence and bliss.

"What's your name, you?" she said through the chin strap, and her neck
blushed hot against my lips.

"Don't make him talk!" said Siggy. "He's Graff."

"I'm Gallen," the girl whispered. "My name's Gallen."

Gallen von St. Leonhard? I said to myself and her neck.

So three-up and wounded, we rode the beast through town, blatting short
echo-shots under the close arches, booming over the high-walled bridge.

"It's your falls, Graff," said Siggy. "It's the Ybbs Falls."

But I was moving to a new spot of neck to kiss. We dodged from sun to
shade, with the stinging air first hot and then cool—bellows to my flaming
feet—and an orchestra of hoots wanted out of me.

"I'm sorry it hurts," Gallen said. "I'll take care of you."

But I couldn't squeeze her hard enough to stop the stinging; I let my eyes
be brushed by the falling goblet-shape of her hair.

"Oh now," she said. "Now, all right."

The cobblestones were blurry; we seemed miles in the air and rising.
There were bears running below me, blowing on the coals that some fiend
had left on my calves.

"It's a castle!" said Siggy. "Why, the *Gasthof*'s a castle!"

But I couldn't be so surprised. With Gallen von St. Leonhard taking care
of me, I could expect a castle.

"Well," Gallen said. "It *was* a castle once."

"It's *still* a castle!" said Siggy, his voice miles away and overrun by
trampling bears. And from forty motorcycle seats distant, he said, "A castle
is always a castle."

And the last things I saw were the little boomerangs of forsythia petals that littered our way and were flung confettilike behind us, hurled in the terrible draft of the cycle's exhaust.

I shut my eyes and went giddy in my Gallen's lovely hair.

Cared For

"Well now," Siggy was saying, "it's a piece of luck our Graff blinked out like that, or he'd have caused some stir, having his pants pulled off."

"You were gentle, though, weren't you?" said Gallen.

"Of course, girl," he was saying. "I put him in the bath with his pants on and did everything underwater." He was saying, "Then I drained the bath out from under him and let him lie."

But I still *felt* underwater, and I couldn't see anything. There were high, hard walls around me, and my legs were wrapped up in slime.

"Oh, help," I whispered, but not a pinprick of light broke my blackness.

And Siggy was saying, "Then I greased some towels with that gunk your auntie gave me, and I swaddled him up like Jesus."

"But where is he now?" Gallen said.

"Oh, where am I now?" I bellowed.

"In the bathtub!" said Siggy, and a harsh doorway of light swung over me; I looked down at myself, at the towels wrapped from shins to belly.

"He's had a fine nap," said Siggy.

"You didn't have to wrap up so much of him," Gallen said.

"Well, I thought you'd want a peek," said Siggy, "and the towels were easier than dressing him."

Their heads looked over the bathtub, but everything was all awhack— as if they were kneeling on the floor, because their chins barely made it to the tub rim.

"Stand up!" I shouted. "Why are you down there?"

"Oh, dear," said Gallen.

"Out of his head," Siggy told her.

It's a monster of a bathtub, I thought. But I said, "Let me down easy, up there!"

"God, Graff," said Siggy, and to Gallen he said, "He's ninny. He needs more sleep."

Then I watched their shadows bent over double and hinged at the ceiling and at the top of the wall; they were moving diagonally to the doorway, and their shadows grew jagged and huge.

"God!" I cried.

"Praise Him!" said Siggy, and they left me to my dark.

It wasn't a bad bit of dark, though; I had the tub walls, cool and smooth, to touch with my tongue, and I could latch hold of the tub rim with both hands, steering myself wherever I felt I must be going—whenever I shut my eyes.

In mad little swirls I was sledding about the bathroom when the door-way-shaped light came at me again, and a shadow unhinged itself, wall to ceiling—grew smaller, fled free-spirited down the other wall, just before the doorway of light closed.

"I saw you," I said to whatever hadn't gotten out. "I know very well you're in here, you frotter!"

"Be quiet, Graff," said Gallen.

"All right," I said, and I listened for her to come nearer; she sounded like she was under the bathtub. Then I felt the silky little shiver of her blouse across my hand on the tub rim.

"Hello, Gallen," I said.

"Are you all right, Graff?"

"I can't see you," I said.

"Well, that's good," said Gallen. "Because I've come to change your bandages and make them right."

"Oh, but Siggy can do that."

"He's got you wrapped too much."

"I feel fine," I said.

"You don't either. I'm just going to take off these old towels and put on a real bandage."

"It's nice that you work here," I said, and her braid end brushed my chest.

"Hush," she said.

"Why are you so far below me, Gallen?"

"I'm above you, silly," she said.

"Well, it must be a very deep tub."

"It's on a platform and seems so," she said.

Then I felt her hands find my chest and skitter down my hips.

"Arch your back, Graff."

One towel unwound, so lightly her hands never touched me.

"Again," she said, and I arched for another; I felt myself tubcool and naked to the knees. When she leaned to catch my big toes for handles, her braid plopped in my lap.

"Your hair tickles," I said.

"Where?"

"Tickles," I said, and caught the braid with both my hands. I swished it over me, and she tugged it back.

"You stop, Graff."

"I want to see the back of your neck," I said.

She was unwinding from my ankles up, and when she got to the hot, sticky places on my calves, she unwound very slowly; they were the most congealed towels.

"Where have you hidden your braid?"

"Never mind," she said. All the towels were off now.

"Can you see in the dark, Gallen?"

"I can't!"

"If you could," I said, "you'd see me—"

"I would, all right."

"—all pink and scattered-hairy, like a baby ape."

"That's nice," she said. "Now stop."

But I was able to reach out and find her head, and slide my hand under her chin, and run the backs of my knuckles across and down her throat to the first knot of her braid, tucked into her blouse.

"I want to see the back of your neck," I said.

She was putting on the new bandages now; the gauze wound lightly and fast. She bound only my calves, and she didn't hobble my legs together; that was Siggy's sort of work.

"I've a clean towel to cover you," she said.

"Is it a monstrous towel?"

"Arch," she said, and she whisked it around me so fast I was fanned by the draft.

"Now give us some light," I said.

"I'm not supposed to be here, Graff. My aunt thinks I'm turning down beds."

"I'll just have a look at your neck, Gallen," I said.

"And you won't grab me, will you?"

"No."

"Or pull off your towel?"

"Of course not!"

"Once a man did—in the hall, my aunt said. He just pulled it off in front of her."

Then she danced the doorway's bright light across us, and she leaned over me. I turned her face against my shoulder, and lifted her rich braid; I folded her ear down, and looked.

Why yes, in the down of her neck was the soft welt I'd given her.

"You're not unmarked yourself," I said, and I pecked her on the spot.

"You're not grabbing," she said, "are you?" And I let my hands lie on the tub floor; I pecked her twice more on the ear. And she touched my chest with her hand, just with the points of her fingers; she wouldn't let her palm lie flush. She kept her face turned against my shoulder; she touched me as stilly as she could. Her weight wasn't on me. She was like a long, lightly stunned fish—made to lie coolly atwitch, but airy in the hand.

"I'm going now," she said.

"Why do I have to stay in the bathtub?"

"I guess you don't."

"Where's Siggy?" I said.

"Getting you flowers."

"Getting me flowers?"

"Yes," said Gallen. "He's got a bowl of water, and he's going to fill it full of forsythia petals."

Then a wood-creek shuddered the walls and crept under the tub, and my Gallen flicked as noiselessly across the room as her shadow; the rectangle of bright doorway drew round its sides on itself, and my light disappeared like a water drop in a sponge.

Out of the Bathtub,
Life Goes On

Notorious Graff,
Lord of the Tub
Where nymphets come to water.
Grabby Graff,
Sly in the Tub,
Leads virgins to their slaughter.
Bottomless Graff,
Fiend of the Tub,
Wooer of beasts and nymphets.
Appalling Graff,
Stealthy in Tub,
Makes virgins into strumpets.

Oh, Graff!
Rotten Graff!
For your ass a briar staff,
To teach you to be kinder.

So writes Siegfried Javotnik, poet of the humdrum and shell-shocked ear —bearer of forsythia petals afloat in a borrowed bowl.

No one ever gave me a poem before, so I said, "I think you cheat on your rhymes."

"You shouldn't have gotten out of the bathtub," said Siggy. "You might have swooned and cracked your oafish head."

"The flowers are great, Sig. I want to thank you for them."

"Well, they're certainly not for you," he said. "They're for our room in general."

"It's a nice room," I said.

We had a large, iron-grate window with a deep ledge; the window swung out and let in the sound of the falls. The old castle had a courtyard that our window opened to; we could see the motorcycle parked by the fullest forsythia bush—a lovely, weaponlike hulk of such purposeful machinery, misplaced in the yellows of the garden.

There were two beds, separated by a carved magazine stand. One bed was turned down. The sheet lay back crisply unwrinkled; the pillow was punched up high and light.

"Did you fix my bed, Sig?"

"No, Graff, I did not. I'm sure it was your nymphet, or perhaps her kindly aunt."

"Her aunt is kindly, is she?"

"A dear old babe, Graff—a loving old soul. Why, she lent me this bowl for the flowers!"

"Well," I said.

"For a small price," said Siggy. "A pittance."

"Which was?" I said.

"My tolerance of her questions," said Siggy. "Where we came from and how we came. And why we came. And what is it we do for work?"

"Work?"

"Work, Graff. That's how we live."

"That's a question, isn't it?" I said.

"But not her best one, Graff. She wished to know which one of us had the eyes for Gallen."

"Well," I said, "a kindly aunt, she is."

"So I eased her mind on that score," said Siggy. "I told her we were both raving queers and she needn't worry."

"Frot you!" I said. "And what did she do then?"

"She lent me her bowl," said Siggy, "so I could pick flowers for you."

Off the Scent

"I'm Frau Tratt," said Gallen's aunt. "We haven't met, as you were carried in."

"A disgrace to me, Frau Tratt," I said.

"How are your legs?" she asked.

"They've had the right sort of care," I told her.

"I take good care of my Graff," said Siggy.

"Oh yes, I can see," said Auntie Tratt, and she left us one menu to share.

The dining room of the Gasthof Schloss Wasserfall overlooked the dam, which added a woozy, bilious sensation to eating and drinking. The great falls spewed a froth on the windows, which made running, delta patterns down the glass. My stomach rolled over and gave me back an old taste.

"I've not seen that Gallen in a while," I said.

"She's probably in our bathtub, Graff. Waiting for you."

And the street lamps came on in the town, although the dark was another rusty evening-hour away. The lamplight flecked the water shot over the falls, filtered through it just at the arc where it bent to fall; the river held a million tiny shapes of dress-up colors reflected from the town.

Siggy was saying, "Unless, of course, she's heard from her auntie that you've no interest in girls."

"And thanks must go to you for that," I said. "I'll have to straighten it out."

"Ah, Graff. You'll find it's quite a mess, straightening out that sort of thing."

"She won't believe it anyway," I said.

And some of the shops blinked their lights across the river; the towers bobbed downstream and toppled over the falls.

"Not hungry?" asked Auntie Tratt.

"I got very full, just sitting here," I said.

"Ah, Frau Tratt," said Siggy. "When you're in love, the other appetites suffer."

"Well, well," said Auntie Tratt, and she took our menu away.

"I don't think you need to carry this much farther, Sig."

"But, Graff! It's sure to put the old madam off your scent."

"And put us out of her *Gasthof* too."

"We can't afford it anyway," he said. "And your baby Gallen can't afford it either."

The Foot of Your Bed

My Gallen was not in the bathtub, so Siggy thought he'd have a bath.

"If you wouldn't mind," he said.

"I'd be happy for you," I told him. I sat on the window ledge while he splashed about and hummed in the tub; he was spanking the water with the flat of his hand, making sharp, beaverlike slaps.

Outside, the courtyard was full of soft yellows and greens; the evenings were taking longer and longer to come on. The falls brought a mist round the castle; I felt the wet of the air on my face.

"Come down here, Graff," said Gallen.

"Where are you?" I asked into the garden.

"On your motorcycle," Gallen said, but I could see the motorcycle looking gruff and shaggy like an old bull under the forsythia—lurking surly in the fairytale light of evening—and my Gallen was nowhere around it.

"No, you're not," I said. "I can see."

"All right, I'm under your window. I can see your chin."

"Step out, then," I said.

"I'm naked all over," said Gallen. "I haven't a thing on."

"You have so," I said.

"You come down here, Graff."

"I won't wear anything either," I said.

"Oh, you better," said Gallen, and she stepped out where I could see her, blousy in her long-sleeved ruffles and her apron full of frills. I thought: God, she can't be more than fourteen.

"Is your auntie with you?" I asked.

"Of course not," she said. "You come down."

So I danced down the prickly carpeted hall. The chandeliers swung overhead, giving me weary winks, as if they were tired of seeing such stealthy evening schemes go padding by underneath them. And the local soccer teams rebuked me from their framed, fixed poses on the lobby wall; year by year, their faces never changed. There was one year when they all shaved off their mustaches. There were the war years, when there'd been a girls' team—but righteous, athletic faces nonetheless. They were faces that had seen you before, had seen countless adventurers and lovers creeping through that lobby, and they'd rebuked them all. Impatient toes stirred their ready, soccer feet. They'd have left their photographs and kicked me, for sure, if only they hadn't seen so many secrets like mine.

The castle let me safely out, and Gallen said, "Who's there?"

"Bright pink Graff," I told her, "as shiny and nude as the Christ Child."

"You step out," she said.

I saw her in the vines along the castle wall; she ducked under the window ledges and waved me after her.

"Come around," she said. "Around here, Graff."

We turned the castle's cornerstone; the heavy spray from the falls met us. The rush of water silenced the crickets, and the gun slits of Waidhofen's towers, lit along the riverbank, were cutting light-slices in the creamy swirls of foam below the dam.

"It's been so long since I've seen you, Graff," said Gallen.

I sat down with her, our backs against the castle; her shoulder overlapped mine just a little. Her braid was coiled on top of her head, and she gave it a pat before she looked at me.

"How did I fix your legs?" she said.

"Oh, I'm fine now, Gallen. May I see your neck again?"

"Why can't you just talk?" she said.

"Words fail me," I told her.

"Well, you must try," said Gallen.

"I wish we had adjoining rooms," I tried.

"I'll never tell you where my room is," she said.

"Then I'll look in every one."

"Auntie has a dog sleep at the foot of her bed."

"Who sleeps at the foot of yours?"

"If I thought you were staying long, I'd have a lion. How long will you stay, Graff?" she said.

"Fate shapes our course," I told her.

"If I thought you were staying long, I'd tell you where my room is."

"Would your auntie give you a dowry?"

"I don't believe you're going to stay another day."

"Where would you go for your wedding trip?" I said.

"Where would you take me?"

"On a cruise in a bathtub!" I said. "A huge bathtub."

"And would Siggy come with us?" said Gallen.

"Well," I said, "I don't know how to drive the motorcycle."

"Here," she said. "See my neck? What you did is going away."

But it was getting too dark to see; I turned her shoulders and pulled her back against me. Oh, she never would give me all her weight; a part of her sat up away from me when I kissed her.

"You'll make it come back, Graff."

"Would you show me how your hair is when it's down and loose," I said.

And she reached up to uncoil her braid; under my fingers I felt the long, hard line of her collarbones, squared up to her shoulders when she raised her arms.

"What a lot of bones you have, Gallen," I said.

She brought her braid over her shoulder and undid the end knot. Then she tugged apart the thick-wound bands of her hair, combing her fingers through it, letting it crackle loose and dance like auburn milkweed in the spray gusts from the falls.

"There's nothing to cover my bones," said Gallen. "I haven't filled out in years."

"Oh, it's ages ago since you were fat," I said.

"Are you kissing or biting?" she asked.

"You're a little filled out," I said, and I put my arms round her waist, touched my fingertips to her long little belly. She seemed to draw herself from under me; I felt I was falling inside her.

"You're scaring me, Graff," she said. "You just want to scare me."

"I don't either."

"And that old Siggy-friend of yours," she said, "he just wants to scare Auntie."

"He does?"

"He did, and he meant to," she said, "because it's certainly not a bit true. And wouldn't I know it, if it were true of you?"

"Oh, you would," I said.

Her hair was wrinkled from the braiding and left a bare place behind her ear. So I kissed her there, and she moved a little more away, and came a little back, and pressed my hands down flush to her sides. "Feel the bones again," she whispered.

She relaxed, and then she didn't; she jounced away from me and stood up. "Oh, Graff," she said. "You mustn't think that I do anything I do on purpose. I don't know what I'm doing at all."

"Don't be frightened of what I might think," I said.

"Are you really pretty nice, Graff?" she asked. "Even though you scare me a little, aren't you really pretty good?"

"Bright pink Graff," I said, "to you."

And there were dramatic lightning flashes across the river, paling the yellows of the garden. The thunder was dry and splintery, far-off and in a world I didn't live in. Gallen's hair was bleached a brighter red in the lightning.

She skipped along the wall to the castle corner. When she got to the cornerstone, she let me come up to her; I put my arms round her waist again, and she leaned back into me. But she wouldn't turn; she just held my hands to her hips. "Oh my, Graff," she said.

"My, your bones," I whispered.

We looked into the courtyard. The few night-lit windows threw the bright squares and crosshatches of their grates over the lawn. Against the crosshatching I saw Siggy's shadow, arms over his head.

"What's that?" said Gallen.

"Siggy's touching his toes," I said. But, oh no, that wasn't it. He had ahold of the window grating; he'd reached over his head and had caught the weave of rungs and bars, and he seemed to press himself out into the courtyard—like some nocturnal enlivened beast, testing the strength of his cage.

"He's not touching his toes at all," said Gallen.

"It's just a stretching exercise," I said. And I hurried her along under the window ledges; I gave her a sudden blurry kiss at the monstrous castle door.

"We've got to watch out for your auntie," I said, and I went into the castle ahead of her.

And did the soccer players seem suddenly interested? Was there a light in their eyes that hadn't shone since the day they were fixed, framed and hung?

But there was no light coming under my own door, and for a long while I waited in the hall—listening to the perfect rhythm of my Siggy-friend's fake snores.

A Blurb from the Prophet

Will you ride with me?
The prison of the Sybarites
Is still fat and secure.

Will you always be such
Easy prey for sycophants?

Will you never admit
There are greater devotions?

Will you ride with me?
While the Sybarites take their sleep
We can set their prisoners free.

"You're a better snorer than a poet," I said. "I think you're more conscious about snoring."

"Did the thunder wake you, Graff?"

"I read your poem in the lightning."

"Ah," he said. "A veritable bolt lit your way."

"And did you summon it?" I asked.

"It was very officious of me," he admitted.

"From the window, Sig? Hanging on the grate, were you? Summoning wayward bolts?"

"Not at first," he said. "At first I was just watching, when old Fate happened along with the nightfall and gave me a second looking-over."

"Listen to that rain that's coming, Sig. Did you have a hand in that too?"

"Nothing to do with it, Graff. It's a slip-up, that rain. And all along the way, Graff, it's the slip-ups that have to be reckoned with."

"I wish I'd seen Fate too," I said. "It must make a fellow very knowing."

"Did you frot her yet, Graff?"

"I didn't," I said.

"You have a natural respect for youth," he said.

"When's leaving day, Sig?"

"Ah, the tearful departure! When can you whip yourself away?"

"You can be a prodding frotter, Siggy. I'd like to have some sleep now."

"So Graff would like to sleep!" he yelled, and he sat up with his pillow. "Sleep then," he said.

"Sleep yourself," I said.

"Like a volcano, Graff. This old Siggy sleeps like a volcano."

"I don't care how you sleep," I said.

"No, it's true you don't, Graff. You don't care a sweet frot!"

"Oh, Christ!" I said.

"He's in the bathroom, Graff," said Siggy, "cooking up what's next for you and me."

What Christ Cooked Up
in the Bathroom

The light was early in our room, even though the rain still puddled the courtyard; I could hear the fat drops *ping* on the pipes of the motorcycle. I propped myself up on my elbows and peered out the window through the grating; the wet cobblestones of the drive looked like a cluster of egg shapes, and I could see Auntie Tratt preparing for the milkman.

She seemed to come into the courtyard from under the castle; she rolled two milkcans in front of her, prodding them with her floppy galoshes. The pink hem of her robe showed under her sacklike raingear; her hairnet slipped down to her eyebrows and made her forehead look like some puffy thing caught from the sea. The short shocks of her calves peeked between her clog tops and the hem of her robe; her flesh was as white as lard.

She set the milkcans on the cobblestones, just in front of the castle door; then she hurried down to the courtyard gate and opened it for the milkman. Only the milkman wasn't there yet; Auntie Tratt looked both ways on the street, and then she pelted back to the castle—flying her soggy hem, leaving the gateway clear.

The rain now drummed on the milkcans; it *pong*ed a deeper sound than it made off the motorcycle pipes.

In a sudden, mad flurry, as doomed as dancing on ice, the milkman arrived.

I saw the crooked-faced horse lurch into the gateway, tilting his blinders against all the possible momentum of the rickety cart and his own swaying body; the hitchmast shunted up along his sagging spine, and the mass of leathery harness and trappings leaned out against the corner this fool horse tried to cut. Then I saw the driver rein and crank up the horse's maw; and the whole cart pick itself up and skitter after the horse, wrenching on the hitchmast and slinging its awkward weight to one side of the animal's rump —as if a rider had flung himself off the horse's back at full gallop, keeping the reins in hand, and weighing as much as the horse.

The driver cried, "Jeee-*sus!*" and the cart hopped sideways on its two wheels, which locked and wouldn't spin.

The horse was waiting for all his legs to come down, and for the cart to follow him. And I waited for the fool driver to stop reining his poor horse's head so high up that the animal saw only the tops of the forsythia bushes, and not his own hooves landing on edge on the wet, egg-smooth cobblestones.

The horse came down on his side, with the hitchmast sliding along his spine and conking him in the ear; the little cart stopped high up on his rump. When his spongy ribs whomped the cobbles, the horse said, *"Gnif!"*

The fool driver pitched out of his seat and landed on all fours on the horse's neck, in a tangle of leather hitchings and the jingling iron rings. The milkcans made a terrible clamor in the slat-sided cart. The breeching slid up and lifted the horse's tail like a banner.

"What was that?" said Siggy.

And the milkman squatted on the horse's neck, jouncing like a spring just burst through an old bed.

"Jeee-*sus!* Horse!" he cried.

"God, Graff!" said Siggy. "What's going on?"

The milkman grabbed the sprawled horse by the ears and lifted the animal's head to his lap. He cradled the head and rocked back and forth on his haunches. *"Oh, sweet mother Jeee-sus, horse!"* he cried.

Then he pounded the horse's head on the cobblestones; he just tugged it up by the ears and flung it down again, leaning his weight after it. The horse's forehooves began to flay through the rain.

All the milkcan covers were tipped forward in the cart, and seemed like round, wet faces peering over the slatted sides. Auntie Tratt was stomping on the stoop to the main door, pushing her heels into her galoshes. She slopped crooked-footed along the drive to the milkman.

"Oh, here!" she said. "What can be the matter with you?"

The milkman, jockeying on the horse's neck, kept hold of the ears, laid his cheek in the hollow under the horse's jaw, and used his own head to batter the animal down. He was more expert at doing it now; he didn't try to lift the horse, he let the horse raise himself—just enough, to where the milkman was perfectly above the head, gripped on the ear handles. There he had the leverage; he could fling down so suddenly on the horse that its head would bounce a little before it lay on the cobbles—frothed over the bit, shook, bucked to raise itself again.

"Well, frotting Graff!" said Siggy. "If you won't tell me what's happening"—and he cloaked himself in the satiny pouf and hopped to the window ledge.

The horse was more frenzied now; the milkman was calm and terrible. The milkcart had ridden over the horse's rump, and the hitchmast bent like a great bow being strung on the horse's spine. And whenever the horse stopped churning, the hitchmast would spring back and over-straighten the unbelievable vertebrae.

But none of this bothered the milkman, he held so fiercely to the neck and ears, his cheek tucked in the jaw hollow.

"Oh my God," said Siggy.

"Berserk!" I said. "His brains must have muddled in the fall."

"*Aaah!*" said Siggy.

And Auntie Tratt moved gingerly about the scene, conscious of her pink hem in the rain.

And Siggy, the pouf cloaked over his shoulders and pinched to his throat —moving past me, one bare foot arched as a cat's back in wet grass— whooped over the magazine stand, was out the door and off down the hall. An utterly graceless pirouette round the stairwell, and his ballooning pouf snagged on the banister, just bending him backward as he took the steps; he let go of the pouf at his throat and went on. And he didn't come back for it. It gave me a satiny wave from the banister, fluffed by the draft from the main door opening wide and fast.

I ran back to my window.

And this is split-second seeing: someone new in the courtyard, a large man with pink knees and hairless legs below his lederhosen—an untucked ascot at the throat of his pajama tops, and very thick-soled sandals. He stood halfway between the main door and where Auntie Tratt was circling the fallen horse; stood with his hands on his hips, his hands stubbing suddenly at the ends of his arms—for he was a more or less wristless man, and a neckless, ankleless man besides.

He was saying, "Frau Tratt, what a terrible racket—it was very late when I got to bed"—and then he turned round to the castle and spread his arms as if someone were throwing him a bouquet from the door.

Siggy ran into him as dead-weight as a sandbag, and the man never closed his arms before he fell, or before Siggy's bare feet padded over his pajama chest.

Auntie Tratt was turning, a gesture beginning in her hands, the palms rolling up. Tiredly she said, "A fool, this driver—a crazy drunk." She just looked up and saw the puffy pink man pillowed on his ascot, his fingers twitching and his head moving very little. "It's going to rain all day," she said, and she caught a bit of Siggy flashing past her; she turned, her hands coming together.

Siggy's dazzling bottom was so sleek in the rain.

And the large, jointless man wet his ascot in a puddle, dabbed his mouth with it, lay just as he was on his back. "No!" he shouted. "No, nothing! He had nothing on *all over, all over.*"

And Siggy mounted the milkman; he worked his hands under the chin to a hold on the throat. Then he tucked his head down close to the milkman and bit into the back of his milky neck.

Down the prickly hall, I was hopping into my pants. Auntie Tratt came bobbing like a pigeon through the lobby; I saw her head jog by below me, just flit in and out of the slot in the stairwell.

Gallen had the pouf; she leaned against the banister, a touch of the satin to her cheek, and watched out the main door into the courtyard, where there were sounds of terrible suffering and pain—where the flaying horse jostled the milkcart about, and where the tumbled man sat up with his ascot hanging out of his mouth, gaping at the open castle door as if he expected a horde of naked men to come trampling him into the grooves of the cobblestones; and where Siggy rode the milkman through the garden, in and out of the forsythia.

"Graff," said Gallen, "my aunt's calling the police."

I took the pouf from her and nudged one of her small, upright breasts with my elbow. "Lovely little bosom," I said. "I'm afraid we'll be leaving you today."

"I couldn't sleep last night, Graff," she said.

But I had the pouf and I ran by her, into the courtyard.

The poor lopsided man made circles with his arms, tipped up his broad bottom and sat again. "He's all around," the man said. "Get nets and ropes." He gagged on his ascot. "Get dogs!" He choked, his arms still circling.

So in and out of the forsythia—the bell-shaped petals drooped with rain —in and out a strange figure was darting, bent over in the back bushes of the thicket, upright and charging by the motorcycle, here and there appearing, four-armed and two-headed; a terror-high, doglike wail marked the spot where I could expect it next to come in view.

The little needlepoints of rain fell icy on my back; I held the pouf like a bullfighter's cape, keeping it out from under my feet.

"Siggy?" I said.

In shiny raingear a hollow-eyed man with transparent ears came lurching between two fat forsythia bushes, spilling the rain from the burst cups of petals, showering the boomerang pieces of flower with his thudding galoshes —with a naked man on his back, fastened by teeth to the milky neck.

"*Blaaah-rooo!*" the fool driver was screaming.

Two bushes away, I crossed between, after the next holler—the next peep of double-man to straighten up and blunder on.

Then they were one bush away; I looked over a squat shrub and could have touched the two heads with my hand, if the shrub hadn't stabbed me when I reached.

"Siggy!" I said.

In the courtyard, on the stoop to the castle door, I heard the tumbled man yelling, "Get the dogs on him! Why aren't the dogs here?"

And now we ran in the same bush row; I followed the wet-streaked, flexed bottom, the long toes bent back and dragged behind the churning milkman, who was staggering more headdown, more slowly now. I could catch them.

Then the milkman was three-headed; he couldn't run, he swayed—his shoulders coming back—and his knees quit.

"Oh, dear God," he moaned. And we were all in a pile in the black garden-muck, the milkman groveling under Siggy, skittering his hips out sideways and thrashing his arms. I had Siggy's head, but he wouldn't come loose. I got under his chin and tried to work open his mouth, but he ground his jaw into my hands until my knuckles were cracking. Then I biffed him in the ears and kneeled on his spine; but he held. And the milkman began some chanting wail, his hands digging back into Siggy's hair.

"Sig, let up," I said. "Let him go!" But he clenched his teeth still, and kept the man from turning his hips.

So I broke a switch of forsythia off a bush, and lashed it across Siggy's rear, and he writhed sideways; but I could still catch him, and did. At the third fanny lash he rolled free of the milkman and sat his smarting rump in the cool, kind mud.

He put his hands under himself and slopped the mud over his hips as if he were dressing himself in it; his mouth made a little puckered *O*. I held out the pouf to him, and he made whistling noises.

"The police are coming, Sig," I said.

And the milkman inched away from us; he scooped up a great splot of mud to the mauve welt on his neck. He made the whistling sounds too.

Siggy wrapped himself in the pouf. I caught him under his arms and pushed him up in front of me—out of the bushes and along the castle wall. Siggy began to march; he took great strides that jogged his head up and down. His feet left spread and terrible toe marks in the ooze. "There's a mound of mud in my ass, Graff," he said; he jiggled.

There was a mound of sorts in the lobby too. Auntie Tratt, sponging, held the fat, dizzy man in a chair. She tried to clean the mud off his lederhosen; my Gallen held the water pail to dip the sponge.

"Well," the man said, "I heard someone coming and I was turning around to see." And Siggy came up the stoop with the pouf draped over one shoulder and down between his legs.

The dizzy man rocked in his chair; he made an odd, fishy gurgle. He hammered his fists in his lap, where his ascot lay puddled like a napkin over his bright knees; his lower lip was as purple and fat as a beet.

"Frau Tratt," said Siggy. "It's raining up a flood, fit to burst the dam. The end of the earth!" And he paraded by her.

The pouf flared out as he swung on the banister, taking the stairs on upward—rhythmically, with flourish, and two at a time.

Massing the Forces
of Justice

Now and then a clod of mud appeared in the air above the forsythia, a long spitter of debris trailing behind it. It was always flung nearly straight up, and followed by unreasonable stamping sounds and violent shakings of the bushes. The milkman was composing himself in the garden.

The poor horse was only making his lot worse. He'd managed to turn himself, still on his side, so that he now lay perpendicular to the hitchmast, and under it; he'd twisted himself so tightly in his breeching that he hadn't room to move any more. A lump the size of a tennis ball swelled on the ridge of his eyebrow and closed one eye. The other eye blinked into the rain, and the horse lay back and wheezed—his tail switching.

"Is it still raining, Graff?" said Siggy.

"Harder now."

"But it's not an electrical storm, is it?"

"No," I said, "not any more."

"Well," he said, "it's not a good idea to have a bath during an electrical storm."

"You're safe," I said.

"It's an enormous bathtub, Graff. I can see how you managed it."

"The milkman's still in the bushes," I said.

"Are you taking a bath after me, Graff?"

"I didn't get that muddy," I said.

"How fussy of you," said Siggy.

"The police are here, Sig," I told him.

The green Volkswagen with the bar of blue lights had some trouble getting through the gate and past the milkcart. There were two policemen, high-booted and in immaculate uniform, the collars of their rain slickers identically curled to a sneer; and perhaps there was a third one, out of uniform—in a long coat of black leather, belted, and under a jaunty black beret.

"They've brought an assassin," I said.

"The police?"

"With a secret agent."

"It's probably the mayor," said Siggy. "A small town, a rainy day—what has a mayor got to do?"

The three went into the castle; I could hear the man who was being sponged, creaking his chair and raising his voice to greet them.

"Siggy?" I said. "How many kicks would it take to start that good motorcycle?"

But he gave me a bathtub song:

> Disaster, disaster,
> We're having a
> Disaster.
> If we try to
> Get away,
> Disaster
> Will run faster.

"Oh, frot your damn rhyming," I said.

"You should have a bath, Graff," said Siggy. He splashed for me.

And one of the uniformed policemen came out in the courtyard, carrying some large hedge-trimming shears. He straddled the horse and squatted on the poor animal's back; then he snipped along the hitchmast, freeing the harness. But the horse just lay there, dizzy, with his old blinky one-eye; the policeman hissed and turned back for the castle.

It was then he saw a mudclot come spinning out of the forsythia, and heard the stamping, battering sounds of the milkman in the garden.

"Hello?" said the policeman. "You! Hello!"

And the milkman spattered handfuls of mud and sticks in the air.

"You!" the policeman shouted. And he advanced on the garden, with the hedge trimmers held in front of him like a water douser's rod.

I could see the milkman darting from bush to bush—crouching, scooping mud and twigs and hurtling them in the air; he lurked, watching his little bombs fall; and with cartoon stealth, he darted on.

"Sig, the milkman's lost his head," I said. And the policeman tiptoed into the forsythia, the great, vicious beak of the hedge trimmers held before him.

Then I heard them gathering in the hall outside our door. The light slot under the door was patched and blurred by sneaking feet; an elbow, a hip or a belly brushed the wood. They were milling, their voices thin and whispery—now and then a word, a phrase, would stand out clearly and be hissed, be hushed:

"as the day he was born"

"there should be"

"live together"

"hoe"

"must be"

"laws"

"dogs"

"unnatural"

"God knows"

And everything else—as if someone were speaking through a fan, and only the quickest speech-pieces made it between the blades—was chopped and whished into a single voice, indistinguishable from the rub of clothes and human weight against the walls and door.

"Sig," I said. "They're out in the hall."

"Massing the forces of justice?" he asked.

"Are you staying in the tub?"

"Why, hello!" he cried. "Look here!" And there was a lot of splashing. "Lash marks!" he said. "Whippings! Pink as your tongue, Graff. You did some job with your switch, you should see."

"I couldn't get you off him," I said.

"My ass is remarkable!" he said. "Veritable grooves!" And I heard him plunking and skidding in the tub.

Then there was a tiny knocking on the door, and the hall was very quiet; there were only two feet taking up the light slot now.

"Graff?" said my Gallen.

"Have they made you our Judas?" I said.

"Oh, Graff," she said.

Then weight came against the door, and someone was trying a key.

"Stand back!" said Auntie Tratt.

"It's unlocked," I told them.

A uniformed policeman booted the door open, springing the knob; he came sideways into the room, and the doorway filled behind him. Anxious Auntie Tratt, her arms crossed; the newly sponged man, pushing his shiny knees into the room; between them was the assassin, or the mayor. And nowhere was my Gallen now.

"Where's the other one?" said the sponged man, walking his knees forward.

And Siggy said, "You should see, Graff," and opened the bathroom door.

He flashed to all of us his stinging, washed bottom. The pink scars glowed across his rump like the tilted smiles of new moons.

"There!" said Auntie Tratt. "Do you see?"

And it was the mayor, all right—the formidable *Bürgermeister,* who hadn't removed his beret for Auntie Tratt, but who removed it now with a precise nod to the fanny poised in the bathroom doorway. A perfect job of doffing, quick enough to catch the fanny before Siggy leapt his hind end back in the bathroom and whomped shut the door.

"I see, Frau Tratt," said the mayor. "We all see, I'm sure." And he barely raised his voice. "Herr Javotnik?" he called. "Herr Siegfried Javotnik."

But we could hear Siggy padding across the bathroom floor; he thumped up on the platform and plunked back in the tub.

The Revealing of Crimes

He wouldn't unlock the bathroom door, so we all waited in the lobby downstairs—all of us except one policeman, who was left behind to search our room.

The very upset pink man said, *"Herr Bürgermeister,* I can't understand why we just don't smash down the door." But the mayor was watching his other policeman, leading the milkman through the courtyard and up the castle stoop.

"Drunk again, Josef Köller?" the mayor said. "Having wrecks and beating your horse?"

The milkman was so muddy it was hard to see his fabulous neck-welt. But the mayor moved closer and examined.

"Taught a small lesson?" he said; he poked around the welt, and the milkman drew himself in like a turtle. "Perhaps a bit more than you had coming," the mayor said.

"And my milk is all froth," said Auntie Tratt.

"Then, Josef," the mayor said, "you'll leave an extra can?"

The milkman tried to nod, but his jowls knotted and he made a winced-up face.

"He's a madman," I told the mayor.

"Bitten on the neck," the mayor said, "and bitten hard enough to break the skin and raise a welt the size of my fist! And *who's* a madman? Running nude in the courtyard! Riding a man! Biting a man! And dallying about in a bathtub, locked in! An exhibitionist and a flagellant!" roared the mayor.

"Worse!" Auntie Tratt said. "A pervert!"

"A screwdriver!" bellowed the pink man. "Just a screwdriver would get you in that bathroom. And if you'd only gotten the dogs here on time, there'd be no mess now."

Then the upstairs policeman appeared on the stairs—the toes of his boots so perfectly together he looked as if he would fall.

"He's still in there," the policeman said. "He sang me a song."

"What did you find?" the mayor asked.

"Saltshakers," said the policeman.

"Saltshakers?" the mayor said—his voice like the high-pitched gnaw of the rain on the castle's hollow-tiled roof.

"Fourteen," said the policeman. "Fourteen saltshakers."

"My God," the mayor said. "A pervert, for sure."

Fetching the Details

What's going on? These interruptions! They're what happens when you stand still long enough to let the real and unreasonable world catch up with you. And listen, Graff—that's not standing still very long.

My father Vratno, Vratno Javotnik, born in Jesenje before there were wheels in that part of Yugoslavia, moved to Slovenjgradec, where he fell in with the Germans—who were doing things with wheels no one had seen before; and with them rolled to Maribor, where a good road ran him straight across the border into Austria. And by himself, for he was sly.

Young Vratno followed the tank-trodden way to Vienna, where my mother was starving stoically and beautifully, and waiting to fall in with someone as sly as him—and not expecting, I'm sure, to play a part in the conception of anyone as born to wheels as me.

Young Vratno, who said across his soup to me, "Harder and harder it's getting, to have a thing going for yourself that isn't somehow the apprenticeship to something that's gone before; and not yours and never will be. And never a thing to make you happy." That's just what the poor fart said, I'm told.

Oh, my father was a splendid, melodramatic troll for mischief all his own; and so am I. And so are you, Graff. And so this world might yet be spared the cool, old drudge of death-by-dullness.

But these interruptions! Digressions. Oh, it's repetitive death every time you let the world catch up with you!

Young Vratno, the ladling spoon a part of his lip and the soup becoming a part of his speech—he said, "Listen, you've got to move in the split-second interim between the time they find you out and the time they decide what to do with you. Just a hop ahead, and you're a cut above!" So he said, or so I'm told.

Siggy's note. Pinned to the bottom sheet of my bed, where my bottom found it—a starchy crumple to make me grope for the light. And I hadn't seen him leave any note.

In fact, when the mayor had me try my hand at getting him out of the bath, and when I'd come into the room again, Siggy was tub-slicked and dressed—all except the duckjacket, to which he was applying the last, thick rubs of saddle soap.

And the mayor's voice came up from the lobby: "If you can't get him out of there, he'll have to pay for the door!"

Siggy had the raingear out of the rucksack, the plastic bags to cover his boots, the rubber bands to wrap the bags tight to his calves, and the saddle soap. The duckjacket took a candle gloss and looked like a thing melted over him. "Don't worry," he whispered. "You draw them off, and I'll be back for you."

"They're down in the lobby, Sig. They'll hear you."

"Then get them up here. I'll be back, Graff—a day, two nights, at the most. You've got the pack and all the money I don't need for gas."

"Sig," I said.

But he opened the window and swung out on the ledge. He put on the goggles and helmet—a parachutist tightening his flyaway parts. Then he stepped his boots into the bags; they ballooned; he looked like a man with his feet in glass pots.

"Siggy?"

"Graff," he said, "we're in need of *details!* After all, Graff, we didn't really have much of a look at the place—what with your sporting with that hippo of a girl, and with the offense we took to it right away—now did we?"

And I thought: What? How your mind can leap—to something the spanning of is beyond me.

He jumped.

And I thought: What a show! You could have climbed down the vines. He made a *splotz* sound in the garden-muck.

I heard the mayor's voice again. "Herr Graff! Is he making up his mind?"

"Oh, I think he'll talk," I called, and I went out in the hall. "Come up now!" I yelled, and I could hear them thudding the stairs.

I could hear the damp-chilled motorcycle too; it made short and engine-like sucks—caught and faltered once, like a bull-voiced man who started a shout, but gagged in mid-holler. Those rounding the stairwell, they heard it all too; we faced each other with the safe length of the hall between us.

Then I ran back to my room and the window; I could hear the stairs being swung down upon to the lobby. The mayor, though, came alongside me; his eager face spasmed from cheek to ear.

Siggy had caught it and held it; thick balls of gray were lobbed from the tailpipes, as weightless and wispy as dust kittens. They seemed like flimsy wads of hair, so tangled that we'd later find them in the garden, strung from the forsythia like mangled pieces of wigs.

Siggy smoothed the engine in one throttling, up and down—and lined up with the gateway, still narrowed by the strewn milkcart.

So it was *before* the policemen were off the castle stoop—and *before* the shoving milkman, the pink-washed man and Auntie Tratt had all shouted themselves out the castle door—that Siggy sped through the gap, posting on the foot pedals. The hunched, waxy duckjacket gleamed like a beetle's back. And even through the rain, I could hear him hit three of his gears.

Oh, a lover of ill weather and of the overall, precarious condition! This was—why yes, the trial marathon to Vienna—Siggy's reconnaissance mission to the Hietzinger Zoo.

The Real and
Unreasonable World

So I read the note more than once, and Gallen saw the light under my door. I saw her foot shadows, creepy and soft.

"Gallen?" I said. "I'm unlocked"—because no one had fixed the knob that the policeman had sprung.

And I expected her in nightgown, unblushing black lace, and sleekly unfrilled.

But she had her apron on; she jingled into my room, hands stuck in the flowery pocket for coins.

"I know," I said. "You want to sleep with me."

"Stop it," she said. "I can't stay a second."

"It'll take hours," I told her.

"Oh, Graff," she said. "They're talking about you."

"Do they like me?"

"You helped him get away," she said. "No one knows what to do."

"They'll think of something," I said.

"Graff, they said you don't have much money."

"So you don't want to marry me, Gallen?"

"Graff! They really mean to get you."

"Come and sit, Gallen," I said. "I really mean to get you too."

But she sat on Siggy's bed; it was so soft and had such a sag in it that her knees were tipped face-up to me—lovely little chin-sized knees.

"Stop blushing, Gallen."

"What are you doing in bed like that?" she said.

"I was reading."

"I'll bet you've nothing on," she said. "Underneath the covers, I'll bet you sleep without a stitch."

"Does it drive you wild to guess?" I asked.

"They're going to get you, Graff," she said. "I just saw your light, so I knew you were up. I thought you'd be dressed."

"Well, I'm hidden," I said. "Come sit on my bed."

"Graff—the mayor and my aunt, they're cooking something up."

"Well, what?" I said.

"They've looked through your stuff, you know. They saw what your money was like."

"I've enough to pay for this room," I said.

"And there's not much left after that, Graff. They can arrest you for not having money."

"I'm a loiterer," I said. "I always knew someone would find it out."

"And you helped him get away, Graff. They can get you for that."

"I can't wait to see what they'll do," I told her.

"They're going to make you get a job," she said.

Well, that was something, all right—a frotting job. Of course, I could just scram, make off for the mountains and fish, and tell Gallen where Siggy could find me when he came back looking; leave the money with her for the *Gasthof* bill.

Now I thought that, but Gallen had her eyes on me—and that one lovely line making the fine, sharp jut to her jaw, putting the slope off her shoulder that ran long to her wrist and the angle her hand made; her fingers were as sensitive as a Braille reader's, I was sure; and her dark lip-color, the rust blush-color on her cheek, and her pale, high-freckled forehead. She went as well together as the different ripe- and sun-spots of a peach.

So I said, "What kind of a job?"

"Just a little job," she said. "Just another way to have someone keeping an eye on you so they'll know when he's coming back."

"So they think he'll be back?"

"I think so too," she said. "Will he be back, Graff?"

"Are you a Judas, Gallen?"

"Oh, Graff," she said. "I'm just warning you what they're thinking they'll do." And she made her braid hide her face from me. "And I've got to know when you'll be leaving. I want to know where you're going so I can write you. And I want you to keep writing that you'll come back."

"Come sit here," I said, but she shook her head.

"They think he'll come back, Graff, because Auntie said you were lovers."

"What sort of a job is it?" I said.

"You've got to bring in the bees," she said.

"What bees?" I said.

"The bee boxes in the apple orchards," said Gallen. "The hives are full and ready to be brought in. It's a job you do at night, and they think that's the most likely time you'd be trying to leave with him."

"And if I won't take the job, Gallen?"

"Then they arrest you," she said. "You're a vagrant, they'll say, and they'll lock you up. You helped him escape, and they can get you for that."

"I could skip out tonight," I said.

"Could you?" she said, and she went round to the other side of Siggy's bed; she sat with her back to me. "If you think you could do that," she whispered, "I could help you do it."

Well, I thought: Is it forsythia that turns the moon so yellow and sends it through my window to your hair—hues the air vermilion above your small, lovely head? "I couldn't do that, Gallen," I said.

She jingled her pocket of coins. "I've got to go now, Graff," she said.

"Would you come and tuck me in?" I asked.

She turned quick and smiled. Oh yes. Oh my.

"Don't you grab," she said. And she came round to my bedside, put off my light. "Get your arms under," she said to the dark.

She tucked once and came round to my other side. I was wriggling an arm out, but she tucked too fast. Then she pounced her hands down on my shoulders; her braids fell in my face.

"Oh, I'm so clumsy," she said, but she didn't let me go.

"Where's your room, Gallen?" I asked.

But by the time I'd untucked myself, she was out the door. Her foot shadows crept out from under the light slot, and I couldn't hear a thing amove in the hall.

I got up and opened my door just a bit, and peeked round the jamb; there she was, just waiting for me—not so angry that she couldn't blush.

"You never mind where my room is, Graff," she said.

So I went back to my sad, saggy bed; I rumpled around a bit, trying to second-guess the world. Well, I thought, the bees are done with their pollinating now; the honey's come full and the hive's fat for tapping. Oh, look out.

Looking Out

I woke up with a sun smell on my pillow. So I thought: Siggy is leaving Vienna now; he's had time to fetch his details, time to skulk in the zoo all night.

I saw him saying goodbye to the animals, trying to cheer them up.

"Bless you, Siggy!" said the fraught giraffe.

And the wallaroo cradled a tear in its fist.

"Graff," said Gallen, under my door. "They're down in the dining room."

Well, I didn't feel very good about any of it; their conspiracy weighed in the air of the hall. It was like they'd left a door open to the cellar-dungeon; I could smell the foul, dank mildew of thoughts left down there to ripen and go moldy, but I couldn't find the door, to close it.

They had a table in the dining room, near to mine: the wily *Herr Bürgermeister,* dear Auntie Tratt, and the cider-smelling one—Herr Windisch, appleman and employer of the needy. He had withered blossoms caught in the cuffs of his pants.

There was another they hadn't let sit with them; he slumped in the dining-room doorway—Keff the tractor driver. Windisch's man. He was burly enough, descended pure from the Java stock, and his leathers smelt fresh from the goat.

And how would they attempt it? Watching me butter my *Brötchen?* Would Keff block my escape at the door? Mush my spine with the meat of his knee?

But, yes, Siggy had written it:

> Just a hop ahead, and you're a cut above!

So I dashed off the breakfast that my Gallen had served me. And I went right up to their table.

"Forgive me if I'm interrupting," I said, "but I thought all of you could advise me. Since I'll be staying awhile, I'd like a job. Oh, just a little something at night, I'd prefer. If you know of anything," I said.

And I heard it all! The dungeon door closing with terrible wrenching clanks; and deep in my ears, sounding all the way from Vienna, the Rare Spectacled Bears were stamping their feet and shaking their heads with a fury that flapped their jowls.

"Oh my," said Auntie Tratt. "Isn't that a fine idea?"

And that had their tableful wondering.

But behind my eyes, and making them water, Siggy was riding faster and faster. The motorcycle screamed beneath him like an animal in pain.

Speculations

I took some beers out in the garden and sat where I could see round the castle to the falls. I found a spot where the motorcycle had dripped oil and clotted the grass. In a while the forsythia would all be gone by; the garden would turn brown- and green-weedy, tropical and over-thick. The river spray made everything a little wet, and the garden made ominous growing sounds in the wind. Only the soil smudge resisted; the spray was as beaded as sweat on the little black clot.

And I thought: He's just stopped for lunch. The pipes are *ping*ing with heat; he's been pushing it. If you spat on the pipes, your spittle would ball up and bounce like waterdrops off a ready griddle. He's had an early start and he's really been pushing it. He's a long way out of the Danube Valley; he may even be following the Ybbs by now. And of course he'll have it all written out in that frotting notebook, with little maps of the cages, and all the details you'd ever need to know.

Eighteen minutes from behind the bush in Maxing Park to the outskirts of Hietzing; eighteen minutes, four up-and down-shifts, two skids, one *Strassenbahn*-crossing and a blinking-yellow light.

And behind you, the din of escaping aardvarks.

Well, I thought, he probably won't even stop for lunch.

And there was Auntie Tratt in my room, airing me out; she shot a smile down to me when she opened my window and beat my pillow.

Well, you old gob, Auntie—he's not going to ride that motorcycle in here for you to see. No, blobby Auntie—my Siggy-friend's brighter than your old fishy eyes.

And there was my Gallen in my window too. Trimming off the corners of my bed, no doubt, just as innocent as milk.

Now which bed does that Graff sleep in? the sly Tratt says.

Well, I don't know, Auntie, but this one looks most recently used.

"Herr Graff?" the Tratt called. "Which bed are you sleeping in?"

"Nearest the bathtub, Frau Tratt," I said. And Gallen breezed past the window without looking down at me.

Well, you're right, Gallen dear, the Tratt is saying—thinking every minute.

And I was thinking too, all right. Frau Tratt on the poke in my room; someone sent to fix my doorknob, secretly, while I was getting a job—so they could lock me in? And those hazy clouds, stealing the yellow from the last, fallen forsythia, squatted like bomb smog in the sky.

And where was Siggy? Out of Ulmerfeld by now? Hiesbach, maybe, or even on the road to St. Leonhard? If he's coming that way. Was he taking a roundabout route?

How many hours away is that Siggy? And what will my Gallen be wearing when she visits my room tonight?

The spray put such a wet weight in the air—and the garden going on with its damn growing, getting all out of hand. Well, as the Old Oaf, Fate—the Great Lout—could tell you: look out, look out.

It's the kind of thing Siggy might have written a poem about. In fact, there's a rough beginning in the notebook:

> Ah, Life—fat bubble fit to burst!
> Fate's got the veritable pin.

But it would have made a terrible poem. One of his worst.

The Approach
of the Veritable Pin

The fat sun, very low, turned everything the color of forsythia—yellowed the squares of last night to fall through my window's grating, blotched my bed and my resting toes.

"He's coming, isn't he?" said Gallen.

"Anytime now," I told her.

"Graff," she said, "if he comes from St. Leonhard, they'll see him. If he takes the road by the orchards, Graff, there's Windisch and Keff who'll be looking."

"Well, he won't just come rolling in on the bike, will he?"

"I'll bet he drives it into town," she said. "Oh, he won't bring it right to the courtyard, but he's not going to walk from St. Leonhard either—if he's fool enough to come from St. Leonhard, and not pick a new way."

"You figure it out, then," I said. "You think of the road he'll take in."

"Graff, you're not even going to say goodbye, are you?"

"Come and sit with me, Gallen," I said. But she shook her head and wouldn't budge from the window ledge. From down on the bed I could peek past her knees; there was a roundness to her leg where the ledge pinched her.

"Stop looking up my skirt!" she said; she drew her legs up and swung herself back-to me. She gave a look out the window. "Someone just ran out of the garden," she said.

Then she got on her knees and leaned out the window.

"Someone's up against the wall," she said. "Someone's scratching the vines, but I can't see."

So I came up beside her on the ledge; we knelt together, leaning out. Her braid slid up her back and over her shoulder; it shaded her face from me. I put my arm round her waist, and she straightened a little. On all fours we were, I draped on her back.

"Oh, damn you, Graff!" she said, and gave me her elbow in my throat. It choked me up so, I had to sit and water my eyes. She sat cross-legged on the ledge in front of me.

"Oh, you Graff!" she said. "Goodbye, you! You just go on and go."

She was getting teary; I had to look away from her. I peeked out the window, but there was nobody there. I was still gagging; it was like swimming, my eyes were so watery.

"Oh, Graff," she said, "don't you cry too." And she pitched forward at me, burrowing round me with her arms. Her face was wet against my cheek. "I could meet you somewhere, Graff. Couldn't I? I've got wages coming, and I never buy anything."

My Adam's apple was so fat in my throat I couldn't talk; I think she'd given it a bat that had turned it around.

"*Gak,*" I said.

And she dissolved; she bit her braid end and shivered herself up small against me.

"Gallen," I managed, "there's nobody out there."

But she wouldn't hear it. She was still shaking when the two strange elbows and the fist-shape of chin came wriggling up on the window ledge, together with animal pants and groans, and followed by the Great Greek Face of Comedy without a hair on his head—which all bore a bald resemblance to my previous Siggy-friend.

"God, give me a hand!" he said. "My foot's caught in this frotting ivy."

So I had to slide Gallen off my lap and drag the terribly disguised Siggy into the room.

"I'm back!" he said.

And he flopped down next to the heap my Gallen made on the floor.

Fate's Disguise

Poor crumpled Gallen couldn't look at him again; and one look was enough
—I agree, I agree.

"Siggy?" I said.

"Right you are, Graff! But I know, you didn't recognize me?"

"Not right away, without the duckjacket," I said, although I meant:
Without any hair! How could I recognize you when you don't have any
hair?

"And the new shave, Graff?" he said. "That was the trick!"

"But your whole head, Siggy?"

"Eyebrows too, Graff. Did you notice?"

"You look awful," I said.

"A walking dome, Graff! A solid pate from chin to uppermost cranial
lump. Did you ever know there were such dents in a skull?"

"In *your* skull," I said. "Mine doesn't look like that." But maybe it did
—little grooves and knots all over, like a bleached peach pit.

He said, "I walked through town, across the bridge. No one knew me,
Graff. I saw the mayor, and he passed me by as if I were a war relic."

A barber's relic, his head was icy to the touch; I jumped. His relic was
spattered with mosquitos, and with larger more smearing flyers who'd run
into his hurtling dome; there was a wing-mash above one ear that might
have been a crow. Of course, he'd ridden here helmetless, letting the wind
cool the barber's mistakes.

I said, "Siggy, you're hideous to behold."

"Of course, Graff. Of course," he said, "and I'm parked in hiding across
the town. Get your stuff."

"Well, Siggy."

"Get it packed and we'll wait for dark," he said. "It's all set, Graff. It's
just perfect."

And my crumpled Gallen huddled on the floor, a fetus dropped madly
into this world and shrouded in a servant's clothes.

"Gallen?" I said.

"It looks like you got her," said Siggy.

"Don't," I said.

"Pack," he said. "I've found the spot."

"What spot?"

"To stash the guard!"

"Siggy."

"I was there all night, Graff. It's all planned."

"I knew it would be," I said.

"I didn't know you had such faith, Graff."

"Faith!" said Gallen.

"Is she going to scream?" said Siggy.

"Faith," Gallen said. "Did he come by the orchard road?" Oh, she wouldn't look at him. "Then they saw his motorcycle!" she wailed. "Oh, everyone's been told to look for it!"

"Why does she care?" said Siggy.

"Did you come from St. Leonhard, Sig?" I asked him.

"Graff," he said. "Look at me and tell me if you see an amateur."

Faith

Well, I heard the first of the wood-creaks edge down the hallway from the stairs—and the sound of the top step being squeaked, the banister being leaned on.

"Who's that?" Gallen whispered.

"It's not about me," said Siggy. "No one's seen me."

So I peeked out in the hall. It was the old Tratt, sagged on the banister, winded from her climb.

"Herr Graff!" she called. "Herr Graff?"

I came out in the hall where she could see me.

"It's Keff," she said. "It's Keff, come to take you to your job."

"Job?" Siggy whispered.

"He's much too early," I told the Tratt. "Tell him he's early."

"He knows he's early," she said, "and he's waiting." And the terrible Tratt and I understood each other for a moment; then she swayed back down the stairs.

But bald Siggy was bent over my Gallen. He had her braid in his fist, and she bit her lip.

"He's got a *job?*" said Siggy. "Has he got a *job,* you damn girl?"

"Siggy," I said.

"Faith!" he said. "You never thought I'd be back, did you? Got yourself a job and a frotting *girl!*"

"They were going to arrest him," Gallen said over her lip.

"I set it all up," said Siggy. "Did you think I'd run out?"

"I knew you were setting it up," I said. "But, Siggy, they were figuring me as a vagrant. They were setting things up, too."

"Keff's waiting," said Gallen. "Oh, it's all fixed, Graff! If you don't go down, he'll come up."

"Sig," I said, "where can I meet you after work?"

"Oh, sure!" he said. "You're telling me you've not frotted this sweet rag of a girl?"

"Siggy, don't," I said.

"You're telling me!" he shouted. "Telling me you're coming with me? But *after* your frotting job! Oh, sure."

"This Keff," I said. "He's looking out for me." And I heard woody little spasms down the hallway: somebody heavy, mounting two at a time.

"Sig, get out!" I said. "You're going to get caught. Say a place where we'll meet."

"Say a place to meet *me,*" Gallen said to him. "Graff's got to go."

"Meet *you?*" said Siggy. "Meet Graff's little raggy drab! Meet you for *what?*"

And big steps were taking up the hallway, huffs like tractor breath stirred the doorway air.

"Get out, Siggy," I said.

"I want my sleeping bag and my toothbrush, Graff. Please can I have my things back?"

"Oh, Christ, Sig!" I said. "Get out of here!"

And *thump!* said Keff to the door. *Thump.*

"Oh! Enter the heavy!" said Siggy. "Enter the crusher of spines!"

Keff thumped.

"I'm coming back for my things," said Siggy.

"Oh, you're crazy!" said Gallen. "You bald goon," she said. "You mean terrible queer!"

"Oh, Graff," he said—he was backing between the beds—"oh, Graff, I had this beautiful plan."

"Siggy, listen," I said.

"Oh, damn you, Graff," he said so softly—he was on the sunset on the window ledge.

"Sig, I'm really going to meet you," I said.

"Oh, Keff!" said Gallen. "Keff." He was thumping very hard.

"Sig, say where you'll meet me."

"Where *did* I meet you, Graff? You watched girls in the Rathaus Park," he said. "You watched me too."

"Siggy," I said.

"You've had a good laugh over me," he said. "You and this tender young slip-in you've made the whole trip for."

And the hinge pins sprouted from the door. Oh, how Keff could thump!

"You got a *job!*" said Siggy. And he jumped, *splotz* in the awful garden-muck.

The sunset struck his terrible, hairless dome. Shadows deepened his skull dents, and the skeleton gape of his mouth—scooped the life from his eyes.

"Graff?" said Gallen.

"You shut up," I said. "You tell me when he comes back, Gallen—if you have to walk the orchards to St. Leonhard, you find me and tell me when he's come back."

"Oh damn, Graff!" she cried. Then she said, "Oh, Keff"—who now appeared round the hinge side of the door, swinging the door with him until the knob side snapped free of the jamb. Surprised, he still held the door—not knowing where to lay it down.

"Oh, Christ!" I said.

But no one spoke up.

Denying the Animal

As the notebooks say:

Hinley Gouch hated animals on the loose, having so long and selfrighteously denied the animal in himself.

But Keff was not one to deny the animal. Not when he carried my kicking Gallen downstairs to her auntie; not when he lifted the hitch end of the iron flatbed and clamped trailer to tractor with one mighty Keff-heff.

I balanced on the flatbed while Keff drove; the iron sang under my feet, and the trailer end swung with the switchbacks. We climbed the orchard road, and for a while the evening grew lighter; we were catching the day's end-glow, which the mountain held last.

When we reached the top of the orchards, near St. Leonhard, Keff waited for a more final dark.

"Been in the bee business long, Keff?" I asked.

"You're a smarty, for sure," he said.

And the scarce neon from Waidhofen, the pale lights along the river, winked at us way below. The fresh white paint on the bee boxes took a greenish cheese-color; the boxes dotted the orchards like gypsy tents—living a secret life.

Keff slumped on the tractor seat, crouched among hand clutch and foot brakes, gearshifts, gauges and iron parts; he sprawled using the great wheels as armrests in some warlike easy chair.

"It's dark, Keff," I told him.

"It'll get darker," he said. "You're the one who's picking up the hives. Don't you want it darker?"

"So the bees will be faster asleep?"

"That's the idea, smarty," said Keff. "So you can sneak up and close the screen door on them. So when you start juggling them awake, they can't get out."

So we waited until the mountaintop was just another sky-shape, until the moon was the only color, and far-off, blinking Waidhofen gave the only signs of night people awake under lantern and bulb.

Keff would do it this way: I balanced on the trailer, and he drove through the tree rows of one orchard and then another. He'd stop at a bee box and I'd creep up to it easy. They had a little entrance the size of a letter slot in a door. There'd be a few sleepy bees on the ledge outside; I'd nudge them into their house, extra gently, and then I'd pull the screening down over their entranceway, and exit.

When you picked up the box, the hive woke up. They hummed inside; like distant electricity, they vibrated your arms.

The boxes were very heavy; honey leaked between the bottom slats when I lifted them up to the flatbed.

Keff said, "If you drop one, smarty, it'll split for sure. If it splits, smarty, I'll drive off and leave you."

So I didn't drop any. When they were on the flatbed, six or so, I had to brace my back against them so they wouldn't slide. First they'd slide toward the tractor on a downhill pitch, then they'd slide to the rear end when we climbed.

"Scramble, smarty," said Keff.

They fitted, fourteen on the flatbed floor; that was the first tier. Then I had to stack. With a second tier on, they didn't slide as easily; there was too much weighing them down. But I had to leave one space off the second tier so that I could load a third tier. I had to stand on a bee box with another bee box in my arms. Then I had to crawl over the second tier to fill out the corners.

"Three tiers is enough, huh, Keff?"

"Don't let your feet fall through," said Keff. "You'll be stuck, for sure."

"For sure I would, Keff." Honey-mucked, knee-deep, a prowler crashed into the home at night.

Keff would do this: I braced the hives and he crossed the road, working one side and then the other, moving down the mountain. He kept the orchards even on each side, but crossing the road was the problem. Coming up out of one ditch and down into the other, the flatbed would tilt enough to rock the second-tier boxes on edge. I braced, and Keff would do this: kill the engine, turn off the headlight, let all the groans and snaps of his tractor part cease and be quiet. Then he listened for cars on the road; if he heard anything, he'd wait.

Well, it took such a long time for the tractor and trailer to cross, and the road was too winding to be safely spotting headlights. So Keff would listen for engine sounds.

"Is that a car, smarty?"

"I don't hear anything, Keff."

"Listen," he said. "Do you want to get broadside in the road and have somebody drive through the hives?"

So I'd listen. To the tractor's manifold singing its heat. To the talkative bees.

I was stung just once. A bee I'd brushed off the doorstoop ledge, and who hadn't gone into the house, got caught in my shirt cuff and got my wrist. It made just a little burn, but my wrist got fat.

And we were four or five boxes away from a full third tier, when Keff stopped the tractor to check the pressure in the trailer tires. "I think they've got him by now, smarty," he said.

"Who?" I said.

"Your queer friend, smarty. He got in to see you, but he won't get out."

"Just voices you were hearing, Keff. Just Gallen and I were in that room."

"Oh, smarty," he said. "There's footprints in the garden, and there's everyone who heard the yelling. See? It makes you dumb to be a queer, smarty."

He read his tire gauge. How many pounds of air does it take to hold a single-axle trailer, two tires a side, carrying what must be tons of honey and bees?

Keff stooped near the space I'd left for standing on the second tier. I could have just hopped up and shoved a whole row of third-tier boxes on him; I hopped up on the second tier.

"What were you doing with that little Gallen, smarty?" He wasn't looking up. "I've been waiting for her to get old enough," he said. "And a little bigger." And his squat, neckless head spun his face up to me, grinning.

"What are you doing up there?" he said. And his feet moved back under his haunches, like a sprinter getting set.

I said, "Why don't we have bee suits, Keff? Why don't we have masks and all that?"

But he was backing up, not taking his eyes off that third-tier row of hives. "Why don't we have what?" he said.

"Bee suits," I said. "Protection, if there's an accident."

"Beekeeper's idea," said Keff, standing up now. "When you're protected, you're careless, smarty. When you're careless, you have accidents."

"Why doesn't the beekeeper get the hives himself, Keff?"

But Keff was still ogling at the third-tier row. "Third tier's almost full," he said. "Once more across the road, and we'll go back to the barns."

"Well, let's do it then," I said.

"Think he'll still be there, do you, smarty? We'll take another load after this one, and you think he'll still be around, fancy-free?"

"Well, Keff," I said, thinking: You almost weren't so fancy-free yourself,

Keff—you almost weren't around any more. Eager bees are in those hives, Keff, and you were almost mired in honey-muck; with bee stings swelling your fat head fatter.

Keff was listening for anything coming.

Well no, of course, I thought. You were always there, safe all along, Keff. And don't you see, Siggy, how I'm drawing the line? And what in hell is it you expect of me, Siggy?

"Someone's coming," said Keff. He kept the engine killed.

Well, even the bees were quieted, listening too.

"Someone's running," said Keff, and he opened the toolbox.

I could hear the breathing down the road; gravel-scuff and the sounds of panting.

"Someone you know, smarty?" said Keff, the open-end wrench in his paw.

Then he twisted the housing round the headlight, opened the face of the light down the road; but he kept the light off. He was just getting ready.

Hush, bees, I thought. Those are little, short steps; those are quick, little breaths.

And Keff turned the light on my Gallen, hair loose and fanning the night as she ran.

How Many Bees Would Do for You?

Coming with the news, she was—rubber-legged from running uphill since Waidhofen. Gallen brought the news of Siggy's great return for his tooth-brush, how he swung apelike from ivy vine to the window's grate to gain another entrance, how he bleated down the hall, rode the banister to the lobby, spoke the epitaphs for them all—for Auntie Tratt, who clucked like a tupping hen in her nook under the stairwell; and for my Gallen too, he gave some screaming metaphor of shattered maidenhood. And for me, he had also spoken for me—Gallen told—a diatribe, a prophecy of my eventual castration.

"Oh, crazy!" she gasped. "Oh he was, Graff. And he pawed up the garden, he threw mud on the castle walls!"

Well, the bees heard it all; they hummed against her where she slumped against them—the bee boxes propping her up all along her long, slight back.

"Don't let her lean too heavy," said Keff. "Don't have her tip a hive, smarty."

Oh, enough of you, Keff. Isn't it entirely enough now? I thought.

"They'll get him for sure," said Keff.

"Oh, he's wild," Gallen said. "Graff, the whole town is out for him. I don't know where he's gone."

"They should box him in," said Keff—and down the road behind him the crazy-twisted headlight startled the trees crouched against the switchbacks. The town blinked noiselessly beyond the dentshapes and reliefs of round tree clumps balled against the night sky.

"Oh, Graff," said Gallen. "I'm so sorry. Please, I am sorry, Graff—if he's your friend," she said.

"Listen," said Keff, but I heard nothing. "Listen, smarty"—down in the town, winding up our way but just a murmur yet—"do you hear the car?"

And some of the tree clumps caught the blinking-blue light, flashing above the road and changing sides with the turn of the switchbacks.

"Listen," said Keff. "That's a Volkswagen. That's the police, for sure."

For sure. Sirenless and stealthy.

There were two in the car, and they didn't stay long.

"We're making a roadblock at the top!" said one, and a black glove snapped its fingers.

"At St. Leonhard!" said the other. "If he comes this way."

And the bees heard; the diminishing blue blinked away from their box houses; they stirred against my poor, propped Gallen, who for the second time this evening had been reduced to a heap on account of me.

And I could only think: For sure, he's not going to try riding that bike out of town. Oh, for sure—at least—he won't be coming *this* way.

And Keff said, "Smarty, we can't just be gawking here all night. If the girl won't fall off, I'd like to get across the road."

"I'll be all right," said Gallen, but her voice shivered as if some kind of wind down the mountains had blown all the way from the Raxalpe, all the way from last January, and caught her warm and precious and vulnerable, just waking up in the morning, coverless. She was so hurt, really, and there was nothing I could think clearly.

"Let's listen, then," said Keff, mounting the great spring-back seat, settling among his iron-clanking parts. We listened and he wrenched the housing for the headlight around, so we were pointed and lit straight across the road. Then he came up with a heavy foot on each wheel brake; he rocked and struggled the tractor out of gear. The trailer shifted; the bees sang.

"I don't hear anything," I said.

"No, nothing," said Keff, and he reached for the startrod.

He was reaching; I said, "Keff?"

"Smarty?" he said, and his hand stopped in air.

"Listen," I said. "Do you hear?"

And he froze himself still, not squeaking the tractor's parts, not gusting his own breath.

"Oh yes," he said.

Maybe not even out of the town yet, but coming—and maybe not even coming our way. In those close arches, maybe—maybe that's what brought on the sound and then suddenly shut it off. Off and on again.

"Why, smarty," said Keff. "That's real good listening."

And now it was out of the town; it took our road. A hoarse man clearing his throat, many closed rooms away—clearing a great hoarse throat, not momentarily but eternally; going on forever, coming toward us forever.

"Oh yes!" said Keff.

Oh yes, I would have known it from a million others. Oh, the good sounds of the throggy beast my Siggy rode!

"Ha!" said Keff. "It's *him,* smarty. It's him, the queer!"

And, Keff, you were almost done then. A third-tier bee box for you, Keff, right where your neckless head looms almost level with the humming stack; right where you lurk on your high seat, Keff, a bee box for you. And perhaps another, perhaps a whole toppling row come down on you, thick Keff. If I dared, Keff, and if I thought it would make any difference or do any good.

How many bees would do for you, Keff? A strapping fellow like yourself —how many bee stings could you take? What's your quota, rotten Keff?

Uphill and Downhill, Hither and Yon

And was it Gallen's cold hand that brought me back? That crouched me by the trailer end, thinking: What now, Siggy? How do I stop you from meeting the mountaintop with the blinking-blue Volkswagen, and the snapping, black-gloved fingers therein, therein?

Up the mountain, where Keff and I had wound down from the gravelly switchbacks are sharper; three S-curves above the bee-wagon was the very best S-curve of them all. It was as sharp as a Z. Well, I thought, he'll have to slow down for that one—even Siggy, even the beast, will have to come down a gear or two for that one. Maybe even first gear; he'd be going slow enough to stop, or at least slow enough so he'd have to see me in the road.

I ran, and I didn't decipher Keff's shouting; no, I didn't heed his woolly voice.

You always think you run so fast at night, even uphill; you can't see how slowly the road slips under you or the trees come by. The old night-shapes loomed and hovered; I could hear the beast rage louder.

Is it looking back that makes me fill in all the pieces, and make the facts come out so tight? Or did I really hear them then? The bees. Their million, double-, triple-million voices, urgent and impatient and abuzz.

But *this* I'm sure of: it was three S-curves up the tumbling mountain, and then the Z. Was it so perfectly worked out that I saw the headlight hit the tree clumps around me, precisely when I turned the Z? Or was it really somewhere in the last S, approaching the Z? Or did I really have to wait in ambush, long before the *throg* and *thump* of valve and tire slap bent into the Z itself?

At least I was there; I saw his rider shape come slithering out of the S below me—could hear that his gear was third—and saw the jerking head-light wash me a moon color and fix me forever to that spot on the road.

Then, hearing the gears come down to first. Into the elbow of the Z— was he coming at me sideways? Was the headlight jogging along all by itself?

"Frotting Graff!" he said, and the beast coughed itself out.

"Oh, Siggy!" I said, and I could have kissed his shining helmet—only it wasn't his helmet. It was his bare dome, bald as the moon and bared for the night of his escape. Cold as a gun.

"Frotting Graff!" he said, and he struggled to kick the bike out of gear. He lifted his foot for the kick starter.

"Sig, they've a roadblock for you at St. Leonhard!"

"You've a roadblock in your brain," he said. "Let me go."

"Siggy, you can't drive out. You'll have to hide."

But he got his foot back again; I joggled him off balance so he needed both legs to hold the bike up.

"Frotting Graff! Messing things up, you ninny-assed lover of that *girl!*"

And he wrestled the bike up steady, kicked back with his starting foot. But I wouldn't let him.

"Siggy, they're laying for you. You can't go."

"Have you a plan, Graff?" he said. "I'd like to hear your plan, frotting Graff!"

Why no, there wasn't any plan. Of course, there wasn't.

But I said, "You've got to stash the bike. Drive off in the orchards, lay low till the morning."

"Is that a *plan?*" he said. "Is there any good plan coming from you, Graff? Until every maidenhead on earth is taken, will you ever have a worthwhile plan?"

And he wrenched the handlebars out of my grip, but I pinned his legs against the bike and he couldn't kick.

"Never a plan from you, frotting Graff! Never a scheme of any greatness from you—not while there are any young upright unfondled diddies left in the world!"

And he shunted the bike around, jerking up on the handlebars, digging in with his heels. But I still had his starting foot trapped.

"Small-minded, immediate Graff!" he roared. "All the unbounced boobies of the world are in your brain!"

And he woggled the front wheel to point downhill. He started his beast rolling; I caught the vent-pocket of his duckjacket and ran close alongside.

"Hysteria for hymen!" he shouted. "You Graff, Graff you!"

Oh, he was rare, he was gone by, all right. And the bike moved along now; he tried to find a gear, he was pulling in the clutch to jump-start his beast on the glide.

"You'll always throw everything away, Graff," he said, strangely gentle.

And I couldn't keep up. I jockeyed on behind him, and the bike wobbled. I flung myself to his back, but he had folded up the foot pedals for the rear rider. He'd thoroughly planned this trip alone.

I felt him find the gear with a chunk.

But I did this: I leaned over his shoulder and dropped the heel of my hand on the kill button. The bike never caught. It made a muted, airy farting behind us, but the gear pull slowed us fast. I was slammed up against him, and he skipped over the gas tank astraddle, his knees wedging up under the handlebars; his feet came off his own foot pedals, and he couldn't reach back for the gears.

And whatever gear we were in didn't hold. The old rampaging, momentum-bent beast slipped into neutral. We were wheeling free, the headlight jogging down the road in front of us; we floated engineless, coasting—the soft whir of gravel-mush sprayed out beside us; the whispering hum-slap of tires jounced us down. We weren't making a sound.

Did even the bees hear us coming?

This S-curve and that one, blurring by faster than the night bolting alongside.

"Move back on the seat!" said Siggy. "I've got to get in gear."

But the pitch was too steep; my weight was fallen forward, on him, on the gas tank. And just when I tried to move, another S-curve was coming at us hard.

"Shift, Graff!" he yelled. "You can reach it, you ninny!"

And he snapped in on the clutch handle; I dug my toes under the foreign little lever, but it wouldn't budge.

The jostling headlight threw us pieces and juts of the broken road, a scare of tree clump and bottomless ditch—of cold, peaceful night sky and the shimmering angelic town, countless switchbacks below. Everything came at us on jagged mirror-sections set askew.

Almost carelessly he said, "Graff, you've got to work it."

My toes ground in pain, but the gear lever made a sudden, ratcheting sound; the engine blatted, cannonlike and horse-whinnying, and I felt myself pelting up Siggy's back, and clawing to get myself down. The front shocks hissed; the bike bent forward.

Siggy's weight was too far front for good leaning; we lumbered heavily and wobbly round the top of an endless S, but we were slowing, a little.

"That's second," said Siggy. "Find me first, slow us down."

The bottom of the S bent in front of us; the bike picked itself up and hopped the crown sideways, but we stayed with the road. We held, and Siggy said, "First gear, Graff. Now *first.*" And my toes were digging again, prying the lever; I thought I could feel it begin to move. And Siggy said, "Don't miss the gear, Graff. Get it all the way in, Graff." And I thought: Almost now, it's almost over—we're coming clean out of this mad little ride. And we came shunting out of the S. I thought: That's it, it's all right, for sure.

But what was Keff doing, just ahead? What were his tractor and bee-wagon doing there, broadside in the road?

And didn't they look surprised? Keff holding the great steering wheel like a world slipping out of his grasp, and Gallen perched on the trailer end, steadying those third-tier bee boxes.

Keff, the great listener, who of course hadn't heard the beginning of our engineless descent. And just what are you going to do, Keff, broadside and taking up all the life in the road?

"Oh," said Siggy, so softly it was either a whisper or a complaint spoken straight into the rush of the wind.

The Number of Bees That Will Do

The headlight was dancing over them; the squat, alive boxes, three tiers high, looming in front of and fast above us. The humming iron bottom of the flatbed—sagging under honey and level with our coming headlight—reflected our unfair arrival back to us.

Siggy's elbow pumped twice, whumped me in the chest and rocked me off his shoulders. But I was already helping him; my hands were already knuckling into the tight squeeze of seat and gas tank between us. I pushed up and off from my wrists, snapped my arms out straight and felt myself move away from Siggy and the beast, very slowly, it seemed—for a hundred miles of down-hill-flying road I was pushing myself up and off; for a hundred miles, I was floating behind and away from the beast, who was still in second gear and would never find first.

The jogging-red taillight pranced below and in front of me. And I thought: I'm going to sit in the air and float this road down to Waidhofen. I'm going to clear these bees by a mile; for a hundred miles I will never come down.

And the taillight moved away from me, sidestepped, tried to make up its mind and direction—had, of course, no place to go.

The longest hundred miles I was ever in the air strangely took no time at all. Not even time enough for the indefatigable Siggy to free his knees from under the handlebars, though time enough for me to see him trying —his dome snapping back and catching all the weird reflections of head-light, taillight, edges and faces of bee box, flatbed, hulking tractor-fender and the iron parts of Keff's open mouth.

The taillight, doing the damnedest dance, fell down on the road and spattered patterns of red-light, white-light pieces—did its dance out and went dark. Siggy, tucking his dome in the shadows, and in his duckjacket, put the old beast on its side.

The headlight pierced under the flatbed to the safe road beyond. The bike, on its side, was taking that route, flowering sparks from the drag of the tailpipe searing along—of foot pedal and kickstand, of handlebar and wheel hub, biting off chunks of the falling-down road.

And won't it surprise you, Keff, to see me fly over the whole damn mess and meet up with Siggy when he ducks out from under the far side of your terrible cargo?

But what did you do, Keff? Just what precisely did you think you were doing—when you lurched forward, Keff, and stalled; when you stalled and then lurched, or whatever the order was? What were you trying to do, Keff? What in your too-late brain could you ever have been thinking? Keff, why did you think you could ever get out of the way?

Why did you move, Keff—so that Siggy slid under the flatbed, but *not* out the other side?

Oh, you didn't move much, Keff, but just enough so that something caught a part of Siggy or his beast—an axle? an inch of tire? the outjutting edge of the flatbed's bottom? God, something said THANG!—a hollow, iron ringing that shook the moon.

You didn't move much, Keff, but you lurched.

Just as I was about to fly over your awesome cargo, you lurched, Keff! And Siggy, or a part of his beast, said THANG! up under the flatbed's bottom; and Gallen, her long, loveless arms only pretending to steady the terrible third-tier bee boxes, jumped! Knew the game was up and that the hives were moving beyond her control. She jumped clear; just as I was about to buzz over your bees, Keff—just then. You lurched, stalled, choked—whatever it is you do, and did, behind your gauges, gears, and ominous iron parts.

And the third-tier bee boxes hung on edge for as long as it had taken me to travel my hundred miles in the air; they fell in slow motion, feathered down to the powder-soft road and the waiting iron edge of the flatbed. The bees and I fell in slow motion, Keff.

Did I decide to put in a landing when I saw them fall? I came down mushy in the road, which was harder than it looked, and chewed all the skin off the heels of my hands.

But the bee boxes fell harder than I did. They were as heavy and vulnerable as water balloons. Their frail sides split, and they spilled their running, spongy hives.

God, what did they say? What did the bees say? Was it "Who's mashed my home in the middle of night?" Or was it "Who's woken me up—crashed into the hive, crushed my babies in their waxy little cells of sleep! *And who blinds me now with this light?"*

Because the beast wouldn't die, would not put out its headlight; it shone up under the trailer, so beautifully amber, on the great gobs of honey that drooled down over the flatbed's edge.

Well, the light caught you too, Keff—coming up the road to me, loping bearlike and swinging your great arms round your head, smacking your pants cuffs and leaping, Keff—yes, leaping—and turning around in the air, hugging yourself, Keff; and bending low; and again loping on toward me.

Did Gallen get to me before you did, Keff? Or did I only imagine her there for a second before you scooped me up like a ball and half carried, half rolled me up the mountain, out of the light that was showing the bees the way?

And did the stinging begin then? I don't remember feeling a thing. I remember hearing a quieted, much duller repetition of the original THANG! the beast, or something, had made against the trailer. I remember it, *thang-whump, thang-whump,* up under the flatbed's bottom.

Siggy, were you trying to lift the trailer off you—still trying to get your poor, wedged knees out from under the handlebars? Your fist, or forearm —your dome?—*thang-whump* and *thang-shump* again; did you know I'd hear you and come running?

I heard you. I came running. And I would have gotten there if the bees hadn't closed my eyes, filled my ears and slowed me to a crawl. Even then I might have gotten there, if Keff hadn't come lumbering down on me, taking me over his hip and up under his arm and bumbling me back up the road.

If I screamed, it was to hear a human sound; to drown out the bee drone —what was it they were saying?

"Here is the breaker of homes, the masher of baby bees! And he can't get away if we follow his light!"

And after that, what was the true order of things?

There was Keff, telling me what I already knew: "Oh, smarty, I *listened.* I *listened!* I heard your engine die, and I listened for it to start up, but it didn't. I didn't hear it, smarty! I said to the girl, 'Just you steady those boxes and we'll finally get across this road.' Oh, smarty, ask her! We *both* listened, and you *weren't* coming. Nobody was coming. How did you get here so fast that I never heard?"

And before that, or during that, or even after that, the blinking-blue Volkswagen came down from St. Leonhard, having heard, they said, the THANG!—even up there.

I was trying to open my eyes, sometime in all of that. But they wouldn't open, and Gallen put her mouth to them and wetted them cool for me.

And again Keff assured me that he had listened.

Then I'm really not sure what I listened for and heard; if there was another *thang-whump* or two, or if I asked Keff, "How many bees, would you guess?" And whether Keff and I had a highly technical discussion on the number of bees per box and the number of boxes that had toppled off —whether it was just the third-tier rows on the trailer's uphill, hind-end side, or was it more or less. And did it matter how many?

And whether Keff answered or guessed; if all of this had happened on the spot, or if my counting of bees hadn't really been later, semi-conscious and semi-sunk in an Epsom salts bath. If any of this was three minutes after the last *thang-whump* I really heard, or three days after—three Epsom salts baths away.

And did the faces of the only true mourners crouch about me there on that down-falling road, in that bee-conspiring night? Did the animals accuse me then, mourn him then? Or was that soaked out of me in Epsom salts too?

The weeping wallaroo, the shaken oryx, the despairing Rare Spectacled Bears. When did I see them mourning him?

Was it there, with my eyes still puffed shut? Or was it countless cathartic baths away, and long after Siggy had reached and surpassed his quota of bee stings?

The Notebook

The First Zoo Watch:
Monday, June 5, 1967, @ 1:20 p.m.

I won't actually go inside until midafternoon. Another hour or so in this
sun won't hurt me a bit; I might even dry out. As you certainly know, Graff,
I left Waidhofen in a considerable downpour. And the roads were slick
almost all the way to Hietzing, even though the rain stopped once I was out
of the mountains.

I wasn't at all sure of the time when I left. When was it that the milkman
first arrived? Everything happened very fast and early; I'm sure I was away
by nine, and I've been at this café just long enough to order—a tea with rum,
because the rain gave me some chill. So then, if I left at nine and it's
one-twenty now, we can figure on four hours—Waidhofen to the Heitzinger
Zoo. And that's with a wet road.

You know the café I'm at? On the Platz, off Maxing Strasse, across from
the main zoo gate. I'm simply resting up and drying out. I'll just saunter
over to the zoo about midafternoon, browse a bit, and find myself a spot
to hide by the time they start ushering customers out and locking up for
the night. That way I'll be inside to see the changing of the guard, if they
have such a thing, and I'll be in a position to observe the habits of the
nightwatchman. I hope I'll have the opportunity to talk with some of the
animals, too, and let them know they've got nothing to fear from me. I'll

stay until the zoo reopens; when there's enough of a crowd I'll just meander out, as if I've been an early-morning, paying customer.

Right now, the café's very nice. My waiter rolled back the awning for me, and I've got a tableful of sun; the sidewalk's warm to my feet. A pretty nice waiter, as waiters in the outer districts go. He's got a Balkan look, and his accent's as light as the chinking of wineglasses.

"Come here after the war?" I asked him.

"Oh, I missed the whole bit," he said.

"What did you miss?" I asked.

"The whole damn war," he said.

I couldn't tell if he was disappointed about it, or if it was at all true. It's true of you, isn't it, Graff? You were all Salzburg people, weren't you? And moved yourselves well west of Zürich before the war, you've said. I'd guess that Switzerland was as well off as any place on the continent. And you had Salzburg to come back to. The Americans occupied Salzburg, didn't they? And from all I've heard, they kept things pretty clean.

My waiter just brought me my tea with rum. I asked him, "The Americans are a marvelously clean people, aren't they?"

"I never met one," he said.

Sly, these Balkans. He's just the right age for the war, and I'll bet he didn't miss a thing. But if you take me, for example, I'm just the wrong age. I was in the right place for the war, all right, but it passed me by when I was in the womb, and on my way there—and again too fresh from the womb to even take part in the post-mortem. That's a bit of what you live with if you're twenty-one in 1967, in Austria; you don't have a history, really, and no immediate future that you can see. What I mean is, we're at an interim age in an interim time; we're alive between two times of monstrous decisions —one past, the other coming. We're taking up the lag in history, for who knows how long. What I mean is, I have only a pre-history—a womb and pre-womb existence at a time when great popular decisions with terrible consequences were being made. We may be fifty before it happens again; anyway, now science has seen to it that monstrous decisions don't need popular support. You see, Graff, in our case, it's the pre-history that made us and mattered to what we'd become. My *vita* begins with my grandparents and is almost over on the day I was born.

My waiter just brought me the Frankfurt newspaper. He opened it to page three and let it fall in my lap. There's a photo from America of a German shepherd dog eating the dress off a Negress. There's an unmistakably white policeman standing by, truncheon raised; he's going to whop the Negress, it looks like, just as soon as the dog gets off her. Quite blurry in the background, there's a line of black people plastered against a storefront by an incredible stream from a fire hose. Didn't I say how these Balkans were sly? My waiter just walked off and left this in my lap. Marvelously clean people, the Americans; they wash their black folk with fire hoses.

I guess if you're twenty-one in 1967, in America, you needn't glut yourself with pre-history; in America I understand that there are crusades every day. But I'm not in America. I'm in the Old World, and what makes it old isn't that it's had a head start. Any place that's lagging, waiting again for The National Crisis—that's an Old World, and it's often a pity to be young in it.

I guess if I cared very profoundly I'd go to America, join the blackest extreme and wash white people with fire hoses. But it's only an idea that pops up every now and then, and I don't really give it much thought.

My waiter came to take his newspaper back.

"All done with it, sir?" he asked, and held out his hand. He's missing an index finger, down to the base knuckle. I gave him back his paper, spreading my thumb on the white policeman's face.

"Well, it's a German paper," I said. "Don't you think it must give some old Germans a kick to see a little racism in America?" Just to nudge him, I said that.

"I couldn't venture a guess," he told me, sly as he could be. Extra spiffy waiters, these Balkans. Half of them appear to have been full professors, before taking up their humble trade.

Vienna puzzles you that way. It's all pre-history—smug and secretive. It leaves me out, every time. But if we're supposed to be the generation that's to profit from our elders' mistakes, I feel I ought to know everyone's error.

My tea's cold, but it's heavy on the rum. A good waiter, no matter what else I say of him. But how did he lose that finger? If you asked him, he'd tell you—as a little boy, he was run over by a tram. Only there weren't any trams in far-eastern, small-town Yugoslavia when he was a little boy; there may not even be trams there now. But I guess if you were in America and asked a fingerless man how he lost it—probably a man who'd slashed it to the bone in a bottleneck—he'd tell you how a red-hot trigger burned it off while he was shooting the enemy in Manchuria.

Some people are proud, and some have their doubts.

And I can look at how left out of these times I feel—how I rely on pre-history for any sense and influence—and I can simplify this aforementioned garble. I can say: all *anyone* has is a pre-history. Feeling that you live at an interim time is something in the nature of being born and all the things that never happen to you after birth.

And once in a rare sometime, there's a grand scheme that comes along and changes all of that.

So I'll tip this good waiter fairly, and be getting myself across the street. There's many an animal I'd like to have a word with.

(BEGINNING)
THE HIGHLY SELECTIVE AUTOBIOGRAPHY OF
SIEGFRIED JAVOTNIK: PRE-HISTORY I

May 30, 1935: Hilke Marter, my mother-to-be, celebrates her fifteenth birthday. Her back against a naked trellis, she lolls in a Grinzing wine garden; some miles below her, the sun is melting its way to the snow's last, Baroque hiding places in downtown Vienna; above her, the meltwater trickles through the Vienna Woods, and the treetops are bobbing in a ground fog as intricate as the lacework in the downtown lingerie. Melt, says the day, and my mother melts.

Zahn Glanz, Hilke's first boyfriend, has such soft and blurry, mudpuddly eyes. But what my mother most admires are the few threads of cornsilk he wears on his bright chin. And Zahn can make his wineglass hum by skidding his tongue round the rim; he can change to an octave higher by the force of his grip on the stem. In 1935, art is still common in glassware, even in public places, and talents as graceful as Zahn's develop, simply, to greatness.

So Zahn thinks he'll be a journalist, or a politician. And he'll never take Hilke to places where the radio doesn't work—or isn't always on, and loud enough—just so he'll be up with the current events.

"Watch you don't jar the trellis," says Zahn, and my mother leans forward, fingers on the table, looks over her shoulder and up to the speaker box wedged in the lattice-work above her head.

Even the waiter is careful he doesn't disturb Zahn's contact with the world outside the wine garden; he tiptoes—a gingerbread man crumbling softly over the terrace.

And Radio Johannesgasse complies with Zahn's readiness. Hitler is quoted as saying that Germany has neither the intention nor desire to interfere with internal affairs of Austria, or to annex or incorporate Austria.

"I'll cut off my trunk," says Zahn Glanz, "if a bit of that's true."

Oh, your what? Hilke thinks. No, you wouldn't. Oh, don't.

The Second Zoo Watch:
Monday, June 5, 1967, @ 4:30 p.m.

Shortly after I came in, I watched them feed the Big Cats. Everyone in the zoo seemed to have been waiting all day for that.

At the time, I was having a look at Bennet's cassowary, a wingless bird, related to emus and ostriches. It has enormous feet, which are said to be dangerous. But what I thought was interesting is that the bird has a bony casque on top of its head, and the information sheet speculated that this was to protect it—"as it bolts through dense undergrowth at amazing speeds." Now why would cassowaries be bolting through dense undergrowth at amazing speeds? They don't look especially stupid. My own theory on the evolution of that head armor is that the cassowaries only grew such helmets after people started trapping them in dense undergrowth, and chasing them at amazing speeds. Perhaps a worry gland produced it. It certainly is nothing they'd need if they were left alone.

Anyway, I was having a look at Bennet's cassowary when the Big Cats started their caterwauling. Well, everyone around me was hopping, and shoving, just dying to get to the spectacle.

Inside the Cat House, it smells very strong. People were remarking on that, all right. And I saw two terrible things.

First, this keeper came and flipped a horse steak through the bars to the lioness; the keeper flipped it right in a puddle of her pee. Everyone snickered, and waited for the lioness to make some derisive expression.

Second, the keeper was more professional with the cheetah; he slid the meat in on a little tray, shook it off, and the cheetah pounced on it, snapping it around in his mouth. Just the way a house cat breaks a mouse's neck. Great roars from everyone. But the cheetah shook his meat too hard; a big hunk flew off and plopped on the ledge outside the bars. Everyone was hysterical. You see, the cheetah couldn't quite reach it, and being afraid someone would steal it, the poor animal set up this roar. Some children had to be taken outside the Cat House when all the other Big Cats started roaring too. They thought, you see, that this cheetah was threatening their own food. All of them were crouched down over their meat hunks, eating much too fast. All down the cage row, the tails were swishing—flanks flexed and twitching. And naturally, the people started hollering too. Someone pranced in front of the cheetah, pretending to make a grab for the meat on the ledge. The cheetah must have lost his mind, trying to jam his head between the bars. Then the keeper came back with a long pole that had a sort of gaffing hook on the end of it. The keeper snared the meat and flung it through the bars like a jai-alai ball. The cheetah reeled to the rear of his cage, the meat caught in his mouth. God, he ate up that meat in two terrible bites and swallows—not one bit of chewing—and sure enough, he gagged, finally spewing it all back up.

And when I left the Cat House, the cheetah was bolting down his vomit. The other Big Cats were padding in circles, envious that someone had a bit left to eat.

And even now, at four-thirty, I don't see any signs of the zoo getting ready to close. I'm under an umbrella in the *Biergarten.* You remember? The Rare Spectacled Bears. They've surely not bathed since the last time we were here; they're reeking worse than ever; they seem very nice, though; they're very gentle with each other. We should decide: either we let both of them out, or we leave them both. It wouldn't do to break them up. That's where the viciousness would come in.

Of course, I don't believe we can do anything for the Big Cats. I'm afraid they'll have to stay. Although I hate to admit it, we do have a responsibility to the *people* of this world.

(CONTINUING:)

THE HIGHLY SELECTIVE AUTOBIOGRAPHY OF
SIEGFRIED JAVOTNIK: PRE-HISTORY I

February 22, 1938: morning in the Rathaus Park. Hilke Marter and Zahn Glanz are sharing a bag of assorted Spanish nuts. They're taking a chilly, head-down walk, and they've kept a tally of how many different, following squirrels have begged and received a nut from the bag. Hilke and Zahn have counted four: one with a thin face, one with a tooth gone, one with a bitten ear, and one who limps. Zahn makes squirrel-summoning sounds. And Hilke says to the thin-faced one, "No, you've had yours. One apiece. Isn't there anyone else?"

"Just four squirrels in the whole park," says Zahn.

But my mother thinks she spots a fifth; they count again.

"Just four," says Zahn.

"No," says Hilke. "The one with the limp is gone." But Zahn believes it's the same, fourth squirrel who's given up limping for leaping.

"That's a different one," Hilke insists, and they approach a squirrel chasing its shadow. But the shadow-chaser isn't after its shadow at all. Zahn kneels, blocks off the squirrel's sun, and Hilke offers it an almond. And the squirrel goes right on unreasonably leaping, in circles.

"Some sort of calisthenics," says Zahn, and Hilke holds the almond closer. The squirrel reels, draws back, leaps—spinning and directionless, like a bronco tossing off its rider.

"It might be a trained squirrel," Hilke says, and sees the pink on its head.

"It's bald," says Zahn, and he reaches. The squirrel spins; its only course is around. And when Zahn has it in his lap, he sees that the baldness has a shape; there's an etching on the squirrel's head. The squirrel shuts its eyes and bites the air; Zahn stops breathing to unfog his view. The squirrel has a pink and perfect, hairless swastika carved on its head.

"My God," says Zahn.

"Poor thing," my mother says, and offers the almond again. But the squirrel appears dizzy and near to fainting. Maybe it was an almond that set the trap before. The scar is edged with blue; it pulses—signals that this squirrel wants nothing more to do with nuts. Zahn lets it go; it goes around.

Then my mother feels like bundling. Zahn tucks her head in the great fur collar of his cavalry coat, which is in style with students of politics and journalism; on snowy days there's such a wet-fur reek in the classrooms that the university smells like a rabbitry.

A line of tramcars comes down Stadiongasse at a tilting jog: the cars wince and tip along, like heavy men with cold, brittle feet. Hands are rubbing the steam from the windows, a few gay hats are waved; some fingertips are spread on the glass and pointed at the couple bundling in the Rathaus Park.

A wind blows up; the squirrels crouch when their fur gets tufted. Mindless of the wind, and of all else, the fifth squirrel goes his own way: around —leaping, maybe, to catch up with the hat it's lost, or to regain whatever sense is only skin-deep for squirrels.

"Someplace warm?" says Zahn, and feels Hilke Marter catch her breath against him. My mother gives a nod that bumps Zahn Glanz's bright, smooth chin.

The Third Zoo Watch:
Monday, June 5, 1967, @ 7:30 p.m.

I confess I've not seen any evidence of actual atrocities being performed on these animals, either by the guards or by the customers. Unhappy arrangements, I've seen, but actual atrocities, no. Of course I'll keep looking, but right now it's best if I don't come out of hiding. It will be dark very soon, and I can investigate more thoroughly.

I had plenty of time to get myself hidden. A little before five a janitorial fellow came through the *Biergarten,* sweeping across the flagstones with a great push broom. Well, I got up and strolled. All over the zoo I could hear the brushing sounds. When you passed a sweeper, he'd say, "The zoo's about to close."

I even saw some people *trotting* for the gates—panicked, it seemed, at the thought of spending the night.

I thought it best not to try and hide with any of the animals; that is, I felt if I got inside a pen with one of the safe creatures, I might be discovered by some after-hours guard whose job it is to come and wash the animals, or give them a bed check—read them a story, or even beat them.

I did consider the lofty shed of the Yukon dall sheep, which sits on top of a fake mountain—a man-made pile of ruins, knit together in cement. The Yukon dall sheep have the best view of the zoo, but I was worried by this after-hours-guard idea, and I also thought the animals might have an alarm system.

So I'm hiding between a high hedgerow and the fence line for the Assorted Antelopes. It's a long, thick hedgerow, but at root level I can find spaces to look through. I can watch down one path to the Cat House, I can see the roofs of the Small Mammal House and the House of Pachyderms; I can look up another path, past the great oryx's private shed and yard, all the way to where the Australian creatures dwell. I can move behind the cover of this hedge, almost fifty yards in two directions.

As far as guards go, they won't be any problem. The sweepers passed my way several times after the official closing. They came brooming along, chanting, "The zoo is closed. Is there anyone in the zoo?" They make a game of it.

After them, I saw what you'd call an official guard—actually two guards, or the same guard twice. He, or they, took more than an hour testing cages; giving a tug here, a clank there, jingling a very large keyring; and then seemed to leave by the main gate. That is, I can't see the main gate from here, but an hour after my last glimpse of anybody, I heard the main gate open and snap shut.

I've seen no one since then. It was a quarter to seven when I heard the gate. The animals are quieting down; someone with a large voice has a cold. And I'll be a while yet behind this hedgerow. I don't think it's going to be as dark a night as I'd like to have, and although it's been almost an hour since I've seen or heard another human being, I know someone's here.

(CONTINUING:)
THE HIGHLY SELECTIVE AUTOBIOGRAPHY OF
SIEGFRIED JAVOTNIK: PRE-HISTORY I

February 22, 1938: afternoon in a *Kaffeehaus* on Schauflergasse. My mother and Zahn rub steam off the window and look out at the Chancellery on the Ballhausplatz. But Chancellor Kurt von Schuschnigg isn't going to come and stand in an open window today.

The guard at the Chancellery stamps his boots and takes a wishful peek at the *Kaffeehaus,* which seems to be thawing; the snow is building ledges on the guard's mustache, and even his bayonet is blue. Zahn thinks the rifle bore is full of snow and no defense at all.

It's only a guard of honor, after all, which was certainly known well enough in 1934, when Otto Planetta walked past the honorable, unloaded gun, and with his own, dishonorable weapon shot and killed the previous Chancellor, little Engelbert Dollfuss.

But Otto's choice for a replacement didn't fare well; Nazi Doktor Rintelen attempted suicide by inaccurately shooting himself in a room at the

Imperial Hotel. And Kurt von Schuschnigg, friend of Dollfuss, moved his slow feet to fill his shoes.

"Does the guard of honor load his gun now?" says Zahn.

And Hilke squeaks her mitten over the window; she touches her nose to the glass. "It looks like it's loaded," she says.

"Guns are supposed to look loaded," says Zahn. "But that one just looks heavy."

"Student," the waiter says. "Why don't you charge the guard, and see?"

"I can't hear your radio," says Zahn, uneasy to be here—a new place with an untested volume, but the nearest warmth to the Rathaus Park.

The radio goes loud enough; it catches the guard's attention, and his boots start to waltz.

A taxi stops outside, and whoever is the taxi's fare dashes into the Chancellery, giving a hand signal to the guard. The driver comes and mashes his face against the *Kaffeehaus* window, fish-nostriled, appearing to have swum a snowy ocean to the farthest, glass end of his aquarium-world; he comes inside.

"Well, something's happening," he says.

But the waiter only asks, "A cognac? A tea with rum?"

"I've got a fare," the driver says, and comes to Zahn's table. He rubs himself a peep sight on the window above my mother's head.

"A cognac's quicker," the waiter says.

And the driver nods to Zahn, compliments him on the elegance of my mother's neck.

"It's not every day I get a fare like this," he says.

Zahn and Hilke make peep sights for themselves. The taxi stands chugging in its own exhaust; the windshield is icing and the wipers slip and rasp.

"Lennhoff," says the driver. "And he was in a hurry."

"You could have finished a cognac by now," the waiter says.

"Editor Lennhoff?" says Zahn.

"Of the *Telegraph,*" the driver says, and wipes his own breath from the window—peers down Hilke's neckline.

"Lenhoff's the best there is," says Zahn.

"He puts it straight," the driver says.

"He sticks his neck out," says the waiter.

The driver breathes like his standing taxi, short huffs and a long gust. "I'll have a cognac," he says.

"You won't have time," says the waiter, who's already got it poured.

And Hilke asks the driver, "Do you get a lot of important fares?"

"Well," he says, "important people like the taxi all right. And you get used to it after a while. You learn how to put them at their ease."

"How?" the waiter asks, and sets the driver's cognac on Zahn's table.

But the driver's eyes and mind are far down my mother's neckline; he takes a while to get back. He reaches over Hilke's shoulder for his cognac, tilts the glass and twirls to coat the rim around. "Well," he says, "you've got to be at ease yourself. You've got to be relaxed with them. Let them know you've seen something of the world too. Now, for example, Lennhoff there—you wouldn't want to say to him, 'Oh, I cut out all your editorials and save them!' But you want to let him know you're bright enough to recognize him; for example, I said just now, 'Good afternoon, Herr Lennhoff, but it's a cold one, isn't it?' Called him by name, you see, and he said, 'It's a cold one, all right, but it's nice and warm in here.' And right away he's at home with you."

"Well, they're just like anyone else," says the waiter.

And just like anyone else, Lennhoff stoops in the cold; his scarf flourishes and drags him off balance; he's flurried out of the Chancellery and swept into the surprised guard of honor, who's been scratching his back with his bayonet and has his rifle upsidedown above his head. The guard avoids stabbing himself by a batonlike brandish of his weapon. Lennhoff cringes before the spinning rifle; the guard begins a slow salute, stops it midway— remembering that newspaper editors aren't saluted—and offers a hand-shake instead. Lennhoff moves to accept the hand, then remembers that this isn't part of his own protocol. The two scuff their feet, and Lennhoff allows himself to be buffeted out to the curb; he crosses the Ballhausplatz to the shuddering taxi.

The driver fires his cognac down, swallowing most of it through his nose; his eyes blear. He swims his way up Hilke's neckline, clears his head, and steadies himself with a touch of Hilke's shoulder. "Oh, excuse me," he says, and gives another complimentary nod to Zahn. Zahn rubs the window.

Lennhoff pounds on the taxitop; he opens the driver's-side door and blares on the horn.

With a miraculous, run-on fumble, the driver finds the right change for the waiter—touches my mother's shoulder again, and gets his chin tucked under his scarf. The waiter holds the door; the snow scoots over the driver's boots and flies up his pants. He slaps his knees together, spreads himself out thin and knifes into the flurry. At the sight of him, the horn blares again.

Lennhoff still must be in a hurry. The taxi reels round the Ballhausplatz, drifts to a curb and caroms off. Then the snow makes the taxi's straightaway journey seem so slow and soft.

"I'd like to drive a taxi," says Zahn.

"It's easy enough to do," the waiter says. "You just have to know how to drive."

And Zahn orders a bowl of hot wine soup. One bowl with two spoons. Hilke is fussy about the spicing; Zahn sprinkles not enough cinnamon and too much clove. The waiter watches the spoons compete.

"I could have given you two bowls," he says.

And Zahn hears the signal blip he knows so well—newstime, Radio

Johannesgasse. He pins down my mother's spoon with his own and wishes the waves in the soup to be still.

Worldwide: French chargé d'affaires in Rome, M. Blondel, is rumored to have suffered some unspeakable insult from Count Ciano; and Anthony Eden has resigned from whatever he's been doing.

Austria: Chancellor Kurt von Schuschnigg has confirmed his new appointments to the Cabinet—Seyss-Inquart and four other Nazis.

Local: there's been a tram accident in the first district, at the intersection of Gumpendorfer Strasse and Nibelungengasse. A driver on Strassenbahn Line 57, Klag Brahms, says he was creeping down Gumpendorfer when a man came running out of Nibelungen. The tram tracks were iced, of course, and the driver didn't want to risk a derailment. Klag Brahms says the man was running very fast, or was caught in a gale. But a woman in the second tramcar says the man was being chased by a gang of youths. Another passenger in the same tramcar refutes the woman's theory; the unidentified source says that this woman is always seeing look-alike gangs of youths. The victim himself is as yet unidentified; anyone who thinks he knows him may call Radio Johannesgasse. The man is described as old and small.

"And dead," the waiter says, while Hilke tries to remember all the old, small men she knows. No one she can think of was ever in the habit of running on Nibelungengasse.

But Zahn was counting up his fingers. "How many days ago was it," he asks, "when Schuschnigg went to Berchtesgaden and visited with Hitler?" And the waiter starts counting his own fingers.

"Ten," says Zahn, with fingers enough. "Just ten days, and now we've got five Nazis on the Cabinet."

"Half a Nazi a day," says the waiter, and spread-eagles a handful of fingers.

"Little old Herr Baum," my mother says, "isn't his shoe-shop on some street like Nibelungen?"

And the waiter asks Zahn, "Don't you think the man was chased? I've seen those gangs around myself."

And Hilke's seen them too, she remembers. In trams, or in the theater, they sprawl their legs in the aisles; arm in arm, they shoulder you off the sidewalks. Sometimes they march in step, and they're great at following you home.

"Zahn?" my mother asks. "Would you like to come home for supper?"

But Zahn is looking out the window. When the wind drops, the guard of honor looms clear and motionless; then the snow gusts him over. A totem-soldier, turned to ice—if you bashed his face, his cheek would break off bloodless in the snow.

"That's no defense at all," says Zahn, and adds, "Now the trouble starts."

"*Now?*" the waiter says. "It started four years ago. Four years ago this July, when you weren't even much of a student. He came in here and had a cup of mocha. He sat just where you're sitting. I'll never forget him."

"Who?" says Zahn.

"Otto Planetta," the waiter says. "Had his cup of mocha, watching out the window, the smug pig. Then a whole truckful of them unloaded outside. SS Standarte Eighty-nine, but they *looked* like Army Regulars. This Otto Planetta—he had his change all counted—he said, 'Why, there's my brother.' And out he went, marched right in with the rest of them, and killed poor Dollfus; he shot him twice."

"Well, it didn't work," says Zahn.

"If I'd known who he was," the waiter says, "I'd have had him where he sat—right where you're sitting." And the waiter fumbles in his apron pocket, comes up with a pair of meat shears. "These would have done him, all right," he says.

"But Schuschnigg took over," says my mother. "And didn't Dollfuss want Schuschnigg?"

"In fact," Zahn says, "when Dollfuss was dying, he asked that Schuschnigg be the new Chancellor."

"He asked for a priest," the waiter says, "and they let him die without one."

My mother can remember more; these are the sad, family pieces of history she remembers over the rest. "His wife and children were in Italy," she says. "His children sent him flowers on the day he was killed, so he never got them."

"Schuschnigg's half of what Dollfuss was," says the waiter, "and you know what's amazing? Dollfuss was such a *little* man. I used to watch him going out and coming in, you know. I mean, he was a *tiny* one—with all his clothes too big for him. Really, he was almost an *elf.* But it didn't matter at all, did it?"

"How do you know," says Zahn, "that it was Otto Planetta who came in here?" Then Zahn notices the waiter's size. He's a very small waiter. And the hand that holds the meat shears is more fragile than my mother's.

The Fourth Zoo Watch:
Monday, June 5, 1967, @ 9:00 p.m.

There's a nightwatchman, all right. But as far as I know, there's just one.

I waited an hour after dark, and I didn't see anyone. Nevertheless, I promised myself I wouldn't come out from behind the hedgerow until I knew the whereabouts of the guard. And a half-hour ago I saw a light I knew was inside the zoo. It was a glow, coming from the Small Mammal House. The light had probably been on since nightfall, but I hadn't noticed it as being actually inside the zoo—and not a reflection from Hietzing. At first I was frightened; I thought the Small Mammal House might be on fire.

But the light didn't flicker. I went along my hedgerow to the corner of the fence line that gave me the best view. Trees in my way, a cage looming up here and there; I couldn't see the doorway, but I could see the eaves under the tiled roof, taking on a glow that had to come from the ground in front of the building. It had to be that; after all, there are no windows in the Small Mammal House.

I may have been sure of myself, but I was careful. Inching along stooped over—at times on all fours—against the cages and pens. I startled something. Something got up right next to me and thrashed into a gallop; snorted or whinnied or harumphed. I went down along the ponds of Various Aquatic Birds—all with fairly high pool curbs and signposts here and there: histories and bird legends. I had good cover round the ponds, and I found a spot with a clear view of the Small Mammal House's door. It was open; there was a light coming down the long hall and landing outside, thrown back up against the building. I think the light comes from an open room round the corner at the end of the hall. You remember the Small Mammal House—all those corridors winding round and round, in the fake night of infrared?

I did some thinking while I waited. It might not have been the night-watchman's room at all; it might have been a light left on to give the nocturnal beasts a chance to sleep—in a daylight as illusory as their infrared night.

I nested in a shrub and leaned my arms on a pool curb. I read the nearest bird legend in the moonlight. It had to do with auks. The Hietzinger Zoo has only one member of the auk family. It is the least auklet, described as small and wizen-faced, and rather stupid; it has been known to wander down the paths, where it can easily get stepped on. In fact, the king of the auk family was such a stupid bird it became extinct. The great auk was last seen alive in 1844, and the last dead great auk, to be seen, was washed ashore at Trinity Bay, Ireland, in 1853. The great auk was both inquisitive and gullible, the legend says. If quietly approached, it would stand its ground. It was a favorite to provision fishing vessels; fishermen stalked the shorelines, approaching quietly and beating the auks with clubs.

Pretentious bird legend! Do they mean that the great auk was stupid—or that stupid men extinguished the great auk?

I looked about for the great auk's surviving kin, but I found no silly least auklet—not wandering down the paths, either, or dolting underfoot.

I was watched for awhile. Something webfooted tottered down the pool curb to me, stopped a few feet away and garbled softly—wishing to know whom I came to see at such an odd hour. It flopped down in the water and paddled past below me, gurgling—perhaps complaining; I believe, from its backswept head, it was an eared grebe, and I'd like to think it was encouraging me.

I got a little stiff and damp among the ponds, but I got to see the guard. He came out in the hallway of light and squinted out the door. Uniformed, holstered, and although I couldn't really see—certainly armed; he took his flashlight for a walk down the dim hall and through the dark zoo—not as dark as I would wish it; there's too much moon.

> But, oh, it's oh
> so easy!—
> Watching
> Watchmen.

(CONTINUING:)
THE HIGHLY SELECTIVE AUTOBIOGRAPHY OF
SIEGFRIED JAVOTNIK: PRE-HISTORY I

March 9, 1938—and every Wednesday teatime—my Grandmother Marter straightens fork tines. Grandfather Marter is impatient with the Pflaumenkuchen; the plum skins are blistered from the oven, and anyone can see the cake's too hot to eat. But my grandfather always burns his tongue. Then he paces in the kitchen; he sneaks more rum in his tea.

"I hate this waiting for the damn cake to cool," he says. "If the cake were started earlier, we'd have it ready with the tea."

And Grandmother aims a fork at him. "Then you'd want to have tea sooner," she says. "Then you'd start your waiting sooner, and move everything up so we'd be having our tea on top of lunch."

Zahn keeps his teacup in his lap; so he's ready when Grandfather comes round the table, sneaking rum. Grandfather tilts the bottle from his hip.

"Watch out for my Hilke, Zahn," he says. "Watch out she's not a know-it-all like her Muttie."

"Muttie's right," says Hilke. "You'd fuss around and burn yourself, no matter when the cake came out of the oven."

"You see, Zahn?" says Grandfather.

"The forks are all straight," Grandmother announces. "Nobody's going to stab a lip now!" she crows. "Real silver, you know, Zahn—it's so soft it bends easy."

"Muttie," says Hilke, "Zahn's got a job now."

"But you're in school, Zahn," says Grandfather.

"He's driving a taxi," Hilke says. "He can drive me around."

"It's just a part-time job," says Zahn. "I'm still in school."

"I like riding taxis," Grandmother says.

"And just when do you do all your taxi-riding?" says Grandfather. "You always take the trams when you're out with me."

Grandmother prods the plum cake with one of her forks. "It's cool enough now," she announces.

"Know-it-alls," says Grandfather. "Everyone's a know-it-all today."

And before he draws a chair up to the kitchen table, he feels obliged—for Zahn's happiness—to jar the static out of the radio.

Zahn is pleased. Here's Radio Johannesgasse, clear for tea, and he anticipates the newstime signal blip. Time is that dependable on Wednesdays; when the forks are straight and the cake's cool, it's time for news.

Worldwide: Steenockerzeel Castle, Belgium, where the Habsburg Pretender lives. Legitimist leader Freiherr von Wiesner calls on all Austrian monarchists to resist Nazi Germany's continued pressure to incorporate Austria into the Reich. Von Wiesner appealed to Chancellor Schuschnigg that a return of the monarchy would offer the best resistance to Germany.

Austria: Tyrolean-born Kurt von Schuschnigg, at a mass meeting in Innsbruck, announced to his native province, and to the world, that in four days' time, on Sunday, the country will hold a plebiscite. The voters may decide for themselves—an independent Austria, or the Anschluss with Germany. Chancellor Schuschnigg ended his speech by shouting in Tyrolean dialect to the twenty thousand assembled in the Maria-Theresien-Platz: "Men, the time has come!" In Innsbruck this had special significance, of course, because one hundred and thirty years ago the peasant hero Andreas Hofer had with the same cry impassioned his countrymen to resist Napoleon.

Local: a young woman identified as Mara Madoff, daughter of clothier Sigismund Madoff, was found this morning hanging in her coat on a coat hook in the second-balcony wardrobe closet of the Vienna State Opera House. Opera custodian Odilo Linz, who discovered the body, says he's sure this particular closet is never used, and at least wasn't being used at last night's performance of *Lohengrin*. Odilo checked the closet sometime during the Prelude; he says nothing was hanging there then. Authorities attribute the cause of death to a star-shaped series of fine-pointed stab wounds in the heart, and estimate the time of death as well toward the end of the opera. The authorities say that the young woman was in no way assaulted; however, her stockings were missing and her shoes had been put back on. Late last night, someone claims to have seen a group of young men at the Haarhof Keller; allegedly, one of them wore a pair of women's stockings for a scarf. But among the young men, these days, this is a common way of showing off.

Also local: spokesmen for several anti-Nazi groups have already pledged their endorsement of Schuschnigg's proposed plebiscite. Karl Mittler has promised the support of the underground Socialists; Colonel Wolff has spoken for the monarchists; Doktor Friedmann for the Jewish community; Cardinal Innitzer for the Catholics. Chancellor Schuschnigg will be taking the overnight train from the Alps and is scheduled to arrive in Vienna by early morning. Some welcome is expected for him.

"Some welcome, for sure!" says Zahn. "He's done something, anyway, to show we're not just Hitler's backyard."

"Know-it-all," says Grandfather. "Just who does he think he is? Another

Andreas Hofer, standing up to Napoleon. Cheers in the Tyrol—*that* I believe. But what do they say about Schuschnigg in Berlin? We're not standing up to a Frenchman this time."

"God," says Zahn. "Give him some credit. The vote's a sure thing. Nobody wants Germany in Austria."

"You're thinking like a taxi driver now, all right," Grandfather says. *"Nobody,* you say—and what does it matter?—*wants,* you say. I'll tell you what *I* want, and how little it matters. I want a man who'll do what he says he'll do. And that was Dollfuss, and he got murdered by some of those *nobodies* you mention. And now we've got Schuschnigg, that's what we've got."

"But he's called for an open vote," Zahn says.

"And it's four days away," says Grandfather, scornfully—and notices the cake crumbs he's sprayed about the table. He grows a bit muttery, and his ears blush. "I'm telling you, student or taxi driver or whatnot," he says, careful of cake, "it's a good thing the world's not flat, or Schuschnigg would have backed off long ago."

"You're such an old pessimist," Hilke says.

"Yes, you are," says Grandmother, herding crumbs off the tablecloth with one of her forks, "and you're the biggest know-it-all there is, too. And got the worst eating manners I've seen, for someone of your colossal age."

"Of my what?" shouts Grandfather, and showers cake. "Where'd you ever learn to say a thing like that?"

And Grandmother, haughtily, moistens a fingertip, dabs at a cake crumb on Grandfather's tie. "I read it in a book you brought home," she says proudly, "and I thought it was very poetical. And you're always telling me I don't read enough, you *know-it-all.*"

"Just show me the book," says Grandfather, "so I won't make the mistake of reading it."

Zahn makes faces at Grandfather, to show his tea is weak on rum. "Well, there's going to be some celebrating tomorrow," he says. "I could make a pile of fares, all right."

And Hilke is deciding what she'll wear. The one-piece, red wool jersey with the big roll collar. If it doesn't snow.

The Fifth Zoo Watch:
Monday, June 5, 1967, @ 11:45 p.m.

The watchman starts his first round at a quarter to nine and returns to the Small Mammal House at a quarter past. He made another round from quarter to eleven till quarter past. It was just the same.

The second time, I stayed behind the hedgerow and let him pass by close to me. I can tell you what he looks like from the waist down. A military snap-flap holster on a skinny ammunition belt that holds twelve rounds; I don't know how many rounds his snubnose revolver holds. The keyring loops through the ammunition belt; it would be too heavy for a belt loop. The flashlight has a wrist thong and is cased in metal; it may make up for the fact that he doesn't carry a truncheon. Gray twill uniform pants, wide at the ankle, and cuffless. The socks are funny; they have a squiggly design, and one of them keeps slipping into the heel of his shoe; he's always stopping to tug it up. The shoes are just black shoes, sort of everyday shoes. He doesn't take his uniform very seriously.

I was in no danger of being spotted. He shone his light along the hedges, but they're too thick to penetrate. Maybe if he'd been down on all fours, shining at root level—and if his eyesight had been very keen to begin with —he might have seen through to me. But you can tell what a good place to hide I've got.

This watchman doesn't seem so bad. He's sometimes inconsiderate as to where he shines his flashlight. He just flashes it around to every little cough or stir, and you'd think by now he'd know the dreaming prattle of his charges, and wouldn't have to be checking up on every little snore. Still, he doesn't seem to be malicious about it. He may be nervous, or bored—and trying to find as much to look at as he can.

He even seems to have his favorites. I watched him call a zebra over to the fence line. "Fancy horse," he said. "Come here, fancy horse." And one of the zebras, who must have been awake and waiting, came alongside him, shoving its muzzle over the fence. The watchman fed it something—certainly, against the rules—and gave its ears a tug or two. Now, any man who likes zebras can't be all bad.

He also has an interesting relationship with one of the lesser kangaroos. I think it's the wallaby, or perhaps the wallaroo; they're rather similar, at the distance I was from them. It wasn't the great gray boomer, certainly; I could have noted the size of that monster, the whole length of the path. Anyway, the watchman called somebody over. "Hey, you Australian," he said. "Hey, you dandy, come over here and box." And somebody thumped; a long, sharp ear sprang up—a stiff tail thwacked the ground. Maybe the guard's tone was a little taunting, and it may have been rude of him to be waking up the Australian's neighbors. But this watchman is a pretty gentle type, I feel. If it turns out that he's the guard we have to nab and stash, I'd want to do the job as politely as possible.

Something strange just happened. A little bell rang in the Small Mammal House; very clearly, I heard it ring. The animals heard it too. There was a tossing, a general turnover—coughs, grunts, startled snorts; a lot of short, wary breathing. There are a number of those noises things make when they're trying to keep quiet; joints snap, stomachs rumble, swallowing is loud.

First the bell rang, then the watchman came out of the Small Mammal House. I saw his flashlight nodding. Then I saw this flashing down one of the paths; I think it came from the main zoo gate, and I think the watchman flashed back to it.

Along the fence line, behind my hedgerow, the Assorted Antelopes are shuffling their hooves. Something's up, all right. I mean it; it's midnight and this zoo is wide-awake.

(CONTINUING:)
THE HIGHLY SELECTIVE AUTOBIOGRAPHY OF
SIEGFRIED JAVOTNIK: PRE-HISTORY I

March 10, 1938: a warm, unsnowy Thursday, perfect for Hilke's one-piece, red wool jersey with the big roll collar.

In the early morning, about the time Chancellor Schuschnigg's train from Innsbruck is arriving at the Westbahnhof—and just after Zahn Glanz has chalked JA! SCHUSCHNIGG! on the black hood of his taxi—a chicken farmer in the outskirting countryside of Hacking begins getting dressed for the celebrations anticipated in the city. Ernst Watzek-Trummer has neglected the eggs this morning and collected the feathers instead. Which is no less strange than the work that kept him up all night—puncturing and wiring together tin pieplates to make a suit of mock chainmail, and then larding the suit to make the surface sticky enough to hold the chicken feathers he now rolls in. Anyone watching Ernst Watzek-Trummer getting dressed would never buy a single egg from him again. But no one sees, except the chickens who squabble out of his way as he rolls back and forth through his feather pile on the henhouse floor. And, moreover, no one could accuse Ernst Watzek-Trummer of being extravagant; this costume hasn't cost him a thing. The pieplates he has plenty of, and they can still be used for selling eggs in; and this is more use than he's ever got out of the feathers before. Why, even the head of his costume is pieplates, a helmet of pieplates, two for the earflaps, one for the top, and one bent to fit his face—with eyeholes, and a breathing hole, and two tiny punctured holes for the wire which fastens on the hammered tin of his beak. A beak sharp enough to lance a man through. And between the eyeholes is a decal of the Austrian eagle, steamed off the bumper of Ernst Watzek-Trummer's truck and reaffixed with lard. So that hasn't cost him either. And it is undeniably an eaglesuit of frightening authenticity—or if not authentic, at least strong. The feathered chainmail hangs to his knees, and the pieplate sleeves are made loose enough for flapping. He leaves the head unfeathered, but lards it anyway —not only to make the decal stick, but to make his whole dome gleam. Ernst Watzek-Trummer, for this day an eagle—and the Austrian eagle in particular—finishes dressing in his henhouse, and clanks fiercely toward the outlying district of the city, hoping he will be permitted to ride on the tram.

And Zahn Glanz, en route to my mother's street, has stopped once, just to let a little air out of his tires to make them squeal, and is now practicing the noise of his cornering in the rotary between the technical high school and Karl's Church.

And Grandfather Marter has decided not to go to work this morning, because no one will be reading in the foreign-language reading room of the International Student House anyway, and so the head librarian won't be missed. Grandfather watches for Zahn's taxi because he can at least indulge the young their optimism, Grandmother has said, and he can certainly indulge himself whatever drink is due a day of celebration.

And Zahn, on his fourth trip around the rotary, sees an early Mass letting out of Karl's Church. Only slightly money-minded, Zahn thinks an early fare would nicely preface his arrival at my mother's. He idles his taxi at the curb in front of Karl's Church, and reads his *Telegraph* spread over the wheel. Lennhoff's editorial praises Schuschnigg's plebiscite, expresses snide curiosity concerning Germany's reaction.

While at the Hütteldorf-Hacking Station for Strassenbahn Line 49, a sour tram driver refuses a ride to a man in an eaglesuit. Ernst Watzek-Trummer adjusts his beak, thumps his breast feathers and struts on.

And on the Ballhausplatz, Chancellor Kurt von Schuschnigg peers from a Chancellery window and spots a banner stretched from the balustrade of St. Michael's, across the Michaelerplatz, to a balustrade of the Hofburg showrooms. The banner is bed sheets stitched together, the lettering is neat and enormous: SCHUSCHNIGG, FOR A FREE AUSTRIA. And the Chancellor guesses that, in order for him to be able to see it at this distance, the comma must be the size of a man's head. It warms him to the tip of his Tyrolean to know that beyond the banner, down Augustinerstrasse, to the Albertinaplatz and still beyond—throughout the Inner City—the throng is toasting him.

It would warm him even more to see the determination of Ernst Watzek-Trummer, who is suffering the humiliation of being thrown from a tramcar at the St. Veit Station—in full view of the children who've been collected along the way from Hacking, and who've been following at a steady, taunting distance. The eagle leaves a few untidy larded feathers; he struts on. But Chancellor Kurt von Schuschnigg can't see over five city districts to witness this unique, patriotic demonstration.

Grandfather Marter would say that the Chancellor has never been particularly far-sighted. My grandfather fancies himself as having a monopoly on far-sightedness. For example, he says to my mother, "Hilke, get your coat, it's Zahn"—while Zahn is still three blocks away, and only now, thinking that early Mass-goers must be walking types, decides to abandon the curb at Karl's Church. But whether it's far-sightedness or plain impatience,

Grandfather and Hilke have their coats on when Zahn turns down their street.

"Don't get in any scuffles," says my grandmother.

"You just read a good book," Grandfather tells her.

And it's midafternoon before Grandfather Marter has a vision through a smeary window of the Augustiner Keller; he sloshes his beer and hides his face against Zahn's collar. He giggles.

"Father!" says Hilke, embarrassed.

"Are you going to be sick?" Zahn asks, and my grandfather snaps his face around to the window again; he still keeps hold of Zahn's lapel, ready to dive back in hiding if the creature of his vision reappears.

"It's the biggest bird I ever saw," he mutters, and then his vision looms round the revolving door—is flown into the *Keller* with staggering, tinny wing flaps, alarming a counter row of men munching sausage; they stumble backward in a wave; a thick slice of meat flaps to the floor, and they all stare at it as if it were someone's heart or hand.

"Jesus!" says Grandfather, and dives for Zahn's lapel again.

The vision with the terrifying wingspan clatters its feathered pieplate breast. *"Cawk!"* it cries. *"Cawk! Cawk!* Austria is free!" And very slowly, after an awesome silence, drinkers, one by one, rush to embrace the national symbol.

"Cawk!" says Grandfather, with dignity again, and Zahn catches hold of the eagle's chainmail, dragging him to their table; his beak nearly stabs my grandfather, who greets the great bird with a bear hug.

"Oh, *look* at you," says Grandfather. "What a *fine* eagle!"

"I came all the way to Europa Platz on foot," the eagle says, "before I was allowed on the tram."

"Who put you off?" shouts Grandfather, furious.

"Drivers, here and there," Ernst Watzek-Trummer says.

"There's very little patriotism in the outer districts," my grandfather tells him.

"I made it all myself too," the eagle says. "I'm just an egg man, really. I've got chickens"—touching his feathers, and tapping the tin underneath —"and I've got these little pans around, for selling eggs in."

"Marvelous!" says Zahn.

"You're beautiful," Hilke tells the eagle, and pokes his downy parts, where the feathers are all wadded up and stuck on the thickest—under his tin-jutting chin, wild across his breast and gathered in his wing pits.

"Take off your head," says Zahn. "You can't drink with your head on."

And a wave of jostling men surges up behind the eagle. "Yes! Take off your head!" they shout, and reach and slosh their way nearer the bird.

"Don't crowd! Show some respect!" Grandfather says.

A violinist skitters to the balcony above their table—a cellist, stooping and grunting, follows. They refold their handkerchiefs.

"Music!" says Grandfather, lording over the *Keller* now.

The violinist tweaks his bow. The cellist creaks a string of finger-thickness; everyone clutches his spine, as if the cellist had struck a vertebra.

"Now quiet!" says Grandfather, still in charge. The eagle spreads his wings.

"Take off your head," Zahn whispers, and the music begins—a *Volkslied* to make the mighty blubber.

Hilke helps the eagle off with his head. Ernst Watzek-Trummer crinkles his old elfish face and sinks a dimple deep in his chin. My mother wants to kiss him; my grandfather does—out of second-joy, perhaps, to find so many gray hairs fringing the eagle's ears. Only a man of my grandfather's generation could be the Austrian eagle.

Ernst Watzek-Trummer is overcome—toasted and kissed by a man of some education, he can tell. He keeps agonized time with the *Volkslied*. His head is reverently passed around; it skids from hand to hand, losing lard and some of its gleam.

The windows frost. Someone suggests they devise a plan to fly the eagle —to hang him and swing him from the balustrade of St. Michael's. If they did it at St. Michael's, then Schuschnigg could see. Suspenders are offered. The eagle seems willing, but my grandfather is stern.

"Sirs," he says, and hands back a broad pair of red suspenders. "Please, sirs." And surveys the puzzled, blurry faces of the men holding up their pants with their thumbs. "My daughter is with us," says Grandfather, and he gently lifts my mother's face to the crowd. They retreat, admonished, and the eagle survives a near-swinging—what might have been a most elastic flight, with the combined snap-and-stretch of strong and weak suspenders.

Ernst Watzek-Trummer makes it safely to Zahn's taxi. At Grandfather's suggestion, the eagle blunts his beak with a wine cork—so he won't give injury on his way through the throng to the door. With beak corked—and a little bit bent, getting into the taxi—he enfolds my mother and grandfather in the backseat, while Zahn reels them through the Michaelerplatz, under the rumpling bed sheets that bless Schuschnigg, and down the *Kaffeehaus* alleys off the Graben.

Zahn announces, with shouts and his horn, the deliverance of Austria. *"Cawk! Cawk!"* he cries. "The country's free!" And the by now weary observers, sobering in coffee and behind hand-rubbed peep sights on steamy windows, pay little attention. They're already tired of miracles. This is only some large bird in a flying taxi's backseat.

And waiting up for them is my grandmother—book open, tea cold. When she sees the eagle led into her kitchen, she turns to Grandfather as if he's brought home a pet they can't afford to feed. "Lord, look at you!" she says to him. "And your daughter with you all the while."

"Cawk!" the eagle says.

"What does it want, Zahn?" Grandmother asks. And to Grandfather: "You haven't bought it, have you? Or signed anything?"

"It's the Austrian eagle!" says Grandfather. "Show some respect!"

And Grandmother looks, not quite respectfully; she peers past the corked beak, into the eyeholes.

"Frau Marter," says the eagle. "I'm Ernst Watzek-Trummer, from Hacking."

"A patriot!" Grandfather shouts, and clomps the eagle's shoulder. A feather falls; it appears to go on falling forever.

"Muttie," says Hilke. "He made the suit himself."

And Grandmother makes a wary reach, touching the plumage on the eagle's breast.

Grandfather gently says, "It's just a little last fling I was having, Muttie. Our daughter's been properly looked after."

"Oh, indeed she has!" says Zahn, and thumps the eagle.

And Grandfather very sadly says, "Oh, it's Austria's last fling too, Muttie." And he genuflects before the eagle.

Ernst Watzek-Trummer covers his eyeholes, trembles his feathers and starts to cry—a grinding whimper into his beak.

"*Cawk! Cawk!*" says Zahn, still gay, but the eagle's helmet is rattling with sobs.

"Oh, there," Grandfather says. "Here now, you're a fine patriot, aren't you? There, there—and didn't we have some evening, though? And Zahn's going to drive you home, you know."

"Oh, the poor thing," says Grandmother.

And together, all of them, they get the eagle to the taxi.

"You'll have the whole backseat to yourself," says Zahn.

"Get his head off," Grandfather says. "He could drown."

And Hilke says to her father: "It's all your fault, you pessimist."

"You know-it-all!" says Grandmother.

But Grandfather is slamming doors and directing imaginary traffic on the empty street. He signals to Zahn that it's safe to pull away.

Zahn drives through the cemetery stillness of the outer districts—Hadik and St. Veit and Hütteldorf-Hacking—where, Zahn can only guess, the ghosts and present dwellers seem as ready or not to welcome the Holy Roman Empire as Hitler.

While the eagle takes himself apart in the backseat. And when Zahn finds the dark farm hiding outside the glow from the night-laying henhouse, there's a disheveled old man in his rear-view mirror, weeping—and feathers are floating all over the taxi.

"Come on," says Zahn, but Ernst Watzek-Trummer is attacking the empty eagle, shouldering it against the frontseat. He's trying to break its back, but the eagle is surprisingly well made; it slumps in a half-sit position, its weave of pieplates stronger than a spine.

"All right, all right now," says Zahn. "Just look at what you're doing to your suit." But Ernst Watzek-Trummer punches, snatches handfuls of feathers and gropes his kicking-foot along the floor—trying to find and squash the fallen head.

Zahn crawls in the backseat after him and wrestles him out the door. Ernst Watzek-Trummer flaps his arms. Zahn shuts the door and steers the egg man.

"Oh, please," says Zahn. "You'll have a good sleep, won't you? And I'll drive out and bring you to the polls myself."

The egg man buckles; Zahn lets him stumble forward but comes round in front of him to hold up his head. They kneel, facing each other.

"Can you remember?" says Zahn. "I'll pick you up for the plebiscite. I'll drive you to the polls. All right?"

Ernst Watzek-Trummer stares hard and lifts his fanny like a sprinter poising up on the blocks; he jerks his head as if to charge, draws Zahn off and scampers round him—on all fours, but running himself upright. He stops and looks back at Zahn. Zahn plots a move.

"Come on," says Zahn. "You'll go to bed, won't you? You won't get in any trouble, will you?"

Ernst Watzek-Trummer lets his arms hang. "There won't be any vote," he says. "They'll never get away with it, you young fool." And he breaks for his henhouse; Zahn starts after him, but stops. A doorway of light opens on Zahn's horizon, and then Ernst Watzek-Trummer closes it after him. The henhouse stoops under its own roof and groans; there's a moment, Zahn is sure, when eggs are caught in the act, half laid. Then there's some squabbling; Zahn sees a hen go winging or falling past a window; the light inside dances or is swung. Another hen, or even the same one, shrieks. Then the light goes out; there won't be any eggs laid tonight. Zahn waits until he's sure that Ernst Watzek-Trummer has found a berth—has put someone off his roost. But whoever is put out is at least being quiet about it.

Zahn wobbles back to the taxi, sits on the running board and has a pull from the cognac bottle Grandfather has left with him. He tries to smoke, but he can't keep lit. And he's almost behind the wheel and driving off when he spots the eagle, uninhabited, leaning over the front-seat. Zahn sits the eagle beside him, but it keeps slumping over; Zahn finds the eagle's head, sits it in the eagle's lap—offers it some of my grandfather's cognac.

"You'll have quite a head in the morning," Zahn tells it, and begins a giggle that turns into a sneezing bout, a fit—a seizure loud enough to cause some clucking in the henhouse. Zahn can't stop; hysterical, he sees himself in the eaglesuit suddenly looming into the henhouse, switching on the light and *cawk*ing till the frenzied hens begin a binge of laying eggs—or never lay an egg again; *cawk*ing so loudly that Ernst Watzek-Trummer lays the greatest egg of all.

But Zahn just offers the eagle's head another drink; when it fails to respond, he pours a shot down the head hole.

It seems to Zahn that they talk for hours, passing the bottle, keeping watch over the darkened henhouse, guarding the sleep of Ernst Watzek-Trummer on his lordly roost.

"Drink up, brave eagle!" says Zahn, and watches the head hole quaffing down the upended bottle.

The Sixth Zoo Watch:
Tuesday, June 6, 1967, @ 1:30 a.m.

The changing of the guard happened at midnight, and things haven't been the same since. Everyone is still awake. Really—this zoo is one restless stir and scuff; no one is asleep. A general insomnia arrived at midnight.

At first, I thought they were on to me. I thought the first-shift guard told the second-shift guard that someone was prowling about. Or, perhaps, the animals passed the word around; along some universal grapevine of tapped hooves, twitters, grunts and such, they told each other about me. And now they're waiting to see what I'll do.

But I don't think that's really why the zoo's awake. It's because of the new nightwatchman. The little bell-ringing prepared everyone; the animals were expecting him. There's some difference in the guards, I can tell you.

He walked by me. This one's got a truncheon; he sticks it in a sheath that's stitched inside his left boot. They're above-ankle, modified combat boots, laced loosely at the calf. The gray twills tuck in the boots. He wears an open holster, cowboy-style, and the barrel of his clip-load handgun is at least six inches long. He does an interesting thing with the key ring. He puts his arm through it and hikes it up on his shoulder; he fastens it under an epaulette—his uniform still has both epaulettes too. All the keys hang under his armpit and jangle against him. It seems awkward to me; if you've a bunch of keys in your armpit, you carry your arm funny. It's his right arm, though, and maybe that puts him in a better position for going at the open holster, which is worn rather high on his right hip. I think, although he looks a bit off balance, he has his hardware fairly well understood. Of course, he's got a flashlight too. He carries that left-handed, and it's on a wrist thong—so it wouldn't interfere if he reached for the truncheon. That's reasonable: if you're close enough to use a truncheon, you don't need a flashlight to see; if you're far enough away to use a gun, you want a flashlight steady in your other hand. I think this watchman takes his job seriously.

He walked the length of my hedgerow. When he'd passed me, I leaned out through a root gap—just enough to see him from the waist up: the key ring, the epaulettes, the crook in his right arm. But I only saw the whole of him back-to, and it had to be a quick look. He's very sudden with his flashlight. He'll be nodding the light out on his boot toes, and then he'll whirl and paint a circle of light around himself.

It's been an hour and a half, and he's still out in the zoo, whirling his light. Perhaps he thinks the first-shift guard is careless. Perhaps, before he settles down to a normal watch, he has to make the place safe in his mind.

It must make the animals very nervous to have this disturbance every night. I see the watchman's sudden circles of light—often three or four times in the same area. And he's very aggressive about checking the locks. Just a tug won't do for him—he trembles the cages.

It's no wonder everyone's awake.

(CONTINUING:)
THE HIGHLY SELECTIVE AUTOBIOGRAPHY OF
SIEGFRIED JAVOTNIK: PRE-HISTORY I

Black Friday, March 11, 1938: at a little after half past five, the early morning priests are setting up the side altars in St. Stephen's and Kurt von Schuschnigg ducks in for a very brief, clear prayer. He's been up and en route to the Chancellery ever since Secretary of Security Skubl phoned him about the Germans closing the border at Salzburg and withdrawing all customs officials. Skubl also mentioned a German troop build-up from Reichenhall to Passau. And at the Chancellery, Schuschnigg finds the sour telegram from Austria's consulate general in Munich: LEO AS READY TO TRAVEL. All this before it's light outside, and before all of the morning's German press has been telegraphed to Vienna for Kurt von Schuschnigg's perusal. They have just a smattering of German sentiment to go on, though it should be enough. The Nazi news agency, D.N.B., claims that hammer-and-sickle flags have been hoisted in Vienna, and that the frenzied citizens have been yelling, "Heil Schuschnigg! Heil Moskau!" in the same breath. D.N.B. says that the Führer might be forced to make an "anti-Bolshevik crusade," on Austria's behalf. Poor Kurt von Schuschnigg must confess that this is particularly creative reporting of his plebiscite. He gets off an urgency phonecall to the British minister, who in turn cables Lord Halifax in London—to inquire if Britain will choose sides. Then Schuschnigg watches the first light, glancing through the sooty windows of the Hofburg showrooms —seeking out the rare old jewels and gold within.

The slow March light is lifting windowshades in drowsy St. Veit, and Zahn Glanz is crowing a welcome to the dawn. It's good for Zahn that it's early, and there's little traffic, because he's not being very consistent at the intersections. The cobblestones are giving him a headache, so he drives in the tram tracks wherever that's possible; he doesn't quite get the taxi to fit in the tracks, but he can usually manage to have one wheel side unjarred.

He's approaching the Inner City on Währinger Strasse when he stops to pick up a fare. A head-down man, nodding out of an early Mass in the Votivkirche, steps into the backseat. Zahn is off with him before the man can properly close the door.

"*Cawk! Cawk!*" says Zahn. "Where to?"

And the man, smacking chicken feathers off his trousers, says, "Is this a taxi or a barnyard?" And looks up at Zahn's bent beak in the rear-view mirror, and sees the spotty-feathered shoulders hunched over the wheel. And rolls out the door he hasn't quite closed.

"Better not leave the door open," says Zahn, but he's looking at an empty backseat awhirl with feathers.

Zahn turns up Kolingasse and stops; he shambles out of the taxi and struts back to the corner of Währinger, where he sees the man limping to the curb. The man must think he's seen a seraph, being so fresh out of Mass.

So Zahn springs back to his taxi, startles a café-owner rolling up his awning to watch whatever weak sun there is. The man lets go of the awning crank; the awning comes rumpling down over him, and the crank spins madly, cracking the backs of his hands.

"Oh, I'm sure up early this morning," says Zahn, and gives a fierce cock call from his taxi's running board. Somehow Zahn's got chicken feathers, cocks' crowing and eagles all confused.

Zahn does feel something is amiss, and decides it's that he's clawless. Whatever bird he is, he should have claws. So he stops at a butcher shop in the Kohlmarkt and buys a whole chicken. Then he crunches the legs off and fastens them in the mesh of his chainmail, just under the wide, forearm-length cuffs. The claws curl over his own hands; as he drives, they scratch him.

But butchers are notoriously unimaginative types, and the Kohlmarkt butcher is no exception. He calls Radio Johannesgasse to report a man in a birdsuit, inexpertly driving a taxi.

"What sort of man, you tell me," says the butcher, "would buy a whole chicken and crunch off the legs on the edge of his taxi's door? Just so— opening and shutting the door on his poor chicken's legs until he had them sawed through. And he threw away the chicken!" says the butcher, who thinks the people should be warned.

But Radio Johannesgasse already has been informed of something feathery—from a worried cab-company man, who phoned after someone was arrested on Währinger Strasse for blasphemous rantings and general disturbances concerning a possible seraph. So the word is out on Zahn, all right. The only one who's heard it on the radio and isn't interested is Kurt von Schuschnigg, for whom this day has too much time.

The next thing to befall poor Kurt is Nazi Cabinet member Seyss-

Inquart, reporting a most unreasonable phonecall from a diatribing Goebbels in Munich. Seyss has been told to seize control of the Cabinet and see to it that Schuschnigg calls off the plebiscite. Seyss-Inquart is almost apologetic about it; perhaps he's not sure if things aren't happening a bit too fast. He and Schuschnigg go along to find President Miklas, after Schuschnigg —or someone near him—has sent a Chancellery pageboy to pick up the fallen mass of bed sheets that is interfering with traffic in the Michaelerplatz.

And Grandfather Marter has again decided that the head librarian will stay at home; in fact, since he heard the first radio report of the taxi-driving, birdlike creature, my grandfather has not left the window. Grandmother brings him his coffee, and Hilke watches the Schwindgasse with him. The sun isn't down on the street yet. It's an occasional sun, anyway, and it strikes, when it does, only the topmost stories and roofs across the street —and is impressive only when it catches the brass ball cupped in the palms of a cupid atop the Bulgarian embassy. There are cupids all over, but only the Bulgarians gave theirs a brass ball to hold; or someone else gave it, perhaps to insult the Bulgarians. Anyway, it's the only embassy building on the Schwindgasse, and it's given Grandfather something to watch while he's waiting for Zahn. Grandfather has noticed that even the Bulgarians are making and receiving phonecalls today. A short, heavy man, who must have hair all over himself, has been stooped at the phone in the front-office window, all the while that Grandfather has been standing watch.

When Grandfather hears the latest news brief of the Kohlmarkt butcher's experience, he asks Grandmother for a tea with rum. The Kohlmarkt butcher has an eye for detail. Radio Johannesgasse broadcasts a picture of a madman in a birdsuit, reeking of cognac, driving a taxi with JA! SCHUSCHNIGG! chalked on the hood.

If Schuschnigg pays any attention to this local affair now, it's only because he has enough imagination to see what the Nazi news agency could do with such an item: A secret Bolshevik society of terrorists disguised as birds, taking over the city's public transportation systems to prevent voters from participating in Schuschnigg's rigged plebiscite. But local disturbances can't seem very important to Schuschnigg now. He's having trouble enough convincing old President Miklas that Germany's demands for Seyss-Inquart should probably be carried out. And old Miklas, so long inactive, is picking this occasion to offer resistance.

Perhaps Schuschnigg has read the writing on the wall, on his early-morning stroll through the dark-paneled offices of the Chancellery; Maria Theresia and Aehrenthal, and the small wood-carved Madonna for the murdered Dollfuss: a gallery of Austria's deciders—always for or against Germany.

No such heavy thoughts are weighing down Zahn Glanz. He's a bird, and flying. He's coming up Goethegasse and almost doesn't stop for the tram coming round the Opernring. It's unfortunate that Zahn makes such a display of last-minute stopping; the squeals attract the attention of some rowdy street workers, waiting for a drill-bit replacement. One of them must have just been near a radio, because the JA! SCHUSCHNIGG! on the hood appears to have special significance. It's lucky for Zahn, though, that they don't conceal their excitement and approach the taxi with stealth. Instead, they raise an awful cry and charge, and Zahn has time enough to feel quite threatened. He shoots the intersection with only one of the workers making it to the running board. And if that worker was pleased with himself—if he's been leering in the window at Zahn—he's not very happy when Zahn reaches the Schillerplatz and startles a drove of pigeons, dung-dropping their terror in flight.

"*Cawk!*" Zahn screams to them, birds of a feather. And the worker is convinced he should be waiting for the drill bit with his friends, and not hanging on to the handle of the locked door, and beating his head on the rolled-up window—receiving, only once and briefly, a terrible glance from the empty eyeholes of the armored eagle.

Round the Schillerplatz and through a close arch of the Academy of Graphic Arts, the worker flattens himself against the taxi and hears the echo of some awful wail he doesn't recognize as his own.

Zahn Glanz, in the clear for a moment, kindly slows his taxi and aims for the last archway of the Academy of Graphic Arts. Then he opens his door. Not too hard; he just lets it swing out, carrying the surprised, clutching worker off the running board. The worker dangles, watching the arch approach; then he lets go of the handle, and Zahn closes the door. In his rear-view mirror, he can see the worker back-pedaling and almost catching up with his own momentum. But he topples over a little foolishly, and somersaults out of Zahn's mirror.

Zahn decides that alley travel is advisable, since he's not sure who's after him. But he runs out of gas in the alley alongside the Atelier Theater. His taxi comes to rest just under the billboard portrait of dark-eyed Katrina Marek, who's been a sensational Antigone for the past two weeks.

"Pardon me," says Zahn, because he bumps Katrina when he opens the door. If it even crosses his mind that it's strange of the actress Katrina Marek to be dressed in a sheet for hailing taxis, Zahn doesn't give it much thought. He's dressed none too smartly himself.

And once again my grandfather is troubled by what he calls his far-sightedness.

"Hilke," he says. "Would you bring me my coat? I think I'll be going out." And although there are two possible entrances to the Schwindgasse, Grandfather settles his gaze on one.

Meanwhile, the eagle is still preferring alley travel; he swoops along the garbage routes, and it's not until he emerges in the Rilke Platz that he realizes he's in my mother's neighborhood. Zahn feels a little weighed down from all his swooping under chainmail. He boards the hindmost platform of a Gusshausstrasse tram, just starting up from behind the technical high school. Zahn thinks it's wise to stay outside the tramcar, but the tram picks up a little speed, and the eagle's pieplates begin to clap. The conductor squints down the aisle; he thinks a piece of the tram is loose and flapping. Zahn hangs back on the handrail and takes one step down the platform stairs. Someone points at him from a pastry-shop window. Zahn rides the platform stairs alone; his tail feathers learn to fly.

And he'd have been all right that way, for at least the block or two farther he had to go, except that a throng of technical-high-school students, sitting in the last car, decide to come out on the platform for a smoke.

"Morning, boys," the eagle says, and they don't say a word. So Zahn asks, "You haven't seen Katrina Marek this morning, have you? She's wearing her sheet, you know."

And one of the student mechanics says, "You wouldn't be that birdman, would you?"

"What birdman?" says another.

"What birdman?" says Zahn.

"The one who's terrorizing people," the student says, stepping a little closer, and one of his friends remembers, then; he steps up closer too.

Zahn is wishing he had his head off so he'd have better peripheral vision —and know, if he were to jump, whether he'd hit a hitching post or a litter basket.

"It looks like my stop coming up," says Zahn, only the tram isn't slowing any. He puts one foot down another platform step, and leans out on the handrail.

"Get him!" shouts the closest student, and brings a lunch pail down on Zahn's hand. But the eagle flies off backwards, losing one of his claws.

Zahn makes an awful clatter, and his pieplates spark on the sidewalk; several little fastening wires gouge the eagle's back. But he is less than a block away from my mother's, and hasn't time to grieve over the pieplates spinning and rolling free down the sidewalk and along the curb.

My grandfather says, "You can shut off the damn radio, Hilke"—having just heard the news brief of the birdman's brutal kidnapping of a worker from an Opernring street crew.

Hilke already has her coat, and she puts her scarf on—loose around her neck. She follows Grandfather to the staircase landing outside the apartment. Grandfather looks up the marble and iron-spiral stairs, tuning his ear to the opening of letter slots and doors. Then he leads Hilke downstairs and through the long lobby to the great door with the foot-length crank-open handle. Hilke peers up and down the street, but my grandfather looks only left—to the corner at Argentinierstrasse. He watches a man who's tamping his pipe bowl with his thumb and standing back-to Argentinier.

Then the man turns round to the corner and ducks his head, thinking he hears the approaching wing beat of a hundred pigeons. And Zahn Glanz, banking on the corner, topples the man and jars himself off balance down a short flight of steps and against the door of someone's cellar cubby. So that Zahn is below sidewalk level and altogether out of sight when the man picks himself up and shakes the pipe tobacco out of his hair; and looks both ways along the street—and seeing nothing at all, bolts down Argentinierstrasse with a wing beat all his own.

Grandfather waves. Zahn is crawling up to the sidewalk when a bustling little laundress opens the cellar-cubby door. She jousts the eagle with a sock stretcher, and prances lively up to the sidewalk; she's going to give the bird a clout, but Zahn lays his limp, cold remaining claw against her indignant bosom. The laundress drops to her knees, convinced the thing is real.

Zahn is winging to my mother. He chooses to fly the last few yards and nearly clears a parked car, getting his beak caught on the aerial and ripping off his whole head. Grandfather gets a grip under the pieplates and clatters Zahn through the great lobby door. Hilke scoops the eagle's head under her arm and covers it with her scarf. Downstreet, the laundress still kneels on the sidewalk, hiding her face in her hands; fanny-up, she seems to be expecting some ungentlemanly visit from a god.

My mother picks up feathers and bits of down; fussily she gets them all, from the parked car to Grandmother's kitchen. Where Zahn slumps against the oven—an almost-plucked bird, wrapped in tinfoil and ready to bake.

"Zahn," says Grandfather. "Where did you leave the taxi?"

"With Katrina Marek," Zahn says.

"Where?" asks Grandfather.

"I ran out of gas right under her nose," Zahn says.

"How far from here, Zahn?" says Grandfather.

"She was wearing her sheet," Zahn says.

"Did anyone see you leave the taxi?" Grandfather asks.

"The proletariat," says Zahn, "they're rising up to destroy the city."

"Did anyone see where you left it, Zahn?" Grandfather shouts.

"Katrina Marek," says Zahn. "I should go back for her."

"Put the poor boy to bed," says Grandmother. "He's totally addled. Get him out of that costume and put him to bed."

"Jesus," says Zahn. "It's been one long day." But my mother is too kind to tell him that the morning's just beginning.

And although I'm sure that Schuschnigg already has guessed the outcome, the day must seem long to him too. It's only nine-thirty when Hitler makes a phonecall and delivers a personal ultimatum to the poor Chancellor: the plebiscite must be postponed for at least two weeks, or Germany will invade Austria this evening. So Schuschnigg and the faithful Skubl confer: the class of 1915 Austrian reservists are called to colors, supposedly to keep order on the upcoming election day; the Socony Vacuum Oil Company of Austria is asked to supply extra fuel to motorize possible troop

movements. And Chancellor Schuschnigg gloomily notices that by noontime the city is preparing a second day of celebrations for Schuschnigg's
Austria. Leaflets for the plebiscite are floating down the streets. The sun is
very warm and bright at noon. The people don't seem to notice the increase
of militia on the fringe of every little fest. And the militia, too, are tapping
their boots to waltzes and patriotic marches, from radios pointed out the
open windows.

Schuschnigg makes his third phonecall to Mussolini, but the Duce is still
unavailable. Someone sends another message to France.

The noontime report on Radio Johannesgasse is somewhat vague with
the worldwide news. It's about the Salzburg border being closed, and the
uncounted troop build-up; a rhino assembly of tanks inching forward in the
night, a daze of headlights peering across the border, and in the morning,
a screen of smoke hanging above the German forests—from a million
cigarettes lit and puffed once and put out on signal. And something about
how Radio Berlin is broadcasting the news of yesterday's and today's
Bolshevik riots in Vienna, where there haven't been any rioting Bolsheviks
since the great siege and capture of the Schlingerhof Palace in 1934.

The local news is more detailed. The kidnapped worker has been found;
he was beaten off the birdman's speeding taxi and miraculously escaped
with scratches. The birdman, the worker estimates, is at least seven feet tall.
That was in the Schillerplatz. The birdman was then spotted on a Gusshausstrasse tram; a brave group of technical-high-school students tried to capture him but were overpowered. And lastly, in the Schwindgasse, the birdman assaulted Frau Drexa Neff, laundress. Frau Neff maintains the
creature is most certainly not human, and she didn't see which way it went
after it attacked her. Authorities in the nearby Belvedere Gardens are
searching the shrubs and trees. And there is still no sign of the apparently
abandoned taxi, with JA! SCHUSCHNIGG! on the hood.

But my grandfather knows where to look. By checking the theater listings
and discovering where Katrina Marek has been astounding as Antigone,
and by realizing that the Atelier Theater is neatly between the castaway
worker at the Schillerplatz and the eagle's first taxiless appearance on the
Gusshausstrasse tram. So Grandfather empties a two-quarter cookie crock
and dampens a sponge; he puts a funnel in his overcoat pocket. Zahn doesn't
have a key on him, so Grandfather hopes the eagle left it in the ignition.
Then Hilke puts the sponge in her pocketbook, and Grandfather carries the
cookie crock under his arm, hefting it up as if it were full; they leave the
Schwindgasse apartment, trusting my grandmother will tend to the undis-
turbed sleep of Zahn Glanz, laid to rest in Hilke's bed.

It's unfortunate that Kurt von Schuschnigg is of a more compromising
nature than my grandfather. At a little after two-thirty, Schuschnigg bows
to one of Germany's ultimatums. He asks that Seyss-Inquart phone Göring
in Berlin and convey the Chancellor's decision to postpone the plebiscite;

Seyss-Inquart also tells Göring that Schuschnigg has not resigned his Chancellorship. Grandfather, of course, could tell Kurt a thing or two about the insatiable nature of Field Marshal Göring's appetite.

But my grandfather isn't available for consultation. He's walking my mother out of the *Tankstelle* on the Karlsplatz, with a cookie crock of gasoline under his arm—just three-quarters full, so he can walk without slopping. My mother is smiling more than a family-outing smile, because Grandfather has told the *Tankstelle* man that the cookie crock is a surprise for an uncle, who eats too much and is always running out of gas.

They cross the Getreidemarkt, whispering family secrets; they slow down to look at the billboards on the Atelier Theater.

"Oh, look," says Grandfather, reading matinee times.

And Hilke says, "I think there's more around the side." And turns up the alley, trying not to be startled by the taxi squatting under Katrina Marek's nose. "Come on," she says to Grandfather. "It's really the best picture I've seen of her."

"Just a minute," says Grandfather, still staring at the matinee schedule. But he moves along, reading, and darts a look up and down the street; he sticks his hand round the corner of the alley and waggles a finger at my mother. She takes the damp sponge out of her pocketbook and rubs JA! SCHUSCHNIGG! off the taxi's hood. Then she stands back to look at Katrina Marek, and moves casually round the taxi, here and there whisking away a flake of chalk. Then she comes back out of the alley and tugs my grandfather's arm.

"Come on, go look," she says. "It's a wonderful picture of her."

"You read this," says Grandfather. "Would you just read this? Isn't that amazing?" And he moves around the corner, pointing back to the matinee schedule. Hilke tosses her head, gets a look both ways; she shakes her bracelet for Grandfather.

From the alley, Grandfather says, "A real beauty, you're right." And removes the gas cap his first trip round the taxi; inserts the funnel while leaning against a fender, gazing fondly at Katrina Marek. "What do you think of that schedule?" he calls, and my mother jingles her bracelet again. Grandfather empties the cookie crock into the gas tank. On his way out of the alley, he passes the driver's-side window and is delighted to see the key in the ignition.

"This is truly incredible," says Hilke, pointing to the schedule. She takes Grandfather's arm, and together they walk on, past the alley and up a block. Then Grandfather makes her a bow, kisses her cheek and hands her the cookie crock. My mother returns the kiss and goes straight on, while Grandfather turns up a side block. He comes out behind the theater and waltzes into the alley, facing the taxi head-on.

My mother tosses herself along, throwing back her hair for the storefront windows to see; she cuddles the cookie crock against her high, light bosom;

she sees herself, transparent, passing through racks of dresses, rows of shoes, swivel displays of cakes and pastries; through the *Kaffeehaus* windows too, she sees herself lift faces from the rims of cups—and pass indelibly, even if transparent, through the mind of everyone who's looking out when my mother looks in. She imagines Zahn Glanz is watching her too, in his dreams brought on by her girlishly perfumed bed. But she's not in such a trance that she forgets her street corners; she slows at Faulmanngasse and Mühl, and hesitates until she recognizes the driver before she hails the taxi coming along.

"Where to?" says Grandfather, chin on chest, and waits until they're under way before he says, "Pretty damn slick father you've got, haven't you? Went all the way down Elisabethstrasse for a full tank of gas, and picked you off this corner just as you got here. I could see you coming. You didn't even have to wait. Some sense of timing, I have."

Hilke tugs her hair around her ears; she laughs a bright, adoring laugh, and Grandfather, nodding his head, laughs along. "Pretty slick, pretty slick —a flawless job, I must say."

Anyone watching them, bobbing up and down in the getaway taxi, must be thinking: Now what could an old man like that have to say, to make such a pretty girl laugh?

My grandfather gets things done—delicately, and with fanfare.

So does Göring—but with much less fanfare, and no delicacy at all. Just twenty minutes after receiving the phonecall of Schuschnigg's first concession, Göring phones back. He tells Seyss-Inquart that Schuschnigg's behavior is unacceptable and that the Chancellor and his Cabinet are asked to resign; that President Miklas is asked to nominate Seyss-Inquart for the Chancellorship. Göring has such an odd way of putting things. He promises that Austria will have German military *aid*, if the Schuschnigg government cannot change itself promptly.

It's a most embarrassed Seyss-Inquart who breaks this news to Kurt von Schuschnigg, and Schuschnigg takes his next-to-last step backward. At three-thirty, or only half an hour after Göring's phonecall, Schuschnigg simply places the resignation of his entire government in President Miklas' hands. And here's an arbitrary matter: it would have looked so much nicer, after the war, if Schuschnigg had held out an hour longer—until Lord Halifax's message was conveyed from the British embassy in Vienna; how His Majesty's government wouldn't want to be taking the responsibility of advising the Chancellor to expose his country to dangers against which His Majesty's government would be unable to guarantee protection.

It's a matter of giving in when you're abandoned, or abandoning yourself when you know you're going to be abandoned. But after the fact, fine hairs are indeed split.

At three-thirty, Schuschnigg doesn't need anything formal to know he's been abandoned. He can anticipate: that Lord Halifax will evade; that

French chargé d'affaires in Rome, M. Blondel, will be told by Count Ciano's private secretary that if the reason for his visit is Austria, he needn't bother to come; and that Mussolini will never be reached by phone—that he's hiding somewhere, listening to it ring and ring.

So Schuschnigg leaves Federal President Miklas with the decision for a new Chancellor. Old Miklas has been this route before. Under the Nazi *Putsch* of four years ago—poor Dollfuss murdered in the sanctity of his Chancellery office, and a courtyard of toughs below, waiting to sway the crowd whichever way the limbo turned; then Miklas turned to Kurt von Schuschnigg. Now Miklas has until seven-thirty. So the old President goes looking for a Chancellor.

There's faithful police head, Skubl, but Skubl declines; he's known in Berlin, and his nomination would be a further irritation to Hitler. There's Doktor Ender, authority on constitutional law, who feels his need to be Chancellor already has been satisfied, as leader of a previous government. And General Schilhawsky, Inspector General of the Armed Forces, says he's an officer, not a politician. So Miklas finds no takers.

Pity that he didn't know my grandfather, who would probably enjoy another intrigue.

Grandfather—who's parked and locked the taxi in the lot at Karl's Church—walks Hilke and the cookie crock home. Ignoring Grandmother's protest, they peek in on Zahn Glanz. Peeled out of his pieplates, disarmed of his last claw, the eagle's feet protrude from the little girl's bed. A chicken feather laces his ear, a pink pouf makes him cozy; he sleeps midst the knickknackery and troll kingdom of my mother's room. Hilke tucks him in again, and he sleeps through supper; he sleeps right up to the seven o'clock report on Radio Johannesgasse. Grandfather can't let Zahn miss the news.

The postponement of the plebiscite is announced, and the resignation of the entire Cabinet—all except Seyss-Inquart, who's staying on in his office as Minister of Interior.

Zahn Glanz is not fully recovered; when he goes wordlessly back to bed, old Miklas is sitting all alone in his office of the Federal President, watching the clock run by seven-thirty. Field Marshal Göring's ultimatum time has expired, and Seyss-Inquart is still not Chancellor of Austria. Miklas refuses to make it *official.*

Then Kurt von Schuschnigg performs the last and most conclusive leap backwards of his career—an executive order to General Schilhawsky to withdraw the Austrian Army from the German border; to offer no resistance; to watch, or perhaps wave, from behind the River Enns. The Austrian Army has only forty-eight hours of steady-fire ammunition anyway. What would be the point of so much blood? Someone phones from Salzburg to say the Germans are crossing the border; it's not true, it's a false alarm, but it's another fine hair to be split and Schuschnigg doesn't wait for verification. He steps back.

At eight o'clock, he asks Radio Johannesgasse for a nationwide broadcasting privilege. The microphone wires are strung up the banister of the grand staircase in the Ballhausplatz. And Grandfather wakes up Zahn again.

Schuschnigg is all sadness and no reproach. He speaks of yielding to force; he begs no resistance. He does say there's no truth to the Berlin radio reports of worker revolutions terrorizing Austria, Kurt von Schuschnigg's Austria isn't terrorized; it's forced to be sad. And in the whole show, the only sentiment that touches Grandfather's skulking heart is the rude outburst of the Commissioner for Cultural Propaganda—the old cripple Hammerstein-Equord, who grabs the microphone when the Chancellor is finished, but before the technicians can pull the contact plug. "Long live Austria!" he burbles. "Today I am ashamed to be German."

It's a sad thing for Grandfather to hear. Even though old cripples like Hammerstein-Equord consider *German* as something in the blood, and look at Germans as a *race* to which Austria must belong.

But my grandfather has never looked at things that way. "Pack, Muttie," he says. "There's a taxi full of gas just around the corner."

And my mother takes the arm of Zahn Glanz; she holds to it tighter than she's ever held a thing alive, and waits for Zahn to raise his eyes to hers; her fingers on his arm are talking: Hilke Marter will not let go, will not pack herself or any of her things, until this eagle can unfuddle enough to make up his mind and speak it clear.

While Miklas, with his mind made up and all alone, refuses to accept Schuschnigg's personal resignation and is still speaking of resistance—without a single soldier of the Austrian Army between the German border and the River Enns. In the Federal President's office, Lieutenant General Muff, German military attaché to Vienna, is explaining that the reported border-crossing by German troops is a false alarm. But the troops *will* cross, says Muff, if Miklas doesn't make Seyss-Inquart the Chancellor. Perhaps old Miklas is less futile in his resistance than it appears; he may even recognize Hitler's apparent need to legalize the takeover. But the patient Muff keeps after him: Does the Federal President know that all the provinces are now in the hands of local Austrian Nazi officials? Does the President know that Salzburg and Linz have given the seals of office to Nazi party members there? Has the President even looked in the corridor outside his office, where the Vienna Nazi youth are lighting cigarettes and jeering over the balcony of the grand staircase; they're curling smoke rings round the head of the wood-carved Madonna in mourning for poor Dollfuss.

At eleven o'clock the patient Muff is still conjuring images. Seyss-Inquart has revised his list for his proposed Cabinet; Miklas, in his tenth hour of resistance, is telling an anecdote about Maria Theresia.

At eleven o'clock my grandfather is arbitrating the matter of silver or china. The china is breakable, and less salable. It's the china that stays in

Vienna, the silver that goes. And whether Zahn Glanz will go or stay is still being perceived through my mother's touch.

"It doesn't necessarily mean they'll come marching in," says Zahn. "And where can you go in my taxi anyway?"

"It *does* mean they'll come marching in," Grandfather says, "and we'll take your taxi to my brother's. He's the postmaster of Kaprun."

"That's still Austria," says Zahn.

"It's the cities that won't be safe," Grandfather says. "The Kitzbühler Alps are very rural."

"Rural enough to starve, is it?" asks Zahn.

"Librarians put away *some* money," Grandfather tells him.

"And how will you get it out of your bank," Zahn asks, "in the middle of the night?"

Grandfather says, "If you decide to stay awhile, Zahn, I could endorse my bankbook to you and have you post a draft."

"To your brother the postmaster," says Zahn. "Of course."

"Why can't we just leave in the morning?" Hilke asks. "Why can't Zahn come with us?"

"He can, if he wants to," says Grandfather. "Then I'd stay until morning, and Zahn can drive you."

"Why can't we *all* go in the morning?" Grandmother asks. "Maybe in the morning, we'll find it's going to be all right."

"A lot of people will be leaving in the morning," says Grandfather. "And Zahn hasn't checked in his taxi for a while. Do you think they might start missing your taxi, Zahn?"

"The taxi better go tonight," Zahn says.

"But if Zahn stays," says Hilke, "how can he get to Kaprun?"

"Zahn doesn't have to stay if he doesn't want to," Grandfather says.

"And why would he want to?" Hilke asks.

"Oh, I don't know," says Zahn. "Maybe to watch what happens for a day or so."

And my mother keeps taking the pulse in his arm. Hilke Marter is speaking through her fingers again: Oh, Zahn, there's nobody outside, there's nobody there at all.

But a little before midnight, in the Ballhaus courtyard, there are forty toughs from SS Standarte 89, of which the assassin Otto Planetta was a member. Perhaps it's then—when Miklas sees them—that the old President shares a bit of Schuschnigg's vision for the slaughter that could be Vienna's. Perhaps it's then that Miklas droops down his chins to Muff the middleman.

Zahn Glanz must feel like a middleman now, with my grandfather's bankbook fat in his pocket. He makes the walk from Schwindgasse to Karl's Church, my mother still fastened to his arm. At the Gusshausstrasse corner they're forced to hop off the curb.

Arms locked, in step, five boys from an alphabetized meeting of Vienna's

Nazi youth come shouldering along. It must have been a meeting of the S's from the fourth district. Freshly sewn, their nametags glow: P. Schnell, perhaps, and G. Schritt, with F. Samt, J. Spalt, R. Steg and O. Schrutt— just to name some ordinary names.

Zahn doesn't say a word to them; my mother has shut off his pulse. He unlocks the taxi in the Karl's Church lot and drives back to the Schwind-gasse another way. It wouldn't do to have the cruising youth club see them so suddenly motorized. Zahn drives lights-out up the Schwindgasse. My grandfather opens both sides of the great lever-handled lobby door, and Zahn backs over the sidewalk and inside the apartment building.

It's late, but the upstairs apartments can't be sleeping very soundly tonight. They certainly must hear the motor before Zahn shuts it off. The garbage truck—do they think?—making some awful collection that can't keep till morning? But no one brings their garbage downstairs. There are no frightened faces over the spiraling banister—only juts of light, from letter slots and doors ajar. Grandfather waits for the last, stealthy ray to leave the stairs; then he stations my grandmother by the banister, and has her listen for the cranking of a phone.

It's one o'clock Saturday morning when they begin to load the taxi.

The Seventh Zoo Watch:
Tuesday, June 6, 1967, @ 2:15 a.m.

Some of the animals are dropping off to sleep. A certain nervous element is still in this zoo, all right, but the watchman's gone back to the Small Mammal house, and some of us feel like sleeping.

When the watchman first went inside, I felt like a short nap myself. I heard the Assorted Antelopes lying down in soft collapses. I really thought I'd sleep awhile, and I was snuggling myself around the roots when the Small Mammal House changed color. That's just the way it happened. Over the tops of cages, the glow was white and it changed to blood-purple. The watchman had switched on the infrared.

There they all are again, with the putting-out of one light and the switch-ing-on of one they can't see; there they are, with their distorted view of how quickly the night falls.

So I went lurking along my hedges, and even out of cover, for a moment, to where I could see the door.

Why did the watchman do it? Does he like looking at them when they're awake? Then it's a bit selfish of him to end their sleep to please himself; he should come during the regular zoo hours, if it matters so much to him. But I don't think that's it.

Especially now that I've had a better look at this watchman, I don't think that's his reasoning at all. What I mean is, I went to have a closer look. I wanted a look at that little room.

I was all set up behind a cage. I couldn't see very far into the cage; the moonlight caught just the outer edges. But I was sure it was a part of the indoor-outdoor Monkey Complex. I was peering down the violet corridor of the Small Mammal House when two very rough hands grabbed my head and jerked me against the bars. I couldn't get free, but I was able to turn my head in the thing's hands. I faced the hairless, bright red chest of the male gelada baboon—powerful, savage bandit from the highland plains of Abyssinia.

"I'm here to help you," I whispered. But it sneered.

"No noise now," I pleaded, but its thumbs sank in the hollows behind my ears; the thing was putting me to sleep with its grip. I reached into my jacket and handed it my meerschaum.

"Would you like to try a pipe?" I asked. It looked. One forearm went a little limp on my shoulder.

"Go on, take it," I whispered, hoping I wouldn't be forced to ram the pipestem up one of its flaring nostrils.

It took; one hand peeled off my neck and covered my fist, pipe and all. Then its other hand came delicately poking for the pipe between my fingers. I lunged my head back, but I couldn't free my fist; the gelada baboon shoved the pipe in its mouth and grabbed hold of my arm with both hands. I wasn't a match for it, but I got my feet against the bars and pushed back with all my weight. I fell out of its reach, away from the cage, and the gelada baboon, munching my meerschaum and spitting it out on the cage floor, knew it had been fooled. It made enormous noises.

It whooped and raced round the cage, leaping off the bars and stamping in the water trough. The indoor-outdoor Monkey Complex understood: a baboon had been outwitted by a lower-species creature.

If there had been animals finally dropping off to sleep, I apologize. They awoke to a clamor of general primate noisemaking; the Big Cats roared back; bears grumbled; all over the zoo was a skitter of hooves, dashing from fence line to fence line. And I was stumbling backward down the path, heading for my hedges again, when I saw the watchman round the end of his lavender hallway.

It surprised me. I expected the infrared to go out; I expected the guard, camouflaged and crawling belly-down, combat-style, to sneak up on me from behind with his truncheon. But he stood and gaped down the blood-colored aisle, frozen and aghast; he would have made an easy target.

I was safe behind my hedgerow before I saw his light come whirling down the path; when his light began to whirl, the zoo was suddenly hushed. He spun from bush to bush, and cage to cage. When he passed the spot where I'd been assaulted, I expected trouble. But the gelada baboon must have gathered together the bits of my pipe and slinked through the back-wall door, losing itself in the parapets and split-level avenues of the Monkey Complex.

The guard seemed to know that this was where it started, though. He stopped and shone his light, from the corners of the cages to the treetops all around him. He timidly kicked the cage where the gelada baboon had been. "Was it you?" he cried, in a high lisping voice.

The zoo was wide-awake and silent; a hundred breaths were being held, and lost in little pieces.

On past the Monkey Complex the watchman skittered—and stopped again at the corner of my hedgerow, the diluted blood-light from the Small Mammal House faintly reaching him on the path. He whirled for us, shaking his light. "What happened?" he shouted.

Something with hooves took a false step, caught itself and held its ground. The watchman's light leapt down to the Australians' area, struck across the sky. The guard fired his light up a nearby tree, seeking leopards or ocelots that might have been lurking there, ready to pounce. "All of you!" he screamed. "You go to sleep now!"

His own flashlight, tilted from his hip and pointed overhead, illuminated him for me. The watchman was lighting up himself.

I saw him head-on, his old face lightly tinged by infrared—with a rich magenta scar, sharp and thin, from the top of his gray crew-cut head, past his ear to his left nostril, where it plunges through the gum. A part of his upper lip is tucked in by it, and appears as a slightly raised hackle—baring all the scarlet of his upper left gum. It was no proper duel that caused it. Perhaps a foil gone berserk.

Head-on, I saw him—that face, and that remarkable uniform-front. It's not only that he hasn't, somehow, lost his epaulettes; his uniform still has a nametag. O. Schrutt, he is—or was once. And if it's not still O. Schrutt, inside that old uniform, why would he have left the nametag on? O. SCHRUTT, with the period very faded. What an edge it seems to give you —to find out someone's name before they've even seen your face. This watchman is O. Schrutt.

Strange, but that's a name I've used before; I've had O. Schrutt on my lips before. It's possible I knew an O. Schrutt; surely I've known one Schrutt or another in my time. Vienna is full of Schrutt families. And I also believe I've used this name in one fiction or another. That's it, I'm sure; I've made up an O. Schrutt before.

But this O. Schrutt is real; he searches the upper tree limbs for ocelots and such. Animals don't sleep when O. Schrutt is on the prowl, and neither do I.

I can't sleep now, although O. Schrutt's gone back to his Small Mammal House. He retreated from my hedges, pretending lack of interest: casually backing down the path—he would then erupt, in circles, exposing each lurking bit of the darkness around him. O. Schrutt makes vowel sounds when he whirls his light. *"Aah!"* he cries, and *"Oooh!"*—surprising the shapes that hide just out of his beam.

Now the animals are dropping off; groans, stretches, sighs, slumps; a brief, shrill-voiced argument in the Monkey Complex, and someone swings a trapeze against an echoing wall. But I can't sleep.

When O. Schrutt emerges for another round, I want to get inside his blood-lit den and see just what it is that makes old O. turn on the infrared. One reason, I can guess: O. Schrutt is not a man who likes to be seen. Even by animals.

(CONTINUING:)
THE HIGHLY SELECTIVE AUTOBIOGRAPHY OF
SIEGFRIED JAVOTNIK: PRE-HISTORY I

Saturday, March 12, 1938: 1:00 A.M. at the Chancellery on the Ballhaus-platz. Miklas has given in. Seyss-Inquart is Chancellor of Austria.

Seyss is in conference with Lieutenant General Muff. They want to make certain that Berlin knows everything is in control, and that the German border troops no longer think of crossing.

Poor Seyss-Inquart, he should know better:

> If you bring lions to your home,
> They'll want to stay for dinner.

But about two o'clock, it's Muff who phones Berlin and attempts the put-off. Perhaps he says, "It's all right, you can take your armies home now; it's all right, we've got our politics just like yours now; you don't have to hang around our border now, because it's really all right here."

And at two-thirty, after a frantic bicker between the War Office, the Foreign Office and the Reich Chancellery, Hitler's personal adjutant is asked to wake up the Führer.

Wake up any man at two-thirty in the morning, says Grandfather—even a reasonable man—and see what you get.

At two-thirty, Zahn Glanz is pressing my mother against the great lobby door, and Grandmother still hasn't heard anyone cranking a phone. Grandfather is bringing out the little things now: a crate of kitchenware, a carton of food and wine, a box of winter scarves and hats, and the crocheted bedspreads.

"If not *all* the china," says Grandmother, "maybe just the gravyboat?"

"No, Muttie," says Grandfather, "just what we need"—and makes the last check of Hilke's room. He packs the eaglesuit in the bottom of a winter army duffel.

In the kitchen, Grandfather empties the spice rack and tumbles all the little jars into the duffel, thinking that anything with enough spice can taste like food; then the radio.

Grandmother whispers from the staircase, "I just looked in that car, and you're going to have a whole seat left empty."

"I know it," says Grandfather, thinking that there's room for one more who's leaving Vienna this morning before light.

It's not Schuschnigg. He leaves the Ballhausplatz, shakes hands with a tearful guard, ignores the Nazi salute from the file of citizens with swastika armbands.

The apologetic Seyss-Inquart drives Schuschnigg home—to ten weeks of house arrest and seven years in Gestapo prisons. All because Kurt von Schuschnigg has claimed he's committed no crime, and has refused the protection of the Hungarian embassy—has not joined the lines of monarchists, Jews, and some Catholics, who've been jamming up the Czech and Hungarian customs posts since midnight.

Grandfather finds the traffic is all going the other way. East. But Grandfather seems to feel that the Czechs and Hungarians will be next, and he doesn't want to have to move again; especially since then there would be no choice of moving east or west, but only east again—and that would be Russia. My grandfather has a picture of himself in nightmares: driven to the Black Sea, hunted by Cossacks and wild-haired Turks.

So driving west, he has no traffic going his way. St. Veit is dark, Hacking is darker. Only the lighted trams are still going in my grandfather's direction; the conductors wave swastika flags; at the stations, men with armbands and nametags are singing; someone *bloops* a one-note tuba.

"Is this the fastest route west?" my grandmother asks.

But Grandfather finds his way. He stops at the only unlighted henhouse in the outskirts of Hacking.

Ernst Watzek-Trummer has plucked and spitted three anonymous chickens over a low-coal fire on the henhouse floor. He gnaws at a bone on his roost. Grandfather and the patriot gather a pail of eggs and water, and hard-boil the eggs. Watzek-Trummer slaughters and plucks his best capon; it's thrown in the pail to boil. Then they hobble four prime hens and a stud champion rooster. Hilke bundles them violently together in a blanket; they go berserk on the floor under the backseat, against the long duffel which separates my mother from my grandmother. Ernst Watzek-Trummer takes the frontseat by Grandfather, each to his own side of the kitchenware crate —the egg pail on the floor between them. Before they leave, Watzek-Trummer sets his chickens loose and lights the henhouse afire. In the glove compartment, he stows his best slaying-cleaver.

The three anonymous chickens, spitted and charred, and the freshly boiled capon, a bit underdone, are hacked and ripped apart by Watzek-Trummer while Grandfather drives. Ernst distributes chicken parts and hard-boiled eggs while Grandfather turns south, through Gloggnitz and Brück an der Mur, then west, and even a little north—skirting mountains. He settles straight-ahead west at St. Martin.

That's a long way from Vienna; that puts them almost due south of Linz and nearly out of gas. The Mercedes, used to taxi-living, bubbles up its radiator once—even though it's March—and Ernst Watzek-Trummer has to cool it off with lukewarm water from the egg pail.

My mother, in the backseat, doesn't say a word. She feels she's still pinching Zahn Glanz's knee between her own, and feels Zahn's despairing weight—making her back take on the grain of the wood in the great lobby door.

Grandmother says, "The live chickens are smelling."

"We need gas," says Grandfather.

And in Pruggern they find there's still a celebration going on. Grandfather rolls down his window and slows for a policeman with his coat uniform open down his chest—and somehow, a swastika armband stretched enough to slip over his head and collar his neck. It's hard to tell whether he put it on himself or had his head held while someone else did the fitting.

Watzek-Trummer sets the glove compartment ajar and holds it half shut with his knee; the slaying-cleaver winks at him. My grandfather shoves a Nazi salute out the window. "I'm glad to see the whole country's not gone to bed on such a night!" he says. But the policeman peers inside, suspicious of the egg pail and scattered chickens.

Ernst Watzek-Trummer clomps my grandfather's back. "His brother's got a seal of office in Salzburg now!" he says. "You should see Vienna, and all the Bolsheviks we've passed along the way—running east."

"Your brother's got a seal?" the policeman says.

"I may be sent to Munich!" says Grandfather gayly.

"Well, bless you," the policeman says. Watzek-Trummer passes him a hard-boiled egg.

"Keep it up!" says Grandfather. "Keep the whole town up till dawn!"

"I wish I knew what was going on," the policeman says. "I mean, really, you know."

"Just keep it up," says Grandfather, and starts to pull ahead, then stops. "You wouldn't have any gas for us, would you?" he asks.

"There's things we could siphon," says the policeman. "You wouldn't have a hose?"

"Just happen to," Watzek-Trummer says.

They find a mail truck in the back buildings of a dark post-office lot. The policeman even does the sucking to get the siphon hose started, so they give him one of the capon's legs.

And my mother bears down on the imagined knee between her own; she rubs the window with the heel of her hand, as if it were a crystal ball to show her every safe, unfoolish move Zahn Glanz will make to get himself out of Vienna.

And the rest is mostly hearsay. That Hilke assumes Zahn finds out—almost as soon as befuddled Muff—the German border troops are crossing anyway. That, as a fact among few, Zahn does forward the draft of Grandfather's endorsed bankbook to the postmaster of Kaprun. That Zahn may have been reading Lennhoff's editorial about the German *Putsch* as late as noon, and then heard of the warm welcome Hitler was receiving in Linz —where the Führer marched to from the border to Passau, with soldiers and tanks, "to visit his mother's grave." And that Zahn, or someone like him, was the one who borrowed or stole the taxi which drove the criminal editor Lennhoff across the Hungarian border at Kittsee—having been turned away by the Czechs. If Zahn Glanz wasn't the driver, why did he never meet my mother in Kaprun? So he must have been the driver. And carried with him half of what I was at that time, because then I was, at best, only an idea of my mother's—half of which, if it didn't cross the Hungarian border at Kittsee, went wherever Zahn Glanz went.

And the rest is simply the seven-year affair of living in the protective shadow of my grandfather's brother, the postmaster of Kaprun, who kept his official post by joining the Nazi party, and because Kaprun was so small then, found the post not demanding, and the Nazi guise quite easy to maintain, except in the presence of the one youth club he supervised—some member of which suspected the postmaster's sincerity and caught him off guard in a poorly insulated latrine stall of the Hitler Youth's barracks, and roasted him with a lightweight SS flamethrower the postmaster had demonstrated just that morning. But that was when the war was almost over, and I don't think my mother or my grandparents suffered or starved so very much, especially owing to the food-hoarding genius of Ernst Watzek-Trummer, and the spices my grandfather wisely added to the last duffel packed in Vienna.

And the rest is all in Göring's telegram to Hitler in Linz, because Göring at his radio in Berlin heard of the Führer's triumphant welcome in that first city. Göring asked, "If the enthusiasm is so great, why not go the whole hog?" And Hitler certainly went ahead and did that. In Vienna alone, the first wave of Gestapo arrests took seventy-six thousand. (And if Zahn Glanz wasn't the driver of the editor's getaway taxi, wouldn't he have been one of these seventy-six thousand? So he must have been the driver.)

And the rest, as far as I was concerned, had to wait for my mother's second suitor. I wouldn't want to say, exactly, that he was a suitor less worthy than the first—or that I've condemned my mother for not letting Zahn Glanz father me. Because even if it wasn't carried in the genes, something of Zahn Glanz certainly got into me. I only want to show how Zahn Glanz put an idea of me in my mother. Even if he put nothing else there.

The Eighth Zoo Watch:
Tuesday, June 6, 1967, @ 3:00 a.m.

Almost everyone is asleep. One of the Various Aquatic Birds is garbling, prophecies or indigestion. I'm certainly awake, and I don't believe that sleep ever comes to O. Schrutt. But everyone else has finally dropped off.

I've been thinking: How do they know the last great auk is dead? The Irishmen at Trinity Bay—did they hear the great auk's final murmur? Did it actually say, "I am the last, there are no more"?

I've heard that Irishmen are always drunk. How could they be sure this great auk washed ashore was the last? It might have been a plot. The great auks might have anticipated their own extinction, and sent a martyr—instructed to identify itself as final. And somewhere, maybe in deserted coastal cottages in Wales, a tribe of great auks are living still, multiplying, and teaching their young about the martyr who washed itself ashore that they might live—and be not gullible.

I wonder if the great auk is a bitter bird. I wonder if their young are warlike, if they're organized in diving teams, scuttling small fishing boats, spreading rumors as old and unbelievable as sea serpents and mermaids—working up to the day when the Great Auk Navy will rule the waterways of the world. *Human* history happens that way. I wonder: do the surviving great auks bear grudges?

I've also been thinking about O. Schrutt. Curious that I should have created his namesake. I thumbed back through my various fictions, true and false, and found the other O. Schrutt. A decidedly more tender-aged O. Schrutt than this nightwatchman. Curious that my invented O. Schrutt should be a bit character, a walk-on part, an alphabetized member of Vienna's Nazi youth. It's *very* curious, isn't it?

Just imagine: if my invented O. Schrutt had lived through all the walk-on parts I anticipated him to play, what would that O. Schrutt be doing now? What more perfect thing could he be than this second-shift nightwatchman at the Hietzinger Zoo?

(CONTINUING:)
THE HIGHLY SELECTIVE AUTOBIOGRAPHY OF
SIEGFRIED JAVOTNIK: PRE-HISTORY II

I can't make my father fit the ethnographic maps of Yugoslavia. He was born in Jesenje in 1919, which at least made him a Croat, and possibly a

Slovene. He was certainly not a Serb, although Vratno Javotnik was such a worldly sort of Yugoslav, I believe he was the only Yugoslav to whom being a Serb instead of a Croat wouldn't have made any difference—and splitting the hair between Croats and Slovenes would have been absurd for him. His politics were strictly personal.

By that I mean he had no affiliations. If he was born in Jesenje, it's likely he was baptized a Roman Catholic. If not, it's at least certain he was in no way near enough Serbia to be Eastern Orthodox. But it couldn't have mattered to Vratno, one way or the other.

One thing seems to have mattered, though. My father was something of a linguist, and Jesenje is less than fifty miles from the University of Zagreb, where my father studied languages. This may have been a premonition on his part—pessimism at a tender age: to master the speech of several occupying armies before they came to occupy.

Whatever the motives, Vratno was in Zagreb on the twenty-fourth of March, 1941, when Foreign Minister Tsintsar-Markovich left Berlin for Vienna, and when the students at the University of Belgrade demonstrated on that Serbian campus—burning German textbooks and picketing all the German classes.

The Croatian reaction in Zagreb was probably sullen—the feeling that the Serbs were sure to get everyone killed by their lunatic defiance of Germany. Vratno only thought they'd missed the point. It didn't matter whose side you were going to be on; when Germany came into Yugoslavia, one day it could save your skin to speak German. Burning your textbooks was certainly unwise.

So the next day my father left Zagreb for Jesenje. It's my belief that he traveled light.

That day the Tripartite Pact was signed in Vienna; Vratno was probably en route to Jesenje when he heard the news. I'm sure he guessed that various Serbian zealots wouldn't accept this welcome to Germany. And I'm sure Vratno turned to practicing his German idioms.

All the way into Jesenje, I can hear him practicing.

In fact, on the next night, while in Belgrade the General Staff of the revolution was in its final, deciding session, Vratno was probably perfecting his irregular verbs. When the bold takeover was in process, and plans for the impossible resistance against Germany were being made, Vratno was making umlaut sounds.

In Belgrade, the quisling government was overthrown; Prime Minister Tsvetkovich was arrested at 2:30 A.M. And Prince Paul was caught later aboard a train in Zagreb; he was exiled to Greece. In Belgrade there were heroes: Lieutenant Colonel Danilo Zobenitsa, tank corps commander and the rescuer of young King Peter; Professor Radoye Knezevich, King Peter's former tutor; Ilya Trifunovich Birchanin, commander of Chetniks, those diehard Serb guerrillas of World War One—the only warriors, they say, who can fight hand to hand with the Turks.

And in Jesenje was my father, making himself universally fluent, preparing for his sly survival.

The Ninth Zoo Watch:
Tuesday, June 6, 1967, @ 3:15 a.m.

A few minutes ago I had this urge to make a bed check on the elephants. I'm sure at one time or another everyone has heard, as I have, that elephants never sleep. So I decided to go check on the elephants, even at the risk of disturbing the other, finally sleeping animals—or even at the risk of catching the awful attention of O. Schrutt, professional insomniac. After all, there aren't many opportunities in this world for testing myths. And the myth of the never-sleeping elephant is one that I've often thought needed testing.

I can tell you, I already had my doubts about the myth. What I expected to find in the House of Pachyderms was a boulder field of heavily sleeping elephants—cages of elephant mounds. I pictured them heaped together, circled like a Western wagon train—their trunks draped over each other, like great pythons sunning on bouldertops.

But if you take this night's example, the myth was substantiated. The elephant quarters were uncannily awake. The elephants stood in a perfect row, and hung their great heads over the fronts of their stalls like restless horses in an ordinary barn. They nodded, and waved their trunks, they breathed in slow motion.

When I walked in front of their stalls, they reached their trunks out to me—they opened and closed their nostrils to me. Their trunks kissed my hands. One of them had a cold—a runny trunk that rattled.

"When I come back for the real thing," I whispered, "I'll bring some medicated cough drops for you."

It nodded: All right, if you can remember. But I've had colds before.

The bored elephants nodded: Bring a lot of cough drops. We'll probably all have colds by then. Everything's very catching here.

It's puzzling to me. Perhaps there's some connection between their sleeplessness and how long they live. Seventy years without a snooze? Although it seems unlikely, perhaps there's a myth snorted trunk to trunk among the elephants—that if you fall asleep, you die.

Someone should find a way to tell them it's perfectly healthy to sleep.

I'll bet there's no one, though, who could convince O. Schrutt of that.

I heard him when I stalked back to my hedgerow from the House of Pachyderms. I heard him taking chances with the animals' sleep. Doors in the Small Mammal House were creaked, and sliding glass was slid.

O. Schrutt, creeping around in the residue of infrared. O. Schrutt is up to no good, I'll bet. But so long as he chooses to stay inside the Small Mammal House, I'll just have to wait my chance.

Or maybe go back and ask the sleep-suspicious elephants, who must be wise: what prompts O. Schrutt to indulge himself with infrared? And: more than twenty years or so ago, just what did old O. Schrutt do?

(CONTINUING:)
THE HIGHLY SELECTIVE AUTOBIOGRAPHY OF
SIEGFRIED JAVOTNIK: PRE-HISTORY II

I wonder where my stealthy father was when the *Luftwaffe* bombed the open city of Belgrade, without a declaration of war. I feel certain that Vratno wasn't observing any protocol either.

On April 6, 1941, Heinkels and Stukas were used simultaneously. The Wehrmacht pushed into Yugoslavia with thirty-three divisions, six of which were panzers and four of which were motorized. The aim was to march on Russia in mid-May, in the dry-weather season—when the roads would still be hard. So the German onslaught against this upstart revolution was fierce. So fierce that on May 4 Germany announced that the Yugoslav State was nonexistent. But on May 10, Colonel Drazha Mihailovich and his band of wild Chetniks hoisted the Yugoslav flag on the mountain on Ravna Gora. Mihailovich and his freedom fanatics went on doing that kind of thing all summer.

Oh, stories got told, you know, how Croat quislings and other Yugoslav capitulators marched with the Germans, hunting down Chetniks. How the Chetniks would disguise themselves as Croat quislings and appear to be hunting for themselves. How Mihailovich was a magician in the mountains —potting Germans throughout Serbia. In fact, in watchful America, *Time* magazine voted Drazha Mihailovich Man of the Year. And the Communist press was most praiseworthy too. After all, the Germans didn't get to march on Russia in mid-May. They were delayed five weeks, and they sloughed in on soggy roads. And they were no longer thirty-three divisions strong; between ten and twenty divisions were left behind as an occupying force— still hunting down those fanatical Chetniks.

But those were heroes, and I'm wondering where my father was. I suspect he summered in Jesenje, mastering the languages of likely victors—even learning the names of foreign wines and soups, brands of cigarettes and movie stars. Regardless, his whereabouts were unknown to me until the fall of '41, when Vratno Javotnik appeared in Slovenjgradec.

The city was full of capitulating Slovenes and Croats who felt reasonably secure to be occupied by Germany, and who resented the wildly resisting

Serbs to the southeast. The only people my father had to fear in Slovenjgradec were a few uprooted Serbs. These called attention to themselves on October 21, 1941, by protesting the somewhat conflicting reports of the massacre at Kraguyevats, where—one broadcast said—2,300 Serbian men and boys were machine-gunned in retaliation for 10 German soldiers killed by Chetniks, and 26 Germans also sniped but only wounded; another broadcast said that at least 3,400 Serbs were shot, which would have been in excess of the retaliation number promised by Germany to combat Chetnik sniping—that is, 100 Serbs per German killed, and 50 Serbs per German wounded.

Whichever broadcast was correct, the womenfolk of Kraguyevats were digging graves from Wednesday to Sunday, and Slovenjgradec, at least, was generally pacified to learn that the Germans had presented the Kraguyevats Town Council with 380,000 dinars for the poor. Who were just about everyone after the massacre. Oddly, the amount of the German donation was estimated to be slightly less than half of what 2,000 to 3,000 dead Serbian men and boys might have had in their pockets.

But the Kraguyevats massacre had all of Slovenjgradec outdoors anyway. Just to hear the conflicting broadcasts and to catch the sentiment of the city from sidewalk talk. In fact, the massacre brought people out in public who might otherwise have stayed aloof.

Namely, my father—out listening to dialects of his native Serbo-Croat, and picking up various German colloquialisms from café to café.

And namely, the entire Slivnica family horde, as they were known—dreaded fiends, all of them, enlisted in the service of the Ustashi terrorist organization, supposedly headed by the fascist Ante Pavelich. It was a hireling of Pavelich's, we're all told, who assassinated King Alexander and French Foreign Minister Barthou in Marseilles in '34.

Fascist Italy was reportedly behind the Ustashi end of this organization; Yugoslavia's neighbors were known to take advantage of the endless tiff between Serbs and Croats. But the Slivnica family horde were Ustashi terrorists of a special kind. Oh, the terror they waged wasn't in the least political; they were simply well fed for their work. In fact, they were feeding when Vratno encountered them, although it was only the lovely Dabrinka who first caught my father's eye.

The Slivnicas were at a long table at an outdoor terrace restaurant above the Mislinja River. Fair Dabrinka was pouring the wine for her two sisters and four brothers. Her sisters were nothing to what Vratno saw in Dabrinka. Only squat, circle-mouthed Baba, and the sulky, melon-round Julka. Dabrinka was a creature with lines and bones—more features than flesh, my father was fond of saying. Dabrinka was a cool, slim trickle—more the green stem than the flower. My father thought she was a waitress, and never guessed her to be a member of that most thick family she served.

One table away, Vratno raised his empty glass to her. "My girl," he said.

"Would you fill me up?" And Dabrinka hugged the wine decanter; she turned away. The Slivnica menfolk turned to my father the linguist, now speaking Serbo-Croat. My father felt the wrath. Oh yes. Four of them: the sturdy twins, Gavro and Lutvo; Bijelo, the eldest—and leader—and terrible Todor, body-awesome.

"What shall we fill you up with?" Bijelo asked.

"Nails?" said Todor. "Or ground glass?"

"Oh, you're all one family," my father cried. "Oh yes, I see."

For the resemblance was striking among them all, excluding Dabrinka. She had their olive-black and -green color only in her eyes, but not their quickly sloping-away foreheads and nothing of the family swarth. Not the flat, pounded cheeks—which even Baba and Julka had—and not the twins' close-together eye slits. Not the exaggerated dimples of Bijelo the eldest; not a bit of the bulk of her big brother Todor, and not his cleft chin, either— the imagined tool work of hours with a rat's-tail file.

"Seven of you!" said my father. "My, what a big family!" Thinking: What inconceivable twosome could ever have mated and conceived them?

"Do you know us?" Bijelo asked. The twins sat mum and shook their heads; Baba and Julka licked their lips, trying to remember; Dabrinka blushed through her blouse; Todor hulked.

"I'd be honored," my father said, in ordinary Serbo-Croat; he faltered to his feet. Then in German he said, "It would be my pleasure." And in English: "Happy to know you, I'm sure." And in the Mother Russian tongue, hoping to arouse possible pan-Slav sympathies: "Extraordinarily glad!"

"He's a languist!" said Tudor.

"A linguist," Bijelo said.

"He's sort of nice," said Baba.

"Just a youngster," Julka breathed, while Lutvo and Gavro still sat mum.

"And you don't know us from somewhere?" said the leader Bijelo.

"But I hope to," my father said, in his straightest Serbo-Croat.

"Bring your wineglass over," Bijelo commanded.

"Perhaps," said Todor, "we could powder the rim of your glass into the finest possible bits, and let you sip the glass dust down?"

"That's enough humor, Todor," Bijelo said.

"I only wondered," said Todor, "what language he would speak with glass dust in his larynx."

Bijelo cuffed a twin. "Give the linguist your chair and get another," he said. Both Gavro and Lutvo went looking.

When my father sat down, Baba said, "Oh, get him!"

"Go on, if you want," said Julka.

Gavro and Lutvo came back with a chair each.

"They're dumb," Baba said.

"Dummies," said Julka.

"They share one brain between them," Todor said. "It's a small allowance to live on."

"Enough humor, Todor," Bijelo said, and Todor sat mum with the twins, who sat puzzling over the extra chair.

When the young Dabrinka turned around, my father felt his wineglass was too heavy to lift.

And that was how Vratno Javotnik met the Slivnica family horde, odd-job artists for the Ustashi terrorists—who had use for a linguist.

The Ustashi had touchy sort of work in mind. In fact, this job was so delicate that the Slivnicas had been surprisingly inactive for the past two weeks, pending the discovery of just the *right* man. The Slivnicas were probably quite restless for work—or for work less random than linguist-looking. Their last job had called on the services of the entire family and had gratified everyone. A French newspaperman, unauthorized in Yugo-slavia, had sought a home experience with a typical Slovenjgradec family —to learn for himself the degree of fascism and Italo-German sentiments in the average Slovene or Croat. The Ustashi were not interested in this sort of publicity, feeling that the French were soreheaded enough about Minister Barthou's assassination. So the Ustashi selected the Slivnicas as the typical family for the French newspaperman.

But this Monsieur Pecile didn't think the Slivnicas were average, or wished, at least, to live with a family that *didn't* have twin mutes and *did* have a living mother and father. Perhaps he doubted, as Vratno had, the possibility of natural genitors; or perhaps he made a pass at Dabrinka—and with Baba and Julka offering it so freely, the Slivnica family feelings were hurt. At any rate, the gleeful twins, Gavro and Lutvo, described in drawings, on the dusty hood of the Frenchman's car, the spectacular rocklike plummeting of Monsieur Pecile into the Mislinja River.

Now there was a job that had involved them all—a real family project. But this linguist hunt had been something else. Todor confessed it to be so tedious that he feared his humor had soured.

Oh yes, the job that Ustashi terrorists had for Vratno was indeed more delicate than the mere disposal of an unauthorized Frenchman. This new subject was a German named Gottlob Wut, as authorized in Yugoslavia as the rest of his horde, and the particular job asked of Vratno—for the moment, at least—was not a disposal. Gottlob Wut was scout-outfit leader of Motorcycle Unit Balkan 4, and the Ustashi weren't looking for any trouble with the Germans. Chiefly, they wanted my father to make a fast friend of Gottlob Wut.

The Slivnicas were to prepare my father for this considerable task; Gottlob Wut, as far as anyone knew, had never had a friend.

Poor Wut had been uprooted by the war, which isn't a thing you could say for all Germans. Gottlob had left an art for a service, and the Ustashi were interested in what Gottlob Wut might reveal of his mysterious past, to a friend, in his presently low-key, nostalgic condition.

It's not clear what the Ustashi had against Gottlob, but I suspect it was an issue of wounded pride. Gottlob Wut had been a racing mechanic for the NSU motorcycle factory at Neckarsulm before the war. The motorcycle world was always saying that Wut had a mystical touch. The Ustashi also thought he had a violent touch, even a certain criminal touch—because a new-model NSU racer surprisingly won the Grand Prix of Italy in 1930, with Britisher Freddy Harrell doing the driving, and the Ustashi figured that Gottlob had more of a hand in the victory than his precise genius with valve control. The Italian counterpart of the Ustashi produced some evidence that Gottlob Wut had tinkered effectively with more than hairpin valve springs. Allegedly, Gottlob Wut had tinkered with the head of the Italian favorite, Guido Maggiacomo, whose body was found after the race in the Grand Prix body shop—lying peacefully beside his highly touted Velocette, which had missed the race. Guido Maggiacomo's temple was severely dented, authorities claimed, by an Amal racing carburetor found at the scene of the crime. It was said of Gottlob Wut, in those days, that he was never without an Amal racing carburetor. The new NSU racer had attained a new speed by successfully tilting these carburetors at a slightly downdraft angle.

Unfortunately, the Italian counterpart of the Ustashi had backed a number of syndicates who put their money on Guido Maggiacomo and his highly touted Velocette. When the betting turnover was tabulated, it appeared that the NSU team of Britisher Freddy Harrell and German Klaus Worfer had made a killing. But the record has it that all the betting was done by the mystical mechanic Gottlob Wut. It was Wut who took away the booty.

But that was in 1930, and if the Ustashi were to reveal this crime to Wut's Nazi superiors, the Germans certainly wouldn't care. Gottlob Wut was a valuable scout-outfit leader of Motorcycle Unit Balkan 4.

This unit itself didn't seem to be very valuable at the moment. The Germans had found their motorcycle scouts rather obsolete in the Yugoslav campaign. They were easy targets to pot off in the Serbian mountains; the way those Chetniks hid and fought, motorcycles were easy to spot. But to keep Gottlob Wut's unit in Slovenjgradec wasn't very vital either. There wasn't a real war in Slovenia or Croatia—just an easy occupation; for police work, there were better means than motorcycles available.

Gottlob's rough riders looked a bit silly in a quiet city.

Of course, the Ustashi had more in mind about Gottlob than an old financial grudge. They thought it would be nice to catch the old mystic at a new crime, and one which could be presented as anti-German. They already knew of a small scandal. If Gottlob Wut didn't have a friend, he did have a woman—a Serbian woman, who was something of a political outlaw in Slovenjgradec. Gottlob Wut, it might be shown, was taking his German blood rather lightly. In fact, he didn't seem to give a damn for the whole war.

All of which was how the get-the-goods-on-Wut campaign began, with my father studying motorcycle memorabilia on the Slivnicas' kitchen table. Vratno learned the names of racers and the dates of races; Vratno learned the bores and strokes, and the significant compression ratios; Vratno distinguished the side-valve model from the supercharged double-overhead-cam twin in sizes 350 and 500 cc. My father had never been on a motorcycle before, so the Slivnicas helped where they could.

Broad Todor went down on all fours, and my father mounted. Todor gave his elbows for handlebars; he demonstrated cornering. Bijelo called out the road conditions.

"Corner sharp right," Bijelo said.

"Lean from your spine," said Todor. "Don't move those elbows, you never want to steer a bike, the handles are just for holding on. You got to lean a bike, hips and head. Now tip me a little right."

"Corner sharp left," Bijelo said, and watched my father gingerly lean left off the broad back, his knees slipping.

"You wouldn't have made that one," said Todor. "You'd have gone wild, Vratno, my boy. Let's feel those knees, now, give me a squeeze."

And Baba giggled. "I'll be the bike," she said. "Let me."

"Todor makes a fine motorcycle," said Bijelo the eldest; he had an eye for bikes, all right. He'd stolen some Italian's Norton, over the border in Tarviso—oh, before he was a responsible head of a family—and had ridden the great chugger over the mountains, back to Yugoslavia, crossing where there wasn't a customs checkpoint because he crossed where there wasn't a road. But he was so carried away to be back in his homeland with it, and finally driving on a real road, that he drove it into the Sava River on the outskirts of Bled, climbed out wet but wildly happy, knowing how he'd do it again if he had the chance—and this time, make it all the way to Slovenjgradec. So he said.

He was a good teacher for my father at least. My father rode Todor Slivnica under Bijelo's critical eye, for hours every evening—with Baba offering her own broad back, should Todor give out, and Julka claiming that she could clamp a gas tank on her brother's rib cage tighter than Vratno could.

My father, riding long hours through the nighttime kitchen, would see his shy Dabrinka maybe once or twice. She poured the wine, she served the coffee, she was pinched by her sisters and she never met my father's eyes. Once, on a corner sharp left, Vratno held a smile up for Dabrinka; he would have waited forever to catch her eyes. But Todor turned his head, the back of which usually pretended to be the headlight and necessary gauges. Todor dumped my father on the corner sharp left.

"You must have leaned too far, Vratno," he said, then leaned himself closer to where my father sat. "I think it should be grownup ladies for you," he said. "You don't have to go outside this house to get it, and you don't have to kill yourself looking for it, either." And Todor made a scissors of his index and middle finger, thick as garden shears, and he snipped his finger scissors just above my father's lap.

Oh, now that the linguist hunt was over, Todor Slivnica's humor was brightening, you could tell.

The Tenth Zoo Watch:
Tuesday, June 6, 1967, @ 3:45 a.m.

Seeing those elephants has made me sleepy, but if they can be insomniacs for seventy years or more, I can hold out for a few more hours. It's just because of the lull in here; for a moment, I was bored.

When I came back from the House of Pachyderms, it was so quiet that I went on by my hedgerow. I went down the path to the oryx's pen. For no good reason, I realized, I'd been putting off visiting the oryx.

It was easy, climbing the pen, but I saw as soon as I set foot inside that the oryx was in his shed. His hind hooves were splayed out the shed door, over the ramp; silky white hairs lay over his fetlocks. He looked like someone who'd been felled with a sledge as he came in his house—ambushed in his doorway. But when I gingerly came up behind him, he raised his head and shoved his face out the doorway into the moonlight; I touched his wet black nose; he sort of mooed. It was a little disappointing, he was so docile; I'd expected to be challenged—to be backed against his shed wall, threatened with horn and hoof, until I proved to him I was the sort he could trust. But the oryx needed no proof; he lay back again, stretched, raised up again, sliding his great hip out from under himself—kneeling, actually! His great ballocks bumped the boards of the ramp. He stood up tiredly, as if to say: All right, I'll *show* you where the bathroom is. You probably can't find it by yourself.

He invited me into his shed; that is, he backed up, completely off the ramp, and with his nodding head, he showed me about his room: This is where I sleep when it's cold—when it's warmer, as you saw, I hang a piece of me out the shed door. And this is where I take my brunch, by the glassless window. And this is where I sit to read.

He knocked about the shed (expecting, I think, that I was going to feed him something), and when I showed him I didn't have anything, he somewhat indignantly walked out of his house. The moonlight bounced off the ramp; his balls wobbled and were shot through by the strobe-light effect of the reflecting moon.

Something more definite should be said for the size. Not basketballs—that's exaggerating, of course. But they're bigger than softballs and—really! —bigger than the elephant balls I saw standing at attention just a while ago. They're volleyball-sized, only too heavy to be perfectly round. They're volleyballs that look sat on, or with the air let out—little dents where the ball collapsed for lack of air. That's as close as I can come, other than to point out that they're dangled in long, loose leather moneybags, and also, that they're a little crusty—owing, I'm sure, to the muck in the poor oryx's slum.

Imagine: the oryx was born in the Hietzinger Zoo! Brainwashed! He thinks his balls are just for lugging around. They never told him; he probably wouldn't know what to make of a lady.

And that's when I got to thinking: Why isn't there an antelope of sorts, a mountain goat or experienced gnu, who could show this poor oryx what his volleyballs are for?

I'm convinced: it's abstinence that's given them their size!

So I made a check of the surrounding pens, looking for a lady who might enlighten the naïve and apathetic oryx. Now this was hard. The blesbok was too small and skittish—would only teach our oryx frustration. I felt the white-tailed gnu was far too hairy; Mrs. Gray's waterbuck looked absurdly virginal; the lesser kudu had little to offer; the hartebeest had too thin a back; and the only female wildebeest had a beard. There was nothing in all of the Hietzinger Zoo as perfect for the oryx as a gentle old madam cow.

So I decided. Rather than corrupt the oryx with a lascivious llama, I'd hope for the best on the day of the bust; that our oryx would escape forever to the Wachau pasture lands along the Danube, plundering queenly cows and lording over the awe-struck herds.

And thus encouraged, I skulked past the Small Mammal House. O. Schrutt was off somewhere in the back streets of the Small Mammal Maze —still creaking doors, I could hear, and sliding the sliding glass.

But along with O. Schrutt's sounds of clumsiness, I could hear something new from my stand just outside the open door. O. Schrutt had woken up his charges; there were shuffles, scratchings, claws clacking on the glass. And just as I began to think of this waking as a preface to O. Schrutt's own sudden emergence in the aisle, and his striking out for the open door—just as I'd turned a bit down the path, and was retreating to my hedgerow— I heard a wail from some lost aisle of the Small Mammal Maze. A cry cut off at full force, as if O. Schrutt had flung open a door on some poor beast's nightmare and slammed the door shut again as quickly as he'd opened it —fearing, perhaps, he'd be involved in the beastly dream.

But the wail was contagious. The Small Mammal House whimpered and moaned. Oh, the screams blared and were cut off again, muffled but not altogether gone. As if a certain zoo train had passed you somewhere, going fast, and the frightened animals' cries had slashed out at you like a passing buggy driver's whip; and the cries hung for a moment all around, like the sting of the whip lingering on your neck after the buggy driver had slashed and passed on.

So I pawed my way through the nearest root gap and crawled under and behind my hedge. Holding my breath.

It wasn't until I exhaled, and heard a thousand exhalations round me, that I realized the rest of the zoo was awake again too.

(CONTINUING:)

**THE HIGHLY SELECTIVE AUTOBIOGRAPHY OF
SIEGFRIED JAVOTNIK: PRE-HISTORY II**

On Sunday the twenty-sixth of October, 1941, Vratno Javotnik was judged by the Slivnicas as being prepared to meet Gottlob Wut, who had Sunday habits convenient for a meeting.

The scout outfit had Sundays off. There was no guard at the Balkan 4 barracks on Smartin Street, and no guard at the motorcycle unit's garage —a nearby block down Smartin Street, flush to the Mislinja riverbank.

Sunday was Wut's day for a leisurely breakfast with his Serbian mistress, whom he'd openly moved to a Smartin Street apartment, halfway between the Balkan 4 barracks and the garage. Wut would cross Smartin Street every Sunday morning, briskly out of the barracks, wearing his bathrobe and unlaced dress shoes, carrying his uniform under his arm; it was the only day of the week he wasn't wearing or carrying his crash helmet. Wut had his own key to the Serbian woman's apartment. All Smartin Street watched Wut let himself in.

Occasionally, one of the scout outfit's members would have stand-by messenger duty on Sundays. In which case, one of the 600 cc. NSU side-valve sidecar models would be parked in front of the barracks. Otherwise, all the bikes were locked up, downstreet at the garage.

Wut had a key for the garage too. He'd leave his mistress in the late afternoon and go down to his motorcycles, letting himself in again, neat in his uniform—this time—his bathrobe under his arm. Then he'd fiddle with the bikes until dark. He'd start them, adjust them, tighten them, bounce on them, leave little tickets tied to several handlebars—stating the nature of maladies he'd discovered, noting ill effects of maladies left uncorrected, sometimes suggesting punishments for the more careless of his drivers.

When fussing, he left the garage door open to vent the exhaust—and to admit his audience; mostly children, they'd stand in the doorway and make revving sounds of their own. Wut let them sit on the sidecar models, but never on the ones that could tip off their kickstands and crush a child. Gottlob brought pastries from the Serbian woman and had a snack with the children before he closed up. But the children who stole—even so little as an insignia—he never let come back. Wut always knew who stole what too.

Gottlob Wut was a stringy, hipless and rumpless man, bent-backed, and stiff in all his twitchy motions; he had a wincing walk, as if it hurt him to unbend his joints. It probably did hurt too. At one time or another, Gottlob Wut had broken all his fingers and half his toes, both wrists and both ankles, one leg and the other elbow, all but the highest rib on his left side, once his jaw, twice his nose, and three times his sunken left cheek—though never his right. Wut had never driven in a race, but he'd tested all the racers before the flaws were gone. NSU discovered flaws through Gottlob Wut. Poor Wut, pinned under one test model or another, his hand lanced through by a front brake handle, fuel sloshing over his chest, the old hand gearshift of a Tourensport stuck in his thigh—while hirelings pull the monster off him, Wut is speaking: "*Ja,* I'd say there is clearly no rear suspension, and we'll have to retain the girder fork in front if we're to have any suspension at all. Because I certainly was totally lacking suspension of any kind, in that corner I missed back there."

But now Wut had a dull job, writing tickets: Bronsky, your tires are forever soft; Gortz, tissue paper will not stop your leak, you've lost a seal in your transmission, and don't you ever put such gunk as tissue in there again; Wallner, you've been laying over too much on your corners, you've skinned your tailpipes and bent your kickstand—such hot-rodding will get you just nothing but a sidecar attached, to slow you down, you fool; Vatch, your tail fender Iron Cross is gone, and don't you tell me it was my children who took it, for I watch them and I know it's some girl that has it or you sent it home and said it was a medal you never got—it's got screw holes in it, you won't be fooling anyone—so get it back on that tail fender; Metz, your sparkplugs are filthy, and I don't scrape carbon for anyone, that unskilled labor like you can do—Monday, instead of your lunch.

Yes, Gottlob Wut had a dull job—survived adventures to be bored to death. He would have liked to tell his best driver, Wallner, how he could skin his tailpipes down to dust, how he could lay over on a corner and really grind his tailpipes down to nothing—only watch out for the kickstand, it can snag you up, which is why you don't put one on a bike you're racing, and often no tailpipes either. But Gottlob wrote tickets on Sunday, and had to write tickets that kept Scout Outfit Balkan 4 intact, even if obsolete; parts and drivers weren't so easily replaced in Slovenjgradec as they were in the old Neckarsulm factory.

Certainly the Sunday of October 26, 1941, was a fine Slivnica sort of choice for a day when my father could attempt to bring some excitement into the dull life of Gottlob Wut.

It was also the fifth and last day of gravedigging for the shovel-sore and weary widows of Kraguyevats.

And it was probably a day of sneaky fighting, like many other days, for the Chetniks of Mihailovich and for the Communist partisans who at this time were supporting the Chetnik forces against the Germans—the Communist partisans being led by a little-known son of a Croatian blacksmith from the village of Klanyets. The blacksmith's son had gone to the Russian front with the Austro-Hungarian Army, but he went over to the Russians and fought with the Red Army through the civil war; then returned home as a leader of the Yugoslav Communist party; then was arrested as a Communist in 1928 and served five years in prison; then allegedly was in charge of the Yugoslav Communist party through the period of illegality, although those involved with the Balkan underground centers in Vienna, at the time, swear they never once heard of this blacksmith's son. Certain members of the Balkan underground claim that the blacksmith's son was actually a member of the Russian secret service, and that he was in Russia until the Germans' delayed invasion got under way. Whatever his real history is, the blacksmith's son was the mystery-man leader of the Communist partisans, who were fighting along with the Chetniks against the Germans—when they weren't fighting against the Chetniks. He was a Communist; he had a large and handsome Slavic head; he was fighting along with Mihailovich before he turned against Mihailovich; he was indeed mysterious.

At the time my father was on his way to meet Gottlob Wut, very few people had ever heard of Josip Broz Tito, the blacksmith's son.

My father certainly hadn't heard of him, but, as I've said, Vratno paid little attention to politics. He was attentive to more constant details: the various uses of Amal carburetors, the advantages of the double-overhead cam, umlaut sounds and verb endings. In fact, by the Sunday of October 26, 1941, my father had learned his introductory lines by heart.

Vratno spoke his German softly to himself; he even spoke made-up lines for Wut. Then he strolled through the open doors of the motorcycle unit's garage, an indigo-blue racing helmet with a red-tinted visor cocked a bit back on his head, chin strap loose and jaunty; and over the ear hole of the helmet, a crossed pair of checkered racing flags with a halo printed above them, reading: AMAL CARBURETORS FINISH FIRST—AND LAST!

"Herr Commander Wut," he said. "Well, yes, I'd still recognize you. You're older, of course. I was only eleven, so of course I'm older too. That wonderful Wut!" Vratno crowed. "If only my poor uncle had lived to meet you."

"What?" said Wut, strewing tools and children. "Who?" said Wut, a socket wrench firm in his puffy old hand—the dirtiest, most knuckle-cut hands that my father had ever seen.

"Javotnik here," my father said. "Vratno Javotnik."

"You speak German," said Wut. "And what are you doing in leathers?"

"Wut," said Vratno, "I've come to join your team.'

"My what?" said Wut.

"I've come to learn all over again, Wut—now that I've found the master."

"I don't have any teams," said Wut. "I don't know any Javotniks."

"Remember the Grand Prix of Italy, 1930?" Vratno asked. "Ah, Wut, you really made a killing."

Gottlob Wut unsnapped his sidearm holster.

Vratno said, "My poor dead uncle took me, Wut. I was only eleven. Uncle said you were the very best."

"At what?" said Wut, holster open.

"Motorcycles, of course, Wut. Fixing them and driving them, testing them and coaching drivers. A genius, Uncle said. Politics got in the way, of course, or my uncle would have joined your team."

"But I don't have any *team,*" said Wut.

"Look," my father said, "I've got a real problem."

"I'm very sorry," said Gottlob Wut, sincerely.

"I was just coming along as a driver," Vratno said, "when my uncle was killed—drove his Norton into the Sava outside the Bled. It ruined me, Wut. I haven't sat on a bike since."

"I don't know what you want," Gottlob said.

"You can teach me, Wut. I've got to learn all over—how to ride. I was good, Wut, but I lost my nerve when poor Uncle sank in the Sava. Uncle said you were the very best."

"How did your uncle know me?" Wut asked.

"The world knew you, Wut! The Grand Prix of Italy, 1930. What a killing!"

"You said that before," Wut complained.

"My uncle was teaching me, Wut. My uncle said I had all the moves. But I lost my nerve, you see. It would take a master to have me riding again."

"There's a war now, you fool," said Wut. "What are you anyway?"

"Croat, I guess—if it matters," Vratno said. "But motorcycles are international!"

"But there's a *war* now," said Wut. "I'm the scout-outfit leader of Motorcycle Unit Balkan 4."

"That's the team I want!" my father said.

"It's not a *team!*" said Wut. "It's a *war!*"

"Are you really in the war, Wut?" Vratno asked. "What will the war do to NSU?"

"Set us back ten years," said Wut. "There won't be any racers made, there won't be any improvements made. There might not be a factory to go back to, and all my drivers could lose their legs. Everything will come back, covered with camouflage paint."

"Oh, you're surely right that these politics have no place with motorcycles," my father said. "Wut, is there any way I can overcome my fear?"

"My God!" said Wut. "You can't have anything to do with a German military unit."

"You can help me, Wut, I know you can. You could make me a driver again."

"Why are you speaking German?" said Wut.

"Do you speak Serbo-Croat?" my father asked.

"Of course not," Gottlob said.

"Then I'd better speak German, don't you think? I was driving all over the continent, you see—mostly amateur events, sure. But I was an alternate for the 1939 Grand Prix races. Pity that NSU wasn't a winner in '39—a bit heavy, your racer model that year, wasn't it? But I picked up some languages when I was touring."

"Before you lost your nerve?" said Wut, who was lost.

"Yes, before poor Uncle drowned with the Norton."

"And you were only eleven at the 1930 Grand Prix of Italy?"

"Eleven, Wut. Merely an admiring child."

"And you found out I was here?"

"I found out, Wut."

"How did you ever find that out?" Gottlob said.

"The world knows you, Wut—the motorcycle world."

"Yes, you said so before," Wut agreed.

"How would you go about overcoming such a fear?" my father asked.

"You're crazy," said Wut. "And you'll frighten the children."

"Please, Wut," Vratno said. "I had all the right impulses, and now I'm frozen."

"You must be out of your head," said Wut, and my father cast a wild eye around the garage.

"Lots of sidecars," he said, "but they're not motorcycles, really. And side-valvers," he said, "lots of low-speed torque, which is all right for the war, I guess, but you don't win races with them, do you?"

"Just a minute," said Wut. "I've got two six hundred cc. overhead valves. They move along all right."

"No rear suspension, though," Vratno said. "Center of gravity was too high, and hurt the handling—if I remember '38."

"Remarkably, you remember," said Wut. "And how old were you then, boy?"

"Just two '38 models, the side-valvers and the sidecar tanks," my father counted scornfully. "I'm sorry, Wut," he said, "I was mistaken. You don't have anything for me here." And he started for the door. "By the end of this war," he added, "NSU will be back to making nothing but mopeds."

"And they don't even send me where the real driving is!" said Wut.

My father walked out into Smartin Street, with Gottlob Wut wincing behind, socket wrench stuck in his boot.

"Maybe," said Vratno, "they thought you were too old for the front. Maybe, Wut, they figured you had your action behind you. Lost your zip, you know?"

"You didn't see the racer in there," said Wut, shyly. "I keep it under a tarp."

"What racer?" Vratno asked.

"Grand Prix racer of '39," said Wut, and stood unbalanced with his feet too close together—his hands locking and unlocking behind his back.

"The one that was too heavy?" Vratno said.

"I can make it lighter," said Wut. "Of course, I had to put some trimmings on it so they'd think it was just a workhorse machine like the others. But I take them off for a run, now and then. You know—the kickstand, toolbox, pack rack, radio mounts and that saddlebag crap; I had to fill it in a little, for the war look, but it's still the '39 Grand Prix racer, five hundred cc. model."

My father came suspiciously back to the doorway. "That's the twin, right?" he said. "The supercharged double-overhead-cam twin? Got the duplex cradle frame, and the boxed plunger rear suspension?"

"Want to see it, huh?" said Wut, and he blushed.

But under the tarp was the racer disguised as a war bike, the camouflage paint a somewhat darker tone because of the black enamel layers underneath.

"What can she hit?" Vratno asked.

"Strip her down and she'll hit one-fifty," said Wut. "Her weight's still high at four eighty-six, but a lot of that's fuel. She puts it away; she's under four hundred when she's dry."

"Roadability?" said Vratno, giving conspicuous little jounces to the front end, as if he knew all about the shocks.

"Oh, still a bit rough," Wut said. "Handles hard, maybe, but the power never fails you."

"I can imagine," said Vratno, and Gottlob Wut looked at the racing flags crossed over my father's ear hole. Then he sent one of the children to the barracks for his helmet.

"Javotnik, wasn't it?" he asked.

"Vratno. Vratno Javotnik."

And Gottlob said, "Well, Vratno, about this fear of yours . . ."

"Overcoming it's the problem, Wut."

"I think, Vratno," Gottlob said, "that good drivers have to transfer their fears."

"To what, Wut?"

And Gottlob said, "Pretend it's a different fear, boy. Pretend it's like the fear when you first learn to ride."

"Pretend?" said Vratno.

"If it's not too hard," said Wut, "you should try to pretend that you've never driven a motorcycle before."

"That shouldn't be too hard," Vratno said, and watched Gottlob Wut doing knee bends—limbering up the old sticky joints before mounting the monster Grand Prix racer, '39.

If you're careless with the spark retard, the kickstarter can kick you back hard enough to slide your ankle joint flush to your knee joint—shove the whole shaft of your thighbone screaming up under your lungs.

Or so claimed Gottlob Wut, the motorcycle master and secret keeper of a Grand Prix racer, '39, who was as unconcerned with politics as my father was; who hadn't yet heard of Josip Broz Tito, either.

The Eleventh Zoo Watch:
Tuesday, June 6, 1967, @ 4:15 a.m.

I can't imagine what O. Schrutt could be doing to them. I still hear them; the whole zoo is listening. Now and then there's a door that opens suddenly on some awful animal music, and just as suddenly closes—muffles the cry.

I can only guess: O. Schrutt is beating them, one by one.

It's clearly anguish. Whenever the cries blare full force, there's an answer for the rest of the zoo. A monkey scolds, a large cat coughs, the Various Aquatic Birds are practicing takeoffs and landings; bears pace; the great gray boomer is viciously shadow-boxing; more subtly, in the Reptile House, the great snakes twine and untwine. Everyone seems in angry mourning for the creatures under infrared.

I can only guess: O. Schrutt is mating with them, one by one.

There's a herd of Miscellaneous Range Animals just behind my hedge-row; they're huddled round each other, conspiring. I can guess what they're saying, nipping each other's ears with their strange, herbivorous teeth: Schrutt's at it again. Did you hear the last one? Brannick's giant rat. I know its terrible bark anywhere.

Oh, the zoo is full of gossip.

A moment ago, I crept out of my hedgerow and down to the empty *Biergarten* to have a word with the bears. They were all in a stew. The most fierce and famous Asiatic Black Bear squatted and roared himself upright, lunging into the bars as I scurried past his cage. I saw his shaggy arms still groping out for me when I was half a zoo block away. The Famous Asiatic Black Bear must have been thinking of his captor, Hinley Gouch—and was interpreting the nameless diabolics of O. Schrutt as no more than another capture of that deceiving Hinley Gouch's kind. For the terrible Asiatic Black Bear, all men must be Hinley Gouch—especially O. Schrutt.

I tried to calm them all, but the Asiatic Black Bear was unfit for reason. I did whisper to the polar bears that they shouldn't take it out on each other, and they floated, though uneasily, thereafter; I did beg the grizzly to have a seat and collect his thoughts, which, after a half-blind charge at me, he begrudgingly did; my gentle pair of Rare Spectacled Bears were so very worried that they hugged each other upright.

Oh, I can only guess: O. Schrutt—mad fetishist!—what is your evil indulgence that frenzies the whole zoo?

But no one can tell me, I'm in some haunted bazaar in someplace more scheming than Istanbul; in their cages and behind their fences, the animals are gossiping in a language more violent and foreign than Turkish.

I even tried a little Serbo-Croat with a Slavic-looking great brown bear. But no one can tell me a thing.

I can only guess what the last shriek meant: O. Schrutt, with ritual slowness, is strangling the coati-mundi. The cry pushes thickly through the lavender maze; now it's cut off like all the rest.

Now sliding glass is slid. And the zoo gives me a Turkish explanation.

(CONTINUING:)
THE HIGHLY SELECTIVE AUTOBIOGRAPHY OF
SIEGFRIED JAVOTNIK: PRE-HISTORY II

The ritual of Vratno learning to drive the 1939 Grand Prix racer was limited to Sundays. My father would wait for Gottlob Wut on the Smartin Street sidewalk in front of the Serbian woman's door. Wut was punctual, bathrobed, helmeted, shoed but unlaced—uniform under his arm. My father, in Bijelo Slivnica's leathers, would polish his indigo-blue helmet while waiting for Wut.

Gottlob Wut required a two-hour bath Sunday mornings. The tub had a ledge for his pastries and coffee. My father ate his breakfast on the hopper, lid down. They talked around and occasionally through the passing bulk of Wut's Serbian mistress, who refreshed the coffee and Wut's bath water —who at times simply squatted between tub and hopper, watching the changing colors of Gottlob Wut's many scars underwater.

Zivanna Slobod was about as effortless a mistress as anyone could come by. Middle-aged, heavy in the jaw and hips, she had a shiny, black-haired, gypsy strength to her. She never spoke a word with Wut, and when my father would compliment her services in Serbo-Croat, she would raise her head a little and show him the fine rippling vein in her neck and all her bright, heavy teeth.

Zivanna took Wut away from my father after the bath; she returned him in half an hour. This was the rubbing-down session, wherein the thoroughly bath-limp Wut would be bundled in towels and escorted from the bathroom by strong Zivanna. Vratno turned up the radio and loudly drained the bath so he wouldn't hear Gottlob Wut's joints being loosened beyond imagination on the great airless mound of bed things in Zivanna's only room with a door that closed. Vratno saw the mound once—the door had been left ajar as he followed Wut to the bathroom one morning. It would have been like sleeping on a ball, because Zivanna's bed, if that's what really was beneath the bed things, was strewn with silks and pelts, fur pillows and large, shiny scarves; a tippy bowl of fruit perched on top of the mound.

God bless Gottlob Wut for his indulgent Sundays. The man knew how to break up the weeks.

And he knew everything about his 1939 Grand Prix racer. He could strip it in ten minutes. It was to Wut's unending sorrow, however, that he hadn't the time to do anything about the camouflage paint. Some appearances had to be maintained. Wut was fortunate enough to have a most agreeable motorcycle unit; they never reported the racer's presence to the overseers of the German scout command. Gottlob kept them happy by giving each his turn on the racer, although this pained him a good deal. Wallner was too cocky with it—had no respect for the power; Vatch was afraid of it and never shifted out of second; Gortz ground gears; Bronsky floated corners, one gear too high; Metz was an utter dolt about the overuse of brakes— he brought the racer back smoking. Even out of Slovenjgradec on a very open road, Gottlob was nervous about anyone else riding his racer. But certain sacrifices had to be made.

With my father, Wut was very cautious. They began by riding the racer double—Wut driving, of course, and carrying steady instructions back to his passenger. "Now see?" said Wut, and would corner neat, with a whining, flawless down shift at the break of the turn. My father's eyes were shut tight, the wind screamed in his ear holes and moved his helmet up and down. "You can even take it up a gear when the curve is banked," said Wut. "Now see?" And would never break the steady, increasing pace when he changed his gears; and would never miss a gear, either. "Never miss," said Wut. "There's too much weight behind you to miss a gear and hold the road." And would give an example: he'd pull in the clutch and freewheel the racer into a turn. "Do you feel?" Wut asked. "You'd never hold this corner out of gear, would you?"

"Oh, my God no!" my father answered, to show as quickly as possible that he felt very surely they wouldn't hold the curve. And Wut would ease the clutch out; they'd feel the sweet and heavy gear pull drawing them back to the crown of the road.

If you were deaf, you would never know when Gottlob Wut was shifting; he was much smoother than an automatic transmission.

"Do you *feel* it, Vratno," Wut was always asking.

"A conditioned reflex," my father would answer. "You're pure Pavlov, Wut."

But they didn't get far into November of '41 before it snowed, so my father had to wait awhile before going beyond the passenger stage. Wut let Vratno get the feel of the gears on the big side-valve model 600 with the sidecar, but he refused to let my father drive a straight bike until the ice was off the roads.

Wut himself was not so cautious. In fact, one Sunday in February of '42, he took one of the straight 600 overheads, 1938, and with Vratno as passenger, drove north of Slovenjgradec to the village of Bucovska Vas, where an elbow of the Mislinja River was reportedly frozen the thickest. My father stood shaking in the pine grove on the edge of the bank while Wut gingerly drove the '38 out on the ice. "Now see?" said Wut, and began to move slowly from my father's left to my father's right—very slowly, with steady first-gear work, Wut cornered and came back, right to left; then he cornered again and came back, left to right—this time hitting second gear. When he cornered in second, his rear wheel slipped and he touched one tailpipe down to the ice; then righted the bike, slipped to the other tailpipe and righted it again. And came back, right to left—now hitting third. "Now see?" he cried, and swung his leg over from the side of the bike that was going down, this time, all the way to the rear wheel hub; he stood two-footed on one pedal and held the throttle steady while the bike righted itself. He remounted and came back, carrying a little farther in both directions each time he turned, so that my father had to come gaping out of the pine grove and stand with his toes on the river's ice heave—just to see the farthest reaches of Wut's fantastic turns. Again and again, the bike rocked over a tailpipe and touched down the rear wheel hub, and Wut swung a stiff leg to right the machine. "Now see?" Wut screamed, and made the frozen river twang and sing beneath him. Back and forth, faster and faster, in a wider and wider radius—letting the bike almost lie flat on the ice, with the wheel hub trying to eat its way down to the running water. In a flourish, Wut tapped his rear brake very lightly—let the bike slip out from under him while he swung his leg; let the bike rest at last, laying it down gently— standing on its gas tank until it had stopped spinning.

Then the only thing Wut had trouble with was getting the heavy old '38 back up on its wheels. Gottlob's feet kept slipping on the ice when he tried to lift. My father came off the bank, and together they righted it, and wiped off the tank where some fuel had sloshed.

"Of course," said Wut, "you've got to feel that just right. But that's how it's done."

"Driving on rivers?" my father said.

"No, you fool," said Wut. "That's how you handle tar or an oil slick. You hold your throttle steady, you get your leg out from under, and if you don't touch the brake, she should come back up on her own."

Then they minced along the ice, walking the old '38 to where the bank was flattest. And from the bank on the far side of the river came a shouting foursome of ice fishermen on a sled with droning runners; out from wherever they'd watched the performance, they brought their strange, mittened applause.

Gottlob Wut, perhaps, had never had such a public audience before; he seemed wholly stunned. He took his helmet off and held it under one arm, waiting for the wreath or trophy, maybe, or for no more than a bearded ice fisherman's kiss. He was bashful, suddenly self-conscious. But when the sledful of fishermen arrived, my father saw that the Slovenians were hopelessly drunk and oblivious to Wut's uniform. They nudged their sled up to Gottlob's left boot; one of the fishermen used his mitten for a megaphone and shouted up to Wut, in Serbo-Croat, "You must be the craziest man in the world!"

Then they all laughed and clapped their mittens. Wut smiled; his kindly eyes begged my father for a translation.

"He said you must be the best in the world," Vratno told Gottlob Wut, but to the drunks on the sled, my father said, in cheerful Serbo-Croat, "Keep smiling, oafs, and bow a little as you leave. The man's a German commander, and he'll shoot your bladders if you say another word."

Vratno had them smiling foolishly up from the sled, their heels slipping on the ice as they backed. The beefiest of them went down on his knees on the river and grunted against the runners. They straddled the sled and hugged each other, hip-to-thigh, looking like children who'd ridden their sled into a place where sleds were absurd, or not permitted.

My father held the motorcycle up for Wut, who waved after his departing fans. Poor, gullible Gottlob Wut, standing helmet-in-armpit, chin-up and vulnerable on the creaking ice.

"That was really great, Wut," my father said. "You were just fine."

The Twelfth Zoo Watch:
Tuesday, June 6, 1967, @ 4:30 a.m.

I was thoroughly chilled and was burrowed down in the roots of my hedge when old O. Schrutt came jangling his keys down the center-doorway aisle; for a second, I came crouching and duck-walking out from my hedge and peered down the path at him. He staggered out of the Small Mammal House and down the blood-glowing stairs.

O. Schrutt drinks on the job! Smokes pot, takes acid or pep pills. O. Schrutt pushes heroin—to the animals! Perhaps.

God, he was awful. He looked ravished. One pant leg was untucked from one combat boot; one epaulette was unbuttoned and flapped; his flashlight was jittery; he carried the keyring like a great mace.

Perhaps his mind is stretched and torn and then mushed back in shape by dark and tidal, almost lunar forces. Perhaps O. Schrutt averages three transformations a night.

But whatever cycle his insanity goes through—whatever phase this was —his effect on me was hypnotic. I crouched almost too long on the path; I would have been dumbstruck at his feet, if he hadn't sent me scrambling back to the cover of my hedge with his sudden barking at the Monkey Complex.

"*Rauf!*" he barked—perhaps still remembering the gelada baboon.

"Raa-ow-ff!" But all the primates kept very still, hating or pitying him.

And when he came on down the path again, he was making growls.

"Aaaaarr," he said softly. *"Uuuuurr."*

While the Parliament meeting of Miscellaneous Range Animals tried to look casual about herding and milling together. But O. Schrutt walked the length of my hedgerow with his eye on them. When he turned down the path to the *Biergarten,* I ran scootched-over behind the hedge—all the way to the far corner, where I could see him move on. Sauntering, a changed man in a minute—cocky, I tell you—he whirled back to face the Miscellaneous Range Animals.

"Awake, eh?" he cried—so shrilly that the tiny kiang, the wild ass of Tibet, bolted out of the herd.

And virtually swaggering then, O. Schrutt walked on to the *Biergarten* —as far as I could see. He stopped a few feet before the Famous Asiatic Black Bear; then O. Schrutt leaned out toward the bear's cage and rang his keyring like a gong against the bars.

"You don't fool me," cried old O. Schrutt, "crouching there like you're asleep and not planning an ambush!" While the Asiatic Black Bear threw and threw himself against his cage—roaring like I've never heard, alarming the Big Cats so much that they didn't dare to roar a challenge back, but only coughed in little rasps, and unbefitting mewing noises: Oh, feed me or forget to—I'll eat old O. Schrutt or anyone else. But whatever you do, God, don't you let that Oriental bear out. Oh please, no.

But O. Schrutt boldly taunted; exhausted, the Asiatic Black Bear slumped against the front of his cage, his great forepaws dragging through the peanut shells on the path, on the cage side of the safety rope—as far as he could reach and still six inches short of old O.

O. Schrutt went on, continuing what must be the aggressive phase of his zoo watch. I heard him plunk a rock in the polar bears' pool.

He's not quite far enough away to suit me yet; I would guess he's only at the ponds of Various Aquatic Birds. I believe that's him I hear, skipping stones across the ponds—bonking, now and then, a rare and outraged Aquatic Bird.

Let O. Schrutt get a little farther off. Let him get to the House of Pachyderms, let him rouse the rhino or echo his keys in the hippohouse. When he's a whole zoo away from me, I'll be in that Small Mammal Maze to see what's what.

And if there's time, old O., I've something else in mind. It's easy enough to do. Just move that safety rope six inches or a foot nearer the Famous Asiatic Black Bear's cage. It wouldn't be hard at all. There's just a rope strung between those posts; they have an awkward, concrete base, but they're certainly not immovable.

How would that fix you, O. Schrutt? Just change your safety line a foot or so—move you closer than you think you are, old O., and when you waggle your taunting head, we'll all watch it get lopped off.

And now, if that's him I hear, O. Schrutt is braying his empathy with the elephants' paranoia concerning sleep. Now he's far enough away.

(CONTINUING:)
THE HIGHLY SELECTIVE AUTOBIOGRAPHY OF
SIEGFRIED JAVOTNIK: PRE-HISTORY II

The 1939 Grand Prix racer 500 cc. could summon 90 h.p. at 8,000 r.p.m., and hit 150 m.p.h. when stripped of unnecessary parts, but my father was allowed no more than 80 m.p.h. when he took to driving the racer in the spring of '42. Vratno carried a necessary part. Namely, Gottlob Wut as passenger—the constant, correcting voice in my father's indigo-blue ear hole.

"You should be in third now. You steered us through that last one more than you leaned. You're much too nervous; you're tight, your hands will cramp. And never use your rear brake on the downhills. Front-brake work, if you've got to brake at all. Use that rear brake again and I'll disconnect it. You're very nervous, you know."

But Gottlob Wut never said a thing about what a good job my father was doing at pretending he'd never driven before. And only after Wut had been forced to disconnect the rear brake did he ask Vratno where he lived and what he did for food. Clerical work, my father told him—occasional translations for pro-German Slovenes and Croats in a subgovernment position. Whatever that meant. Wut never asked again.

Although it wasn't exactly fair to call the Ustashi pro-German, they were pro-winning—and in the spring of '42, the Germans were still winning. There was even a Ustashi militia who wore Wehrmacht uniforms. In fact, the Slivnica twins, Gavro and Lutvo, had Wehrmacht uniforms of their own, which they wore only for dress-up, or for going out at night. The twins weren't part of any unit Vratno knew of, and once Bijelo scolded them on their manner of acquiring the uniforms; it seems they had several changes. The Ustashi overseer for the Slivnicas was alarmed, and called the twins a "relationship risk."

"Our family," said Todor, "has never been afraid to risk relationships of any kind."

But Todor was often snappish in the spring of '42. After all the work, the Ustashi had either lost interest or given up their hope that Gottlob Wut would betray anything vital enough to make him touchable. At least, as long as the Germans were winners—and as long as the Ustashi were pro-winning

—Wut seemed quite safe from revenge. About all Wut was guilty of was the keeping and disguising of a Grand Prix racer in a motorcycle unit meant to have slower and less delicate war models. And Zivanna Slobod, Wut's ritual-minded Serbian mistress, turned out to be a Serb more by accident than inclination—and a "political outlaw," as she was called on record, only because her list of lovers included every political or apolitical type imaginable. So they couldn't very well incriminate Wut on her account either. And Sundays were free; what Wut did with the racer and my father, he did on his own time. It could even be argued that Wut's Sundays demonstrated extra effort on the part of the motorcycle unit's leader—a kind of keeping-in-shape exercise. The Ustashi simply had nothing they could ever make stick on Gottlob Wut.

"We could steal his pet racer," Bijelo suggested. "That might make him do something foolish."

"We could steal the Serbian woman," said Todor.

"Great cow of a woman," grumped jealous Baba, a titter-minded toad of a girl—as my father has described her. "You'd need a van to move her."

"It seems to me," said Julka, "that Wut is more fond of the motorcycle."

"Certainly," my father agreed. "But stealing it would do nothing. He'd have perfectly good military means for recovering it, or at least for looking. And I'm not so sure that the German command would even mind him having a racer."

"We'll just kill him, then," said Todor.

"The Ustashi," Bijelo said, "are in need of being legal, to a point."

"The Ustashi are boring me to death," said Todor.

"They have to stay on the right side," Bijelo said. "Wut is a German, and the Ustashi are siding with the Germans now. The idea is to make Wut be a bad German."

"Impossible," said Vratno. "He doesn't think one way or the other about being a German, so how could he be a bad one?"

"Well," Bijelo said, "I don't think the Ustashi are so very much interested in Wut any more. People are changing sides all the time, and the Ustashi have to come out with the winner. That's no longer so easy."

Because there were too many side wars within the war; whole sides were changing sides. In the spring of '42, the worldwide Communist press suddenly changed its mind about the Chetnik colonel Drazha Mihailovich—who was now a general. A suspiciously Russian-located station called Radio Free Yugoslavia was reporting that Drazha Mihailovich and his Chetniks were siding with the Germans. Radio Free Yugoslavia—and through them, even the B.B.C.—was saying that a certain blacksmith's son had been the only freedom fighter all along. Josip Broz Tito was the leader of the real resistance, and the defenders of Yugoslavia were Communist partisans, not hairy Chetniks. It seemed that Russia was looking ahead; with remarkable optimism, they appeared to be looking past the Germans to a more crucial issue in Yugoslavia.

Who would run the country when the war was over?

"Communists," said Bijelo Slivnica. "It's quite obvious, really. The Chetniks fight the Germans, the partisans fight the Germans, and in a little while the whole Red Army will be here—fighting Germans. In between Germans and after Germans, partisans and the Red Army will fight Chetniks— claiming that Chetniks side with the Germans. Good propaganda is what counts."

"A divine scheme," said Todor.

"Publicity's the thing," Bijelo said. "Look: the Chetniks beat the Germans in Bosnia, right? But Radio Free Yugoslavia broadcasts that it was partisans who did the beating, and that they discovered Chetniks in Wehrmacht uniforms."

At the mere mention of which, Gavro and Lutvo went to change into their uniforms.

"Utter dummies," said Julka; while in the kitchen, fine Dabrinka washed wineglasses. My father didn't dare to watch her any more.

"Which brings us back to Wut," Bijelo Slivnica said.

"I don't at all see how," said Todor.

"Because the Ustashi need to be sure," Bijelo said. "Wut is a German. Germans kill Chetnik-Serbs, and lately, partisans. Partisans kill Chetnik-Serbs, and lately, Germans. The Ustashi will kill whatever the Germans want killed, but they don't want to kill partisans, if they can help it."

"Why not?" my father asked.

"Because," said Bijelo, "the Ustashi will soon enough be killing Germans *for* the partisans, because in the end the partisans will win."

"So what?" said Todor.

"So who does just about everyone want to kill?" Bijelo asked.

"Serbs!" said Todor.

And Bijelo Slivnica finally said, "Then a Serb should kill Gottlob Wut. Because the Ustashi will support the German percentage proclamation and kill one hundred Serbs for the one German, Wut. So the Germans are appeased, and when the Red Army and the partisans team up and drive the Germans from Yugoslavia—there's the Ustashi, having a good reputation for killing Serbs, nasty Chetnik-types. So the partisans are happy to have the Ustashi along. And the Ustashi stay happy; they pick winners. And, of course, they get to settle the score with old Gottlob Wut. Now I ask you," said Bijelo, "how's that for thinking?"

"What *Serb* is ever going to kill Wut?" my father asked.

"You," said Bijelo, "only you make it look like the job was done by Zivanna Slobod, who really is a Serb. Then you'll have to kill her too. So the Ustashi and the Germans will round up ninety-nine other Serbs and bump them—to make the forewarned ratio come out right. One hundred to one, see?"

"Bijelo has a touch for making everyone happy," said Todor.

But my father said, "I don't think I want to kill Gottlob Wut."

Julka brought her thighs together. *Flap!* they said. In the kitchen, Dabrinka broke a wineglass.

"Oh, dear," said Baba.

And my father said to Bijelo, "Well, if it happens like you say, the war will get old Wut anyway, won't it? And the Ustashi aren't so very interested in Wut, you said so yourself, anyway."

The twins came in, in their uniforms, and paraded for everyone.

Bijelo, very calmly, said, "Look, it would be on a Sunday. See the twins' uniforms? You carry one with you in a paper bag. Wut's having his endless bath, you see. And the lid on the flush box behind the toilet? It's porcelain, right? And very, very heavy. So when Zivanna goes to get her pastries from the oven, you drop the flush-box lid on the bathing, unsuspecting Wut. Should submerge him quite handily. And where's Wut's sidearm holster? Hung on the bathroom mirror, isn't it? So you take the gun and shoot Zivanna when she brings back the pastries. Then you put on Gavro's or Lutvo's uniform, and call the German scout command. It's Sunday, remember; the motorcycle unit has the day off. It's spring, remember; they won't be sweating inside their barracks, either. German command takes you for one of Wut's regular drivers—you know their names, so give one. Just watch your irregular verbs. You tell a few tales about the Serbian woman —how you heard of a plot to kill Wut but you arrived too late. There are more than two million Serbs in Slovenia and Croatia. Surely the Ustashi and the Germans can round up ninety-nine in downtown Slovenjgradec. Shoot them all the same day too—I wouldn't be surprised."

But Vratno said, "I *like* Gottlob Wut."

"Sure," said Bijelo. "I like him too."

"We all like Gottlob Wut," Todor said. "But you like your job with us, don't you, Vratno?"

"Of course he does," said Bijelo. "Now why don't you try on a uniform, Vratno?"

But my father backed into the kitchen doorway; over his shoulder he could hear the squeak of a dishtowel on glass—the high, nervous sounds of Dabrinka's fast finger work.

"Why don't you try one on, now?" Todor said, and grabbed Lutvo, the nearest twin, and snatched down Lutvo's pants to his ankles, jerked up and dumped poor Lutvo on the floor.

Webfooted Baba prodded her still-uniformed brother Gavro toward the upturned face of the naked Lutvo—where Gavro behaved as a perfect twin and undressed himself. Todor then gathered the uniforms and flung them to my father in the kitchen doorway.

"Pick a uniform," he said. "Either one should do."

My father, backing into the kitchen, heard the gentle Dabrinka break another wineglass, and was turning to lend assistance when Dabrinka's slim wrists skated over his shoulders; her fine, girlish fingers lightly pricked my father's jugular with the needlepoint of the wineglass's splintered stem.

"You try on one of those uniforms, please," she said in Vratno's blushing ear. Which marked the first and only time there were ever words between them.

The Thirteenth Zoo Watch:
Tuesday, June 6, 1967, @ 4:45 a.m.

There's something funny going on here, all right.

When O. Schrutt was teasing the insomniacs in the House of Pachyderms, I went inside the Small Mammal House. Very spooky in there—with those infrared-exposed animals, thinking they live in a world with a twenty-hour night. They were all wakeful, most of them sort of shifty in their glasshouses—crouched or even pacing in the corners of their cages.

But I couldn't see that anything in particular was wrong! There wasn't any blood, and no one looked beaten or ravished or at Death's Door. They were just watchful, suspicious, and too alert for nocturnal creatures supposedly put at ease in nocturnal surroundings. Take, for example, the spotted civet cat—who was panting on its belly, its hind legs spread out behind it like a seal's tailflipper. It swished its tail, waiting for the mouse or madman who would any second now burst through the closed back door of its cage.

The back doors of these cages, I found, lead into alleys that divide and are shared by the two opposing faces of cages in each block of the Small Mammal Maze. The alleys are more like chutes for coal—a guard would have to kneel to make his way between and behind the cages, checking each labeled door. It is very nifty. A guard or feeder or cage-cleaner could creep along this passageway and know which animal's house he was invading, just by reading the tags on the door. Very wise. You wouldn't want to be unprepared—to carelessly dart your head inside a cage, expecting the wee Brazilian pygmy marmoset and finding instead the great curved fighting claws of the giant anteaters, or a brash, ill-tempered mongoose.

From the alley, you can get some idea of what the outside looks like to the animals. I opened the back door of the ratel's cage, thinking that a ratel must be a wee sort of rat, and to my surprise, discovered that the ratel is a fierce, badgerlike creature of Afro-Indian heritage, silky-furred and long-clawed; but before I slammed the door in his snarling face, I got a peek at how he saw the world. Darker than dark, like a solid rectangle of black, blacker than the entrance to a cave, there was a void drawn down like a shade beyond his front window glass.

When I closed the door, I had the awful feeling that if O. Schrutt had sneaked back to his lair, he could have been watching the ratel, and would have seen me suddenly loom in the ratel's back doorway and quickly slam the door on my own frightened face. I crept out of the chute, expecting at any moment to meet—if not O. Schrutt grunting on all fours—an ape specially trained for routing things out of the alleyways.

So when I got out in the main maze again, I went straight ahead with my business, with no more dallying. I went to O. Schrutt's room, the nightwatchman's layover spot. A percolator coffeepot, a cup with dregs, a ledger on the messy desk—the master sheet for the zoo animals, with columns for special entries, things to be on the lookout for. Like:

The giant forest hog has ingrown tusk; is caused some pain. Give aspirinated salt cubes (2), if suffering.

The ocelot is expecting, any day now.

The binturong (bearcat of Borneo) has rare disease; better watch out for it.

The bandicoot is dying.

And each animal had a number; on the master plan of the zoo, the cages were numbered in an orderly, clockwise fashion.

My God. A *rare disease!* Is that all—just watch out for a rare disease? The binturong has nameless, incurable suffering. And the bandicoot is dying! Just like that—dying; the rare little leaper. Keep an eye on it, sweep it out when it's through.

Into a world like this, the ocelot is giving birth. My God. Stop the whole process.

O. Schrutt's den. This ledger, this murky percolator, and hanging by a leather thong to a hook just inside the door—an electric cattle prod; beside it was a pole with a gaffinglike hook on the end.

For the life of me, I can't tell what O. Schrutt has done in here.

I looked around as long as I dared. And then I heard him coming by the bears again. I heard the famous frustration of the Asiatic Black Bear, lunging just short of O. Schrutt's combat boots. I realized I'd missed my chance, this time, for moving the safety rope about a foot in the unsafe direction. I made my break then, down by the Monkey Complex.

This time, I didn't come too close. I saw the frotter, this time. The gelada baboon, waiting for me, crouched motionless on the dark, outside terrace of his cage—hoping I'd come too close to the bars again. And when he saw I saw him, and that I wasn't coming anywhere near him, he leapt to the nearest trapeze and swung himself howling through the half-dark, landing high up on the bars, facing me. He just screamed, and the scheming Monkey

Complex broke out in unison, in a banter that got all the zoo heated and talking again.

O. Schrutt came, bobbing his flashlight along, but I was easily ahead of him and under my hedge before he'd even got to the Monkey Complex.

And again, when he arrived, there wasn't so much as a spider monkey on the outside terrace. They were all swinging silently within the complex; once or twice, a thump of a trapeze, or dry slaps—as if an ape were rolling over and over, beating his chest and knees, aping laughter in a pantomime of loud and huge delight.

"You did it again!" O. Schrutt screamed. "What are you up to?" And he lost a shade of his aggressiveness; he began again to back away, darting his flashlight through the treetops, jerking his head back from imagined, claw-carrying shapes he saw hurtling down on him. "What's out here?" cried old O. Schrutt. And backing farther off, leaning toward the security of the Small Mammal House, he shouted, "You damn baboon, you can't fool me! I'm not monkey enough to fall for your games!"

Then he turned and ran for the door of the Small Mammal House, looking back over his shoulder as he stumbled headlong up the stairs.

I thought: If only at this moment, *there* was the Asiatic Black Bear, or a mere vision of him, in the doorway—if just for a second, precisely as O. Schrutt gave a last look over his shoulder before going inside, there would be the terrible Oriental bear laying a gruff paw on the back of O. Schrutt's neck—old O. would die of fright, without a word.

But he got back inside. I heard him swearing. Then I heard doors being creaked, and at least I knew now what doors they were, and where they led. And I again heard sliding glass being slid. I thought: What glass? There was no glass I saw that slid.

But it was very soon thereafter that the cries and snarls reached me in their piecemeal fashion again, and I knew that I simply had to see the Small Mammal House while O. Schrutt was still *inside* and up to his dirty work.

I feel I have to risk it. If only because the bandicoot is dying—and the glossy ocelot is expecting, any day now.

(CONTINUING:)
THE HIGHLY SELECTIVE AUTOBIOGRAPHY OF
SIEGFRIED JAVOTNIK: PRE-HISTORY II

The Slivnicas were a rare family for foresight. The plan for sinking Gottlob Wut in his bathtub was approved by the Ustashi. And the penalty of one hundred to one being carried out on Serbs for the death of a German was not unfamiliar with the Ustashi either. They'd been setting up Serbian massacres since the middle months of '41. There had been some countermassacres as well, but the Ustashi were numerically far ahead; they had a percentage proclamation just like the Germans'—one hundred Serbs for each Ustashi killed. If anything was accomplished by this, by the summer of '42, it was the feeling among Serbs that all Slovenes and Croats were Ustashi terrorists—among Slovenes and Croats, that all Serbs were hairy Chetniks. A fine muddle was made, as Bijelo Slivnica wisely foresaw, and Tito's partisans were growing stronger on the fringes of every mess. The Germans were spread out thin, from Slovenjgradec en route to Moscow, and the Italians now held the Dalmatian coast of Yugoslavia and royally supported the Ustashi.

"Wut is nicely settled," said Bijelo Slivnica through a huge sandwich. But my father had a bit of foresight himself.

On a Sunday morning in August, known as Wut Sunday among the Slivnicas, my father sat in the bathroom while Gottlob Wut soaked. When Zivanna Slobod went to check her oven, Vratno said, "There's a strange car across the street from us, Wut—a strange, large family on some sort of outing."

"That so?" said Wut.

My father lifted up the flush-box lid and held it in his lap.

"Need exercise?" said Wut.

"I'm supposed to kill you," Vratno said. "I'm supposed to sink you under this toilet top and shoot your lady when she brings in the pastries."

"Why's that?" said Wut.

"Oh, it's a real mess," my father said.

"Are you a Chetnik," Gottlob asked, "or a partisan?"

"I'm presently employed by the Ustashi," my father said.

"But they're on our side, now," said Wut.

My father explained: "They were also on the side of Guido Maggiacomo at the Grand Prix of Italy in 1930. So I imagine it's awkward for them too."

"Oh, dear, I see," said Wut. "Of course, it must be very difficult for them, I'm sure." He stood up, embarrassed in his tub; his countless, indented scars held the bath water and dripped like wounds still open.

When Zivanna Slobod came back to the bathroom, she noticed that her ritual had been upset and she dropped her pastries in Gottlob's abandoned bath. Wut himself was putting the toilet top back in place, and Vratno was getting into a Slivnica Wehrmacht uniform. Wut then uniformed himself, while the blubbering Zivanna was fishing a nut loaf out of the bath water. Surprises did not become her.

Surprises weren't very becoming to the Slivnicas, either. When Gottlob Wut, all alone, came out on Smartin Street and wandered leisurely toward the motorcycle unit's garage, Bijelo Slivnica simply must have said: sit tight. Because the carload of the whole family sat there, watching Wut and waiting for Vratno to make a dash.

They waited all the while it took Wut to start one of the 600 cc. sidecar models and roll it into the open doorway, pointed out—to go. Then Wut took the carburetors out of all the remaining motorcycles in the garage, except the 1939 Grand Prix racer. Wut put all the carburetors into the waiting sidecar—along with a toolbox, points, plugs, cables, assorted engine parts, a primary and a drive chain, topographical maps of Slovenia and Croatia, and two dozen grenades; he cupped one grenade in his hand and started up his racer.

The Slivnicas were still waiting when Gottlob Wut came back up Smartin Street on the Grand Prix racer, stripped of trimmings, and they must have thought Wut was having trouble with his bike, because he was riding bent over and had one hand cupped under his gas tank—where his fuel line might have come loose. The Slivnicas watched Wut weave up the street toward them, head down and fumbling under the gas tank, and quite possibly they never saw him roll the unpinned grenade under their car.

I believe that Bijelo Slivnica and his unpleasant family were still sitting tight when the car blew up.

The noise of which brought my father bolting out on Smartin Street and up behind Wut on the racer. Gottlob turned back to the garage and established Vratno on the running, warmed-up sidecar model 600.

"Why'd you do it, Wut?" my father asked.

"For some time now," said Gottlob Wut, "I've wanted to be on the road again."

But whatever the reason Wut gave, there was this understood: they were even. My father had not submerged Gottlob Wut, and Gottlob had not abandoned my father.

They weren't followed. Scout Outfit Balkan 4 was hard to find on Sundays, and when found, they were hard to mobilize—owing to a lack of carburetors.

When they got to Dravograd, Wut and my father heard the carefully censored news. A well-liked Ustashi family of six had been killed—sabotaged on Smartin Street, Slovenjgradec. Ustashi and German troops seized Zivanna Slobod, notorious Serbian prostitute—and the murderess responsible for this crime. In accordance with German and Ustashi proclamations, one hundred Serbs will be shot for each German or Ustashi murdered. In Slovenjgradec, Serbs were being sought to answer for the crime. Six Slivnicas equals six hundred Serbs—Zivanna Slobod and five hundred and ninety-nine others.

And in Dravograd my father was thinking: But there were *seven* Slivnicas. Bijelo, Todor, Gavro, Lutvo, Baba, Julka, and Dabrinka makes seven. Whichever one escaped saved the lives of one hundred Serbs, but my father, who was unconcerned with politics, wasn't comforted by that thought.

"I think it was Dabrinka who wasn't blown up," Vratno told Wut. "She had the least flesh to get in the way of flying stuff."

"Doubtful," said Wut. "It must have been the driver. He was the only one who might possibly have seen it coming, and he had the wheel to hold on to—to keep himself from going through the roof."

They discussed it further over a urinal in a Dravograd dive.

"Who would have been the driver?" asked Wut.

"Todor always drove," said Vratno. "But he also had the most flesh to get in the way of flying stuff, if you go by my theory."

"I don't go by any theories," said Gottlob Wut. "It's just very pleasant to be on the road again."

The Fourteenth Zoo Watch:
Tuesday, June 6, 1967, @ 5:00 a.m.

I'm stalling. But I have my reasons!

One thing, it's beginning to get light out—as if this moon hasn't been light enough. And foremost, I don't see how I can get into the Small Mammal House without O. Schrutt seeing me. If I were inside and O. Schrutt came in, that would be a different matter; then I could listen to where he was and avoid him in the maze. But I don't like the idea of making a dash up those stairs and coming through that doorway, when I can't be sure what part of the maze O. Schrutt is in.

So I've decided: I have to wait for the plotting gelada baboon to come outside again. Now that it's getting light, I can see the outside terrace of the Monkey Complex from the end of my hedgerow. When that gelada baboon comes out, I'll make my move.

It's simple. I'll station myself behind the children's drinking fountain, near the entrance to the Small Mammal House. Then I'll get that baboon's attention; I'll lob rocks at him; I'll leap out from behind the fountain and make rude, insulting gestures. That will set him off, I know. And when he's raging, O. Schrutt will come pelting down those stairs, fit to kill. And when O. Schrutt is going through his paranoiac ritual at the Monkey Complex, I'll streak silent and barefoot into the Small Mammal House; I'll get myself well back in the maze. O. Schrutt may come out so fast that he'll leave the bloody evidence this time. And if not, then at least I'll be in there when he starts up again.

At least, there's been no indication that he'll let up. The fiend seems bent on keeping everyone up till the zoo opens. No wonder the animals always look so drowsy.

You may think, Graff, that I sound extreme. But if there's an ulterior motive behind this zoo bust, it would certainly be the exposing of old O. —even if I don't know exactly what he is, yet.

I know where he's come from, though. Twenty or more years ago—it's common history what various O. Schrutts were up to. I know the route O. Schrutt has been, and I'll bet there are those along that route who'd be surprised to hear of O. Schrutt again. At least, there are those who'd be more than interested to find an O. Schrutt who still wears his nametag and has kept both epaulettes.

Ha! After how many atrocities to previous small mammals, how very fitting that old O. should end up here.

(CONTINUING:)

THE HIGHLY SELECTIVE AUTOBIOGRAPHY OF SIEGFRIED JAVOTNIK: PRE-HISTORY II

My father and Gottlob Wut spent two years in the mountains of northern Slovenia. Twice they were lonesome and planned trips. The first one, to Austria, ended at the Radel Pass along the mountain border. The Austrian Army guards appeared very formal and thorough with their rifles and paper work at the checkpoint. Wut decided that they'd have to abandon the motorcycles to make a crossing feasible, so they drove back into the Slovenian mountains that same night. And the second trip, to Turkey, ended just southeast of Maribor at the Drava River, where the Ustashi had accomplished another massacre of Serbs the night before; an elbow of the Drava was clogged with corpses. My father would always remember a raft snagged in some deadfall along the bank. The raft was neatly piled with heads; the architect had attempted a pyramid. It was almost perfect. But one head near the peak had slipped out of place; its hair was caught between other heads, and it swung from face to face in the river wind; some faces watched the swinging, and some looked away. My father and Gottlob again drove back to the Slovenian mountains, near the village of Rogla, and that night slept in each other's arms.

In Rogla, an old peasant named Borsfa Durd kept them alive for the privilege of having rides on the sidecar model 600. Borsfa Durd was scared of the racer—he never understood what kept it upright—but he loved to sit toothless in the sidecar while my father bumped him over the mountains. Borsfa Durd got them fuel and food; he raided the Ustashi depot at Vitanje —until the August of '44, when he was returned to Rogla in a fellow-villager's mulch wagon. The terrified villager said the Ustashi had stood the kicking old Durd on his head on the wagon floor and shovel-packed mulch all around him; only the soles of his shoes were visible at the peak of the mulch mound, when everyone tried to extricate him for a proper burial in Rogla. But the mulch was too wet and heavy, too hard-packed, so a certain mass of mulch was chopped and rolled off the wagon into a hole; the hole was circle-shaped because that was the appropriate cut of the mulch mass, which was said to contain Borsfa Durd. Although no one really saw more of him than the soles of his shoes, the fellow-villager who'd brought him back, in his reeking wagon, testified that it was Borsfa Durd without a doubt —and Gottlob Wut said he recognized the shoes.

So Borsfa Durd was buried coffinless in a chunk of mulch, which ended the fuel-and-food supply for the runaway motorcycles and their keepers. My father and Gottlob Wut thought they'd better move; if the Ustashi at the depot in Vitanje were at all curious as to why Borsfa Durd had been raiding their supplies, Vratno and Gottlob could be expecting a visit. So they left, taking what Borsfa Durd had owned for clothes.

Relying on the topographical maps, they went over a route in the daytime, dressed as peasants and scouting on foot—the motorcycles were always stashed in brush; they'd walk five miles down the mountains, spotting the villages for small armies of any kind, and then five miles back to the motorcycles—out again on the bikes at night, this time in their Wehrmacht uniforms. By checking the route in the daytime, they not only knew how far away they were from villages, but they could drive most of the time with their headlights out and be reasonably confident of where they were going. They had some fuel left over from Borsfa Durd's next to last raid at Vitanje, but there's no doubt it would have been safer to abandon the motorcycles; they'd have run little risk, dressed as peasants and traveling on foot. This alternative, however, was never mentioned; it must be understood that the scout-outfit leader of Motorcycle Unit Balkan 4 had deserted the war in order to devote his time to motorcycles, not to escape anything in particular —especially on foot.

In fact, Gottlob Wut was such a bad walker that they couldn't for long keep up their routine of five miles out and back in one day. Wut developed shin splints, or water on the spine, or an ailment stemming from early childhood—when he had somehow cheated on his learning-to-walk responsibilities, and depended, even at that time, on wheels. Actually, he confessed to Vratno, it was just one wheel at first. Wut had been the unicycle champion of Neckarsulm Technical High School for three straight years. As far as Gottlob knew, he still held the school record for the unicycle: three hours and thirty-one minutes of steady wheeling and balancing with no rest and without touching the ground with heel or toe. This performance was recorded on Parents' Night too, on the speaker's platform—when hundreds of weary elders drooped and shifted on hard benches, praying for three hours and thirty-one minutes that Wut would fall and break his boring neck.

But Gottlob Wut simply needed a wheel or two under his spine, in order to stay even moderately upright for any length of time.

They were a long time in the mountains, with only one incident. They were in the habit of fishing for food, or raiding, at night, the villages they'd spotted in the daytime. But on the third of September, 1944, they'd been two days with nothing but berries and water when they fell in with an odd crew. Croats, they were—a ragged peasant army—on their long way to join Mihailovich and his diehard Chetniks. Gottlob and my father, fortunately in Borsfa Durd's old clothes, were ambushed by them in a valley below Sv. Areh. The ambush was all shouts, a stick or two, and a very old gun fired in the air. The Croats were, among other things, lost, and they offered Vratno and Gottlob safe passage for good directions out of where they were. It was a very odd crew—Croats wanting to join up with Serbs! They had apparently all been unwillingly involved in a recent partisan-Ustashi massacre of Serbs, and had seen for themselves how the Serbs were abused. Of course, their position was hopeless; there couldn't have been any organized Chetniks of any account in Slovenia. But my father and Gottlob spent a day and an evening with them, eating off a captured cow and drinking a wine so new it was pulpy. Vratno told the Croats how Gottlob hadn't been able to talk since he was shot in the brain. Which excused old Wut from the Serbo-Croat.

The Croats said the Germans were losing the war.

The Croats also had a radio, which was how Vratno and Gottlob discovered the date as September 3—and were able to confirm their guess that the year was '44. And that evening they heard a Communist communiqué on Radio Free Yugoslavia, concerning a partisan victory over the Germans at Lazarevats. The Croats wildly protested, saying they'd had it from Serb sources that the Chetniks were surrounding Lazarevats and therefore must have been responsible for the victory and the capture of some two hundred Germans. The Croats insisted there were no partisans within miles of Lazarevats; then one of them asked where Lazarevats was, and the poor, befuddled Croats bemoaned again how lost they were.

That same evening, Vratno excused Gottlob and himself. And plodded back to the motorcycles. He explained to the Croats how Gottlob's muteness caused him pain, and they had to find a doctor. The poor Croats were so hopeless; not one of them even had the sense to notice that my father and Gottlob went off in the opposite direction from how they'd been headed at the ambush.

Vratno gave Wut a translation of the radio broadcast.

"Mihailovich is a goner," Wut said. "The trouble with the Chetniks and all those fool Serbs is that they've got no idea of propaganda. They don't even have a party line—not so much as a slogan! There's nothing to grab on to. Now these partisans," said Wut, "they've got the radio controls, and a simple, unswerving line: defend Russia; communism is anti-Nazi; and the Chetniks really side with the Germans. Does it matter if it's true?" Wut asked. "It's repeated and repeated, and it's very simply principled. The very essence," said Wut, "of effective propaganda."

"I didn't know you had any ideas," my father said.

"It's all in *Mein Kampf*," said Wut, "and you certainly have to agree. Adolf Hitler is the greatest propaganda artist of all time."

"But Germany's losing the war," my father said.

"Win or lose," said Gottlob Wut, "look at how much that little fart got going. Look at how far the fart has gone!"

The Fifteenth Zoo Watch:
Tuesday, June 6, 1967, @ 5:15 a.m.

O. Schrutt has gone too far!

Oh, my part was easy. When that sulking baboon came out on the prowl again, I tore around the Monkey Complex and broke cover—for a moment —going full-tilt for the children's drinking fountain. I didn't even have to cause a stir; the old gelada saw me coming before I got behind the fountain. He brayed, he barked, he crowed; in a frenzy, he chomped the chain of his trapeze. And, of course, the zoo joined in again.

And, of course, O. Schrutt left some small mammals in the midst of their various agonies and stormed out the door.

He went off the deep end this time; this time, he went inside the Monkey Complex. I waited only a second, horrified at the din O. Schrutt and the monkeys made; it all squeezed out a small, open skylight in the Monkey Complex, like one tremendous lungful blown in a flute and squeezed out through only one shrill finger hole. And before O. Schrutt came outside again, I dashed up the stairs and into the Small Mammal House.

I didn't stop to look in the cages. I pelted down the nearest aisle, took a left and then a narrower right—considered entering a chute, but thought against it—and finally stopped where I felt it quite safe; I was within listening distance of the main door, and I was around several corners from whatever way O. Schrutt might come; there were corners and turnoffs enough between us, so that I could hear him coming and have time to plot my next, avoiding move.

I saw briefly that I'd stopped alongside the aardvark's glasshouse. But it wasn't until I'd made an effort to control my panting that I realized the aardvark wasn't alone.

There was a stand-off! In one corner of his home, the aardvark backed himself up on the root of his tail—balancing, and holding his foreclaws out like boxing gloves; in the opposite, diagonal corner, facing the aardvark, was the small but vicious Indo-Chinese fishing cat—a nasty little item, hackles up and back arched high. They hardly moved. It didn't appear that either one would attack, but each time the aardvark would slightly lose and then catch his balance on the root of his tail, the fishing cat would snarl and hiss and lower its chin to the sawdust floor. And the aardvark—old sluggish earth pig—would snort a low sort of snort. I was trying to weigh all the odds in my mind when I heard O. Schrutt.

He sounded like he was just outside the Monkey Complex, but his bullying voice was coming my way. "There's nothing here, you fake of a baboon! You try me once more, and I'll have you go a round with my little jaguarundi! I'll give you something to scream about, I will!"

While beside me the fishing cat yowled, faked a spring; and the aardvark grunted, stiffened up on his hind legs and the thick root of his tail. They stood off each other—my God, for how long?

O. Schrutt! He makes his own theater! He creates a late show all for himself!

O. Schrutt came roaring into the Small Mammal House. I heard him taunt someone; and then I heard the combat boots walking round a corner closer to me, one aisle to my left and one up; I traced an aisle to my right, padding coolly barefoot on the cement. I waited for O. Schrutt's next move.

Only twice did I actually see O. Schrutt in the maze.

Once, when I was crouched flush to a cage wall, but below a cage window —out of the infrared reflected through the glass, I think, and a whole aisle-length away—I saw old O. approach one of his productions. He slid back the glass to the cage! That's the glass that slides, the whole damn window face slides back. O. Schrutt's got a little key that lets him unlock the sliding glass—it makes sense; if someone heavy died, or someone vicious was sick and wouldn't come out, you wouldn't want to fool around with that little back door off the chute—but O. Schrutt opens the glass to urge his gladiators on! If he thinks a stand-off is much too calm, he slips his cattle prod inside and touches off one of his contestants. And, of course, they can't see him, standing in the void—inserting his electric arm; it comes groping at them out of the dark, and jolts them neatly, once or twice.

I saw him conduct the vocal levels up, then slide the glass back—cutting off the complaints. Then he watched, with interest, the Tasmanian devil skittering side to side and yelling as if it were running over hot coals—kept at bay by the surly ratel. O. Schrutt watched quite calmly, I thought—his raving mind at ease, or drugged.

And once more I saw O. Schrutt. This time, I was perfectly safe in observing him. He'd gone in one of the chutes, so I just watched a whole glassy row of animals, looking for which cage would suddenly exhibit old O. at the back door—from where, I knew, he had the animals' perspective, and couldn't see a thing beyond the front glass.

I watched him break up a stand-off that looked like it had been running over-long. Two tired giant anteaters looked as if they had taken all they could stand from a wildly pacing, panting jaguarundi—long, low, lean, little tropical cat. O. Schrutt is sly! He doesn't want any blood. O. Schrutt's overseers would be suspicious of mangled small mammals. O. Schrutt is a careful director; he keeps the matches at an exhausting standstill; he's there with his cattle prod to break up anything that gets out of hand.

I saw enough, I'll tell you. O. Schrutt operates on all scales.

The slow loris exchanges terrified glances with a lemur. The Malayan tree shrew is aghast at the startled leaps of the kangaroo rat. I was so ashamed to see: even the dying bandicoot is forced to endure the antics of the flying phalanger. And the expectant mother ocelot lies haggard in her cage corner, listening to the grunts and scuffles in the chute behind her back door.

O. Schrutt knows no bounds.

I waited until he was off in one end of the maze, and then I fled his house of organized horror.

I lay back in my hedgerow, thinking: Whatever gave him the idea? Where did O. Schrutt first develop his perverse habit of playing small mammals off against each other?

It's getting lighter all around me now, and I'm still without an overall scheme. But I can tell you, I have plans for old O. Schrutt.

(CONTINUING:)

THE HIGHLY SELECTIVE AUTOBIOGRAPHY OF
SIEGFRIED JAVOTNIK: PRE-HISTORY II

On the fourteenth of October, 1944, the Red Army entered Belgrade, with ex-quisling Marko Mesich leading the Yugoslav contingent. Well, times change; it was a hard war to go through if you stayed on the same side you began with.

On the twenty-fourth of October, 1944, a Russian partisan group were surprised to find Chetniks engaging a force of twenty thousand Germans at Chachak. While the Russians and Chetniks were making a pincer attack on the Germans, a Russian officer observed that the partisans were attacking the Chetniks from behind. After the battle, the Chetniks turned over forty-five hundred German prisoners to the Russians; the following day, the Russians and partisans disarmed the Chetniks and arrested them. Chetnik Captain Rakovich escaped, and the partisans made a most sincere hunt for him throughout the Chachak area.

My father and Gottlob Wut were still in the Slovenian mountains, west of Maribor, when the hunt for Chetnik Captain Rakovich began.

There was no hunting at all in the Slovenian mountains. The Germans were on the defensive now, and the Ustashi were biding their time, middle-of-the-road. The Red Army wasn't as far west as Slovenia, and the partisan forces weren't at their strongest; the Ustashi weren't really fighting *for* the Germans any more—not wanting to turn the partisans against them—but it wasn't quite safe enough for the Ustashi to fight *against* the Germans either. At least not in Slovenia.

And Gottlob Wut was getting depressed. His legs and back and general walking apparatus were pitifully shot, and there were very few roads in the mountains where Gottlob could wheel his motorcycle peacefully and freely. And by November the mountains were very cold; the motorcycles needed a lighter oil.

It was some time in mid-November that the staff radio in the 600 sidecar model began to burble; up to that time, Vratno and Gottlob had figured the radio was dead, or that any mobilized German effort was out of broadcasting range. Gottlob eavesdropped over his radio; for two days the burble grew louder, but it was all some sort of number code. On the third day, however, Gottlob Wut recognized a voice from Motorcycle Unit Balkan 4.

"That's Wallner!" Gottlob said. "That hot-rodding punk, he's got my old job!" And before my father could knock him away from the radio, poor Wut flipped on the transmit switch and shouted, "Piglet! Incompetent piglet!" Then Vratno tackled him off the seat, scrambled back to the radio and flipped off the transmit switch, leaving the dial at listen-in. Where they heard a motorcycle idling, almost stalling.

Then Wallner's voice whispered or gasped, "Wut! Herr Commander Wut?" While Wut tore the grass on the ground. "Commander Wut?" the voice said again.

There was only the rough idle coming over the radio when Gottlob said, "Listen to that engine! It's so far out of tune, it would burn up if you ever had to push it."

But the transmit switch was left off; Wallner was given no opportunity to confirm what he thought he heard. Radio Wallner said, "Bronsky, are you switched on? Come in, come in." And there was nothing, so Wallner said, "Gortz, listen in! Listen in, Metz! It's the commander, didn't you hear him?" And then he shouted, "Vatch, are you there, Vatch?" Then the motorcycle stalled and Wallner grunted some untender oath. Vratno and Gottlob could hear him jumping on the kick starter.

"He's got the choke full on," said Wut. "Listen to him draw the air."

And they heard the kick starter ratcheting up and down; far away from catching, his engine sucked.

"Listen in, you bastards!" Radio Wallner screamed. "You're supposed to be switched on!" And he labored on the kick starter, panting into the radio. "You pricks!" he screamed. "I heard old Wut!"

"*Old* Wut!" said Wut, but my father held him back from the transmit switch.

"Old Wut is around!" Wallner screamed to the radio.

"Where are you, Wut?"

"Up your ass," said Gottlob, still tearing grass.

"*Wut!*" Wallner screamed.

And another radio voice said, "Who?"

"Wut!" said Wallner.

"Wut? Where?" the other voice said.

"That's Gortz," Wut told my father.

"Bronsky?" said Wallner.

"No, Gortz," Gortz said. "What's this Wut shit?"

"I heard Wut," said Wallner.

A third radio voice said, "Hello?"

"That's Metz," said Wut.

"Bronsky?" Wallner asked.

"No, Metz," Metz said. "What's up?"

"Wut's around," said Wallner.

"I didn't hear him," Gortz said.

"You weren't switched on!" Wallner screamed. "I heard Wut!"

"What'd he say?" asked Metz.

"Oh, I don't know," Wallner said. " 'Piglet,' I think. *Ja,* 'piglet'!"

"I've heard him use the word," said Metz.

"*Ja,* two years ago," said Gortz. "I didn't hear anything."

"You prick, you weren't switched on!" Wallner shouted.

"Hello," said a fourth.

"Bronsky," Wut said to my father.

"Vatch?" said Wallner.

"Bronsky," Bronsky said.

"Wallner heard Wut," said Metz.

"Wallner *thinks* he did," Gortz said.

"I heard him, very loud!" said Wallner.

"Wut?" Bronsky said. "Wut, around here?"

"Around *where,* I'd like to know," my father said to Gottlob.

"It was crystal clear," said Wallner.

"Hello," Vatch said, the last to switch on.

"Vatch?" said Wallner.

"Yes," said Vatch. "What's up?"

"Its very complicated," Gortz said.

"Pricks!" said Wallner. "I really heard him!"

"Heard who?" Vatch asked.

"Hitler," said Gortz.

"Churchill," said Metz.

"Wut!" Wallner screamed. "You're out there, Wut, you piglet yourself! Speak up, Wut!" But Gottlob sat grinning on the grass. He listened to the ragged motorcycles and the mad Wallner, his cronies dropping off the radio, one by one.

Then a voice Wut didn't know came from some further distance—carrying static with it: more numbers. And Wallner answered, "I heard my old commander. Wut, the deserter—he's out here." And the numbers answered him back. "No, really! Wut is out here," said Wallner. And a staticful voice from a further distance said, "Use your numbers, Commander Wallner." And Wallner babbled numbers.

"*Commander* Wallner," Gottlob scoffed. He and Vratno listened longer, until there was no more transmitting; the radio crackled and hummed.

"Where do you think they are?" said Vratno.

"Where are we?" Wut asked. Together, they went over the maps. They were maybe five miles above the Drava River and the Maribor road.

"A movement?" said Wut. "They're pulling out of Slovenjgradec, maybe? Going east to fight the Russians? North to join the Austrians?"

"A movement, anyway," Vratno said. "On the Maribor road."

And that night they listened at the radio again. There were more numbers, staticful and distant. It was after midnight when they heard Wallner again.

"Wut?" the radio whispered. "Can you hear me, Wut?"

And Gortz must have been at his radio, because he said, "Come on, Wallner, take it easy. Get some sleep, man."

"Get off your radio," Wallner snapped. "Maybe he only talks to me."

"*That* I believe," said Gortz.

"Get off!" Wallner said, and said again, "Wut?" in a whisper. "Come in, come in. Damn you, Wut, come in." And was drowned out by numbers.

Then the unrecognizable authoritative voice came back: "Commander Wallner, go to sleep. I must ask you, when you use the radio, to use your numbers, please." Wallner spewed numbers and got no reply.

Vratno whispered to the giggling Gottlob Wut, "When he's alone, now, that's when. When you're sure he's got the radio to himself, give it to him then." And Wut, still leaving the dial at listen-in, flipped on the transmit switch.

Later, Wallner whispered numbers. There was no reply. "Balkan Four," whispered Wallner then. "Balkan Four." And got no reply. Then he said, a little louder, "You old prick, Wut. Wut, come in." Gottlob waited for someone else to come in. There was no reply, and Wallner said, "Wut. You traitor, Wut. Gutless prick, Wut."

Then Gottlob said softly, "Goodnight, *Commander* Wallner." And flipped the transmit switch off, still keeping the dial at listen-in.

"Wut!" Wallner hissed. "*Wooooooooot!*" he screamed. and there was more static—and brushing, thumping sounds. Wallner must have had the radio off the motorcycle mounts and in a tent somewhere; they heard the tent flap, they heard radio parts crackle. Wallner must have lugged the radio out of his tent like a football hugged to his chest, because his shouts seemed farther away now, as if his mouth weren't near the speaker hole: "He's around, listen in! You pricks, switch on and hear him!"

And Gortz whispered loudly, "Wallner! For God's sakes, man."

And the unknown authoritative voice said, "Commander Wallner, that's quite enough. Use your numbers or lose your radio, Commander." And almost rhythmically, Wallner came on with his numbers; musically, he crooned his numbers into the night.

Vratno and Gottlob sat and dozed; they woke and hugged each other—laughing down their two-year beards—and dozed again, keeping the radio at listen-in. Once they heard Wallner murmur, asleep or still feebly trying, "Goodnight, Commander Wut, you prick." But Gottlob just grinned in silence.

Before first light, Wut and Vratno packed the bikes and moved four miles north, above Limbus. Then they camouflaged their gear and bikes, and carried the unmounted radio, walked a quarter of a mile, north along a ridge line—caught the sun coming over the right of the church spire at Limbus, and camped themselves less than a mile from, and in full view of, the Maribor road.

They were there the next day and night without a bite to eat or a glimpse of a motorcycle scout. At night they tuned in on Wallner, but heard only numbers—none of them in Wallner's voice. It was the next morning that they heard louder numbers, coming from Gortz, and once, shortly before noon, Gortz said, "It's too bad about Wallner." Bronsky answered that poor Wallner had always been too highly strung.

Then the overhearing, unknown voice said, "Commander Gortz, you'll use your numbers, please." And Gortz said he would.

It was that afternoon when Gottlob spotted sloppy Heine Gortz on one of the '38 600 models, without sidecar. Bronsky followed him, with soft tires that Wut could see all the way from the ridge.

And that night a large force moved through Limbus, observing blackout conditions. With the tail end of the movement barely out of town, my father made a raid on a Limbus dairy and came back with milk and cheese.

They stayed two more days above Limbus before spotting a second, following, German movement—this one, with unidentified motorcycle scouts. Not Balkan 4, anyway; they were some outfit down from Austria, maybe. They scouted for a ragged force, a straggling crew—no panzers, just some trucks and jeeps. And they were preceded by no number series. Some of the soldiers marched with their helmets off; many sprouted most un-German beards. It was a likely bet, and my father and Gottlob Wut took the odds. They joined the movement on the Maribor side of Limbus, meeting them on the road and saying they'd had motor trouble which dropped them out of Balkan 4. They were fed—the bikes had an oil change—and they wheeled into Maribor, not knowing whether they were on a retreat or headed for a front.

It didn't really matter. When the barracks' assignments were given out, Gottlob said that he and his man were hooking up again with their old outfit.

For a fee, they stashed their motorcycles in an outdoor prostitute's booth in what was called the Old City; then they rolled and robbed a German officer in an uptown district—cleverly done, disguised in Borsfa Durd's well-worn clothes; next they found a *saunabad* which uncurled their beards and made them glossy. Uniformed now, they turned out on the town—two soldiers out for a night of fun.

But oh, dear. In all of Maribor, you'd have thought Gottlob Wut would have found a night spot that wasn't the topmost choice for the other remnants of Balkan 4.

Perhaps Wut thought his two-year beard made him unrecognizable. Whatever, he was jaunty among the soldiers in the Sv. Benedikt Cellar. There was a *Turkish* belly dancer with the suspiciously Yugoslav name of Jarenina; her dancing belly was Caesareaned. The beer was thin. Surprising was this: there were no Ustashi troops in Wehrmacht uniforms to be seen. But there was a blown-up photo above the bar, riddled with darts—Ustashi in Wehrmacht uniform, marching with *partisans!* somewhere in Croatia.

My father was careful to be accurate with his umlaut sounds; he felt their beards brought them under suspicion.

It was very late when Vratno followed Wut's wincing walk to the unheated men's room. The urinal steamed; the tiles were cracked around the terrible hole for the standup crapper. A man weaved on his heels, pants down to his ankles, and leaned back over the crapper's chasm—clutching to the handrail that kept him from falling in. Four men steamed over the urinal; another two came in with Gottlob and my father.

Heads bowed over the trough, breath held against the rising steam and stench, eight men fumbled and peed. One dropped a cigarette down the sluiceway.

Then the man spanning the crapper gave a cry, and must have tried to tug himself upright with a wrench on the handrail.

"Wut!" the man screamed, and Gottlob, turning fast and peeing down my father's leg, saw sloppy Heine Gortz rip the handrail from the rotting, tiled stall's wall and pitch backward, pants snug at his ankles, fanny-first down into the crapper's chasm. "Oh dear God!" moaned Heine Gortz, and feet-up, his pocket change falling down on him, he cried again, "Wut! For God's sakes, Bronsky, it's Wut! Wake up, Metz! You're peeing next to old Wut!"

And before my father could stop his own peeing, Bronsky and Metz had spun poor Gottlob around and bent him backward over the urinal. Heine Gortz clawed himself up out of the hole. My father fumbled himself back in his pants, but sloppy Heine Gortz said, *"You!* Who are you with Wut?" But Gottlob didn't even look at Vratno; they didn't appear to recognize each other.

My father said—enunciating every German syllable, perfectly—"I just met the man. We had beards in common, you see. Just a mutual admiration."

And Bronsky or Metz said, "Old Wut! Would you just look at him!"

"Filthy traitor," said Heine Gortz. And one of them brought a knee up under him—buckled him—and someone tugged him along by his beard.

They moved him into the stand-up crapper stall. Then they upended him, and sent him head-first down into the breathless bog. Balkan 4 worked as a team. New-leader Heine Gortz, beshitted from his spine to the backs of knees, with his pants still down at his ankles, had Wut by one leg and stuffed poor Gottlob down the crapper's chasm.

While my father fastened his fly, exchanged shrugs of shoulder and tilts of head with the perplexed others still standing at the steaming urinal.

"Wut?" said one. "Who's this Wut?"

"We just had beards in common," Vratno said. "Just a mutual admiration, was all," he emphasized, although my poor father could scarcely talk —he was struck so dumb by the terrible teamwork of Balkan 4—and it seemed to him that he had to shout to get his words out in front of his rising stomach.

When my father quietly left the Sv. Benedikt Cellar's men's room, only the soles of Wut's shoes were showing above the awful hole; like poor Borsfa Durd, Gottlob Wut was buried coffinless; like Borsfa Durd, Gottlob Wut could finally be recognized by no more than the soles of his shoes.

The Sixteenth Zoo Watch:
Tuesday, June 6, 1967, @ 5:30 a.m.

I recommend that we do it just as I've done up to now. We get behind this hedgerow late one afternoon; we just sit tight through the first-shift night-watchman's watch. When O. Schrutt takes over, we'll let him go through a round or two. We'll have to be on our guard for the gelada baboon too, although that could be made to work out in our favor.

I can't decide whether we should drive O. Schrutt babbling mad, subtly; or simply feed him to the Famous Asiatic Black Bear—at the first possible opportunity.

Handling O. Schrutt in the latter fashion could present some problems. The Asiatic Black Bear might also get the keyring, and there'd be no taking it away from him, I assure you. Also, O. Schrutt might just have time enough to pull his gun and get a shot off. Whether he'd save himself or not, there'd surely be a policeman in Hietzing with an ear open for trouble in the zoo.

But even if we used the gelada baboon to drive O. Schrutt over the edge, there's no telling what form his final madness would take. He might run amuck in the zoo.

So this is a problem. I believe we'll have to nab O. Schrutt very neatly, in the Small Mammal House. Disarm him, tie and gag him—lead the frotter along a chute and tumble him into a glasshouse for safekeeping.

We'll toss him in with the giant anteaters! They should keep him still.

With what O. Schrutt knows about matchmaking, he should know exactly how quiet and inoffensive he has to be to keep the giant anteaters at ease with him. But then, it would be unfair of us not to share O. Schrutt a little. I'm sure the Indo-Chinese fishing cat would love to babysit with O. Schrutt awhile. I'm sure the ratel and the jaguarundi would love to have O. Schrutt visit their homes, all trussed up like a goose for the roasting pan—cooing dovelike through his gag, his face in the sawdust, saying, "Nice, nice ratel —*ooooh!* Aren't you a nice little ratel, though? And you don't have any hard feelings, do you, ratel?"

Better yet, we could blindfold him and let him guess which animal he's been thrown in with—which snuffling, deep-breathing animal is laying a cold, movable nose against old O.'s ear.

Tit for tat, O. Schrutt.

(CONTINUING:)
THE HIGHLY SELECTIVE AUTOBIOGRAPHY OF
SIEGFRIED JAVOTNIK: PRE-HISTORY II

My father laid low in Maribor. He paid a rather high rent for the prostitute's outdoor booth in the Old City, but thereby garaged the motorcycles safely out of sight. Not that he trusted the prostitute, a witchy thing who wouldn't tell him her name; in fact, one night when Vratno came back to the booth to sleep with the bikes, he found an old Serb siphoning gas out of the sidecar model 600. The Serb wouldn't give himself a name, either, but my father talked to him in Serbo-Croat and the old Serb gave way to senile utterances —choosing a theme of general disillusionment: first, with traitorous King Peter, who, after all, Mihailovich had rescued and sent to London. Did my father know the song the Serbs sang? No, since it had to do with politics; the old Serb sang it for him:

> *Kralju Pero, ti se naše zlato*
> *Churchill-u si na čuvanje dato . . .*

> King Peter, you are our gold,
> We sent you to Churchill to keep you for us . . .

But then, the old Serb ranted, the chicken-hearted King had been bullied by the British into *what was best for Yugoslav unity.* King Peter announced on September 12, 1944, that support of Marshal Tito's People's Army was the best chance for Yugoslavia. The King denounced Mihailovich and Chetniks—called all those "Traitors to the Fatherland" who wouldn't join the partisan army. Did the King know, the old Serb asked, that only six days before his betrayal of his people, Chetniks had risked their lives in the night to honor the King's birthday—bonfires on every mountaintop and singing aflaunt their love for the King, under blackout conditions too?

Did my father even know that? And Vratno confessed he'd been tied up for a time in the mountains himself—but not in Serbian mountains.

Well, then, did my father know what the Serbs sang now?

> *Nećemo Tita Bandita—*
> *Hoćemo Kralja, i ako ne valja!*

> We don't want Tito the Bandit—
> We want the King, though he is no good!

So you shouldn't want him, then, my father told the Serb. But the old man changed in Vratno's face:

> *Bolje grob nego rob!*
> Better a grave than a slave!

"No," my father said. "Anything's better than a *grob.*" Undoubtedly thinking: Especially as fresh a grave as the one that received Gottlob Wut.

But Vratno didn't kill the old Serb for siphoning. He made a deal. The sidecar model 600, with twenty-three leftover grenades, for some of the Serb's underground handiwork—a transit permit, with name and photograph, that would enable my father to cross the Austrian border on the racer. Because he was going to Berlin to kill Hitler, he said.

"Why don't you kill Tito?" the Serb asked. "You wouldn't have to drive so far."

But they made the deal. A certain Siegfried Schmidt was issued German-command special-messenger transit papers by the very undermanned but efficient Serb underground of Maribor. And one cold but bright morning in mid-December of '44, Siegfried Schmidt—formerly, Vratno Javotnik—crossed into Austria and over the Mur River on a 1939 Grand Prix racer, stripped of its warlike fanfare (for special-messenger service), and fled north toward the city of Graz on what is now called Route 67.

And I choose to believe that it was the same cold but bright morning of December '44 when Chetnik Captain Rakovich was finally caught by the partisans and dragged back to Chachak—where his body was rearranged and displayed in the market plaza.

But concerning what happened to my father after the cold, bright morning of his entry into Austria, I can only guess. After all, Siegfried Schmidt was not protected for long by his Wehrmacht uniform, his Grand Prix racer, and his special papers—which were special only as long as the Germans held Austria.

One morning my father fled north to Graz, but he was never clear about how long he stayed in Graz—or when it was, exactly, that he drove north-northeast to Vienna. He wouldn't have stayed long in Graz, for sure, because Yugoslav partisans were crossing the Austrian border quite soon after him, without the need of special papers. And Vienna couldn't have been too safe for Siegfried Schmidt, motorcycle messenger, either; on April 13, 1945—just four months after my father left Maribor—the Soviets captured Vienna with the aid of Austrian resistance fighters. The Soviets were supposed to be liberating the city, but for a liberating army they did a surprising amount of raping and such. The Soviets obviously had difficulty considering Austria as a real victim of Germany; they'd seen so many Austrian soldiers fighting with the Germans on the Russian front.

But whatever the conditions, on the thirteenth of April, 1945, Siegfried Schmidt must have gone underground.

And on the thirtieth of April, French troops crossed into Austria over the Vorarlberg; the following day, the Americans entered from Germany; and when the British came into the country a week or so later, from Italy, they were surprised to find Yugoslav partisans running amuck in the Carinthian and Styrian provinces.

Austria was overrun—and Vienna stayed indoors; learned it wasn't wise to welcome the liberators with open arms.

And there's very little that's clear in my father's account of this. Abandoned apartment houses were the best places—though popular, too often crowded, and not wanting the company of some fool who wouldn't leave his incriminating motorcycle behind. Vratno would remember: quarter-faces slanting through letter slots—"No room for soldiers, you hide somewheres else."

Food would get you temporary entry, but food could get you killed too.

Vratno would remember warm-weather months indoors; recalled a week spent in trying to trap a Russian and get his uniform—for in Wehrmacht cloth, my father's language abilities wouldn't be convincing enough.

Foremost, he would remember this one summer night. A sector near the Inner City, floodlights caught his flight at every roaring alley end—the Grand Prix racer bolting zigzag and hard-to-hit. He remembered what must have been the Belvedere Gardens—soldiers in the trees with flashlights, and Vratno running the racer almost flush to the high concrete wall, where he must have made a poor target but tore his elbow and knee against the jagged bomb tears in the concrete. He recalled a fountain that wasn't turned on; that would have to be the Schwarzenberg Platz. And remembered being forced to double back when he ran into a daze of floodlights and Russian voices.

Vratno would always remember: Gottlob Wut behind him, whispering into the indigo-blue ear hole—and weaving to Wut's flawless directions, my father jumped curbs and traveled down sidewalks, close to the building walls and dodging the occasional door that jutted out; skidding lightless down darker and darker streets, waiting for the wall or door he wouldn't see coming to smack him head-on.

Vratno always remembered a great lobby door, one side twisted off its hinges—the inner lobby where he skidded to, dark as a cave and marble-cool. He recalled daring his headlight once, and seeing the spiraling staircase going up at least four landings—to what he hoped were abandoned apartments. He remembered, forever: lifting his front wheel to the first step, revving, and jouncing madly up the wide but shallow marble stairs to the first landing, where he popped the clutch of the fierce Grand Prix and battered into the first apartment. And opened his eyes then, killed the engine—waited for the shot. Then he set the lock bolts back in place and closed the sprung door of the apartment.

Remembered then are floodlights coming down the street and into the lobby. Voices in Russian were saying, "There's no bike been ditched in here."

At dawn, cigarettes all over the floor, and what might have been good china was smashed; a rank, bleached corner of the kitchen where other hideaways, from this or an earlier occupation, decided to make their toilet. Cupboards empty, of course. Beds with knifed mattresses—occasionally peed-in beds. And only one of many stuffed animals still had its eyes unplucked—on the window sill of what must have been a young girl's room.

Vratno remembered: how odd it was, in a city apartment, to see an occasional chicken feather lacing the floor. But above all, he would cling to this—for days, the one bright spot on the whole dark street: a brass ball that caught the sun for a while each day; the ball was held in a cupid's hands; the cupid had half of its head bombed off, but still perched angelic above what used to be the Bulgarian embassy—in fact, the only embassy building on the Schwindgasse.

The Seventeenth Zoo Watch:
Tuesday, June 6, 1967, @ 5:45 a.m.

You know, Graff, once before there was a zoo bust in Vienna. Its failure is little-known history now. And the details are not the clearest.

No one seems to know just what went on in the zoo during the late years of the war. There was a time, though—let's say, early '45, when the Russians had captured the city, but before the other powers had agreed on the terms of occupation—when there wasn't anything to feed the people. There's no telling what the animals did for food. There are some accounts of what the people did for food, though—since there wasn't the manpower, or the concern, to keep the zoo well guarded.

But four men, say, even if they were unarmed—and almost everyone who moved about was armed then too—could do a pretty slick job of making off with a fair-sized antelope; even a camel, or a small giraffe.

And that happened. There were raids, although some city-guard outfit was supposedly protecting the zoo; they had the future in mind—a kind of emergency rationing.

For you, and you and you—you get the left hindquarters of this here kangaroo. And you get this rump steak of hippo; just remember, you got to boil it a good long while.

But regardless of the city-guard outfit, there were successful raids. One bold, hungry crew made off with a wild Tibetan yak. One man, all alone, stole a whole seal.

I suppose there were plans for a full-scale raid. I suppose it was only a matter of time, before some well-organized group of citizens or soldiers, from *any* army, would decide there was a profit to be made in large meat-locker operations in a starving city.

But nothing that well organized came off.

There was also in the city a would-be noble hero, who thought the animals had suffered enough; he foresaw a grand slaughter and figured a way to thwart the butchers. No one knows who he was; he's only known by his partial remains.

Because, of course, the animals ate him. He busted in one night and let loose every animal he could find. I think he is reputed to have opened just about all the cages before he was eaten. Naturally, the animals were hungry too. He should have thought of that.

And so his good intentions backfired. I don't know if any animals even got outside the main gate, or whether they were all attacked within the general confines. I suppose animals ate other animals too, before the mob got wind of what had happened and swooped into the chaos with old grenades and kitchen utensils.

The details are cloudy. With so many small mammals underfoot all over the city, who was going to keep accurate records on animals? But the confusion must have been really something, and I imagine the Russians got in on it sometime during the long night—thinking, perhaps, from all the fierce clamor, that they had a revolution on their hands, already.

I believe that neither tanks nor planes were used, but everything else must have been fair game.

I hope everyone who ate an animal choked on it. Or exploded when his bowels seized up.

After all, it wasn't the animals' war.

They should have been eating all the O. Schrutts.

(CONTINUING:)

THE HIGHLY SELECTIVE AUTOBIOGRAPHY OF

SIEGFRIED JAVOTNIK: PRE-HISTORY II

The Americans occupied the Salzburger province, which includes Kaprun —such a peaceful spot that it made the few Americans who came all the way into the village very friendly. In fact, about the only unpeaceful thing I was told of—and this, before the Americans came—was the setting afire of my grandfather's brother, the postmaster of Kaprun. In general, though, it was so relatively comfortable in Kaprun that I can't speak too well for the wisdom of my grandfather's taking his family and Ernst Watzek-Trummer back to Vienna. Or at least they should have waited to see how the four-way occupation of the city was going to work out.

But in the early summer of '45, my mother had an interest in returning to the *liberated* city. This was before the other Allies had arrived at a definitive agreement with the Soviets too. Even the reports of the Russian occupation should have been enough to dissuade them from going back so soon.

It had something to do with Hilke's idea about Zahn Glanz. Now that the war was over, she felt that Zahn would be sure to look her up. And my grandmother, of course, wanted to see how her little apartment and her abandoned china might have fared. And Grandfather, perhaps, was anxious to return some fourteen books—seven years and three months overdue—to the foreign-language reading room of the International Student House, where Grandfather had been the head librarian. I can't think of any reason Ernst Watzek-Trummer might have had for going back—other than his protective feelings toward the Marter family, and perhaps to take out more books from Grandfather's library. Watzek-Trummer, living seven years with my grandfather, had begun to value an education.

Whatever—or all things combined—it was very poor timing of them to leave Kaprun when they did, in the first week of July, '45.

Also, Grandfather's trip was made difficult by the deplorable state of Zahn Glanz's old taxi. The trip was made easier, however, by Grandfather's political record—vouchsafes, in letter and visa form, from resistance leaders who knew that the Nazi role of Grandfather's brother had been a disguise, and sympathized with the family for the postmaster's flaming death. Watzek-Trummer, too, had a record of some note—mostly, a clever bunch of train derailments and subtle arson jobs at the depot in Zell am See.

So in the early morning of July 9, 1945, Grandfather Marter and his crew made an inconceivable journey through rubble and occupying armies, and entered Vienna in the late evening—having had more trouble with the paper work of the Soviets than with anyone else's red tape.

That was the day the Allies resolved the sectioning of the city. The Americans and the British grabbed up the best residential areas, and the French wanted the shopping areas. The Russians were long-term realistic; they settled themselves in the worker-industrial areas, and crouched themselves around the Inner City—near all the embassies and government buildings. The Russians, for example—and much to Grandfather's uneasiness—occupied the fourth district, which included the Schwindgasse.

And sixteen out of twenty-one districts had Communist police chiefs. And in the Soviet-established Renner provisional government, the Minister of Interior, Franz Honner, had fought with the Yugoslav partisans. Renner himself, however, was a veteran Austrian socialist, and had his own premonitions about the suspiciously forward-looking occupation of the *liberating* Soviets.

So did my grandfather have his anxieties, as he drove down a Schwindgasse darker and more windowless than he'd ever seen.

Watzek-Trummer said, "It's a ghost-town street, like the cowboys are always finding."

Grandmother, in the backseat, hummed or moaned to herself.

When Grandfather drove over the sidewalk and into the lobby, some Russian soldiers in the former Bulgarian embassy put the floodlights on them from across the street. Papers were shown again, and Grandfather spoke a little dated Russian—relying on his experience from the foreign-language reading room to send the soldiers away. Then, before they unpacked the taxi, they went up to the first landing, found the keyhole rusted, and shoved against a previously weakened lock bolt—springing open the door.

"Oh, they've been peeing in here, the bastards," Watzek-Trummer said; in the dark he cracked his shin on a large, heavy metal thing a few feet inside the doorway. "Give a light," he said. "They've left a cannon here, or something."

Grandmother crunched on what must have been her china; she moaned a little. And Grandfather put the flashlight on a very battered and muddy motorcycle, sagged against an armchair because it had no kickstand to hold itself up.

No one spoke, no one moved, and from down the hall, out of my mother's room, they heard someone who'd held his breath too long finally let it go—exhale what might have been interpreted as a last despairing breath. Grandfather put his flashlight out, and Hilke said, "I'll get the soldiers, right?" But no one moved; my mother heard her old bed creak. "In my bed?" she said to Grandfather, and then broke his grip on her arm —bumped the chair and motorcycle, moving down the hall toward her room. "Zahn?" she said. "Oh, Zahn, Zahn!" And bolted in the dark for the open door of her room. Watzek-Trummer got the flashlight from Grandfather and caught Hilke before she reached the doorway. He snapped her back up the hallway, and peeking round the jamb, blinked the light into her room.

On the bed was a dark, long-bearded man—a white paste on his lips, like a man with a thirsty, cotton-filled mouth. He sat dead-center on the bed, held his motorcycle boots in his hands and stared at the light.

"Don't shoot!" he cried, in German—and then repeated himself, in Russian, in English and in some unrecognizable Slavic tongue. "Don't shoot! Don't shoot! Don't shoot!" He waved the motorcycle boots above his head, conducting his own voice more than he was threatening.

"You have papers?" said Grandfather, in German, and the man threw a billfold to him.

"They're not right!" the man cried, in Russian—trying to guess his captors behind the dazzling light.

"You're Siegfried Schmidt?" my grandfather said. "A special messenger."

"Up yours, messenger," said Watzek-Trummer. "You're too late."

"No, I'm Javotnik!" said the man on the bed, sticking with Russian—fearing they were only trying to trap him with their German.

"It says Siegfried Schmidt," my grandfather said.

"Fake!" said my father. "I'm Vratno, Vratno Schmidt," he mumbled. Then he said, "No, Javotnik."

"Siegfried Javotnik?" Watzek-Trummer asked. "Where'd you get your dirty Wehrmacht suit?"

And my father fell to ranting in Serbo-Croat; those in the doorway puzzled at him. My father chanted:

Bolje rob nego grob!

Better a slave than a grave!

"Yugoslav?" said Grandfather, but Vratno didn't hear him; he bundled on the knifed mattress, and Grandfather walked in the room and sat beside him on the bed. "Come on, now," Grandfather said. "Take it easy."

And then Watzek-Trummer asked, "Which army are you hiding from?"

"All of them," my father said, in German—then in English, then in Russian, then in Serbo-Croat. "All of them, all of them, all of them."

"War paranoid," announced Watzek-Trummer, who'd read and remembered a number of things from Grandfather's overdue books.

So they went back to the taxi for their food and clothes, and got water from the inner courtyard well pump behind the main lobby. Then they fed and washed my father and dressed him in one of Watzek-Trummer's nightshirts. Watzek-Trummer slept in the taxi, keeping a wary guard; Hilke and my grandmother slept in the master bedroom, and Grandfather watched over the war paranoid in Hilke's old bed. Until three or four A.M., July 10, 1945, when my mother came to relieve Grandfather at his watch.

Three or four A.M., it was—very scarce predawn light and a light rain, Watzek-Trummer remembered, sleeping in the taxi. Three or four A.M., and Hilke, covering my father's sleeping beard with her hand, notices his forehead is somewhat the age of what she imagines Zahn Glanz's forehead to be—noticed how his hands were young too. And Vratno, waking once and bolting upright in my mother's old, knifed bed, saw a slim, sad-mouthed girl—more the green stem than the flower—and said, "Dabrinka! I told that foolish Wut it would have to be you who wasn't blown up." In German, in English, in Russian, in Serbo-Croat.

Limiting herself to one language, Hilke said in German, "Oh, you're all right now. You're safe here, hush. You're back, you—whoever." And gently shoved my father back down on her bed on his back, and lay over him herself—it being a damp, chilly, light-rainy night for both their summer nightshirts.

Many languages were whispered; though the rain was light, it lasted long, and many drops fell. Tireless Ernst Watzek-Trummer, sleeping light as the rain, remembers the rustling on the old, knifed bed that sent me giddily on my long way into this scary world. In very scarce predawn light. With a light rain falling. At three or four A.M., July 10, 1945, when Ernst Watzek-Trummer was sleeping unusually light.

Old Watzek-Trummer, historian without equal, has kept track of the details.

The Eighteenth Zoo Watch: Tuesday, June 6, 1967, @ 6:00 a.m.

The rarely diseased binturong is coughing; the shambling bearcat of Borneo suffering from his peculiar, unnamable disorder.

And O. Schrutt is waiting to be relieved of his command. His own unmarketable narcotics have finally soothed him. It's peaceful in the Small Mammal House, the infrared is off, and a lazy, docile-appearing O. Schrutt is greeting the dawn with a cigarette—puffed like a luxury cigar. I see great smoke rings rise above the ponds for the Various Aquatic Birds.

And it's clear to me, with it growing so light out—so quickly too—that we'll have to do most of our work when it's still dark. We'll have to have O. Schrutt safely tucked away—have the keys in hand, and some prearranged order of releasing—before it's light outside.

And clearly the chief problem is this: though it's simple enough to unlock the cages, how do we get the animals out of the general zoo area? How do we get them out the gates? Put them at large in Hietzing, and hopefully guide them in the countryside direction?

This is crucial, Graff. It's why, among other things, the earlier zoo bust failed. What do you do with forty or so animals loose within the confines of the whole zoo? We can't lead them out the main gate, or into the Tiroler Garten, one at a time. That way, some cluck in Hietzing would be sure to spot one and give the alarm before we're finished up inside. They have to leave all at once.

Can we expect them to stand in line?

It seems we'll have to divide them in some orderly fashion. We'll have to save all the antagonists till last, and maybe we'll release the bigger ones through the back gateway and into the Tiroler Garten; they can sneak away through predawn Maxing Park.

I think I must admit it will be a case for Fate.

See us now: the elephants are playing water sports in the ponds for Various Aquatic Birds; countless Miscellaneous Range Animals are chomping the potted plants along the paths; all the wild monkeys are teasing the zebras, scattering after the back-and-forth clattering, bewildered giraffe; some of the small mammals could easily get lost.

If it's still around, surely the least auklet will get stepped on.

When they're all on the loose, how do you get their attention? How do you say, "All right, out the gate, and make it snappy"?

Some of them may not even leave.

It's one reason I've always doubted Noah's neat trick of pairing up the gangplank to the ark.

So I think this calls for faith. I think there's no point in discussing further the possibilities for chaos, because it's a matter of the mass frame of mind. We either convey the spirit to them or we don't.

And you can't draw the line anywhere, either. Not this time.

(CONTINUING:)
THE HIGHLY SELECTIVE AUTOBIOGRAPHY OF
SIEGFRIED JAVOTNIK: PRE-HISTORY II

On August 2, 1945, my mother had her suspicions confirmed by a Soviet Army doctor; she was married to Vratno Javotnik in St. Stephen's, in what was a small but noisy ceremony—throughout which my grandmother hummed or moaned, and Ernst Watzek-Trummer sneezed; Ernst had caught a cold, sleeping in a taxi.

And there were other noises—the dismantling work at one of the side altars, where a crew of U.S. Army engineers were sweatily removing an unexploded bomb which had been dropped through the mosaic roof of St.

Stephen's and was wedged between some organ pipes. For some months after the bombing, the organist had been too nervous to play either loudly or well.

As in any other wedding, after the oaths my mother shyly kissed my father's newly shaved face. Then they were clumsily followed up the aisle and out of the cathedral by several burly Americans bearing their bomb like a very heavy, just christened child.

The wedding party was held in the newly established American hamburger spa on the Graben. The young couple were most secretive. In fact, most of what I know of their relationship is a sparsely documented tale—relying on the interpretations, if not actual witness, of Ernst Watzek-Trummer, Ernst maintains that the most he ever heard the couple say in public was the discussion concerning Hilke's wish that Vratno shave for the wedding. Which was very shy talk, even for such a domestic matter.

Nevertheless, the record has it. August 2, 1945, Hilke Marter was given in marriage by her father, an ex-librarian with fourteen books overdue for seven years and three-plus months; Ernst Watzek-Trummer was best man for the groom.

Record also has it that August 2, 1945, was the last day of bickering at Potsdam, and the only day in which Truman and Churchill slumped a bit off their mark. The British and Americans had come prepared to Potsdam —this time aware of Russian means and motives of occupation, as observed in the Balkans and in Berlin. But Churchill and Truman had been thinking hard since July 17, and Potsdam's last day marked a slacking off. It was on the issue of *war booty*, and Russian claims in Eastern Austria—the Russians declaring that they had been most heavily damaged by the war and that Germany would have to make it good. Russian statistics are always staggering; they claimed 1,710 cities and 70,000 villages destroyed—a loss of 6,-000,000 buildings, making 25,000,000 homeless, not to mention the damage to 31,850 industries and enterprises. The losses to be made good by Germany were losses for which certain Austrian *war booty* could be seized. A language confusion was operative; the Russians spoke of Austria's liberation in the same breath as they spoke of Austria's co-responsibility with Germany for the war.

Later, Soviet representative of the Potsdam Economic Commission, Mr. I.M. Maisky, confessed that *war booty* meant any property that could be moved to the Soviet Union. But aside from letting this vague phrase slip by, Churchill and Truman were prepared for Stalin's aims, this time.

Vienna herself was not unprepared, either—by the time of the Potsdam conference. She'd simply been caught by surprise before then, but made some strongly independent gestures thereafter.

On September 11, 1945, the Allied Council had their first meeting in the Soviet-occupied Imperial Hotel on the Ringstrasse, under the chairmanship of Russia's Marshal Koniev.

And Vratno Javotnik was not unprepared, either—even for pending family life. My grandfather got him some legitimate refugee papers and a job as interpreter-aid to himself—Grandfather having landed fat work as a documentor for the supposedly kept-up-to-date minutes of the Allied Council meetings.

Just fourteen days after the first meeting, Vienna held its first free parliamentary elections since the Anschluss. And much against the grain of all previous Soviet efforts, the Communist party won less than 6 percent of the total vote—only four seats out of one twenty-five in the National Rat. The socialist and People's parties about split even.

What Vienna really wasn't prepared for was what bad losers the Soviets could be.

What Ernst Watzek-Trummer was totally unprepared for was the recorded assumption of the Hacking district police who had listed Watzek-Trummer as deceased, since March 12, 1938—the victim of a fire which consumed his henhouse. I doubt if Watzek-Trummer could seriously have been offended by the lack of faith shown in him by the Hacking district police. But whatever, Ernst refused to find a job, and at Grandfather's suggestion, made himself busy with apartment repairs and modifications on the Marters' Schwindgasse home.

In the daytime, then, Watzek-Trummer and the womenfolk had the Schwindgasse to themselves. When laundry ladies would chide him for his laziness, his puttering-about at home, Trummer would say, "I'm legally dead. What better excuse for not working is there?"

The first thing Watzek-Trummer did was to partition a section of the kitchen into his private bedroom. Next he took the fourteen overdue books underarm and went to find the foreign-language reading room of the International Student House, which was no longer operating—which had, in fact, been bombed and looted. So Watzek-Trummer tore all the library labels out of the books and took them home again—giving up the idea of trading them for fourteen he hadn't read. Grandfather did bring him new books, but books were very scarce, and the bulk of the literature in the Schwindgasse apartment was Grandfather's and Vratno's homework—the minutes of the Allied Council meetings, which Watzek-Trummer found evasive and dull.

But despite Watzek-Trummer's discontent with his reading material, he did a most charitable thing—as a wedding present for Hilke and my father. He scraped all the camouflage off the 1939 Grand Prix racer, and stripped it further—of all warlike insignia, traces of radio mounts and obvious machine-gun creases—and painted it glossy black; thereby he made it a private vehicle, not so easily subject to Russian confiscation as *war booty,* and gave my mother and Vratno a luxury. Although fuel was precious, and travel between the sectors of occupation was tedious—even for an interpreter-aid with a paper-work job on the Allied Council.

So Watzek-Trummer provided the shy newlyweds a means to get off by themselves, where they must have relaxed and talked more easily to each other than they ever did in the Schwindgasse apartment. Watzek-Trummer insists that they were always shy with each other, at least in public or on any occasion Trummer had to observe them. Their talking was done at night, with Ernst Watzek-Trummer sleeping characteristically light behind the light walls of his partitioned bedroom in the kitchen. Watzek-Trummer maintains that they never raised their voices—nor did he beat her, nor did she ever cry—and the rustling that Watzek-Trummer heard through and over his thin partition was always gentle.

Often, after midnight, Vratno would go into the kitchen and serve himself a sandwich and a glass of wine. Whereupon, Watzek-Trummer would pop out from behind his partition and say, "Blutwurst tonight, is it? What is there for cheese?" And together they'd hold a conspiracy of snacking, silently spreading bread, cautiously cutting sausage. When there was brandy they'd stay up later, and my father would speak of a highly fantastical motorcycle genius, with whom he once had beards in common. And much later, when there was both wine and brandy, Vratno would whisper to Ernst Watzek-Trummer. "Zahn Glanz," Vratno would say. "Does the name ring a bell for you? Who was Zahn Glanz?" And Watzek-Trummer would counter: "You knew a Wut, you said. What was it about this Wut you knew?" And together they'd politic into the night, often interpreting the Soviet-sponsored newspaper, the *Österreichische Zeitung* of November 28, 1945, for example, which told of Nazi bandits in Russian uniform bringing disgrace to the Soviets by a series of rural rapes and murders, not to mention a few isolated downtown incidents. Or the edition of January 12, 1946, which told of a certain Herr H. Schien of Mistelbach, Lower Austria, who was arrested by the Soviets after he'd spread false rumors about Russian soldiers plundering his home. Or, occasionally, they would discuss my father's and grandfather's homework, the minutes of the Allied Council meetings—one in particular, dealing with an incident on January 16, 1946, which occurred on the U.S. military "Mozart" Train that ran American troops between Salzburg and Vienna. A United States Army technical sergeant, Shirley B. Dixon, MP, turned away a Russian train-boarding party, including Soviet Captain Klementiev and Senior Lieutenant Salnikov. The Russians went for their guns, but Technical Sergeant Shirley B. Dixon, U.S.A., MP, quick-on-the-draw, shot both Russians—killing Captain Klementiev and wounding Senior Lieutenant Salnikov. In the Allied Council meeting, the Soviets claimed that their men had been victims of a language confusion, and Marshal Koniev demanded fast-gun Shirley B. Dixon's punishment. Dixon, however, was said, by a military court, to be doing his duty.

Watzek-Trummer, who'd indulged himself in a rash of American Western movies, claimed that the name Shirley B. Dixon rang a bell for him. Wasn't that the gunfighter-turned-deputy in the one about poisoning water holes in Wyoming? But my father thought that Shirley was usually a girl's name, which prompted Watzek-Trummer to remember the one about the great-breasted lady outlaw who straightened- or flattened-out in the end, by marrying an effeminate pacifist judge. So they concluded that Shirley B. Dixon, the fastest gun on the Mozart Train, was actually a Wac.

And Vratno would ask again, "Zahn Glanz? You must have known him."

But Watzek-Trummer would counter: "You never said what happened after you and Gottlob Wut got to Maribor. Did this Wut have a lady friend there? Why didn't he come with you?"

And Vratno: "Which one of you was this mythical eagle? Frau Drexa Neff, the laundress across the street—and she's Muttie Marter's friend, I've talked to her—why is she kept in the dark about it? She's always talking about this great bird, and all of you get funny faces. Who was the bird, Ernst? Was Zahn Glanz that eagle? Was he? And what happened to this Glanz?"

Then Watzek-Trummer, historian without equal, keeper of every detail—Watzek-Trummer would ramble on: "All right, all right, I'm with you, to a point. But after all those Slivnicas were blown up, minus one, and after the bit with the radio in the mountains—when Borsfa Durd was already dead and buried, in his way, I mean—and after you let Balkan Four go by and you'd marched to Maribor with that other outfit. When you were in Maribor, Vratno—is what I mean—what happened to this Gottlob Wut?"

On and on they went, a snacking merry-go-round, until my mother would rustle from the other room and my father would eat up, drink up, talk up and leave Ernst Watzek-Trummer to keep track of the rest of the night. Which he did, with increasing insomnia—perhaps owing to the growing discomfort of my mother's pregnancy, because she tossed about rather loudly from February into March. And Ernst gave up his partitioned bedroom; he sat by the kitchen window instead, poured my mother a glass of milk whenever she came sleeplessly waddling into the kitchen; otherwise, he watched the nightwatchmen on the Schwindgasse—the hourly floodlights from the former Bulgarian embassy, and the hourly check of the house doors along the street.

A Russian officer who carried a revolver walked flush against the buildings—a poor target for flower vases or boiling pasta pots; he tried each lobby lock. He was covered by a Russian infantryman, a machine gunner, who walked just off the curb in the street—himself a poor target for heaved windowboxes, because it would take considerable determination to launch anything very weighty that far into the street. The machine gunner watched windows; the officer first felt his hand around the jambs before stepping into doorways. The floodlights from the former embassy moved in front of them. There wasn't a curfew, exactly, but even a light left on after midnight was suspicious, and therefore Watzek-Trummer settled for a candle on the kitchen table and kept the windowshade drawn to an inch above the sill. So Watzek-Trummer had his window inch from watching Russian watchmen; Ernst insists he kept a kind of peace on the Schwindgasse by casting a hex, a pox, a jinx, a trance or even blessing over the machine gunner as he passed. Because the first thing Watzek-Trummer noticed about the machine gunner was that he was too nervous; he watched the windows behind himself more than he watched those coming into the moving floodlight ahead—and he clicked on and off the safety on his gun. So Ernst contends that his duty at the window inch was to keep the gunner calm; and be available for the morning exodus of the laundress Frau Drexa Neff, another nighttime window-watcher, who would bob up from her cellar cubby and holler across the street to Ernst, "How's her coffee look to you, Herr Trummer? Low enough, is it, so I should pick up hers with mine?" And Watzek-Trummer would usually say, "No, the coffee's fine, but we could use some fancy almonds, or the best French brandy the rations man has today." And feisty Drexa: "Ha! You need some sleep, Herr Trummer. Ha! That's what, all right."

So that was February and most of March, 1946, with Drexa—as March came on and on—asking Watzek-Trummer if Hilke had had me overnight, and with no other incidents except this: on Plösslgasse, two blocks south of Watzek-Trummer's window inch, a man was machine-gunned for peeing out a window into an alley (because, it turned out, his toilet was stopped up), after midnight. The noise of which had the Schwindgasse machine gunner wheeling himself around and around in the street, clicking his safety on and off—checking the night sky for hurtling windowboxes, kitchen utensils and wet, wadded socks. Which never came, or he'd have surely opened up.

And this incident too: the Soviets seized the entire Danube Shipping Company assets under the heading of *war booty*. Which was disputed in an Allied Council meeting or two.

But nothing else until I was spectacularly born.

Watzek-Trummer remembers a bit of light snow, recalls my mother waddling to the kitchen sometime past midnight and not being pacified by her usual glass of milk. He remembers Grandfather and Vratno getting dressed and calling out the lobby door to the Russian hangout at the former Bulgarian embassy. And three of them, then, in a Russian squad car, batting off to the Soviet-sector clinic.

That would have been early morning, one or two A.M. of March 25, 1946. It was three or four, Ernst remembers, when Grandfather phoned back to the apartment to tell Watzek-Trummer and my grandmother about me— a boy! Nine pounds, nine ounces, which was big, I might add, considering the diet of that occupied year. And my grandmother took up the candle and whirled across the kitchen to the windowshade drawn to one inch above the sill—and she flung up the shade, candle in her hand, and cried across the street to her friend the laundress, "Drexa! It's a boy! Nearly ten pounds too!"

Watzek-Trummer recalls: he was midway from the phone to Grandmother, off his feet, he believes—spread out in the air and reaching to put out the candle—when the floodlights came into the kitchen and Grandmother was propelled toward him and right past him. Their paths crossed; he recalls looking over his shoulder as she was flung by him—her very surprised face, not even bleeding yet. In fact, Watzek-Trummer doesn't remember *hearing* the machine-gunning until after he recrossed the kitchen to her and tried to sit her up.

It's Drexa Neff who has told Watzek-Trummer the details, really. How the gunner was a few feet past the window and looking over his shoulder, as he would do forever, when Grandmother Marter scared the wits out of him with her ghostly candle and her screaming in a language the Russian didn't understand. And after he shot her—Drexa is very clear about this —the whole street was floodlit, but you couldn't see the faces that were in every window, just inches above the sill. At least not until Watzek-Trummer started screaming, "They killed Frau Marter! She was just saying she was a grandmother now!" And how the street rained kitchenware and bits of pottery; how it was downstreet, only a few doors from where Frau Marter was shot, that the machine gunner caught in his neck the first piece of well-aimed crock or lead or silver; and down on one knee, weaving a downed boxer's weave, he opened up his machine gun again and took out a row of third-story windows from the Argentinier corner of the Schwindgasse halfway to Prinz-Eugen-Strasse. And would have gone the whole block length if the Russian officer hadn't got in the way—or had not been able to get out of the way; whatever, the gunner blew his officer down the sidewalk and stopped his sweep shot then. He covered his head with his arms and made a ball of himself in the street; everyone's kitchenware— some of which Drexa could identify, and even told Watzek-Trummer where it was bought and for how much—covered the Russian gunner, lying kitty-corner across from the former Bulgarian embassy, out of which no one ran to try and fetch him.

So I was born on March 25, 1946, and my birth was overshadowed not only by this aforementioned mistake. Because although I weighed nine pounds, nine ounces, and my mother had a short labor and smooth delivery, no one would ever remember. Although there was even a significant argument concerning my name—whether I be a *Zahn,* but my father asked, "Who was *Zahn?*" and got no answer, or whether I be a *Gottlob,* but my mother asked, "What was he to you?" and got no answer, so that Grandfather's suggestion was approved, because no questions and answers were necessary concerning a *Siegfried,* the name that carried Vratno to safety— even though there was this pertinent discussion, hardly anyone would associate me with the date of my birth. Because not only was my grandmother machine-gunned within moments of my delivery—which wouldn't be remembered by many, either—but because on the twenty-fifth of March, 1946, Tito's partisans finally hunted down and captured the Chetnik general Drazha Mihailovich, the last honest and stupid liberator or revolutionary left in the world.

The Nineteenth Zoo Watch:
Tuesday, June 6, 1967, @ 6:15 a.m.

Well, I know, Graff, I may seem to you to be turning my back on old principles. Well, there are some things, I see now, that you just can't split the hair over.

I mean, you always end up arbitrating in the end, don't you? What's the good of being so selective if you end up with more animals left in the zoo than animals that make it out? Now I'm certainly not advocating any slaughter, and I think we ought to save the bigger, rougher ones for last. But what kind of zoo bust would it be if you kept everything big or a little bit dangerous in its cage?

I tell you, I understand these animals—they know what the whole thing's for; or they *will* know, if you just point the way.

Now I don't mean to apply this to other things, but it's the liberators with unswerving principles who never get the revolution off the ground.

I'm sure. If you let these animals know you're for *all* of them, even the gelada baboon, even if we have to save him for near the end—I mean, *all* of them get let out of the cages—they'll be up at those gates, one hundred percent. Nobody trusts favoritism!

I really mean it; even the frotting gelada baboon. I'm not going to be the one to let a little personal experience run my mind amuck.

(CONTINUING:)
THE HIGHLY SELECTIVE AUTOBIOGRAPHY OF
SIEGFRIED JAVOTNIK: MY REAL HISTORY

Nothing was done about Grandmother Marter's death. The minutes of the Allied Council meetings are full of incidents much less understandably accidental than that one. The obviously premeditated ones, for example, were thought to be the work of hirelings for the Upravlenye Sovietskovo Imushchestva v Avstrii, or USIA—the Administration for Soviet Property in Austria. Which, under the label of *war booty,* made off with four hundred Austrian enterprises; foundries, spinning mills, factories for machinery, chemicals, electrical equipment, glass and steel, and a motion picture corporation. Hired killers made off with the Austrians who resisted the USIA.

The majority of these weren't killings of my grandmother's type. Wild shootings, rapes and bombings were more up the alley of the Russian soldier. It was the abductions that bothered the Allied Council, and these seemed to be carried out by the notorious Benno Blum Gang—a cigarette-smuggling ring, also black-marketing nylon stockings. For the privilege of operating in the Russian sector, the Benno Blum Gang deftly did away with people. Benno Blum's Boys would waylay people all over Vienna, and skulk back to the Russian sector when the heat was on—although the Soviets claimed to be hunting down Benno Blum too. In fact, about twice a month some Russian soldier would shoot someone and say that he'd thought it was Benno Blum. Although no one ever saw Benno Blum, to know what he looked like—or if he existed.

So there was a rather general illegality about the Soviet-sector operations in Vienna, which diverted any interest the Allied Council might have taken in my grandmother's commonplace machine-gunning.

But Watzek-Trummer helped my grandfather. He varied his nights between his kitchen partition and the master bedroom—going from time to time to sprawl beside Grandfather on the master bed; head-by-head, they indulged each other's anger—sometimes ranting so loudly that the floodlights from the former Bulgarian embassy would linger at the remembered kitchen window and blink, as if to say: Go to sleep in there, and stop your complaining. It was an accident. Don't plot against us.

But there were enough incidents that clearly weren't accidents to bring about the New Control Agreement on June 28, 1946, which eliminated Soviet veto power over the elected Parliament. This dissolved the Russian Booty Department, although Benno Blum, perhaps revenge-bent, appeared to be more active than ever, snitching a third of the anti-Soviets in Vienna —and causing Chancellor Figl to say, in a sad speech in Upper Austria, "We have had to write down against a very long list of names simply the word 'disappeared.' "

"Like Zahn Glanz, huh?" said Vratno. "Is that what happened?"

And irritable Watzek-Trummer said, "Ask your wife, or do you only talk bed talk in bed?"

Not that they had soured on each other, really. It was only that it had been hashed out so much before, they'd come round to this so many times.

But they did have it out once, all right—although I've no right to remember it as well as I do, since I wasn't quite four months old at the time. I guess Ernst Watzek-Trummer has remembered it for me, like most important things.

Anyway, one night in the summer, the seventeenth of July, 1946, my father came home in a drunken babble, having heard the news that Drazha Mihailovich had been executed by a partisan firing squad. And Watzek-

Trummer said, "What about this Mihailovich? What was he, really?" But Vratno cried, "He was abandoned!" And began to describe a ghastly vision for Watzek-Trummer, concerning a fantastical motorcycle mechanic who was gulped down a stand-up crapper in Maribor. Vratno talked not about Mihailovich but about Gottlob Wut, with whom my father once had beards in common. Vratno called to mind the sloppy Heine Gortz's question "Who are you with Wut?" And speculated how he might have kicked Heine Gortz down into the crapper, and then grabbed Bronsky, or Metz, or *both,* bending them back over the urinal while Gottlob freed himself and cracked their skulls with his concealed Amal racing carburetor.

And suddenly Watzek-Trummer said, "You mean you *didn't* do all that? You didn't even *try* to do any of that?"

"I said we just met," my father told him, "and Gottlob was a good enough sport to go along with it."

"Oh, he *was,* was he?" Watzek-Trummer roared.

"Well, I told you now, Trummer!" Vratno said. "Now you tell me, O.K.? Tit for tat, Trummer. Who was Zahn Glanz?"

But Watzek-Trummer stared at my father and said, "I don't consider the information equal."

My father screamed at him, "Zahn Glanz, damn you!" And the floodlights came on across the street, scanning windows near and far.

Then my mother was out of her room, with her nightgown open so wide that Ernst Watzek-Trummer looked away from her. She said, "What was that? Who's here?"

"Zahn Glanz!" Vratno shouted at her. "Zahn Glanz is here!" And with a flourishing gesture to her room, he said, "Zahn Glanz! What you call me in there sometimes—and they're usually the *best* times too!"

So Watzek-Trummer sent a blow across the kitchen table—with his former cleaver hand, his chicken-chopping hand—and belted my father up against the sink, where his elbow struck a faucet and started the water running.

Grandfather Marter came out of his master bedroom and whispered, "Oh, please, don't any of you get near the window. You know it's very dangerous this late at night." He looked at all of them, perplexed; they all sulked, eyes down. My grandfather added, "Better not run the water so hard. It's summer, you know, and there's probably not an awful lot of water."

Then Watzek-Trummer remembers that I started to cry, and my mother went back to her room to me. Funny, how wailing babies bring people to their senses. Even the floodlights went out with my crying. Babies cry; that's perfectly all right.

But that was when it all came out, one way or another. On the seventeenth of July, 1946, when Drazha Mihailovich was shot as a traitor. Which prompted the *New York Times* to suggest that the Russians build a statue of Mihailovich in Red Square, because Drazha Mihailovich was, among other things, the ironical Saviour of Moscow.

Watzek-Trummer, who still read everything he could get his hands on, tried to make peace in the kitchen by remarking, "Isn't it amazing? The Americans have so many good afterthoughts!"

Which was true enough, of course. Very like the Russians in this respect: they react best to statistics and have little interest in details.

For example, it happened—was even witnessed—that one twenty-nine-year-old Viennese social worker, name of Anna Hellein, was dragged off her train by a Soviet guard at the Steyregg Bridge checkpoint on the United States—Soviet demarcation line, where she was raped, murdered and left on the rails. She was decapitated by a train shortly thereafter. But this in no way produced action by the Allied Council so much as did Chancellor Figl's *list* of eleven recent murders by men in Soviet uniform. Now, you see, it was the *numbers* that impressed them. But Figl's request that the Austrian police be armed, and be permitted to defend themselves and other citizens from men in uniform—of *any* army—was postponed a bit because the Soviets produced a *list* of their own; from some anonymous source, the Soviets counted thirty-six hundred "known Nazis" within the police force. *Numbers* again, you see.

Actually, the problem with the police was *decommunizing* it, which went on slowly for about five years. Actually arming the police—or, that is, making the police worth having—was a somewhat slower process. As late as March 31, 1952, when I'd just had my sixth birthday, the Soviets prevented the police chief in their sector from sending any armed force to quell a horde of rioting Communists attacking the Greek embassy—protesting the recent execution of Beloyannis and three other Greek Communists. In fact, the rioters were brought to the scene in Soviet Army trucks.

Even later, when there was a riot due, the Soviets disarmed the police in their sector, taking away their rubber truncheons—which proved too effective in quelling riots, even though they were never quite what Chancellor Figl had in mind by "arming" his policemen.

But the Soviets were losing Vienna, and that made them unreasonable; in fact, there were setbacks all over.

In June of '48 the Yugoslav Communist party was expelled from the Cominform—Tito didn't need his crutches any more—and in November of '48, Soviet soldiers attempted to arrest someone on Sweden Bridge in downtown Vienna and were beaten back by angry crowds, rushing to the defense. Angry crowds were doing the Russians harm, even in their own sector.

And because of their tiff with Yugoslavia, the Soviets withdrew their support of Yugoslav claims in Austria's southland, Carinthia and Styria, and consequently, the Yugoslavs had to drop the whole idea of expanding into Austria.

This brought an odd number of Yugoslavs to Vienna, by the way; strange Yugoslavs—some Ustashi, I'm told, who were in the thick of plots and counterplots along the Austro-Yugoslav border when they were cut off. And the implication is that they found work with Benno Blum, who still had use for good abductors and roughies in general. Even though the records claim that Benno Blum was virtually washed up by March 10, 1950, when gangmember Max Blair was the subject of an Allied Council meeting, there's some evidence that a bit of Benno survived thereafter.

At least Ernst Watzek-Trummer claims so, and I take my history from him.

Ernst was there, anyway—March 5, 1953. When I was twenty days short of being seven, Joseph Stalin died. My grandfather and Watzek-Trummer had a celebration of their own, a little brandy round the kitchen table and spirits higher than their portions. But my parents were out, so I have to rely on Watzek-Trummer's account of their affairs. Not that I wasn't usually with my parents, only not for this celebration. And even I must admit— though Watzek-Trummer has certainly influenced me in this—that my parents had a relationship which struck me, at best, as being shy and unspoken. I was out with them from time to time—most memorably, sunny drives on the Grand Prix racer with my mother's arms around my father and myself, locking me against his stomach and pushing my knees tight against the gas tank I straddled. My father whispering Wutlike maxims of motorcycle-riding in my ear.

But on March 5, 1953, Joseph Stalin died, and Vratno and Hilke took a night out together, to celebrate, and they left me behind—to the old men's celebration at the kitchen table. I don't even remember my mother coming home, though it certainly must have been startling.

Because she came home alone, more puzzled than upset, and sat round the kitchen table with my grandfather and Watzek-Trummer (and maybe, with me too), wondering out loud whatever could have possessed Vratno.

Because, she said, they were comfortably wined and dined and sitting in a Serbian restaurant that Vratno frequently enjoyed, somewhere up by the Südbahnhof—still in the Russian sector—when all at once, in comes this man, dark-skinned, bearded, small but fierce-eyed. Though he was friendly, Mother insisted to Watzek-Trummer. This man sat down with them at their table.

"The killer is dead!" he said to them, in German, and they toasted one with him. Then the man pinched Vratno's arm and said something my mother said sounded like this:

Bolje grob nego rob!

Better a grave than a slave!

And Vratno looked startled, but not very—only a little; perhaps because he hadn't thought that he looked very much like a Yugoslav of any kind, sitting talking German, as he was, with a Viennese lady.

But the man went on: a little Serbo-Croat, and a little German now and then—he was being polite to Hilke. He also put his arm around my father and, my mother guessed, wanted him to come for a drink somewhere, alone. But Vratno said, in German, how he didn't really want to leave his wife, even for a short while, or for a drink or two—or even to meet some more homelanders. But the whole thing was very gay until the man said something my mother said sounded like this:

Todor.

Just that, once or twice—all by itself, or in sentences of Serbo-Croat. Vratno looked startled again—this time, even very startled. But the man kept smiling all the time.

It was then that Vratno very rudely tried to whisper to my mother without the other man hearing; it was something about how she should go to the ladies' room, find an open phone and call Watzek-Trummer just as quick as she could. But this man kept laughing and slapping Vratno's back, leaning over between my father's face and my mother's—so they couldn't really whisper with success.

It was then, my mother said, that the *other* man came in.

Hilke Marter-Javotnik has maintained that he was the biggest man she ever saw, and that when he came in, my father leaned across the table and kissed her hard on the mouth; got up, then, looked down at his feet, hesitated—but the first, smaller man said in German, "Your wife is very lovely, but she'll be safe—with me." And Vratno looked up at the huge man and walked past him, right out the door.

The big one, whom the little one called Todor, went right out after my father.

The worst thing about the big one, my mother said, was that his face was lopsided—sort of chewed or blown off—and flecked with bluish scars; some, jagged, stuck like gum on his face, and some were of sliver thinness, deep enough to tug and wrinkle the surrounding skin.

There wasn't anything wrong with the little one. He stayed and had a drink with her; then he went to bring back Vratno, he said, but never came back himself. And neither did my father.

My mother said that the Grand Prix racer was still parked in front of the Serbian restaurant, so Ernst Watzek-Trummer and Grandfather walked up to get it, chatting with Russian soldiers along the way.

"A big man," Grandfather said to the soldiers. "I think his name is Todor Slivnica. He's got bad scars, was grenaded in a car once. He's with my son-in-law, and maybe with another man too." But no one had seen a soul —except, earlier, my mother walking home with a Russian soldier, the most gentlemanly-looking one she ran across; she'd dared to ask that he walk her home. He was a young one; in the last block, he'd held her hand, but I guess that was all he wanted.

The soldiers along the way had seen no one else all evening.

And when Grandfather and Watzek-Trummer got to the Serbian restaurant, there was the racer outside, and inside there was a singer singing Serbo-Croat, and couples or dark groups of men clapping and singing along from their tables. Very gay.

But Watzek-Trummer thought the whole Serb joint was in league. He shouted, "Todor Slivnica!" And the singer stopped; she wrung her hands. No one accused Watzek-Trummer of being rude; the waiters just shook and shook their heads.

They were about to leave when Grandfather said, "Oh my God, Ernst." And pointed out an enormous man sitting alone at a table by the door; he was beginning to eat a custard out of a little glass dish. They'd walked right by him when they came in.

So they moved in on the man, whose face the candlelight made as multicolored and multi-shaped as a semi-crushed prism.

"Todor Slivnica?" Watzek-Trummer asked. The big man smiled and stood up—an awesome yard, it seemed, above Grandfather and Ernst. Todor tried to bow, as if he were little.

My grandfather, not knowing any Serbo-Croat, could only say, "Vratno Javotnik?"

And Todor let the blood flush his scars, made his whole face blink neonlike; taking up the little glass dish, he scooped the jiggling custard into his paw and spread his fingers out flat, with the custard quivering like a rare gift under Grandfather's nose, and then brought his other fist down on it —*fop!* and *squeech!*

Then Todor Slivnica sat down and smiled, a dollop of custard sliding into one of his deeper-grooved scars. And he gestured—to the custard on the walls, to the custard all over the table, all over Grandfather and Ernst, and even smoking on the pulled-low overhead lantern. Everywhere there was custard, Todor Slivnica pointed and smiled.

Where is Vratno Javotnik? Why, he's here, on your nose, and here, on the lantern overhead—and even here! In space.

So Watzek-Trummer has remembered that, has kept it all straight in his mind, to interpret—the riddle of where my father went is tied up in Todor Slivnica's symbolic gestures. Todor, among other things, was known for his sense of humor.

The Twentieth Zoo Watch:
Tuesday, June 6, 1967, @ 6:30 a.m.

An interesting thing. O. Schrutt has changed his clothes! Or not changed them, exactly, but he's disguised them. He's got a rain slicker on; it covers his nametag and epaulettes. And he has neatly, purposefully untucked his pants from his combat boots. It almost looks like he's wearing regular shoes —or, at least, just lifters.

O. Schrutt is getting ready for full daylight, and for the keepers who'll relieve him. O. Schrutt is not stupid; he takes good care of his indulgences. O. Schrutt will not likely be appearing as an addict in public. He's had his fix; he can outwardly endure a nonviolent day.

At the risk of sounding polemical, I'd like to say that there are two ways to live a long time in this world. One is to trade with violence strictly as a free agent, with no cause or love that overlaps what's expedient; and if you give no direct answers, you'll never be discovered as lying to protect yourself. But I don't exactly know what the other way to live a long time is, although I believe it involves incredible luck. There certainly is another way, though, because it's not *always* the O. Schrutts who live a long time. There are just a few survivors of a different nature around.

I think that patience has something to do with it too.

For example, I'll bet there are a few survivors among O. Schrutt's previous small-mammal charges. If they've been patient enough to *live,* they'll finally get to see the fellow they've been so patient for. They'll jar their trancelike faces over a newspaper, they'll twitch their old bashed hands in their exhausted laps—a spasm will fling them out of their TV-watching chairs: O. Schrutt is news again, they'll see—recognizing him through twinges in a scar that's been numb for twenty years or more. Their crippled feet will uncramp enough to stagger them to a phone; they'll lose their speech impediments, talking to the operator; they'll breathe twenty back years of patience into the mouthpiece.

That's right, dear Franz, it's him, I seen his picture, and for God's sakes, call Stein right away—to cheer him up, at last. O. Schrutt it was, I'm sure —kicking and screaming with a bunch of wild animals; their keeper, of course. And of course he had the night shift, and his uniform on too. Yes, the nametag still—right on the TV! I got to go tell Weschel, he's got no phone —and with his eyes, no paper or TV. But you call poor Stein, quick as you can. Oh, he'll be tickled to hear!

Because nobody stops looking for the disappeared. It's only the surely dead who flatly can't end up as you'd want or expect them to.

It's got to be my good faith, O. Schrutt; it's got me believing that some of your small-mammal charges will survive even you.

(CONTINUING:)
THE HIGHLY SELECTIVE AUTOBIOGRAPHY OF
SIEGFRIED JAVOTNIK: MY REAL HISTORY

March 25, 1953. For my seventh birthday, my mother took me on the train to Kaprun—just twenty days after the death of Stalin, and the custardlike disappearance of my father. Ernst Watzek-Trummer and Grandfather met us in Kaprun on the Grand Prix racer, which had slowly and inexpertly made a nervous trip from Vienna.

And so what was left of us settled in Kaprun, a village very small at the time; this was before the hydroelectric power dam in the mountains, and before the big ski lift brought less-hardy skiers to the town.

My grandfather became the postmaster of Kaprun; Watzek-Trummer became the town handyman, and he delivered the mail—in the winter, towing it in rough brown bags on a sled that was mine when there wasn't any mail. I would occasionally ride the mailbags on top of the sled and allow Ernst to skid me over the steep winter streets. My mother made red cord tassels to tie up the bags, and a red cord tassel with a ball of wool on the end was attached to my stocking hat.

In the summers, Ernst Watzek-Trummer delivered the mail in a high two-wheeler cart that was mounted to the rear fender of the Grand Prix racer. Which must have made Gottlob Wut roll over in his grave, if you could call it a grave.

We were quite happy in Kaprun; we were in the American sector now, of course, and within broadcasting range of Salzburg. In the evenings we listened to the American station that played all the Negro music—with rich-voiced women wailing, and yodeling trumpets and guitars: groin-blues. I remember that music without Watzek-Trummer's help, I really do. Because once at the Gasthof Enns, in the village, an American Negro, a soldier on leave, accompanied the radio with his harmonica, and sang, like a great iron bucket left out in the rain. It was winter; against the snow he was the blackest thing in Kaprun; people touched him to see if he felt like wood. He walked my mother home from the Gasthof Enns, and pulled me behind them on the mail sled. He sang a line or two, then he signaled to me and I honked his harmonica up from the sled—through the little Y-shaped village, quite late at night, I think. Grandfather could talk English with the soldier, and later the Negro sent Watzek-Trummer a book of photographs about civil rights in America.

Much else, I don't remember, and Watzek-Trummer's selective memory hasn't found anything important in these years—when I was eight, and then nine. There's just this: when the last Soviet soldier left Vienna on September 19, 1955, my grandfather suffered a small stroke—pitching backward into a stack of loose mail. People saw little squares of him falling through their side of the mailboxes in the post-office cage. But Grandfather recovered quickly. Only one thing: his eyebrows went from gray to white, overnight. And that's another one of those details which I may have remembered myself, or which Watzek-Trummer may have remembered for me—or, more likely, it was some combined, repetitive remembering from the two of us.

I remember the only important thing, though—all by myself, I'm sure.

Because Watzek-Trummer either finds this hard to remember himself, or at least hard to remember out loud to me.

I was ten and a half on the twenty-fifth of October, 1956—Flag Day, the first anniversary of the official end to the occupation. Grandfather and Ernst had been nine steady-drinking hours at the Gasthof Enns when they started going through old trunks in the post-office basement—our family storage center too. I don't know whatever could have possessed him, but my old grandfather found (or was looking for, all along) the eaglesuit—completely featherless, because the lard had long ago given out: a slightly greasy, gleaming suit of partially rusted pieplates; the head, and beak in particular, was solid rust. But my grandfather put the thing on, insisting to Watzek-Trummer that it was his turn to be the eagle, since both Ernst and Zahn Glanz once had a crack at it. And what better day for the Austrian eagle than Flag Day?

Except that this Flag Day was somewhat marred. At least for my mother. Only two days before, the streets of Budapest had been suddenly bled; fortunately, the Hungarians at least had a cleared route of escape, because Austrian officials, after the Russian withdrawal from Vienna, had removed the barbed wire and picked the minefields along the Austro-Hungarian border. A good thing. Because the Hungarian political police and the Soviet Army had driven more than 170,000 refugees across the border, where Vienna—sympathetic to occupied peoples—had taken them under her eagle's wing. And they were still coming across on Flag Day.

I can only guess that why this affected my mother so strongly was rooted back in March of '38, when Zahn Glanz either crossed the Hungarian border at Kittsee or he didn't cross at all. And if you choose to think of Zahn as crossing, then you might think of him as crossing back—with, perhaps, 170,000 other refugees from Hungary.

I only think this because such things must have been on Hilke's mind to make her react as she did, to Grandfather—striding, magnificent, into our Kaprun kitchen, and shrieking under his bald bird helmet. *"Cawk!"* he cried. "Austria is free!"

My mother moaned; she dug her fingers into me, where I was being made to model for a knitted sweater. Then she was up and charging the surprised, featherless eagle in the doorway, and caught him there, up against the jamb. She ground her knee between his legs, lifting the hem of his chainmail dress; she tugged and tugged to get his helmet off.

"Oh God, Zahn," she whimpered, so that Grandfather pulled roughly away from her and took the eagle head off himself. And couldn't look at her straight, but sort of turned his face away and mumbled. "Oh, I just found it in the P.O., Hilke. Oh, I'm so sorry, but my God, Hilke, it's been *eighteen years!*" But he still wouldn't meet her eyes.

She stayed sagged against the doorjamb; her face was ageless, even sexless —showed nothing at all. She said in a radio-announcing voice, "They keep coming in. More than one hundred seventy thousand now. All of Hungary is coming to Vienna. Don't you think we should go back now—in case he tries to look us up?"

"Oh, Hilke," Grandfather said. "No, oh no. There's nothing back in the city for us."

Still radio-announcing, she said, "Editor Lennhoff *did* successfully escape to Hungary. That's a fact."

Grandfather tried to stand still enough so his pieplates wouldn't rattle, but she heard his noise and looked up at him; her real voice and face came back.

My mother said, "You left him there once, you know. You made him stay behind for your bankbook, when he could have come with us."

"You watch it, girl," said Watzek-Trummer, and caught her hair in one hand. "You just get hold of yourself now, you hear?"

"You left Zahn in Vienna!" my mother screamed at the bird, who rattled under his pieplates and turned away from her altogether. Watzek-Trummer yanked my mother's hair.

"Stop it!" he hissed. "Damn you, Hilke, your Zahn Glanz didn't have to stay so long as he did. He didn't *have* to drive any editors to Hungary, did he? And what makes you so sure he *did,* anyway?"

But my mother tore her hair free of him and weaved back to me, where I balanced on the modeling chair, somewhat crucified in a thus far unseamed sweater, fastened on me with pins.

Watzek-Trummer took the huddled eagle back to the post-office basement, and that night my mother woke me very late—rubbed her cold, wet face across my own and tickled me down under the covers with a fur-collared coat she only wore for trips. And then she took one. Leaving behind no symbolic gestures to be interpreted—that we might guess, for example, how long she would be gone, or how and with whom she would end up.

Leaving us not so much, even, as custard on the walls, or soles of shoes to be recognized as final.

Although my grandfather didn't need any evidence to know she wouldn't be back. Less than two weeks later, in November '56, Kaprun and the surrounding Salzburger mountains had their first snowfall—a wet, heavy storm that turned to ice at night. So after supper, Grandfather took the mail sled and—although no one saw him—put on the eagle's pieplate armor; he hiked two miles and a half up the glacier field toward the summit of the Kitzsteinhorn. He had a flashlight with him, and when he'd been gone several hours, Watzek-Trummer got up from our kitchen table and looked out the window up the mountains. And saw a faint light, almost motionless, blinking midway up the glacier, under the black peak of the Kitzsteinhorn. Then the light came down—the sled must have been careening, because the light shot straight down, leapt, zigzagged, steered to a route more roundabout than it had climbed: a logger's swath cut across the lower mountain, below the glacier field. The old skiers called it the Catapult Trail. It bent very steeply through fourteen S-curves, three and one quarter miles down to the village.

Now, of course, there's an aerial tramcar that takes you up there, and the new skiers call the trail the Suicide Run.

But Grandfather took the mail sled down what was then called the Catapult, and Trummer and I followed the light of his descent from our kitchen window.

"That's your grandfather, boy," said Ernst. "Just look at him go."

We followed him through eight, then nine S-curves in the timber—he must have been sitting up and steering with his feet—and then his flashlight-headlight became so blurry it looked like a whole line of speeding traffic on the freeway. Though Watzek-Trummer claims he counted that Grandfather made one more S-curve before we lost sight of him altogether. That would have made ten out of fourteen, which isn't a bad percentage for a mail sled at night.

Ernst told me I wasn't to come and shut me up in our kitchen, from where I watched a tiny band of flashlights combing the mountain under the Kitzsteinhorn until dawn. When they found my grandfather, who'd been catapulted off the Catapult by striking a log the new snow had almost hidden. The mail sled, by some mystical steering I'll never understand, made it back to the village all by itself.

In fact, when they got Grandfather out of the forest, it was the mail sled Watzek-Trummer wanted found. And when they'd found it and brought it up to him, Watzek-Trummer laid my grandfather on it and eased him down the mountain and through the village to the Gasthof Enns. Where Ernst drank four brandy coffees and waited for the priest. Who was upset that Watzek-Trummer refused to remove the eaglesuit. Watzek-Trummer vowed that Grandfather would be buried just as was, in armor—featherless but masked. Ernst was given little debate. Grandfather had made his point clear some time ago, that the Catholics would never have their way with his body after what that traitorous Cardinal Innitzer did in '38. So to end all discussion, Watzek-Trummer said, "You remember Cardinal Innitzer, Father? He sold out Vienna to Hitler. He encouraged all his flock to endorse the Führer."

And the priest said, "But the Vatican never endorsed it."

"The Vatican," said Watzek-Trummer, "has a history of being fashionably late." Because old Ernst was still reading, all he could get.

Then I was sent for, and together, Ernst and I, we straightened poor grandfather's pieplates and packed snow around him—so he'd keep cool while the coffin was being made.

Watzek-Trummer said to me, "It was a stroke, of sorts; it was his heart, one way or another. But at least this is a better burial than some I've heard of."

After which, we went home, Ernst and I. I was a confident ten; if I felt at all abandoned by my family, I at least felt in good hands. You couldn't have much better than Ernst Watzek-Trummer. Keeper of the family album —egg man, postman, historian, survivor. Responsible, finally, for seeing that I would survive to understand my heritage.

The Twenty-first Zoo Watch:
Tuesday, June 6, 1967, @ 6:45 a.m.

The cage-cleaners were admitted a little after 6:30. O. Schrutt opened the main gate for them, and he left the gate open. He put a chain across the entrance, though; there's a sign hung on it, probably a NO ADMITTANCE sign—although it's hung in such a way that I can't read it.

The cage-cleaners are a sour, shaggy lot; they went in the House of Reptiles and came out with their paraphernalia, and then went en masse to the House of Pachyderms.

Then I thought that if O. Schrutt would only move away from the gate, I could leave straightaway. I wanted to be casually outside the zoo when O. Schrutt left. Perhaps I could see where he went!

Does O. Schrutt eat a *normal* breakfast?

But some sort of morning watchman met O. Schrutt at the gate. There were very few words between them. Perhaps the new watchman chided old O. about wearing the rain slicker in so much sun. But O. Schrutt simply vanished; he stepped over the chain across the gateway, and I didn't even see which way he turned.

I had to wait for the new watchman to slowly make a half-hearted round. When he finally went into the Small Mammal House, the cage-cleaners were still in the House of Pachyderms. But before I left my hedgerow and made it out the main gate, I saw the new watchman turn on the infrared! Funny, but I can't remember when O. Schrutt turned it off. This watch has worn me out, I guess.

And when I got outside the gate, I couldn't see a trace of O. Schrutt. I went across Maxing Strasse to the café. I sat at a sidewalk table and was told I'd have to wait till seven to be served.

My interesting Balkan waiter was setting ashtrays out on the tables. He must work mornings and afternoons—takes the night off, for cooking up sly reports to make the next day.

He eyed me with immeasurable slyness. He let me catch his eyes, and then showed me, with a side glance, that he noticed how my motorcycle was parked in exactly the same place it was yesterday afternoon. That was all; he just showed me he knew *that* much.

And suddenly I began to get a little nervous about coming back to

Waidhofen—about this frotting waiter recognizing me on the day of the bust. I should have a disguise! So I decided to cut all my hair off.

But when this waiter brought an ashtray to my table, and sort of dealt it across the tabletop like a playing card, I got a little bolder and asked him if he'd been around Hietzing when they had a zoo bust—twenty years or so ago.

He said he hadn't been around.

So I said, "You must have heard about it, though. They don't know who it was that had the idea. He was never identified."

"I understand," he said, "that whoever it was ended up like a lamb chop."

See? Sly frotter. He knew it all along.

So I asked him, "What sort of fellow would ever try such a thing?"

"A madman," he said. "A real psych case."

"You mean," I suggested, "someone with inherited flaws? Or someone who had a background heaped with insecurities and frustrations—a type from a broken home?"

"Why, sure," he said—still humoring me, the frotter. "That's what I meant, all right."

"A case of transference," I added.

"An error of judgment," he pronounced.

"A lack of logic," I said.

"A total *loss* of logic," said the waiter; he beamed at me. His armload of polished glass ashtrays threw little sharp triangles of sun up to his face.

But I have my own idea of who the mad zoo buster might have been. After all, it's perfectly fair to have your own theory on this matter; it's an open question. And I can think of the perfect man for the job; at least, from all I've heard about him, he would have been ripe for it—both for the divine idea and the flaw in his youthful foresight that caused him to be eaten. He was somehow related to me too; he was rumored to have driven a hunted newspaper editor to Hungary, and rumored not to have gotten back. But everyone knows that the editor was saved, and so it's possible to assume that the driver might have gone to Hungary *and* gotten back—at a time when those he most wanted to see were unavailable. Well, it's possible. This person *did* love animals. I happen to know he once expressed grave concern over a park squirrel who'd been tattooed—so deeply that its mind could only dance in circles.

It could have been him, as easily as it could have been another—say, some guilt-ridden relative of Hinley Gouch.

Then that sly Balkan waiter said, "Sir, are you all right?" Trying to make me think I wasn't, you see; suggesting that I'd been doing funny things with my hands or mouth, maybe.

You have to watch out for these Balkans. I once knew of one who failed to recognize his best friend over a urinal.

But I wasn't about to let a frotting Balkan trick me. I said, "Of course I'm all right. Are you?" Seeing, already, what would happen to his armload of ashtrays, one morning soon, when he'd raise his sly eyes and lose his smug composure—in the face of a charging Rare Spectacled Bear from across Maxing Strasse.

"I only thought, sir," the waiter said, "that maybe you wanted some water. You seemed to be dizzy, or at loose ends—as they say."

But I wasn't going to let him get the best of me. I said:

Bolje rob nego grob!

Better a slave than a grave!

Then I said, "Right? That's right, isn't it?"

Incredibly sly, like a stone, he said, "Would you like anything to eat?"

"Just coffee," I told him.

"Then you'll have to wait," he said, thinking he'd fix me good. "We don't serve till seven."

"Then tell me where's the nearest barbershop," I said.

"But it's almost seven now," he said.

"I want a barber," I told him, nastily.

"They won't cut your hair till seven, either," he said.

"How do you know I want my hair cut?" I asked him, and that shut him up. He pointed round the Platz off Maxing Strasse; I pretended I didn't see the barber's striped pole.

Then, just to confuse him, I sat at the table past seven o'clock—doodling in my notebook. I pretended I was sketching his portrait, keeping my eyes on him and making him nervous while he served a few other early people.

At seven o'clock they open the zoo. There's no one who goes that early, though. There's just a fat man with a gambler's green eyeshade, smug as a sultan in the ticket booth. Over the booth, from time to time, the giraffe's head looms.

THE HIGHLY SELECTIVE AUTOBIOGRAPHY OF SIEGFRIED JAVOTNIK: EPILOGUE

I grew up in Kaprun, a well-read child because Watzek-Trummer knew the value of books; a child with historical perspectives too, because Ernst filled me in as I went along—leaving gaps here and there, I assure you, until I was properly old enough to hear it all.

Before he sent me to the University of Vienna, Watzek-Trummer saw to it that I learned to drive the Grand Prix racer, 1939—suggesting to me that the bike was an almost genetical inheritance. So I was certainly deprived of nothing; I had my hot rod. First thing I did was to strip it of that degrading mail cart.

But after I'd done some thinking about Gottlob Wut, I began to consider the Grand Prix racer as something really too special for me to waste on my adolescence, and getting all the details from Ernst, I made my first trip out of Kaprun. That was in the summer of '64. I was eighteen.

I drove the Grand Prix racer to the NSU factory at Neckarsulm, where I tried to speak with one of the manager types concerning the prize-worthy motorcycle that had been my inheritance. I told a mechanic first, as that was the first type I met in the factory—how this had been the bike of Gottlob Wut, the masterful, mystical mechanic of the 1930 Italian Grand Prix. But the mechanic hadn't heard of Wut; neither had the young manager type I finally found.

"What you got there?" he said. "A tractor?"

"Wut," I told him. "Gottlob Wut. He was killed in the war."

"No kidding?" said the manager. "I heard that happened to a number of people."

"The Grand Prix of Italy, 1930," I said. "Wut was the key man."

But the young manager only remembered the drivers, Freddy Harrell and Klaus Worfer. He knew no Wut.

"Well, get to it," he said. "How much you want for that old thing?"

And when I mentioned that perhaps it was a museum piece—and did NSU have a place where they honored their old racers?—the manager laughed.

"You'd make a great salesman," he told me, only I didn't tell him that I'd planned to give it away—if they had a nice place for it.

The bike shop was full of awful, spiteful motorcycles that made spitting sounds when they were revved. So I started up my racer and—in my mind —loosened all their frotting aluminum parts.

I drove back to Kaprun and told Watzek-Trummer that we ought to keep the motorcycle in storage somewhere, and drive it only for emergencies. Of course, with *his* historical perspective, he agreed.

Then I went to Vienna and attempted to join in the university life. But I met no one very interesting; most of them hadn't even read as much as I had, and none of them knew as much as Ernst Watzek-Trummer. There was one student I remember fairly well, though—a Jewish kid who was a part-time spy for a secret Jewish organization that hunted down old Nazis. The kid had lost all eighty-nine members of his family—disappeared, he said—but when I questioned him as to how he knew, then, that he even belonged to this family, he confessed he had "adopted" them. Because as far as he really knew, he had no family. He remembered no one, except the RAF pilot who flew him out of the Belsen area after the camp was busted. But he "adopted" this eighty-nine-member family because on the records he's seen, that looked like the largest single family who had vanished without a leftover. It was for them, he said, that he made himself the ninetieth member of the family—the survivor, at least in name.

He was fairly interesting, with his part-time apprentice spying, but apparently he became very good at his job and was so boastful that his picture got in one of the Vienna papers, as being single-handedly responsible for the discovery and arrest of a certain Richter Mull, a Nazi war criminal. But that publicity made the kid nervous, and his secret Jewish organization disowned him. He used to sit around in the university *Kellers;* remembering what had happened to America's Wild Bill Hickok, he never sat back-to a window or a door. When I told Ernst Watzek-Trummer about him, Ernst said, "A war-paranoid type." It was something he'd read.

And then there was my good friend Dragutin Svet. I met him on a ski trip to Tauplitz my second year at the university. He was a Balkan studies fellow, a Serb by birth, and we did a lot of skiing together. He always wanted to meet Watzek-Trummer.

But we had a falling out. A silly thing. I went with him once to Switzerland, skiing again, and while we were there, we overheard a group of men speaking Serbo-Croat in our gasthaus lobby. It turned out there was a sort of convention of exiled Serbs, a mean-looking crew of old folk, for the most part, and a few young, idealistic-looking, soldierly chaps. Some of the old ones—so the word was—had fought side by side with the Chetnik general Drazha Mihailovich.

We got to go in their dining room, though our age and nervousness put us under suspicion. I was trying to remember some witty Serbo-Croat when this one old fellow said, in German—nastily leering at me the length of their table—"Where are you from, boy?" And I said, truthfully, "Maribor, by way of Slovenjgradec." And several men put down their cocktails and said severely, "Croat? Slovene?" Since I didn't want to embarrass my friend Dragutin Svet, the Serb by birth, I blurted the only Serbo-Croat I could remember:

Bolje rob nego grob!

Better a slave than a grave!

Which, as Watzek-Trummer later explained, was precisely the opposite of what I should have said; it was my own father's unheroic improvising that got me in trouble with the diehard Chetniks. Because there was a deeply insulted man at the head of the table who leaned over a long way toward me; he had only one hand and used it remarkably well, to toss a shot glass of Scotch in my face.

My friend Dragutin Svet refused to understand the accident, and he thought me in bad taste for making such word play with a slogan the Serbs take so seriously. And I didn't see much of Svet thereafter.

I got a job with a certain Herr Faber, to keep my hand in—and my eyes open for—motorcycles. Also, I needed to finance my education, which appeared to be taking longer than it should have. All because my thesis project was rejected by a certain Herr Doktor Ficht.

This thesis was to be my HIGHLY SELECTIVE AUTOBIOGRAPHY, as I thought it was well enough detailed, and even creative. But this Ficht was furious. He said it was a decidedly biased and incomplete picture of history, and flippant besides—and there were no footnotes. Well, in trying to calm him down, I discovered that Herr Doktor Ficht used to be Herr Doktor Fichtstein, Jew, who'd lived a wharf rat's life on the Dutch coast during the war—having been caught only once; escaping after they'd injected his gums with some tooth-mortifying chemical too new and experimental to be safe. The previous Fichtstein was enraged that I should be so pretentious as to dash through the war with so little mention of the Jews. I tried to explain that he should really look at my autobiography as what is loosely called fiction—a novel, say. Because it's not intended to be *real* history. And I added, besides, that I thought the Doktor was making a rather Russian-American value judgment by claiming that no picture of atrocity can be complete without the millions of Jews. Numbers again, you see. Ficht, or Fichtstein, seemed to miss my point altogether, but I confess, statistics have a way of getting the best of you. They can make almost anything, all by itself, seem not in the least atrocious.

But that run-in made my university career look a bit long-term. That is, I'd have to stay around until I mastered some academic subject or other—rather than show them what I already knew and have done with it.

Watzek-Trummer, of course, doesn't understand universities at all. He declares that they all must have read too much before they were interested in anything, which prevented them, later, from becoming interested in anything they read. He's rather perplexing on this issue. Self-educated men, you know, are unbudging.

Ernst still reads like a demon. I see him every Christmas, and I never come without a stock of books for him. Unlike most old people, though, his reading has become more selective; that is, he no longer reads everything he can get his hands on. In fact, he's often unimpressed with the books I bring him. He begins, he browses, he stops at page ten. "I know it already," he says, and lays it aside.

Actually, I go home for Christmas more to read the books Trummer has than to flatter myself into thinking I'm bringing him any favors.

Watzek-Trummer is a retired postman now, and very venerable in the town. He keeps three rooms in the Gasthof Enns; he's even something of a tourist attraction, when he permits it.

One of Trummer's rooms is all books; one room stores the Grand Prix racer, 1939; one room has a bed, and a kitchen table—even though Ernst eats all his meals in the *Gasthof* now. The kitchen table is for sitting at, leaning on and talking over—a habit he says he can't break, even though he's alone now.

Whenever I'm home, I sleep in the room with the 1939 Grand Prix racer. And I enjoy my Christmases very much.

Believe me, Ernst Watzek-Trummer can tell you a thing or two.

The Twenty-second and Very Last Zoo Watch: Tuesday, June 6, 1967, @ 7:30 a.m.

I've stopped for a coffee in Hütteldorf-Hacking, not more than a mile west of Hietzing. There's some countryside here, though it's mostly small vineyards; you've got to go a mile more if you want to see cows.

At the minimum, then, the oryx has a two-mile trip before his first lay.

Hütteldorf-Hacking is taken aback with me. I got a winner of a haircut back in Hietzing.

Following that sneaky waiter's directions, I went round the Platz off Maxing Strasse and was Hugel Furtwängler's first customer.

"Shave or haircut?" said little Hugel Furtwängler. You could tell he wanted to give me both, or at least the haircut—since shaves are cheaper.

"Just a shave," I said. "But a *total* shave."

And pretentiously nodding as if he understood me, he packed some hot towels around my cheeks. But I said, "Get the eyebrows too, won't you?" And that stopped him from looking so know-it-all.

"Eyebrows?" Hugel said. "You want your eyebrows shaved?"

"A *total* shave, please, Hugel," I said. "And no nonsense now."

"Oh well," he said. "I worked at the hospital once. We'd get them sometimes after fights, and you'd have to shave their eyebrows then."

"Everything," I said. "Just shave my whole head, please."

And that threw him off again, although he tried to pretend he wasn't baffled.

"You mean you want a haircut," he said.

"Just a whole shave," I insisted. "I don't want my hair *cut,* I want it shaved off altogether—smooth as the end of my nose." And he gawked at my nose as if it would help him to understand me.

"If I'm going to *shave* your head," he said, "I have to *cut* the hair first. I have to cut it down close *in order to* shave it."

But I wasn't going to have him talking to me as if I were a child, or a madman to be humored along. I said, "Hugel, you do whatever you think is necessary to get the job done. Only, no gashes in my head, please. I'm a bleeder, you know—there's been a touch of hemophilia in our family for years. So no cuts, please, or I'll be bled like a steer in your chair."

And Hugel Furtwängler gave a phony laugh—humoring me again, thinking he was in control.

"You're a real laugher, aren't you, Hugel?" I said. And he kept right on.

"Such a sense of humor you have," he said. "And so early in the morning!"

"Sometimes," I told him, "I laugh so loud that I bleed through my ears." But he still kept up his giggle, and I could see he was set in his ways of belittling me. So I changed the subject.

"Lived in the zoo long, Hugel?" I asked. And he harumphed over that.

"Did you ever see a zoo bust, Hugel?" I asked. And he snuck down behind my head in the mirror, pretending he was trimming the base of my neck.

"There *was* one, you know," I said.

"But they didn't get out," he said—knowing all along, the frotter.

"You were here, then?" I asked.

"Oh, such a long time ago," he said. "I don't remember where I was."

"Were you always a barber, Hugel?" I asked.

"It runs in the family," he said, "—like your bleeding!" And he thought himself so funny that he almost cut my ear off.

"Watch it," I said, going stiff in my chair. "You didn't break the skin, did you?" And that sobered him some; he worked with great care.

But when he'd given me no more than what looked like a normal haircut, he said, "It's not too late. I can stop here."

"*Shave* me," I said, staring stonefaced at the mirror. And he did.

He was starting up his giggles again, while I inspected my head front-and-back in the mirror, when his second customer came in.

"Ah, Herr Ruhr," said Hugel. "I'm ready for you right away."

"Morning, Hugel," said heavy Herr Ruhr.

But I leapt back from the mirror and stared at Herr Ruhr. He looked a little alarmed, and I said, "This barber's a laughing fool. I ask for a shave and look what he gives me."

Hugel gave a little pip of a cry, razor in his tiny hand—shaving cream on the backs of his knuckles.

"Watch out for him, Herr Ruhr," I said, running my hand over my gleaming head. "He's a dangerous man with that razor." And Herr Ruhr stared at the razor in little Hugel's hand.

"He's crazy!" cried Hugel Furtwängler. "He *wanted* me to do it!" But dancing with his razor, and his face so bright red, Hugel looked a little crazy himself. "And he's a bleeder too!" Hugel shouted.

"Hugel's got blood on his mind this morning," I said to Herr Ruhr. Then I paid Hugel for a shave.

"Shave *and* a haircut!" cried the flustered little Furtwängler.

But I turned to Herr Ruhr and said, "Would you call *this* a haircut?" And again I slicked my hand over my dome. "I only asked for a shave."

Herr Ruhr looked at his watch and said, "I don't know where the time's gone to this morning. I'll just have to skip it, this morning, Hugel."

But Hugel waved his razor and made an awkward attempt to block Herr Ruhr at the door. Herr Ruhr dodged quickly into the street, and I followed him out, leaving Hugel Furtwängler bespattered with shaving cream and waving his razor after us.

In somewhat the same condition, I thought, that poor Hugel will be in when he sees the stiff-bristled aardvark come lumbering across the Platz for a shampoo.

Then I snuck up on the motorcycle without that plotting Balkan waiter spying my new head, and quickly put my helmet on so that when he did notice me pumping the kick starter, he wouldn't realize I was much changed. But I only rode as far as Hütteldorf-Hacking with the helmet on, because it was very irritating—not fitting me any more, and bouncing all over my stinging head; Hugel had not rendered my dome absolutely cut-free.

I tied the helmet by its chin strap to the waist cord of my jacket, because I don't need a helmet any more. I have one of my very own.

Then I had a coffee, smelling the sun cooking the little grapes in the vineyards across the road, and trying to figure out exactly where it was from here that a certain fellow I know once had a henhouse; a laboratory, actually, wherein a much talked-about bird was invented. But I lost my bearings among so many buildings that look new, or at least rebuilt.

And it would be hard to spot the property I have in mind now, because the henhouse was burned down long ago.

It doesn't matter. There's an important issue at hand right now.

I'm on my way, Graff, and don't you worry. I'll be careful. I'll come into Waidhofen a sneaky new way; I'll leave the bike a bit out of town and walk in without my duckjacket, and without my old recognizable head. Thinking all the time, see.

And don't you worry either, Graff—about going to Italy. We'll go, all right. Maybe some of them will follow us!

We'll get to see your frotting beaches, Graff. We'll get to see the sea.

In fact, there's an interesting place I know of in Naples. They've a big aquarium where they keep all the wondrous fishes, in stale sea water under glass. I've seen pictures. The place is just off the harbor.

In fact, it would be an easy job. We wouldn't have to wriggle the fishes very far, or keep them out of water too long. Just across a street or two—and maybe there's a small park before the sea wall, if I remember rightly. And then we'd launch them free in the Bay of Naples.

In fact, Graff, it will be even easier than the Hietzinger Zoo.

Setting Them Free

P. S.

Of course, there's more to the notebook than that. And, of course, the zoo watches and the autobiography don't appear together in the original; it was my idea to interleaf them. Because, I felt, it was almost impossible to endure either the verbosity of Siggy's souped-up history or the fanaticism of his frotting zoo watches—if you were to read them whole. At least, it was for me; I found myself skipping back and forth, though part of that may have been due to my discomfort at being forced to read in Auntie Tratt's bathtub, where I spent a week, or almost that long, soaking my bee stings.

But I still feel the two journals demand separation, if only for literary reasons. And certainly Siggy made some obscure connections between his awesome history and his scheme for busting the zoo; though, for my own part, I can't speak too well for the logic in that.

Again, if only for literary reasons, I couldn't see the sense in reproducing the other memorabilia in the notebook. All those frotting poems and proverbs. All his exclamation points, addresses and phone numbers, reminders of due dates for library books; and what constitutes his ill-kept bibliography.

I'm afraid that Doktor Ficht was at least right in griping about poor

Siggy's failure to footnote. He obviously drew as heavily from Watzek-Trummer's library as he did from old eyewitness Ernst himself.

To mention a few of Siggy's jottings:

I'm quite pleased with Brook-Shepherd's *Anschluss*. B-S really knew what was the matter.

D. Martin goes to the heart of it in *Ally Betrayed!*

Poor L. Adamic is a hopeless propagandist in *My Native Land*.

All the info is in Stearman's *The Soviet Union and the Occupation of Austria*. But his footnotes are longer than the text.

There's a lot of emotional writing in Stoyan Pribichevich's *World Without End* and G.E.R. Gedye's *Fallen Bastions*.

And other entries, without his pronouncements:

Kurt von Schuschnigg's *Austrian Requiem,* and Sheridon's *Kurt von Schuschnigg*.

The Schmidt Trial Protocols, esp. the testimonies of Skubl, Miklas and Raab; and *The Nuremburg Testimonies,* esp. of Göring and Seyss-Inquart.

The official Minutes of the Meetings of the Allied Council and Executive Committee, 1945–55.

Plamenatz's *The Truth About Mihailovich.*

Vaso Trivanovich's *The Treason of Mihailovich.*

Colonel Zivan Knezevich's *Why The Allies Abandoned the Yugoslav Army of General Mihailovich.*

And countless references to:

What Ernst Watzek-Trummer said.

It was some days, however, before I could read any of this—confined to the bathtub as I was. Epsom salts, with the tub water changed hourly.

Of course, they brought me all of Siggy's honey-covered things. I was some time separating the pages of the notebook; I had to steam them open, over my bath water. And then I had to wait a few days before I could see clearly to read—until my bee swellings had come down enough to let me hold my eyes open. I ran a fever too, and vomited a bit—the poison in my system excessive as it was.

But if my bee dose was excessive, I wouldn't have wanted any part of the overdose that must have been poor Siggy's lot. And no one would tell me

if it had been his head I heard go THANG!—and put him out before the
bees filled him up—or if I'd only imagined his struggling under the flatbed,
after he'd toppled the hives. As the notebook says:

God knows. Or guesses.

But when I did get down to reading, I can assure you there were spots
that gave me twinges more considerable than my bee wounds. There was
this:

Today I met and bought a motorcycle with Hannes Graff.
He's a nice person. At loose ends, though.

And despite his countless recovering baths, I can tell you that Hannes
Graff was at loose ends still.

And there were more twinges from the notebook:

What Drazha Mihailovich said at his trial: "I wanted much . . . I started much
. . . but the gale of the world blew away me and my work."

Well, Siggy, I'm not so sure. I don't think it was the gale of the world
that got *you*. Like so many other unfitted parts of your history and your
scheme, I'm not convinced by any logic to your comparisons—only hinted,
or leapt to, and not clear.

It was no gale of the world that got you, Sig. You made your own breeze,
and it blew you away.

Loose Ends

The honeybee, polliniferous: Any of certain socially-minded, honey-pro-
ducing bees (genus *Apis* and allied genera), especially the species *Apis
mellifera,* native to Europe, raised for their honey and wax and pollinating
services in much of the world.

The honeybee has several parts.

Most of which, in varying mashed and torn conditions, I discovered—
as Siggy might have put it:

In my trouser cuffs
And socks.

> In my underwear
> And armpit hair.
> Little bee bits,
> Here and there.

A thorax part in the spiral binder of Siggy's notebook; a hairy pair of posterior legs on the bathroom floor—where, I guess, I was shucked out of my clothes and dunked for the first time in soothing salts; antennae, eyes and heads, nasty abdomens and lovely wings, in countless folds and pockets of Siggy's honey-ruined duckjacket.

I found whole bees too. One of which I slowly drowned in the bathtub, but I think it was already dead.

For a few days, Hannes Graff soaked all his loose ends, and was not allowed visitors. Frau Tratt tended to me.

Ironic, I thought, that she who'd taken such great offense to Siggy's startling nakedness should be at ease with mine. Insulting, I thought. But Auntie Tratt excused herself on account of her age.

"Someone's got to tend to you," she said. "Could you afford a doctor? There's already some debt outstanding to me, you know. And I could be your grandmother, you know. It's just another little bare bottom to me."

And I thought: There couldn't have been so very many little bare bottoms for you, at any time.

But she was daily there, with soups and sponges; my general puffiness going down under her eyes.

"They took a liking to your neck," she said—the cruel old bitch—and she evaded my questions about what they were doing with Siggy. If they were treating the body or anything.

Of course, I didn't need to be told he was dead. There was just this endless bringing back of his parts to me. His duckjacket, his pipes, his notebook.

Formally, Frau Tratt would inquire, "Where is he to be sent?"

This before I'd read enough of the notebook to have visions of his relatives.

Later, when I could read, I pictured a weary Watzek-Trummer, tired of burial responsibilities. In one way or another, on hand for two generations of deaths in a family—endings direct and absolute, and endings only implied.

Siggy certainly had to go to Kaprun, but I couldn't imagine him there —for a few days beflowered, resting in the room with the Grand Prix racer, 1939.

"Well, anyway, you're lucky," the old Tratt said. "This kind of thing can be expensive, but Keff's building the box for him."

"Keff?" I said. "Why Keff?"

"I am sure I don't know," said Frau Tratt. "It's just a box, though—real simple. You don't get much for nothing, you know."

Not from you, surely, I thought. But I said, "Where's Gallen?"

"What do you care where she is?" said Auntie Tratt.

But I wouldn't give her the satisfaction. I sat hunched over on my bed of towels, drying off from my last bath of that day and trying to prepare myself for the old Tratt's rough hands going over me—tingling me, in spite of myself, with that good, nut-scented witch hazel.

The Tratt said again, "What do you care where she is? Is Gallen a part of your plans now?"

But I told her, "I just wondered where Gallen was keeping herself. She hasn't once come to see me."

"Well," the good Frau said, "she won't be visiting until it's comfortable for you to wear some *clothes* again." And when she said *"clothes,"* she splashed that icy witch hazel on my back, and as I gasped half upright under her hand, she ground down her forearm on my neck and shoved my head down between my knees. She slopped some down my shoulders, and slicking her hands over me in her slaplike fashion, she got some witch hazel in one of my ears. Then her voice came at me, half underwater, prying, as if I were an eel to be coaxed out from under some rock—for the final stew. "But you don't have any plans for the moment, Herr Graff?" she snooped.

"No plans," I said quickly, and realized that this was the first hopeful thing to come into my head since the frotting bees. Remembering, of course, what Siggy had once said about plans. He had once had *the way not to spoil it. No planning, Graff. No mapping it out. No dates to get anywhere, no dates to get back.* And in a grating sort of way, I started laughing—really, it was so funny; that this should be his foremost, solemn ingredient for a good trip between us. How funny, really, his crazy and elaborate scheme for the zoo bust looked alongside that previous notion.

"Am I hurting you, Herr Graff?" said the Tratt, who must have felt my odd quivers even through her gross, insensitive calluses.

But I just laughed out loud at her. "No plans, Frau Tratt!" I said. "I don't have any. And I won't! No plans. Frot plans! Frot me!" I bellowed at her, "if I so much as start to make any plans."

"Well, goodness," the rare old Tratt said. "I only asked to make a little conversation."

"You lie," I told her, and she backed off—the sweet witch hazel drying on her hands so fast you could see it disappear, like the white under your thumbnail goes back to pink as soon as you unclench your fist.

Where Gallen Was

Eventually, by my bath- and bedside—after I'd healed sufficiently to wear at least a loincloth equivalent, and after I'd adequately insulted the Tratt, to make necessary someone else's waiting on me—Gallen cared for me, again.

I was permitted to show her my less-private bee welts, still a bit reddened, even after my tedious treatments. Because, I'm told, my poor antibodies had fled my bloodstream on the thirty-fifth or -sixth sting, leaving my general resistance rather low.

"How are you, Graff?" Gallen asked.

"My resistance is low," I told her, and we discreetly discussed my poor antibodies.

She said, "What are you going to do now?"

"I've not made any plans," I said quickly, and she hung by my bed, hands folding and unfolding, in a mock-casual stance. She was growing too tall and forcing too much shape in her little-girlish clothes. Puffed shoulders and frilled cuffs on this outfit—a high-buttoned and forbidding blouse. The old Tratt's choice, I could be sure. A further, plotting defense of hers against me. May she rot.

"Sit down, Gallen," I offered, and slid over for her.

"Your resistance is low," she reminded, saucily; as if she were so old and frotting worldly—a favorite guise of hers—under the clothes.

"What have you been doing?" I asked.

"Thinking," said Gallen, and pulled down her chin with her hand. As if she'd just started this minute, to convince me.

"What about?" I asked.

"About what you're going to do now," she said.

"No plans," I repeated. "But I've got to do something with Siggy."

"Keff built a nice box," said Gallen.

"How thoughtful," I said. "How does he seem to you?"

"Oh, Keff feels very bad," said Gallen.

"I meant, how's Siggy?" I said. "I couldn't care less about Keff."

"Keff's very sorry, really," she said. "He keeps asking about you."

"How's *Siggy*?" I asked. "How's he look?"

"Well, I haven't *seen* him," she said. But the way her shoulders shook when she said *"seen,"* I believe she'd taken a peek.

"All puffy?" I said, a bit nastily. "Like two of me?" And I pinched up a fair-sized welt on my bare witch-hazeled stomach.

"Keff wouldn't let anyone see him," said Gallen.

"Frotting Keff!" I said. "What's he taken an interest for? Does he enjoy it that much?"

"He's been very nice, Graff," she said.

"And seeing a bit of you too," I said. "No doubt."

So she told me about the aftermath. How the armored beekeeper had finally been the one to extricate poor Siggy from under the flatbed. They'd all taken him for the doctor to poke—and see if he'd deflate—and then the mayor had pronounced over the body. Afterwards Keff had asked for him, and said he'd build the box.

"Where's he going to be sent?" said Gallen. "Keff says to ask you that."

"To Kaprun," I said, "if Keff can tear himself away from the body."

"It wasn't Keff's fault, Graff," she said. And added how she thought that Siggy must have been crazy. So I told her about the mad notebook, and the ultimate, unreasonable scheme; and all the conclusions leapt to, concerning O. Schrutt and the Famous Asiatic Black Bear. I said I agreed with her, that poor Siggy had perhaps gone off his rail somewhere. Then I sat up in bed and pulled her down to sit beside me.

Since we were closer and I'd got her talking about it, I asked her what the doctor said he'd died of. "Cause of death," I said stiffly. "Precisely what?"

"A heart attack," said Gallen, "which could have been the shock."

"Or too many bees," I said, thinking that too much bee gunk went inside him and sent a sort of thrombus to clog his heart. Then I got dizzy, sitting upright; I began to itch all over.

"Witch hazel, Graff?" said Gallen.

But feeling the need for at least an immediate sort of plan I said—as quickly and officiously as possible, "Tell Keff there's to be no fanfare, and no flowers or anything. And the coffin should be sealed. Just the name, no engraving. And put him on the train to Kaprun—to a man named Ernst Watzek-Trummer. Who'll pay for it, I'm sure. Then you bring me a telegram form. I'll send off something to precede the body."

"Keff wonders if you want anything to read," said Gallen. As if I hadn't read enough.

She spread the witch-hazeled washcloth over my eyes, which made it easier for me to answer her back—not being able to see her bent over me. "Just some sex book or other," I said. "I'm sure Keff knows where to find that sort of thing, if he's not too busy—fiddling so much with Siggy and you."

When I took the washcloth off my face, and caught an unscented breath, Gallen had left me alone in the room. With my doubts of her. And with my horror thoughts of Keff's possible necrophilia.

What Keff Was Doing

Keff bought a book and sent it to me with Gallen, though it was an honorable, scholarly sort of sex book—the wholesome teamwork of a pair of Danes—called *The ABZ of Love*.

"It's got drawings in it," said Gallen, not looking at me. Probably afraid I'd turn into one of the sketches before her eyes.

"Read it cover to cover already, have you?" I asked.

"I have not," she said distinctly, and left me with Keff's odd gift.

Actually, it's a very sane, clean book, concerned with potting the old taboos, and encouraging us to have good, healthy fun. But I just randomly flipped it open, and was given a misleading picture of the book at first reading—because of this queer anecdote.

During the last century a lady woke up one night, feeling she was being pushed. Somebody went in and out and hands touched her every now and again. As she was not expecting anybody and had fallen asleep alone, she was so terrified she fainted. Much later she came to her senses and by the light of the dawning day saw that her butler (who, incidentally, was a genuine sleepwalker) had laid dinner for fourteen people on her bed. But of course this sort of thing is rather unusual, especially nowadays when so few people have servants.

Which totally puzzled me about Keff and his intentions.

But I read on and momentarily rid my mind of a certain planless dark. I put off further the empty telegram form for Ernst Watzek-Trummer. These startling lines were my distraction:

Letting off a thoroughly good sneeze is a natural, spontaneous, frank action of which some people really are a little afraid in the same way that they are afraid of being spontaneous and letting themselves go in their sex life.

It had been contended that there must be a direct connection between a person's ability to have a thoroughly good sneeze and the ability to have a satisfying orgasm.

Which was so fascinating to me that I made a point of not falling asleep until Gallen came back to see if I needed more witch hazel.

"Like your book?" she mumbled.

"It's lowered my resistance even more," I said, feeling nice and playful. And just waiting for her to come near me with that nut-scented washcloth. But she handed it to me to do for myself, and sat herself down on the edge of my bed, at the foot. She crossed her nice legs, kicking up—for just a second—her long apron-like skirt.

So I saw her burns—two perfect fist-sized burns on the insides of her legs between each ankle and calf, just where mine had been from the bike.

"How'd you get those?" I said, sitting up fierce and letting her know I frotting well knew what they *had* to come from.

"Keff fixed the motorcycle," Gallen said. "He's teaching me to drive." And when I stared at her, she said, "I can do it very well, except the starting. I don't have enough kick, Keff says." But I gaped at her, so she went on. "I just stalled it, Graff, and when I tried to start it again, I pulled it over on me. While I was kicking, you know."

"Gallen," I said. "Just what's going on, please?"

"Well, that's how I was burned," she said. "Really! When the pipes touched me, you see."

"What is rotting Keff teaching you to drive for?" I shouted.

"So somebody knows," said Gallen. "So one of us can, when you take me with you, when you go—if you want to, Graff."

And she didn't jump up and go this time, when I sat forward to touch her.

"Only if you *want* to take me with you, Graff," she said. But when I leaned so far forward that I could tuck her head down in the crook of my neck, Keff's sex book slipped off my lap to the floor. Where both of us stared at it and broke our kind of trance over each other.

When she was still looking down at *The ABZ,* I reared up in bed and gave out with a tremendous sneeze—harumphing so, it snapped her eyes back up to my face.

Well, she blushed so much I knew she'd read the book before giving it to me. Anyone would have remembered the sneezing part. And when she flashed out of my room, I only hoped I hadn't scared her away from her plan.

Well, it wasn't really a *scheme* sort of plan—or hardly more of a plan than Siggy and I had started off with. Rationalizing, and welcoming it, I thought it was at least so much better and less defined a plan than the one I'd just read about. And would, I hoped, lead my mind out of poor Siggy's zoo notions.

Anyway, it was a pleasure to let Gallen run through my head that way. It was pleasure enough to keep me another night from composing Watzek-Trummer's telegram.

I even slept, and dreamt the coward's dream of impossible isolation. The landscape unidentified, and no wildlife other than our own—Gallen and I, in daylight lasting only as long as we'd care to have it, in weather of our whim; on forest floors, not damp, and lakeshores free of biting insects. Unbelievably uninterrupted, we danced through the poses I remember from the faint, indistinct sketches in *The ABZ of Love.*

While Siggy, in Keff's box, couldn't intrude on us with his awesome details. And all beasts threatening my perfect peace were snug in the Hietzinger Zoo.

What Ernst Watzek –Trummer Received by Mail

In Keff's sealed and simple box, Siggy left Waidhofen for Kaprun on the Saturday evening train, June 10, 1967. My telegram preceded the body by hours enough for Ernst Watzek-Trummer to be warned to meet the train on Sunday noon.

I wrote several drafts of the telegram. I began:

Herr Watzek-Trummer/ I am informed that you were the guardian of Siegfried Javotnik/ a friend/ who was killed on a motorcycle/ and who arrives in Kaprun on this Sunday noon/ Hannes Graff/ who will write you at a later date/

And rewrote, to this:

Dear Herr Watzek-Trummer/ Arriving Sunday noon is your charge/ Siegfried Javotnik/ who was killed on a motorcycle/ He was my friend/ I will get in touch with you/ Yours/ Hannes Graff/

And this:

My Dear Watzek-Trummer/ I am grieved to say that your charge and my friend/ Siegfried Javotnik/ was killed in a freak motorcycle accident in Waidhofen/ He will arrive in Kaprun on Sunday noon/ I will see you myself soon/ Hannes Graff/

And finally decided on this:

Dear Ernst Watzek-Trummer/ I am very sorry to tell you that my very good friend and your relation/ Siegfried Javotnik/ was killed on a motorcycle while performing a secret mission/ the details of which I will explain to you when you hear from me soon/ You may be proud of his work/ My condolences/ Hannes Graff/

And sent that, not hopeful of much better coming from me, and not daring to think further of when I must go meet this Watzek-Trummer, to whom,

I was sure, it would be hard to lie. But at the moment, I simply couldn't have faced another of Watzek-Trummer's sort of funerals.

And I was thinking how Ernst would be dimly impressed with me—as someone who couldn't possibly have the remotest idea of what family griefs of his kind were like. Because if Siggy ever got anything right, he was right about this one thing: my family and I *did* miss the whole war, which, strangely, I felt a bit guilty about.

I remember one thing from the war. In Salzburg, at the close of the American occupation, my mother, who was something of a bopper for her time, remarked on how sad she was that Salzburg would have to go back to the *old* music now—since the Americans took their Negro-horn radio station with them.

I believe that was the only thing my family lost from the war. And my mother wouldn't have had it in the first place, if there hadn't been a war.

So I couldn't very well feel at ease with Watzek-Trummer, with such scanty horrors of my own. Frot me if I wasn't thinking that my unwillingness to go with Siggy's body had to do with my belief that I didn't have nearly enough calamities on record to hold a candle to Watzek-Trummer —and his ghastly burial duties, direct and indirect, certain and implied, one by one.

So I left it all to Keff and said I'd go see Watzek-Trummer someday soon; but I made no *plans*. I wouldn't. I'd seen what schemes for things could do.

Frotting Siggy! What really got me was how, for all his scheming, he would have doomed himself if he'd ever had the chance to go through with it. He'd gone so totally paranoid at the end, what with his prying the Balkan waiter and little Hugel Furtwängler, that if he'd really tried the zoo bust, those two would have put the word on him. Asking so many smart questions about the other zoo bust, he was practically confessing before the crime. And shaving his head was a dumb disguise, to say the least.

We simply mustn't call attention to our extremities, I'm convinced.

And frot me if we ever would have gone to Italy, simply to play on the beaches—planless, as he'd promised first. If there's an aquarium in Naples, there's probably a zoo in Rome. And wouldn't that have been the total, flying finish—knocking over all the animal pens on the continent, until the Regent Park in London would be laying on extra keepers, waiting for the notorious zoo busters to strike there?

But sitting up in my room on the bed, looking out through that nighttime forsythia, I really missed him not popping up on the window ledge any more. For it was a little bit like sitting there waiting for him to come back from that reconnaissance mission. And I began to think that if he *had* gotten by the roadblock, or if I'd just left with him when he first came crawling in over the ledge, I guess I *would* have gone along with it. I mean, it was a doomed idea, and bad that he lost all reason to the plan—deciding *all* the beasts would get the open door, even the eaters—but I don't think I could have let him try it alone. I would have gone along to introduce my strain of caution, my vein of limitless common sense—to see if there wasn't some way I could get *him* safely out again, unclawed, and maybe even spring an antelope or two in the process.

That was the funny feeling, that came hazy and yellow to me from the forsythia garden, clinging with spray from the falls: I *would* have gone with him, but only because he obviously needed looking after.

I mean, thinking coldly, it was a brainless, impossible plan.

But I'd go along with Gallen right now, for virtually the same reasons that I would have indulged Siggy. Though, I had to admit, there hadn't been much in that for me. So far. And, I confess, knocking over Gallen seemed to me as impossible as my knocking over the Hietzinger Zoo.

What Keff Also Did

Keff did all the planning. I would have nothing to do with it, and Gallen told him as much.

So I was still sitting on the bed, Saturday evening, the tenth of June, 1967. I was trying to guess where Siggy was, but I didn't know the way the train lines ran. Whether Siggy would ride in Keff's box to Salzburg, before turning south, or whether he'd be turning south as soon as Steyr—in which case, he would be turning south by now, since Steyr was just a bit west of Waidhofen and Siggy had left an hour ago.

I imagined a most melodramatic race. Siggy, riding rigid in his box—a determined traveler—and I wondered if they'd sent my telegram out of Waidhofen yet, although it didn't matter; it would, at some point along the way, leap over Siggy wherever he was and be the first of them to touch down in Ernst Watzek-Trummer's rooms at the Gasthof Enns.

Watzek-Trummer, of course, would be sitting at his unnecessary kitchen table. While Siggy was hurrying prone.

And then I heard the crawling, clawing sounds in the vines under my window, and I think all my bee stings stung me over again. I saw the paws come groping over the window ledge; I heard grunts. Backing out of my bed, I screamed, "All right! I'll go with you! We'll let them out, if that's what you want!"

But it was Keff. Looking very surprised at my shouting. I couldn't move to help him in, and he appreared to take that as a rebuke; he looked shyly away from me when he swung his thick legs in.

"I didn't mean to scare you," he said sadly. "But we're ready, smarty."

"Why go?" I said, finding it hard to trust enormous Keff.

"Because they've got you on the spot now," he said. "You're good for taxes. The more you stay, the more you owe—for your room, for one thing. And then there's the accident. Windisch says you owe him for the bees, you see. They're going to take it out of you, smarty. They'll fine you to death if you don't go." And he wouldn't look at me; he swayed his lowered ape's head.

"Where's Gallen, Keff?" I said.

"In the orchard," said Keff, "on the town side of the mountain."

"With the bike?" I asked.

"It's registered new, in my name," said Keff. "So they won't know how to trace it, if they care enough to look that hard. I'll stay here after you're gone. If old Tratt comes, I'll hold her here till morning. That gives you some distance, you see."

"What's in it for you, Keff?" I said, and watched him knot his eyebrows; tennis-ball-sized, they welted out from his head.

"Aw, smarty," he said. "Please, I do mean it good for you." But then he looked at me—a faint menace in his eyes. "Your nice girl's waiting now, and you're going to go if I have to lug you, smarty."

"You don't have to," I said, and packed what there was. Notebook, sleeping bags, helmets—in the rucksack or tied on top. There was nothing worth saving the duckjacket for, and I gave Siggy's pipes to Keff. Then I gave him back *The ABZ of Love*.

"Aw, smarty," he said.

"It wasn't your fault, Keff," I said, and actually gave a squeeze to the bit of his arm I could get my hand around.

Then Keff caught me under my shoulders and lowered me by the armpits, half down the castle wall—so I wouldn't have so far to drop, and plop so loud in the garden when I landed. For a moment, I thought he wasn't going to let me go. He held me straight down and a little away from the wall; I couldn't even hear him breathing. Hanging, I said up to him, "Keff, it's too bad you never knew Todor Slivnica. Because I'll bet you could have taken him."

Then I looked straight up above me and saw him giving down his puzzled little *O*-shaped grin, above his three, thick chins.

"O.K., smarty," said Keff, and he dropped me. I fell softly in the garden and broke straightaway for the forsythia. In the grove still in the courtyard, I peered out the gate and all around me. Waiting for an absolutely empty landscape, and not a sound on the cobblestones.

But before I made my break for the road, I threw a look back to my previous window and saw Keff pressed against the grate—the enormity of his shadow blotting out whole shrubs and garden plots below. His shadow, segmented by bars, loomed so much bigger than Siggy's had, and although the great Keff had turned so gentle to me, his caged shadow struck me as even more violent and determined than what Siggy once had cast.

And the Gallen I was headed for now seemed altogether different-promising, too, than the girl of the first evening, when I'd lightly held her; whom I'd left standing in the spray of the falls while I hurried to my Siggy's room to inquire why he aped caged animals at the window grate.

So I jogged up the dark orchard road with this clutter in my skull, doing my fighting best to keep the slightest plan from taking the slightest root in my stung head.

While Siggy, unresisting, was being carried further and further away from the scene of his schemes—while, I imagined, O. Schrutt's watch had not yet begun, and the Famous Asiatic Black Bear, taking his brief rest when he could get it, slept as stonily as Siggy.

But I cut the imagining there. I broke out of my jog and ran full-out on my bathtub-tired legs, digging for Gallen, with no more in my head than the most immediate of plots. Only the essentials.

Would she be there—where Keff said? Would the bike start? And since she'd had the lessons to make her be our driver, where would I put my hands when I held her as she drove us away?

The Feel of the Night

I had to be careful where I put my hands. This girl was skittish of them, and a nervous driver anyway. Gallen had been well enough taught the mechanics of it—the gearing and leaning—but she had this caution about her that was carried a little too far. She startled easy, at stuff in the road that wasn't there.

"Well, Keff didn't teach me at *night*," she said—the helmet so funny, high up on her head, and her braid whipping side to side, as she kept looking for *things* off the road. About to leap out at us, I guess.

So I didn't want to add to her nervousness any, and I was moderate about my hands; I stayed around her waist—except when we were coasting, when I'd let them rest, just lightly, on her hips. She wore her brown leather ladies' jacket, with an old belt Keff gave her to sash it shut. Around her waist, I let my hands go under the jacket and flattened my palms against her warm blouse. But they were the tightest tummy muscles I'd ever felt, so I didn't move against her any.

I once said, in her helmet's ear hole, "Gallen, you drive very well."

But she startled at that too. Turning her head around, she said, "What?" And almost dumped us.

When we slowed for the little towns, I could talk more easily. I said, "It's getting late. We could find a campsite." But she was convinced we should ride through the night and get out of the Waidhofen vicinity—well up in the mountains to the southeast. So if they did care enough to look very hard for us, we'd be hard to find.

But I don't think she wanted to sleep out that night with me. In fact, I wondered if she'd make a travel plan that would have us never sleeping in the dark. For as long as we were together, I foresaw, we'd be nervously driving every night, throughout the night; even if we liked a place well enough to stay awhile, we'd still go off and drive in circles—until the dawn.

But then she surprised me. She stopped in the biggest town we'd come to so far, still before midnight. Mariazell, it was—big and touristy. The whole place was a sort of summerized ski lodge, and the loudest club still open had a young, dancing crowd of smart dressers—rock-and-roll music mashing down the flowers in the windowboxes.

My Gallen kept us idling awhile, out in front of the place; she just stared in the open windows and looked over all the couples, smoking on the outside steps. They looked us up and down, as well.

It was then I realized that Gallen von St. Leonhard hadn't been out of Waidhofen, ever; this was city life to her, and awesome. *Attractive* to her.

It was killing, really, though unnerving, that there was such a world lust, even in her.

And when we were out on the road again, I dared to let my fingers dig at her tummy; just a little kneading, you might say. I thought her muscles weren't quite so tensed. I kissed her, awkwardly, through her helmet's ear hole, and she let some of her weight rest back against me.

Out of town, she pulled the bike into a flashy lay-over on a corner and scared me so much that she had me digging into her tummy harder, which she felt, of course, and knew she'd had the edge on me for a moment. I felt her belly chuckle.

But still she wouldn't stop. We drove straightaway south now, and every coming town was darker. She even developed a feel for speed. And the whole night was wondrously eventless, as if we had stepped out of the gale of this world, as Siggy's old Chetnik hero would have claimed—out in limbo —and were moving nowhere.

Present, somewhere in my mind, was the unnecessary and elbow-worn kitchen table, and Siggy hurrying prone in the box. But I got through most of the night without actually seeing them. It was only when we headed east, through Stübming, that my peace was jarred.

Another drunken town frotter peeing in another town fountain, as if someone had arranged it: that I would always be the one to catch them at it. Only this one didn't dive for cover; perhaps Gallen drove not quite so bomblike as Siggy. This one simply gawked, his cold part held out in his hand. We struck him numb in our headlight and then batted past him; I felt Gallen's tummy tighten, just a bit.

But the memory was enough to spoil my last hour of traveling darkness. For the next hour before daylight, it was my turn to see *things* off the side of the road—like the night Siggy had called the blackout to mind, and we saw *things* come to the roadside to watch us.

Once, I thought I saw—standing motionless in the deep vines—an old bull oryx, with moss on his horns. Once, more startling, an eagle in a chainmail suit of pieplates—standing as if he'd grown there, or had fallen down wingless and taken up roots, years ago.

We crossed the Mürz River at Krieglach, with the daylight hitting us, and a suddenly strong wind came off the river and blew the bike out over the centerline of the road. Gallen lurched us back to our side of the crown, and the wind fell in behind our backs.

But it's the frotting gale of the world, I thought. If it's not blowing against you, head-on, it's behind you and shoving you faster than you want to go. It even does the steering, maybe.

But I kept it to myself, and let Gallen think she was our pilot.

What Gallen Did, Finally

She stopped us for a long and gluttonous brunch at the top of the Semmering Pass. Somehow she'd wound us south, then east and even a little north, so that although we now were southeast of Waidhofen, we were far enough east to be almost straightaway south of Vienna, and straightaway north of either Italy or Yugoslavia—though we had no plans to leave the country; or, that is, *she* had no plans as such. I made it clear I had no plans at all, when we discussed our money—we had maybe two weeks' worth, of traveling as we were. I did figure that much of our plans. That if we bought no more than one meal a day, and stayed far enough in the country to fish for another—slept out and never bought a room—we'd make it two weeks, fuel and food, and then there'd have to be a job.

And jobs meant not leaving Austria. What with the problems of working permits for foreigners, which we'd be if we went out.

That talk was good for mind-occupying, and I'd have gotten along all right if we hadn't been up on the pass at noontime, when the church bells all through the Semmering Valley so formally announced it was noon.

When Siggy gets to Kaprun, I thought—where most of his family retreated to, at one time or another. And I saw old Watzek-Trummer with the crude, prone box.

"Don't you want another beer, Graff?" Gallen said.

And I said, "He's there now. I should be too."

"Come on, Graff," she said.

But I could only think that the old Trummer had been in on too many burials to take on the last one alone. And that was just too sickish-sweet a thought to have in the touristy Semmering Pass Motel and Restaurant, where they piped in the Old World music—to quiver us over our soup.

So Gallen suggested that I learn to drive the bike, since both of us should know. And she led me out of the restaurant, and wound us northwest into the valley. Then we climbed up higher than the Semmering Pass, to Vois, where I bought two bottles of white wine and a butter pat.

We found a pine-needled bank of the fast black Schwarza River, out of tiny Singerin Village. There was room to practice driving; there was running water to chill the wine, and get some fish for Freina Gippel's pan; and we were well off the road, to be sure of a private night.

I started driving down the bank—with Gallen up behind me, saying, "Keff said it's the feel for the gears that comes first." But I wasn't really listening to her. All of a sudden, it was broad Todor Slivnica beneath me, and worldly Bijelo was saying, "Corner sharp left, Vratno, my boy." And then I was pelting up and down the bank, with Gallen meekly saying something, but it was Gottlob Wut who was doing my driving, dictating loud and clear: "See? Like this!" And then I was mounting a marble staircase, when I was the hunted Siegfried Schmidt, special messenger and alley traveler of Old Vienna. But I hit some root that jarred me forward on the gas tank, with poor Gallen sliding up snug behind me—and I had to stretch my toes back to reach the gear lever. Then I saw again the downfalling orchard road, and Siggy said, "First-gear work, here, Graff. You've got to work it."

I was aware of my knees up under the handlebars, hooking me forever on the old beast—and a honey-gunked crown of bees settling on my smarting head—when I went tearing through our unmade campsite and rode right over our rucksack.

"God, Graff," said Gallen. "You're a bit out of control."

But when she got off behind me and came around front, probably wondering why I hadn't shut the engine off, she must have got a look at my dreaming eyes. "Oh, now, Graff. Come on. That's enough," she said.

And when I didn't answer her, and just kept raising the idle higher and higher—letting the bike scream itself silly beneath me—she tapped the kill button and shut me off. The noise died. "Show me," she said, "how you catch fish, Graff."

So I did, though the river was too fast here—with no good bank to get off, and get down in the water. I was hooking and losing them for a while, before I eked out three smallish trout—light enough to jerk right up on the shore.

"Well," I said, "it's always a good thing to go to bed a little hungry."

"Why?" said Gallen.

"And on two bottles of wine too," I said, and grinned.

But she pouted away from me, skittish again.

They were good trout, though. They made Gallen sneeze—a *snit* of a sneeze, half caught in her hand. And I said, "Ha!"

"What do you mean, '*Ha*'?" she said.

And I reminded her: " 'Letting off a thoroughly good sneeze is a natural, spontaneous, frank action of which some people really are a little afraid.' " And stopped there, to see what she'd do.

She said, "Graff." And spilled her wine.

"There's more," I said. "There's a second bottle in the river."

"Thought of everything, didn't you?" she said, but not angrily.

So I thought a bit more, in my way—an immediate sort of plotting. Remembering how Siggy had bought the two sleeping bags at the same place, at the same time; how they made a pair, and zipped either separate or together. They could make a double.

It's the double for you, Gallen, I thought. But it wasn't even dark yet, and we still had a bottle to go, in the river.

So I said, "Gallen, fetch us that second bottle, and I'll build up this fire. It cuts down on mosquitoes, you know." But there weren't any mosquitoes, anyway, thanks be. We were too high up; it was cold.

And would be colder after dark, I knew, looking at the winter sort of river, that even in summer was hard to imagine without frills of thin ice on the outskirts of the current, and shuddering deer coming down off the bank for a lick, picking their hooves up high and shaking them, as if deer could get cold-footed. Though maybe they can.

Anything's possible, Siggy said somewhere. And I had a sort of seizure at the fire, bending down.

If anything's possible, Siggy could get lost on the train; they could send him to Munich or Paris. I saw Siggy stacked upright in a warehouse in Paris.

Or, I thought, there could be trouble in Ernst Watzek-Trummer's tiny rooms. Surely, he'll put Siggy in the room with the racer; and there's sure to be candles. A candle was burning too close to the Grand Prix racer. And they surely left a bit of gas in the tank, to prevent the tank from rusting. I saw the Gasthof Enns blow up.

But I had no feelings about any of the things I saw, seeing them all in the time it took an ash to rise from the fire, or in the time it took Gallen to fetch the wine. I was just numb to reacting to any of it, even to the ashes I tossed in the air. They floated down straight; there wasn't any wind.

So the gale of the world dies down at night, I thought. And I thought: So what if it does? Because I had totally benumbed myself with either too many related or unrelated things.

And all this happened in the time it took ashes to rise, or Gallen to get the wine—or it seemed to; although it was somehow dark before I was aware that Gallen had brought back the wine, and drunk half of it herself. And dark by the time I said, "It's time to fix the sleeping bag." *The bag,* singular, I said—because I was plotting for us in the double.

"I've already done it," said Gallen. *It,* she said—singular. And I realized how she'd zipped them together—perhaps, to make things easier for me. Out of pity, I hoped not.

I went down to the river and washed the fish off my teeth. Then I crept to the bag, which Gallen was warming. But she was dressed. That is: still the corduroy slacks, and her blouse. At least she'd taken her bra off; I saw where she'd tried to hide it under her jacket, just outside the bag.

Little things make a difference, I'm sure.

But when I slipped in beside her, she said, "Goodnight, Graff." Before I'd even stretched out! And I'd been discreet enough to leave my miserable, sagging boxer shorts on.

The river was so fast it made a racket. And frog tones came up, across the river. There's always a swamp where you least expect it.

I was thinking like that—little philosophies popping up all by themselves. Gallen had her back to me—balled, with her knees drawn up. "Why, you must be tired, Gallen," I said, bright and snappy.

"Yes, very, goodnight," she said again—faking a groggy voice, as if she'd fallen into an instant sleep. So I just pushed toward her, my shoulder against the warm back of her blouse—and she stiffened. "You took your clothes off," she accused.

"I've got my hangies on," I said.

"Your what?" said Gallen.

"My hangies." I told her. "My boxer shorts."

For a moment I thought she'd call for a light to look at my miserable hangies; I would have expired for the shame. She sat up in the bag.

But she said, "Isn't it a lovely night, Graff?"

"Oh yes," I said, crouching back in my corner of the bag—just waiting for her to lie down again.

"And isn't the river loud?" said Gallen.

"Oh yes," I said, in my bored way. I just lurked in my part of the bag for her. I watched how her blouse was fluffed by the wind.

And I remember waiting a long time for her to lie down, and finally getting myself sleepy because she sat up so long. I thought: She's probably going to put her bra back on.

So I let myself be carried away with the water in the fast, black, winter river. I dozed downstream; I woke for short spurts and swam against the current. But always restfully, without any struggle. I let myself be coaxed into letting it carry me—past towns brightly lit over the water; paddling past a typical sort of sawmill, with pitch-smelling logs jamming up along the bank; past young girls doing their sheer laundry. And then I was traveling, muffled, through steep riverbanks of snow, and it was almost dark, or almost light, and the deer were coming down to drink. A great buck with a harem of does all meekly herded after him; the buck looked, I admit, a bit like the oryx. He dared walking out on the thin frills of ice offshore. He eased down his great weight; lightly, he placed his carefully aimed, sharp hooves. The herd of does brushed warmly together. I stopped floating by; I treaded water in place.

The does brushed too loudly together, I thought. But it was Gallen, sitting up above me—getting into her frotting bra, no doubt. Except that her legs behaved foolishly beside me in the bag. She is bicycle-pedaling in this bag, I thought. What next? She's getting into her chainmail pants, which are padlocked. This girl takes no chances.

But then she slipped into the bag, out long alongside me, and I felt her knee draw up and lightly touch my hand.

She'd taken *off* her clothes! I faked sleep.

"Graff?" Gallen said, and her feet clapped like hands round my ankle. I squiggled a little toward her, still sleeping. Of course.

"You, Graff," she said. "Wake up, please." But except for our feet touching now, she held off my tummy with her hands. Then she moved; she was touching me nowhere. And then she came down from the roof of the bag on top of me; it was her hair, unbraided and falling loose, that fell over me first. Our skin touched very hot or cold; we were flush in a moment. I felt the ice frill break from the bank and cast the great buck adrift.

Gallen said, "Wake up now, please." And hugged herself so tight to me I couldn't move.

"I'm awake," I said, down in my throat. But I gurgled so meekly, I tried to get my neck off her shoulder bone so she'd be sure to hear me.

But before I could croak again, she crawled down on me a bit and kissed over my mouth. So I gurgled again. Her face was wet against mine; she was crying down over me, of all things.

I was confused, I confess. I said, "Don't do me any favors—if it's just because you feel sorry for me."

"I don't at all," she said—fierce for her.

"You don't?" I said, hurt—and held her at elbow's length off my chest. Her hair covered her face and mine. Then she kneed me and I doubled up into her, where her body seemed to know I'd be coming—because she caught my shoulders and swung herself off me, and brought me down over her.

Now she was crying out loud and I kissed over her mouth to stop it. We rolled to get leg room in the frotting bag.

I felt obliged to—I said, "I love you, Gallen, really." And she told me the same.

It was the only part that felt at all forced—or seemed remembered from a history of necessary prefixes that we didn't use quite naturally between us.

She tied her hair around my neck; she bound my head on her chest—so high and thin and fragile, I thought I'd break through it and fall inside her. I closed one eye on the pulse in her throat; it was running light and fast.

Like the winter river, bearing downstream the daring buck, who rode the ice flow that melted beneath him; his does ran apace with him, safe on the shore.

And Gallen said, "What are these? What did you call them?"

"Hangies," I said, but softly. I wouldn't, for this world, have interrupted her pulse.

"Well, then," she said (and her hip bone jabbed me; she was turning under me), "these of mine are called huggies." No more tears, but she was stalling. Then she said, "Take them off."

I thought: If only a poor soul could see in this frotting bag.

But when I looked, I saw the buck, in the balance—his ice cake almost gone beneath him.

And if I hooked my thumbs just over the front of Gallen's waist, and touched down the heels of my hands where her hips began—and if I squeezed, hard—my middle fingers touched, or seemed to, on her backbone. So I lifted her.

And she babbled, as if she were blurting it out in midstream of the running, winter river, "You, Graff, where did you put my huggies, you—they're bought new for this trip."

Then she lifted herself when I lifted her. The does ran in step.

Gallen said, "You, Graff!" And something squeaked in her throat, an inch behind her pulse and stepping it up.

I saw the buck's hard forehoof break through the ice; his chest fell first and split the lace-thin cake in two. He floated down; he passed towns brightly lit over the water, and sawmills smelling thick with pitch—the river dark and musty with slabs of bark. He emerged between spotless banks of snow, saw his does wanting him ashore. He took an easy stroke or two, in no hurry, brushing the frills of ice that fingered out into the current.

I was confused again, I held my breath, for I'd stopped treading water and had sunk too long ago. I got my footing on the blanket-soft river bottom. As I pushed off, the buck reached shore.

Then I sneezed, of all things. I had surfaced.

From out of the sawmill smell of the bag, Gallen brought her hands against my ears and rang my head. The buck staggered, dizzy, up the bank. Gallen kissed over my mouth, and my head cleared. Solidly ashore now, the buck loped for the warm does.

Then Gallen let her hands fall lightly away from my ears, my pulse came down, and the only real sounds came back to me.

The river storming along. And frog tones from the swamp that you'd least expect to find here.

What Gallen Did, Again

I woke up early, feeling guilty that I'd slept at all. Because I knew that Ernst Watzek-Trummer had spent the night at elbow height above his kitchen table, had even outlasted the dishwashers downstairs in the Gasthof Enns.

Gallen was already awake, inching about for her huggies and trying to snare her bra, outside, without my seeing any of her. Thanks be, she took my guilty look for herself. Because she said, "Graff, it's all right. I feel fine." And she tried to look very gay—but not at me; her eyes shiny and shying away.

So I said, "Just so you're fine, then." To keep her thinking I'd been thinking of her. Then I did think of her, and kissed her, and started to hunch myself out of the bag, very lively.

But Gallen said, "Wait, your hangies are right here." She turned her back so I wouldn't have to contort myself down deep in the sweet, pitch-smelling bag.

"This bag could stand some air," I said.

"Is that me?" she said. "Do I smell like that too?"

"Well," I said, and we both looked around. I was hoping for some small, unusual animal to come on the scene, or a wild-colored bird, about which I could say, "Heavens, Gallen. Would you look at that." And thereby change the subject neatly. But I saw nothing except the dew-covered motorcycle and the river, heaped in fog. The morning air was cold.

"Let's have a swim," I said bravely.

But she didn't want to get out of the bag until I'd fetched her the bra. Which she wouldn't ask me for, either, so I popped out and groped around for it, finding it and holding it aloft. "Why, what's this odd article?" I said.

"O.K., give it here," said Gallen, hair over her eyes. Then I went down to the river and waited for her.

Lord, the water was fierce; it made my teeth tinkle like glass, and nearly tugged my miserable hangies off. Gallen didn't swim; she just dunked in and out. With her hair wet, I saw how sleek her head was. Her ears were a little funny—too long, and even pointed, slightly. Her jaw was trembly from the cold. When she climbed out, her bra was full of water. In such the nicest way, she squeezed herself; she sort of wrung out her breasts and made her bra cling to her. Then she saw me watching her and she danced over the bank, back-to me, conscious of how tightly her huggies hugged her.

I came up the bank, forced to walk somewhat apelike because my frotting hangies were stuck all over me, almost down to my knees. And when she saw what a figure I cut, she laughed at my vain bones. "I think you need smaller-sized hangies," she said.

Then I leapt toward her, hooting self-conscious, and danced around her, pointing. "Look!" I shouted. "You've got two schillings in your bra."

Because that's just what her nipples looked like, size- and color-wise— a lovely off-brass color, just glorious. Two schillings, for sure.

So she stared at herself and then spun away from me. I thought: Please laugh, Gallen—even at your own parts. A little humor is essential, I'm convinced.

"Do you have a shirt I could wear?" said Gallen, seriously worried. "My blouse would wet through, and I didn't pack any towels."

And when I brought her my fabulous red-and-white-striped soccer jersey, she was hiding her schillings with her hands—but smiling wide, with a slash of hair in the corner of her mouth, stuck wet against her cheek; she pushed it away with her tongue.

"Breakfast?" I said. "If you can make a fire, I can ride to Singerin for eggs and coffee."

"I can," she said, laughing at something funny to her now, "if you can help me with this first," and I came around behind her to help unhook her bra, under the soccer shirt. She wiggled, sliding the wet thing down to her waist; behind her, I just came up with my hands for a moment—around her wet, cold, hard breasts. She was like a statue just hosed down.

"Let me brush my hair," she said, but she didn't try to get away. She leaned back into me.

The river rose; it seemed to wash over us. But it was only a wind that came up and moved the fog our way. I saw deer in the forest, docile as sheep. Except the forest was hemmed in by something. Rivers on all sides, maybe, or even a fence. And standing off to one side of the deer, like a shepherd —though he didn't have a staff—Siggy was saying, "Sit tight, my deer. I'll have you out of here, don't you worry."

Then Gallen said, "You're hurting me, Graff—just a little." I'd bitten a ring-shaped, fire-bright spot on her neck, through a strand of her hair. And when she saw me looking guilty again, she thought it was just because I'd bitten her.

"Well, I'm all right," she said. "Graff, I'm not so delicate, really."

I went along with it, letting her think I wore my odd look for her sake. She brushed her dark wet hair, bringing the red back into it. So I ducked into the woods to change out of my impossible wet hangies.

Then I drove to Singerin for eggs and coffee. And when I came back, she had a fire going, with too much wood to cook on. But she'd also spread open the sleeping bag and dragged it back up into the woods, way above the water. Embarrassed, I saw she'd hung my hangies on a stick—a spear stuck in the ground and the hangies waving, as if the wearer lay buried under this crude marker.

We ate a lot. I found a very old loaf of bread too—in the rucksack, where it must have been stashed a week or so ago. But it toasted very well in the grease in Freina's pan. Because I make it a policy never to really clean the pan. That way you remember all the good meals you've had.

Gallen still dried her hair. She brushed it down over her face, then she gave a puff and blew a strand of it away from her—baring just her mouth and nose. Her hair danced alive by itself; she played with it across from me, and I gave several fake moans and crawled up in the woods, plopping down on the bag. Bigger than any bedspread, set better than any tablecloth—with trees all around it, and pine needles packed under it. Soft as water; you sank in it.

But Gallen went futzing around with the fire, and washing her hands in the river. She'd changed back in her corduroys again, and hadn't been so bold as to fly her huggies in the same way she'd chosen to immortalize me.

I faked some more exhausted grunts from my great bed in the woods. Then I shouted down to her, "Aren't you sleepy, Gallen? I could sleep all day, myself."

"But you wouldn't," she said, "if I came up there with you."

Well, such conceit seemed to demand some firm resolve on my part, so I bolted out of the woods and charged her on the riverbank. She raced into the field. But I never knew a girl who could really run. It's their structure, I'm convinced; they're hippy, whether there's much flesh or not, and that structuring forces their legs to swivel out sideways when they move.

Besides, I'm tireless in short bursts. I caught her when she tried to double back to the woods to hide. She said, all out of breath and as if she'd been thinking on it all along, "Where do you think we should go next? Where do you want to go?" But I wasn't to be that easily thrown off. I carried her back to the sleeping bag; she tied me up in her hair again, even before I set her down. But I noticed how she genuinely winced when I rolled over her.

"Gallen, are you sore?" I said. She looked away from me, of course.

"Well, a little," she said. "It's not anything wrong with me, is it?"

"Oh no," I said. "I'm sorry."

"Oh, I don't hurt a lot, anyway," she said. Meaning it, because she didn't untangle her hair from around my neck.

Lord, in the daylight, I thought—embarrassed, myself. But she surprised me.

"You don't have any hangies on under," she said.

"I've just got one pair," I said, sheepish.

"Graff, you can wear mine, you know," said Gallen. "They stretch."

"These are blue!" I said.

And Gallen said, "I have a green pair, a blue pair and a red pair."

But she only had that one bra, I knew—having seen some of the packing.

"You can have my soccer shirt," I told her.

And seeing the shirt off to the side of our spread, I remembered a loon

of a boy who was on my old soccer team in high school. He hated the game
as much as I did, I'm sure, but he had this special knack in that awful
situation when you're running to kick the ball and the other man is running
toward you, to get the ball first. You don't know who'll get to kick it, but
if he does he'll probably kick it in your face or you'll catch his toe in your
throat. But this loon I knew would always start yelling when he got in that
situation. He wouldn't shy off, he'd dig hard for the ball, very serious—but
yelling as he ran, *"Yaaii! Yaaaiii!"* He'd scream right in the face of the
fellow opposite. He terrified everyone, just by showing them how scared he
was.

He was a very good player because of it, I'm convinced. He beat everyone
to the ball. It sort of took your edge off to have him blubbering like that,
as if he were charging a machine gunner's nest.

And I thought: That's true. We should all be loudly afraid when we are
—just so no one confuses the hero with the loon. It's the loon who makes
you laugh, and makes you think he's crazy. But it's the hero who's stupid.
He's full up with platitudes and vague notions, and he doesn't really care
if he gets to the ball first. Now take me—I'm the loon, I thought.

And Gallen said, "Graff?" Probably embarrassed that I *wasn't* looking
at her, having prepared herself to have me see.

She was no statue; she was soft, despite the bones around. Someone
shouted, above the river:

Bless the green stem before the flower!

It must have been Siggy, speaking prone—droning in the candlelight by
the Grand Prix racer, '39.

"Why do you have hair there?" said Gallen.

There's always a swamp where you least expect it, I thought. And I lay
my head down quickly between her high, small breasts. This time, I wanted
no distractions. No frotting deer by the winter river, or tended to by a
shepherdlike Siggy. I thought—and surprisingly, not until now—I might be
going mad. Or just bizzare.

It frightened me so, I wouldn't close my eyes. I looked down her long
waist; I saw where her pelvis moved, if that's a pelvis. I looked up her neck
—saw the pulse beating at the thin-skinned spot, but didn't dare to feel it.
Her mouth opened and her eyes looked down at me—still surprised, no
doubt, at where I had hair and where I didn't.

Then I was over her mouth and so close to her eyes I could count all her
lashes; saw her squeeze water down over them, but not crying, really.

And I didn't have any inappropriate visions—only her face and her
flooding hair. The hands over me were absolutely the hands of Gallen von
St. Leonhard; there were no distractions. No sound effects, either, except
what I caught of Gallen's breathing.

Her eyes closed; I nipped a tear off her cheek. She covered my ears in her fashion again. My head rang, but I knew precisely what caused it.

I had sneezed. This time she had too. Because her eyes opened very frightened. She said, "Graff?" I thought: No, that wasn't anything wrong. That was perfectly proper. But she said, "Graff, did you feel that? Did I hurt myself?"

"No, you just sneezed," I said, making light. "That's good," I said, like a frotting doctor. But this time I heard her every word and breath, and I knew I hadn't traveled beyond the bag. I was sane: I knew Gallen and I were alone there together, and everyone or everything else was either dead or not with us. For that moment.

"It was something that fell out of me, though," she said. "Graff? It was, I think."

"You simply sneezed," I said. "And nothing fell out that won't be back."

I thought: A sense of humor is essential, Gallen. This is so important. Please smile now.

But Gallen said—still nervous, and I hadn't left her—"Graff, do you think of other things when you do this? Do you ever?"

"How could I?" I said. And I didn't dare take my eyes off her, or dare to close my eyes, either—because I knew that the woods around us were full of deer and oryxes and shepherds, just waiting to catch my mind. Frot them.

Gallen smiled; she even laughed a little, under me. "I don't think of anything, either," she said. "I can't even get anything on my mind right now."

Well, you're a very healthy girl, I thought. But you'd better watch out for me. Hannes Graff is known for his loose, straying ends.

Noah's Ark

Later that afternoon, Gallen said, "Do you think it's come back yet? It still *feels* gone."

"What does?" I said, and because she was talking, I dared to close my eyes.

"What I thought fell out of me," said Gallen. "You know."

She was a little too glum about it, I thought.

"Look," I said. "Some girls never sneeze all their life. You're lucky."

"Will I ever again?" she said. "Is what I mean."

"Of course you will," I said.

"When?" said Gallen, more brightly—even playful. With her one wet bra still drying, she certainly tossed my soccer shirt around when she moved.

"Hannes Graff needs time to recover," I said.

And that's true enough, I thought—my eyes still closed. I could move my head back and forth—into a spot where the sun hit my face and changed my darkness from black to red. Then back to black, with the frame of my darkness edged in red and white stripes, like the soccer shirt.

Keep talking to me, please, Gallen, I thought.

But she must have been imagining the degrees of my recovery—a silent wonder, I've often thought myself.

My eyes still closed, I moved my head, black to red, red to black—a simple trick, with lighting effects—but the core of my darkness was opening like the shutter-eye of a camera. It was really premeditated; I could have stopped it by just opening my eyes wide and talking fast to Gallen. But I compromised, to test myself. Eyes still shut, I said, "About where we'll go. Have you given it any thought yourself?"

"Well, I've been thinking," said Gallen.

But my shutter-eye opened wider now, on the frotting winter river—like a movie beginning, with no titles and no characters yet onstage. Please *think* out loud, Gallen, I thought. But she didn't say a word, or if she did, it was too late for me to hear her—for the speed of my traveling.

This river went everywhere; it passed every place in the world. But I was just a camera-eye, not in the picture. In spots, there were crowds on the banks, all with their suitcases. And there were animals too—on the ark, that is. I neglected to mention it: a rather poorly put-together raft. Someone ran a collection service; he wore an eaglesuit and was in charge of the ship— or he ran about, breaking up squabbles on board, thrusting an oar between cats and wombats, separating the bears and shrieking birds. *People* tried to swim out and board the ark. They tried to hold their suitcases above water; their children were sinking.

The ark and the river went through a city. The man in the eaglesuit welcomed strange animals aboard. Cows huffed alongside—escaped from the slaughterhouses. A taxi drove into the river.

Siggy said to the cows, "I'm terribly sorry, but we already have two of you. This is an arbitrary business."

The taxi was still afloat. An impossible number of passengers unloaded, treading water in place. Someone tipped the driver, and he sank with his cab.

And then I was watching myself, making my way through the water with my suitcase overhead; my fellow-passengers from the cab were chatting.

One said, "There's no proof at all that the driver was actually Zahn Glanz."

"Whoever he was, you overtipped him," said a woman, and everyone laughed.

When I came alongside the ark, Siggy said, "I'm sorry, but I believe we already have two of you."

I said, "For God's sake, Sig, a sense of humor is essential."

"If you're really with us, Graff, you may board," said Siggy. But a vicious Oriental bear was protesting. "I mean *really*, Graff," Siggy said. "We can't give up the ship."

Then Gallen put her arm around my waist, dragging me under. "I've been thinking where we should go, Graff," she said.

"All right! I'm with you!" I screamed, and bolted upright off the sleeping bag, into her arms and the movable soccer shirt.

"Graff?" she said. "Graff, I just said I thought about where we could go."

"Well, I've been thinking too," I told her, and clung to her.

I had my eyes open as wide as they'd go. I counted the stripes on the soccer shirt. They were nice, broad stripes—two white and one red, from the collar to where her breasts began and unstraightened the striping; five red and four white, from her breasts to the hem on her thigh. I lay my head on her hem.

These stripes were more restful than counting sheep.

"Or walruses, Graff," said Siggy, somewhere. "Wallowing, frolicsome walruses."

"All right, that's enough. I'm with you," I said.

"Well, of course you are, Graff," said Gallen.

Plans

Just before nightfall, I reenergized myself and took a long walk upstream to a good fishing spot, where I could wade out within easy casting range of the rocky pools on the far bank. I pulled them in very handily there, while Gallen rode to Singerin for beer.

Before she was back, I had a fire going and six trout cleaned for Freina's super-flavored pan.

My head was clear. It's always good to have a few money plans forced on your mind; it keeps you from having notions of other, vaguer plans.

We'd talked over where we should go next, and Gallen thought that Vienna might be best—because I knew my way around the job spots there; but mainly, I think, since her glimpse of Mariazell, Gallen had her eyes on the city life—as she imagined it. I was worried it might make her stickish, but I had to admit that Vienna did seem the likeliest place for either of us to get a job. Now, what I'd argued with her, though, was this: you'd also *spend* more money in Vienna than anywhere else around us, while you were *looking* for a frotting awful job. And what would keep us fed and well slept for two weeks in the country wouldn't hold us for five or six days in Vienna —if we wanted to eat. We could still drive out past the suburbs each night and camp in the vineyards—if we weren't eaten by watchdogs. But you couldn't catch your meals in Vienna, for sure.

On the other hand, in the wilderness we were in, there were too many places for *things* to hide—and be popping out at me. There's less daydreaming in a city, all right, and Hannes Graff could stand to have less of that.

So Sunday evening, after we'd eaten, we sat with our beers and talked it over again.

"I've been thinking," said Gallen.

Well, thinking's good for you, I thought—at least, this fussy kind. Also, this business at hand seemed to have taken her mind off her first sneeze. And no one should ponder on that subject for very long, I'm convinced.

"The trouble is, Graff," she said, officiously, "—as I seem to understand it—we need more money than we have now, if we're to give ourselves enough job-hunting time in the city. Until the first pay check."

"That's precisely what the trouble is," I agreed. "I think you've got it."

"Well, then, it's solved," she said, and brought her long auburn braid over her shoulder—holding it out to me, the way a vendor shows you his vegetables and fruit.

"Very nice hair," I said, puzzled.

"Well, I'll sell it," said Gallen. "There's good money in selling your hair for wigs."

"Sell it?" I said. It struck me as a perverse sort of whoring.

"We'll just find some classy *friseur* in the suburbs," said Gallen.

"How do you know about wig makers?" I said.

"Keff told me," said Gallen.

"Frotting *Keff?*" I said. "And just what does he know about it?"

"He was in Paris for the war," she told me. "He said it was big business, even then—ladies selling their hair."

"In Paris for the war?" I said. "I understood they were snatching hair, not buying it."

"Well, some maybe," said Gallen. "But it's a very classy business now. And real hair makes the best wigs."

"Keff told you he was in Paris?"

"Yes," said Gallen. "It came up when we were talking about my hair."

"Oh, *were* you?" I said, and tried to imagine Keff in Paris. It wasn't a pretty picture. I saw a very young, swaggering, bullish Keff—in the ladies' hair business, or somehow connected with hair. In his off-duty hours.

"Well, we were talking about money too," said Gallen. "That's when he mentioned my hair."

"Did *he* want to buy it?" I said.

"Of course not," said Gallen. "He just said I'd get a good price for it, if we were short." And she stroked her hair, as if she were petting a cat.

"Gallen, I love your hair," I said.

"You wouldn't love me without it?" she said, and snatched it up above her head, showing off her ears and the long back of her neck. She made her face sleeker, and her shoulders more slight; she seemed even more fragile. I thought: Frot Hannes Graff—the girl would cut off her hair for him.

"I'd love you without any hair," I said, but I was sure I wouldn't. I saw her bald, gleaming at me; she had her own helmet, spotted with speed-struck insects, pitted as a peach stone. I took Gallen's braid in my hands.

Then Siggy snapped at me, out of the fire, "No nonsense now. Just a total shave, please." And I dropped Gallen's hair.

She must have noticed my faraway-traveling eyes, because she said, "Graff? It's not that you don't want to go to Vienna, is it? I mean, if you'd rather go somewhere you've never been before—if you don't want to see any old stuff you remember, or might, you know—I wouldn't care, Graff. Really, if Vienna's a bad place for you now. I just thought it would be easier for money—in the long run."

In the long run? I thought.

"You know," said Gallen. "It would just probably give us enough to get someplace to stay, indoors. Just a room, maybe, at first."

At first? I thought. Oh, frot me if she doesn't have some overall plan.

"Wouldn't you just like a room with a great big bed in it?" she asked, and blushed.

But this girl's schemes were sounding dangerous to me—this vague, long-term stuff never works. This was too much planning in front of ourselves—for sure.

I said, "Well, let's just go to Vienna and get one or both of us a job, at first. Then maybe we can do whatever we want. Maybe we'll want to go to Italy then," I said hopefully.

"Well," she said, "I thought you'd like the room with the bed."

"Well, let's just see what heppens," I said. "What's the matter? Don't you like our sleeping bag?"

"Well, of course I like it," said Gallen. "But you can't sleep outside forever, you know."

Maybe *you* can't, I thought. And who said anything about *forever?*

"Well, just thinking practically," she said, sounding too much like her frotting Auntie, "it will be cold in a few months, and you can't sleep outside and drive a motorcycle in the snow."

Well, the truth of that was startling. *A few months?* I'll have to get the bike down south *before* it snows, I thought. And suddenly *time* was involved in any plans you made or didn't. For example, tomorrow was Monday, June 12, 1967. A real *date*. And one week ago tomorrow, Siggy was leaving Waidhofen in the rain—past the fallen horse and milkwagon, headed for the Hietzinger Zoo. And today was Sunday, Siggy was in Kaprun with old Watzek-Trummer; they were respectively prone and sitting, above the dinner guests in the Gasthof Enns.

"Well, we'll leave for Vienna, early tomorrow," I said. And I thought: Maybe it will rain like a week ago.

"Do you know the suburbs?" said Gallen. "Where we might find some classy *friseur.*"

"I know *one* suburb," I said. "It's called Hietzing."

"Is it hard to get to?" she said.

"You go right through it on your way downtown," I said.

"Well, that's easy then," said Gallen.

"That's where the zoo is," I told her, and she was very quiet.

"Fate shapes the course!" Siggy popped from the fire.

Frot that myth, I thought. I'm doing this all by myself.

"Oh, Graff," said Gallen, making light. "Come on, now. We don't *have* to see the zoo."

"Well, you shouldn't go to Vienna," I said, "without seeing how spring has struck the zoo."

And although the first-shift watch was the only chance the animals had to sleep, I saw them all wake up and cock their various ears to this talk.

But you animals misunderstand me, I thought. There's no point in getting your hopes up. I'm just coming to look. But they were all awake and staring through their bars, accusing me. I shouted aloud, "Go to sleep!"

"What?" said Gallen. "Graff? Do you want to think or something? I'll go up in the woods, if you want to be alone—if you don't want to talk to me or anything."

But I thought: You're giving up your hair for me, for Christ's sake don't do anything more. So I tackled her when she tried to stand and leave me. I burrowed in her lap, and she lifted her soccer shirt to tuck my head under it, face-down on her warm, ribby tum. She hugged me; she had little, alive pulses everywhere.

I thought: Hannes Graff, gather up your loose ends, please. This living girl is vulnerable to being let down by just about everything.

More Plans

Just out of Hütteldorf-Hacking, in the outskirts of Hietzing, we found a first-class *friseur,* name of Orestic Szirtes—a Greco-Hungarian, or a Hungarian-Greek. His father, he told us, was Zoltan Szirtes; his mother was the former beauty Nitsa Papadatou, who sat and watched us from her throne in the best barber chair.

"My father's gone," Orestic said, and not just out for lunch, I gathered —by the way the former Nitsa Papadatou shook her glossy black mane and rattled the bright gems on her long black robe; lowly V-necked, her jeweled robe exposed her fierce cleavage and the rump-sized swell of her mighty, unfallen breasts. A former beauty, for sure.

Gallen said, "Do you buy hair?"

"Why should we buy it?" old Nitsa said. "There's no need—it's all over our floor."

But it wasn't, really. It was a spiffy place—a light, tasteful perfume hit you when you walked in the door. But the air turned more to musk the nearer you got to Nitsa. And the only hair on the floor was under Nitsa's chair, as if no one were allowed to sweep under her while she was enthroned.

"The girl means for wigs, Mama," Orestic said. "Of course, yes, we buy hair." And he touched Gallen's braid, sort of flicked it to see how it behaved when provoked. "Oh, lovely, yes," Orestic said.

"I think so," I said.

"Young hair is best," he said.

"Well, she *is* young," I said.

"But it's *red,* " said Nitsa, shocked.

"All the more in demand!" I claimed. While Orestic stroked the braid.

"How much?" said Gallen, world-wise and tough as cork.

Orestic pondered over her braid. His own hair was as thick and shining-clean as damp black saw grass in a marsh. I wandered to the rows of speared heads in the window; each head, wigged and necklaced, had an upturned nose without any nostrils.

"Two hundred schillings," said Orestic. "And for that I trim her after —any kind of cut she wants."

"Three-fifty," I said. "Your window sales start at seven hundred."

"Well," said Orestic, "I have to do a bit of work to make a wig out of it, you know. She's got scarcely more than a hairpiece here." And with that, he swished her braid away.

"Three hundred, then," I said.

"Two-fifty," said Nitsa, "and I'll pierce her ears for free."

"Pierce her ears?" I said.

"Mama pierces ears," said Orestic. "How many ears has it been now, Mama?"

Probably all saved in her chest of drawers, I thought.

"Oh, I lost count long ago," old Nitsa claimed. Then she looked at Gallen. "So, how's two-fifty and your ears in with it?"

"Graff," said Gallen, "I always did want to—especially since I'm in the city."

"For God's sake," I whispered. "Not here, please. You might lose them altogether." I said to Orestic, "Three hundred, without ears."

"And you'll fix my hair up after?" said Gallen. "All right?" She tossed her braid over her shoulder; it teased poor Orestic like a charming-snake.

"All right," he said.

But the former Nitsa Papadatou spat on the floor. "Weak!" she told her son. "Just like your miserable father, you've got no spine." She straightened up in the best barber chair and whumped her backbone with her hand; Nitsa had a spine, all right. She huffed out her frontispiece at us; her wondrous cleavage opened wider, closed tighter, opened wide and closed again.

"Mama, *please,*" Orestic said.

But when Orestic ushered my Gallen into the vacant, lesser barber chair. Nitsa was a welcome distraction. Because it pained me to see Orestic feverishly undoing Gallen's braid, then brushing—crackling her hair out full and over the back of the chair, nearly to the seat. Then he snatched it up above her head and with sure, heavy strokes brushed it upward, stretching it—as if he were coaxing it to grow another inch or two before he claimed it. I was sitting directly behind Gallen, so I couldn't see her face in the mirror, thanks be; I didn't want to see her eyes when Orestic gathered up a great horsetail of hair and sheared it off at the roots—it seemed. I looked slantwise at the mirror, down the full, reflected cleavage of Mama Nitsa.

Orestic swished the auburn tail around; then I had a sudden shiver, as if I'd just watched a beheading; Gallen held both hands to her scalp. Slick Orestic put her hair on a cushion in the windowseat, and came back, dancing round her—his razor *tzik* ing over her ears and up the back of her long, bare neck.

"Now! What to *do* with it!" he said. "Leave you bangs, or none?"

"No bangs," said Gallen. He cut a little, but left enough to brush back; he trimmed off her forehead, swept it over only the points to her ears, left it fairly full on the back of her head, but brought it up close on her neck. Near the roots, though, the auburn shone richer.

"No thinning," he said. "We'll leave it nice and thick." And he seized up a handful, as if he were going to tear it out. "Oh, it's thick as a *pelt!*" he cried excitedly. But Gallen just stared at her new forehead; she sneaked a look, now and then, round the sides of her head to her startling ears.

It was the turning in the swivel chair that disconcerted me, I guess. I was just thinking how it wasn't so bad, really; how she was spared disgrace by very nice bones in her cheeks and jaw, and by her neck being so nice naked —when Orestic began swiveling her around in the chair, taking his finishing looks.

"See?" he said proudly to me. "How even? All around." And spun her a little faster, so flashes of her caught the mirror and flashed back at me double, on both sides of the chair, as if we were suddenly in a full barbershop —with a spinning row of dizzy customers, and madmen barbers, conducted by the old fortunetelling woman in the best barber chair. It was funny; I relaxed my eyes.

But then he shampooed her and—before I knew how long I'd watched the row of customers spin themselves bald—he stuck her head in a large chrome hair dryer; he tipped her head back in the chair, back toward me, and I watched the humming dome gleam.

"I only asked for a shave," someone said. "Would you call *this* a haircut?" And somehow, Nitsa's cleavage, spreading everywhere, was reflected on the back of Gallen's domish hair dryer.

"Would you like *your* ears pierced?" Nitsa asked me. "But I know, the men usually like just *one* ear done."

"Not in *this* country, Mama," Orestic said.

And little Hugel Furtwängler, with a barbers'-union flag, leered over the wigged heads in the window. He said, "He's a lunatic! He *wanted* me to do it!"

Oh, I'm off, I thought—just because this hair dryer is steaming up this room, unhealthily.

Nitsa Szirtes plucked her robe a bit away from her stuck-together breasts and blew a thin-lipped jet of breath down her cleavage.

Then I asked Orestic, "Have you been here long—in this country? Or just since the war."

"Since and before," said old Nitsa. "His father, Zoltan, took us back and forth to Hungary—a wretched place, if I ever."

"My father's gone," Orestic reminded me.

"He was a cruddy, hairy man," said Nitsa.

"Mama, *please*," Orestic said.

"I should never have left Greece," said the former girl-Papadatou.

"Oh yes, we've been here awhile," Orestic told me, and lifted Gallen's dried and shrunken head out of the shiny dome. He made her keep her head thrown back while he brushed, furiously. An odd angle, I had, looking over the back of Gallen's tilted chair; I could see no more of her face than the sharp bridge of her nose. Except what I caught misreflected in the hair dryer —her enlarged ear.

Which blushed when it heard me ask Orestic, "Then were you here when that man broke into the zoo?"

"Ha! He was eaten!" said Nitsa.

"Yes, he was," I said.

"But we weren't here, Mama," said Orestic.

"We weren't?" she said.

"We were in Hungary," Orestic said.

"But you've heard about it, obviously," I said.

"We were in Hungary," he said, "when all those things were going on here."

"What *other* sort of things?" I said.

"How do I know?" he said. "We were in Hungary."

"Then we must have been wretched," said Mama Nitsa, "with that cruddy, hairy man."

"Hair's done," Orestic said. Gallen nervously touched the top of her head.

"Well, two-fifty we owe you," said Mama Nitsa.

"Three hundred," I said.

"Three hundred," said Orestic. "Be fair, Mama."

"Weak!" She snorted. As weak as the cruddy, hairy man, no doubt. Poor blasphemed Zolton Szirtes must have rolled in his grave to hear her—if he had a grave or was in it yet; or if those in their graves can roll.

"Anything's possible!" Siggy called, out of the hair dryer's gleaming dome—or out of Keff's box, alongside the Grand Prix racer, 1939.

I checked my watch. Time was a part of my life again. It was nearly lunchtime, Monday, June 12, 1967. Which would put us perfectly on schedule, if we left straightaway, parked the motorcycle off the Platz, down Maxing Strasse; went to the Balkan waiter's café; went into the zoo that afternoon.

We'd be sure to find the same conditions that were written down, one week ago this Monday.

"I like your hair, Gallen," I said. She was sort of sheepish, but trying to be proud. Her new hair was tufted close to her head, like a bobcat's.

And trying to be casual—not thinking about her choice of words—she asked me brightly, "What's the plan now?" Which forced my cluttered mind to admit, if only to myself, that I *did* have one.

How the Animals' Radar Marked My Reentry

I drove far enough down Maxing Strasse to park opposite Maxing Park.

"Is this the zoo?" said Gallen.

"No," I said. "It's up a block or two, off the Platz."

"Then why are we parking so far away?" she said.

"Oh, it's a pleasant walk," I told her. And while she was fussing with her new hair in the side-view mirror, and pressing against her head to try to make her ears lie flat, I unloaded our pack and sleeping bag and tied everything all together in a gross lump, with our helmets strapped on top. Then I crept off in Maxing Park's deep hedges and stashed the whole mess out of sight.

"Why are you unpacking?" Gallen asked.

"Well, we don't want to be robbed," I said.

"But we won't be gone long, will we? Graff?"

"Everyone's out to rob you, these days," I said, and I didn't let her see me tuck the notebook under my shirt and jacket.

It's just common sense. If there's an available instruction manual for a job you're doing, you should certainly bring it with you.

"Oh, it's lovely here," said Gallen.

We passed the Tiroler Garten, and I said, "There's a mile of moss and ferns in there, and you can take off your shoes."

"But that's just like the country," she said, disappointed. She was much more impressed by the overhead maze of tram wires, when we got to the Platz. "Is that the café you mean?" she said.

Of course, it was, but we were on the zoo side of the Platz, and from there I couldn't distinguish the Balkan waiter among the other white coats round the café.

We were about to cross over when I heard a Big Cat behind us, starting an uproar in the zoo.

"What's that?" said Gallen.

"A lion," I said. "Or a tiger, a leopard, a puma or cougar—a jaguar, cheetah or panther."

"God," said Gallen. "Why don't you just say *cat*? A large cat."

But I was suddenly too impatient to bother with the frotting Balkan waiter. Knowing what a sly one he was, I also thought he might make me tip my hand. So I said, "There's a better place inside the zoo. It's a *Biergarten*, and much better than this café."

Then maybe I turned her around too fast, and set off at too quick a clip, because Gallen said, "Graff? Are you all right now, really? Do you think you should come back here?"

I just dragged her on; I couldn't look at her. I think I would have seen her with all her guards down, and I was sure there'd be a better time to break my plan to her.

"Well, yes," I said. "The Hietzinger Zoo."

Still gated by stone. Admission still granted by the man with the gambler's green eyeshade. Over whose stall the giraffe's head loomed.

"Oh, Graff!" said Gallen. "Oh, look at him! He's beautiful!"

"Well, look at his chin," I said. "It's all scraped up from the fence."

"Oh, look how he *moves!*" said Gallen, not even noticing that the poor giraffe's chin was damaged on account of his captivity. "Oh, what's in *here?*" she said, and darted off for the walrus's pool.

What really *is* here? I thought. She was much too gay; I couldn't watch her tottering so happy on the edge of that belching giant's slimy tub.

"Does he talk?" said Gallen, and flashed her new, sharp face back to me. "Do you talk?" she asked the walrus. *"Grrumph!"* she said. And the walrus, an old hand at doing favors for fish, rolled his great bulging head and belched for her.

"BROP!" said the walrus.

"He talked!" Gallen cried.

And said more than I have to say, I thought.

I felt the notebook go clammy against my stomach; when I moved, it scraped me. The pages of zoo watches pressed against me. It was as if I'd eaten a whole magazine; and the paper, in shreds, was wadded in my belly.

"Oh!" said Gallen—a general statement, while looking around for what came next.

Hannes Graff, I thought, please do get rid of your stomach disorder. This zoo is a place to enjoy. Nothing more.

Not ten feet away from me was an iron litter basket. I rapped my belly with my knuckles. I took a light step, my first. Then something happened with the giraffe.

He began to canter; he loped along, his great neck arching his head over the top of the storm fence like a live antenna, a kind of radar.

My God, he's recognized me, I thought.

"What's happening?" said Gallen.

The giraffe clattered excitedly. The walrus raised his head up above the rim of the pool; for just a second, he held his mass erect and goggled at me. I heard nearby skitters from pens and cages throughout the zoo. My presence, and my step toward the litter basket, was passed along the animals' grapevine. From half a zoo away, I heard the bar-slamming, roaring Asiatic Black Bear.

"What's happening?" Gallen said again.

"Something must have startled one of them," I answered, defeated.

"BROP!" said the walrus, rising again.

BROP yourself, I thought.

"BROP!" he repeated, his throbbing neck straining to keep himself up —and in sight of me. While the great cantering giraffe zoomed his neck in on me.

"Where's the *Biergarten?*" said Gallen, so frotting eager.

And down by the *Biergarten* that my Gallen wanted to see, the terrible Asiatic Black Bear deafened the zoo.

"God, what's *that?*" said Gallen.

"BROP!" said the endlessly belching walrus. "That's our terrifying leader. That's who that is."

The giraffe now transfixed me with his neck. "How could you?" his radar asked. "How could you have even considered it?"

"BROP!" said the tiresome walrus. "Weren't you forgetting O. SCHRUTT?"

Gallen tugged my arm. "Come *on,* Graff," she said.

And as I stumbled, half-blind, toward the *Biergarten,* I saw again my loon of a soccer mate on my old high-school team. Down the path was the ball, and ahead of it, coming full tilt, the Famous Asiatic Black Bear, who wouldn't allow O. Schrutt to be forgotten, appeared to have a step or two on me; he was going to get to the ball first.

Past the Monkey Complex then; my eyes were blurred by the frotting bear's speed. I began, low down in my throat: *"Aaii, aaii,"* I cried softly, *"Aaaiii!"* I screamed.

"Graff!" said Gallen. "What's the matter with you?"

"Aaaiii! Aaaiii!" wailed a monkey or two, old hands at mimicry.

And Gallen laughed, with all her guards clearly down, even more vulnerable than I'd imagined—to my inevitable surprise.

"I didn't know, Graff," she said, taking my arm, "that you knew how to talk to monkeys."

But I thought: It's clearly a matter of them knowing how to talk to me. And make me one of them.

How, Clearing the Ditch,
I Fell in the Gorge

The Rare Spectacled Bears sat upright and stared, seeing me ensconced in
the *Biergarten* with a new partner. Gallen shone a rich wine-brown, her new
neck pale and perhaps prickly in the sun bearing straight down on her. She
sat outside the fringe of our Cinzano umbrella; she pushed herself back from
our table—the better to view me at a distance, with awe.

"You mean, you've been thinking you'd do it all along?" she said. "Then
you *tricked* me into coming here with you."

"No, not exactly," I said. "Not at all, really. I don't know when I really
knew I was going to go through with it."

"You mean, Graff," she said, "you're going to creep around in here all
night? You're going to let them out? And it was *you* who told me it was
a crazy idea! You *said* so, you *did,* Graff. You agreed he must have been
crazy to even think of such a thing."

"No, not exactly," I said, with the frotting notebook rising up under my
shirt and against my belly, like a gorged feast I couldn't possibly keep down.
"Not at all, really," I said. "I mean, yes, I think it's a crazy idea—I think
he lost his sense over it, sure. But I mean, I think there's a proper way to
go about it. And basically, I think, it's a sound enough idea."

"Graff, you're crazy too," she said.

"No, not exactly," I insisted. "Not at all, really. I just think there's a
reasonable way to go about it. I think his error was to even imagine that
he could get them *all* out. No, this is the point, you see: *reasonable selection*
of animals, Gallen. Naturally, I agree, you'd have to be mad to let them
all loose. That would be unmanageable, I agree."

"Graff," she said. "Graff, you're even *talking* like him. You are, really.
More and more. I've noticed. You sound just like he did."

"Well, I haven't noticed any such thing," I said. "And so what if I do?
I mean, he went too far—I'd be the first to admit. But there's a proper
perspective to put this in, I think. What I mean, Gallen, is let's put it in
a new light. It *could* be kind of fun, if it's done with some taste."

"Oh, *fun,* yes," said Gallen. "Oh, with *taste,* sure. All these lovely
animals out biting people and each other. That's fun, sure. And that really
has taste, Graff, I have to admit."

"*Reasonable selection,* Gallen," I insisted; I wasn't going to let her bait
me into a fight.

"Oh, you're out of your head, Graff," she said. "You must be." And she stood up. "I'm not staying in here for one minute more," she said.

But I said, "Oh, fine. Just where will you go?"

"Oh, Graff," said Gallen. "We're fighting already." And she held her ears —remembering, no doubt, that I was the cause of them being so exposed. I went round the table and squatted down next to her; she crouched, sniffling in her hand.

"Gallen," I said. "Just think of it, please—just for a minute."

"I wanted to go *shopping* with you, or *something,*" she said. "I've never been."

"Gallen," I said. "Just a *few* animals, really. Just a few of the gentle types. And just a little scare for old O. Schrutt." But she shook her head.

"You're not even *thinking* of me," she said. "You just *took* me!" she whispered, fierce and dramatic. "You have *had* me! I was just taken along," she accused, with ridiculous flourishing of her pointed elbows.

"Oh, frot," I said.

"You're crazy and mean," she said.

"All right," I said. "Frot me, I am." And then I whispered these fierce dramatics of my own: "Siggy's dead, Gallen, and I never took him seriously —we never even got to talk about anything at all." But that didn't sound like what I meant, really, so I said, "I hardly got to know him. I mean, really, I didn't know him at all." But that led to nothing logical either, so I said, "it all started out very light and funny—just easy, going nowhere in particular. We were never very intimate, really—or serious. We'd only gotten started." And I saw no conclusions leaping at me out of that, either. So I stopped.

"How could *anyone* take Siggy seriously?" she said.

"I *liked* him, you bitch." I stopped. "It was his idea and it's crazy, maybe. And maybe, so am I."

But she took my hand, then, and sneaked it under the soccer shirt to her hot, hard tummy; she sat back down in her chair, holding my hand to her. "Oh no, you're not crazy, really," she said. "I don't think you are, Graff. I'm sorry. But I'm not a bitch, either, am I?"

"No," I said. "You're not. And *I'm* sorry." She held my hand against her a long while, as if she were telling my fortune on her tummy.

Anything's possible.

"But what will we do afterwards?" she asked.

"I just want to get this over with," I said.

"And then what?" said Gallen.

"What you want," I said, and I really hoped so. "We'll go to Italy. Have you seen the sea?"

"No, never," she said. "Really, though—what I want to?"

"Whatever you want," I said. "I just want done with this business here."

And she sat so frotting trusting in her chair, my hand snug in her lap.

The Rare Spectacled Bears relaxed too. They slumped in their fashion, against the bars and each other, as if they'd been not so much interested in that outcome as in any, even over-simple settlement of our squabble.

Oh, don't fight among each other, their sighs implied. Never fight among each other. We know. In close quarters, it's not wise. You'll find there's no one else. Passively, they hugged each other.

But I thought: This is strange. This isn't quite right. It's the wrong mood for it. I want to restore this idea to its proper larklike light. But I saw too many alternatives to be fair to either Siggy or Gallen.

The *attitude* for zoo-busting wasn't right yet. It was just something I was getting over with—I'd even said so—and Siggy wouldn't approve of the unhappy tone in that: such a piddling, compromising gesture.

The Big Cats roared. But I thought: No, I'm sorry, Big Cats, but I'm not here for you. Just for a harmless, trivial few. Thus the notebook warns:

Most decisions are anticlimatic.

So, oddly, after all, it hardly seemed worthwhile, at least as I had rear-ranged it—the reasonable selections of Hannes Graff. That only seemed of any consequence when I looked across the table at my Gallen. Who de-served, at least, a *little* reason.

Passively sad but accepting anything, the Rare Spectacled Bears repeated their sighs: At the very least, we must get along with each other.

But there was one to refute them. The Famous Asiatic Black Bear wasn't familiar with compromise.

I thought—with considerable surprise: Why, they're all *different*—these animals! Just like people, whose sad history shows they're all impossibly different too. And not equal, either. Not even born that way.

About that, the notebook says:

How incomplete. How funny. How simple. And also, a great pity.

I stood up from the table; on the facing of the service counter, the *Biergarten* staff had hung an old funhouse mirror, salvaged somewhere; if you were weary of animals, you could look up skirts at unidentified bits of bloomer and thigh. Remarkably, I caught myself in it—or caught part of myself, weirdly segmented, and parts of other people and things. Legs of unassociated chairs, and unmatching shoes. In the strange mirror, I was generally unfitted; my parts didn't go together, at all.

While the sweaty notebook on my belly made such a unit—a solid bulk of perfect lunacy.

"Oh, look," I said to Gallen, or to anyone. "How nothing goes together."

And she stood in the mirror with me, her parts no more together than mine, but easier to pick out—from chairs and more people-pieces. Because all her parts were simply beautiful; a mirror fragment of broad, thin mouth and long, downy throat; crease of blousy soccer shirt between one breast and a half. She laughed. I didn't.

She said, "How do we start?" Whispering, so frotting eager and trusting me, all of a sudden. "Do we let them out in the dark? What do we do about the guard?" And when I kept looking for my scattered self in the mirror, she said, with mock stealth, "No good attracting attention like that, Graff. Shouldn't we slip off somewhere and go over the plan?"

I watched the mirror-section of her mouth, talking all by itself. I didn't even know if she was baiting me, or if she was serious. I squinted. Somewhere in the frotting mirror, I had lost my head and couldn't find it.

Following Directions

It was easy. We poked about till late afternoon, and scouted out the hedge-row by the long pen for Miscellaneous Range Animals; the hedge was every bit as snug as Siggy said it was. Shortly before we ducked behind it, and listened to the cage-cleaners and sweepers calling for stragglers, I showed Gallen the Small Mammal House—and noted, for myself, the closed door of the room that had to be the watchman's lair. In fact, we had time to look at everything—before we went in hiding behind the hedgerow.

I was only disappointed that the oryx had been thinking in his shed—travel plans, perhaps—and Gallen hadn't seen him and his fierce balloons.

But the skulking part was easier than easy, and we got to feel quite cheery about it—lying close against the fence line, peering through the hexagonal holes at the shuffling Assorted Antelopes and their miscellaneous kin. I'll admit, though, I didn't totally relax until all the daylight had left us.

By eight-thirty or so it was dark, and the animals were dropping off—breathing more even and making those comfortable, unconscious noises. A paw flapped in a water dish, and someone briefly complained. The zoo dozed.

But I knew the guard was due for another round at a quarter to nine, and I wanted us to do it just as Siggy had—and be down on the ponds for the Various Aquatic Birds, when the guard started out.

It was very easy getting there too. I dipped my fingers over the pool curb; sleeping ducks floated by, heads tucked, webbed feet dragging. Occasionally, a foot would paddle in sleep. Unaware, the duck would turn like a rowboat pulled by one oar, and bump the pool curb; wake and squabble with the cement; churn off, doze, paddle and sleep again. Oh, the rhythms of that first-shift watch were lovely.

Gallen's heartbeat was no more than a flutter on my palm, as if some elf inside her were blowing softly on the pale skin under her breast.

"It's so quiet," said Gallen. "When does Schupp come?"

"*Schrutt,*" I said, and woke a duck. He croaked like a frog.

"Well, when does he get here?" said Gallen.

"Not for a while," I said, and watched the casual first-shift guard stretching and yawning in the good, white light coming out the Small Mammal House door.

"This is the good guard?" said Gallen.

"Yes," I said, and immediately had kindly feelings toward him—seeing him go off through the zoo, softly clucking his tongue to special friends. The boxing Australian, and his cherished zebra horde.

"This is the one who leaves the red off?" said Gallen.

"Infrared," I said. "Yes, this one's all right."

And when he was being considerate enough not to wake anyone in the House of Pachyderms, we went back to our hedgerow and snuggled along the fence line, legs scissoring—with each other's elbows for pillows on the roots.

"Now," said Gallen, "this guard has another watch at eleven?"

"Quarter to eleven," I said.

"All *right,*" she said, and lightly bit my cheek. "Eleven or quarter to. What's the difference?"

"*De*tail," I said. "*De*tail is the difference." Knowing myself that details are, of course, essential to any good plan. And, of course, knowing the need for a plan.

I was working on one; like every good plan, I was taking first things first, and first was O. Schrutt—the nabbing and stashing thereof. After which, I do confess, my thinking was still a little too general. But under the hedge I was calm again, and Gallen seemed so much in this anticlimax with me that I at least had an easier conscience toward her.

In fact, after the guard's round at a quarter to eleven, with the zoo sleeping heavily around us, I initiated suggestive nuzzles in Gallen's rich, thick hair—patted her behind, and attacked with suchlike ploys—because I thought our hedgerow was just too snug to abuse, or not use at all.

But she turned away from me and pointed through the hexagonal holes in the fence, indicating the sleeping, overlapping mound of Miscellaneous Range Animals huddled in the center of the pen. "Not with *them* there, Graff," she said. And I thought: Really, this animal business has been carried far enough.

I even felt foolish, but I got over it; Gallen was all of a sudden climbing on me with nervous ploys of her own, and I thought she'd changed her mind. But she said, too sweetly, "Graff, don't you see how nice it is in here? What do you want to do anything for?" She performed disgusting nibbles on my chin, but I wasn't to be so easily fooled.

I admit I was a bit defensive; I drew back in the hedges. She whispered after me, "Graff?" But I kept backing down the fence line from her, on all fours, getting all bushed over in the hedge. So she couldn't see me, and she said, too loudly, "Graff!"

There was a violent clubbing sort of sound from the Monkey Complex, and some heavy, hooved animal clattered back and forth. One or two Big Cats cleared their throats, and Gallen said, "All right, Graff. Come on, it was just an idea."

"Been your idea all along, hasn't it?" I said, peering from deep in the hedge. "You just stayed with me to try to talk me out of it."

"Oh, Graff!" she said, and what was left of the range herd picked themselves up and cantered down to the opposite fence line.

"Shut up, Gallen!" I whispered, hoarse.

"Oh, Graff," she whispered back, and I could hear her take her little catch breath, setting up a good sob. "Graff," she said, "I just don't know what you *want* to do, even. Really, I can't imagine why."

Really, I can't either, I thought. It's hard to make any decisions when you're as reasonable as I am. But for decision-making, little helpful things, like swamps, come when you least expect them.

I was suddenly aware that the zoo was awake—and not, I thought, from Gallen's slight blurting. I mean, it was *really* awake. All around us, creatures were balancing in frozen crouches, three-legged stances, anxious suspension from the squeaking trapezes in the Monkey Complex. I checked my watch and realized I'd been too casual for the occasion. It was after midnight. I hadn't heard the bell for the changing of the guard, but the first-shift watchman was gone. The zoo was poised. I listened to the footfall on the patch along our hedgerow. I saw his combat boots, with pants tucked in. And the truncheon in the sheath that's stitched so neatly in the left boot.

There wasn't time to warn Gallen, but I could see her silhouette up tight against the fence line, hands over her ears; I could see the profile of her open lips. Thanks be, she saw him too.

And when he'd passed by us, spinning his light once or twice and jolting himself off balance so his keyring jangled under his armpit, I dared a headlong look out in the path, through a root gap, and saw him strutting robotlike—his head and epaulettes above the horizon line the hedgerow made against the night. He turned a military corner on the path; I waited, and heard his keyring ringing in the empty *Biergarten.*

"Graff?" said Gallen, in her accomplice voice again. "Was that Schupp?"

"His name is *Schrutt,*" I said, and thought: So that sudden phantom was old O. Schrutt.

Whose reception was instantly flung through the zoo, in echos bouncing off the ponds; the Famous Asiatic Black Bear's nightly rage. Gallen scurried down the hedgerow to me, and I held her through this second phase of zoo-watching, on this week-old anniversary of poor Siggy's unreasonable conclusions; in the Hietzinger Playhouse with everyone playing his own separate role, of not living very well with each other; where I was decision-making—there were just these three choices: the anticlimax, no climax at all, or the raging, unreasonable but definite climax demanded by the Famous Asiatic Black Bear.

First Things First

When O. Schrutt finished his first round, he went back to the Small Mammal House and turned on the infrared.

"Graff," said Gallen. "Please let's get out of here." And I held her behind the hedge. Coming through the root gaps, far down the fence line, there was a purple light reflected on the wire hexagons.

When the first muffled complaints from the Small Mammal House came to us, Gallen said, "Please, Graff. Let's just get the police." And for a moment I thought: Why not? How easy that would be.

But I said, "How would we explain our being here?"

"They'd understand, Graff," she said. And although I'm not absolutely sure they wouldn't have, I didn't consider it further. My own variations on the theme were anticlimactic enough.

And besides, I remembered, if one was to even come close to Siggy's absolute faith, the idea for the zoo bust existed before O. Schrutt.

O. Schrutt was simply an added feature. Who happens to come first in any overall plan.

"O. Schrutt comes first," I said to Gallen, and going over the plan once more, I sent her on her way to the Monkey Complex while I passed by the complex myself, and took a stand behind the children's drinking fountain.

The gelada baboon didn't see me. Unlike Siggy's evening, on this occasion the baboon was not on guard for anything. So when I waved back to the corner of the complex, Gallen began her business in the brush just outside the trapeze terrace. I listened to her, shaking the bushes and making low, girlish grunts of an inappropriately erotic nature. Perhaps, though, not inappropriate for the old gelada male and his fiery red chest, which suddenly flashed between the dark terrace bars—catching a bit of the blood-lit reflections coming out the Small Mammal House door.

Then I couldn't see the old primate; I could hear him huffing and wrenching down on the trapezes, one by one, which he used to swing himself from one long end of the terrace to the other. Where Gallen must have had some fright, thinking he'd sail right through the bars and get her.

The trapezes tangled and clanged on the wall. The gelada baboon wailed his frustration; he ranted, doglike and crowlike—all sounds of all animals were compressed and made one in this frotting baboon.

And, of course, the zoo joined in. And Gallen slipped out of those bushes; I saw her—just a bit of her nice leg flicking out in the doorway path of blood-purple light from O. Schrutt's research center.

Then there was old O. himself, his scar stretched over his face like a worn-thin spot on a balloon. And when he went bleating past me, flashlight aimed at the gelada baboon's corner, I ducked behind him and ran the other way, into the Small Mammal House. And in lurking fashion, hid myself behind the door of his office room.

Around me, I surveyed: the gaffing-hook thing, the electric prod, the zoo ledger open on the desk.

The binturong was still rarely diseased; the ocelot was still expecting; the giant forest hog still suffered from his ingrown tusk. But there was nothing entered concerning the bandicoot who had been dying—who was either dead or better.

Most likely dead, I thought—as I heard O. Schrutt cursing the gelada baboon, his voice on a pitch with the shriller monkeys, his key loop ringing the terrace bars like a gong.

I took up the electric prod and waited for Schrutt's surly footfall coming down the aisles of the maze.

When O. Schrutt came in his room, I stepped up behind him and snatched his revolver out of the handy open holster, and as he turned round to me, grabbing for the truncheon in his boot, I zapped him with the prod across the bridge of his nose. He fell back, blind for a moment. He threw his flashlight at me; it hit my chest. But before he could go for the truncheon again, I zonked his wet lips with the neat, electric prod. That seemed to buzz him properly; he spun around and tripped himself; he was down, sitting on the floor, his arms wrapped round his head, making a spitting sound—as if he were trying to get that electric fuzz off his gums.

"O. Schrutt," I said. "If you open your eyes again, I'll clean out your sockets with this electricity. And shoot off your elbows with your own gun." And I clicked the safety on and off, just so he'd remember that I really had it.

"Who?" he said, his voice furry.

"O. Schrutt," I said, in a deeper and older voice than my own—an ancient voice, I attempted. "At last I've found you, old O. Schrutt," I droned.

"Who are you?" he said, and went to move his hands off his eyes. I just skittered the prod over his fingertips. He howled; then he held his breath, and I held mine. The room was tomb-still; down the maze, even the small mammals were hushed.

"It's been a long time, O. Schrutt," I said, in my creaky voice.

"Who?" he said, in a little huff. "Zeiker?" he said, and pressed his eyes so hard that his blotchy knuckles whitened.

I laughed a low, gritty laugh.

"No. Beinberg?" he said, and I held my breath for him. "Who are you?" he screamed.

"Your just reward," I said, with pomp. "Your final justice."

"*Final?*" said old O. Schrutt.

"Stand up," I said, and he did. I snatched the truncheon out of his boot and lifted his chin up with it. "Eyes closed, Schrutt," I said. "I'll guide you with this beating stick, and see you don't move odd or I'll bash you. In the old fashion," I added, not knowing what that might be but hoping it might ring bells for him—or have him imagining an old fashion of his own.

"Zeiker!" he said. "It *is* Zeiker, isn't it?" but I just poked him through the door and out in the maze. "Is it Zeiker?" he screamed, and I bopped him lightly on his head.

"Quiet, please," I said, tapping his ear with the truncheon.

"Zeiker, it's been too many years for this," he said. I said nothing; I just led him through the aisles, looking for a cage.

Empty was the biggest glasshouse of all, the home of the giant anteaters —missing, off on a Schrutt-sent mission of terror. I found the chute behind the cage rows, opened it and prodded old O. Schrutt inside.

"What are you doing?" he said, feeling his hands along the chute. "Some of these animals are vicious."

But I just poked him along until the label on the chute door said: GIANT ANTEATER, PAIR OF. Then there was the problem of cramming Schrutt down into the pitlike cage, where he groveled in the sawdust, covering his eyes and throat. And when nothing attacked him straightaway, he sat up for me so I could lash him all together in a lump—in his thick, multi-buckled ammunition belt, I crossed his arms and feet on his rump, and trussed him up, face-down in the sawdust.

"Keep those eyes shut, Schrutt," I said.

"I'm sorry, Zeiker," he moaned. "Really, that was a terrible time for us all, you know." And when I didn't answer, he said, "Please, Zeiker, is it you?"

He was still asking me when I crept back in the chute and locked the door behind me. He could yell all night in there, and as long as the glass frontis-piece wasn't slid back, no one would hear him. His cries would be as muffled as his mistreated neighbors'.

Out in the aisle, then, I paused to watch him under infrared. He peered at the blank glass; he must have known I stood there, watching him. His scar pulsed double-time, and for that moment I might have pitied him, but across the aisle I noticed a new sadness. The expectant ocelot was wary of her forced company, the frightened wombat, *Vombatus hirsutus*—a small bearlike creature with a rodent's sort of nose, or a huge hamster, looking like a toothy bear's runt cub.

First things first, again, I thought. And ran into the doorway aisle of the Small Mammal House.

"Gallen!" I cried, and the zoo responded—thumps and outcries bolder than my own. "All clear!" I shouted, and the monkeys mimicked. I could almost sense the Big Cats purring.

And when I said. "The ocelot is a waiting mother," Gallen was helpful and unwary about the delicate business of separating O. Schrutt's luckless charges. She even paused at O. Schrutt's cage and stared at him awhile— her eyes the closest they could come to hating, a sort of horror-struck glare through the one-way glass. While old O. flopped nervously about in the sawdust, anticipating company.

But Gallen got her caution back, once the mother ocelot was bedded by herself and somewhat relaxed in her crib of straw. "Graff?" she said. "Don't you think it's illogical of you to separate these animals now, because they scare or even hurt each other, and then to let them all loose in the same mess, when they're sure to *really* hurt each other?"

"I said I wasn't going to let them *all* go," I told her, and felt a little let down by that reminder to myself.

Perhaps as an added gesture, then—after Gallen had left the Small Mammal House to scout down the paths for me, to see if our disturbance had brought anybody snooping around—I thought I shouldn't leave old O. to himself in the cage. And having no place to put the giant anteaters, anyway —having removed them from the cages of ratel and civet, respectively—I allowed O. Schrutt to *know,* before the chute door was opened, just who was returning home.

The giant anteater measures seven feet from nose to tip of tail; it's sort of two-fifths tail and two-fifths nose, and one-fifth hair. With no body to speak of.

And O. Schrutt surely knew them by their peculiar grunts—and how they sent their long noses inquiring into the cage, before they allowed me to budge them with a shove down into their rightful home. Which was not trespassed in by old O. Schrutt, whom the anteaters regarded distastefully from the other side of the cage. And seeing, I suppose, that Schrutt was without gaff or prod, and had himself trussed up in a lump, they were not afraid of him. In fact, they clawed up a little sawdust and grunted at him; they began to circle him—although the anteater is no meat hunter at all and wouldn't be interested in eating people, preferring bugs—while old O. said, "No! I didn't *mean* to come in here. I'll leave you alone. Please don't you feel threatened by me, oh no, sir!" And then whispered, a different pitch, "Here now, isn't this cozy, sort of? Wouldn't you say so? Oh, I would." But they shuffled around and around him—now and then a long tongue flying out and testing his cheek, tasting how sacred he was.

When I left, he might have been saying, "Here now, did you have a nice visit with ratel and civet? All for fun, I hope you know—and exercise, which you need. And there's no harm done, now, is there?" But I assured myself that the anteaters wouldn't eat him, or even pound him very severely with their leaden tails; or claw through him, the way they can claw through trunks of trees, or at least thigh-thick roots.

I *could* have left him with the Chinese fishing cat, I thought. And if you're not a good O. Schrutt, I will.

Then I walked out of the Small Mammal House, going over again in my mind just what few animals I would select as safe. But I saw Gallen looking rather frightened outside the door, and when I entered the real night again, I heard the din the zoo was making. The Big Cats sputtering like barges on the Danube, the monkeys reeling, thumping loud against the bars, the birds all calling their praise of me; and over it all, in a low-voiced monotone, the Famous Asiatic Black Bear.

All of them greeted me as I stepped out in the zoo I now had total charge of. *All* of them. Every different, frotting one of them—awaiting Hannes Graff's decision.

My Reunion with the Real and Unreasonable World

"Graff," Gallen said, "someone's sure to hear all this." And I wondered if perhaps there were loud nights in the zoo, anyway; if the conditioned suburb folk of Hietzing wouldn't just roll over and mildly complain: the animals are having a restless night. But I couldn't convince myself that there ever was a clamor like this. They were stomping, shaking the bars and bellowing delirious. And my frotting fellow-primates were the worst.

I'd left the infrared on because I didn't want anyone sleeping now; they had to be ready; and I wanted O. Schrutt kept in the dark, you might say. So I stayed a moment in the pathway of purple light from the Small Mammal House and I tried to read the key labels off the keyring. Finding the Monkey Complex key, I skirted the outside terrace, where shriveled and savage faces poked through the bars, ushering me inside with wails. I didn't dare an overhead light, thinking some passer-by outside the zoo might notice something different and report. I went from cage to cage with O.

Schrutt's flashlight, glimpsing the rows and rows of black, leathery hands clutching the bars. I was being careful; I read the names of animals.

Monkeys: howler, lion-tailed, proboscis, rhesus, spider, squirrel and woolly—all small ones, so I let them out.

Then the snarling baboons: smiling, snowy-haired hamadryases, and the dog-faced geladas; my red-chested male, now forgetting his grievances. And the chacma baboons, the biggest; and perhaps I shouldn't have let out that old hundred-twenty-pound male.

Then gibbons, a whole horde. And chimpanzees, all six—one potbellied, who shoved the others and bit a spider monkey's tail. But I passed over, ashamed, the male, two-hundred-pound orangutan, and the quarter-ton lowland gorilla from the Gulf of Guinea. They couldn't believe it; they let me get almost to the door before they cried out, enraged and very envious. The orang-utan tore his swinging tire off the rope and crammed it through the bars, squishing it up as thin as a bicycle tube. The lowland gorilla folded his tin water dish, as neatly as an envelope.

And the primates I released were not quiet, the frotting ingrates. I could hear my primates smashing ashtrays off the tables in the *Biergarten*.

"Graff," said Gallen, "you've got to calm them down or get us out."

"These antelope types are safe enough," I said, "and they might distract the monkeys." So I bolted for the pens—stretching from the Monkey Complex to the Australian's Little Colony—turning loose the aoudad, the anoa and the addax; letting go the gerenuk, the gemsbok and the gaur. I should have thought twice about the frotting gaur—tallest of wild oxen of the world—but I just read the name and didn't see him lurking in the dark. This bull stood six-foot-four at the shoulders, and I *thought* the gaur was a sort of diminutive goat. When he thundered out the fence gate past me, Gallen screamed, "What's that, Graff?" And it tore by her, smashing down hedges, frightened blind. "What was it, Graff?" said Gallen, pinned down alongside the waiting zebra. "You promised, Graff!" she cried.

"My mistake!" I cried. "You let out those zebras now!" While I promptly loosed the sleek impala and the knobby Siberian ibex; all the Australians, and selected others.

But the zoo wasn't getting any quieter. The elephants blatted their brassy notes—resounding in the ponds of squabbling birds.

What harm would an elephant do? I thought. Just one, of course. And I could pick a docile one, certainly.

So I was off, scattering a conspiracy of gibbons cowering by the house for Big Loud Cats, and by the mysteriously silent hippohouse, where the hippo, I could only guess, was underwater and oblivious to this activity. Just as well, for sure, I thought—with his great plant-reeking mouth.

Inside the House of Pachyderms, the elephants were swaying, lifting their leg chains and thudding their trunks against each other's sides. I selected an old, large and chewed-eared African, and set my key in his shackles. He was so nice; I had to lead him by his trunk, out the Pachyderm House door, through which he barely fitted and where his presence scattered those conniving gibbons. But apparently, the elephant was a little deaf and had appeared so docile inside because he hadn't *heard* the rumpus. Because, outside, he jerked his trunk out of my hand and moved off at a steady, sideways trot, gathering speed, crushing shrubs and flattening down the iron rails along the paths.

I thought: Please don't let Gallen see him, God. And heard more ashtrays crash in whatever game the scheming monkeys played at the *Biergarten.*

Then I passed the tall, screened ruins where the giant birds of prey were perched, and thought: Not you. You'll eat the smaller monkeys. And for a second, thought: Which would at least keep them quiet.

But I went on back to the Small Mammal House, to collect my thoughts and see how old O. was doing with the anteaters. I met Gallen on the steps; she crouched in the purple light.

"I saw an elephant, Graff," she said. "I want to leave right now."

"Just one elephant," I said, dashing inside to spy O. Schrutt rumpled in a corner, his eyes watering with sawdust. The giant anteaters sat happily in the center of the glasshouse, spiraling their tongues around their long snouts, calmly watching over old O.

This will never do, I thought—O. Schrutt must be kept on his toes. And I crawled back in the chute again, enticing and prodding the anteaters out of there—telling Schrutt, before I opened the chute door, that if I saw his eyes looking at me, I'd bring in the Chinese fishing cat.

Of course, I didn't. I exchanged the anteaters for the ratel—a surly, snarling badgerlike oval of hair and claws, with a long memory concerning Schrutt, I was sure. But the ratel was too small, I knew, to ever initiate a full-scale assault on old O.—even in the lumped and trussed condition.

I just popped open the chute door and called down to Schrutt, "Here's little ratel!" And nudged the fat snarler inside. I watched them from the glass front; they respected each other from opposite corners, before the ratel grasped the situation Schrutt was in and boldly began a strutting show of himself, across the center of the cage.

But when I began lifting glass fronts elsewhere in the maze—releasing small and reasonable animals—I had to contend with Gallen again.

"You're not going to do a thing to that mother ocelot," she said.

"Of course I won't," I said, displaying my common sense for her to see —turning loose the casual sloth and the dour wombat, but passing by the lean, low, liver-colored jaguarundi. And letting go the zippy coati-mundi.

Of course, the anteaters were a nuisance—just blocking traffic in the aisle where they sat, watching the ratel and old O. Schrutt.

Gallen said, "Please, Graff. Can't we leave now?"

And I said. "We've got to muster them together, at one gate or another." Then I turned the mongoose loose, of which Gallen disapproved, and freed the reluctant slow loris and the ring-tailed lemur, feeling more reasonable every minute.

Just to show you how reasonable I was, I did not free the poor binturong —the bearcat of Borneo—not wanting other animals to catch his rare disease.

And I gave a silent bow to the empty glasshouse of the bandi-coot, already escaped this world.

But when I shook off nagging Gallen and emerged on the steps outside again, I was greeted by those animals I hadn't selected. And they weren't cheering me now. They were tyrannical; they raged their envy. Forever present gibbons were sitting at the step bottom, shrugging shoulders and spitting. When I reached the path, they chattered accusations. They threw stones at me; I threw some back. I swung at one gibbon with the keyring, and he danced to the path rail and flung himself into the brush. Then I was assaulted with weed clods, sticks and general earth.

"You're free to go!" I screamed. "Why don't you? Don't ask for too much!" And responding to my voice was what sounded like the utter demolishment of the *Biergarten.* I pelted down there, through a crunchy dust of littered ashtrays. This was a primate sort of destruction, for sure; a vandalism of a shocking, human type. They had shattered the one-time funhouse mirror; chunks of it lay all over the *Biergarten* terrace. I kept looking down at my puzzlework reflection, looming over myself.

"Just one more and that does me," I said. And moved to the reeking cage of the Rare Spectacled Bears, who were hiding behind their drinking-and-dunking pool when I opened their cage. I had to shout at them to make them come out. They came shoulder to shoulder across the floor, heads lowered like whipped dogs. They turned circles through the destroyed *Biergarten,* running too close together and butting themselves into umbrellas and hissing monkeys.

This is enough, I thought. Enough, for sure. And I was winding through the other, roaring bear cages when Gallen screamed. Schrutt's out! I thought. But when I squinted through cage corners and down the dark paths toward the Small Mammal House, I saw a man-shaped figure, loping more or less on all fours, turn the corner by the Monkey Complex— followed by another just like him, though not as thick in the chest. The orang-utan and the lowland gorilla, in cahoots.

I thought: But how the frot did *they* ever get out? And saw then— cantering sideways behind them—the house-sized blur of the African elephant, carrying a cage wall in his trunk; a great rectangle of bars bent every which way.

When he flung the cage wall down on the path, it rang off the cement —as if the bell in St. Stephen's had broken loose and dropped straight down the steeple, striking the organ pipes behind the center altar.

Then all running forms stood still: I stood trying to hold my breath. The zoo was church-still; a new hope brings silence. And I started up slowly, past the polar bears and brown bears and American grizzly; I turned up the path by the Famous Asiatic Black Bear, who stood like an assassin in his cage. But I was forced to leap over the Oriental's safety rope and crash against his wrist-thick bars—when the elephant blurred up in front of me on the path and charged on by me after I'd crumpled against the terrible bear's cage door; the elephant tore through the *Biergarten,* squashing umbrellas and grinding up fallen mirror-bits under his mammoth feet. And I was almost up and away again, when the Famous Asiatic Black Bear seized me round the chest and hugged me back against his bars. I took a breath and held it; I was back-to him and could feel his foul breath stir my hair. I thought, calmly: When he realizes he can't fit his great head through the bars to eat me, then he'll rake up my belly with his claws and gobble me innards-first. But instead, he turned me to face him; his head seemed buffalo-sized. But when I dared to look him in the eye, I saw that he eyed the keyring looped over my shoulder.

"Oh no!" I told him. He hugged me; I was chest to chest with him, the bars grooving my ribs. I felt the claws plucking at my spine. "Squash me, then," I grunted at him. "Just get your eyes off that keyring, because I'm not ever letting *you* out." He roared all over my face; he bellowed up my nostrils, so loud I almost choked. "Never!" I squeaked. "You have to draw the line somewhere!"

But then Gallen screamed again. I thought: That elephant has loosed O. Schrutt! Or: That virile orang-utan has got my Gallen—surely, the best he's ever had.

I moved my hand for the keyring; the Asiatic Black Bear let my spine move out a notch. I fumbled, reading in the dark for the key I thought would probably be labeled: NEVER USE! But it said simply: ASIAN BEAR. Such understatement, but I fitted the key to latch; the bear held me, unbelieving. I felt the door swing into me; the bear and I swung out together on the opening frame of bars. And for a moment, he still squeezed me, not really believing he was free. Then he let me go; we both plopped to all fours.

Now he'll run around this door and eat me whole, I thought. But both of us heard the Big Cats then, a brief upcry noticeably louder than before, as if—at the very least—their general house door had been opened. And then I heard the *terrible* Big Cats, purring close-by. The Big Cats were *prowling,* on the loose. I crept backward from the door. But the Oriental took no notice; oddly, he crouched very still, his nose lifting up now and then—salivating, and quivering the long, coarse hair on his flanks.

The Famous Asiatic Black Bear is *thinking!* I thought. Or plotting.

And I didn't wait a moment more—for him to make up his awful mind. I bolted round his open cage and back to the path, past the ponds, to the Small Mammal House. Where I found my poor Gallen huddled in the doorway aisle of the maze, watching down the blood-bathed path to where a tiger, his stripes tinted crimson and black in the infrared, was squatting over a large and tawny, deep-chested antelope with spiraled horns; with a large brain-shaped mass of intestines spilled over his side. And with a hind hoof bent or drawn up under his thigh, over which sprawled his unmistakable, familiar balloons of volleyball size.

"Oh, Siggy, it's the oryx," I said.

"It's a tiger," said Gallen, colder than the winter river. "And I'm *not* Siggy."

And just as coldly, I said, "You screamed?"

"Oh, you heard?" she said, with a demented brightness to her voice. "Well, I got over whatever it was, without you."

"Where did the apes go?" I asked. But she sat mum and hard-faced, so I didn't press her.

Down the maze, a muffled voice was naming names. I went to see: old O. Schrutt upright against the glass, the ratel almost playful with his odd snarls—boastful in the center of the cage. And old O. was naming names, or asking them.

"Zeiker?" he called. "Beinberg? Muffel? Brandeis? Schmerling? Frieden?" Name by name, O. Schrutt was leaving his mind behind.

So I went back to Gallen, just in time to hear the final thunder: the Famous Asiatic Black Bear's deciding roar. At last, adjusted to the surprise of his freedom, the bear had made up his mind. The zoo pitch of the other creatures hit hysteria, as if this bear were a griffin and what they feared was more his myth than his reality—all of them knowing what he thought for so long about Hinley Gouch, and how that had warped his mind.

"You let that bear out too," said Gallen.

"No!" I said. "I mean, I *had* to. He caught me. He wouldn't let me go. I had to make a deal." But she stared at me as if I were as foreign to her as the fallen oryx, whom she'd never seen when he was so wondrously whole and upright.

"Oh, Graff," she whispered. Her eyes glazed.

I looked out the doorway of the Small Mammal House and saw the Asiatic Black Bear mounting the stairs, four at a time. Gallen was benumbed; she never even flinched when he rushed at us, and by us, echoing through the maze. But he stopped, silent, when he saw O. Schrutt. Who was saying: "Weinstürm? Bottweiler? Schnuller? Steingarten? Frankl? Little Frisch?"

And I thought: Why not Wut? Javotnik? Marter? Watzek-Trummer? Or loose-ended Hannes Graff, too?

Having found what he came for, the Famous Asiatic Black Bear sat down at the glass front, perplexed, and rapped the hopefully foot-thick frontispiece once or twice, with a curious, pecking sort of claw. O. Schrutt stopped reciting. "Who's there?" he said. "I know it's Zeiker!" But the Asiatic Black Bear was not one to further endure O. Schrutt's yelling at him. He reared up and thudded against the glass; backed away; thudded again; then sat down, puzzled.

And O. Schrutt said, "Come on! Who are you? I know you're out there!"
And the Asiatic Black Bear began to roar. A gathering din that gained force
through its own echo in the maze. O. Schrutt flopped backward in the
sawdust, rolling into the ratel, who snapped, but who backed away himself
—at the chute door, the two of them quaking at the close-range roar
familiar to all the inmates of the Hietzinger Zoo.

O. Schrutt screamed, "No! Not *you!* Don't let him in! Not him! Not ever!
No! *Please!* Zeiker? Beinberg? Frankl? Schnuller? Schmerling? Little
Frisch? *Please!*"

And I hustled Gallen out the door—the roaring seemed to shove us out
—into a zoo that was bolting; hearing, no doubt, the rage of the animal no
one dared to challenge. Not Big Cats, and not the elephant, either; nor apes
running somewhere—for the main gate, it seemed. Along with everyone
else. They were organized; the zoo was mustering. The Asiatic Black Bear
was out, and nobody wanted his unreasonable company.

But when Gallen and I turned round the ticket taker's booth and headed
for the main gate, I saw outside the zoo a daze of headlights, parked in rows
—and heard the blurry, human sounds of a crowd in waiting. And saw a
stream of animals, hooved, padded, clawed and dashing, splashing through
the ponds for Various Aquatic Birds, setting the night aflight—all of them
making for the rear gate that opened to the Tiroler Garten. Where there's
moss and ferns, all the sweet way to Maxing Park.

There was a jam at the gate, but the elephant had obliged and left a
passable hole for all but himself. He'd managed to spring one hinge, but the
bottom corner of the gate had held, and the bottom hinge had swung the
whole gate crosswise in the exit.

Gallen and I sneaked by the elephant's trapped and blundering shape,
plunging through little mustering teams of monkeys.

But in the Tiroler Garten there was also a crowd, a predawn army of
more citizens than police—of suburb folk in nightwear, blinking flashlights.
We were not noticed in the mayhem; we jogged alongside housewives,
shriller than monkeys.

It was only when we reached the larger, darker shrubs of Maxing Park
that a sense of outcome loomed clearly in my mind against this chaos.
Through the shrubs, I saw them hiding. Anonymous men with ancient
weapons—with fireplace tridents, grub hoes and gleaming bucksaws; pitch-
forks, sledges and moon-shaped sickles. And *people's* voices, now, were
raised above the Asiatic Black Bear's din—left behind me.

And when I'd dragged Gallen as far as she could go, I knelt over her,
sobbing on a stone park bench, and saw how the hiding men seemed
uniformed and old and starving; an army of diehard meat-eaters, all these
years of nights in the parks round the Hietzinger Zoo. Ever since Zahn
Glanz, or whoever he was, was eaten.

I heard a shot or two; the trees shook with birds and monkeys. Beside us, on the park bench, a comfortably seated gibbon ate a candy-bar wrapper.

I said to Gallen, "Will you promise me to stay here with this gibbon?" Her face was as calm, or numb, as the gobbling primate's.

I dashed for Maxing Strasse, tracing down the curb for the bike, and spotted the bush where our lumpish rucksack was stashed.

It was still dark, but all the houses were lit along the street and headlit cars tore by; cabs unloaded customers carrying *things*—sticks, brooms, mops and shish kebabbers. Men stepped out into the battle sound. A din like they hadn't heard in years.

I lashed the pack on the motorcycle and drove down Maxing Strasse, yelling for Gallen. I didn't know if I could be heard above the clamor—the wailing police-green Volkswagens sounding behind me in Maxing Platz. And over the trees of the Tiroler Garten, their blinking-blue bars of light. Streams of people pouring into Maxing Park, and streams of animals pouring out.

I saw Gallen on the curb, standing as if she were catching a bus she always caught at this hour, in this customary traffic. Mounting numbly behind me, she was slightly bumped by a Siberian ibex, stumbling blindly and goatlike over the curb—a chunk of his hide torn open and flapping down over his shoulder; the gash was sort of hoe-shaped.

And I listened and listened for him—the Famous Asiatic Black Bear— for some final roar of despair or satisfaction. But I could never have heard him above the din the *people* made; not even him.

Gallen sat like a puppet behind me, and I pulled us out in the traffic of Maxing Strasse. The police were now cruising Maxing Park; I saw the bobbing, single headlights and pearl-white fairings of their BMW's—weaving through the shrubs, trying to rout the mob. Inside a fast-closing circle of motorcycle headlights, the great gray boomer was beating up a man, who'd lost his grip on his garden shears; they shone in the grass, pinned under the boomer's hunting claw.

The mob was around us for five suburb blocks of driving. In a doorway on Wattmann Gasse, I saw the snow leopard panting and licking one paw. And in Sarajevo Platz, I saw a team of five successful hunters trying to crouch down out of my passing headlight, thinking I was a police cycle; behind them, they attempted to conceal the dragged, bloodied and unprotesting gaur. Who, when he was upright, was six-foot-four.

The low, sturdy zebra herd came in a noiseless wave across the lawns, weaving through shrubs—shifty, and able to fool the three-some of hunters with a net and two-man saw. The zebras came out over the curb in front of me, their hooves sparking off the cobblestones. Their own clatter startled them; they veered and zigzagged between parked cars, crossing the far sidewalk and bolting down tiny Wolter Gasse, where onrushing headlights turned them back—again across Maxing Strasse—and once more drove them into Maxing Park.

Then Gallen and I were in the Lainz suburbs, in the eerie outlying hospital district. We passed them altogether—the Old People's Home, the Invalids' Home, and City Hospital; the floodlit lawns, and stark, beige stucco. On the balconies, rows of wheelchairs gleamed; on the lawns and in the windows, cigarettes and pipes were glowing. The old and sick and maimed were listening to the clamorous zoo, like people in the country watch the lighting effects in a city being bombed.

And for a moment I idled low, listening with them, and watching, as they were, for the one brilliant animal who might any second appear—having run the best possible obstacle course. For the one superb gibbon, maybe, who would come handspringing over the hospital grounds—be surrounded by nurses, showered by wheelchairs off the balconies; be finally snagged in rubber breathing tubes, and strangled with a stethoscope. A capture for which all the hospital staffs and patients would take proud credit.

But no one made it that far. Gallen slumped more heavily on my back; I felt her start shaking against my neck. So I turned us past the waiting hospitals, toward the country west of the suburbs, with Gallen's wet cheek sliding against my own, and her hands plucking at my shirt; and her teeth in my shoulder, biting me fierce.

But I didn't mind it, and wished for all this world that she could bite much deeper and hurt me more. While I alternated driving fast with driving slow; fast so the din would fade behind me, and slow so that if there were any who successfully escaped, they might overtake me and lope before me in my headlight—serve me for that moment kindly, as guides I would be happy to believe in.

But no one overtook me; there was no traffic headed in my direction. All the traffic I met was going the other way. Family autos, farmers' wagons, clattering with tools and weapons—in the early morning dark, the people poured eagerly into the calamity area.

For every headlight I met, I saw again my old soccerball situation. And I was beaten to the kick, every time.

Making New Plans

The beginning daylight found us out of the city, in the countryside above the Danube, south of Klosterneuburg. Where there still were monks.

I don't know how long I'd been pulled off the roadside, sitting down in the ditch, before I noticed the country folk coming wearily back from the wondrous, city-type excitement in the Hietzinger Zoo. Truck and whole wagonloads of them, mostly; some of the loutish younger farmers whistled at Gallen, who sat in a ball on the other side of the road from me.

We hadn't spoken. I thought: It's not wise of me to let her do so much thinking by herself. But I had nothing to say, so I kept the peace of the road between us. Until these farmers started coming back.

Then I thought: We look suspicious. Although O. Schrutt never got a look at us, and probably would never be coherent again, there was that Balkan waiter and little Hugel Furtwängler who might have had something to say about a big, ragged motorcycle, and a madman who spoke zoo talk.

O. Schrutt, I thought, at least was found with his nametag on—and his epaulettes buttoned down sharp. That's something.

But it wasn't enough, for sure. Because the last of the pickup trucks to pass us had a load in the back—a lump under a tarp, hanging down off the tailgate. I saw a bit of leg and hoof protrude; I recognized the brownish-red and creamy-white striping, running from hock to shank. Heavens forfend all evil from the previous bongo, handsomest of antelopes—about to be eaten and have his rack mounted over the mantle of the humble peasant dwelling. For later generations of hunters to ask: Was he once native to Austria?

Oh yes. A slave boat to Austria brought the first of them.

But extinct now?

Oh yes. They were a damaging lot—to the gardens. And dogs were gored.

By *them?*

Oh yes.

But he has such a thin, gentle face.

Oh yes. But he was actually fat and very tasty.

Him?

Oh yes.

And when the last of the caravan had passed us, I thought I should try to salvage Gallen out of this. She sat across the road from me and stared over my shoulder, or through my chest. But I couldn't face her; I looked down my pant leg and discovered, wadded and clinging to my sock, a little mesh of fur.

Oh, I *am* sorry, Siggy, I thought. But you were more than illogical. You were wrong.

Then Gallen crossed the road to the bike and stood over the lumpish rucksack, for a moment, before she began to take her things out.

She'd done entirely too much thinking, for sure.

And since I had nothing to say, I said, "Well, what do you want to do now?" She just gaped at me. So I said, "We'll do whatever you want." But she just pulled her things out faster; she made a sack of her ladies' leather jacket; I saw her stuff her silky blue panties up one sleeve. And that hurt me.

I thought: She's going to give me back my soccer shirt. But she gave no signs of taking it off. At least, she was sparing me the little gestures.

"Where are you going?" I said.

"To Vienna," she said. "May I have my hair money, please?"

"To Vienna?" I said.

"Aren't you interested in going back and reading all about it?" she asked. "Don't you want to know, *exactly,* just what happened? Aren't you interested in all the *de*tails, Graff?"

But she wasn't going to get a rise out of me; I had no place to come up from. And casualty statistics were of no interest to me, for sure. After the oryx, there was no need to keep count of disasters.

I said, "Really, please. Why is it Vienna?"

"Because," she said, "it's the one place I can think of where you wouldn't try to come along with me."

And I got some footing, suddenly—to rise from. I said to her, "You won't ever sneeze again, I hope you know." And she just glared at me. "Well, you won't," I said. "Whoever gets you."

"It was *my* hair," said Gallen. "You give me the money now, please." So I did. She took it like suspected bait, as if she were afraid I'd touch her.

"Wherever will *you* go, Graff?" she said, in a bright, cold, clear-sky voice. But I wouldn't allow myself to be taunted.

I said, seriously, "To Kaprun." And she looked away. "When I come back," I said, "how can I find you?"

"*If* you come back," she said, still turned away.

"I will," I said. "And where will you be?"

"Oh, I'm very fond of *zoos,*" she said, in the cold, bright voice again. "I expect I'll visit the zoo often. You might find me there, when you decide to try it again—with a *new* plan."

But I wasn't going to have us go out this way. I said, "I'm going for a while to Kaprun, and I know I'll want to see you again."

"You mean, when you're all better?" she said, mock-sweet. "When you're all done with it?" But I knew that wasn't the way it worked, and was the wrong attitude to carry off with me. You can't rush getting over anything. Even the notebook is clear on this:

The figures make a certain sum, no matter how you add them up.

Officious, as ever. Another half-truth, as always.

I said, "Gallen, I'm sorry. And I won't forget about you."

"Then come to Vienna with me, Graff," she said, and I couldn't tell what kind of edge her voice had now.

"I have to go to Kaprun," I said.

"Then how will you find me?" she asked—my question. And it was her unsharp, thick and natural voice again—a genuine query.

"Kahlenberg," I said, "is a place you'll hear about when you're in the city. Take any Grinzing tram and a bus up through the Vienna Woods. Go there Wednesday evenings," I said. "There's a view of the Danube, and all Vienna."

"And you'll come some Wednesday, I suppose," she said.

"You be there every Wednesday," I said. But this was pushing her too hard, and roundabout from where she'd first taken a stance.

She said, "Maybe." With a touch of that bright coldness in her voice.

"I'll take you to the buses in Klosterneuburg," I said. "The first outlying tram stop is in Josefdorf."

"I don't want to ride with you," she said. "I'll just walk."

And because I felt I was losing again, I said, "Well, sure. You're a strong-legged girl, I know. It won't hurt you."

"You said *Thursdays?*" she asked.

"Wednesdays," I said quickly. "Any *Wednesday night."*

"You'll come then?" she asked.

"For sure," I said, and she started to go. I said, *"Wednesday."*

"Maybe," she said, and kept her fine legs strutting away from me.

Trying to make light of it all, I said, "I'm going to watch your sweet behind till you're out of sight."

But she wasn't exactly smiling when she turned round to me. "Not a long, *last* look, though?" she said. "Or is it?"

"No," I said—so quickly that her mouth came close to smiling. She kept walking away from me; I watched her almost to where the road turned. Then I called *"Wednesday!"*

"Maybe," she called, in an uninterpretable voice, and didn't turn around.

"For sure!" I hollered, and she was gone.

I sat in the road ditch, letting her get all the way into Klosterneuburg; I didn't want to pass her on the road.

Around me the morning was coming on stronger. The domestic life of the trimly hedged and fenced fields. The borders separating cows from corn; the property lines orderly and unmistakable in the sun. All cows were belled; all sheep were ear-notched.

All men have names, and specific places where they're allowed to go.

A wind picked up and blew the roadside dust in my face. I watched the motorcycle brace against the little gale and shudder on its kick stand. I saw the mirror mounted on the handlebars, reflecting some anonymous patch of tar-smeared gravel of the roadside—and a petal-part of a flower, grown too close to the road. But when I looked behind the motorcycle, I just couldn't say, for sure, which flower lent its part to that reflection. Or just which stretch of tar-smeared gravel.

Things didn't piece together any better than before.

And that should have been no surprise to me. I knew. All the figures in your frotting column make the sum, but the figures are in no way bound to be otherwise related. They're just all the things you've ever paid for. As unfitted to each other as toothpaste and your first touch of warm, upstanding breast.

Gallen was in Klosterneuburg. Where there still were monasteries. And monks making wine.

And Gallen, who might some Wednesday meet me in Kahlenberg, was now of the nature of Todor Slivnica's custard—to be interpreted from wherever it all lay spattered.

Congratulations to All You Survivors!

Hannes Graff, I thought, is too split-haired and loose-ended to ever rise up out of this road ditch and ride his beastly motorcycle out of this deceptively ordered countryside.

And orderly, too, were the towns I'd go through. If only I could get myself started.

An easy plan. Through Klosterneuburg, Königstetten, Judenau and Mitterndorf; through Hankenfeld or Asperhofen, Perschling, Pottenbrunn and wee St. Hain; to the big town of Amstetten and three hours west on the Autobahn—where you can easily drive faster than the frotting wind. Then there would still be an hour south of Salzburg, through the little Lofer Range; and I know a place to eat in Fürth. And after-dinner coffee in Kaprun, across that well-worn kitchen table—a second pair of elbows, speaking. Now, at least, with something to say. Something needless and lunatic enough to hold the attention of doughty Watzek-Trummer. Surely, I thought, Ernst Watzek-Trummer has had enough experience with pointless schemes to be sympathetic.

But I thought, too, that I wouldn't rise up from the road ditch, just yet. Or if I did, there was no need to hurry my visit to Kaprun.

Let the grave mound grow a little grass, I always say. Grass is nice, and it will not hurt you, Siggy.

So I'd move along in the general direction of Kaprun, for sure. But I'd creep up on it slowly, you might say; I'd have myself more familiar with this frotting memorabilia I was trucking to Watzek-Trummer.

But what deadened me in the road ditch was that *none* of my ideas was very stirring, and there seemed to be no excitable planning called for—for *this* trip.

Something new to get used to, I thought. How Hannes Graff was rendered inert. What worse awareness is there than to know there would have been a better outcome if you'd never done anything at all? That all small mammals would have been better off if you'd never meddled in the unsatisfactory scheme of things.

And I surveyed once again this unalterable countryside around me—namable and controlled. A pasture down the road with three white fences and one brown; with nine ewes, one ram and one watchful dog. A pasture up the road with one stone wall, one briar hedge, one wire fence, and one forest—the boundary at the rear; with one horse, and six splotched dairy cows—and, conceivably, an old bull in the woods behind. But not an oryx, surely.

Across the road was a forest, through which the old wind tunneled, furrowing the pine needles.

Then the watchful sheepdog barked over the road at the forest. So, someone's coming, I thought, and I got on the motorcycle—thinking I'd better leave, ready or not, because I looked pretty foolish, just sitting there.

The dog barked more. At someone coming on a well-walked path through the tidy forest, and probably someone who'd come this way, at this time, for years and years—and for years and years, this dog has always barked. A domestic chore, connected to wagging the tail. Which the dog will do next, I thought—at any moment now, when this farmer's wife or daughter breaks out of the forest and up on the road. And shouldn't see me here, suspiciously inert.

But when I tried to pump the kick starter, my legs were spongy; the heel piece of my boot wouldn't grip the lever. And I forgot to open the gas line. I leaned over and sniffed the carburetor, filled my mind with woozy thoughts of fuel sloshing loose in my skull. I had all I could do to keep the bike upright; I tottered back and forth.

So whoever it is will just have to see me here, I thought; I'll be a non-routine blob on the landscape. Someone will sick the dog on me. Or perhaps the dog is really barking *at* me; only he's got this crazy habit, derived from sheep, of looking in another direction from what he's barking at.

But the dog was barking furiously now. And I thought: Whether it's me or not he's barking about, why didn't he bark at me before now? If that's the sort of dog he is—given so easily to woofling at the slightest thing.

The dog was berserk; he snapped around his sheep and drove the flock into a tight circle. He's lost his head, I thought—familiar with the symptoms. The sheepdog is going to eat his sheep!

He was the most unreasonably behaving dog I have ever seen.

I was still watching him, and shaking on the motorcycle, when the shoulder-to-shoulder pair of Rare Spectacled Bears tumbled out of the forest and huffed across the road, not more than twenty yards from me. The dog dropped flat down on his belly—paws spread, ears tight to his head.

But the Rare Spectacled Bears were not looking for sheep, or dogs—or cows in the next field, or a possible bull in the woods. They were running steadily together; they came down in my road ditch and up over the fence, into the sheepdog's field. He howled by the huddled flock, and the bears pushed on—not at unreasonable speed; not even hurrying, really. They just headed for the woods at the far end of the field—where, more than likely, they would still keep running. The inexhaustible, remarkable, and very Rare Spectacled Bears, running back to the Andes in Ecuador. Or at least to the Alps.

But when they reached the end of the field, they stopped and cocked their heads back toward me. I wanted to wave, but I didn't dare. I wanted them to go on. If they'd ever waved back to me, or had shouted "Hello!"—if they'd said "Thank you!" or "Frot you!"—I wouldn't have been able to believe they were really there. They just paused, though, and went on again; they ran shoulder to shoulder into the woods.

I was so thankful that their escape didn't take on the custardlike quality of too many other endings.

And I suddenly didn't dare stay there any longer. In case, I thought, the Famous Asiatic Black Bear comes next. Or even gibbons. Or Siggy astride the oryx—the remaining flesh and ghosts of the Hietzinger Zoo. That would have spoiled this little token offered me by these Rare Spectacled Bears. That would not have allowed me to believe in them, either.

So I worked the kick starter this time. The bike made a ragged, suffering idle under me. I was still shaky. Even so, I couldn't stay there—until, perhaps, the Rare Spectacled Bears passed by me again, this time followed by some more of those who had temporarily escaped. Vratno Javotnik on the Grand Prix racer, '39—leaving Gottlob Wut behind. And other selected mammals.

I looked nervously to the woods behind the field, and was happy to see that the Rare Spectacled Bears were gone—leaving the pastures at least not quite the same, at least not for this moment. Cows fretted; the sheep still obeyed the panting dog. A little something had been harmlessly disrupted, and I certainly don't imply that it made things all frotting rosy. Only that I was able to sincerely imagine coming this way again, some Wednesday. And meeting someone from the area, who would tell me: There are bears in Klosterneuburg.

Really?

Oh yes. Bears.

But they've done no harm?

Not these bears. They're strange bears.

Rare Spectacled Bears?

Well, I don't know about that.

But they're multiplying?

I don't know about that, either. But they're very friendly with each other, you know.

Oh yes. I know.

And that was a little something to know, anyway. And enough to get the motorcycle running under me. I listened to my idle coming smoother; it still had rough edges, of course. But I braced my feet on each side of the old beast, and it sat steady; it waited for me, now. Then I identified all its parts in my head; there's a certain confidence in having names for things. I called my right hand Throttle, and turned it up. I called my left hand Clutch, and pulled it in. Even my right foot responded to the gear lever, and found first —and it's not a particularly impressive right foot.

The point is, everything worked. Oh, sure, for a while I would have to be careful, and keep a sharp eye on the mechanics of things. But for that moment, at least, everything was functioning. My eyes too; I saw no more bears, but I could see the grass they'd bent down for a path across the field. Tomorrow the grass would be sprung back in place, and only the watchful dog might remember them with me. And he would forget before I would, for sure.

As for those casualties back at the Hietzinger Zoo—even for old O. Schrutt's mind, left behind, name by name and roar by roar—I will admit to being responsible. For sure, I will turn myself over to Ernst Watzek-Trummer. Historian without equal, and the keeper of details. He should make a fine confessor, for sure.

So I felt the clutch in my left hand; I controlled the throttle and front brake with my right. I put myself in gear and was properly balanced when I came out of the gravel at the roadside. I was steady, shifting up, when I rode into the full-force wind. But I didn't panic; I leaned to the curves; I held the crown of the road and drove faster and faster. I truly outdrove the wind. For sure—for the moment, at least—there was no gale hurrying me out of this world.

For sure, Siggy, I'll have to let your grave mound grow a little grass.

For sure, Gallen, I'll look you up some Wednesday.

For sure, I expect to hear great things of the Rare Spectacled Bears.

The Water–Method Man

for
SHYLA

ACKNOWLEDGMENTS

The author is grateful to the director Irvin Kershner for a valuable and exciting film experience in 1969 and 1970, and to the Rockefeller Foundation for their assistance in 1970 and 1971.

Especially, the author is indebted to Donald Harington. A vital passage in this book is his.

1

Yogurt & Lots of Water

Her gynecologist recommended him to me. Ironic: the best urologist in New York is French. Dr. Jean Claude Vigneron: ONLY BY APPOINTMENT. So I made one.

"You like New York better than Paris?" I asked.

"In Paris, I dared to keep a car."

"My father is a urologist, too."

"Then he must be a second-rate one," Vigneron said, "if he didn't know what was wrong with you."

"It's nonspecific," I said. I knew the history of my ailment well. "Sometimes it's nonspecific urethritis, once it was nonspecific prostatitis. Another time, I had the clap—but that's a different story. Once it was just a common germ. But always, nonspecific."

"It looks very specific to me," Vigneron said.

"No," I said. "Sometimes it responds to penicillin, sometimes sulfa does the trick. Once, Furadantin cured it."

"There, you see?" he said. "Urethritis and prostatitis don't respond to Furadantin."

"Well, there," I said, *"you see?* It was something else that time. Nonspecific."

"Specific," Vigneron said. "You can't get much more specific than the urinary tract."

He showed me. On his examination table I tried to be calm. He handed me a perfect plastic breast, as lovely a one as I've seen: realistic color and texture, and a fine, upstanding nipple.

"My God . . ."

"Just bite on it," he said. "Forget about me."

I clutched the rare boob, looking it straight in the eye. I'm sure that my father employs no such up-to-date devices. When you're erect, the nasty glass rod goes in a bit easier. I recall I pulled a muscle, trying not to cry.

"*Very* specific," said Jean Claude Vigneron, who responded in sly French when I told him it was at least unusual to hold a breast whose nipple one could bite without reserve.

Vigneron's diagnosis of my ailment is best understood with some historical perspective. Odd and painful peeing is not new to me.

Seven times in the last five years, I have suffered this unnamable disorder. Once it was the clap, but that's another story. Usually, the apparatus is simply stuck together in the morning. A careful pinch sets things right, or almost right. Urinating is often a challenge, the sensations always new and surprising. Also, it's time-consuming—your day spent in anticipation of the next time you'll have to pee. Sex, typically, is unmentionable. Orgasm is truly climactic. Coming is a slow experience—the long, astonishing journey of a rough and oversized ball bearing. In the past I had given up the act altogether. Which drives me to drink, which makes the pee burn: an unfriendly circle.

And *always* the nonspecific diagnosis. Terrifying new strains of possibly Asian venereal diseases are never substantiated. "Some kind of infection" is carefully not named. Different drugs are tried; one eventually works. *The Medical Encyclopedia of the Home* reveals vague and ominous symptoms of cancer of the prostate. But the doctors always tell me I'm too young. I always agree.

And now, Jean Claude Vigneron puts his glass rod on the problem. Specifically a birth defect. Not surprising—I have already suspected the existence of several.

"Your urinary tract is a narrow, winding road."

I took the news pretty well.

"Americans are so silly about sex," Vigneron said. From my own experience, I felt unfit to argue. "You think everything is washable, but the vagina remains the dirtiest thing in the world. Did you know that? Every unexposed orifice harbors hundreds of harmless bacteria, but the vagina is a superior hostess. I say 'harmless'—but not to you. *Normal* penises flush them out."

"But not my narrow, winding road?" I said, thinking of its odd crannies, where hundreds of bacteria could lead a secret life.

"You see?" said Vigneron. "Isn't that specific?"

"What's the recommended treatment?" I still held the plastic breast. A man with an invulnerable nipple can be brave.

"You have four alternatives," Vigneron said. "There are lots of drugs, and one will always work. Seven times in five years is not surprising, considering such a urinary tract as yours. And the pain isn't severe, is it? You can live with this periodic inconvenience to your peeing and your screwing, can't you?"

"I have a new life now," I said. "I want to change."

"Then stop screwing," Vigneron said. "Consider masturbation. You can wash your hand."

"I don't want to change *that* much."

"Remarkable!" Vigneron cried. He is a handsome man, big and cocksure; I gripped the plastic breast tightly. "Remarkable, remarkable . . . you are my tenth American patient to face these alternatives, and every one of you rejects the first two."

"So what's remarkable about that?" I said. "They're not very attractive alternatives."

"For *Americans!*" cried Vigneron. "Three of my patients in my Paris days chose to live with it. And one—and he wasn't an old man, either—gave up screwing."

"I haven't heard the other two alternatives," I said.

"I always pause here," said Dr. Vigneron. "I like to guess which one you'll choose. With Americans I've never guessed wrong. You are a predictable people. You always want to change your lives. You never accept what you're born with. And for you? For you, I can *sense* it. It's the water method for you!"

I found the doctor's tone offensive. With breast in hand, I was determined that the water method would *not* be for me.

"It is a fallible method, of course," Vigneron said. "A compromise, at best. Instead of seven times in five years, maybe one time in three years—healthier odds, that's all."

"I don't like it."

"But you haven't tried it," he said. "It's very simple. You drink lots of water before you screw. You drink lots of water *after* you screw. And you go easy on the booze. Alcohol makes bacteria happy. In the French Army, we had an ingenious test-cure for the clap. Give them the normal dose of penicillin. Then give them three beers before bedtime when they tell you they think they're cured. If they have a discharge in the morning, more penicillin. You just need lots of water. With your curious tract, you need all the flushing you can get. After intercourse, just remember to get up and pee."

The breast in my hand was only plastic. I said, "You expect me to perform the sexual act on a full bladder? That's painful."

"It's different," Vigneron agreed. "But you'll have bigger erections. Did you know that?"

I asked him what the fourth alternative was, and he smiled.

"A simple operation," he said. "Minor surgery."

I sliced my thumbnail into the plastic nipple.

"We simply straighten you out," said Vigneron. "We widen the road. It doesn't take a minute. We put you to sleep, of course."

In my hand was an absurd synthetic mammary gland, an obvious fake. I put it down. "It must hurt a little," I said. "I mean, *after* the operation."

"For forty-eight hours or so." Vigneron shrugged; all pain appeared equally tolerable to him.

"Can you put me to sleep for forty-eight hours?" I asked.

"Ten out of ten!" Vigneron cried. "They always ask that!"

"Forty-eight hours?" I wondered. "How do I pee?"

"As fast as you can," he said, poking the upright nipple on the examination table as if it were a button summoning nurses and anesthetists— bringing him the polished scalpel for this surgical feat. I could imagine it. A slender version of a Roto-Rooter. A long, tubular razor, like a miniature of the mouth of a lamprey eel.

Dr. Jean Claude Vigneron eyed me as if I were a painting he was not quite finished with. "The water method?" he guessed.

"You're ten for ten," I said, just to please him. "Did any of your patients ever choose the operation?"

"Just one," said Vigneron, "and I knew he would, from the start. He was a practical, scientific, no-nonsense sort of man. On the examination table he was the only one who scorned the tit."

"A hard man," I said.

"A *secure* man," said Vigneron. He lit a foul, dark Gauloise and inhaled without fear.

———

Later, living with the water method, I thought about his four alternatives. I thought of a fifth: French urological surgeons are quacks, seek another opinion, seek lots of other opinions—any other opinion . . .

I had my hand on a real breast when I phoned Vigneron to tell him of this fifth alternative that he should offer his patients.

"Remarkable!" he cried.

"Don't tell me. You're ten for ten?"

"Ten out of ten!" he hollered. "And always about three days after the examination. You're right on time!"

I was quiet on my end of the phone. In my hand her breast felt like plastic. But only for this quiet moment; she came to life when Vigneron boomed at me.

"It's not a matter of another *opinion.* Don't kid yourself. The geography of your urinary tract is a *fact.* I could draw you a map, to scale . . ."

I hung up. "I've never liked the French," I told her. "Your gynecologist must have it in for me, recommending that sadist. He hates Americans, you know. I'm sure that's why he came here, with his goddamn glass rods . . ."

"Paranoia," she said, her eyes already closed. She's not a big talker, this one. "Words," she says, in her harumphing way. She has a gesture for what she thinks of words: she lifts one breast with the back of her hand. She has good, full breasts, but they need a bra. I'm very fond of her breasts; they make me wonder how that fake boob of Vigneron's had any effect on me. If I had it to do again, I wouldn't take the tit. Well, yes, I would. *She* wouldn't ever need a device like that, though. She's a practical, no-nonsense, gut-level, secure person. Offer her those four alternatives and she'd take the operation. I know; I asked her.

"Surgery," she said. "If something *can* be fixed, then fix it."

"The water's not so bad," I said. "I *like* water. It's good for me too, in lots of ways. And I have bigger erections. Did you know that?"

She lifts the back of her hand and one breast stands up. I really like her very much.

Her name is Tulpen. That means tulips in German, but her parents didn't know it was German, or what it meant, when they named her. Her parents were Polish. They died peacefully in New York, but Tulpen was born in an R.A.F. hospital outside London during the blitz. There was a nice nurse whose name was Tulpen. They liked the nurse, they wanted to forget everything Polish, and they thought that the nurse was a Swede. Nobody found out what Tulpen meant until Tulpen took German in high school, in Brooklyn. She came home and told her parents, who were very surprised; it wasn't the cause of their death, or anything like that; it was just a fact. None of this is important; these are just facts. But that's when Tulpen talks: when there's a fact. And there aren't many.

Following her example, I began with a fact: my urinary tract is a narrow, winding road.

Facts are true. Tulpen is a very honest person. I am not so honest. I'm a pretty good liar, in fact. People who've really known me tend to believe me less and less. They tend to think I lie all the time. But I'm telling the truth now! Just remember: you don't know me.

When I talk like this, Tulpen lifts a breast with the back of her hand.

What in hell do we have in common? I'll stick to the facts. Names are facts. Tulpen and I have the carelessness of our names in common. Hers was a mistake, which doesn't matter to her. I have several; like hers, they're all pretty accidental. My father and mother named me Fred, and it never seemed to bother them that almost no one else ever called me that. Biggie called me Bogus. That was the invention of my oldest and dearest friend, Couth, who coined the name when he first caught me lying. The name stuck. Most of my old friends called me that, and Biggie knew me then. Merrill Overturf, who is still lost, called me Boggle. Like any name, there were vague reasons. Ralph Packer named me Thump-Thump, a name I despise. And Tulpen calls me by my surname, Trumper. I know why: it's the closest to a fact that you can come to in a name. Male surnames don't often change. So most of the time I'm Fred "Bogus" Trumper. That's a fact.

Facts fall out of me slowly. So I don't get lost, I'll repeat them. Now there are two. One: My urinary tract is a narrow, winding road. Two: Tulpen and I have the carelessness of our names in common. And possibly not much else.

But wait! I am reaching for a third fact. Three: I believe in Rituals! I mean, there have always been things like the water method in my life; there have always been rituals. No particular ritual has ever lasted very long (I told Vigneron I have a new life, that I want to change, and this is true), but always I have moved from one ritual to another. Right now it's the water method. Some historical perspective on my rituals will take a little time, but the water method is clear. Also, Tulpen and I share an early morning ritual, of sorts. Although the water method has me getting up a little earlier—and a few times in the night—Tulpen and I have persisted in this routine. I get up and pee and brush my teeth and drink a lot of water. She starts coffee and puts on a stack of records. We meet back in bed for yogurt. Always yogurt. She has a red bowl, I have a blue one, but if we have different flavors we often trade the bowls back and forth. A flexible ritual is the best kind, and yogurt is a sensible, healthy food which is very kind to your mouth in the morning. We don't talk. This is nothing new for Tulpen, but even *I* don't talk. We listen to the records and eat our yogurt. I don't know Tulpen very well, but apparently she's always done this. An addition to her ritual was introduced by me: when the yogurt is all gone, we make love for a long time. After that, the coffee's ready and we have it. We don't talk as long as the records play. The only variation caused by the water method is minor, and falls somewhere after love and during coffee. I get up to pee and drink a lot of water.

I haven't lived with Tulpen for very long, but I've a feeling that if I'd lived with her for years and years, I wouldn't know her any better.

Tulpen and I are both twenty-eight, but she's really older than I am; she has outgrown having to talk about herself.

It's Tulpen's apartment, and all the things in it are hers. I left my things, and my child, with my first and only wife.

I said to Dr. Jean Claude Vigneron that I have a new life, etc.; I said that some historical perspective on my rituals will take a little time; I also said that I'm not so honest. But Tulpen is. She helps me keep things straight by raising one breast with the back of her hand. In no time at all, I learned not to talk as long as the records play. I learned to say only what's essential (though people who've known me would tend to say that I am lying even now. Fuck them! I say, for such pessimism).

My urinary tract is a narrow, winding road, and right now there's yogurt and lots of water. I'm going to stick to the facts. I want to change.

2

War-Built Things

Among his other kicks, Fred Bogus Trumper likes to remember Merrill Overturf, the diabetic. In Trumper's Iowa phase, his memories of Overturf are especially sweet. It helps, for accuracy, that some of Overturf is tape-recorded.

Such escapism. Listening to Merrill, in Vienna—while Trumper looks out his Iowa window, through a rusty screen and a fat katydid's wing; he sees a slow-moving, beshitted truck, brimming with hogs. Over the complaining pigs, Bogus listens to the ditty Merrill composed at the Prater—later used, Merrill claimed, to seduce Wanga Holthausen, a singing coach for the Vienna Boys' Choir. The background music is from the Prater go-kart track, where Merrill Overturf once held the 20-lap record. Possibly, he still holds it.

There are faint distortions on the tape; then Merrill is telling his swimming story, the one about there being a tank at the bottom of the Danube. "You can only see it in a full moon. You must block the moon with your back," says Merrill, "which cuts the reflection." Then, somehow, you arch out of the water and hold your face "approximately six inches above the surface—all the time keeping a land-sight on the dock at the Gelhafts Keller." Somehow you hold this position without stirring the water, "and if the wind doesn't make a single ripple, the tank's barrel swings up to where you think you could almost touch it, or it's perfectly aimed to blast you. And in a straight line off the Gelhafts dock, the tank's top hatch opens, or flutters in the water, or *seems* to open. But that's as long as I've ever been able to hold my face approximately six inches above the water surface . . ." Then, thinking diabetically, Merrill announces that this exertion always influences his blood sugar.

Bogus Trumper flips the switch that says REWIND. The hog truck is gone, but on the other side of the screen, the katydid still holds out its wings, more perfect and complicated than some Oriental silkscreen, and Trumper, squinting through this lovely mesh, sees Mr. Fitch, a retired neighbor, scratching his dry and overraked lawn. *Scritch-scritch* goes Mr. Fitch, urging the last ant out of his grass. Through a katydid's wing is the only way to make Fitch-watching bearable.

The car that now labors to the curb—the one that Mr. Fitch waves his rake at—carries Trumper's wife, Biggie, his son, Colm, and three spare tires. Trumper regards the car, wonders if three spare tires are enough. His face mashed to the window screen, he startles the katydid, whose sudden wing-whir startles Trumper—who lurches off balance, his head pushing the rotting screen free of the frame. Catching himself, Bogus jars the frame loose too, and what his startled wife sees is her husband's precarious dangle—his waist, the axis for his unexplained teetering on the window sill.

"What are you doing?" Biggie screams to him.

And Bogus finds the tape recorder with his foot, dragging it toward him like an anchor. He restores his balance by kneeling on the control panel. The recorder is confused; one knee says FULL SPEED FORWARD, the other says PLAY. In a high voice, Merrill Overturf blurts, ". . . off the Gelhalfts dock the tank's top hatch opens, or flut—!"

"What?" says Biggie. "What are you doing?"

"I'm fixing the screen," Trumper says, and waves reassuringly to Mr. Fitch, who waves his rake. Not in the least distressed at window-dangling or odd shrieks, Fitch is used to various demonstrations of imbalance from this house.

"Well," says Biggie, with one hip cocked out, making a seat for Colm. "Well, the diapers aren't done. Someone will have to go back to the laundromat and take them out of the dryer."

"I'll go, Big," Bogus says, "just as soon as I fix this screen."

"That won't be easy!" hollers Mr. Fitch, leaning on his rake. "War-built!" he cries. "Damn war-built things!"

"The screens?" Bogus asks from his window.

"Your whole house!" Fitch shouts. "All these jiffy one-stories the university put up! War-built! Cheap materials! Woman labor! Junk!" But Mr. Fitch isn't really being unpleasant. Anything vaguely connected with the war effort sets him off. A bad time for Fitch; he was too old to go, even back then, so he fought the home front with the women.

At the see-through curtains of his front-porch window, Fitch's tiny wife is stirring nervously. *Do you want to have your fifth stroke, Fitch?*

When Trumper examines the rotten screen, he finds the accusation to be true. The wood feels like sponge; the mesh is rusted brittle.

"Bogus," says Biggie, straddling the sidewalk, *"I'll* fix the screen. You're terrible at that kind of thing."

Trumper slides back inside, moves the tape recorder to the safety of an upper bookshelf and watches Mrs. Fitch at her see-through curtain waving Mr. Fitch inside.

Later, Bogus goes to get the diapers. On his way home, his right headlight falls out and he drives over it. Changing his right front tire, he thinks he'd like to meet a man who thinks he's got a worse car. *I would trade with him in an instant.*

But what Trumper thinks he'd really like to know is whether there was anyone under the top hatch of that tank. Or if there really is a tank, at all; if Merrill Overturf really saw it; if, even, Merrill Overturf knows how to swim.

ॐ

Old Tasks & Plumbing News

Bogus Trumper
918 Iowa Ave.
Iowa City, Iowa

Sept. 20, 1969

Mr. Cuthbert Bennett
Caretaker / The Pillsbury Estate
Mad Indian Point
Georgetown, Maine

My Dear Couth:
How are you keeping the seventeen bathrooms, now that all the Pillsburys have left you with their plumbing? And have you decided in which master bedroom, with which sea-view, you will spend your winter?

Biggie and I appreciated your convincing the Pillsburys we were safe guests for the boathouse. That was a nice revival week for us, Couth—and a break to be able to leave my genitors.

It was a curious summer we had with my genitors. Great Boar's Head is the same summer scene as ever—a convalescent home for the dying, who seem to think that three months of wheezing in the salt air will preserve their lungs for another winter. My father's business thrives in the summer. He once told me something about old people: their bladders are the first to go. A urologist's heaven on the New Hampshire shore!

But it *was* something for the old boy to open his basement to us for July and August. Since my disinheritance, Mother has obviously been feeling grandmotherly urges; their summer offer must have stemmed from Mom's desire to see Colm, not Biggie and me. And my father seemed to unbend his previous financial ultimatum—though the unbending was no more appealing to me than his cutting me off. Also, he charged me rent on the basement.

When we left to come back here, the good doctor orated, "Let's leave it like this, Fred. You're going on four years of doing it on your own, and I must tell you: I'm impressed. Let's see you tie down that Ph.D., and keep your grades, and I think Mom and I might be able to help you and Biggie and little Colm toward a nest egg. That Colm *is* a dandy."

And Mom kissed Biggie (when my father wasn't looking), and we all bundled back to Iowa City. Three tires and two fan belts later, we were back in our war-built one-story. The old man didn't give me so much as a dime for the tolls.

Which brings me to something important, Couth—if you could spare a little. The tolls alone ran us twenty bills, and I haven't even paid the credit-card companies for the trip east in July. And in Michigan City, Indiana, we had a Holiday Inn Experience which will probably mean the early retirement of my Gulf Card.

But! There is a thin shard of sunlight in this gloom. My thesis chairman, Dr. Wolfram Holster, has given me some of the Comparative Literature Kitty, as he insists on calling it. For my piece of the kitty, I run the tapes in the language lab for freshman German. My officemate, and fellow tape-runner in the lab, is a sly little pedant named Zanther, whose interpretation and "supra-literal" translation of Borgetz is being heralded in this month's issue of *The Linguist.* I showed Zanther the bulk of my summer's writing on my thesis; he read it all in one afternoon and told me he didn't think anyone would publish it. I asked him what the circulation of *The Linguist* was; we haven't spoken since. Following my period of proctorship in the language lab—when I know Zanther is coming on duty—I artfully misfile the tapes. He left me a note about it. "I know what you're doing," the note said; it was stuck in what he knew to be my favorite tape. I left him a note, too. It said: "*No one* knows what *you're* doing." Now communication is impossible between us.

Even so, it's a small kitty and I've got a small bite of it. Biggie's back with her old job at the hospital, bed-panning the elderly between 6 A.M. and noon, five days a week. Colm, therefore, is with me. The child gets up about the time Biggie leaves. I fight him off in bed until almost seven. Then his repeated news of what's wrong with the toilet prompts me to rise and call Krotz the plumber again.

We've seen quite enough of Krotz. I sublet the house this summer, you know, to three football players taking a summer make-up course in world culture. I knew football players might be rough types, that they might break a chair or split our bed; I was even prepared to find a raped and castaway girl; but I was sure they'd be *clean.* You know athletes—all that showering and deodering. I was sure they couldn't live in filth.

Well, the apartment was clean, all right, and there wasn't even a raped girl. There was a pair of Biggie's panties nailed to our door, and the more literate of the three had pinned a note to the panties, saying "Thanks." Biggie was a bit resentful; she'd packed all our clothes very neatly, and it disturbed her to imagine football players riffling through her underwear. But I felt enormously encouraged; the house had survived and the athletes' scholarships had paid their rent. Then the plumbing problems started, and Biggie concluded that the only reason the place looked so clean was because the football players had *flushed* all the crud away.

Krotz has sent his Roto-Rooter down our john four times. Among other things, he's retrieved six athletic socks, three whole potatoes, a crushed lampshade and a small girl's bra—clearly *not* Biggie's.

I phoned the Athletic Department and bitched. At first, they were very concerned. A man said, "Of course it doesn't do to have our boys getting a name for themselves with the local landlords." He said he'd take care of it. Then he asked me my name, and what property it was that I owned. I had to say that I didn't *own* it, really—that I rented it, and had sublet to the athletes for the summer. He said, "Oh, you're a *student?*" I should have seen the put-off coming, but I said, "Right—getting my Ph.D. in Comp. Lit." And he said, "Well, son, get your landlord to put the complaint in writing."

And since my landlord told me that I was responsible for any subletting, all bills from Krotz the plumber are mine. And believe me, Couth, Roto-Rootering is costly.

I'm afraid you know what I mean . . . if you've got some to spare.

I really think you've got the life, Couth. Better the caretaker than them who need to be cared for. Thanks be, though, it's the last damn year of this. My father says, "With your Ph.D. you'll have a profession that's dependable. But every professional man must suffer his training."

My father—as I'm sure he's told you before—didn't marry Mom until *after* college, *after* med school, *after* interning and *after* he'd established himself in Great Boar's Head, New Hampshire. The only urologist at Rockingham-by-the-Sea Hospital. After a six-year engagement to good old Mom—two thousand one hundred and ninety nights of masturbating ago —my father saw the time was ripe to marry.

I said to him this summer, "Well, look at Couth. He's set for life. A mansion to himself for nine months of the year, his expenses paid. And a mere three-month summer of fussing for the Pillsburys, tidying their ample grounds, caulking their boats and washing their cars; and they treat him like one of the family. Can you beat that?"

My father answered, "Couth doesn't have a profession, though."

Well, Biggie and I agree that you look quite professional to us.

Flush all seventeen of the johns once for me.

Love,
Bogus

4

Iowa Evening Rituals

Since his father disinherited him, he had learned to hoard little injustices, wishing they might merge and leave him with one significant wound, for which he could guiltlessly martyr himself forever.

Bogus flips the record switch. "A keeper of petty injustices," he tells the microphone unconvincingly, "I was exposed to self-pity at a tender age."

"What?" says Biggie—a low, groggy voice down the hall.

"Nothing, Big," he calls to her, and notices he's recorded this too. Erasing, he tries to think: From what did he catch his self-pity? He can hear his father saying, "From a virus." But Bogus is sure he invented the whole thing himself. "I made it all myself," he says, with surprising conviction, then notices that he's failed to record it.

"You made *what* all yourself?" Biggie asks, suddenly alert in the bedroom.

"Nothing, Big." But her astonishment at the possibility of his doing something himself is painful.

Blowing hair off the control panel, he gingerly fingers his forehead; for some time he has suspected that his hairline will one day recede far enough to expose his brain. But would that be a significant humiliation?

Into the microphone he records: "There's a danger in dwelling on small emotional things."

But when he attempts to play this back, he discovers that he's jammed the announcement too close to one of his father's hospital reports—recorded in the good doctor's den at Great Boar's Head, with a live audience of Biggie and his mother listening to a description of an honest day's fortune. Bogus is sure he's erased this once, but apparently he missed a bit of it. Or perhaps certain parts of his father's speeches are capable of reproducing themselves. Bogus is not beyond believing this.

"There's a danger in dwelling on small emotional . . . *bladders which can be easily infected, though the major key is some kidney complication.*"

STOP. REWIND. ERASE.

With a brief titter, Bogus records: "I resolve to be more careful how I pee."

It's well past midnight when Bogus sees a light go on in Fitch's house, and Mr. Fitch minces down a hallway in broad-striped pajamas. His bladder, Trumper thinks. But Fitch appears on the front porch, gray-faced from the nearest streetlight. *Fitch can't leave his lawn alone! He's worried that a leaf has crashed in the night!*

But Mr. Fitch just stands on his porch, his face lifted, his mind beyond his lawn. Before he goes back inside, he looks up at the lighted window, where Bogus sits frozen. Then they wave to each other, and Fitch stealthily sidles into his eerie hallway and kills the light.

These night encounters. Bogus remembers Colm, sprouting a new tooth at Great Boar's Head. Colm was always a miserable teether; he kept Biggie and Bogus's mother up half the night. Once, when Bogus relieved them, he slipped off for a walk on the beach, passing each dark cottage until he smelled the pot in front of Elsbeth Malkas's porch. *Elsbeth is turning her parents on!* A childhood friend, he had grown up with her (once, in her hammock). Now she is a lady college instructor, referred to as "the poetess" at Bennington, where she returned to teach, three years after graduating.

"It's incestuous, really," she once told Biggie.

And Biggie had said, "I wouldn't know anything about it, really."

The mark of a child's acceptance these days, Trumper thought, is to be so successful that you can turn your parents on. He tried to imagine his own luck with that. In doctoral robes, he delivers the commencement address, then forces a joint on his father!

Bogus crept up to see this generational wonder, but the Malkases' house was dark, and Elsbeth, spotting Trumper's crouching silhouette against the lighter background of the sea, sat up in her porch hammock. Elsbeth Malkas had a chunky, oily body, nude and damp in her hammock gasping grass.

From the safe distance of a ledge beyond the porch, Bogus discussed Colm's habit of breaking new teeth in the night. There was a moment, later, when he could have discreetly left—when she went into the house to get her diaphragm. But the old-fashioned charm of this device touched him; he imagined the diaphragm crammed with erasers, pencils and postage stamps —tools of this poetess, who needed a deskful of receptacles—and he was too fascinated to leave.

He wondered, vaguely, if he would catch from Elsbeth what he'd caught from her long ago. But in the hammock he only expressed his disappointment that the diaphragm had been inserted while Elsbeth was inside her house. "Why did you want to *see* it?" she asked.

He couldn't very well mention the erasers, pencils and postage stamps, or even perhaps a torn, tiny scrap of an unfinished poem. After all, with a poetess, one might make fertile her very words.

But he had never liked Elsbeth's poetry, and afterward he walked almost a mile along the beach before he plunged in the ocean, to make sure she wouldn't hear his splash and feel insulted.

Bogus informs the tape recorder: "I resolve to go a fair bit out of my way to be polite."

Some dawn light falls on Fitch's manicured lawn, and Bogus sees the old man pad restlessly out on his porch again, just looking. What future is there for me, Trumper thinks, if Fitch, at his age, is still an insomniac?

5

A Dream to Me Now

I am not an insomniac anymore. Tulpen has seen to that. She knows better than to leave me to my own devices. We go to bed at a reasonable hour, we make love, we sleep. If she catches me awake, we make love again. Despite lots of water, I sleep very well. It's in the daytime that I look for things to do.

I used to be very busy. Yes, I was a graduate student, getting my Ph.D. in Comparative Literature. My thesis chairman and my father were in agreement about specialization. Once, when Colm was sick, my father wouldn't write him a prescription. "Is a urologist a pediatrician?" Well, who could argue? "See a pediatrician. You're in graduate school, aren't you? Surely you know the importance of specialization."

Indeed I knew it. My thesis chairman, Dr. Wolfram Holster, admitted that he'd never been exposed to such specialization as mine.

I had a rare thesis topic, I confess. My thesis was going to be an original translation of *Akthelt and Gunnel,* a ballad in Old Low Norse; in fact, it was going to be the *only* translation. Old Low Norse is not well known. It's referred to, scornfully, in some satirical poems in Old East Norse and Old West Norse. Old East Norse is a dead language, North Germanic, which grew into Icelandic and Faroese. Old West Norse is also dead, and also North Germanic. It grew into Swedish and Danish. Norwegian evolved out of something between Old East Norse and Old West Norse. But the deadest of them all, old Old Low Norse, came to nothing. In fact, it's such a crude dialect that only one thing ever was actually written in it: *Akthelt and Gunnel.*

I was going to include in my translation a sort of etymological dictionary of Old Low Norse. That means a dictionary of the origins of Old Low Norse. Dr. Holster was very interested in such a dictionary; he felt it would be of some etymological use. That was why he approved the thesis topic; he actually thought *Akthelt and Gunnel* was junk, though he was hard pressed to prove it. Dr. Holster didn't know any Old Low Norse at all.

At first, I found the dictionary part very hard. Old Low Norse is pretty damn old, and the origins are rather obscure. It was actually easier to look *ahead,* at Swedish and Danish and Norwegian, to see what those Old Low Norse words would *become.* Mainly, I discovered, they were just bad pronunciations of Old West Norse and Old East Norse.

Then I found a way to make the dictionary part easy. Since no one knew anything about Old Low Norse, I could make things up. I made up a lot of origins. This made the translation of *Akthelt and Gunnel* easier too. I started making up a lot of words. It's very hard to tell real Old Low Norse from made-up Old Low Norse.

Dr. Wolfram Holster never knew the difference.

But I had some difficulty finishing the thesis. I would like to say that I stopped out of reverence for the main characters. It was a very personal love story and no one knew what it meant. I would like to say that I stopped because I felt Akthelt and Gunnel should be allowed to keep their privacy. But anyone who knows me at all would say that was a shameless lie. They would say I stopped simply because I hated *Akthelt and Gunnel,* or because I was bored, or because I was lazy, or because I had made up so much phony Old Low Norse that I could no longer keep the story straight.

There are elements of truth in what they would say, but it's also true that I was deeply moved by *Akthelt and Gunnel.* To be sure, it is an awful ballad. It's impossible to imagine anyone singing it, for example; for one thing, it's much too long. Also, I once characterized its metrics and rhyme scheme as "multiple and flexible." Actually, it has no rhyme scheme; it tries to rhyme when it can. And metrics were simply not known to its anonymous Old Low Norse author. (I imagine that author, by the way, as a peasant housewife.)

There is a false assumption usually made about the ballads of this period: that since the subjects were always kings and queens and princes and princesses, the authors were always royalty too. But peasants wrote about those kings and queens. The royalty was not alone in thinking that kings and queens were somehow better; part of being a peasant was thinking that kings and queens were better. I suspect that a fair portion of the population still thinks that way.

But Akthelt and Gunnel *were* better. They were in love; they were two against the world; they were formidable. And so was the world. I thought I knew the story.

I started out being faithful to the original. My translation is literal through the first fifty-one stanzas. Then I followed the text of the story fairly closely, just using my own details, until stanza one hundred and twenty. Then I translated pretty loosely for another hundred and fifty stanzas or so. I stopped at stanza two hundred and eighty and tried a literal translation again, just to see if I'd lost the hang of it.

> *Gunnel uppvaktat att titta Akthelt.*
> *Hanz kniv af slik lang.*
>
> *Uden hun kende inde hunz hjert*
> *Den varld af ogsa mektig.*
>
> Gunnel loved to look at Akthelt.
> His knife was so long.
>
> But she knew in her heart
> The world was too strong.

I stopped reading with this wretched stanza and gave up on *Akthelt and Gunnel.* Dr. Holster *laughed* at this stanza. So did Biggie. But *I* didn't laugh. The world *is* too strong—I saw it all coming!—the author was trying to foreshadow the inevitable doom! Clearly Akthelt and Gunnel were headed for grief. I knew, and I simply didn't want to see it out.

Lies! they would be shouting at me, those who knew me then. Old Bogus's mush-minded ability to read his own sentimentality into everything around him! The world was too strong—for *him!* He saw *himself* headed for grief—the only one we knew who could see a lousy movie and love it, read a rotten book and weep, if it had a flicker or a jot to do with *him!* Muck in his mind! Goo in his heart! What do you think he's called Bogus for? For *truth?*

Never mind them, the heartless *schlubs.* I live in another *varld* now.

When I showed Tulpen stanza two hundred and eighty she reacted in her solemn fashion. She put her head down to my heart and listened. Then she made me listen to hers. She does this when she recognizes a vulnerable situation; there are no sarcastic breast-flips when she's moved.

"Strong?" she said. I was listening to her heart; I nodded.

"Mektig," I said.

"Mektig?" She liked the sound; she went off playing with the word. Playing with the words was one of the things I really liked about Old Low Norse.

So there. Yogurt and lots of water, and a certain sympathy when sympathy matters. I'm all right. Things are straightening out. There is the matter of my urinary tract, of course, but in general things are straightening out.

Prelude to the Last Stand

Bogus Trumper
918 Iowa Ave.
Iowa City, Iowa

Oct. 2, 1969

Mr. Cuthbert Bennett
Caretaker / The Pillsbury Estate
Mad Indian Point
Georgetown, Maine

My Dear Couth:

Am in receipt of your fine encouragements and most generous check. They have Biggie and me down and under at Iowa State Bank & Trust; I relish the feeling of plunking your check on them. If Biggie and I are ever in the chips, you'll be our honorary caretaker. In fact, we'd love to take care of you, Couth—to see that you eat enough during your long, alone winters; that you brush your mane forty strokes before sleep; and to provide a fine young fire for your sea-drafty bed. In fact, I know just the fine young fire for you! Her name is Lydia Kindle. Really.

I met her in the language lab. She takes freshman German, but little else has touched her. She approached me yesterday, chirping, "Mr. Trumper, are there no tapes with *songs?* I mean, I *know* the conversation. Aren't there any German ballads, or even opera?"

I stalled her; I browsed through the files with her bemoaning the lack of music in the language lab, and life in general. She's as shy as a cat underfoot; she fears her skirt might brush against your knee.

306 – The Water-Method Man

Lydia Kindle wants German ballads whispered in her ear. Or even *opera,* Couth!

I harbor no such musical illusion for my new job, my most degrading employment to date. I sell buttons and pennants and cowbells at the Iowa football games. I lug a large plywood board from gate to gate around the stadium. The board is wide and tippy with an easel-type stand; the wind blows it down; tiny gold footballs are scratched, buttons chip, pennants wrinkle and smudge. I get a commission: 10% of what I sell.

"Just one dollar for this Hawkeye pennant! A bell for two bucks! Big badges only seventy-five cents! It's a dollar, madam, for the pins with the little gold footballs attached. The kids love them; the footballs are just small enough for the wee ones to swallow. No, sir, this bell is *not* broken! It is simply a little bent. These bells are unbreakable. They'll dong forever."

I get to see the game for free, but I hate football. And I have to wear this bright-yellow apron with a fat change-pocket. A large, shiny badge on my coat says: HAWKEYE ENTERPRISES—GO HAWKS! Every badge is numbered too; we communicate around the stadium by numbers. Competition is fierce for the best stand. On Saturday Number 368 said to me, "This is my post, 501. Lug off, will you?" He wore a tie with red footballs on it; he sold many more pennants and buttons and cowbells than I did. I cleared just enough for a three-month packet of birth-control pills for Biggie.

Root for Iowa, Couth. Next game I might clear enough to have myself sterilized.

I was told that if Iowa ever won a football game, we would all sell many more things. The psychology of the fans was outlined to us in our Warm-Up Meeting by the concession sales head of Hawkeye Enterprises, Mr. Fred Paff, who told us that Iowans were proud folks, in need of a winner before they'd adorn their aerials and sprout badges and pins on their coats. "Nobody likes to be associated with a loser," Paff said, and to *me* he said, "Well, we're both Freds, you know. How about that?"

"I know another Fred in Spokane, Washington," I told him. "Perhaps we should try to get something going."

"A sense of humor!" Fred Paff cried. "You'll do well here. A sense of humor is essential with the fans."

Let it be known, Couth, that you have more loyal and constant fans than these Iowans. Biggie and I appreciated your photographs almost as much as your money. Biggie especially liked your "Self-Portrait w/Seaweed." I frankly suspect it's illegal to send such photographs through the mail, and I don't mean to insult your body, but I preferred "Dead Gull No. 8."

Please dip into your darkroom and print one like that for me; in fact, make it *of* me. Make me prone and sort of sallow; fold my hands in the appropriate fashion and place the ready coffin near my figure; crack the casket's lid ajar, waiting for Fred Bogus Trumper, who at any moment now could easily be tempted by that plush velvet liner. Destroy the negative. Print only one 8 × 10. Superimposed, include the faces of my family: Biggie solid with grief, but not bitter, and Colm at play with the casket's ornate handle. Please underexpose my father and mother. Move my father's mouth; in fact, *blur* it. He orates over the dead. The caption reads: "A professional man must suffer his training . . ." Then seal it in a black matboard and mail the whole thing to the University of Iowa Business Office, with a curt note of apology for the failure of the deceased to pay his tuition. Which has been raised again, by vote of the trustees, to include an additional recreation fee. To pay, no doubt, for new gold football cleats and a Homecoming Day parade float: millions of yellow roses, shaped to form a giant ear of corn.

You're lucky to have a darkroom, Couth. I see you naked in your eerie safelight, awash in chemicals, developing, enlarging; you print yourself on a clean white sheet. Sometime, if there ever is time, you must teach me photography. The control of it amazes me. I remember watching you bathe your prints; I saw the images emerging and defining underwater; it was more than I could stand! As if so many ameboid things swam into place and made a man.

I think of this while translating the eighty-third stanza of *Akthelt and Gunnel.* It's the last word that bothers me: *Klegwoerum.* My thesis chairman thinks it should be "fertile." I say "fecund." My friend Ralph Packer suggests "rank." And Biggie says it doesn't really matter. There is a hurtful ton of truth in Biggie.

I think she's cracking, though. It's not like her, but she's taking it personally that some octogenarian in the hospital gooses her when she empties his bedpan. But do you know, Biggie never cries. Do you know what she does do, though? She finds a hangnail and tugs it slowly down her finger; I've seen her tease one past the first joint. Biggie bleeds, but she never cries.

Couth, I have felt close to you ever since I caught your clap from Elsbeth Malkas. Or we both caught and shared what Elsbeth had to start with. The details of who began it have never seemed to me essential for our friendship.

Once more, flush all seventeen of the johns for me. It would do my heart good to know that somewhere there are toilets which are not clogged with jockstraps. Choose a foggy night, open all the windows—sound bounces best off water in the fog—and flush away! I will hear you and rejoice.

Biggie sends her love. She's in the kitchen peeling her fingers. She's pretty busy, otherwise I'd ask her for a hangnail to enclose, a shred of her Trumpering fortitude boldly traveling from Iowa to Maine.

Love,
Bogus

7

Ralph Packer Films, Inc.
109 Christopher Street
New York, New York 10014

Tulpen and me at work. She does the editing; actually, Ralph is his own editor, but Tulpen assists him. She also does some darkroom work, but Ralph is his own developer too. I don't know anything about developing and not much about editing. I'm the sound tracker; I tape in the music; if there's sync-sound, I get it right; if there's a voice-over, I lay it in; if there's offstage noise, I make some; when there's a narrator, I often do the talking. I have a nice big voice.

The film is nearly finished by the time it's brought to me, with most of the unusable footage cut out, and the sequence of shots pretty much the way Ralph wants it, at least rough-spliced—more or less the way Ralph will finally edit it. Ralph is very close to a one-man band, with some technical help from Tulpen and me. It's always Ralph's script and his camera-work; it's *his* movie. But Tulpen and I have great technique, and there's a Ralph Packer Fan Club kid named Kent who runs errands.

Tulpen and I are not members in The Ralph Packer Fan Club. The kid named Kent is a one-man band at that. I don't mean to suggest that Ralph Packer's films are unknown. His first film, *The Group Thing,* won first prize in the National Student Film Festival. My nice big voice is in that film; Ralph made it when he was a graduate student in the Cinematography Workshop at Iowa.

I met him in the language lab. In a lull between lab sections, I was editing tapes for freshman German when this shuffling man of hair came in. Possibly twenty, or forty; possibly student, or faculty, Trotskyite or Amish farmer, human or animal; a thief lumbering out of a camera shop, laden with lenses and light meters; a bear who after a terrible and violent struggle ate a photographer. This beast approached me.

I was still doing my translation of *Akthelt and Gunnel* then. I felt myself confronted by Akthelt's father, Old Thak. As he came closer a musk moved with him. One hundred glints of fluorescent light, off his lenses, buckles and polished parts.

"You Trumper?" he said.

A wise man, I thought, would confess it all now. Admit the translation was a fraud. Hope Old Thak goes back to the grave.

"*Vroog etz?*" I asked, just testing him.

"Good," he grumbled; he understood! He was Old Thak! But all he said was "Ralph Packer," freeing a white hand from an arctic mitten, pushing this toward me out of the cuff of his Eskimo parka. "You speak German, right? And you know tapes?"

"Right," I said cautiously.

"Ever done any dubbing?" he asked. "I'm making a film." A *pervert,* I thought; wants me in his blue movie. "I need a German voice," he said. "Some kind of clever German slipping in and out of the English narration."

I knew those film-making students. Passing by Benny's and seeing through the window a terrible fight, a girl with her bra torn off, holding her tits. I rush inside to this lady's aid, only to spill a cameraman from his dolly, tangle my feet in extension cords, jar a man with his hands full of microphones. And the girl says tiredly, "*Easy,* hey. It's just a goddamn *movie.*" She gives you a look to say: Because of nuts like you, I'm on my fourth bra today.

". . . well, if you like playing with tapes and recorders," Ralph Packer was saying, "jamming voices, jumbling time. You know, sound montage. There's just a couple of things I want done, then you can play with it—you know, do what you want. Maybe give me some ideas . . ."

It was such a shock at the time: to be a football-pennant salesman, and here's someone suggesting I might even have *ideas!*

"Hey," said Ralph Packer, looking at me. "You speak English too, don't you?"

"What do you pay?" I asked, and he whomped his arctic mitten down on my tape stack, sending one reel flopping like a stunned fish.

"Pay *you!*" he shouted. A great shrug of his shoulders sent a zoom lens around his neck swinging. Scenes of Old Thak in a rage sprang to mind.

> Though well into his dotage, and weak
> With the arrow sunk deep in his chest,
> Which was wider than Gurk's wine cask,
> Old Thak strode up to the assassin-archer
> And strangled him with his own bowstring.
>
> Then, with his great palm, hardened
> By holding the reins for a hundred horses,
> Thak drove the arrow through his own chest
> And drew it out his back, groaning mightily.
>
> With the shaft still slimy with the old one's gore,
> Thak slew the treacherous Gurk—a disemboweling
> Thrust! Then did the Great Thak thank Gwolph
> And blessed the banquet laid before him bloodily.

Thus did Ralph Packer storm about the listening booths of the language lab, and a frightened gathering of freshman German students cowered in the door while he ranted on.

"Sweet fuck! I should *pay* you? For an *experience?* And an *opportunity!* Look, Thumper"—a titter from my disloyal students—"you should pay me for giving you the chance! I'm just getting started, I don't even pay *myself!* I sold fifteen hundred fucking football pennants for one wide-angle lens, and you want to be paid for your education!"

"Wait! Packer!" I cried; he was heading out the door, the students scampering.

"Fuck you, Thump-Thump," he said. And turning fiercely on the freshman Germans: "Fuck him, I say!" For a moment, sensing their blind dread, I feared the lot of them would rush me and impulsively obey his command. But I ran after him. I found him watering himself with deep, greedy draughts at the drinking fountain in the hall.

"I didn't know you sold football pennants," I said.

Later, when he was pleased with my sound-tracking games, Packer told me he'd be able to pay me one day. "When I'm able to pay myself, Thump-Thump, there will be work for you."

So Ralph Packer was true to his word. *The Group Thing* was a mild success. That part where the "Horst Wessel Song" is played over a beery crowd at Benny's? That was my idea. And the part with the Math department meeting at the University of Iowa, with German dubbed in and the subtitles reading: *"First* you arrest them with the proper court order, *then* you start arresting so many that group trials become acceptable, *then* you've got them so worried about the detention camps that they don't bother you about having to have a court order any more, so then . . ."

It was a kind of propaganda film. The evil was the innate hostility directed at the individual by groups. It was not a political film, however; all groups were equally misrepresented. The enemy was any unified crowd. Even a classroom with nodding heads: "Yes, yes, I see, I agree, *jawohl!"*

Everyone thought that *The Group Thing* was "innovative." Only one major complaint was ever leveled against it, and it came to Ralph in the form of a letter from the German American Society of Columbus, Ohio. They said the film was anti-German; it "raked over a lot of old coals," they said. There wasn't anything especially *German* about groups, they said, and there wasn't anything wrong with groups, either. Ralph was referred to as a "nut." The letter was not actually signed by anybody, by any real person. It was stamped, with one of those ink stampers: THE GERMAN AMERICAN SOCIETY.

"Another fucking group," said Ralph. "Over five hundred people wrote that letter. And shit, Thump-Thump, I didn't really *mean* anything. I mean, I don't *know* what I meant . . ."

This is still true of Ralph; it has been the major criticism of his films. They are nearly always called "innovative," often "unpretentious," usually "truthful." But *The New York Times,* for example, notes "a certain lack of resolution . . . he fails to commit himself to a point of view." *The Village Voice* finds that "the visions are always striving to be personal, authentic and fresh, yet Packer fails to really deal with the issues . . . a simple portrait of the action seems to satisfy him." I think it satisfies me too.

"Shit," says Ralph. "They're just *pictures,* Thump-Thump."

In fact, their lack of "meaning" I find especially refreshing.

The Group Thing was his only propaganda film; it was the only one to win a prize, too. His next two films, I wasn't in on; I was leaving my wife and mind behind.

Ralph went on a long lam, from Iowa to New York. *Soft Dirt* was about a rock group. Ralph just followed them around when Soft Dirt was on a concert tour. Interviews with their girls, shots of the guys cutting each other's hair, shots of the leg-wrestling competition organized among the girls, shots of what the winners won. The high point of the film comes when the leader's dog gets accidentally electrocuted by an amplifier. The group canceled a week of concerts; out of sympathy, fans donated about fifty dogs. "They're all very nice dogs," said the leader, "but they're just not like old Soft Dirt." That had been the name of the dog too.

The third film was about a small traveling circus, which Ralph followed through an endless series of one-night stands. There's a lot of footage of the tent going up and coming down, and interviews with the trapeze girls.

"Is the circus dead?"

"God . . . why would you ever think that?"

And a very long vignette about the elephant keeper who lost three fingers on his right hand when the elephant stepped on him.

"Do you still like elephants?"

"Sure, I love elephants."

"Even this particular elephant who stepped on your hand?"

"Especially this particular elephant. He didn't *mean* to step on my hand. He didn't even know what he was stepping on. I just put my hand where he was stepping; he would have stepped there anyway. And he really felt awful about it."

"The elephant felt awful? He *knew* he'd stepped on your hand?"

"Christ, of course he knew. I yelled, 'You're stepping on my fucking hand!' Sure, he knew all right, and he just felt terrible."

Then there follows an episodic series of shots of the elephant, trying to convey how sorry he was. It was Ralph's worst film, I think. I can't ever remember the title.

But now that I'm back as his sound tracker, his films should improve—soundwise, at least. We're working on one now called *Down on the Farm.* It's about a hippie commune called the Free Farm. The Free Farmers want everybody to use the land—any land. They think private property is bullshit.

The land should be free to them who'd *use* it. They run into a little trouble, from some real farmers up in Vermont. The real farmers think private property is okay. The Free Farmers try to tell the real farmers how badly they're being screwed by not having any free land. They appear to be headed toward a confrontation. A small liberal arts college in the area lends a certain intellectual confusion to the situation. Ralph goes up to Vermont every weekend to see if the confrontation has occurred yet. He comes back with reels and reels, tapes and tapes. "It's still building," he says.

"When the winter comes along," I tell him, "maybe the kids will get cold and hungry and just walk off the land."

"Then we'll film that," he says.

"Maybe there won't be any confrontation," I suggest.

"Maybe there won't," Ralph says, and Tulpen tips her tit with the back of her hand.

This irks Ralph. Tulpen was already working for Ralph when I came to New York; Ralph gave her the job because she was sleeping with him. Oh, long ago. Tulpen didn't know anything about editing film, but Ralph showed her. When she learned to do it very well, she stopped sleeping with him. Ralph didn't fire her because she's a fantastic editor, but sometimes Ralph gets mad about it. "You only slept with me to get this job," he tells her.

"You only gave me the job because I slept with you," Tulpen tells him, unperturbed. "Don't you like my work?" she asks him. "I like the job."

There is this understanding stalemate between them.

The kid named Kent, who runs errands, is another story.

Tulpen and me in the darkroom, sipping coffee, wondering where the doughnuts are. Tulpen is trimming some of Ralph's stills, hot off the dryer, cropping them in the big paper cutter. *Chomp!* And it's been two weeks since I've heard a word from that damn Biggie. Are the other kids kind to Colm in school? Does he still bite?

"Anything wrong?" Tulpen asks.

"My prick," I say. "I think it's getting gummed up again. Wretched water method . . ."

"See your doctor, Trumper," she says casually. "Have the operation."

Chomp! goes the terrible paper cutter; visions of Vigneron blood fill my mind.

In comes Kent. "Hey!" *Hey yourself, Kent.* "Hey, you seen the new footage? He's really got it now."

"Got what, Kent?"

"Great *light* in the new stuff. It's getting cold up there now. Even the weather's closing in on them. Somebody's going to make a move. I mean, the fucking camera is *anticipating* it."

"That doesn't mean it has to happen, Kent."

Ralph comes in with a huff-puff of cold air. Sealskin boots, arctic mittens, Eskimo parka, though it's only fall. Trying to imagine Ralph alive in a tropical climate presents a problem: he would have to change his fur image.

He could wear wicker and straw and reeds wrapped around him: a giant basket!

"Hey!" Kent says to him. "I saw *White Knees* last night."

"Whose?" says Ralph. We all know Kent doesn't get much.

"You know, hey. *White Knees,*" Kent insists. "It's the new Grontz film."

"Oh, yeah, yeah," says Ralph, unmittening, debooting, emerging from his wool.

"Well, it's just another lousy one," Kent says. "More of the same, like his earlier shit. Heavy, you know?"

"Yeah, yeah," says Ralph, unmuffled, looking around. Something is missing.

"I looked at your new footage this morning," Kent tells him. Ralph is thinking, What's missing? "It's just great, Ralph," Kent tells him. "Even the fucking weather—"

"Kent?" Ralph says. "Where are the doughnuts?"

"I was just waiting for you to get here," Kent says, flushing.

"Two jellies, one cream puff," Ralph says. "Tulpen?"

"*Two* cream puffs."

"Thump-Thump?"

"A cruller."

"Two cream puffs, two jellies and one cruller, Kent," Ralph says.

When Kent leaves on his mission, Ralph asks us, "Who in hell is Grontz?"

"Search me," says Tulpen.

"*White Knees,*" I say. "God knows . . ."

"Does Kent smoke?" Ralph asks. No one has any idea. "Well, if he doesn't," Ralph says, "he should try some. And if he does, he should stop."

Back comes Kent, a mine of mystery and information.

"Two jellies, two cream puffs, one cruller."

"Thank you."

"Thank you."

"Thank you, Kent."

"Wardell's new one opens Friday night, at the Beppo," Kent informs.

"It won't last a week," I tell him, then look at Tulpen: Who is Wardell? Her look back at me says, Where is the Beppo?

"Right, right," says Ralph.

We watch Kent cramming the coffeepot. "Don't make it waterproof, Kent," says Tulpen.

Ralph is visibly upset with his two jellies. "*Red* jelly," he says, prodding with a cautious finger. "I like the purple."

"Grape, Ralph," I say.

"Yeah, grape," he says. "This red shit is uneatable."

Kent is worried. "I heard that Marco is out on the Coast," he tells us, "doing the riots."

"How's the cruller, Thump-Thump?"

"An excellent cruller, Ralph."

"Two crullers, Kent," says Ralph. "Can you eat another one, Thump-Thump?"

"No," Tulpen says. "He's getting fat."

"*Three* more crullers, Kent," says Ralph, poking the foul red jelly.

"You're *already* fat," Tulpen tells him. "Trumper can still be saved."

"Three crullers, Kent," says Ralph.

A static friction in the room escapes when Kent opens the door. Ralph listens for Kent's cloddy walking sounds out on the sidewalk. Something conspiratorial and special is being saved for our ears alone; we can always tell. Ralph goes a fair bit out of his way to avoid anything too personal with Kent. A kind of professional self-protection, I assume.

"Boy, Thump-Thump," he says; his broad arms draw Tulpen and me together. "*Boy,* you should have seen the tail I met last night . . ." But he is watching Tulpen, waiting for her to raise one breast with the back of her hand. She's subtle with him; she turns away. Moving toward the door, her elbow lifts a little behind her.

"I saw that!" Ralph shouts. But she's gone; the door to the editing room closes, and I am left alone with Ralph Packer, who—in spite of (perhaps, *because* of) never knowing what he means—is a vanguard in underground film.

We are waiting for crullers.

8

Other Old Mail

Fred Trumper
918 Iowa Ave.
Iowa City, Iowa

Oct. 3, 1969

Humble Oil & Refining Co.
Box 790
Tulsa, Oklahoma

Dear Sirs:

I am in receipt of your reminder. Regarding that, I *do* consider my credit with you as a "privilege," and I have every intention of avoiding the "embarrassment" you speak of.

Enclosed is my check for $3.00. My Balance Due is thereby reduced to $44.56, which of course I shall be forwarding to you shortly.

You see, my son has been very sick.

Gratefully,
Fred Trumper
(Esso card # 657-679-896-22)

Fred Trumper
918 Iowa Ave.
Iowa City, Iowa

Oct. 3, 1969

Mr. Harry Estes
Dept. of Collection
Sinclair Refining Co.
Box 1333
Chicago, Illinois

Dear Mr. Estes:

You will find my check for $15.00 enclosed. And although this may be, in your eyes, "another drop in the bucket," it constitutes a considerable effort for me. And despite the fact that my Balance Due, still outstanding, is $94.67—and I *can* "appreciate" your concern—it is also with great effort that I control myself from responding as I would like to your rude note.

We are both aware that your company is perhaps not so well known as some. Perhaps you might be advised by my long and good experience with other credit-card companies, who demonstrate a degree of cheerfulness and tolerance that your own company would do well to imitate. Perhaps you don't know what it is that makes a well-known company so well known? Well, I'll tell you. It's *patience.*

Alas, if more of the values we esteem in individuals would be incorporated into our business values, I'm sure each of us would be more pleased with one another.

I had the highest hopes for your organization when you first came out with that big warm friendly green dinosaur. I retain the highest hopes that you will eventually live up to your image.

Respectfully,
Fred Trumper
(Sinclair card # 555-546-215-91)

Fred Trumper
918 Iowa Ave.
Iowa City, Iowa

Oct. 3, 1969

Iowa-Illinois Gas & Electric
520 Jefferson St.
Iowa City, Iowa

Dear Sirs:

Enclosed is $10.00 to reduce my Balance Due; the remainder, I realize, is enough to warrant your assessing me with an extra service charge. I will responsibly assume this charge, but I sincerely hope that you recognize the seriousness of my intentions to settle this balance, and that you will not discontinue my service.

Speaking for that service, I will say, in all sincerity, that Iowa-Illinois has provided the best electricity my wife and I have ever known. Seriously, we once lived in a part of the world where the lights were *always* going out.

We've also appreciated your policy of giving small children lollipops, if accompanied by their parents, at your downtown office and appliance center.

Thankfully,
Fred Trumper

Fred Trumper
918 Iowa Ave.
Iowa City, Iowa

Oct. 3, 1969

Northwestern Bell Telephone Co.
302 South Linn St.
Iowa City, Iowa

Dear Sirs:

In regard to my present Balance Due of $35.17: I will not pay one penny of this until you delete from my bill the sum of $16.75, and the corresponding tax—for a call I never made to Georgetown, Maine. I don't know anybody in Georgetown, Maine, and to my knowledge no one in Georgetown, Maine, knows me. This has happened before, if you remember, on a previous bill. I was charged for talking one hour and forty-five minutes to Vienna, Austria—which you finally acknowledged was an error, a foul-up involving the other half of my two-party line. About the other half of my two-party line, I could write you another letter, but your previous explanation of "Oversea Cable Operator Confusion" is not especially satisfying. In any case, it should not be my responsibility to tell you what I owe you.

Frankly,
Fred Trumper
(tel. 338-1536)

Fred Trumper
918 Iowa Ave.
Iowa City, Iowa

Oct. 3, 1969

Mr. Milo Kubik
Peoples Market
660 Dodge St.
Iowa City, Iowa

Dear Mr. Kubik:

Your meats are a taste of the big city, a breath of the best kitchen wind! You're the only place in Iowa City for a decent kidney, tongue, blood sausage and a good heart. And all the little foreign jars, the exotic little tins of food in translation! We are especially fond of the Ragout of Wild Boar in Médoc Sauce. My wife and I, Mr. Kubik, can make a meal of your hors d'oeuvre counter.

I hope you'll forgive us for overindulging ourselves with your quality items this month. I am able to make this $10.00 deposit (enclosed), but the remaining balance of $23.09 I will have to leave outstanding for just a short time.

Next month we will more carefully budget ourselves against your fine temptations, you can rest assured.

Honestly,
Fred & Sue Trumper

Fred Trumper
918 Iowa Ave.
Iowa City, Iowa

Oct. 3, 1969

Mr. Merlin Shumway
President / Iowa State Bank & Trust Co.
400 Clinton St.
Iowa City, Iowa

Mr. Shumway:

Enclosed is Mr. Cuthbert Bennett's check to me, for $250.00, endorsed to the bank, for deposit in my account (checking: 9 51 348). This should amply cover my minus balance.

I am really appalled that the bank saw fit to bounce my wife's check back to the clothier, Sumner Temple. Had you covered this check, my account would have been delinquent by no more than $3.80 plus Service Charge. This small gesture of courtesy would have spared my poor wife an unpleasantry with Mr. Temple over the phone; a needless embarrassment for such a piddling sum.

I can only suppose that you are holding the matter of my educational loan against me. But whatever your reasoning, I am tempted to move my account across the street to the Iowa First National. I will certainly do so if you continue to treat me with such suspicion. I simply had no idea I was overdrawn. As you see, I had in hand the available income to cover the deficit immediately.

Sincerely,
Fred Trumper

Fred Trumper
918 Iowa Ave.
Iowa City, Iowa

Oct. 3, 1969

Sears, Roebuck & Co.
Central States Office
1st Ave. & Kalona St.
Cedar Rapids, Iowa

Dear Sears:

Last June I purchased for my wife one Model X-100, Standard-Plus vacuum cleaner, which, at the suggestion of your sales office in Iowa City,

I elected to pay for under the terms of the Sears Easy-Payment Installment Plan.

At this time, there is no need for me to go into my shock at the rather steep service rates under this "boon" of a plan. At the moment I only want to know *how many* payments you have recorded for me, and why it is that you don't include my current Balance Due in this month's Easy-Packet Payment Envelope. Each month I receive this handy envelope from you, and the enclosed note simply says, PAYMENT DUE: $5.00.

But it seems I have been paying out $5.00 for an awfully long time. How much further do I have to go? Understandably, I am not about to pay this next installment until I receive some notice from you concerning how much I still owe.

I would offer you this piece of advice, so that you will not sully your great reputation among humble folk everywhere. Be forewarned: it would be a shame if Sears, because of its bigness and far-reaching tendrils into the homes and minds of young masses, forgot, or tramped on, the simple needs of the "little person." After all, isn't it us "little people" who make Sears so big?

> A Concerned Little Person,
> Fred Trumper
> (Easy-Payment-Installment Invoice No. 314-312-54-6)

> Fred Trumper
> 918 Iowa Ave.
> Iowa City, Iowa
>
> Oct. 3, 1969

Consumers Union
Edt. Offices of *Consumer Reports*
Mt. Vernon, New York

Dearest Sirs:

From one nonprofit organization to another, let me tell you that you are noble and good and a great consolation in the face of creeping capitalism everywhere!

Where experience permits me an opinion, let me say that I am in complete agreement with your 1968 uncoverings concerning false advertisement all around us. You are to be congratulated. Keep giving them hell! Don't ever be bought!

However, I beg to differ with you in regard to Sears, Roebuck & Co. Most of your listings for their products and service range from "fair" to "good." I have great faith in your research, and I'm willing to admit that your sphere of sources is far greater than my own. But I feel I should add to your findings this consumer's reaction to a certain Model X-100 Standard-Plus vacuum cleaner. Have you ever looked into *that* mechanical wonder? Well, go pick one up under Sears Easy Payment Installment Plan.

You do such healthful, splendid work that I would hate to see this oversight hurt your reputation.

Yours in nonprofit,
Fred Trumper

_____

Fred Trumper
918 Iowa Ave.
Iowa City, Iowa

Oct. 3, 1969

The Business Office
University of Iowa
Iowa City, Iowa

Dear Business:

I'm afraid that this month I'll be forced to assume the $5.00 Penalty Charge for late payment of tuition.

However, although I accept this $5.00 charge, I will deduct $5.00 from my tuition bill as a refusal to pay the newly added Recreation Fee (also $5.00), a school expense for which I am *not* willing to assume responsibility.

I am a graduate student. I am twenty-six years old. I am married and I have a son. I am not at the University of Iowa for "recreation" of any kind. Let them who recreate pay for their own fun. I'm not having any fun at all.

The only reason I'm telling you this is that I thought there might be some misunderstanding on your part when you eventually receive my payment of tuition. You see, it might look as if I have ignored the Penalty Charge for late payment. *That* $5.00 I will pay; it is the *other* $5.00 that will not be included in my check. (Which I will get to you soon.)

It *is* confusing, there being several $5.00 figures involved, but I hope I have made myself clear.

Seriously,
Fred Trumper
(student ID 23 345 G)

Fred Trumper
918 Iowa Ave.
Iowa City, Iowa

Oct. 3, 1969

University of Iowa Educational Placement Service
Student Union Bldg.
University of Iowa
Iowa City, Iowa
Atten. Mrs. Florence Marsh

Dear Mrs. Marsh:
Having paid my Service Fee to you some time ago, I expected that your services would be at least reasonable. Your current enclosure for "Available Positions" does not strike me as reasonable in any way. I specified to you —in an endless form, filled out in triplicate—my capabilities, my field of interest, my degrees, and where (in what region of this country) I sought a teaching position.

In regard to your current information, I do *not* want to meet an interviewer from Carother's Community College of Carother's, Arkansas, "offering a position at their Maple Bliss campus, for five sections of freshman rhetoric at $5,000 per annum." Do you think I am utterly mad?

I told you: New England, Colorado or Northern California; at a college where I'd have some opportunity to teach more than freshman-level courses; for a salary of at least $6,500, plus moving expenses.

Some service you offer, I must say.

Dismally,
Fred Trumper

Fred Trumper
918 Iowa Ave.
Iowa City, Iowa

Oct. 3, 1969

Shive & Hupp
Loan Associates, Farm & Town
U.S. Route 69, West
Marengo, Iowa

Dear Mr. Shive & Mr. Hupp:
Sirs, I repeat: I am unable at this time to make my interest-due payment to you. Please refrain from sending me further form letters about your

famous Rising Rate Scale, and your awkwardly veiled threats of "constables."

Just do what you have to do. That's all *I'm* doing.

Truthfully,
Fred Trumper

Fred Trumper
918 Iowa Ave.
Iowa City, Iowa

Oct. 3, 1969

Addison & Halsey Collection Agency
456 Davenport St.
Des Moines, Iowa
Atten. Mr. Robert Addison

Dear Bobby,
    Cram it.

Best,
Fred

Mice, Turtles & Fish First!

Tulpen takes care of the bills now. I don't even see the checkbook. I contribute, of course, and every week or so I ask her how our money is.

"Are you hungry?" she says. "Do you have enough to drink?"

"Well, sure, I have enough . . ."

"Well, is there something you need?"

"Well, no . . ."

"Well, the money's just fine, then," she says. "*I* don't need any more."

"*I'm* fine," I tell her.

"Was there something you wanted to buy?" Tulpen asks.

"No, no, Tulpen—really, everything's fine with me."

"Well, everything's fine with *me,*" she insists, and I try to force myself never to bring it up again.

But I just can't believe it! "How much do we have?" I ask her. "I mean, just to get an idea of some rough figure . . ."

"Does Biggie need money?"

"No, Biggie doesn't need a thing, Tulpen."

"You want to send something to Colm—a truck, a boat or something?"

"A truck or a boat?"

"Well, some special toy, is that it?"

"Jesus, never mind," I say. "I was just wondering, that's all . . ."

"Well, honestly, Trumper, you should say what you mean."

Indeed, I should stick to the facts. That's what she means.

But I honestly think my avoidance of the facts has as much to do with my distrusting the relevance of them as it has to do with my lying a lot. I don't think the statistics in my life have ever meant very much.

When my mother used to write me, she'd ask about the stuff we had. She was concerned about whether we had a toidy pot for Colm. If we had one, we were all right. My father also suggested snow tires; with snow tires, we'd be happy all winter. I imagined their friends asking them how we were; my father would mention our winter driving, and my mother would bring up the toidy pot. How else could they have answered?

Most recently, in a terse phone conversation with my father, I was asked how I paid my bills. "With checks," I told him. (I guess that's how Tulpen does it.) "You shouldn't send cash through the mails." But he asked me as if that was all he needed to know—and knowing that, he would know about me.

Rituals are more revealing than facts!

For example, I once kept a tape recorder who was my friend. Also, I wrote letters to my wife; I mean, I wrote to Biggie while I was still living with her. Of course I never gave these letters to her; they weren't really letters, then; it was the ritual of writing them that mattered.

I showed one to Tulpen.

Iowa City
Oct. 5, 1969

Thinking of you, Colm—my only child. And you too, Biggie—those hospital smocks don't become you.

The way you arise at six: your fine, firm, muscular lunge for the alarm; your warm collapse back against me.

"Another day, Big," I mumble.

"Oh, Bogus," you say. "Remember how we used to wake up in Kaprun?"

"All the snow piled against the window," I mumble, by rote. "Some of it blown under the sash, a little puff of it on the sill—"

"And the breakfast smells!" you cry. "And all the skis and boots in the downstairs hall—"

"Talk softer, Big," I say. "You'll wake up Colm . . ." who just then begins his cooing down the hall from our room.

"Don't shout at him when I'm gone," you say, Big—and you're out of bed, tucking me back in. Prancing over the cold floor, your large, upstanding boobs peek at the dawn; they point across the hall to the kitchen window (what symbol intended by that direction, I cannot guess).

Then your bra, Big, seizes you like the bit shocks the horse. That damn hospital smock crinkles coldly down over you, and my Biggie is gone, anesthetized, sanitized; you're garbed as shapeless as a dextrose jug, which you'll see later this morning, upended, and dripping down its sugary strength to the elderly.

You grab a bite at the hospital cafeteria, chatting with the other nurses' helpers. They talk about what time their men came home last night, and I know you tell them, "My Bogus is in bed with our Colm. And last night he slept with me."

But last night, Big, you said, "Your father's a prick."

And I've never once heard you use the word quite like that. I agreed with you, of course, and you said, "What is it he wants you to prove to him?"

I said, "That I'm capable of falling flat on my face."

"Well, that's where you are," you said, Big. "What more does he want?"

"He must be waiting," I said, "for me to tell him he was right all along. He wants me to crawl across the floor and kiss his powdered doctor's shoes. Then I am to say, 'Father, I want to be a professional man.' "

"It's not funny, Bogus," you said. And I'd thought I could always count on a laugh from you, Biggie.

"It's the last year, Big," I told you. "We'll go back to Europe. You can ski again."

But all you said was, "Fuck." I've never once heard you use the word quite like that.

Then you just flounced in bed alongside me, leafing backward through a ski magazine, though I must have told you a hundred times that it's a poor way to read.

When you read, Big, you set your chin on your high chest; your thick, honey, shoulder-cut hair juts forward, covering your cheeks, and all I can see is the tip of your sharp nose peeking out of your hair.

But it's always a ski magazine, isn't it, Biggie? Nothing mean intended, perhaps, but just a reminder to me of what I've robbed you of, isn't it? When you find the inevitable Alpine scene, you say, "Oh, look, Bogus. Weren't we there? Wasn't that near Zell, or—no! Maria Zell, isn't it? Just look at them piling out of that train. God, look at the *mountains,* Bogus . . ."

"Well, we're in Iowa now, Big," I remind you. "We'll take a drive tomorrow out in the corn. We'll look for a slight hill. We might more easily find a hog with a sloped back. We could coat him with mud, I could prop up his snout and you could ski between his ears, down to his tail. Not much of a run, but . . ."

"I didn't *mean* anything, Bogus," you say. "I just wanted you to look at the picture."

But why can't I leave you alone?

I keep at you: "I could tow you behind the car, Big. You could slalom through the cornstalks, routing pheasants! Tomorrow I'll simply install four-wheel drive in the Corvair."

"Come on," you say; you sound tired. Our bedside lamp blinks, crackles, goes out, and in the dark you whisper, "Did you pay the electric bill, Bogus?"

"It's just a fuse," I tell you, and leaving the warm groove you put in our bed, I pad down to the basement. It's just as well I'm here, because I've not been down in the basement today to spring the mousetrap that you insist on setting for the mouse I don't want to catch. So I spare the mouse once more and replace the fuse —the same one that always blows, for no reason.

Upstairs, Biggie, you shout down to me, "That's it! It's on again! You got it!" As if some marvel has been performed. And when I come back up to you, you've got your strong, blond arms folded and you're kicking your feet under the sheets. "No more reading now," you say, a fierce twinkle about your eyes, and those heavy feet swishing.

Oh, I know you mean only the best for me, Big, but I know too that the thing with the feet is an old skier's exercise, good for the ankles. You don't fool me.

I tell you, "I'll be right there, Big. Just let me check on Colm."

I always watch him sleep for a while. What I mind about children is that they're so vulnerable, so fragile-looking. Colm: I get up in the night to make sure your breathing hasn't stopped.

"Honestly, Bogus, he's a very healthy child."

"Oh, I'm sure he is, Big. But he just seems so *small.*"

"He's good-sized for his age, Bogus."

"Oh, I know, Big. That's not exactly what I mean . . ."

"Well, please don't wake him up, with your damn checking on him."

And some nights, I cry out, "Look, Big! He's *dead!*"

"He's *sleeping,* for Christ's sake . . ."

"But look how he's just lying there," I insist. *"His neck is broken!"*

"You sleep like that yourself, Bogus . . ."

Well, like father, like son; I'm sure I'm wholly capable of breaking my neck in my sleep.

"Come back to bed, Bogus." I hear you calling me to your groove.

It's not really that I'm reluctant to go there. But I have to check the stove; the pilot light is always going out. And that furnace sounds funny; one day we will wake up baked. Then check the lock on the door. There's more than hogs and corn in Iowa—or there *might* be.

"Will you ever come to bed?" you shout.

"I'm coming! I'm on my way, Big!" I promise.

Bogus Trumper was just checking and double-checking. You may call him improvident, but never blasé.

––––––––

Tulpen was unimpressed with my letter for no one. "God, you haven't changed at all," she said.

"I've a new life," I said. "I'm a different man."

"Once you worried about a mouse," she said. "Now it's turtles and fish."

She sort of had me there. My silence made her smile and lift, just slightly, a breast with the back of her hand. Sometimes I could really whap her when she does that!

But it's true. I *do* worry about the turtles and fish. Not in the same way that I once worried about the mouse, though. That mouse lived in constant peril; it was my responsibility to keep him out of Biggie's trap. But Tulpen was already taking care of these fish and turtles when I moved in. Her bed is framed on three sides by bookcases, waist-high; we are walled in by words. And all along the tops of the cases, in a watery U around us, these gurgling aquariums sit. They bubble all night long. She keeps them lit with underwater neon rays. I'll admit that it helps when I have to get up to pee.

But the aura around the bed takes getting used to. In a half-sleep, you actually *feel* underwater, in spooky color, turtles and fish circling you.

She feeds the turtles with a single chunk of steak tied on a string; all night they gnash at the dangling meat; in the morning, the chunk is gray, like a dead thing, and Tulpen removes it. Thank God she feeds them only once a week.

And once I imagined that the man in the apartment above us was building a bomb. (He does something electrical at night; odd hums and crackles are heard, and the lights in the aquariums dim.) If that man's bomb blew up, there's enough water in those aquariums to drown us in our sleep.

One night, with such a thought, I considered calling Dr. Jean Claude Vigneron. For one thing, I have a complaint: the water method isn't quite working out. But more important, I just wanted to hear the voice of a confident man. And maybe I'd ask him how he got to be so cocksure. I think it would have pleased me more, though, to find a way to shock him, to fluster that confidence of his. I thought of calling him very late. "Dr. Vigneron?" I would say. "My prick just fell off." Just to see what he'd say.

I told Tulpen my plan. "You know what he'd say?" she said. "He'd say, 'Put it in the refrigerator and make an appointment with my secretary in the morning.'"

Even though I suspect she's right, I was glad she didn't doff her boob to me then. She's more sensitive than that. That once, she turned out the aquarium lights.

10

Let's Not Lose Track of Certain Statistics

It grieves him to remember lovely little Lydia Kindle, enraptured with freshman German, wanting ballads, or even opera, hummed to her in the *Muttersprache*. He obliged her; he made a tape for her of her very own. Deep-throated Bogus Trumper lulling her senseless with his favorite songs. It was to be a surprise.

He gave her the tape one afternoon in the language lab.

"Just for you, Miss Kindle. Some lieder I knew of . . ."

"Oh, Mr. Trumper!" she said, and scurried off to her earphones. He watched her big-eyed little face concentrating over the rim of the listening booth. At first she seemed so eager; then she scrunched up her pretty face critically; she stopped the tape—broke his rhythms!—played it back, stopped it again. She took notes. He went over to ask what was wrong.

"That's wrong, isn't it?" she asked, pointing to her elfin scribbles. "It's not *mude*, it's *müde*. But the singer missed the umlaut sound, every time."

"I'm the singer," he said in pain. It's so hard to be criticized by the young. And he added quickly, "German isn't my best foreign tongue. I'm really involved more in the Scandinavian languages—you know, Old Low Norse? I'm afraid my German is a bit rusty. I only thought you'd like the *songs.*" He was bitter with the heartless child.

But she said, then, so high and birdlike, as if her throat were pinched, or being kissed, "Oh, Mr. Trumper. It's a *beautiful* tape. You only missed *müde.* And I just *loved* the songs. You've such a nice big voice." And he thought: A *big* voice?

But all he said was, "You may have the tape. To keep." And retreated, leaving her stunned in the listening booth. Under the earphones now she dreamed.

When he closed the lab for suppertime, she skipped after him—careful, though, that she didn't touch him with her silky little clothes.

"Going to the Union?" she chirped.

"No."

"I'm not going there either," she said, and he thought: She eats her supper in birdfeeders, hopping from one to the other all over town.

But all he said was, "Where *are* you going?"

"Oh, anywhere, nowhere," she said, and tossed her light, fine, nervous hair. When he said nothing, she coaxed him: "Tell me. What's Old Low Norse like?"

He said some words for her. *"Klegwoerum, vroognaven, okthelm, abthur, uxt."* She shivered, he thought. Her shimmery little dress hugged her snug for a moment, then breezed loose again. He hoped she was sincere.

Being so frequently insincere himself, Trumper suspected the motives of others. His own motives struck him as bottomless. To be diddling this farm child in his mind while his own wife—Lady Burden, the Mistress of Cope—suffers more banal encounters.

Biggie waiting in line at the A & P, in the check-out aisle marked EIGHT ITEMS OR LESS. She has less than eight items; she couldn't afford more. She lolls over the sparse cart, feels something old and athletic stirring her: an urge for the giant slalom. She puts her feet close together, one slightly ahead of the other, and shifts her weight to the downhill ski and bends her knees into a springy lock position. Still leaning on the market cart, she wedels ahead in line. Behind her, a soft and shapeless housewife glowers indignantly at Biggie's broad waggling; through Biggie's stretch pants, her rump is round and taut. The housewife's husband tries not to look, pretends he's outraged, too. Inside Biggie's cart, Colm has already opened a box of Cheerios.

Now the confrontation with the check-out girl, tired and sweaty with this Friday-night rush to consume. She almost doesn't notice Biggie's check, but the name is a hard one to forget. Trumper is one of the suspicious ones. The girl checks an ominous list and says, "Hang on a second, will you, ma'am."

Bring on the manager, now, in a short-sleeved, drip-dry summer shirt, the kind so thinly materialed that a few of the pubic-like hairs on his chest are poking through the loose weave. "I got your name on my list, lady," he says.

Biggie wedels. "Huh?" she says.

"Got your name on this list," says the manager. "Your check's no good here. Better empty that cart . . ."

"Of course my check's good here," Biggie tells him. "Come on. You're keeping all these people waiting." But they don't mind waiting in line now; something ugly is being revealed. Perhaps the staring housewife and her husband are somehow feeling vindicated. That shapeless lady is probably thinking, Maybe my ass is running down my legs, but my checks are good.

"Please empty your cart, Mrs. Trumper," the manager says. "You're welcome to shop here—with cash."

"Well, then, cash my check," says Biggie, who never grasps things right off.

"Now, look, lady," says the manager, encouraged; he feels the line of shoppers is on his side. Colm pours the Cheerios on the floor. "Have you got the cash to pay for that cereal?" the manager asks Biggie.

And Biggie says, "Now look, you, yourself . . . I've got a good check . . ." But the manager elbows himself up next to her and starts emptying her cart. When he separates Colm from the Cheerios, the child starts to howl, and Biggie—a good two inches taller than the manager—grabs the bossy bastard by his short-sleeved, drip-dry summer shirt, probably tugging the crispy hairs on his chest. Biggie shoves him hard against the counter, shovels Colm out of the cart and mounts him sidesaddle on her good high hip; with one hand free, she takes back the Cheerios.

"Last time I shop in this dump," she says, and snatches her checkbook away from the check-out girl.

"Now get out of here," the manager whispers, but he's addressing himself to Colm, not Biggie.

Who speaks: "Get out of my way, then . . ." which the manager tries to do, pressing himself against the counter while Biggie squeezes past him, grinding her hip against him. You'd rarely see the person who could fit with Biggie in one of those skinny aisles.

And she holds her dignity very well, out the hissing electric doors— swaggering through the parking lot, a wake of Cheerios behind her. If she's thinking at all, it goes like this: If I were on my old skis, I would execute a tight kick-turn in that aisle. My edges I keep sharp. Through his drip-dry shirt, one outside edge would cut that nasty fucker's nipples off.

But all she does is inform Bogus of her opinion about the root of the money problem: "It's your father, the prick . . ."

. . . and I can't help but agree when we're all home together, Colm groveling in the Cheerios. The light down the hall in our bedroom crackles, blinks and goes out. Biggie doesn't seem to notice that it's the *only* light that's gone out; the others have stayed on. "They've shut us off!" she cries. "Oh, my God, Bogus, you'd think they'd wait until morning, wouldn't you?"

"It's probably just the bulb, Big," I tell her. "Or that damn fuse." And in my bumbling fashion I try to wrestle with her a moment to make her happy, but it's then that she seems to notice the mess poor Colm and the Cheerios are in. She shoves me off and I'm left to investigate the nightly basement alone.

Down the damp stone stairs, remembering I must spring the trap so the mouse won't be guillotined. And calling up again to Biggie, "A smart mouse we got, Big. He's sprung it again without getting caught."

But this time I notice he's actually sprung it himself—sneaked in and snatched the cheese without leaving his soft little head behind. It makes me sweat to think of him taking such chances. I whisper to the musty basement,

"Look here, Mouse, I'm here to help you. Be patient; let *me* spring the trap. Don't take such a risk, you've got everything to lose."

"What?" says Biggie from upstairs.

"Nothing, Big," I call up. "I was just swearing at that damn mouse! He's done it again! He got away!"

For a long time, then, I huddle by the fuse box, long after the fuse is replaced and Biggie has shouted down to me that I've got it, that the light's on again. I can hear the electric meter ticking through the outside wall. I think I hear the mouse, his little heart beating. He's thinking, God, what are the great awful trappers up to now? So I whisper into the darkness, "Don't be frightened. I'm on *your* side." After which the mouse's heartbeat seems to stop. I'm on the verge of crying out, frightened almost the way I'm frightened when I think Colm's breathing has stopped in his sleep.

Biggie shouts, "What are you *doing* down there, Bogus?"

"Oh, nothing, Big."

"What a long time to be doing nothing," Biggie says.

And I catch myself thinking, What a long time indeed! With nothing you could ever call real hardship or suffering. In fact, it's been quite a light pain, and sometimes fun. It's just the nightly things—all little—that seem not to have amounted to something very *big*, or finally serious, so much as they have simply turned my life around to attending almost solely to them. A constant, if petty, irritation.

"Bogus!" Biggie shouts. "What are you doing?"

"Nothing, Big!" I call up again, meaning it this time. Or seeing, a little more clearly, what it is like to be doing nothing.

"You must be doing *something!*" Biggie hollers.

"No, Big," I call up. "I'm really doing nothing at all. Honest!" Bogus Trumper isn't lying now.

"Liar!" Biggie shouts. "You're playing with that damn mouse!"

Mouse? I think. Are you still here? I hope you haven't gone upstairs, thinking it was your big chance. Because you're better off in the basement, Risky Mouse. There's nothing petty down here.

That's it! What I object to is that my upstairs life is so cluttered with *little* things—errors of judgment, but never crimes. I don't face anything very severe; I don't live with anything that's as basic to avoid or as final to lose to as that mousetrap.

"Bogus!" Biggie screams; I hear her flounce in bed.

"I've got it!" I call up. "I'm coming now!"

"The mouse?" says Biggie.

"The mouse?"

"You've got the mouse?"

"No, Jesus, not the mouse," I say.

"Well, Jesus, *what* then?" says Biggie. "What have you got that's taken you all this time?"

"Nothing, Big," I say. "I've got nothing, really . . ."

... and so another night puts Trumper at his window for the witching hour, which seems to lure old Fitch, the lawn-watcher, out of his bed for his brief front-porch constitutionals. Perhaps he's bothered by another Iowa fall; all that ominous dying going on.

But this night Mr. Fitch doesn't get up. Gently pushing his ear to the war-built screen, Trumper hears a sudden dry rush of leaves, and in the yellowing streetlight sees a small scattering of dead autumnal rubble flicker upward in the wind around Fitch's house. Mr. Fitch has died in his sleep! His soul momentarily rebels, once more raking over his lawn!

Bogus wonders if he should ring up the Fitches just to see who answers.

"Mr. Fitch just died," Trumper says aloud. But Biggie has learned to sleep through his voice at night. Poor Fitch, thinks Bogus, genuinely moved. When asked, Fitch had said he used to work for the Bureau of Statistics. *Now have you at last become one, Mr. Fitch?*

Trumper tries to imagine some excitement in Fitch's long career in the Bureau of Statistics. Poised over the microphone, he thinks that the bureau would want him to be brief and objective. Vowing to limit himself to only the most vital statistics, he flips the RECORD switch and begins:

"Fred 'Bogus' Trumper: born March 2, 1942, Rockingham-by-the-Sea Hospital, Portsmouth, New Hampshire; delivered by his father, Dr. Edmund Trumper, a urologist and substitute obstetrician.

"Fred 'Bogus' Trumper was graduated from Exeter Academy, 1960; Vice-President of Der Unterschied (the school's German-language film society); Poetry Editor for the *Pudendum* (the school's underground literary magazine); he lettered in track (pole-vaulter) and in wrestling (a problem with his concentration span: he would be beating his opponent, and well ahead on points, when he would find himself inexplicably pinned). Trumper's grades and College Board scores? Undistinguished.

"He attended the University of Pittsburgh on an athletic scholarship (for wrestling); his potential was considered 'vast,' but he must learn to conquer his regrettable concentration span. His scholarship was revoked at the end of the academic year when he left Pittsburgh. His wrestling performance? Undistinguished.

"He attended the University of New Hampshire. Major? Undeclared. He left at the end of the academic year.

"He attended the University of Vienna, Austria. Field of concentration? German. Span of concentration? Well, he met Merrill Overturf.

"He reattended the University of New Hampshire and was graduated with a B.A. in German. His aptitude for foreign languages was referred to as 'vast.'

"He was accepted at the State University of Iowa, in the Graduate School of Comparative Literature. He was granted full academic credit for a research-absence, in Austria, January through September 1964. He was to discover and prove that the dialect ballads and folk tales of Salzburgerland

and the Tyrol were descendants, via an early North Germanic tribal movement, of Old Low Norse. He found no such thing to be true. He made further contact with Merrill Overturf, however, and in a village in the Austrian Alps called Kaprun, he met and impregnated a member of the U.S. ski team. Her name was Sue 'Biggie' Kunft, of East Gunnery, Vermont.

"He returned to America and presented this large pregnant athlete to his father at Great Boar's Head; father fond of referring to Sue 'Biggie' Kunft as 'that great blond German ship'; father unrelenting, even when told that Biggie's father was a German Vermonter.

"Fred 'Bogus' Trumper was cut off by his father, 'until such a time as responsibility toward the future is demonstrable.'

"Married in East Gunnery, Vermont, September 1964. Sue 'Biggie' Kunft was forced to split her mother's (and her mother's mother's) wedding gown with a razor and insert a flap of suitable material, expandable, to conceal some months of gestation. Biggie's father was only upset that a skiing career was wasted. Biggie's mother thought that girls shouldn't ski anyway, but she was upset about the dress.

"Trumper returned to the State University of Iowa with an acceptable M.A. thesis on the connection between the dialect ballads and folk tales of Salzburgerland and the Tyrol with Old Low Norse. He received permission to return to Austria to follow up this interesting information. He did so, after the shocking birth of his first child (he was treated at the State University of Iowa hospital in March of 1965 for a fainting spell, following the first look at his gory, swaddled son. 'It's a boy!' the nurse, fresh and dripping from the delivery room, informed him. 'Will it live?' asked Trumper, sliding gelatinous to the floor).

"He actually returned to Austria to relive his romance with his wife and to find his old friend Merrill Overturf. Failing both, he returned to Iowa and announced that he had disproved his M.A. thesis and would select a new topic for his Ph.D. He thus began the translation of *Akthelt and Gunnel* from Old Low Norse. He has been doing this for almost four years . . .

"He still seeks reconciliation with his father's income. He still wonders if his child will live. And he considers the advisability of being married to a former professional athlete who can do more sit-ups than he can. He is, for example, afraid to wrestle her, for fear that he will be handily beating her and suddenly find himself inexplicably pinned. And when he told her that he used to be a pole-vaulter, she told him she had tried that once too. He is afraid to ask for comparative heights . . ."

––––––––––

. . . at which point, dramatically, the tape whips to an end, whirs and frays off the empty spool, *tzikity tzikity tzikity tzat!*

"Bogus?" Biggie groans from the bedroom.

"Nothing, Big."

He lets the sleep come back to her, and then quietly replays his recorded statistics. He finds them lacking in objectivity, brevity, honesty and sense, and he realizes that Mr. Fitch and the Bureau of Statistics will reject all information concerning this fraudulent Trumper, and make no entry of his name. Looking out his window at Fitch's dark house, he recalls that Fitch is dead. Strangely relieved, he goes to bed. But in the morning, with Colm bouncing on his chest, he turns his head on the pillow and squints out his bedroom window. Seeing the ghostly vision of Fitch at work on his lawn, Trumper lets his child bounce on the floor.

"My God, Bogus," Biggie says, stooping down to the wailing child.

"Mr. Fitch died last night," Bogus tells her.

Looking blandly out the window, Biggie says, "Well, he looks better this morning." So it's morning, Trumper decides, trying to wake up; he watches Biggie lie back down on the bed with Colm.

And if Biggie isn't at the hospital, he thinks, then it's Saturday. And if it's Saturday, then I sell football pennants, pins, buttons and cowbells. And if Iowa loses again, I'll change to a school with a winning team . . .

There is a sudden thrashing and general upheaval of child and wife on the bed beside him; Biggie is getting up again. He turns to nuzzle her breast before she can go, but it's her elbow.

He opens his eyes. Nothing is as it seems. How could there be a God? He tries to remember the last time he thought there was one. In Europe? Surely God gets to travel more than that. It wasn't in Europe, anyway; at least there was no God in Europe when Biggie was with me.

Then he remembers Merrill Overturf. That was the last time God was around, he thinks. Therefore, believing in God went wherever Merrill went.

11

Notre Dame 52, Iowa 10

God *may* be dead, for all I know, but Our Lady's Eleven seemed to have some twelfth and ominous player on the field, making things fall their way. I could sense some Holy Power believing in them, even before the game. I sold two Notre Dame pennants to every Iowa one—a sure sign that some faith was abroad in the land. Or else some pessimism, a defensiveness on the part of the hometown rooters; fearing the worst, they were not going to be further humiliated by being seen with an Iowa pennant. They filed empty-handed into the stadium, a subtle green tie here and green socks there: If Iowa lost, they could always claim to be Irish, and there would be no Hawkeye button or cowbell to incriminate them.

Oh yes, you could tell by the concession sales: The Fighting Irish—Mary's Team, the Pontiff's Maulers—had something special going for them.

But I missed the game; I was spared that pain. I had a disaster of my own.

With my awkward plywood board (a weak hasp holds an easel stand behind it, but the whole thing is too unsteady to resist the wind), I am hawking my wares by the end-zone gate. And since only students and last-minute ticket-buyers get end-zone seats, it is not the concession stand available to the upper crust of pennant, button and cowbell buyers.

I am selling my sixth Notre Dame pennant when I see little Lydia Kindle, swaying along with an utter *Glork* of a boyfriend. I swear the fierce wind died for a second, heavy with the scent of her hair! And I stop my insane clamoring with a cowbell; I cease chanting, "Pennants! Buttons! Cowbells! Satisfying stadium cushions! Rain hats! Say it for Iowa or Notre Dame!"

I watch Lydia flutter along; her boyfriend scuffs beside her; the wind buffets her against him, and they're laughing. It would be more than I could stand if she should see me blue-cold and huddled by my garish showboard, hawking junk in loutish English, without a lilting trace of Old Low Norse on my tongue.

I dart behind my showboard, crouched with my back against the thing; the wind performs alarming unbalancing feats. Just in case, I unpin my hideous Hawkeye Enterprise button, No. 501, and cram it, with my yellow change apron, into the side-pouch of my parka. Then I lurk quietly behind the board. As her *Glork* announces, "Hey, whattaya know, Lid? Nobody watching the old board here. Have a button." And I hear her giggle.

But *Glork* doesn't quite have the knack for removing a pin from the cloth strips that swaddle the board, and he must be anxious to do his deed and run, for I can feel him tugging and wrenching so hard that I have to hug the easel stand to keep the whole apparatus from falling. Then I hear one of the cloth strips rip, and out the corner of my eye I see a string of Iowa buttons flap in the wind. Yes, the wind, or the combination of the wind and Lydia Kindle's boyfriend's last hard yank: I feel my balance lost, my dignity in motion. The showboard is falling.

"Look out!" cries my bright-voiced Lydia. "It's coming over on you!" But the *Glork* doesn't quite step back in time, not before he's trapped by the descending, seven-foot rectangle of what he suspects is only light plywood. He puts up a casual hand to catch it; he doesn't know I'm riding it down on him, like a 180-pound raft. And when it pins him to the cement, he lets out a terrible yell; the board, I feel, is splitting along my spine; I can feel him weakly scratching through the wood under me. But paying him no mind, I simply look up to Lydia.

"Klegwoerum," I tell her. *"Vroognaven okthelm abthur, awf?"*

She gawks while the board struggles under me. I change my language and garble German up to Lydia: *"Wie gehts dir heute? Hoffentlich gut."*

A muffled grunt under the board. I sit up slowly, with a lofty air about me, and say a little overseriously, as if rudely awakened, "What's going on here, Lydia?"

Immediately defensive, she says, "The board fell over." As if I didn't know. I stand up, and the *Glork* scuttles out from under my fallen wares looking like a little crushed crab.

"What in hell are you doing there?" I ask him, just to put him on the defensive.

"Suffering shit!" he cries. "I was just taking one mucking pin!"

Fatherly, almost, I take Lydia's arm, pronouncing over the kneeling *Glork,* "Watch your language, kid . . ."

"What?" he hoots. "Is this *your* board?"

"Mr. Trumper runs my language lab," Lydia tells him icily—as if this makes impossible any connection I might have with these cheap wares.

But the *Glork* isn't convinced. He straightens up, visibly in pain, and says, "Well, what were you doing behind this damn board?"

"Why . . . the vender . . ." I say, "the vender had to leave it here a moment. Passing by, I offered to watch it for him while he was gone." And attempting to divert this conversation from scrutiny, I point out to the *Glork* that this vender would surely be upset at the condition of his board. Didn't the *Glork* think he should make amends?

A momentous moment. Worshipful Lydia Kindle, adoring me—a man of my talents and tastes, big and unsnobbish enough to stoop to help the most lowly vender. A humanist comes into young Lydia's life! At this peak of glory, I am even not above lifting the showboard upright while the *Glork* fumes beside it, fumbling the button out of his pocket, murmuring, "Come on, Lid, we'll miss the game."

Then I see Fred Paff, hawkish concession sales head for Hawkeye Enterprises, cruising the end-zone gate. Seeing how things are selling, no doubt. And he spots me and my mauled board. And I'm not wearing my proper identification pin, and I am not girdled in my stunning yellow change apron.

"I say, your boy's right, you know," I tell Lydia quickly. "Better get going or you'll miss the kickoff."

But her adoration is too great; she just gapes at me.

"Go *on!*" I beg them, and the *Glork* takes Lydia's elbow.

But it's too late; Fred Paff is upon us. I smell his approaching tweeds nearby; I hear his jowls flapping in the wind; he is athletically deodorized and powdered, sucking big-winded breaths beside me, robust, on the prowl.

He booms, "Trumper! So where's your Hawkeye pin, boy? Where's your change apron? And what in filthy hell has happened to your *board?*" I can't look at him as he flicks at the string of buttons trailing on the ground. He draws in his scented breath at the sight of that fine cloth strip that's been ripped. I simply can't talk. Fred Paff clomps on my shoulder. "Trumper?" he says, almost brotherly. It's more than I can bear; he's fondling me like a wounded dog. He gropes in my parka pouch, pulls out the awful evidence —my yellow change apron and my ID badge, No. 501. "Fred?" he says gently. "Fred, what's *wrong* with you, boy?"

"Ha!" cries the *Glork. "He's* the vender!"

And Paff asks, "Fred? Do these people want to buy something? Aren't you selling today, Fred?"

If only Lydia Kindle had hoo-roared at me too I could have stood it. If only she'd been the true compatriot of her *Glork,* I could somehow have borne up to this. But I felt her there, a sympathetic shiver beside me.

She said, "Oh, Mr. Trumper. You shouldn't be *ashamed.* Some people have to work, you know, and I think it's very strong of you, really!"

It's such stupid and innocent pity that hurts me.

Paff says, "My God, Fred, get hold of yourself." Even Paff! That he should care about what's wrong. (In our orientation meeting he told us he looked out for all his "boys," but I never believed he *meant* it!) It's too much.

They're around me, Paff and Lydia, and out in front of my board is that leering *Glork.* Him I can understand! And behind him, I swear, is a gathering throng. Seeing this drama before the game, better than a half-time show. The crowd is thinking, after a crowd's fashion, Now, if they would only put on something like this during the half. If only they displayed the venders, fed them to Iowa hogs, let them humbly try to defend themselves with their goofy showboards—*that* would be genuine half-time entertainment!

I bolt.

I tackle my tray of wares and batter myself and the board into and over the wailing *Glork.* Off into the vile crowd, then; I shift the board, carrying it like a broad knife through the masses. I shift again; I bear it on my back, stooped and pitched forward; my shield protects me from rear attack. I see terror-struck faces loom up ahead of me, veer out of my charging path; insults are hurled after me. Sometimes my shield is struck or, more often, *picked* at. I am being picked clean from behind! I feel them like predatory birds, snaring a button here, a pennant there. There is a terrible jangle: all my cowbells are gone in a swoop.

Rounding the last edge of the end-zone gate, I see—too late to avoid him —an awestruck campus cop. I can only lower my head; I hear his breath sucked right out of him, and I watch his blue face dipping away from me, floating down between my pumping knees. Somehow I avoid stepping on his chest badge. Running on, I wait for his bullet to pierce my shield and shatter my spine. But I'm safely at the home-team gate and nothing happens. Perhaps, I think with dread, my board decapitated him; perhaps, when I saw his head falling, it was falling unattached.

I batter into the stadium concession room, sagging to my knees under the board. Someone is kind enough to lift it off me. It's No. 368, wearing his football tie. "God! 501!" he says, looking at my bare board. "You really cleaned up! Where was your stand?"

Others mill around me. The head counter starts to tally up my board, determining sales and percentage. I'm too weak to explain. He discovers I've "sold" all but one pennant, all but four of the big GO HAWKS! buttons, every one of the little Iowa pins with the little gold footballs attached, and all my cowbells. He announces, then, that I've "sold" more than three hundred dollars' worth of wares. He's tallying up the mathematical wonder which is to be my "commission" when I hand over my actual earnings: $12.75.

"I was picked clean," I confess. "They got me."

"*They?*" says 368, shocked.

"The mob," I groan, and struggle off my knees. "Mad fans," I tell them. They steady me; their concern destroys me.

"501," says 368, "you mean they *took* all your things?" And I weakly gesture to my ragged board, and to my tattered, gravel-embedded knees.

But feeling my wind return, I realize I should be moving along. Fred Paff will no doubt be here in a jiffy. There's a roar above me: kickoff time. Most of the other venders scatter; even 368, an avid fan, is tempted to leave me. In fact, I gesture that I'm all right, that he needn't stay to support me.

"We've got to *do* something about this," he mumbles, but his mind is really on the kickoff return. If I weren't so weary, I'd tell him that we must unionize all hawkers. I'd speak to him about profit sharing and the victimization of the proletariat. Give a primer to the man in the football tie! Freshman Marx! Hawkers of the world, unite!

But at this moment, five yards deep in his own end zone, the Notre Dame kickoff and punt-return specialist—fleet No. 25—receives the ball like a solid touch from a magic wand. And 368 says, "We should have two men with every board."

"Then you'd have to split the commission," says the head counter.

"Hell, no," says 368. "You'd *double* the commission. Don't tell me someone's not making any money off this junk . . ." No doubt 368 is a business major who picked up his football tie dirt-cheap.

But this speculation is cut off. The stadium above us gives off an animal din. No. 25 of Notre Dame has burst up the middle, over his own 40, a very solid and gold-helmeted patron saint blocking in front of him. And our own 368 takes off down the sidelines of the stadium underground, heading for the nearest ramp, while the head counter dashes to a dungeonlike portal in the back of the concession room.

Wishing I had the speed of 25 of Notre Dame, I make my timely escape. This time the traffic is heavier. The masses who've missed the kickoff are flooding the gates. A cross-body block on a soft man swaddled in blankets squirts me loose from the underground panic, out the press-box gate, as free as No. 25 of Notre Dame who now finds himself all alone, across midfield, one Iowa lineman lagging behind and nothing but the Iowa end zone in front of him. The hometown roar stifles to a death rattle and a shrill fringe cheer goes up from the rabid Catholics in the stands. The Fighting Irish Band sends out a bright green note.

I simply run away, down toward the other end zone—away from where No. 25 is drawing first blood, away from where I suspect the campus cop lies headless, and where an army of R.O.T.C. volunteers is mustering to rout me out. I cross the intramural soccer field sucessfully, except for whacking my knees on the bumpers of all the parked cars and having to avoid the stare of the R.O.T.C. car-parker, wearing his suspicious eyes low, barely showing under his white M.P. helmet. Why do they wear "M.P." just to park a car?

Then I'm weaving through the deserted upper campus, wending down to the Iowa River, past the appallingly quiet university hospitals. In front of the Children's Hospital entrance, several farmers sprawl on the hoods and front fenders of their pickups, waiting for their wives and kids who've gone inside for this social service the university offers. Treating pigbite and miscarriages and countless strange animal diseases that somehow are communicated to the farmers and their families.

I run blindly for an instant, struck with an awful, senseless image of Colm mauled by one of those demented sows who gobble up their own piglets.

Past the quadrangle of boys' dorms now. I hear only one phonograph in operation, playing a Scarlatti harpsichord piece defiantly—harsher and more religious than shattered stained glass. Obviously not a football fan. There's no one to see me stop and listen, or see me take up my pace again, when I hear steps behind me.

They're scuffed steps, all tired out. Perhaps the upended campus cop, with his precarious head held by a sinew. Even so, he couldn't be as tired as I am. I stop. I wait for the steps coming up behind me, and when a hand lights gently on my arm, I kneel; I touch my forehead to the sun-warmed cement in the dorm quadrangle and feel the Scarlatti play up and down my spine—as this hand does, too. I see one fine, fragile pair of legs. When the legs see that I'm looking at them, they draw together; two knees come down, like the bright cheeks of a baby's fine bottom. A weak hand tries to lift my head; I help. I lay my gravel-pocked chin in the hem of her skirt.

And Lydia Kindle says, "Oh, Mr. Trumper," in a sad little voice. And brightening her tone, she adds, *"Wie gehts dir jetzt? Hoffentlich gut . . ."*

But I can hardly match her songster German. I revert to Old Low Norse. *"Klegwoerum,"* I tell her thickly. She slips her cold, brittle hand under the collar of my parka, down the back of my neck, and squeezes as best as she can.

Then, from the towering, near-empty dorms around us, I hear the harpsichord cut off. The last chord hangs above me so long that I half expect it to crash on both of us. I help myself and Lydia up, and hold her flush against me; there's so little thickness to her that I can feel her heartbeat at her spine. She lifts her young, wet face to me: such a fine-boned face. If I had a face that angular, I'd be afraid to roll over in my sleep, fearing I'd break off a piece. Yet she lifts her vulnerable face to me.

My mustache doesn't bear such close scrutiny, so I kiss her quickly. She can't keep her lips still, so I back off, keeping her hand. When I start to walk her along, I pull her closer beside me. Down the boardwalk to the river, I feel her slight, sharp hip jab me; she tries to fit her angles and her springy step to my bearlike swaying. Over the river and into town; after wordless practice, we finally walk well together.

I see our reflection in the storefront windows. We are superimposed over a mannequin with flowered panties and a matching bra, a purse on her arm. Then our image changes. See the next frame: we are superimposed, over the face of a sullen beer drinker, over the pale neon of a flashing pinball machine, over the heaving back of the pinball player, who appears to be furiously mounting the machine. Next frame: we are superimposed over nothing at all—over a dark and vacant storefront window, with only a sign in the bottom corner of our image. The sign says: TO LET. I've read it twice before I realize I've stopped walking and am aiming our faces at this storefront glass. Her face and mine, close together. She looks surprised at herself, but happy.

But see me! My hair is wild, my eyes are mad, my mouth is uncontrollably grinning; my face is a grimace, as tight-skinned and as blotchy as a clenched fist. Behind our faces a small crowd slows and gathers, pausing just long enough to squint into this storefront, to see what's caught our eyes; they hurry on as soon as they see our unmatched faces—practically bolting away, as if my askew features scare them.

"I can see you anytime," says Lydia Kindle, speaking down to the sidewalk. "Just you tell me when."

"I'll call you."

"Or you can give me a note," she says, ". . . in the language lab."

"Sure, a note," I say, thinking: Jesus! *Notes in the language lab?*

"Or anything."

"Sure, anything," I say, and she fidgets a moment, waiting for me to take her hand again.

But I don't. I manage a smile—a dissected face in the storefront, with a grin as convincing as a skeleton's. Then I watch her swish off the curb, dally to the crosswalk, turning to give me a wave; I watch the window glass and see me raise my arm stiffly, from the elbow, as if the wires which help me to bend are somehow overwound or crossed.

Then I dally along behind her, pretending aloofness to the proud flick of her rump. But I notice people staring at my knees, and when I stoop to wipe off the tatters, the blood and gravel, I lose sight of Lydia.

Oh, sympathy and comfort. It's a queer thing that when you're given a little, you only want a lot.

Because I went home to Biggie and caught her stooped in the hall outside the bathroom door, flopping braless in one of my T-shirts, crammed into a pair of my Levis, so tight on her that she couldn't do up the fly. Colm played in the hallway between us, intent on smashing together two trucks. And Biggie, rolling a pail of ammonia cleanser out the bathroom door, caught me looking at her as if her *strength* at that moment had overcome me and left me gaping at her as if she were some animal, ugly and scary and able to eat me whole.

"What are you gawking at?" she asked.

"Nothing, Big," I said. But I was aware of the vision of myself in the storefront window and couldn't meet her eyes.

"Well, I'm sorry if I don't look *pretty* enough for you," she said, and I winced. She advanced on me, down the hall, prodding the ammonia pail along with her foot, having to bend her body to do this and sending one of her boobs askew—one swung out at her side while the other rode high and straight at me. As if I wasn't already intimidated enough.

She said, "Bogus? What's wrong with you, anyway? Did they call off the game?" She lifted my face up with her broad hand.

Then I saw her mouth go slack, and at first I thought it was the sight of my storefront face that shocked her. Not recognizing, at first, that it was an angry look she gave me, and not tasting—until just that moment, with my tongue licking over my dry lips—Lydia Kindle's pale-orange lipstick at the corners of my mouth and on the bristles of my mustache: tangerine love.

"You bastard!" said Biggie, and brought up from the pail a soggy cleaning rag, first swatting my face with it, then wiping it smarting across my mouth. Perhaps it was the ammonia that started my eyes watering, with those fumes so strong under my nose.

I blubbered, "I lost my job, Big." She gaped at me, and I repeated, "I lost my *job,* Big. I lost that fucking job . . ." And I felt myself dropping down to my raw knees, brought to them, I felt, too many times in just one day.

Biggie started to brush by me, but I caught her around the hips and hugged her, repeating over and over, "I lost the job, the job!" But she snapped her knees up and caught my chin; I bit my tongue and felt the sweet blood trickle down my throat. I grabbed for her again, looking for her face, and found her suddenly close to me, down on her knees too, and saying in her quiet, calm way, her *other* way, "Bogus? What was the job to you, Bogus? I mean, it was a bad job, wasn't it? And it was never bringing in enough so that we'll notice it's gone . . . Right, Bogus?"

But that ammonia is strong stuff. I was beyond the hope of talk; I could only grab the waist of Biggie's T-shirt to dab my gory mouth. Biggie pressed me against her; she's so solid I hardly made a dent, but I found my usual spot, hugged snug between bosom and thigh. I let Biggie croon to me there in her low, flat-sung voice, "It's all right, Bogus. Now, really, it's okay. It's all right . . ."

Perhaps I would have contested the point with her if I hadn't seen Colm, all through with bashing his trucks and coming our way—quite curious to know what sort of helpless creature his mother was mothering now. I hid my face against Biggie and felt Colm lightly poking my back and ears and feet to try to find exactly where I must have hurt myself. For the life of me, I can't say for sure where it was.

"I've got a present for you . . ." Biggie's rich voice drifts down the hall, comes back, sinks in. She hands it over. *A job-losing present for the oddly unfaithful!* Colm paws at the label while I translate the Hungarian. From Milo Kubik's Peoples Market one precious eight-ounce tin of my favorite Ragout of Wild Boar in Médoc Sauce. Milo Kubik, the refugee gourmet. He escaped from Budapest with memories, and actual tins of this and other ragouts. Thank God he made it, I say. I know that if I had been in Budapest —a bottle of boar-marinade in my pocket, a snifter of paprika in my crotch —I would have been *caught.*

12

Do You Want to Have a Baby?

Tulpen went home early, but Bogus and Ralph Packer stayed late at the Christopher Street studio, playing with the sound track of *Down on the Farm.*

The hippie commune called the Free Farm had taken over about four acres of undeveloped land belonging to a local liberal arts college. They planted a garden and invited real farmers in the area to come share their harvest and plant gardens of their own. The college had several hundred acres of undeveloped land. The college authorities asked the Free Farmers to leave, but the Free Farmers said they were simply using unused land. Unused land was a crime against humanity; all over Vermont there are farmers without enough land. The Free Farmers would stay on the college land until the pigs threw them off.

Ralph screened some new shots of the latest developments; Bogus played with the sound.

(Medium shot; no sync sound; interior, day; general store. The Free Farmers are shopping, fanning out through the store aisles, picking up things and putting them back, as if these foodstuffs and hardware were rare gifts)

NARRATOR *(Bogus, voice-over)*: The Free Farmers buy wheat germ, honey, brown rice, milk, oranges, apple wine, cigarette paper, corncob pipes, Camels, Marlboros, Winstons, Luckies, Salems . . .

(Medium shot; sync sound; exterior, day; general store. The Free Farmers mill around their psychedelic Volkswagen panel truck parked outside the store. The boy holding the grocery bag has long hair tied back in a ponytail; he wears a pair of farmer's overalls. He is pawing around in the bag, pulling things out)

BOY: Whose Salems? *(He holds up the pack)* Come on! Who got the Salems?

Then they view the scene with the president of the local college. The president is useful to the movie because he blatantly foreshadows what's going to happen.

(Medium shot, moving; no sync sound; exterior, day; college campus. We follow the college president across the parking lot, up a path through the campus mall. He is sharply dressed; he nods graciously to several passing students)

NARRATOR *(Bogus, voice-over)*: The president is forty-three, once-divorced, now remarried, B.S., M.S., Ph.D. in botany, Yale. He has four children of his own. He is the chairman of the State Democratic Committee . . .

(The president follows a group of students into a building; the students walk on in, but the president stops to wipe his feet)

NARRATOR *(v.o.)*: He is opposed to having the police on campus; although he believes firmly in private property and has repeatedly asked the Free Farmers to leave, he will not call in the police . . .

(Medium close-up; sync sound; interior, day; president's office. The president speaks directly into camera)

PRESIDENT: Why call in the police? The real farmers around here will take care of it . . .

The bulk of the new footage has to do with the leader of the Free Farm, a character named Morris. One night a lot of real farmers come to the Free Farm and maul Morris. The police interview the nameless girlfriend of Morris, a witness to the mauling.

(Medium shot; sync sound; interior, night police station. Morris's girl wears farm overalls over a great soft pair of breasts in an old T-shirt that we've previously seen Morris wearing. The girl is talking to a police sergeant in the station, and a police secretary is taking notes)

GIRL: . . . then I couldn't tell what they were doing to Morris, 'cause one of them knocked me down—you know, talking dirty to me. And one of them reached under me—I was lying on my stomach—and he pinched me in the tit. *(She lifts her breast to display the part pinched)* It's clear it's what they really want from us, of course. Just fucking! That's really all. They pretend they hate us, but they really want our asses, man. Oh, sure, they hit me, knocked me down and all, but what they were really after was a cheap feel. You know, their wives with bras and girdles on all the time, and their hair in curlers—it's natural for them to go around wanting it all the time. But they just feel so threatened by us—at least they responded that way to Morris . . .

POLICE SERGEANT: Exactly how did they respond to Morris?

GIRL: They just beat the shit out of him, man.

POLICE SERGEANT: Did Morris provoke them?

GIRL: Morris? You've got to be kidding! Morris asked them to turn on with him! Morris just doesn't know how to fucking provoke anybody . . .

There follows a lot of dismal footage of the mauled, hospitalized Morris in traction. Finally, the rest of the Free Farmers have to get police protection because the real farmers raid them again and shotgun all the tomato plants. "Police protection" entails the police removing all the Free Farmers from the Free Farm.

When Morris is released from the hospital, he goes around the village conducting a kind of autopsy on the deserted Free Farm. He asks all the town farmers whether they really would have shot anybody, or whether in time they might have grown to tolerate the Free Farm. This is all pointless, since there is no more Free Farm, but apparently it is important for Morris to get the answers.

(Medium shot—fade in, from dissolve; no sync sound, music-over; exterior, day; village firehouse. Morris, on crutches, is with his girl. They are talking with the fire chief, but there is no sync sound. The music is Neil Young's "After the Goldrush." Although Morris is doing all the talking, the fire chief keeps looking at Morris's girl. Medium shot; no sync sound, music-over; exterior, day; farmer's house. Morris and the girl are talking with one of the real farmers, possibly involved in the mauling. The girl holds up her breast, probably referring to the pinch. Morris is friendly; the farmer is cautious. Medium shot; no sync sound, music-over; exterior, day; general store. Morris and his girl sit on the steps of the general store. They are drinking Pepsi;

Morris talks enthusiastically, but the girl seems fed up with him. Another angle—to include the kids' psychedelic Volkswagen panel truck; sync sound, music fades. Morris and his girl, about to depart. They are getting into the truck. Morris talks directly into camera; his girl holds his crutches for him)

MORRIS: They wouldn't have shot us. Maybe they would've beaten us up again, but they absolutely would not have shot us. I feel we're much closer to them now; there's some communication happening. *(He turns to his girl)* You can just feel it, can't you?

GIRL: They would have blown your goddamn head off, Morris . . .

The plan of the film is to close with the college president's comment.

(Medium shot, moving; sync sound; exterior, day; Parents' Day picnic. Through a formal picnic spread, past many neatly attired parents, all smiling, nodding hello, the president moves like a Pope bestowing blessings. He is eating fried chicken, and manages to do so in an unmessy way. The camera moves closer to him, coming in over his shoulder. He suddenly turns and faces camera. At first he is startled; then he turns on the charm, speaking seriously, as if renewing an old, tireless subject)

PRESIDENT: Do you know what really encourages me, even with such things going on all around us? Well, I'll tell you something about these kids . . . and it's very encouraging, really. They live and learn, that's what they do. They really do . . . and that's what encourages me. They just live and learn, like all kids, anywhere, anytime . . .

Then Kent came in with the beer and cheese. He'd been cameraman for a lot of the new footage and was eager to see how he'd done.

"Did you show it already?" he asked.

"It stinks," Ralph said. "The whole thing. It's just awful."

"It isn't very good," Trumper agreed.

Kent unwrapped the cheese as if it were his failing heart. "The *camera* was bad, huh?" he said.

"The whole thing is terrible," said Ralph.

They sat there, wondering what went wrong.

"It was the fucking camera, wasn't it?" said Kent.

"It's the entire concept," Ralph said.

"The *people* are awful," Trumper said. "They're so obvious."

"They're simple," said Ralph. "There's nothing complex about the people."

"How about the girl with her tit-thing, though?" said Kent. "That was great, wasn't it?"

"It's the politics and the cuteness and the rotten humor that make it awful in every way," Ralph said. "At least that's *part* of it."

"Can I see the footage, please?" Kent said. "At least I should see the damn stuff."

"*You* won't even like your camerawork, Kent," Ralph said.

"You didn't like it, Ralph?"

"I didn't like *any*thing," Ralph said.

"How's the editing?" Kent asked.

"No fair talking about editing when Tulpen isn't here," Trumper said.

"It hadn't really been edited yet, anyway, Kent," Ralph said.

"Yeah, *Jesus,* Kent," Trumper said.

"Okay, Thump-Thump," Kent said. "How's the *sound?*"

"Adequate," said Ralph. "Thump-Thump gets better and better, technically speaking."

"Right," said Trumper. "It's my imagination that goes nowhere."

"Right," said Ralph.

"Look," Kent said. "Can I please just see the fucking footage for myself?"

So they left him rewinding reels in the studio and walked out onto Christopher Street, headed for coffee at the New Deal.

"All I want to do in a film is describe something worthwhile," Ralph said. "I hate conclusions."

"I don't believe in endings," Trumper said.

"Right, right," said Ralph. "Just good description. But it has to be *personal* description. Everything else is journalism."

"If the New Deal is closed," Trumper said, "I will absolutely shit."

But it was open; they sat with two mugs of black espresso with lemon peel and rum.

"Let's scrap the film, Thump-Thump," Ralph said. "It's the same old thing. Everything I've done is extroverted, and I need to make an introverted film."

"Well, it's up to you, Ralph," Trumper said.

"You're a bundle of opinions, Thump-Thump. That's what's so exciting about you."

"It's your movie."

"But suppose *you* did the next one, Thump-Thump. What would it be?"

"I have no plans," Trumper said, observing the lemon peel in his coffee.

"But what do you *feel,* Thump?" Ralph asked him.

Trumper cupped his coffee mug with his hands. "Heat," he said. "At the moment, I feel heat."

What *do* I feel? he asked himself later, groping through Tulpen's dark apartment, encountering her clothes with his bare feet.

A bra, I feel a bra under my left foot there. And pain? Yes, pain; my right shin goes *ker-crack* against the bedroom chair: that's pain.

"Trumper?" from Tulpen, turning over in bed. He crawled in beside her, reached out for her, held on.

"A breast," he said aloud. *I feel a breast.*

"Correct," Tulpen told him, wrapping herself around him now. "What else do you know?" she whispered. *Pain?* Well, yes, her teeth nipping his belly; her kiss rough enough to turn his navel inside out. "I missed you," he told her. They usually left work together.

But she didn't answer him; her mouth shut on his sleepy life; her teeth worried him, and her thighs suddenly seized his head so tight that in his temples he felt his pulse pick up. His tongue touched her, and in her mouth he reached for her brain.

Then they lay lapped by the cold neon lights from the aquariums. Odd fish darted past them; slow turtles surfaced, keeled over and sank sideways. Trumper lay trying to imagine other ways to live.

He saw a tiny, translucent, turquoise eel, its inner organs visible and somehow functioning. One organ looked like a little plumber's helper; it plunged down, sucked up, and the eel's mouth opened to belch a tiny bubble. As the bubble rose to the surface, other fish investigated it, nudged it, sometimes broke it. A form of speech? Trumper wondered. Was a bubble a word or a whole sentence? Perhaps a paragraph! A tiny, translucent, turquoise *poet* reading beautifully to his world! Trumper was about to ask Tulpen about this odd eel, but she spoke first.

"Biggie called you tonight," she said.

Trumper wished he could send up a perfectly lovely bubble. "What did she want?" he asked, envying the eel's easy communication.

"To speak to you."

"She didn't leave a message? There's nothing wrong with Colm, is there?"

"She said they were going off for the weekend," Tulpen told him. "So if you called and no one was there, not to worry."

"Well, that's what she called for, then," Trumper said. "She didn't say anything was wrong with Colm."

"She said you usually called on the weekend," Tulpen said. "I didn't know that."

"Well, I call from the studio," Trumper said. "Just to talk to Colm. I thought you'd just as soon not hear . . ."

"You miss Colm, Trumper?"

"Yes."

"But not her?"

"Biggie?"

"Yes."

"No," Trumper said. "I don't miss Biggie."

Silence. He scanned the aquarium for the verbose eel, but couldn't find him. Change the topic of the bubbles, he thought. Quick.

"Ralph wants to scrap the film," he said, but she was staring at him.

"You know, *Down on the Farm?*" he said. "The new footage was awful. The whole idea is so simple-minded . . ."

Tulpen said, "I know."

"He talked to you already?" Trumper asked.

"He wants to do a *personal* film," she said. "Right?"

"Right," he said; he touched her breast, but she moved away, turned her back to him, tucked into a ball.

"Something complex," Tulpen said. "Introverted and non-political. Something more *private,* right?"

"Right," Trumper said, worried. "I guess he told you more about it than he told me."

"He wants to make a film about you," Tulpen said.

"Me?" he said. "What *about* me?"

"Something personal," she mumbled into the pillow.

"What?" Trumper cried. He sat up and roughly rolled her over into his lap.

"About how your marriage busted up," Tulpen said. "You know, good description? And about how we're getting along . . . now," she said. "And interviews with Biggie, how's *she* living with it, you know? And interviews with *me,*" Tulpen said. "About what I think . . ."

"Well, what *do* you think?" he shouted; he was furious.

"I think it sounds like a good idea."

"For whom?" he said nastily. "For me? Like some kind of therapy? Like going to a fucking shrink?"

"That might not be a bad idea, either," she said; she sat up beside him and touched his thigh. "We've got enough money for it, Trumper . . ."

"Christ!"

"Trumper?" she said. "If you really don't miss her, what's going to hurt about it?"

"It's got nothing to do with hurting," he said. "I've got a new life now. Why go back?"

"What sort of new life?" she asked. "Are you happy, Trumper? Are you going anywhere? Or are you happy where you are?"

"I've got you."

"Do you love me?" she asked. And he thought of the turquoise eel's bubble for that!—a terrible whirlpool rising, the other fish getting out of its way.

"There's no one else I'd rather be with," he said.

"But you miss Colm. You miss your son."

"Yes."

"Well, you can have another one, you know," she said angrily. "Do you want a baby, Trumper? I mean, I *could* produce one, you know . . ."

He looked at her, shocked. "You want a baby?"

"Do *you?*" she yelled at him. "I can give you that, Trumper, but you've got to really *want* one. You've got to let me know what you want of me, Trumper. You can't just live here if I don't even know you!"

"I didn't know you wanted a baby."

"That's not exactly what I said, Trumper."

"I mean," he said, "you seemed sort of aloof, kind of independent—like you didn't want me too close."

"Which is how you want it, isn't it?"

"Well, no, it's got nothing to do with how I want you to be."

"But how *do* you want me?" Tulpen said.

"Well . . ." he said, fumbling, a bubble too heavy to rise. "Well, just like you want to be, Tulpen."

But she turned away from him. "You want things cool, right?" she said. "Sort of detached, not committed, free . . ."

"Goddamn!" he said. "Do you really want a baby?"

"You first," she said. "I'm not putting out something for nothing. I could put out, Trumper. I *can* get involved," she said, looking up at him. "But can you?"

Trumper got up and walked around the aquariums, looking through the tanks at her. A fish darted down her cleavage, algae moved in her lap.

"You're not *doing* anything," Tulpen said to him. "You've got no direction, there's not a plan in your life. There's no plot to it, even."

"Well, I'd make a bad movie then, wouldn't I?" he said. He was looking for the turquoise eel and couldn't find him.

"Trumper, I'm not at all interested in what kind of movie you'd make. I don't care about the damn movie, Trumper." Looking at him staring at her through a fish tank, she snatched the sheet around herself angrily. "Stop looking at my crotch when I'm trying to talk to you!" she screamed.

He bobbed up above the tank, peering down at her. He was genuinely surprised; he'd just been looking for the eel. "I wasn't looking at your crotch," he said, and she fell back on the bed as if she were finally exhausted from sitting up.

"You haven't wanted to go away for a weekend," she said. "People just don't live in New York without at least wanting to go somewhere."

"You know that little see-through eel?" he said, poking around in one of the tanks. "The turquoise one, the very small one?" She popped up from under the sheet and stared at him. "Well, I can't find him," he said to her. "I think he was talking . . . I wanted to show you . . ." But her stare cut him off. "He talked in bubbles," Trumper told her.

Tulpen just shook her head. "Jesus," she whispered. He went over to the bed and sat down beside her. "You know what Ralph says about you, Trumper?" she asked him.

"No," he said, angry. "Tell me what fucking old Ralph says."

"He says you don't come across, Trumper."

"Come across?"

"No one knows you, Trumper! You don't *convey* anything. You don't do much, either. Things just sort of happen to you, and they don't even add up to anything. You don't make anything of what happens to you. Ralph says you must be very complicated, Trumper. He thinks you must have a mysterious core under the surface."

Trumper stared into the fish tank. *Where is the talking eel?*

"And what do *you* think, Tulpen?" he asked her. "What do you think's under the surface?"

"Another surface," she said, and he stared at her. "Or maybe just that one surface," she said, "with nothing under it." He was angry, then, but he stood up lightly and shook his head and laughed. She kept watching him, though.

"Well, you know what *I* think?" he said, and he peered into the tank, wondering what he really did think. "I think," he said, "that the tiny turquoise eel is gone." He grinned at Tulpen, then, but she was not amused and turned away.

"Then that's the second one I've lost," she said coldly.

"Lost?" he said.

"Well, I put the first one in another tank and he disappeared."

"Disappeared?" Trumper said; he looked around at the other tanks.

"Well, something ate him, obviously," Tulpen said. "So I put the second one in a different tank so he wouldn't be eaten by whatever ate the first one. And, obviously, something else ate this one."

Trumper put his hand in the tank, groping all around. "So they *ate* him!" he shouted. He looked and looked, but there wasn't a shred of turquoise, not even a dollop of the strange plumber's helper which had inspired the little eel's poetry. Trumper slapped his hand hard on the water surface; the other fish bolted, fled in terror, collided with each other and glanced off the glass walls. "You bastards!" Trumper screamed. "Which one of you did it?" He stared fiercely at them—the lean yellow one with a blue fin, the evil-red round one. He stabbed into the tank with a pencil.

"Stop it!" Tulpen yelled at him. But he stabbed and stabbed, trying to lance one of them against the glass. They had killed the poet! The eel had been pleading with them—bubbles for mercy! And they had eaten him, the fuckers.

Tulpen grabbed Trumper around his middle and pulled him over on the bed. He thrashed out at her and snatched the alarm clock off the night table, flinging it at the murderous fish tank. The aquarium was thick-walled; it cracked and began to leak, but it didn't shatter. As the water ran out, the smaller fish were pulled up against the crack by the current.

Tulpen lay still under Trumper, watching the water level fall. "Trumper?" she said softly, but he wouldn't look at her. He held her still until the tank had emptied over the bookcase and the killer-fish lay flopping on the dry aquarium floor.

"Trumper, for God's sake," she said, but she didn't struggle. "Let me move them to another tank, please."

He let her up and watched her gently scoop them into another aquarium. In the turtle tank, a bright blue-headed turtle ate the thin yellow fish immediately, but left the evil-red round one alone.

"Shit," said Tulpen. "I never know who's going to eat whom."

"Please tell me why you want a baby," Trumper asked her very quietly, but when she turned to face him, she was calm, her arms folded over her breasts. She coolly blew a lock of her hair out of her eyes and sat down beside him on the bed; she casually crossed her legs; she watched the survivor-fish.

"I guess I *don't* want a baby," she said.

13

Remember Merrill Overturf?

Learning to ski, I quickly realized Merrill Overturf's failure as a coach. Merrill is not a deft skier, though he has mastered the stop. At the children's slope in Saarbrücken, I assaulted the backbreaking rope tow. Aside from the children, it was fortunately unpopulated; most adults were at the races in Zell am See to see the women's downhill and giant slalom.

I mastered the bindings with only three cut knuckles. Merrill flayed a path through the children, leading me to the awesome rope tow; the rope slithered uphill a mere foot above the ground, the proper, comfortable height for five-year-olds and other three-foot dwarfs skiing there. But my knickers did not bend well at the knees, and I could barely stoop to reach the tow, then scoot uphill in the painful position of a coolie bearing a trunk. Holding the rope behind me, Merrill shouted encouragements during the endless journey. If it's this hard going up, I thought, what will it be like going down?

I liked the mountains, all right, and I thrilled to the giant cable-cars carrying you way up where the big skiers go; also, I liked the cable-cars going down—empty, with all the window space to yourself, excepting the leering lift operator who always remarked on the absence of your skis.

"We're almost there, Boggle!" Merrill lied. "Bend your knees!" I watched the bouncy children dancing on the rope in front of me while I carried the mountain on my back—the rope bunching my frozen mittens, my chin hitting my knees as my skis skated uncontrollably in and out of the ruts. I knew I had to straighten up or never use my spine again.

"Bend, Boggle!" Merrill hollered, but I straightened up. All that grief off my back for one lovely moment; I lifted the rope chest-high and leaned back. Above me I saw the little children, their skis completely off the ground, hanging from the rope, swinging like little puppets. Some dropped off, littering the path in front of me; it was clear that they wouldn't struggle out of my way in time.

At the top of the hill, a befurred lift attendant shouted unkindly at me. Below us, the gentle thud of mothers stamping their boots. "Let go of the rope, Boggle!" Merrill shouted. I watched the approaching tangle of children in the path, skis and poles clashing; stuck to the ascending rope were several of their tiny bright and frozen mittens. The lift attendant suddenly dashed for the control house, perhaps thinking the mittens were hands.

I was surprised at how cleverly I kept my balance as I skied over my first child. "Let *go*, Boggle!" said Merrill; I shot a quick look over my shoulder at the child I'd just trampled and watched him groggily rise up and catch Merrill in the solar plexus with his junior crash helmet. Merrill let go of the rope. Then I was surrounded by the tiny creatures, jabbing with their poles and yelping German for God and their mothers. In the midst of them, I felt the rope jerk to a stop in my hands, and I sprawled into a milling nest of them.

"*Es tut mir leid.*"

"*Gott! Hilfe! Mutti, Mutti . . .*"

Merrill steered me out of the rope-tow ruts and onto the slope which had looked so slight and gentle from below.

"Please, Merrill, I want to *walk.*"

"Boggle, you'd make holes for the other skiers . . ."

"I'd like to make one big hole for all the other skiers, Merrill."

But I let Merrill Overturf guide me to center slope and aim me in the general direction of the bottom, where the children appeared to be further dwarfed and the cars way below in the parking lot looked like the children's toys. Overturf demonstrated the snowplow stop, then showed off a wobbly stem-turn. Larkish little children flew by us, poling and zigzagging and falling as lightly and safely as little wads of wool.

My skis felt like long, heavy ladders on my feet: my poles were stilts.

"I'll follow you," said Merrill, "in case you fall."

I began slowly enough; children passed by me with obvious scorn. Then I noted I was picking up speed. "Lean forward," called Merrill, and I went a little faster, my skis clicking together, swaying apart. What if one ski crosses the other? I thought.

Then I passed the first wave of surprised children as if they were standing still. That'll show the little bastards. "Bend your knees, Boggle!" came Merrill's voice from miles behind me. But my knees seemed locked, ramrod stiff. I came up on a bright-capped little blond girl and hipped her neatly out of the way, like sideswiping a squirrel with a train. *"Es tut mir leid,"* I said, but the words were blown down my throat; my eyes watered. *"Snow-plow,* Boggle!" Merrill was screaming. Oh, yes, that stopping device. But I didn't dare move my skis. I attempted to *will* them apart; they resisted me; my hat flew off. Ahead of me, a gaggle of children poled and veered and terror-scampered; an avalanche was after them! Not wanting to gore anyone, I dropped my poles and bludgeoned through them. By the tow shelter at the bottom, an attendant came caterwauling out with a shovel; he had been packing down the tow ruts, but I suspected he would not hesitate to swat me. The lift line broke up; spectators and skiers burst for cover. I imagined an air raid, from the point of view of the bomb.

There was a flat shelf at the base of the slope; surely, I thought, this would slow me down. If not, there was an enormous bulldozed mound of snow piled up to prevent skiers from zipping down into the parking lot. I tried to think of the mound as soft.

"Use your edges!" Merrill screamed. Edges? "Bend your fucking knees!" Knees? "Boggle, for God's sake, fall down!" In front of the children? Never.

I remembered the man at the rent-a-ski place, telling me about the safety bindings. If they were so safe, why didn't they *do* anything?

I hit the flattened shelf off balance and felt my weight fling me back on my heels; the tips of my skis were raised like the bow of a boat. The looming snowbank which protected the parking lot from the likes of me came up awfully suddenly. I saw myself drilled into it like a rifle grenade; they would dig for hours, then decide to blast me out.

The surprise has rarely been equaled: to discover that skis can *climb.* I vaulted the bank. I was launched into the parking lot. Below me, during my descent, I saw a family of sturdy Germans getting out of their Mercedes. Father Round in stout lederhosen knickers and a feathered Tyrolean hat; Mother Heft in hiking boots and swinging a walking stick with an ice-ax point; children: Dumpling, Dumpier and Dollop, with a baffling armload of rucksacks, snowshoes and ski poles. The opened trunk of their Mercedes waited for me to come down. A great whale's maw waiting for the flying fish to fall. Into the jaws of Death!

But sturdy Father Round, the German, precisely closed his trunk.

. . . after which I'm forced to rely on Merrill Overturf's description. I remember only a surprisingly soft landing, the result of my warm, fleshy collision with Mother Heft, wedged between my chest and the taillights of the Mercedes. Her sweet words were hot in my ear: "Aaarp!" and "Hee-urmff!" And the mixed reactions of the children; Child Dumpling's word-less gape, Child Dumpier's sudden avalance of his belongings on Child Dollop, whose ear-splitting wail was shrilly clear from under the rucksacks, snowshoes and ski poles where he lay cringing.

Father Round, said Merrill, quickly scanned the skies, no doubt looking for the *Luftwaffe*. Merrill came clambering down the snowbank to where I lay dazed. Mother Heft's great wind had returned and she prodded me with the ice-ax tip of her walking stick.

"Boggle! Boggle! Boggle!" Merrill ran shouting. While on the lip of the bank above the parking lot, a crowd of those who'd survived me came to see if *I'd* survived. They are reported to have cheered when Merrill held up one of my broken skis and failed to find the other. My safety bindings had released. From the bank the lift attendant savagely hurled my ski poles into the parking lot, across which Merrill gingerly supported me. Insane applause and jeering from the snowbank, to see that I was somewhat marred.

It was then, Merrill claims, that the American couple drove up in their new Porsche. They were apparently lost; they thought they had come to the races in Zell. The man, a frightened one, rolled down his window and stared with considerable insecurity at the yelling crowd on the bank. With pity he smiled at Merrill helping the injured skier away. But the man's wife, big and fortyish, with a jutting chin, slammed her door and strode around to her husband's side of the car.

"Well, dammit," she said to him, forcing him to roll down his window. "You and your rotten German and your lousy sense of directions. We're late. We've missed the first event."

"Madam," Merrill said to her as he dragged me past them. "Be glad that the first event missed *you.*"

But I have to take Merrill's word for this, and Merrill is suspect. By the time we were back at the Gasthaus Tauernhof in Kaprun, Merrill was in worse shape than I was. He was having an insulin reaction; his blood sugar was down to zilch. I had to help him to the bar and explain his exploring eyes to Herr Halling, the bartender.

"He's a diabetic, Herr Halling. Give him an orange juice, or something else with lots of sugar."

"No, no," Halling said. "Diabetics aren't supposed to have any sugar."

"But he's had too much insulin," I told Halling. "He's used up *too much* sugar." And as if to demonstrate my point, Merrill fumbled a cigarette in front of us, lit the filter end, disliked the taste and ground it out on the back of his own hand. I knocked it away from him, and Merrill stared with some puzzlement at what might have been a dull pain coming from the burn. *Do you suppose that's my hand?* With his other hand, he picked it up and waved it to Herr Halling and me as if it were a flag.

"*Ja,* orange juice, immediately," Herr Halling said.

I propped Merrill up against me, but he skidded dizzily off his bar stool.

When he recovered, we watched a rerun of the women's races at Zell on television. The Austrian, Heidi Schatzl, won the downhill as expected, but there was an upset in the giant slalom. The first American girl to win an international race beat out Heidi Schatzl and the French star, Marguerite Delacroix. The video tapes were beautiful. Delacroix missed a gate in her second run and was disqualified, and Heidi Schatzl caught an edge and fell. The Austrians in the Gasthaus Tauernhof were glum, but Merrill and I cheered loudly, in the interests of international hostility.

Then they showed the tape of the American girl who'd won. She was nineteen, blond and very strong. She came through the upper gates smoothly, but a little slow. When she hit the mid-mark, her time was a bit long and she knew it; she bore down on those lower gates like a skidding bus, skating off one ski and then the other, dropping her shoulder and cutting so close to the flags that she left every one flapping. At the last gate, she performed a ballet on that ice-hard, overpacked snow: she lost her balance and managed to hold her cut with one ski off the ground, like a wing out beside her at her waist. Then she righted herself, touched that wild ski down as soft as a kiss, threw her great ass back over her heels and sat on the backs of her skis down the straightaway across the finish line, snapping herself out of that deep squat as soon as she crossed the line. She cut a wide, soft, snow-throwing turn just in front of the safety rope and the crowd. It was very clear that she knew she'd won it.

They had an interview with her on television. She had a smooth, handsome face with a mouth as wide as her cheekbones. No make-up, just the white stickum of Chap Stick on her lips; she kept licking them, laughing all out of breath and bold-faced, clowning into the camera. She wore a one-piece stretch-suit as sleek and tight on her as skin; it had a big gold zipper running from her chin to her crotch, and she'd let it open down to her cleavage, where her big, high, round breasts pushed out her soft velour pullover. She shared the winner's circle with second-place finisher Dubois of France—a petite, darting, ratlike lady with snap-out eyes; and third-place finisher Thalhammer of Austria, a dark, glowering, shapeless, hulking wonderwoman whose chromosomes, you can bet, were half male. The American was a head taller than either of them and an inch above the interviewer, who was as impressed with her bosom as he was with her skiing.

His English was awful. "You haf a Cherman name," he said to her. "Vy?"

"My grandfather was Austrian," the girl said, and the locals in the Gasthaus Tauernhof cheered up a little.

"Then you speak Cherman?" the interviewer asked her, hopefully.

"Only with my father," the girl said.

"Not just a little wit me?" the interviewer teased.

"*Nein,*" said the girl, whose face now betrayed a certain tough irritability; she must have been thinking, Why don't you ask me about my *skiing,* twerp? A bouncy American teammate popped up over her shoulder and held out an unwrapped stick of gum. The big girl stuck it in her mouth and started to soften it up.

"Vy do all American jew cum?" the interviewer asked her.

"All Americans *don't* 'jew cum,' " the girl said. Merrill and I cheered. The interviewer knew he wasn't getting anywhere with her, so he tried to get snotty.

"Itz too bat," he said, "dis is the last race uf dis season, dough it mus be an honor to be the *erst* American to vin vun."

"We'll 'vin' lots more," the girl told him, chewing with little savage snaps.

"Nex year, maybe," the interviewer said. "Vill you ski nex year?"

"I'll see," the girl said. Then the video tape was cut and jumped out of sequence, causing Merrill and me to boo loudly. When the picture was clear again, the interviewer was trying to keep up with the girl, who was striding away from him, carrying her skis lightly on her shoulder. The camera was hand-held and unsteady, the sound track crunched with snow.

"Did it take anyting avay from you fictory," he was asking her, "to vin because Heidi Schatzl fell town?"

The girl turned to him, almost clipping his head with her skis. She didn't say a word, and he added a little nervously: ". . . or to vin because Marguerite Delacroix mist a gate?"

"I'd have won anyway," the girl said. "I was just better than they were today," and she started off again. He had to duck under the backswing of her long skis and jog to catch up to her, his legs getting tangled in the microphone cord.

"Zu 'Biggie' Kunft," the interviewer mumbled after her, stumbling along. *"Die Amerikanerin aus Fermont, U.S.A.,"* he said. He caught up with her, and this time remembered to crouch low under her skis when she turned to him. "Wit the conditions today," he said, "wit the snow zo iczy and fast, do you tink your veight helpt you?" He waited smugly for her reply.

"What about my weight?" she asked him; she was embarrassed.

"Does it help you?"

"It doesn't *hurt* me," she said defensively, and Merrill and I felt angry. "You got great weight!" Merrill shouted. "Every pound of it!" I said.

"Vy do they call you 'Biggie'?" the interviewer asked her. She was upset, you could tell, but she moved right up close to him, heaving out her breasts and cracking her broad mouth into a smile. She looked down on him; she seemed to be trying to push him backward with her tits.

" 'Vy' do you 'tink' so?" she asked.

The bastard interviewer looked away from her and beckoned the camera closer, beaming into the lens and rolling out his sly German, *"Mit mir hier ist die junge Amerikanerin, Zu 'Biggie' Kunft . . ."* he was announcing as she turned away from him suddenly and caught him beautifully in the back of his head with her swinging skis. He dropped out of frame and the camera attempted to trot after her, putting her in and out of focus and finally losing her in the crowd. But her voice, offstage, came back to us, angry and hurt:

"Please leave me the fuck alone," she said. *"Please . . ."* The announcer didn't bother to translate this.

Then did Overturf and I loudly praise the virtues of this skier, Sue "Biggie" Kunft, fending off the strongly nationalist arguments of several Austrians drinking with us in the Tauernhof.

"A rare girl, Merrill."

"An athletic lay, Boggle."

"No, Merrill. She's clearly a virgin."

"Or a man, Boggle."

"Oh, never, Merrill. Her glands are quite unmistakable."

"I'll drink to that," said Merrill, who was under great pressure from the limitations of his diabetic diet; not a well-disciplined person, he frequently substituted booze for food. "Did I eat my dinner tonight, Boggle?"

"No," I told him. "You missed dinner because you were in a trance."

"Good," he said, and ordered another slivowitz.

With TV-skiing over, the local Tauernhof clientele returned to their usual peasant savagery. The regular Hungarian group from Eisenstadt performed: an accordion, a tortured zither and a violin to make the mighty cringe.

With the great privacy afforded us by speaking English in a German-speaking tavern, Merrill and I discussed international sports; Hieronymus Bosch; the function of the American embassy in Vienna; the neutrality of Austria; Tito's remarkable success; the shocking rise of the bourgeoisie; the boredom of televised golf; the source of Herr Halling's halitosis; why the waitress wore a bra, were her armpits shaved or shaggy, and who would ask her; the advisability of chasing slivowitz with beer; the price of Semperit radial tires in Boston, of bourbon in Europe in general, of hashish in Vienna in particular; possible causes of the scar on the face of the man who sat by the door; what a worthless instrument a zither was; whether the Czechs were more creative than the Hungarians; what a stupid, backward language Old Low Norse was; the inadequacies of the two-party system in the United States; the challenge of inventing a new religion; the small differences between clerical fascism and Nazism; the incurability of cancer; the inevitableness of war; the general and overall stupidity of man; the pain in the ass of diabetes. And the best way to introduce yourself to girls. One way, Merrill claimed, was the "boob loop." "You hold the ski pole thus," said Merrill, holding it upside down, his fingers meshed in the basket weave, the point against the heel of his hand. He raised the end with the wrist-thong and waved it like a wand; the wrist-thong made a loop. "That's where the boob goes," Merrill said. He was watching the waitress clear the table next to ours.

"No, Merrill."

"A mere demonstration?"

"I think not here, Merrill."

"Perhaps you're right," he said, letting his weapon hang innocently. "The secret to the boob loop lies, in part, in the boob. The lack of a bra is a must. Also, a proper angle. I usually go over the shoulder; that way, they never see it coming. Under the arm, from the side, is good too, but that takes rare positioning."

"Merrill, have you ever done this before?"

"No. I just brought it up, Boggle, because I thought it would make a great introduction. Reel them in, then introduce yourself."

"They might think you forward."

"Aggressiveness is essential these days."

The waitress eyed Merrill's dangling loop with suspicion, but she offered a small target, at best. Also, Herr Halling, at the bar, could fairly have been termed "moralistic." Merrill forgot about his boob loop, swooned in his slivowitz, revived with beer and considered the possible need of checking his blood sugar by doing his usual urine test. But his test tubes and little vials of sugar-sensitive solutions were three floors up in the Tauernhof, and the men's room would be crowded this time of night; he would be forced to pee in the sink, a habit he knew I despised. Therefore, he went *off,* in his own peculiar fashion, sitting right where he was. He was simply away somewhere. As long as he wasn't hurting himself, I always left his trances alone. He was smiling. Once he said, "What?" "Nothing," I told him, and he nodded. Agreed: there had been nothing.

Then you walked in, Biggie. I recognized Sue "Biggie" Kunft right away. I elbowed Merrill; he didn't feel a thing. I pinched a tight roll of flesh on his belly and gave him a hard, painful twist under the table.

"Nurse . . ." Merrill said, "it's starting again." Then he looked over my shoulder at the sharp little faces and tiny antlers of the chamois trophies along the wall. "Hi! Sit down," he told them. "Shit, it's good to see you."

Sue "Biggie" Kunft had not yet decided to stay. She kept her parka on, though she unzipped it. She wasn't alone; two other girls were with her, obviously teammates. They all wore those parkas with the Olympic insignia and little U.S.A. stickers on the sleeve. Stunning Biggie Kunft, with two unattractive teammates, had shunned the hip and sporty crowds in Zell am See; had they come for local color—for local men, with whom they might remain anonymous?

One of the girls with Biggie Kunft announced that the Gasthaus Tauernhof was "quaint."

Her friend said, "There's no one under forty here."

"Well, there's *that* one," said Sue "Biggie" Kunft, meaning me. She couldn't see Merrill, who'd laid himself down on the far end of the long bench at our table.

"Nurse?" he asked me. I stuffed a ski hat under his head, trying to make him more comfortable. "I don't mind the sleeping pill, nurse," he said in a groggy voice, "but I refuse to have another enema."

The girls were making up their minds while Herr Halling and a few others took turns recognizing this great-boobed blonde. Should they take a table alone or sit at the far end of mine?

"He looks a little drunk," one girl told Biggie.

"What a funny body he has!" said the other.

"I think it's an interesting body," Biggie said, and she slipped her parka off her shoulders and tossed her thick, shoulder-bobbed hair; she bore down on my table with a self-sure swagger, a way of walking which was almost male. A big strong girl, she knew that the grace she had was an athletic sort; she didn't try to fake a kind of femininity she knew she didn't have. Knee-high, big fur boots and dark-brown jersey stretch pants, very snug; she wore a deep-orange velour V-neck, and the white of her throat and cleavage was a shock under her tanned face. Those two outstanding orange breasts were floating down on me, like some drunken double vision of a sunset. I lifted Merrill's head by his ear and bounced him lightly on the ski hat, then harder, on the bench.

"Aggressiveness is essential, nurse," he said. His eyes were open; he was winking at all the chamois on the wall.

"*Ist dieser Tisch noch frei?*" asked Sue "Biggie" Kunft, who on television had said she spoke German only with her father.

"*Bitte, Sie sollen hier setzen,*" I mumbled for them to sit down. That good big one right across from me; the other two hanging back, awkward jocks trying to look lithe and bouncy and girlish. They sat on her side of the table too, across from where Merrill Overturf lay unnoticed; no need, I felt, to make them uncomfortable by calling him to their attention. No need, either, to stand up politely and let Sue Kunft see that she had an inch on me; sitting down, we were equally tall. I've a fine torso; only my legs fall short.

"*Was möchten Sie zum trinken?*" I asked her, and ordered cider for the two nowhere girls and a beer for Biggie. Watching Herr Halling navigate the dark Keller, announcing over the girls' shoulders, "*Zwei Apfelsaft, ein Bier . . .*" His mind took a long drink down the cleavage of the winner of the women's giant slalom.

I continued a distant German prattle with the champion across from me, while the tragic girls at the cold end of the table did fussy things with their hands and mewed together. "Biggie" spoke a sort of homemade German, learned and heard from only one parent, who had given her a perfect accent and no regard for grammar. She could tell I wasn't from around Kaprun or Zell because I didn't use the dialect, but she never guessed I was American, and I saw no reason to speak English; it would have allowed the girls at the end of the table to join in.

However, I wanted Merrill to join in. I reached out to slap his face, but his head was gone.

"You're not from around here?" Biggie asked me.

"*Nein.*"

Merrill's head was not on the bench any more. I groped around for the rest of him under the table with my foot, behind the bench with my hand, smiling and nodding all the while.

"You like skiing here?" she asked.

"*Nein,* I didn't come to ski. I don't ski at all . . ."

"Why are you in the mountains if you don't ski?"

"I used to be a pole-vaulter," I told her, watching her repeat the German softly to herself, then nodding; she understands. Now I watch her thinking of the relationship between being in the mountains and having been a pole-vaulter. Did he imply he came to the mountains because he used to pole-vault? She thinks this was implied. How will she handle this, I'm wondering. Also: Where the hell is Merrill?

"A pole-vaulter?" she said, in her cautious German. "*Sie springen mit einem Pol?*"

"I used to, yes," I told her. "But not now, of course."

Of course? you could see her thinking. But all she said was, "Wait. You used to be a pole-vaulter, but not anymore, right?"

"Of course," I said, to which she shook her head and went right on.

". . . and you're here in the mountains *because* you used to be a pole-vaulter?"

She was admirable; I did love her perseverance. In such casual circumstances, most people would have given up trying to understand.

"Why?" she said insistently. "I mean, what does having been a pole-vaulter have to do with coming here to the mountains?"

"I don't know," I said innocently, as if *she* had proposed such a notion all by herself. She looked utterly confused. "What possible relationship could there be between mountains and pole-vaulting?" I asked her then. She was lost; she must have thought it was a problem with her German.

"You like heights?" she tried.

"Oh yes, the higher the better." And I smiled.

She must have sensed the nonsense in this talk, because she smiled too and said, "You bring your poles with you?"

"My pole-vaulting poles?"

"Of course."

"Of course I bring them with me."

"To the mountains . . ."

"Of course."

"You just sort of lug them around, huh?" She was having fun now.

"Just one at a time."

"Oh, of course."

"It beats waiting in lift lines," I said.

"You just vault right up?"

"It's harder coming down."

"What do you *do?*" she asked. "I mean, *really.*"

"I'm still making up my mind," I said. "Really." I was being serious.

"So am I," she said. She was serious too, so I dropped the German and went straight into English.

"But there's no one thing I can do," I told her, "as well as you can ski."

Her two friends looked up, surprised. "He's American," said one.

"He's a pole-vaulter," Biggie told them, smiling.

"I used to be," I said.

"He's been putting us on," one of the uglies said, with a hurtful look at Biggie.

"He's got a nice sense of humor, though," Biggie told the girl, and then —to me, in German so they wouldn't know—"I miss a sense of humor, skiing. There isn't anything humorous about it."

"You haven't seen *me* ski," I told her.

"Why are you here?" she said.

"I'm taking care of a friend," I said, and gave a guilty look around for Merrill. "He's drunk and he's got diabetes, and right now he's lost. I really ought to try and find him."

"Why haven't you, then?"

I kept on, privately, in German, "Because you came in, and I didn't want to be away for that event."

She smiled, but looked away; her friends seemed angry with her for speaking in German, but she continued. "It's a funny place to pick up girls in," she said. "You couldn't have been trying very hard or you wouldn't be in a place like this."

"That's true," I said. "There's no chance of picking up girls in here."

"No, there *isn't,*" she said, with a look to say she meant it. But she smiled. "Go find your friend," she said. "I won't go away yet."

And I was just about to do that, wondering where to look first. Under the darker Keller tables, where poor Merrill might be lurking insane or lying in a diabetic coma? Upstairs in the Tauernhof, conducting a drunken urine test, botching his test tubes over the sink?

Then I noticed how quiet the table behind the girls was—how some men sat intent on some intrigue. The silhouette of a large dog crept up behind the girls, approaching our table. Herr Halling, poised at the bar with his finger to his lips, about to spitshine a shot glass, was pretending not to notice anything. Then, into the dull light, at a level with our table, a dark shadow of a ski pole extended slowly, the wrist-thong end dipping like a wand toward the space between the elbow (on the table) and the breast of the winner of the women's giant slalom.

"This friend," I said shakily to Biggie Kunft, "is not himself."

"*Find* him, then," she said, truly worried.

"I hope you have a nice sense of humor too," I told her.

"Oh, I do," she said, smiling very warmly. And she leaned a little closer to me across the table, and touched the back of my hand a little awkwardly. Conscious of what big hands she had, she usually kept them folded. "Please go make sure that your friend's all right," she said. Then, into the exaggerated gap between her breast and her elbow, the wrist-thong of a ski pole came dancing; leaning forward, as she was, her breast pushed tight against the velour, she was a target only a fool could miss.

"I hope you'll forgive me," I said, and touched her hand.

"Of course I will," she laughed, as the snare seized her and the wrist-thong tugged her breast up into her armpit, oddly askew, and Merrill Overturf, behind her, weaved up to his knees, his ski pole bending like a fishing rod with a heavy catch, his eyes all glazed and terrible.

"Boob loop!" he screamed.

Then the girl athlete from Vermont demonstrated her catlike coordination and wonder-mother strength. Biggie slipped her breast free of the wrist-thong and seized the end of the pole, swinging her legs out from under the table and across the bench top, where her heavy thighs jarred Merrill Overturf off balance and dropped him on his rump. She was up on her feet, then, and obviously experienced at handling a ski pole, which she thrust repeatedly at Merrill who writhed on the floor, trying to free his twisted fingers from the pole's basket, trying to fend off the gouging pole point with the bleeding heel of his hand.

"Oh, *blood,* Boggle! I've been stabbed!"—while Biggie finally pinned him, one of her tall fur boots resting heavily on Merrill's chest, the point of the pole puckering Merrill's belly.

"It's a game, it's a game!" Merrill shrieked at her. "Did I *hurt* you? Did I? Not on your life I didn't. No, I did *not* hurt you . . . no, no, *no!*" But Sue "Biggie" Kunft poised over him, with just enough weight on the pole to keep Merrill pinned and threatened with disemboweling, while she flashed me an angry, betrayed look. "*Talk* to her, Boggle," Merrill pleaded. "We saw you on TV," he told her. "We *loved* you."

"We hated the interviewer," I told her.

"You were simply beautiful," Merrill said. "They tried to make your winning sound just lucky, but you were clearly above that bullshit." She stared at him, amazed.

"It's his blood sugar," I told her. "He's all mixed up."

"He wrote a poem about you," Merrill lied, and Biggie looked at me, touched. "It's a nice poem," Merrill said. "He's a real poet."

". . . who used to be a pole-vaulter," Biggie said suspiciously.

"He used to be a wrestler too," Merrill said suddenly, crazily, "and if you hurt me with that ski pole, he'll break your goddamn neck!"

"He doesn't know what he's saying," I told Biggie, who was watching Merrill holding up his bloody hand.

"I may die," said Merrill. "There's no telling what that pole's been stuck in."

"Poke him a good one and let's get out of here," one of Biggie's skimates told her.

"And keep the pole," the other one said, glowering at me.

"There are vital organs just under the belly lining," Merrill said. "Oh, God . . ."

"I'm not aiming for your belly," Biggie told him.

"When you were being mocked, we loved you," Merrill told her. "In that ugly, self-serious, competitive world, you had dignity and humor."

"What happened to your humor?" I asked her. She looked at me, stung. She was tender about that; it seemed to matter a lot.

" 'Vy' do they call you 'Biggie'?" Merrill asked her boldly. " 'Vy' do you 'tink' so?" he asked me.

"It must be her *heart,*" I told him. Then I reached out and took the pole from her. She was smiling, and she blushed a hue resembling that deep-orange of her V-neck velour. *I suspect you are velour all over!*

Then Merrill Overturf stood up too fast. What remained of his consciousness had been used to a prone position. When he bounded to his feet like that, I think he left his brain lying down. We saw only the whites of his eyes, though he smiled at everyone. His hands dialed telephones in the air.

"Gob, Doggle," he said.

I noticed he was standing on his ankles just before he fell, like wet snow.

14

Fighting the Good Fight

In my married phase, at 918 Iowa Avenue, optimism was reserved for Risky Mouse. For five nights running, he made his own daring thefts of the baited trap. I warned him again about it. I brought him a fatty portion of Biggie's steamed brisket, which I displayed in an alluring fashion, not in the trap itself, but several feet away. Making it clear that I'd take care of him. He needn't risk his furry, finger-sized neck in Biggie's overlarge trap designed for weasels, woodchucks, wombats and mammoth rats.

I never knew exactly what it was that Biggie had against the rodent. She only saw him once—surprised him on the cellar landing when she went to fetch her skis one night. Perhaps she thought he was getting too bold, that he had intentions of invading the upstairs. Or that he meant to gnaw her skis, which she moved to the bedroom closet. Occasionally, they fell on me in my morning-grope period. Their evil-sharp edges could gash you up good. It was one of the sources of friction between Biggie and me.

So one night Risky Mouse was given brisket, about which I had my doubts. Do mice eat meat?

Then I took a bath with Colm. He was so slippery in the tub that I had to keep my thumbs in his armpits or else he'd giggle under. Baths with Colm relaxed me, except that Biggie always came in and watched.

And with genuine concern, she'd always ask, "Will Colm have as much hair as you do?" Implying, How soon will the horrible growth start ruining him for life?

With some irritation I'd always say, "Would you prefer me hairless, Big?"

She'd back down, saying, "It's not that, exactly. It's more that I wouldn't want Colm to be as hairy as you."

"Relatively, Big, I'm not so hairy as most men."

"Well, *men,*" she'd say, as if the only thing about me that bothered her was that I was one.

I knew what was on her mind, though: skiers. Blond and somewhat male (or if not blond, at least tanned); no tobacco stains on their teeth; hairless, linen-white muscles under their down underwear; smooth all over, from too much time in sleeping bags. The only repulsive part of skiers is their feet. I think skiers only sweat through their hot, cramped, layered feet. All those thick crusty socks! That's their only health gap.

I was the first and only nonskier Biggie ever laid. It must have been the novelty that impressed her. But now she wonders. Remembering all that snowbound cleanliness.

Is it my fault that I never had the silky chafe of down underwear to rub off all my hair? My pores are too big for skiing; the wind gets inside me. Is it my fault if I'm given to excess oil? Can I help it if baths don't quite work for me? I can step glowing from a tub, powder my groin, anoint my pits, slaver my fresh-shaved face with some scented astringent, and ten minutes later I start to sweat. I sort of gloss over. Sometimes, when I'm talking to a person, I see them start to stare; they're uneasy about something. I've figured out what it is. They suddenly see my pores opening, or maybe their attention is fixed on just *one* pore, opening in slow motion and sort of peeking at them. I've experienced the sensation myself, in mirrors, and I can sympathize with the observer; it's unnerving.

But you'd expect your wife not to ogle when your metabolism shows, especially in troubled times. Instead, she dispenses suggestions to improve my funny hair. "Get rid of your mustache, Bogus. It's really pubic."

But I know better. I need all the hair I can grow. Without hair, what would cover my terrible pores? Biggie never understood that; she doesn't *have* any pores. Her skin is as sleek as Colm's bum. What she hoped for, I knew, was that Colm would have her pores—or, rather, her lack of pores. Naturally, this hurt me. But I thought of the child. Frankly, I wouldn't wish my pores on anyone.

Even so, those bathtub confrontations grieved me.

I took a walk to Benny's, thinking that Ralph Packer, the polemicist, might be holding court there or otherwise formulating maxims. But Benny's was unusually empty, and I made use of the silence by making a mindless phone call to Flora Mackey Hall for Women.

"Which floor?" someone wanted to know, and I pondered which floor Lydia Kindle would live on. High up, close to the eaves, where the birds nest?

Different extensions were tried. A girl with a suspicious voice said, "Yes?"

"Lydia Kindle, please," I said.

"Who's calling, please?" the voice wanted to know. "This is her floor sister."

A floor sister? Hanging up, I imagined wall brothers, door fathers, window mothers, and I wrote on the plaster above Benny's urinal, FLORA MACKEY WAS A VIRGIN TO THE END.

In the crapper stall, someone seemed to be in trouble. Under the door peeked thonged sandals, purple socks, a pair of fallen bell-bottoms and obvious grief.

Whoever he was, he was crying.

Well, I know how it can hurt to pee, so I could sympathize. At the same time, I didn't wish to look further into this. Perhaps I could buy a beer from the bar, slip it to him under the door, tell him it's on me and quickly leave.

The urinal flushed—Benny's famous self-flushing urinal. To save the strain on the water pump, it is rumored, it is electrically timed to flush semiannually. To think that I was on hand for the rare event!

But in the crapper stall, he heard it too; he felt someone was there; he stopped crying. I tried to tiptoe to the door.

His voice came weakly from the stall: "Please tell me, is it dark out yet?"

"Yes."

"Oh, God," he said. "Can I leave now? Have they gone?"

A sudden fear was upon me! I looked around for *them. Who?* Peering under the urinal for strange, wet men lurking there. "Who's they?" I asked.

The stall door opened and he came out, hitching his bell-bottoms up. It was the thin, dark boy who is a poet and tends to wear lavender clothes; a student who works in Root's Bookstore, he is alternately assumed to be a great lover or a fag, or both.

"God, have they gone?" he said. "Oh, *thank* you. They told me not to leave until it was dark, but there aren't any windows in here."

A closer look at him revealed the savage beating he had taken. They had jumped him in the men's room and told him he belonged in the lady's room instead. They proceeded to roll him in the urinal; they scoured his nose with the deodorant cake, which graveled up his face and left him smarting, as if he'd been rubbed with a pee-soaked pumice stone. A terrible confusion of odors clung to him; in his pocket, a bottle of Leopardess toilet water had smashed. If perfume were poured in a privy, it could not smell worse.

"Jesus," he said. "They happen to have been right. I *am* a fag—but I might *not* have been. I mean, they had no way of knowing I was. I was just taking a leak. That's normal enough, isn't it? I mean, I don't hustle guys in men's rooms. I get all I want."

"What about the toilet water?"

"They didn't even know I had it," he said. "And it's not for *me,* for Christ's sake. It's for a girl—my sister. I live with her. She called me at work and asked me to pick up some for her on my way home."

He had trouble walking—they'd really stomped him around—so I said I'd help him out of there.

"I live right around here," he said. "You don't have to come with me. They might think *you're* one."

But I walked him out of Benny's on my arm, past two leering couples in a booth by the door. See the boyfriends! One of whom drank a bottle of perfume and then pissed his pants.

Benny himself posed with his shining beer steins at the bar in studied, cultivated ignorance of everything.

"Your urinal flushed itself, Benny," I said. "Mark the calendar."

"Goodnight, boys," said Benny, and a wispy artist at the corner table sank his nose into the head of his beer to drown our passing odor.

"I knew Iowa would be awful," the fag told me, "but I never knew it would be *this* awful."

We were outside his walk-up on downtown Clinton Street. "You've been very nice," he said. "I'd ask you in, but . . . I'm very attached, you understand. I've never been so faithful before, really, but *this* one . . . well, you know. He's just very special."

"I'm not like you," I told him. "I mean, I might have been, but you happen to be wrong."

He took my hand. "It's all right," he said. "I know. Some other time, we'll see. What's your name?"

"Forget it," I said; I was walking off, trying to leave his reek behind. There on that shabby street in his bright clothes, he looked like some gay knight just entering a town wiped out by the plague: brave, silly and doomed.

"Don't be too proud!" he shouted after me. "Don't ever plead, but don't be too proud."

Rare advice from the strangest of seers! Down dark Iowa Avenue, a horde of fag maulers lurked in every shadow. Would they leave me alone if I showed them I was straight? If I meet a girl, should I rape her? Watch me! I'm normal!

Or I could have left the curtains open when I came home to Biggie, my great tawny lioness, propped in our well-grooved bed, lying on and under a wealth of magazines and little pillows with stitched-on Alpine scenes.

"My God, smell you!" said Biggie, staring at me. And the horror of an explanation struck me then as strong as the lush steam of perfumed urine wafting off me from my contact with the Root's Bookstore employee. I was a diluted version of his fragrance.

"What's that all over you?" said Biggie. "*Who's* that? You prick . . ."

"I just went to Benny's," I said. "There was a fairy in the men's room. The one who works at Root's, you know?" But Biggie came bounding off the bed, sniffing me all over, catching up my hands to her nose. "Really, Big," I said, and tried to nip her cheek, but she stiff-armed me away from her.

"Oh, you prick, you bastard, Bogus . . ."

"I haven't been illicit, Big, I swear . . ."

"God!" she cried. "You even bring her smell back to my own house!"

"Biggie, it was this damn fag in the men's room. He got rolled in the urinal, broke some toilet water he had in his pocket . . ." *Shit*, I thought. That doesn't even sound possible, not to mention true. I said with hopeless calm, "It was very strong-smelling, it rubbed off . . ."

"I'll *bet* she's strong-smelling!" Biggie screamed. "Like some bitch in heat, she's got her damn scent all over you!"

"I didn't do anything, Big—"

"Something exotic, I'll bet," said Biggie. "One of those Hindus in robes, with their twitchy things. And smelling like a whole harem! Oh, I know you, Bogus! You always went for that, didn't you? Always ogling the blacks and those kinky Orientals and swarthy Jewesses! Goddamn you, I've seen you!"

"For Christ's sake, Big—"

"It's true, Bogus!" she yelled. "You really go for that, I know. Hairy ones and whorish ones . . . fucking gaudy dirt!"

"Jesus, Big!"

"You always wanted me different," she said; she bit her fist. "Look what you buy me for clothes. You buy me terrible things. I tell you, I'm not like that! My thighs are too big. 'Don't wear a bra,' you tell me. 'You got great boobs, Big,' you say. And if I don't wear a bra, I flop like a cow! 'Looks great, Big,' you say. Jesus, I know what I look like. My *nipples* are bigger than some girls' tits!"

"That's true, Big. They are. And I love your nipples, Biggie—"

"You don't!" she cried. "And you're always saying how you don't like blondes. 'I don't like blondes, as a rule,' you say, and then you pat me some place rude. 'As a rule,' you say, with your little nudges, giving me a feel—"

"I'll give you a little feel right now," I said, "if you don't shut up."

But she stepped back and put the bed between us. "Don't you touch me, goddamn you," she said.

"I haven't done anything, Big."

"You reek!" she screamed. "You must have done it in a *barn!* Wallowed with some sow in . . . in mulch!"

I tore off my shirt and bellowed at her. "*Smell* me, damn you, Biggie! It's just my hands that stink—"

"Just your hands, Bogus?" she said with icy calm. "In the barn," she said slowly, "did you finger-fuck a goat on the side?" I could see this was beyond reason, so I jerked off my boots, yanked down my pants and hopped at her, trying to get my underwear unsnaggled from my ankles.

"You animal!" she yelled. "You keep your thing away from me, Bogus! Oooogh! There's no telling what you've caught! I won't have any, thank you just the same." She dodged to the foot of the bed as I lunged at her, catching the bottom hem of her absurd, ballooning nightie—that wretched cotton-flannel one—ripping the thing up to the seam running around her neck and spinning her back on the bed. I had her almost strait-jacketed in the thing when she landed a high, skier-strong kick to my chest, leaving me holding the tatters of her nightie as she sprinted for the hall. I caught her from behind in the doorway, but she reached over my shoulder with one hand sunk in my hair; between her legs with her other hand, she gouged toward my vitals. I worked a neat back-heel trip—a better one, surely, than in my entire wrestling career. I was sure she'd be stunned, but she slashed an elbow back into my throat and bucked up to her hands and knees under me. With Biggie, you've got to control her legs. I tried a late body-scissors as she came up to her feet, but she bore me on her back across the room, tottering toward the dresser, in front of which she expertly tucked and rolled, driving my head and shoulders into the lingerie drawer.

I saw stars then, and tasted my tongue, which, despite half biting off in every wrestling match I ever had, I've never learned to keep inside my mouth. I clung to her hip as she strode away from the dresser, deftly blocking her fierce uppercut with my forehead, and while she raged over the pain in her hand, I pivoted behind her knee and dropped her with a side-leg dive—this time scissoring her near leg and barring her far arm in my tightest cross-body ride (a desperate hang-on maneuver I often used in my career). She thrashed well, groping with her free hand for something to hurt. I seized this moment to press my advantage and barred both her arms, spinning out at a right angle to her body and jacking her up on the back of her neck. Her fearsome legs crashed all around me, though she was stacked up good; in fact, I had her pinned, but there was no referee to slap the mat and call us quits. The double arm-bar hurt her, I knew, so I slithered my pale stomach up alongside her head, laying my navel against her hot cheek, watchful for her bite. I was careful not to lose my hold; it was at peak moments like these that I had developed the habit of getting myself inexplicably pinned. I inched my vulnerable part up close to her wild eye, ever mindful of her good teeth, just out of reach.

"I'll bite that damn thing off, I swear it," Biggie grunted, and she heaved against my double arm-bar, which held her like a vise.

"Be kind enough to smell it first, Big," I said, brushing my belly on her smooth cheek; her heavy knees sailed around my ducked head and thumped my back. "Just smell me, please," I told her, "and give me your honest impression of the scent. Whether my important part has any *foreign* odor, any reek of harems, Big. Or whether what you smell is strictly me." Her knees pumped slower; I saw her nose wrinkle. "In your estimation, Biggie," I said, "in your wealth of experience in this matter of my odor, would you say that you detect the faintest presence of anything unusual? Would you venture a guess as to whether this belly has slid against some other belly and taken on a different reek?" I could feel her cringe—a disarming shiver against the double arm-bar—and I let her turn her face a little and slide her nose where she would; my frightened part rested on her cheek now. *He put his life on the line to save his marriage.*

"What do you smell, Big?" I asked her softly. "Is there a stench of old stale sex?" She shook her head. My nervous part lay under her nose, across her upper lip.

"But your hands . . ." Her voice had a thin crack in it.

"I touched a poor beat-up fag all covered with pee and perfume, Big. I walked him home. We shook hands."

I had to sit her up against me before I could unlock the double arm-bar and plant a bloody kiss on her neck, my tongue still bleeding sweetly down my throat. Above my left ear, my scalp stretched tightly over the swelling knot where the dresser had clouted me. I imagined the damage to the lingerie drawer. Were the panties shaken up by the blow—unfolded and flung into the deepest corner of the drawer, where they lay worried? Wondering, Whatever it is out there, I hope it doesn't want to wear *me*.

Later, in a gentler battle on our bed, Biggie said, "Move your arm, quick. No, there . . . no, not there. Yes, there . . ." And making us both comfortable, she began to glide under me in a way she has that always makes me feel she's going to get away. But she never does, and she doesn't mean to. It's almost as if she's rowing us somewhere, and I'm just pacing myself to the easy strength of her stroke. The secret is in her tireless, driving legs.

"This must be good for skiers," I told her.

"You know, I have some muscles," said Biggie, rocking easily, like a broad boat moored on a choppy sea.

"I love your muscles, Big," I said.

"Oh, come on, not *that* muscle. I mean, that's not even a muscle, really," she said. "I mean, I've got a lot of muscles for a girl."

"You're all muscle, Big."

"Well, not *all* muscle . . . No, come on, *that's* not a muscle, you know damn well."

"It's better than muscle, Big."

"I'm sure you think so, Bogus."

"And this is better for you than skiing, Big. And more fun too . . ."

"Well, I'd hate to have to choose," she said, and I gouged her for that.

Heavy as she is, Biggie can roll with momentum, like a boat caught and borne along by a breaker. I floated her—a slow ride. Apparently we weighed nothing at all. Then the sea shifted and pitched us suddenly ashore, where our weightlessness went out of us and I lay as beached and leaden as a log under sand, and Biggie lay under me as calm as a pond.

Later she said, "Oh, bye-bye for a while. Bye-bye." But she didn't move.

"Bye," I said. "Where are you going?"

But all she said was, "Oh, Bogus, you're not such a bad person, really."

"Why, no, I'm not, Big," I said, intending to sound flippant. But it came out all hoarse and thick, as if I hadn't spoken for a long time. *Oh, the slow, furry voice of the successfully laid. I remember how I met you, Biggie . . .*

15

Remember Being in Love with Biggie?

Through the quaint gloom of the Tauernhof Keller, I carried the swooned Overturf toward the stairs. I wasn't worried about Merrill. The mismanagement of his diabetes had him frequently fading out and in again—his system alternately empty and too full of sugar.

"Too much alcohol," Herr Halling said sympathetically.

"Too much insulin, or too little," I said.

"He must be crazy," Biggie said, though she was concerned. She followed us upstairs, ignoring the harping from her ugly teammates.

"We should go now," one said.

"It's not our car," the other told me. "It's the team's car."

Crossing the landing with Biggie alongside me, I was conscious of her seeing how short I was. She looked a little down on me. To compensate, I pretended Merrill was no strain to carry; I tossed him around like groceries and took the next stair flight two at a time, letting Biggie see: he is not tall, but he is strong.

Marching Merrill into his room, I cracked his head on the doorjamb, which I had veered into thanks to blind spots induced by breathlessness. Biggie winced, but all Merrill said was, "Not now, please." He opened his eyes when I dumped him on his bed, and he stared at the overhead light as if it were the ultra-high beam over an operating table where he lay rigid, awaiting surgery.

"I have no feeling, no feeling," he told the anesthetist; then he went limp and sleepy and closed his eyes. "If you're going to take everything out of that suitcase," he grumbled, "you're going to put it all back, too."

While I got out all the sugar-sampling vials and set up the test-tube rack above the sink, Biggie whispered with the harpies in the doorway, about the fact that the racing season was over, that there was no curfew, that the team's car had been lent in good faith, that it must be returned.

"Merrill has a car . . ." I told Biggie in German, "if you would like to stay."

"Why would I like to do that?" she asked.

Recalling Merrill's lie, I said, "I'll show you my poem about you."

"I'm sorry, Boggle," Merrill murmured, "but they were such great boobs —Jesus, such a target—I just had to take a crack at them." But he was sound asleep, out of the fray.

"The car . . ." said one of the uglies. "*Really,* Biggie . . ."

"We've simply got to take it back," the other one told her. Biggie looked around Merrill's room, looked *me* over too, with a cool, questioning gaze. Where does the former pole-vaulter keep his pole?

"No, not now, please," Merrill announced to everyone. "I have to pee, oh, yes."

Juggling the vials and tubes for his urine test, I turned to the girls in the doorway, repeating to Biggie in German: "He has to pee." And I added hopefully to her, "You could wait outside . . ." *You warm solid hunk of velour!*

Then I was shut off from their mumbles in the hall outside Merrill's door, where I could hear only the harsh whisperings of the unwanted teammates and Biggie's quiet, solid indifference.

"You *know* there's a breakfast meeting . . ."

"So who's missing breakfast?"

"They'll ask about you tonight . . ."

"Biggie, what about Bill?"

Bill? I wondered, as I led Merrill unsteadily to the sink, his arms flopping in the wild take-off motions of some weak, ungainly bird.

"What *about* Bill?" Biggie hissed in the hall.

Right! Tell old Bill she's taken up with a pole-vaulter!

But Merrill's precarious stance at the sink needed all my attention. On the glass shelf where the toothpaste goes was the test-tube rack with the gay-colored solutions for testing sugar in urine. Overturf gazed at these in the way I'd seen him ogle the bright bottles behind a bar, and I had to keep his elbows from slipping on the sink while I aimed his floppy prod into his special pee mug, a beer stein he'd stolen in Vienna; he liked it because it had a lid and held almost a quart.

"Okay, Merrill," I told him. "Let it come." But he just gawked at his test-tube rack as if he'd never seen it before. "Wake up, baby," I told him. "Fill 'er up!" But Merrill was squinting through the test-tube rack at his own death-gray face reflected in the mirror. Over his shoulder he saw me looming behind him—pressed evilly close to him, struggling to hold him up. He stared at my reflection with great hostility; he didn't know me at all. "Let go of my prick, you," he told the mirror.

"Merrill, shut up and pee."

"Is that all you ever think about?" Biggie hissed at her friends in the hall.

"Well, what are we going to tell Bill?" a harpy asked her. "I mean, I'm not going to lie—if he asks me, I'm going to tell him."

I opened the door, then, holding Merrill around the waist, pointing his pecker down into the pee mug. "Why don't you tell him even if he doesn't ask you?" I said to the appalled harpies. Then I closed the door again and steered Merrill back toward the sink. Somewhere along the way, he began to pee. Biggie's sharp laugh must have touched some nervous part of him, for he twitched, loosening my thumb's grip on the stein's lid, and found himself clamped in the pee mug. Wrestling away, he peed all over my knee. I caught up with him at the foot of his bed, where he spun about, still peeing in a high arch, his face with a child's look of bewildered pain. I stiff-armed him over the footboard and he landed limp on the bed, peed a final burst straight up in the air, then threw up on his pillow. I set the pee mug down, washed off his face, turned his pillow over and covered him with a heavy puff, but he lay rigid in the bed with his eyes like fuses. I washed the pee off me and used the medicine dropper to take pee from the pee mug and plunk it into the different test tubes: red, green, blue, yellow. Then I realized that I didn't know where the color chart was. I didn't know what color the red was supposed to change to, or what color was dangerous for the blue to change to, and whether the green was supposed to stay clear or get cloudy, and what yellow was for. I'd only watched Merrill test himself, because he'd always come around in time to interpret the colors. I went over to the bed where he now seemed to be sleeping and hit him a good one in the face; he clenched his teeth together, grunted and went right on sleeping, so I tagged him a really solid blow in his stomach. But it just went *thok!* Merrill didn't flinch.

So I started tearing through his rucksack until I found all his syringes, needles, injector-bottles of insulin, bags of candy, his hash pipe and, at the bottom, the color chart. It said it was okay if the red got orange, if the green and blue became the same, and if the yellow got cloudy-crimson; it was not okay for the red to change "too quickly" to cloudy-crimson, or for the green and blue to behave differently, or for the yellow to turn orange and stay clear.

But when I turned back to the test-tube rack, the colors had already changed, and I realized that I had forgotten which ones were which colors to begin with. Then I read the color chart to find out what to do if you estimated your blood sugar to be dangerously high or low. You were supposed to get in touch with a doctor, of course.

There was silence from the hall outside the door, and I grieved that Biggie had gone away while I was in here fumbling with Merrill's pecker. Then I got a little worried about him, so I sat him upright by hauling him up by his hair; then I held his head and delivered a good roundhouse slap to his gray cheek, and then another and another, until his eyes rolled open and he pulled his chin down on his chest. He spoke to the closet, or to some spot over my shoulder: a high-spirited, defiant holler in the face of pain. "Fuck you!" Merrill shouted. "Fuck you to death!"

Then he called me Boggle in a perfectly normal voice and said he was terribly thirsty. So I gave him water, lots of it, and poured all the crimson, blue-green, orange pee-colors down the sink and rinsed the test tubes out so that if he woke up in the night, berserk, he couldn't drink those too.

When I finished cleaning up, he was asleep, and because I was furious with him I wrung the washcloth out in his ear. But he never moved, and I dried his ear for him, turned out the light and listened in the dark to his breathing, just to be sure he was all right.

He was the great illusion of my life. That such a self-destroying fool could be so indestructible. And though I was sad to have lost that big girl, I liked Merrill Overturf a lot. "Goodnight, Merrill," I whispered in the dark.

As I eased myself out in the hall and latched his door behind me, he said, "Thank you, Boggle."

And there in the hall, all alone, was Biggie.

She had her parka zipped up; there was no heat in the upstairs of the Tauernhof. She stood a little stiffly, putting one foot on top of the other, shuffling; she looked a little bit angry and a little bit shy.

"Let me see the poem," she said.

"It's not finished yet," I told her, and she looked at me aggressively.

"Finish it, then," she said. "I'll wait . . ." Meaning she'd been waiting all this time, with a look to tell me I had some good work ahead of me to salvage this.

In my room, next door to Merrill's, she sat on the bed like an uncomfortable bear. Little crannies and confined places took her grace away. She felt too big for that room and that bed, and yet she was cold; she kept the parka zipped up and wrapped herself in the puff while I goofed around by the night table, pretending to be scribbling a poem on a piece of paper with words already on it. But they were German words, left by the last guest in this room, so I crossed them out as if I were revising my own work.

Merrill thumped his head against the wall between our rooms; his muffled hoot came through to us: "Oh, he can't ski, but he's sharp with his pole!"

On the bed, without a change of expression, the large girl awaited her poem. So I tried one.

> She is all muscle and velour
> crammed in a vinyl sheath;
> her feet, set in plastic,
> clamped to her slashing skis;
> under her helmet, her hair
> stays soft and hot . . .

Hot? No, not hot, I thought, aware of her there on the bed, watching me. No more hot hair!

> The woman racer is not quite soft.
> She is as heavy and firm as fruit.
> Her skin is as sleek as an apple's,
> and as tough as a banana's. But
> inside, she's all mush and seeds.

Ugh! Can bad poetry improve? By my bed, she'd found my tape recorder, was shuffling the reels, fondling the earphones. Put them on, I indicated, then dreaded what she might hear. Expressionless, she punched buttons and changed reels. *On with the poem!*

> See! How she holds her poles!

No, good God . . .

When she cuts the mountain, she's
packed like a suitcase, neat and hard.
Contained, her metal leather plastic
parts perform; her grace is strong.

Her legs are long? God, no!

But just open her, out of the cold.
Unbuckle, -zip, -strap and unpack her!
Her contents are loose and strewn
things, stray things and warm things,
soft and round things—surprising
unknown things!

Be careful. She was playing through the reels of my life, divining it, rewinding it, stopping it, playing it back. Hearing the ditties, dirty stories, conversations, polemics and dead languages on my tapes, she was probably deciding to leave. Suddenly she turned the volume down, wincing. At least I knew which tape she was on: Merrill Overturf revving the engine of his '54 Zorn-Witwer. *For God's sake, hurry with the poem before it's too late!* But then she took the earphones off—had she reached the part where Merrill and I reminisce on our shared knowledge of the waitress in the Tiergarten Café?

"Let me see that poem," she said.

All muscle and velour, she shared the puff and read it sitting up straight —jacketed, panted, booted, wrapped and occupying the bed like a large trunk you'd have to deal with before you could go to sleep. She read seriously, her lips shaping the words.

"All mush and seeds?" she read aloud, with a stern look of disgust for the poet. In the cold room her breath smoked.

"It gets better," I said, not at all sure that it did. "At least, it doesn't get any worse."

Her grace is strong. The puff was a difficult size to share; she became aware that it was, at best, a three-quarter bed. Removing her boots, she tucked her feet under her and begrudged more of the puff to me. She tore apart a stick of gum, gave me the bigger half; our mutual wet smacking disturbed the quiet room. There wasn't enough heat in the room even to frost the windows; we had a third-floor view of the blue snow under the moon, and of the tiny lights strung out on the glacier—way off to the lift-station huts where, I imagined, rough and big-lunged men were getting laid. Their windows were frosted.

Her contents are ". . . loose and strewn things?" she read. "What's this strewn shit? My mind, you mean? Like scatter-brained?"

"Oh, no . . ."

"Stray things and warm things . . ." she read.

"It's just part of the suitcase image," I said. "Sort of a forced metaphor."

"Soft and round things . . ." she read. "Well, I suppose . . ."

"It's a pretty bad poem," I admitted.

"It's not that bad," she said. "I don't mind it." She took off her parka, and I hunched a little closer to her, my hip to hers. "I'm just taking off my parka," she said.

"I was just getting more of the puff," I said, and she smiled at me.

"It always gets so weighty," she said.

"Puffs?"

"No, sex," she said. "Why does it have to be so serious? You have to start pretending I'm so special to you, and you don't really know if I am."

"I think you are," I said.

"Don't lie," she said. "Don't get serious. It *isn't* serious. I mean, you're not special to me at all. I'm just curious about you. But I don't want to have to pretend that I'm impressed or anything."

"I want to sleep with you," I said.

"Well, I know that," she said. "Of course you do, but I like you better when you're funny."

"I'll be hilarious," I said, standing up with the puff like a cape around me and walking unsteadily on the bed. "I promise," I said, "to perform comic stunts and make you laugh all night!"

"You're trying too hard," she said, grinning. So I sat down at the foot of the bed and covered myself completely in the puff.

"Tell me when you're cold," I said, my voice muffled under the puff, hearing her gum snap and her short laugh. "I'm not looking," I said. "Don't you think this is the perfect opportunity for you to undress?"

"You first," she said, so I began, secretly under the puff, handing items out to her, one by one. She was silent out there, and I imagined her readying herself to bash me with a chair.

I passed out my turtleneck, my fishnet shirt, a wad of knee socks and my lederhosen knickers.

"My God, what heavy pants," she said.

"Keeps me in shape," I said, peeking out at her.

She sat fully clothed by the headboard, looking at my things. When she saw me, she said, "You're not undressed yet."

I went back under the puff and struggled with my long underwear. When I got it off, held it in my lap awhile, then delicately handed it out: a rare gift. I felt her moving on the bed then, and waited in my tent as tense as a tree.

"Don't look," she said. "If you look, it's all over."

Unbuckle, -zip, -strap, and unpack her! Or better, let her do it herself. But why is she doing this?

"Who's Bill?" I asked.

"Search me," she said, then peeked into the puff. "Who are *you?*" she said, sitting knee to knee with me, Indian style. She snatched half the puff around herself, shading her tawny body from the light. She still had her socks on.

"My feet get cold," she said, willing my eyes to stay on her eyes and look nowhere else. But I took her socks off for her. Big broad feet and strong peasant ankles. I tucked her feet in the hollows of my knees, pinched them with my calfs and held her ankles with my hands.

"You have a name?" she asked.

"Bogus."

"No, really . . ."

"Really, it's Bogus."

"That what your parents called you?"

"No, they said Fred."

"Oh, *Fred.*" The way she said it, you could see it was a word for her like *turd.*

"That's why it's Bogus," I said.

"A nickname?"

"A truth," I admitted.

"Like Biggie," she said, and smiled self-consciously; she looked down to her golden lap. "Boy, I'm big, all right," she said.

"Yes, you are," I said, with an appreciative run of my hand up her long thigh; a muscle tightened there.

"I was always big," she said. "People were always fixing me up with giants. Basketball and football players, great big awkward sorts of boys. Like it was necessary we be matched or something. 'Got to find someone large enough for Biggie.' Like they were finding a *meal* for me. People always fed me too much, too; they just assumed I was hungry all the time. Actually, I have a really small appetite. People just seem to think it means something if you're big—like being rich, you know? They think if you're rich, you only like things that cost a lot of money. And if you're big, you're supposed to have some special attraction to big things."

I let her talk. I touched her breast, thinking of other big things, and she ran on, not meeting my eyes now, but watching my hand with a sort of nervous curiosity. What will it touch next?

"Even in cars," she said. "You're in the back seat with two or three other people, and they don't ask the smaller person if she has enough room; they always ask if you have enough room. I mean, if three or four people get stuffed into a car seat, nobody has enough room, right? But they seem to think you're some sort of expert at not having enough room."

She stopped and caught my hand where it moved across her belly, holding it there. "You should say something, don't you think?" she said. "I mean, I think you should say something to me. I'm not a whore, you know. I don't do this every day."

"I never thought you did."

"Well, you don't know me at all," she said.

"I want to know you, seriously," I told her. "But you didn't want me to be serious. You wanted me to be funny." She smiled, and then she let my hand move up to her breast and rest under it.

"Well, it's okay to be a little more serious than you're being now," she said. "You have to at least talk to me a little. I mean, you must wonder why I'm doing this."

"I *do,* I *do,*" I said, and she laughed at that.

"Well, I don't know, really," she said.

"*I* know," I said. "You don't like big people." She blushed, but now she let me hold both her breasts; her hands, light on my wrists, took my pulse.

"You're not that small," she said.

"But I'm shorter than you are.

"Well, yes, but that's not so small."

"I don't mind being smaller."

"God, I don't either," she said, and ran one hand along my leg, where I had her feet trapped. "You've certainly got a lot of hair," she said. "I'd never have guessed it."

"I'm sorry."

"Oh, it's all right."

"Am I your first nonskier?" I asked.

"I haven't been to bed a lot, you know."

"I know."

"No, you don't," she said. "Don't say you know when you don't. I mean, I once knew someone who wasn't a skier."

"A hockey player?"

"No," she laughed. "A football player."

"He was still big, though."

"You're right," she said. "I don't like big people."

"I'm awfully glad I'm small."

"You play things, don't you?" she asked. It was a serious question. "Those tapes. There's really nothing on them, is there? You don't do any one thing, you said."

"I'm your first nobody," I said, and fearing she might take me too seriously, I leaned forward and kissed her—her mouth dry, her teeth shut, her tongue lost. When I kissed her breasts, her fingers found my hair; they hurt me a little—she seemed to be pulling me away.

"What's wrong?"

"My gum."

"Your what?"

"My gum," she said. "It's stuck in your hair." Nestling eye to eye with her nipple, I realized I must have swallowed mine.

"I swallowed mine," I said.

"Swallowed it?"

"Well, I swallowed something," I said. "Maybe your nipple."

She laughed, lifting her breasts up to cup my face. "No, it's still there," she said. "Both of them."

"You have two?"

Then she stretched out on her stomach, across the bed, reaching for the ashtray on the night table, where she deposited the gum and a wad of my hair. I bore the puff over my shoulders like a cloak and stretched out over her. Pumpkin Rump! It was impossible to lie flat on her.

She turned so that we could tangle sideways, and when I kissed her, her teeth were parted. In the blue light that glowed off the snow, we pressed down under the canopied puff and told each other stories of our vague education and more vague experience with books, friends, sports, plans, politics, preferences, religion and orgasm.

And under the hot puff (one, two, three times) the drone of a low, coming airplane seemed to carry us loudly beyond that frosted room, *wung* us out over those blue miles of glacier, where we exploded, and our burnt, melted pieces were flung far apart, snuffed out like matchheads in the snow. We lay separate and barely touching, the puff kicked back, until the bed seemed to cool and harden like a slab of the glacier itself. Then we bundled against the perishing dark and lay scheming under the puff as the first shot of sun glanced off the glacier. Gradually its bright, metallic glint cut slow rivulets through the frost on the windowpane.

Also there, in the harsh sunlight, looming beside our bed in a puff of his own, Merrill Overturf stood shaking and swaying, his face the color of city snow, his hand holding aloft a frail phallus—his hypodermic syringe, with 3 cc's of cloudy insulin to clear his bad chemistry.

"Boggle . . ." he began, and in an ice-thin voice gave a fearsome account of his ill sleep; in a hot dream he had thrown aside his puff and lay naked and uncovered through the cold night, wetting his bed and waking to find his hip fastened to the bedsheet with frozen pee. And when he filled his morning hypo with insulin his hands were shaking too much to give himself the shot.

I sighted down the needle to a spot on his blue thigh and took a gingerly poke, which glanced off. But he never felt it, so I cocked back my arm and flicked my wrist like a dart thrower the way I'd seen doctors do it, and drove the needle in a bit too deep.

"Jesus, you got a muscle," Merrill said, and not wanting to hurt him any longer than necessary, I snapped my thumb down on the plunger to get the stuff into him quick. But it resisted force, and the murky fluid seemed to move into him like a wad of dough. He appeared to swoon and attempted to sit down before I could pull the needle out, and the syringe separated from the needle, leaving the needle in him. He lay across the bed moaning while I found the needle and removed it. Then I looked him all over for frostbite while he looked at Biggie, actually seeing her for the first time; in German, forgetting she spoke it too, he said, "You got her, Boggle. Good work, good work."

But I just smiled at Biggie. "She got me too, Merrill."

"Congratulations to both of you," he said, which made Biggie smile. He seemed so frozen and vulnerable that we stuffed him under the puff with us, letting the warm musky air trapped in there waft over him and pressing him between us as he shivered fiercely. We held him until he began to sweat and make obvious wriggling movements and suggest that he would feel better if he could be facing Biggie instead of me.

"I'm sure you would, Merrill," I told him. "But I believe you're better now."

"His *hands* are all better," Biggie said. "I can tell you that."

Later, his hands were occupied with the steering wheel. While Biggie and I fed him oranges from the back seat, Overturf drove the sputtering Zorn-Witwer, '54, through the crunching main street of Kaprun. No one else was about except a postman walking, for warmth, beside his mail sled, coaxing the furry horse, whose breath steamed like diesel exhaust. Higher up, the sun was thawing the crust on the glacier, but all the valley villages would stay frozen until midmorning, a layer of silver dust over everything, and the air sharp enough to breathe only in careful bits. Kaprun seemed seized in such a brittle cold that if we'd blown our horn a building would have cracked.

Outside the skiers' inn in Zell, Merrill and I waited for Biggie to finish her business, watching a growing number of the men's team forming on the steps of the hotel, looking us over. Which one is Bill? They all looked the same.

"You better get some air," Merrill said.

"Why?"

"You smell," said Merrill. Yes! Biggie's rich wild-honey scent was on me! "The car smells," Merrill complained. "Jesus, everything smells like it just got laid."

On the steps, the skiers looked at Merrill, thinking he was the one.

"If they attack us," Merrill said, "don't think I'm going to take the credit for something I didn't do." But they just looked us over; some of the women's team came out on the steps and milled around too. Then a clean, natty man, older than the others, came out and stared at the '54 Zorn-Witwer as if it were an enemy tank.

"That's the coach," I said as he came down the steps and walked around to Merrill's window, a plastic flap which snapped together like a baby's rubber pants. Merrill unflapped it and the coach poked his head inside the car.

Always of the opinion that no one spoke that language but himself, Merrill spoke German. "Welcome to the vagina," he said, but the coach appeared to have missed it.

"What kind of car is this?" he asked. He had a face like the football players on those old bubble-gum cards. They all wore their helmets, and their head-shapes were all alike, or maybe their heads *were* helmets. "A Zorn-Witwer, 'fifty-four," said Merrill.

The coach showed no recognition. "You don't see many of them around anymore," he said.

"You didn't see so many around in 'fifty-four, either," Merrill said.

Biggie was coming down the steps with an airline flight bag, a U.S. Ski Team bag and an enormous duffel. A member of the men's team carried her skis. I got out to open the Zorn-Witwer's trunk. The bearer of her long skis: Was this Bill?

"This is Robert," Biggie said.

"Hello, Robert."

"What kind of car is this?" Robert asked.

The coach came over to the trunk. "What a big trunk," he said. "They don't make them like that anymore."

"Nope."

Robert was trying to figure out how to put Biggie's skis on the roof rack. "I've never seen a ski rack like this before," he said.

"It's *not* a ski rack, you idiot," the coach told him, surprisingly loud.

Robert looked hurt and Biggie went up to the coach. "Please don't worry, Bill," she said. *The coach was Bill.*

"I'm not worried at all," he said, and he started back to the hotel. "You have a copy of the *Summer Exercise Manual?*" he asked her.

"Of course."

"I should write to your parents," he said.

"I can do that," Biggie said.

Bill stopped and turned back to us. "I didn't know there were two of them," he said. "Which one is him?"

Biggie pointed to me. "Hello," I said.

"Goodbye," said Coach Bill.

Biggie and I got into the car. "I've got to stop at the Hotel Forellen," she said, "where the French team is staying."

"Au revoir?" said Merrill.

"There's a girl on the French team I was going to stay with," she said. "In France, you know—she was going to take me home with her for a visit."

"And what a marvelous opportunity to learn the language," Merrill bubbled. "Culture shock . . ."

"Shut up, Merrill," I said.

Biggie looked sad. "It's all right," she said. "I didn't really like the girl anyway. I think it would have been awful."

So we waited outside the Forellen for Biggie, and observed the similar milling habits of the French men's team. They all kissed Biggie when she went into the hotel, and now they scrutinized the Zorn-Witwer.

"How do you say 'What kind of car is this?' in French?" Merrill asked me, but none of them approached us, and when Biggie came out of the hotel, they all kissed her again.

When we were under way, Merrill asked Biggie, "How about the Italian team? Let's go say goodbye to them. I've always liked Italians." But Biggie was glum and I kicked the back of Merrill's seat. He was quiet, then, through Salzburg and out on the Autobahn to Vienna, the old Zorn-Witwer skittering along like a spider over glass.

Biggie let me take her hand, but she whispered to me, "You smell funny."

"That's *you,*" I whispered.

"I know," she said. But we hadn't whispered soft enough.

"Well, I think it's disgusting," Merrill said. "Expecting an old car like this to endure such an odor." When we didn't respond raucously to this, he was silent until Amstetten. "Well," he said, "I hope to see you guys around in Vienna. Maybe we can make the Opera one night, if you have the time . . ."

I caught his face in the rear-view mirror, just enough of a glance to see that he was serious. "Don't be absurd, Merrill. Of course you'll see us around. Every day." But he looked sullen and unconvinced.

Seeing him in a slump, Biggie came out of hers. She was always good that way. "If you ever wet your bed again, Merrill," she said, "you can always come get warm with us."

"Speaking of smells," I said.

"Sure," said Merrill, driving on.

"When you freeze in your pee, we'll thaw you out, Merrill," I said.

I saw him catch Biggie's eye in the mirror. "If I thought that," he said, "I'd wet my bed every night."

"Do you two live together?" Biggie asked us.

"We used to," Merrill said. "But it's a small place, so I'll go out every night and leave you two alone."

"We don't want to be that alone," said Biggie, leaning forward, touching his shoulder. And she looked back at me, a little frightened, as if she meant this. We should only go out in crowds; being alone was too serious.

"You're not any fun to be with," Merrill told me. "You're in love, you know," he said. "And that's no fun at all . . ."

"No, he's not in love," said Biggie. "We're not in love at all." She looked at me for reassurance, as if to say, We're not, are we?

"Certainly not," I said, but I was nervous.

"You certainly are," said Merrill, "you poor stupid bastard . . ." Biggie looked at him, shocked. "Jesus, you too," he told her. "You're both in love. I don't want anything to do with either of you."

And he had sweet little to do with either of us, by God; we hardly ever saw him in Vienna. We were too vulnerable to his humor; he made us aware how our casualness was faked. Then he drove the Witwer down to Italy for an early spring and sent us each a postcard. "Have an affair," the cards said. "Both of you. With someone else." But Biggie was already pregnant then.

"I thought you had a fucking intrauterine device," I said. "An I.U.D., right?"

"I.U.D." she said. "IBM, NBC, CBS . . ."

"N.C.A.A.," I said.

"U.S.A.," she said. "Well, sure, I had one, dammit. But it was just a device, like any other . . ."

"Did it fall out?" I asked. "They can't break, can they?"

"I don't even know how they work," she said.

"Obviously they *don't* work."

"Well, it used to."

"Maybe it fell in," I said.

"God . . ."

"The baby's probably got it in his teeth," I said.

"It's probably in my lungs," she said.

————

But later she said, "It couldn't *hurt* the baby, could it?"

"I don't know."

"Maybe it's inside the baby," she said. And we tried to imagine it: a plastic, unfunctioning organ next to a tiny heart. Biggie started to cry.

"Well, maybe the baby won't get pregnant," I coaxed. "Maybe the damn thing will work for the baby." But she was not amused; she was furious with me. "I'm just trying to cheer you up," I said. "It's just something Merrill would say."

"It's got nothing to do with Merrill now," she said. "It's us, in fucking love, and a baby." Then she looked at me. "Okay," she said. "It's me in love, anyway. And a baby . . ."

"Of course I love you."

"Don't say that," she said. "You just don't know yet."

Which was true enough. Though at the time, her long body was a blotter of my pain. And though we left before Merrill got back from Italy—if that's really where he was—we did not escape his influence. His example—maybe all examples—of surviving your own self-abuse. That impressed us, and we convinced ourselves that we wanted the baby.

"What will we call it?" Biggie asked.

"Aerial Bombardment?" I said, the shock of it settling upon me. "Or something simpler? Like Megaton? Or Shrapnel?" But Biggie frowned. "Flak?" I said.

But after my father disinherited me, I thought of another name, a family name. My father's brother, Uncle Colm, had been the only Trumper to take pride in being a Scot; he put the "Mac" back in front of his name. If he came for Thanksgiving, he wore a kilt. Wild Colm MacTrumper. He farted proudly after dinner and suggested that grave psychological insecurities had compelled my father to specialize in urology. He always asked my mother if there were any advantages in sleeping with such a specialist, and then always answered his own question: No.

My father's first name was Edmund, but Uncle Colm called him Mac. My father hated Uncle Colm. By the time my son was born, I couldn't think of a better name.

Biggie liked the name too. "It's like a sound you'd want to make in bed," she said.

"Colm?" I said, smiling.

"Mmmmmm," she said.

At the time I was assuming that someday we would be seeing a lot more of Merrill Overturf. If I'd known otherwise, I'd have called our baby Merrill.

16

Fathers & Sons (Two Kinds), Unwanted Daughters - in - Law & Fatherless Friends

918 Iowa Ave.
Iowa City, Iowa

Nov. 1, 1969

Dr. Edmund Trumper
2 Beach Lane
Great Boar's Head, New Hampshire

Dearest Dad & Doctor:

I have noticed in myself lately all the forbidding symptoms of terminal *Weltschmerz,* and I wonder would you send me some penicillin? I still have some of the old penicillin you gave me, although I understand that it increases its strength with age and requires refrigeration, and would by now be unsafe to use.

Do you remember when you gave it to me?

When Couth and Fred were fifteen, Elsbeth Malkas went to Europe and brought back the world in her crotch. Their older, former playmate had outgrown them; it was their first notion that summers at Great Boar's Head were changing. They looked forward to starting prep school in the fall, while Elsbeth prepared for college.

Couth and Fred were not prepared for the way Elsbeth's crinkly black hair affected their toes; it made them curl. Occasionally, they'd notice too that the pads of their fingertips tapped on their palms. It was enough to convince them of evolution, this surely being a primate sort of instinct— derived, they guessed, from the stage when monkeys curled their parts to grip the boughs of trees. It was an instinct concerning balance, and whenever they saw Elsbeth Malkas, they felt they were going to fall out of a tree.

Elsbeth brought new and strange habits home from Europe. No tanning on the beach during the day, no dates at the casino by night. She spent the day in the hot garret of her parent's beach cottage, writing. Poems about Europe, she said. And painting. Couth and Fred could see her garret window from the waterfront; usually, they were throwing a football in the surf. In her window, Elsbeth stood motionless, a long brush in one hand.

"I'll bet she just paints the walls of that dumb room," Fred said.

Couth heaved the football out to sea and plunged through the waves after it, calling back, "I bet not!" Fred saw Elsbeth at her window, looking out. *Is she watching Couth or me?*

At night, they watched *her.* They lay in the sand, halfway between her house and the waterfront, to be ready when she'd come out all white and heated from the garret, wearing a paint-blobbed blue denim workshirt that hung to midthigh; until she bent over to snatch up a stone to throw, you didn't know there was nothing underneath. At the water's edge she'd throw the shirt off and plunge in; her great black hair floating behind her had as much of a life of its own as the tangled kelp abob in the surf. When she slipped the workshirt back on it would cling to her; she never bothered to button it as she walked back to the house.

"You still can't really see it very good," Couth would complain.

"A flashlight!" said Fred. "We could shine it on her up close."

"She'd just cover herself with the shirt," Couth said.

"Yeah, the damn shirt," Fred said. "Shit."

So one night they took the shirt. They ran down to the wet sand and snatched it up while she was out in the surf, but they were back-lit by the cottage lights and she saw that they'd run behind the hedges near her porch, so she just walked right up to them. Rather than look at her, they attempted to conceal themselves under the shirt.

"Freddy Trumper and Cuthbert Bennett," she said. "You horny little bastards." She walked right past them onto her porch, and they heard the screen door slam. Then she called out to them, "You're going to be in a lot of trouble if you don't bring my shirt in here quick!" Imagining her naked in the living room, where her parents sat reading, Couth and Fred clumped up the porch and peered in the screen door. She was naked, but alone, and when they gave her the shirt back, she didn't even put it on. They didn't dare look at her.

"It was just a joke, Elsbeth," Fred said.

"Look!" she said, making a pirouette in front of them. "You wanted to look, so *look!*" They looked, then looked away.

"Actually," Couth said, "we wanted to see what you were painting." When Elsbeth laughed, they both laughed with her and stepped inside. Fred promptly bumped into a standing lamp, knocking off the shade and stepping on it when he tried to pick it up. Which made Couth hysterical. But Elsbeth tossed her shirt lightly over her shoulder and took Couth's hand and pulled him upstairs.

"Well, you must come see the paintings, Cuthbert," she said, and when Fred started up after them, she said, "You wait down here, please, Fred." Couth looked back over his shoulder, frightened and clowning and stumbling upstairs after her.

When Couth returned, Fred had completely ruined the lampshade with his reshaping efforts and was cramming it in a wastebasket under the desk.

"Here, let me fix it," Couth said, and pawed the mangled shade out of the wastebasket. Fred stood watching him, but Couth nervously shoved him upstairs. "Jesus, go *on,*" he said. "I'll wait for you."

So Fred climbed to the garret, unknotting the drawstring of his bathing suit as he went, critically sniffing his armpits and smelling his breath hugged into his cupped palms. But Elsbeth Malkas didn't seem to care about any of that. In a cot in her garret, she stripped his bathing suit off and told him that when she used to baby-sit for him, he would peek when she used the bathroom. Did he remember that? No.

"Well, please remember not to tell," she said, and then laid him so fast he scarcely noticed that every canvas in her room was white, all white; that any stroke or color put upon those canvases had been painted over white. The walls were white too. And when he joined Couth down in the living room, he noticed that the lampshade had been stuck back on the lamp all scrunched up and crushed, so that the light bulb was burning brown a part of the shade which touched it; the whole crazy lamp looked like a man whose head had been driven down between his shoulders, and in an effort to tug up the head, his glowing brain had been exposed.

Out on the blowy beach, Couth asked, "Did she tell you the bit about peeking at her in the bathroom when she used to baby-sit for me?"

"She used to baby-sit for me," Fred said, "but she's wrong; I never did that."

"Well, *I* did it," Couth said. "Boy, did I ever . . ."

"Where were her parents?" Fred asked.

"Well, they weren't home," Couth said, and they walked down to the sea and swam naked, then walked along the wet sand until they were opposite Couth's cottage.

Tiptoeing into Couth's hall, they were surprised to hear the murmurs of a lot of people in the kitchen, and Couth's mother crying. Peeking, they saw Elsbeth's parents and Fred's mother consoling Couth's weeping mother, and Dr. Trumper, Fred's father, seeming to be waiting for them at the door. *Their sin already discovered! She had told them, said she was raped or pregnant! She would marry them both!*

But Fred's father pulled him quietly aside and whispered, "Couth's father died, a stroke . . ." Then he stepped quickly after Couth, intercepting him before he got to his mother.

Fred couldn't look Couth in the eye, for fear that Couth might see how relieved he looked.

No such relief, however, did he see in his bathroom mirror on the morning there was no hole to pee out of. At first, a little pinch would open it. Then it began opening and closing all by itself; he seemed to have no influence over it. He took aspirin and rationed his water.

But on the morning he shyly shared the bathroom with his father (turned away from his father's looming lathered presence shaving at the mirror), Fred straddled the hopper and peed what felt like razor blades, bent bobby-pins and ground glass. His scream opened a messy gash on his father's chin, and before he could hide the evidence, his father shouted, "Let me see that!"

"What?" said Fred, clutching what he was sure was only a remnant of his former part.

"What you're holding," his father said, "that's what."

But Fred wouldn't let go, fearing it would fall at his feet; he knew that if he let go, they would never be able to put it back. He held on fiercely while his father raged around him.

"Stuck together, is it?" the good doctor roared. "A little discharge now and then? Something like nails in the way of your passing water?"

Nails! So that's what he'd felt! My God!

"What have you been into lately?" his father bellowed. "Sweet Jesus! Just fourteen and you've been into it already!"

"I'm fifteen," Fred said; he felt more nails wanting to come out.

"Liar!" boomed his father.

Down the hall, his mother called, "Edmund? He *is* fifteen! What a lot of shouting over such a silly issue!"

"You don't know what he's been into!" his father shrieked at her.

"What?" she asked. They could hear her coming toward the bathroom. "What have you been into, Fred?"

But this made his father conspiratorial. He locked the bathroom door and called to his wife, "Nothing, dear." Then, all pink-foamed, his shaving cut bleeding through his lather, he bent over Fred. "What was it?" he whispered grimly, and the way he said it made Fred want to say, A sheep. But the pink-frosted face was frightening, and after all his father was a urologist; expert advice on peeing was something he couldn't afford to turn down. He thought of iron filings floating down from his bladder; he saw the stout snout of a chisel pushing its way down his urinary tract like a raft.

"God, what's in me?" he asked his father.

"Feels like it's rusted shut, doesn't it?" the good doctor said. "Now let me see it."

Fred let his hand drop to his knee, listening for the *plop* on the bathroom floor.

"Who was it?" his father asked, touching the tip of his life.

"Elsbeth Malkas!" he crooned, hating his betrayal of her but finding nothing delicious enough in his memory of her to make protecting her worthwhile.

Elsbeth Malkas! His toes stuck out so straight he thought he'd fall. Elsbeth Malkas! Bring her in here, stretch her out, discover what in hell she hides in that deceptive snatch of hers . . .

"Clap," his father said, and like most things his father said, it sounded like a command. And Fred thought, *Clap?* Oh no, please be careful. No one should clap anywhere near it now. God, don't anyone clap, please . . .

Then his mother came to the bathroom door and called his father to the phone. "It's Cuthbert Bennett," she said.

"For Fred?"

"No, for you," she told the good doctor, following him down the hall, looking anxiously back at Fred, who was as white as an Elsbeth Malkas canvas. "Edmund," she followed, chirping, "be nice to Cuthbert. He's just lost his father, and I think he wants your advice."

Fred came grimacing after them down the hall, watched his father pick up the phone, slumped against the wall and waited.

"Yes, hello, Cuthbert," his father said in a kindly tone, plastering the mouthpiece with blood-pink shaving lather. "Yes, of course, what is it?" Then his whole face changed and he shot a look at Fred like a killer-dart. Far off, in a tiny sound of panic, Fred heard Couth's hysterical voice; his father stared down the hall at him, shocked, as the voice over the phone went on and on. "No no, not here. I'll see you in my office," his father said irritably, and Fred simply had to smirk, a breaking grin. "In an hour, then," his father said, holding in his rage. "All right, in *half* an hour," he said, louder. Fred slouched haughtily against the wall, then dissolved in a cackling fit as his father shouted into the phone, "Well, don't pee, then!" Hanging up, he glared at Fred, now laughing uncontrollably against the wall.

"Why can't Cuthbert pee?" his mother asked, and his father wheeled on her, his wild head in a gory froth.

"Clap!" he shouted at her. He frightened the poor woman; she began to clap.

918 Iowa Ave.
Iowa City, Iowa

Nov. 3, 1969

Dr. Edmund Trumper
2 Beach Lane
Great Boar's Head, New Hampshire

Dear Dr. Trumper:

As I understand your feelings, if Fred had *not* brought me back pregnant from Europe and married me, you would have continued to support him through graduate school. You have never made it clear, however, that if I *hadn't* been pregnant, you might have continued your support of Fred. Well, frankly, this all strikes me as both insulting and unfair. If Fred didn't have a wife and child to support, he would not really need your money. He could pay for himself through graduate school with part-time jobs and scholarships. And if I hadn't been pregnant, *I* could have gotten a job to support the remainder of his studies. In other words, the situation we are now in requires your support more than both situations you claim you would have supported us in. What exactly is it you don't approve of? That I was pregnant? That Fred didn't wait to do things in the order *you* did them in? Or is it just me in particular whom you simply don't like? It's like some moral punishment you are handing out to Fred, and don't you think that someone over twenty-five shouldn't be treated this way? I mean, you had this money set aside for Fred's education, and I can understand you not being willing to support his wife and child too, but isn't it sort of childish to refuse to pay for his education as well?

Yours,
Biggie

918 Iowa Ave.
Iowa City, Iowa

Nov. 3, 1969

Dr. Edmund Trumper
2 Beach Lane
Great Boar's Head, New Hampshire

Dear Dr. Trumper:

Fred's letters to you have, I think, been what you'd call "hints." I am not going to hint around. *My* mother and father give us what they can so that Fred can finish his goddamn Ph.D., and I think that you should give us at least what you were planning to give Fred for his education before I came pregnantly along and upset your plans for him. I also think that your wife would agree with me, but you bully her.

Biggie

918 Iowa Ave.
Iowa City, Iowa

Nov. 3, 1969

Dr. Edmund Trumper
2 Beach Lane
Great Boar's Head, New Hampshire

Dear Dr. Trumper,

You are a prick. Please forgive my language, but that's what you are. A prick for making your own son suffer and casting aspersions on his manner of marrying me and having Colm and all. Just because he wasn't a doctor when he did it. Even so, your Fred has done quite well for Colm and me. It's just that this last year, with all the pressures on him to finish his thesis and look for a job, he is getting very depressed. And you haven't helped him any—with all you've got, too. My own parents haven't half your luxury, but they contribute something. Did you even know, for example, that your Fred has sold football pennants and borrowed no small sums from his friend Couth, who obviously cares more for us than you do? You prick with your principles, you. A fine fucking father you are, is all I can say.

Your daughter-in-law,
(Like it or not!)
Biggie

That muddy November afternoon, I sat in my window watching Fitch, the grim raker, standing soldierly on his immaculately dying lawn. Fitch was on guard, his rake at the ready; he scanned the mess of leaves on all his neighbors' lawns, waiting for one to stray his way. In the rain gutters of his house, leaves lurked above him, waiting for him to turn his head; then they would swoop down. But I sat there with intolerant thoughts toward the harmless old fool. May your entire yard cave in, Fitch.

In my lap were the carbons of Biggie's three letters, and she sulked over my shoulder. "Which is the best one?" she asked. "I couldn't decide."

"Oh, my God, Big . . ."

"Well, it's high time somebody told him how it is," she said. "And I didn't notice that you had anything to say."

"Biggie . . . oh, Christ," I went on. "A prick, Biggie? Oh, my God . . ."

"Well, he *is* a prick, Bogus. You know very well . . ."

"Of course he is," I said to her. "But what is the effect of telling him?"

"What's been the effect of *not* telling him, Bogus?"

" 'You prick with your principles, you,' " I read in horror. "That's *two* pricks, Big. That's twice you've said it . . ."

"Well, do you like the other letters better?" she asked. "What do you think of the reasonable one, or the short one?"

"God, Biggie, which one did you send?"

"I told you, Bogus," she said. "I couldn't make up my mind—"

"Oh, thank God!" I groaned.

"So I sent all three of them," Biggie said. "Let the prick take his pick."

And I felt the wind blow down Fitch, sweep him light as a leaf down the block and cram him under a parked car!

> 918 Iowa Ave.
> Iowa City, Iowa
>
> Nov. 4, 1969

Mr. Cuthbert Bennett
Caretaker / The Pillsbury Estate
Mad Indian Point
Georgetown, Maine

My Dear Couth:

In the afterglow of your nice phone call, Biggie and I are sitting up tonight, spending imaginary fortunes and considering the alternative: a hara-kiri duet. See the two of us, squatting across from each other on the newly waxed linoleum floor. Biggie is carving out my stomach with the bread knife; I prefer the steak slicer for disemboweling her. We're quite absorbed in our work. We're being careful to smother our screams, not wanting to wake up Colm.

Colm, we agree, will go to Biggie's good parents in East Gunnery, Vermont. He'll grow up to be a skier and a wood-chopper, ruddy and craggy and so strongly mired in his New England nose-tones that he'll never care to trouble himself with another language—like Old Low Norse. The mumbled tongue of his ancestors, close and far.

It's not that I don't agree with everything Biggie told my father. It's only that I wish she hadn't blown her tact. Because I fear my father has to be treated like a Pope before he'll bestow blessings, and if you call the Pope a prick, will he still pray for you?

In the meantime, Biggie and I sit tracing her letter eastward. I see Biggie's blunt truth tilting a mail van in Chicago, her heavy message felling a postal employee in Cleveland. An ember of its heated feeling cools in the sea breeze on the coastal route between Boston and Great Boar's Head, where our mail is invariably delivered in the early afternoon. My mother will be home to open it, but Biggie swears it was addressed to my father alone, *not* to Dr. & Mrs., in which case, recalling my mother's awe of the good doctor, she will not open it. She'll lay it on the counter below the liquor cabinet.

My father will come home at four, having just removed a bladder spigot or told some octogenarian that such an operation is advisable; having just fussily shaved himself in his tidy office-bathroom; having removed from his hands all traces of the surgical powder that helps the gloves slide on and off. He will allow my mother to peck his clean-shaven cheek; he'll fix himself a neat Scotch—after holding up the glass to light, to make sure it's been properly washed. Then he'll see the letter. He'll pinch it all around, to see if there's a check enclosed, and my mother will say, "Oh no, dear. It's from Iowa City. It's not a patient; it's from Fred, don't you think?"

My father will take off his suit jacket, loosen his tie, meander through the den to the sunporch window and remark on whether the tide is high or low, as if, mystically, it will influence where he sits. It never seems to.

He'll sit down in his same red-leather throne, crush the same hassock under his heels, sniff his scotch, sip it, and *then* he'll read Biggie's letters.

If it went out in the noon mail yesterday, it's at least past Chicago today, if not already through Cleveland, and through Boston by tomorrow, and in Great Boar's Head tomorrow or the day after.

At which time, Couth, if you'd be so kind, please enter your darkroom and print two absolutely *solid* photographs, one all-white and one all-black; one is hope and the other is doom. Mail them both to me. I will return to you the one that doesn't suit my occasion.

> Wishing you, Couth, infinite varieties
> of Hope and Freedom
> from the Fear of Doom.

> Love,
> Bogus

Imagining good Couth by the rainy sea, his wild hair sailing in a nor'easter blowing Bar Harbor to Boothbay. Couth with one of his fuddy sea prayers for my letter held aloft, the empty Pillsbury mansion behind him, a ramble of rooms for his lonely play.

I remember the end of that one funny summer when we moved into the boathouse with its crammed little bunk beds.

"Top or bottom, Big?"

"Get up there . . ."

While Couth lolled in the Big House after the Pillsburys had gone home for the fall.

Some younger son phoned to say he might be coming. "My mother gone, Couth?"

"That's true, Bobby."

"Aunt Ruth won't be there, will she?"

"Right again, sir."

"Well, Couth, I suppose you've moved into the Big House now. I wouldn't want to put you out, so we'll take the boathouse."

"Who's we, Bobby?"

"A friend and myself, Couth. But I'd appreciate your telling Father I was alone for the weekend."

"Sorry, Bobby, there are people in the boathouse. Friends of mine. But another couple of bedrooms in the Big House could easily be . . ."

"One bedroom will do it, Couth. With a double . . ."

In the poolroom, while Biggie helped Colm build a fire, Couth and I racked up the balls.

"It won't be so private this fall," Couth said sadly, "now that some of the Pillsbury kids have reached fucking age. They'll be bringing their lays up for the weekends. But after November it'll get too cold for them."

The great mansion still was heated strictly with coal, wood stoves and fireplaces. Couth loved the winters best, with the whole run of the house to himself, fussing with wood and coal all day, banking the fires at night, trying to keep the chemicals from freezing in his darkroom. With Colm after supper, Couth worked down there on a series of Colm pulverizing a clamworm on the dock. Colm grinding it with a sneaker, halving it with a piece of shell; Colm requesting a replacement worm.

In the darkroom, Colm refused to talk; he just watched his image emerging from Couth's chemical baths. He was not at all amazed at his underwater development; he took miracles for granted; he was more impressed by being given a second chance to view the mangled clamworm.

Couth also printed from a double negative: one of Colm on the dock, the other of just the dock from the same angle. The structure was slightly out of focus around the edges, since the two docks did not quite mesh, and Colm appeared to be both on the dock and under it, the grain of the wood spread over his hands and face, his body laid out in planks. Yet he sits up (how? in space?). I was stunned by the image, though I shared Biggie's dislike for it; the boy with the wood imposed over him was strangely dead. We mentioned to Couth the incredible paranoia one felt about one's own children. Couth showed the image to Colm, who disregarded it since it was not a clear reproduction of the worm.

The girl whom Bobby Pillsbury brought "home" for the weekend thought it was "almost like a painting."

"Nell is a painter," Bobby told us all.

Seventeen-year-old Nell said, "Well, I work at it."

"Some more carrots, Nell?" Couth asked.

"It's such a lonely photograph," she told Couth; she was still staring at the picture of Colm with his face under the dock. "This place, you know —in the winter, I mean—it must pretty well sort of collaborate with your vision."

Couth chewed slowly, aware that the girl was gone on him. "My vision?" he said.

"Yeah, well," said Nell, "you know what I mean. Your world-view, sort of."

"I'm not lonely," Couth said.

"Yes, you are, Couth," Biggie said. Colm—the real Colm, his face un-grained with wood—spilled his milk. Biggie held him in her lap and let him touch her boob. Beside her, Bobby Pillsbury sat in love with Biggie.

"It's a very untypical photograph for Couth," I told Nell. "Seldom is the image so literal, and almost never does he use such an obvious double exposure."

"Can I see more of your work?" Nell asked.

"Well," Couth said, "if I can find it."

"Why not have Bogus just tell her about it," Biggie said.

"Up yours, Big," I said, and she laughed.

"I've been working on some short stories," Bobby Pillsbury announced. I took Colm from Biggie and stood him on the table, aimed at Couth.

"Go get Couth, Colm," I said. "Go on . . ." And Colm began to walk with a brute glee across the salad, avoiding the rice.

"Bogus . . ." Biggie protested, but Couth stood up at his end of the table, his arms held out for Colm, now bearing down on him through the mussel shells and corncobs.

"Come to Couth," Couth said. "Come on, come on. Want to see some more pictures? Come on, come on . . ."

Colm went sprawling over a basket of rolls, and Couth swept him up and bore him dizzily off to the darkroom, the girl named Nell followed devotedly.

Bobby Pillsbury watched Biggie push her chair back from the table. "Can I help you with the dishes?" he asked her. I gave Biggie a gleeful pinch under the table; Bobby thought her blush was meant for him. He began to clear the table in clumsy swoops, and I retired to the dark-room to watch Couth dazzle Bobby's girl. As I left her with this bum-bling would-be lover, Biggie caught my eye with a comic look of mock lust for Bobby.

But later, in our boathouse racks, as Couth slept with Colm in the master bedroom of the Big House, and Bobby Pillsbury and his young girl Nell were or were not reconciled, Biggie was cross with me.

"He was a perfectly nice boy, Bogus," she said. "You shouldn't have left him alone with me."

"Big, you're not telling me you grabbed a quickie in the kitchen?"

"Oh, shut up." She shifted in the bottom bunk bed.

"Did he really try, Big?" I asked her.

"Look," she said coolly, "you know nothing happened. It's just that you made it awkward for the kid."

"I'm sorry, Big, really. I was just fooling . . ."

"And I'll admit I was flattered," she said, and then paused a long time.

"I mean, it was sort of nice," she said. "A young kid like that really wanting me."

"You're surprised?"

"Aren't you?" she asked me. "You don't seem that interested."

"Oh, Biggie . . ."

"Well, you don't," she said. "You might pay more attention to who's interested in me, Bogus, and not abuse it."

"Biggie, it was just a dumb evening. Look at Couth with that girl Nell—"

"That brainless twat . . ."

"Biggie! A young girl . . ."

"Couth is the only friend you've got that I like."

"Well, good," I said. "I like Couth too."

"Bogus, I could live like this. Could you?"

"Like Couth?"

"Yes."

"No, Big."

"Why?"

I thought about it.

"Because he doesn't own anything?" Biggie asked, but that was stupid; that didn't matter at all to me, either. "Because he doesn't seem to need any other people around him?" She was edging around it. "Because he lives on the ocean all year round?" Which has nothing to do with anything we're talking about, I thought. "Because he can put a lot into his photographs and not need to put much into his life?" She was a prodder, Biggie was. I forgot the question.

"So you could live here with Couth, Big?" I asked her, and she was quiet for a long time.

"I said I could live like this," she said. "Not with Couth. With you. But like Couth lives."

"I'm not handy with anything," I said. "I couldn't be a caretaker for anything. I couldn't even replace a fuse in a complicated house like this, probably . . ."

"That's not what I mean," she said. "I mean, if you could be content like Couth. You know, *peaceful?*"

I knew.

In the morning, from Biggie's lower bunk we watched Couth and Colm out of the boathouse porthole. On the low-tide mudflats, Couth was taking Colm exploring, carrying his camera and a burlap potato sack to gather the odd sea-leavings off the mud.

In the breakfast nook of the Big House, Biggie served blueberry pancakes to a silent Bobby Pillsbury, a nervous Nell, Couth and Colm, a bubble of display. The contents of the potato sack were for us all to enjoy: a razor-clam shell, a skate's tail, the transparent, paper-thin skeleton of a sculpin, a dead gull, the severed head of a bright-billed tern and the jutting lower jawbone of what might be a seal, a sheep, or a man.

After breakfast, Couth arranged the carnage on our plates and photographed it, suggesting some weird, cannibalistic meal. Though Nell's interest in Couth's photography seemed to end with this, I watched Biggie watching Couth patiently arranging his table settings. Colm appeared to find Couth's work the logical extension of child's play.

"Do you ever do nudes?" asked Nell.

"Models are expensive," Couth said.

"Well, you should ask your friends," Nell told him, smiling.

"Biggie?" Couth asked, but he looked at me. I was balancing Colm on his head on the pool table.

"Search me," I told him. "Ask *her.*"

"Biggie?" Couth called. She was in the kitchen with the breakfast pans. Bobby Pillsbury and Nell handled the long pool cues at the end of the living room. "Will you model for me, Biggie?" I could hear him asking her in the kitchen.

Bobby Pillsbury flexed his pool cue like a fly-fisherman's rod. Nell bent hers like a bow, and I was suddenly aware of how red in the face poor upside-down Colm was. I righted him dizzily on the pool table, and heard Couth add cautiously, "I mean, you know, naked . . ."

"Yeah, just a minute, Couth," said Biggie. "Let me finish these dishes first."

———————

But Couth envied children more than wives. He used to tell me that he thought more of offspring than of mates. Though Biggie touched him, I think Colm got to him more. He used to ask me what I did with Colm; he was amazed that I had to think hard for an answer. All I could tell him was that children changed your life.

"Well, sure, I'd think they would," he said.

"But, I mean, they make you paranoid."

"You were always paranoid."

"But with children, it's different," I said, not knowing how to explain what was so different. I once wrote Merrill about it. I said that children gave you a sudden sense of your own mortality, which was clearly something that Merrill Overturf had no sense of; he never answered me. But I simply meant that you noticed how your priorities had changed. For example, I used to like motorcycles; I couldn't ride one after Colm was born. I don't think it was just responsibility; it's just that children give you a sense of time. It was as if I'd never realized how time moved before.

Also, I had this feeling about Colm that seemed unnatural. That is, I desired to bring him up in some sort of simulated natural habitat—some kind of pasture or corral—rather than the gruesome real natural habitat itself, which seemed too unsafe. Bring him up in a sort of dome! Create his friends, invent a satisfying job, induce limited problems, simulate hardships (to a degree), fake a few careful threats, have him win in the end—nothing too unreasonable.

"You mean, sort of graze him, like a cow?" Couth said. "Well, but he'd become a little bovine, wouldn't he?"

"Cattle are *safe,* Couth, and they're *content.* "

"Cattle are cattle, Bogus."

Biggie agreed with Couth. When Colm was allowed to tricycle around our block, I fretted. Biggie said it was necessary to give the child self-confidence. I knew that; still, I lurked in the bushes around the block, following him unseen. I had a notion of the father as guardian angel. When Colm would see me peeling back a branch and peering out at him from the hedge, I'd tell him that it was actually the hedge that interested me. I was looking for something; I'd try to interest him in such safe scrutiny too. Better than riding your tricycle into danger! Come live a placid life in the untroubled hedge.

I even found a place I thought was suitable for a controlled environment: the Iowa City zoo. No life and death struggles or failures there.

"We always come here," Colm would complain.

"Don't you like the animals?"

"Yes . . ." But in winter there were only four or five animals. "Mommy takes me *there,* " Colm would say, pointing across the river to downtown Iowa City and the university buildings.

"There's just people there," I'd tell him. "No raccoons." Just people; if we went there, we might see one of them crying—or worse.

So coming home from People's Market, I'd take Colm through the zoo. In November, when the monkeys had gone south or indoors, and Biggie and I had been waiting a week to hear from my offended father, Colm and I brought the breakfast bread home through the zoo, and left most of it there.

Feeding the vile raccoons, an entire snarling clan of them in their stony cell, Colm was always concerned that the smaller ones got no bread. "That one," he'd say, pointing to a cowardly one, and I'd try to reach the little bastard with a wad of bread. Every time, some fat and surly one would get there first, bite the coward in the ass, steal the bread and wait for more. Is this good for a child to see?

Or the molting American bison, looking like the last buffalo? His legs as thin as some awkward wading bird's, his mottled coat falling off in hunks, like old furniture in need of reupholstering; a giant, tottering sofa with the stuffing hanging out.

Or the cold, wizened bear, in a brick pit with a swinging innertube he never played with, surrounded by his own awful reeking flaps.

"What's the tire for?" Colm asked.

"For him to play with."

"How?"

"Oh, swing on it, bat it around . . ."

But the tire, unbatted and unswung, hung over the ever-sleeping bear like a taunt. The animal himself probably lived in dread of what it was for. I had growing doubts about the fitness of this zoo habitat for Colm; perhaps the downtown streets would be better for the child, after all.

And then, that November, there was the disaster in the duck pond, where usually I felt most at ease with Colm. The soot-white domestic ducks scrounged the breaded pond; we awaited the striking visitations at this time of year from the bold, bright, wild ducks flying south. Iowa lay in a Midwest flyway, and the pond at the Iowa City zoo was perhaps the only place a duck could rest between Canada and the Gulf without being shot at. We used to watch them land there, a cautious flying wedge with a scout sent down first to test the landing; then he would quack the safe news up to the rest. Such color was a new thing in the zoo; the dull inhabitants were stirred up by the arrival of these real-world travelers: red-eyes, mallards, canvasbacks, blue- and green-winged teal, and the splendid wood ducks.

That November I held Colm's hand and watched the lowering V in the sky, imagining this tired and crippled gaggle coming in to rest, blasted over the Great Lakes, shot down in the Dakotas, ambushed in Iowa! The scout landed like a skater on glass, gave a brazen quack at the old-maid ducks ashore, thanked God for the wonder of no artillery, then called his flock down.

In they came, breaking their flight patterns, splashing down in a great reckless dash, astonished at all the floating bread. But one duck hung back in the sky. His flying was ragged, his descent unsure. The others seemed to clear the pond for him, and he dropped down so suddenly that Colm grabbed my leg and clung to it as if he were afraid the duck was going to bomb us. It appeared that the bird's landing gear was fouled, his wing controls damaged, his vision blurred. He came in at too steep an angle, attempted to correct his position with a weak veer, lost all resemblance to a duck's grace and struck the pond like a stone.

Colm flinched against me as a choral quack of condolences came from the ducks ashore. In the pond, the downed duck's little ass protruded, a spatter of feathers floating around him. Two of his former flock paddled out to prod him, then left him to float there like a feathered bobber. His mates quickly turned their worried attention to the bread, anxious that at any moment a thrashing dog would swim out to retrieve their comrade. Were they shooting with silencers now? The irony of death descending on the Iowa City zoo.

All I said to Colm was, "Silly duck."

"Is he dead?" Colm asked.

"No, no," I said. "He's just fishing, feeding on the bottom." Should I add: They can hold their breath a long time?

Colm was unconvinced. "He's dead."

"No," I said. "He was just showing off. You know, you show off some-times."

Colm was reluctant to leave. Clutching the maimed breadloaf, he looked over his shoulder at the crash-landing duck—former stunt pilot, bizarre bottom-feeding bird. Why this suicide? I wondered. Or had he been wounded, bravely carrying gunshot for many troubled landings, at last losing control here? Or was it just some midair seizure of natural causes? Or drunk, having last fed in a fermenting soybean bog?

"I wish, Bogus," Biggie said, "that when you know you'll be going to the zoo, you'd buy *two* loaves of bread so there'd be one left for us."

"We had a wonderful walk," I said. "The bear was asleep, the raccoons were fighting, the buffalo was trying to grow a new coat. And the ducks," I said, nudging the ominously silent Colm, "we saw this silly duck land in the pond . . ."

"A dead duck, Mommy," Colm said solemnly. "He crashed up."

"Colm," I said, bending down to him. "You don't know he was dead." But he knew, all right.

"Some ducks just die," he said, being irritably patient with me. "They just get old and die, is all. Animals and birds and people," he said. "They just get old and die." And he looked at me with worldly sympathy, obviously feeling sad to be stunning his father with such a hard truth.

Then the phone rang and visions of my own terrible father blotted all else from my brain: Daddy with a five-minute speech prepared, an analysis of the emotional imbalance in Biggie's letters, puffing his pipe at his end of the phone. I believe there was supreme rationality in his tobacco. Suppertime in Iowa, after-dinner coffee in New Hampshire; a phone call timed on his terms, like him. But also like Ralph Packer, inviting himself for supper.

"Well, answer it," Biggie said.

"*You* answer it," I said. "You wrote the letters."

"I'm not picking that thing up, Bogus, not after what I called him, the prick."

As we faced the ringing, unanswered phone, Colm slid a kitchen chair over and climbed up to reach it.

"I'll get it," he said, but both Biggie and I lunged for him before he picked it up.

"Let it ring," Biggie said, looking frightened for the first time. "Why not just let it ring, Bogus?"

We did just that. We rode out the ringing.

Biggie said, "Oh, can't you just see him? Breathing into the phone!"

"I'll bet he's just livid," I said. "The prick."

But later, after Colm had fallen out of bed and bawled—and needed trundling to Biggie's broad chest, and some reassurance about a peculiar nightmare involving a zoo—I said, "I'll bet that was just Ralph Packer, Big.

My father wouldn't call us. He'd write us—he'd write a fucking opus."

"No," Biggie said. "It was your father. And he'll never call again." She sounded glad.

———————

That night Biggie rolled back against me and said, "Let it ring."

But I just dreamed. I dreamed that Iowa was playing out of town and took me with them. They used me for the opening kickoff. From yards deep in my own end zone, I ran all the way upfield for a miraculous touchdown. Of course I was horribly jarred along the route, even chopped, quartered, halved, ground, gouged and swiped; but somehow I emerged, severely crippled but upright, churning into the enemy's virgin end zone.

Then there's the aftermath: I am carried off the field by the Iowa cheer-leaders and toted along the sidelines, past the seething, jeering enemy fans. Little sweatered nymphs bear me along; my near-limp and bloodied arm brushes one of their cold, pink legs; somehow I sense both the smoothness and the prickle. I look giddily up at their young tear-streaked faces; one brushes my cheek with her hair, perhaps trying to remove the grass stain on my nose or dislodge the cleat embedded in my chin. I am light to carry. These strong young girls bear me under the stadium, through a bowel-like tunnel. Their high voices echo, their shrill concern for me pierces me more than my pain. To some linen-covered table, then, where they spread me out, remove my encrusted armor, marvel and wail over my wounds. Above us the stadium throws down its muted din. The girls sponge me off. I go into shock; I shiver; the girls lie across me, fearing that I'll chill.

I am so cold that I have another dream; I'm in a duck blind in the New Hampshire salt marshes with my father. I am wondering how old I am; I don't have a gun, and when I stand on tiptoe, I can just reach my father's throat.

He says, "Be quiet." And, "Jesus, see if I ever bring you with me again."

I am thinking: *See if I come!*

Which I must have dreamed aloud, because Biggie said, "Who asked you?"

"What, Big?"

"Let it ring," she said, asleep again.

But I lay awake contemplating the horror of having to look for a real job. The notion of earning a living . . . The phrase itself was like those other obscene propositions offered on a men's-room wall.

17

Reflections on the Failure of the Water Method

The procedure for making an appointment with Dr. Jean Claude Vigneron is unpleasant. The nurse who answers his phone does not care to hear a description of what ails you; she only wants to know if this is a convenient time for your appointment. Well, no. Well, she's sorry. So you tell her you'll find the time.

The waiting room at Vigneron's office is comfy. A former Norman Rockwell cover for *The Saturday Evening Post* is framed on the wall; also, a Bob Dylan poster. Also, you can read *McCall's, The Village Voice, The New York Times, Reader's Digest* or *Ramparts*—but no one reads. They watch Vigneron's nurse, whose thigh, rump and swivel chair protrude into the waiting room from her typing alcove. They also listen when the nurse asks for a description of what ails you. A certain pattern is evident.

"What are you seeing the doctor for?"

Incoherent whispers.

"What?"

Louder incoherent whispers.

"How long has your urine been this way?"

What way? everyone pretending to read is dying to ask.

Urology is so awesomely foul and debilitating a specialty that I took Tulpen with me for support. The office presented its usual puzzle. A child the color of urine sat cramped beside her mother; perhaps she had not peed for weeks. A stunning young girl, dressed entirely in leather, sat aloof with *The Village Voice.* No doubt, she was infected. And an old man quaked by the door, his tubes and valves and spigots so ancient and malfunctioning that he probably pissed through his navel into a plastic bag.

"What are you seeing the doctor for?"

"The water method has failed." Intense curiosity is provoked in the waiting room.

"The water method?"

"Failed. Utterly."

"I see, Mr. . . . ?"

"Trumper."

"Do you have pain, Mr. Trumper?" I sense that the mother with the swollen child is anxious; the girl in leather grips her paper tight.

"Some . . ." A mysterious answer; the waiting room is on edge.

"Would you tell me, please, just what—"

"It's stuck."

"Stuck?"

"Stuck shut."

"I see. Shut . . ." She looks through my record, a long history of being stuck shut. "And you've had this trouble before?"

"The world over. Austria to Iowa!" The waiting room is impressed by this worldly disease.

"I see. It's what you saw Dr. Vigneron about before?"

"Yes." Incurable, the waiting room decides. Poor fellow.

"And have you been taking anything?"

"Water." The nurse looks up; the water method is clearly unknown to her.

"I see," she says. "If you'll have a seat, Dr. Vigneron will see you in a moment."

Crossing the waiting room to Tulpen, I saw the mother smile kindly at me, the child stare, the stunning young girl cross her legs, thinking, If it's stuck shut, stay away from me. But the poor old man with his faulty tubes did not respond; hard of hearing, perhaps, or totally deaf, or peeing through his ear.

"I should think," Tulpen whispered, "that you've had enough of this."

"Enough of what?" I said too loudly. The mother tensed; the girl flapped her paper; the old man shifted uncomfortably in his chair, his terrible insides sloshing.

"*This,*" Tulpen hissed, tapping her fist in her lap. "This," she said, with a careful gesture taking in this collection of the urinary-wounded. There's always a rare fraternity in doctors' offices, but in the office of a specialist the intimacy is worse. There are clubs for veterans, for people with high I.Q.'s, for lesbians, for alumni, for mothers who gave birth to triplets, persons in favor of saving the elm, Rotarians, Republicans and Neo-Maoists, but here was a forced association: people who have problems peeing. Call us Vigneronists! We could meet once a week, have contests and exhibitions—a kind of track and field meet of urinary events.

Then Dr. Jean Claude Vigneron came into the waiting room from the secret innards of his office, wafting over us the swarthy smell of Gauloises. We Vigneronists sat in great awe: Which of us would be called?

"Mrs. Cullen?" Vigneron said. The mother stood up nervously and cautioned her child to be good while she was gone.

Vigneron smiled at Tulpen. The untrustworthy French! "You waiting to see me?" he asked her. An outsider among these assembled Vigneronists, Tulpen stared back at him, unanswering.

"No, she's with me," I told Vigneron. He and Tulpen smiled.

When the doctor went off with Mrs. Cullen, Tulpen whispered, "I didn't think he'd look like that."

"Look like what?" I asked. "What should urologists look like? Bladders?"

"He doesn't look like a bladder," Tulpen answered, impressed.

The child sat there timidly listening to us. If her mother was the patient, I thought, why did the child look so swollen and yellow? I determined that her appearance was the result of not being allowed to pee. About Colm's age, I thought. She was worried about being alone, and restless too; she peeked at the nurse and watched the old man. She was getting upset, so I tried some reassuring conversation. "Do you go to school?"

But it was the stunning young girl in leather who looked up. Tulpen simply stared at me and the child ignored the question.

"No, I don't," said the surprised leather girl, with a look right through me.

"No, no," I said to her. "Not you." Now the child stared at me. "I mean *you,*" I said to her, pointing. "Do you go to school?" The child was embarrassed and felt threatened; obviously she had been told never to talk to strangers. The young girl in leather regarded the child-molester icily.

"Your mother will be right back," Tulpen told the little girl.

"She's got blood in her pee," the child informed us. The nurse swiveled into view, with a quick look at me which said that my brain must be stuck shut too.

"Oh, your mother will be all right," I told the child. She nodded, bored.

The stunning young girl in leather looked at me as if clearly to inform me that she did not have blood in her pee, so don't ask. Tulpen stifled a giggle and pinched my thigh; I examined the roof of my mouth with my tongue.

Then the old man who had been so silent made a strange sound, like an oddly suppressed belch or a pinched fart or a massive, creaking shift of his whole spine, and when he tried to stand up, we saw a stain the color of burned butter spreading on the loose stomach of his shirt and making his pants cling tight to his skinny thighs. He lurched sideways, and I caught him just before he fell. He weighed nothing at all and was easy to hold upright, but there was an awful reek to him and he clutched at his belly; there was something under his shirt. He looked grateful, but terribly embarrassed, and all he could say was, "Please, the bathroom . . ." flopping his bony wrist in the direction of Vigneron's inner office. Against the stain which his shirt soaked up like a blotter, I could see the outline of a curious little bag and a hose.

"The damn thing is always spilling," he told me as I steered him as fast as I could to the nurse, who was just swiveling out of her chair.

"Oh, Mr. Kroddy," she said scoldingly, plucking him out of my arms as if he were a hollow doll. She muscled him down the long hallway, waving me irritably back to the waiting room and continuing to reprimand him. "You simply have to empty it more often, Mr. Kroddy. There's just no need to have these little accidents . . ."

But he kept crooning over and over, "The damn thing, the goddamn thing! There's just never any place to go, people get so upset, in men's rooms you should see all the looks . . ."

"Can you unbutton your shirt by yourself, Mr. Kroddy?"

"The goddamn fucking thing!"

"This isn't at all necessary, Mr. Kroddy . . ."

In the waiting room, the child looked frightened again, and the tight-assed, snotty girl in leather stared straight at her paper, smug, superior and harboring what awful secret between her legs. No one would know. I hated her.

I whispered to Tulpen, "The poor old guy was all *hoses.* He had to go into this little sack." That damned girl in leather looked coolly up at me, then down at her paper while we all listened to what sounded like the nurse flushing old Mr. Kroddy away.

I looked straight up at that aloof leather lady and asked her, "Do you have the clap?"

She didn't look up; she froze. But Tulpen gouged me hard with her elbow and the child looked up gratefully. "What?" she asked.

Then the young woman looked hard at me. But she couldn't hold her fierce expression; for the first time something human broke over her face —her lower lip curling under, her teeth trying to hold her lip still, her eyes suddenly aswim—and I just felt cruel and awful.

"You shit, Trumper," Tulpen whispered, and I went over to the girl, who now held her face down on her knees, rocking in her chair and crying softly.

"I'm sorry," I told her. "I don't know why, really, I said that . . . I mean, you seemed sort of insensitive . . ."

"Don't listen to him," Tulpen told the girl. "He's just crazy."

"I just can't believe I've got the clap," the girl said, sobbing. "I don't go doing it all around, you know, and I'm not dirty . . ."

Then Vigneron came back, returning the mother to her swollen child. He had a folder in his hand. "Miss DeCarlo?" he asked, smiling. She stood up quickly, wiping her tears.

"I have the clap," she told him, and he stared at her. "Or maybe I *don't* have it," she added hysterically as Vigneron peered into her folder.

"Please, in my office," he said to her, guiding her quickly past us. Then he looked at me, as if somehow I'd given this girl her disease while she was in the waiting room. "You're next," he said, but I stopped him before he could move.

"I'll have the operation," I said, shocking both him and Tulpen. "I don't need to see you. I just want an appointment for the operation."

"But I haven't examined you."

"No need to," I said. "It's the same old thing. The water didn't help. I don't want to see you again except for the operation."

"Well," he said, and I was delighted to see that I'd ruined his perfect record—he wasn't ten for ten with *me*—"ten days or two weeks," he said. "You'll probably want some antibiotic in the meantime, won't you?"

"I'll stick with the water."

"My nurse will call you when we've set a time at the hospital, but it will be at least ten days or two weeks, and if you're at all uncomfortable . . ."

"I won't be."

"You're sure?" Vigneron said; he tried to smile.

"Still ten out of ten?" I asked him, and he looked at Tulpen and blushed. *Vigneron blushed!*

Matter-of-factly I gave Vigneron's nurse the phone number for Ralph Packer Films, Inc., and the number at Tulpen's. Recovering, Vigneron handed me a packet of some capsules, but I shook my head.

"Please, no nonsense," he said. "It's better to operate when you're free from any infection. Take one of these a day, and I'll have to see you the day before we operate, just to check." Now he was being strictly business-like. I took the capsules from him, nodding, smiling, waving over my shoulder, and walked Tulpen out of there. I think I must have swaggered.

And I didn't think, until I was out on the street, about whatever happened to old Mr. Kroddy. Was he having a hose replaced? I shivered, drew Tulpen up against my hip and jostled her along the sidewalk, warm and bouncy, her breath close enough to smell, sweet with candy mints, and her hair whipping my face.

"Don't worry," I said. "I'm going to have a fine new prick, just for you."

She slipped her hand in my pocket, rummaging through change and my Swiss Army knife. "Don't *you* worry, Trumper," she said. "I like the old prick you are."

So we abandoned work for the day and went back to her apartment, though we knew that Ralph expected us at the studio. It was always a touchy time for Ralph when he was dropping one project and picking up another; we noticed late salary checks and signs above the phone: PLEASE ENTER IN THE FUCKING BOOK (↓) YOUR LONG-DISTANCE CALLS!

Tulpen might have guessed that there was more involved in skipping work than my want of her. I didn't care for the subject of Ralph's new film, the subject being me. A tedious outline of interviews with Tulpen and me, and a little gem later in which Ralph planned to include Biggie.

"I must tell you, Ralph, that my enthusiasm for this project is not what it might be."

"Thump-Thump, do I have integrity or do I not?"

"It is your point of view which remains to be seen, Ralph."

For weeks we'd been handling some dull distribution for other film makers, and giving special showings of *Ralph Packer: Retrospective!* for film societies, student groups, museums and the Village matinées. It was better to be on a project again, even this project, and the only really nasty argument Ralph and I'd had so far was the title.

"It's just a working title, Thump-Thump. I often change the title when we're finished."

Somehow I doubted his flexibility about this one. He was calling the film *Fucking Up.* It was a common utterance of his, which made me suspect that he liked it far too well.

"Don't worry, Trumper," Tulpen told me, and in that long afternoon at her apartment I didn't. I changed the record stack; I made Austrian *Tee mit Rum,* swizzled with a cinammon stick and heated on a hot plate by the bed; I ignored the phone, which woke us once at dark. Vacuum-sealed from the city, we didn't know whether it was supper, a midnight snack or an early breakfast we were hungry for; in that kind of timeless dark which only city apartments can give you, the phone clamored on and on.

"Let it ring," Tulpen said, scissoring me fast around my waist. It occurred to me that this line should be a part of *Fucking Up,* but I let it ring.

18

One Long Mother of a Day

It begins, actually, the night before, with an argument, wherein Biggie accuses Merrill Overturf of childish, escapist pranksterism and further claims that I have been able to heroize Merrill only because he has been missing from my life for so long—implying, harshly, that the real Merrill, in the flesh, would even put me off, at least at this moment in my life.

I find these accusations painful and counterattack by accusing Overturf of courage.

"Courage!" Biggie hoots.

She goes on to imply that I am no reliable authority on courage, having no courage myself—having cowardice to spare, in fact. The example given for my cowardice is that I am afraid to call my father and have it out with him about my disinheritance.

Which witlessly prompts me to bluster that I will phone the old prick, anytime—even now, though by the dark Iowa night around us, I vaguely suspect that it's a poor hour for a phone call.

"You will?" says Biggie. Her sudden respect is frightening. She gives me no time to change my mind; she's thumbing through papers, looking for the one on which we once wrote down the Great Boar's Head number.

"What will I say, though?" I ask.

She is starting to dial.

"How about, 'I called to ask you if your mail was being delivered.' "

Biggie frowns and dials on.

"How about, 'How are you? Is the tide in or out?' "

Grimacing over her fast fingerwork, Biggie says, "At least we'll *know,* for God's sake . . ." and hands me the ringing phone.

"Yes, at least we'll know, all right," I say into the mouthpiece, and it echoes back as if it were being spoken to me by some operator of uncanny perception. The phone rings and rings, and I give Biggie what must be a relieved look: A-ha! He's not at home! But Biggie points at my wrist watch. Back East, it's after midnight! I feel my jaw slacken.

Biggie says sternly, "It'll serve the prick right."

Far from groggy, my father curtly answers the phone. Of course doctors are used to being called up in the middle of the night. "Dr. Trumper here," he says. "Edmund Trumper. What is it?"

Biggie is balancing on one leg as if she's got to pee. I can hear my watch tick, and then Daddy says, "Hello? This is Dr. Trumper. Is anything wrong?"

In the background, I hear my mother murmur, "The hospital, Edmund?"

"Hello!" my father shouts into the phone.

And my mother hisses, "You don't suppose it's Mr. Bingham? Oh, Edmund, you know his heart . . ."

Still teetering on one foot, Biggie glares at me, appalled by the cowardice she sees in my face; she grunts fiercely at me.

"Mr. Bingham?" says my father. "Can't you get your breath again?"

Biggie stamps her foot, utters a small-animal cry.

My father advises, "Don't try to breathe too deeply, Mr. Bingham. Listen, you just hold on. I'm coming right over . . ."

Scurrying in the background, my mother calls, "I'll get the hospital to send the oxygen, Edmund—"

"Mr. Bingham!" my father yells into the phone as Biggie kicks the stove, emitting a snarl from her curved mouth. "Bring your knees up to your chest, Mr. Bingham! Don't try to talk!"

I hang up.

Convulsed with something almost like laughter, Biggie lunges past me, into the hall, into the bedroom and slams the door. Her sucking sounds, her crazy lip noises, sound like choking, something like poor Mr. Bingham with his real and faltering heart.

———————

Unnoticed by the night watchman, I spent the night in the Iowa Library Ph.D. thesis alcoves, in one of a long fourth-floor row of cubbies which are usually crammed with sweaty scholars, each with his Coke bottle. A dollop of Coke in each bottle, honey-thick, with several cigarette butts floating. You can hear them hiss when they're plunked in, several cubbies down from your own.

Once, his thesis near the finishing point, Harry Petz, a graduate student from Brooklyn who was reading documents in Serbo-Croatian, heaved himself backward in his chair on casters and shot out of his cubby in reverse; peddling his feet faster and faster down the aisle, he whizzed past all of us, the entire length of the cubby row. He smashed against the fourth-floor thermopane at the end of the aisle, cracking both the glass and his head, but not careening four floors to the library parking lot below, where Harry Petz must have had visions of himself splattering on the hood of someone's car.

But I would never do such a thing, Biggie.

There is a touching scene in *Akthelt and Gunnel* when Akthelt is dressing and arming himself to go out and fight the ever-warring Greths. He is donning his shin pads and shoulder pads and kidney guards and tin cup, ritualistically shielding and spiking his vital parts, while poor Gunnel is wailing at him not to leave her; ritualistically, she is taking off her clothes, unbraiding her hair, unbuckling her anklets, unsheathing her wrists, un-thonging her corset, while Akthelt goes on collaring his throat with chains, fastening his coccyx-spikes, etc. Akthelt is trying to explain to Gunnel the object of war *(det henskit af krig),* but she doesn't want to listen. Then Old Thak, Akthelt's father, bursts in on them. Old Thak has been arming and dressing himself for the war too, and his chest zipper, or something, is stuck and he needs help with it. Of course he is embarrassed to see his son's lovely young wife all distraught and half nude, but he remembers his own youth and realizes what Akthelt and Gunnel have been arguing about. So Old Thak attempts an ambiguous gesture; he wants to try to please them both. He gives sweet Gunnel a lusty goose with his thorny old hand, at the same time saying wisely to Akthelt, *"Det henskit af krig er tu overleve"* ("The object of war is to survive it").

Which struck me as the object of graduate school—and possibly my marriage. Such comparisons struck me hard in those days.

Walking through the library parking lot in which Harry Petz tried to land, I spy young Lydia Kindle lurking for me near a sea-green and arklike Edsel. She wears a pear-colored suit, snug, short-skirted and rather grown-up.

"Hi! That's my Edsel there!" she says. And I think, This is much too much.

But there's a kind of safety at the midthigh of her skirt and I know her knees, so they don't frighten me. It's a relief to feel her leg rise and fall under my head, her foot busy at the brake and accelerator.

"Where are we going?" I ask in a doomed tone and turn a little in her lap, which there's so little of.

"I know," she says, and I look up her suit-front, past her slight breasts to her chin; I see her teeth gently holding her lower lip. At the throat of her suit, her blouse is a deep rust-yellow; it gives that tint to her jaw, like a buttercup. And I remember Biggie and me in a field below the monastery at Katzeldorf, with a bottle of the monks' wine in the buttercups. I held a handful of the flowers to her nipple; it turned her vivid orange and made her blush. Then she held a cluster under my own sunny part. I believe it turned me strictly yellow.

"Actually, this isn't my Edsel," says Lydia Kindle. "It's my brother's, but he's in the service."

New perils everywhere I turn. Lydia Kindle's strapping brother, a punchy Green Beret, coming after me with deft chops to the clavicle, his terrible vengeance brought down on me for defiling his sister and his Edsel.

"Where are we going?" I ask again, feeling her hard thighs bounce under my head on what must be a rough road. I see dust swirl by the windows; I see a flat sky not bent by a single tree, not laced with any powerlines.

"You'll see," she says, and her hand strays off the wheel to brush my cheek—with the faintest, most innocent perfume at her wrist.

Then into a low ditch and out again; I can tell that we've even left the dirt road because there's no dust at the windows and the car dips deeper on a softer surface; occasional snapping sounds, which in Iowa can only be corn stubble or hog bones. We're headed in a different direction too, because the sun warms my kneecaps from a new slant. Then there are some tire-slipping noises, like a squeegee on wet grass. I fear we'll be stuck miles from anywhere, that overnight we and the Edsel will settle forever in some soybean bog. "With only the ducks to cry over us," I say, and Lydia peers down at me, looking slightly alarmed.

"A fellow took me here once," she says. "Sometimes there's a hunter or two, but no one else. Anyway, you can always see the hunters' cars."

Some fellow? I think, wondering if she's already been defiled. But she guesses my thinking and says hurriedly, "I didn't like him. I made him bring me back. But I remember how we got here." And her tongue darts out a moment, to wet each corner of her mouth.

Then shade, and an incline; the ground is firmer and bumpier; I hear rustling under the Edsel and smell pine pitch—in Iowa, of all places! A branch lashes the car, which makes me jump and bump my nose on the steering wheel.

When Lydia stops, we're in a dense grove of new pine, old deadfall, flat-leafed fern and spongy, half-frozen hunks of moss. Mushrooms are about. "See?" she says, opening her door and sliding her legs out. Finding it wet and cold out there, she sits, her back to me, dallying her feet above the ground.

We're on a knoll, in a scruffy thatch of tree and shrub. Behind us are cut corn and soybean fields; in front and well below, what must be part of the Coralville Reservoir lies frozen at its fringes, open and choppy in the middle. If I were a hunter, I'd take my stand on this hill, deep in the ferns, and wait for the lazier ducks to fly this shortcut between one feeding ground and another. They'd come over low to the ground here, especially the fat, sluggish ones, their bellies bright with a glance of the sun off the lake.

But leaning against the Edsel's armrest, I extend my foot to the small of Lydia Kindle's back, and for just a moment feel like propelling her out her open door. But I just touch her spine, and she looks over her shoulder at me before she swings her legs inside and shuts the door.

There's a blanket in the car-boot, and an older-looking girl in her dorm has bought beer, she tells me. There's a nice cheese, too, and a warm circle loaf of pumpernickel and apples.

Climbing over the front seat, she lays this picnic spread in back, and we hunch the blanket over our shoulders, tentlike and cozy. Under the blanket, a bit of cheese sticks to a tiny blue vein on Lydia's wrist. She snares it with her fast tongue, watching me watch her; her legs are crossed under her in such a way that her knees face me.

"Your elbow's in the bread," Lydia whispers, and I giggle witlessly.

She squirms her legs and shakes the blanket around us for crumbs; I watch the bread roll to the floor; I see her skirt lift to her hipbone as she pulls me further up in her lap. She has baby-pink and baby-blue flowers on her slip, flowers too reminiscent of one of Colm's early crib blankets. She says, "I think I love you." But I hear a measure to each word, so deliberate that I know she's practiced saying this. As if she too feels it didn't sound quite right, she amends it: "I think I know I love you." Pressing her fine, thin leg against my side, she shifts to one hip and gently tugs my head to her thigh. My heart hits her knee.

There are the same damn flowers on her panties, too. A baby in her bunting; such frilly, flowered things for Junior Misses.

She squirms again and gives a weak pull on my ears, aware that I've seen her flowers. "You don't have to be in love with me," she says, and again I hear the practiced measure. Somewhere, I know, in Lydia Kindle's dormitory room, there's a piece of notebook paper with this conversation written out like a script, scribbled on, revised, perhaps footnoted. I wish I knew what responses she has written for me.

"Mr. Trumper?" she says, and as I kiss her under her hem, I feel a tiny muscle slack. She tugs my head up to her bird's breast, her suit jacket open, her blouse a thin shiver over her cool skin.

"*Vroognaven abthur, Gunnel mik,*" I recite. Old Low Norse is safest in such circumstances.

With the slightest shudder, she sits up against me, but even an ark like an Edsel is awkward, and there's much wriggling before she's free of her suit jacket. My hunting-coat snags on the rear-window handle; sitting back against her, bobsled style, I manage to unlace my cloddy boots while her hands braille-read my shirt buttons. Turning back to her, I find she's unbuttoned herself, but she is hunching on her knees, arms folded over her bra; she shivers as if she was undressing for some unsure dip in a winter river.

Almost relieved, she stalls against me, happy to be hugged still semi-clothed, her skirt unzipped but only half down one hip. Her damp hands skitter across my ribs and pinch the unfortunate fold that curls slightly over my belt.

Lydia Kindle says, "I never have, you know . . . I have never . . ."

I drop my chin to her sharp, bony shoulder and brush her ear with my mustache. "What does your father do?" I ask, and feel her sigh, both let down and relieved.

"He's in burlap," she says, her fingers finding my kidneys. And I think, He's in burlap! All the time? Wrapped in it, dressed in it, sleeping in it . . .

"He can't be very comfortable," I say, but her hard collarbone is numbing my jaw.

Lydia says, "You know—feed bags, grain sacks . . ."

Imagining Lydia Kindle's huge father, hefting a hundred-pound burlap duffel of onions and swinging it against my spine, I wince.

Lydia straightens up on her knees, pulling away from me, her hands at her hips, working down her skirt; she has the smallest bulge of a tummy under her flowered slip. Seeing her hands so busy, I slip her bra straps off her shoulders. "I'm so small," she apologizes in a tiny voice as I drop my pants down to my ankles. Hoisting my feet over the front seat, my clumsy heels strike the horn; with all the windows closed, it sounds as if it's from another car, and Lydia suddenly crouches against me, allowing me to unhook her bra. The label reads: A YOUNG PETTY-PIECE UNDERTHING. How true.

I feel her hard breasts pushed against me and I shrug off my shirt, aware that the fly of my boxer shorts is gaping, and how she's staring down at me; she's rigid, but her hips help me get off her slip. There's a mole, and the brief V of flowers, baby-pink and baby-blue.

She says, "You've got such tiny nipples." Her fingers wonder over them.

I cup her small, round breasts—just oranges to the touch—with her nipples as hard as the knuckle that is digging into my leg. Slowly I lay her down, getting one glimpse of her body, taut and ribby, and one look at her up-poking breasts, a tint of powder in her narrow cleavage. Then she pulls my head down to the powder spot, but I feel my stomach tighten at the scent. It reminds me of Colm's baby shampoo; the label says: NO TEARS!

She says, "Please . . ."

Please what? I think, and hope she won't make this my decision. I have such trouble with decisions.

Kiss a soft, straight line down to her navel; see the marks her panties' waist band has grooved on the small swell of her belly. It bothers me that I can't remember when or how her panties came off. Was it her decision or mine? It strikes me as an important bit of forgetting. My rough chin rests on that fluffed fringe. When I move, when she first feels my kiss, she scissors my head hard and gives my hair two quick painful tugs. But then her thighs relax; I feel her hands slide off my head and cup my ears, so that I can hear the sea in stereo—or the Coralville Reservoir rising, making our odd hill an island; to maroon us under the dusk-flying ducks, over the dust-choked odor drawn up like groundfog from the soybean fields.

One of my ears is released; the sea rings one-sided, monaural. I catch a flash of Lydia's free hand swooping along the floor and fumbling in her pear-colored suit jacket. What is in the sleeve? She says, "There's a rubber. A girl in my dorm . . . had one."

But I can't fit my hand up her jacket cuff, and she's obliged to shake her suit, saying, "There's a secret pocket in the lining of the wrist . . ." What for?

Her breasts are parted: I see her lip held in her teeth; I see her ribcage quickly lift, hold itself up and slide the tinfoil-wrapped rubber down her belly to my forehead; then her ribs fall, and the queer, small swell to her belly quivers; her hips shake. Out the corner of my eye I see her arm swinging free, her wrist slack; wadded in her palm, like a sponge ball, is what must be the heart of the pumpernickel, torn from the center of the fresh loaf. Her thighs tense and slap my face hard, then fall flush to the seat, and the hand that holds the bread-heart lets the dark wad fall.

I hear the tinfoil tear and crinkle; I wonder if she hears it too. I lay my head on her breasts and hear the flutterstep of her heart. Her elbow is propped on the seat, her forearm dangled over the floor. Her wrist is so sharply bent that it looks broken; her long fingers point down, unmoving, and the cloudy sun through the window is just strong enough to glint off her high school ring; it is too big for her finger and has slipped askew.

I shut my eyes in her powdered cleavage, noting a sort of candy musk. But why does my mind run to slaughterhouses, and to all the young girls raped in wars?

Her thighs close gently on my shielded part, and she asks, "Aren't you going to do the *other?*"

And my frail part shrinks in its thin, pinching skin; it recedes when Lydia Kindle flexes her thighs.

Again she says, "Please . . ." And in a very small voice, "What's wrong?"

Slowly I raise myself off her, kneeling between her legs; I feel her fingers stronger on my shoulders; there's a blue, thread-thin vein that's pulsing in her cleavage, a diagonal between her far-parted breasts. As if she's conscious of her heartbeat showing, she drops one arm across herself, and with the other hand hides her crotch. A YOUNG PETTY-PIECE! saved, for a while. And for whom?

I feel the rubber roll up. While Lydia Kindle, swinging her legs off the seat, says, "I never even asked you to be in love with me or anything. I mean, I've never done this before, or that *other,* and it just didn't even matter what you really thought of me—I mean, to me. Don't you even know that? Oh, my God . . . Shit, and I thought *I* was pretty naïve . . ."

As if she's got the cramps, she bends over, her face on one knee, a lash of hair in the corner of her mouth, and in that familiar angle between her elbow and her knee, the breast nearest me is simply too small and perfect to swing; it points like a thing painted on her, too perfect to be real.

"It's complicated," I try to tell her. "No one should ever leave things up to me."

I fumble with the latch and open my door for the cold, reviving pain of the air. Standing cold and naked in the wet, crunchy moss, I hear Lydia rummaging through the car. Turning, I duck my boots; she's on all fours in the back seat, shoveling my things out the door. Wordless, I gather each article as it falls and make a ball of my stuff and clutch it to my chest. Brainless, Lydia Kindle tosses her own clothes from the back seat to the front seat, and from the front seat to the back seat, and then from the back seat to the front seat . . .

I say, "Let me drive you home, please."

"Please?" she shrieks, and over the knoll, like stones thrown over my head, a low rush of ducks wings by, black in the dusk; startled, they veer off, honking to see this naked fool with his clothes held over his head.

Now watch Lydia, dashing nude around the inside of the Edsel. She is locking all the doors. Still nude, she slips behind the steering wheel, her fine nipples brushing the cold ring of the horn. The Edsel convulses, belches and blurts a thick gray wad of exhaust out its rusted pipe. For a second, though I make no effort to move, I believe Lydia is going to run over me, but she surges in reverse. Jacking the wheel, she spins herself back into the tire ruts that mark our coming here. Wrenching the hard-to-turn Edsel, her breasts at last move like live things. I fear for her nipples on the horn ring.

It's not until I watch her Edsel rocketing over the soybean bog that I realize my predicament. *He died of exposure on the duck-flown shores of the Coralville Reservoir!*

———

So I began to slog through the soybeans, keeping my jogging eyes on the spattered Edsel churning through the far field of corn stubble. I could barely make out the pale line of the road by which we must have come. Running nude and slippery through this swampland, I gambled that if I cut along the shore line of the reservoir, I might intersect the road ahead of her and be able to flag her down. By then, she might be in more of a mood to be flagged down. Flag her down with what? I wondered. With my strangely clad part?

My clothes bundle high and dry in my armpit, I dug through the painful saw grass and spongy muck along the thin-iced edge of the reservoir. A black burst of coots took flight in front of me; once or twice I sank to my knees, feeling terrible oozy and decaying things in the bog slime. But always I kept my clothes bundle high and dry.

Then I was into some uncut corn, bent broken stalks, the running painful on the crinkling cornhusks underfoot, as dry and sharp and brittle as thin pottery. There was a slight pond between me and the flat line of the road; it was not so firmly frozen as it looked, and I crashed waist-deep, striking a downed fence underwater, the fenceposts just visible at either side of the pond, with the barbwire slanting under. But I was too numb to feel any of the cuts.

By now I could foresee our lucky collision. Lydia's seagreen Edsel had a dust tail like a kite trying to leave the ground. Reaching the ditch of the road just ahead of her, I was too exhausted to wave; I simply stood there, my bundle of clothes casually under one arm, and watched her roar by, her breasts as straight in front of her as headlights. She didn't even turn her head, and her brake lights never flickered. Stupefied, I jogged a little in her dusty wake—so thick a dust that I stumbled off the road's crown and had to grope my choked way along.

I was still trotting as her Edsel increased the distance between us when I saw, so close I almost ran into it, a shabby red pickup truck parked along the side of the road. I sagged against the truck's door handle, seeing that I wasn't more than six feet from a hunter busy cleaning a duck on the pickup's hood. He had the floppy neck of the bird draped over the arm of the side-view mirror while blood and clotted parts spilled to the road, and down feathers stuck to his gutting knife and thick thumb.

When he saw me, he almost cut his wrist off, with a sudden wrench that squeegeed the duck over the hood and skidded it wetly down the fender away from him, and he cried out, "Holy shit, Harry . . ."

I panted. "No," I gasped, convinced that I wasn't a Harry yet, not seeing the man in the driver's seat of the truck; his elbow wasn't more than a few inches from my ear.

"Holy shit, Eddy . . ." the driver answered, so close to me that I jumped.

I took a minute more of panting to compose myself, then asked casually, "Are you going to Iowa City?"

They gaped at me for a long time, but I was too proud and too weary to unwrap my bundle and dress myself.

Then Harry said, "God, are *you* going to Iowa City?"

"They won't let you into Iowa City like that," said Eddy, still holding the gory duck.

Dressing in the road beside their truck, I noticed that my condom was still attached. But if I'd removed it, it would have been too much like admitting to these hunters that I really did wear such a thing. I dressed right over it, simply ignoring it.

Then we all got in the truck, amid much changing of seats and bickering about who'd drive. Eddy finally took the wheel and said, "Jesus. We saw your little friend go by."

"If she *was* your friend . . ." Harry said to me. But wedged in between them, I didn't answer. I could feel my feet warming and bleeding in my boots beside the bloody ducks.

Cautious Harry kept the guns between the door and his knee, putting them far from my reach, understandably not trusting a runaround nudist and madman.

"Jesus," said Eddy, as if still trying to convince himself. "She was just batting like hell down that old road . . ."

"She almost swiped you," said Harry.

"Well, Christ, I was staring so hard," Eddy told him, leaning across my lap, "I almost forgot to get out of her way." He paused, then added, "Holy shit, she had such a nice little pair on her, setting right up there, behind the wheel. It was almost like she was *driving* with them . . ."

"Well, God, I was up here in the cab," Harry said. "I could see her whole *thing*. Shit! I was looking right down in her lap!" He paused, then added, ". . . such a nice little bush . . ."

Envious Eddy said defensively, "Well, I saw her pair, anyway. I got a good look."

I almost entered the conversation then; I wanted to say, "I got a pretty good look myself." But I looked down at the floor at a duck's slack neck and upturned downy belly; the feathers near the neat slit, the careful gash, were soaked with the blood.

Then, loud beside me, Eddy said, "Sweet Jesus, here she is again!" All of us stared at the sea-green Edsel parked at the side of the road ahead.

"Slow down," Harry said, but I thought, Please don't slow down too much.

Slowly we cruised past her, three gawking faces turning to look her over. Harry and I turned around and watched the Edsel shrink behind us while Eddy used the mirror, swearing softly, "Shit shit shit, oh, shit . . ."

"Oh, shit," echoed Harry.

But I was relieved to see Lydia Kindle dressing behind the wheel, applying the finishing touches, buttoning up under our gapes; it showed me she was somewhat sane again.

And how sane she looked! There was such a cold, unrecognizing look in her face—unsurprised to see me in the truck, or not even noticing; or poised enough, in an awful adult way, to pretend, with frightening composure, not to notice any of us.

The violation was complete; Lydia Kindle was defiled more perfectly than any pervert could have planned it.

I shifted my throbbing feet, Eddy farted and Harry answered him. Inches from my boot, the viscous eye of the duck was drying up, the shine dulled.

"Jesus," I said.

"Yeah, shit," said Eddy.

"Yeah, Jesus," Harry said.

Grief shared; we were a threesome of disappointment.

On Interstate 80, the sea-green Edsel hurtled past us. Eddy honked his horn and Harry cried, "Go, you little honey!"

And I thought: Lydia Kindle will probably transfer to another section of freshman German language lab.

Eddy took the Clinton Street exit, bringing us in by City Park. As we crossed the river, Harry began to pluck a duck, savagely seizing great clumps of down in his fist and stuffing the feathers out the side-vent window. But half the feathers blew back inside, and his sloppy speed tore the duck's oily skin. Harry didn't seem to mind; fiercely intent, he ravaged on. A feather stuck to Eddy's lip; he spat and rolled down his window, creating a cross gale. Suddenly the cab was awhirl with feathers. Harry hooted and threw a handful of them at Eddy, who swerved onto the shoulder of the road and swiped at mad Harry's throttled bird, reaching across my lap and clucking like a loon.

Along the riverbank, several cold strollers watched with alarm the giddy flight of this enormous leaking pillow careening into town.

When we had passed the park, all the streetlights came on and Eddy slowed down, gazing at the row of lamps lit all the way up Clinton Street as if he'd witnessed a miracle. "Did you see?" he asked, like a child.

Embedded in his duck Harry hadn't seen anything, but I told Eddy, "Yes, they all came on at once."

Turning to look at me, Eddy choked, opening his mouth, gagging and shouting, "You've got feathers in your mustache!" Reaching across and grabbing Harry's knee, he shrieked, "Christ, would you look at his mustache!"

The duck a near pulp in his lap, Harry stared at me with hostility before seeming to remember who I was and how I'd got there. Not giving him time to respond with what I feared might be a pawful of feathers crammed down my throat, I turned back to Eddy, and in a small voice, very faint, asked, "Would you mind letting me out here? This is fine."

Eddy slammed on the brakes with a great grinching noise and a jolt that lurched busy Harry headfirst into the dash. "Christ!" he shouted, holding the duck like a bandage against his forehead.

"Thank you very much," I said to Eddy, and waited for Harry to slide out of the seat. Sliding after him, I caught a brief vision of my feathered mustache in the rear-view mirror.

Standing on the running board, Harry offered me the duck. "Go on, take it," he begged. "We got a shitload."

"Christ, yes," Eddy said. "And better luck next time."

"Yeah, fella," Harry said.

"Thank you very much," I said, and not knowing exactly where to hold the sorry duck, I gingerly took it by its rubbery neck. Harry had plucked it quite cleanly, though it seemed to be internally crushed. Only the wing tips and head were still feathered: a lovely wood duck with a multicolored face. There weren't more than three or four pellet wounds in it; the ugliest wound was the naked slit where it had been dressed out. His great feet felt like armchair leather. And there was a dried, see-through bead of blood, like a small dull marble, on the tip of his beak.

On the curb, along the riverbank sidewalk, I waved to those generous hunters. And heard, just before the slamming of the door, Harry saying, "Jesus, Eddy, did you smell the cunt on him?"

"Shit, yes," said Eddy.

Then the door slammed, and I was stung with sand spray from the pickup's whining tires.

————

All down Clinton Street, the dust of their leaving rises and billows under the hoods of the streetlights, while across the river, on the bank that looks like an Army barracks—stacked with the war-built Quonset huts, now called Married Student Housing—two neighborly wives snap their sheets off a shared clothesline.

Slowly, I get my bearings and decide which way home lies. But when I take my first step I totter off the sidewalk and howl. It's my feet; they've thawed. Now I can feel each gash from the underwater barbwire, each shard of corn stubble in my soles. Trying to stand, I feel a pelletlike object under the arch of my right foot; I suspect that it's one of my severed toes, rolling loose in my blood-warm boot. I scream again, provoking mute stares from the two women across the river.

More people scuttle from the Quonset huts, like bomb survivors; student fathers with books in hand or children riding on their wife-sized hips. Someone from this tribe yells over to me, "What the hell's the matta, fella?"

But I can think of nothing that would pinpoint it. Let them guess: A man who's been ravaged by the ravaged duck he holds?

"What are you screaming for?" cries one Mrs. Sheet, veering about on the riverbank like a ship tipped by her sail.

I search their gathering for the most likely Samaritan. Scanning beyond them, I spot a friend weaving between the Quonset huts on his racing bicycle: Ralph Packer, frequent illicit visitor to these depressed areas of Married Student Housing. Smooth-pedaling Ralph on his racer, stealthily gliding among the harried wives.

"Ralph!" I hoot, and see his front wheel wobble, watch him flatten himself over the handlebars and dig for cover, darting out of sight behind a hut. I shriek, "Ralph *Paaack*-er!" The racer is propelled like a shot; Ralph runs a slalom course between the clothesline posts. But this time, he looks across the river, trying to identify his would-be assailant; no doubt, he is forever imagining student husbands with dueling pistols. But he sees me! Why, it's just Bogus Trumper, out waiking his duck.

Ralph weaves among the onlookers, haughtily pedaling down to the shore. "Hello!" he calls. "What are you doing?"

"The most awful screaming," says the woman under sail.

"Thump-Thump?" Ralph calls.

But all I can say is "Ralph!" I detect a witless sort of ecstasy in my voice.

Ralph balances, back-pedals, then lunges forward, raising his front wheel off the bank and slithering ahead. "Up, Fang!" he commands. If there's a man who can leave rubber smoldering with a bicycle, it's philandering Ralph Packer.

The bridge rails cut him up and paste him together, a collage of feet and spokes crossing the river to me. Oh, help is here. I put my weight on one knee and gently wobble to my feet, but I don't dare take a step. I hold my duck up.

Staring at the plucked bird and at my feathered mustache, Ralph says, "Jesus, was it a fair fight? From here, it looks like a draw."

"Ralph, help," I say. "It's my feet."

"Your *feet?*" he says, and rests the racer against the curb. As he tries to steady me someone over the river starts hollering, "What's the matta with him?"

"It's his *feet!*" Ralph shouts, and the crowd stands under the clotheslines, troubled and murmuring.

"Easy, Ralph," I tell him, tottering to his bike.

"This is a very light bicycle," he tells me. "Be careful you don't bend the crossbar."

I don't see exactly how I can avoid bending it, should it decide to bend, but I perch as weightlessly as possible under the sloped-back handlebars and wedged between Ralph's knees.

"What do you mean, your feet?" he says, wobbling us down Clinton Street. Some of the married students wave.

"I stepped on lots of stuff," I say vaguely.

Ralph warns me not to dangle my duck so far over the handlebars. "That bird could snag in my spokes. Thump-Thump . . ."

"Don't take me home," I say, thinking that I should clean myself up a bit.

"Benny's?" says Ralph. "I'll buy you a beer."

"I can't wash my feet at Benny's, Ralph."

"Well, that's true."

Unsteadily, we arrive downtown. It is still light but growing darker; Saturday night begins early here because it's over so soon.

Shifting my weight on the crossbar, I feel my forgotten condom crinkle. Attempting to adjust myself, I neatly insert my toe between the chain guard and the rear wheel; the pain makes the sky pitch. Lying toppled on the pavement in front of Grafton's Barber Shop, Ralph makes a loud vowel sound. Several sheeted men raise their shaved skulls above the backs of their barber chairs, watching me writhe on the sidewalk as if they were owls— and me, a club-footed mouse.

Ralph releases unspeakable pressure by removing my boots, then whistles at the multitude of flaklike wounds, boil-sized swellings and punctures caked with mud. He takes charge. Back on the bicycle, he holds my boots, laced together, in his teeth, while I balance myself and the duck on the crossbar, fearful of my bare feet in the terrifying spokes.

"I can't go home like this, Ralph," I plead.

"What if that duck has friends?" he asks, my laces slipping through his teeth, causing him to lunge with his mouth as if he meant to eat the boots. "What if that duck's friends are looking for you?" he grunts, turning up Iowa Avenue.

"Please, Ralph."

But he says, "I have never imagined feet like yours before. I'm taking you home, baby." Our timing is perfect. My rotten car is smoking by the curb; Biggie is just back from shopping, and the car is trying to breathe again, throbbing and overheated from its mile-long journey at twenty miles an hour.

"Slip me into the basement, Ralph," I whisper. "There's an old sink in there. At least I can wash my face . . ." I am remembering the scent which the hunters found so gloriously a part of me. And the feathers in my mustache? There's no need for Biggie to think that I plucked this duck with my mouth.

We totter over the side lawn past my retired neighbor, Mr. Fitch, still raking so that the snow will have clean, dead grass to fall on. I wave the duck at him unthinkingly, and the old codger says brightly, "Ho! I used to do some hunting myself, but I don't get around like I used to . . ." He stands like some brittle ice carving, propped on his rake, not at all puzzled by the absence of a gun. In his day they probably used spears.

Ralph scoops me off by the cellar-door, and though it's quite clear to Mr. Fitch that I'm in no condition to walk on my own, he doesn't seem troubled; in his day, no doubt, casualties were to be expected on a rugged duck hunt.

I am carried into the cellar like a bag of coal, wearing my boots like a yoke on my shoulders, and finding the cool slime of the cellar floor most soothing to my feet. Ralph's ursine head looms through the opening. "All right, Thump-Thump?" he asks, and I nod. As he closes the flaps quietly, he slips in some last words. "Thump-Thump, I trust some day you'll tell me about this . . ."

"Sure, Ralph."

Then I hear Biggie's voice from the kitchen window. She says, "Ralph?" and I creep deeper into the cellar.

"Hi, Big!" says Ralph cheerfully.

"What are you doing?" There is cold suspicion in her voice. That's my good Biggie, never fraternizing with the likes of lecherous Ralph Packer. Though it's a foolish moment for it, I feel proud of her.

"Um," says Ralph.

"What are you doing in our cellar?" Biggie asks.

"Well, I wasn't exactly *in* your cellar, Biggie."

I grope blindly toward where I think the cellar sink is, knowing there's little time before I'm discovered, making up whole novels in my mind.

"Playing a game, Ralph?" says Biggie, more playfully than I like. I can't help thinking, Don't let up on him, Big. Be merciless.

Ralph laughs unconvincingly just as I step directly on the trap that's always laid for Risky Mouse, the fierce wombat trap, the crusher of small spines. I think it sprung directly on one of those boil-like wounds the barbwire made, because the whole cellar seemed to light up and I could see everything around me for a moment, just as if the light switch by the stairs had gone on. I couldn't stop the scream, because I didn't realize what I'd stepped on until it was at a crescendo. Its forceful volume must have shattered poor Fitch into thousands of tiny ice cubes beside his rake.

"What was that?" Biggie shouted.

Ralph, the coward, surrendered instantly. "Thump-Thump. He's in the basement . . ." He added gratuitously, "It's his feet," as through the cellar window I saw him sprint across the lawn to his getaway bike.

Mr. Finch, in a voice miles away, said, "Good hunting!"

To Fitch, Biggie said, *"What?"*

"Good hunting!" Fitch repeated, while I wore the mousetrap like a shoe to the sink, opened the rusty faucet and frantically sloshed my face in the dark.

"Bogus?" Biggie called; she thumped on the kitchen floor above me.

"Hi! It's just me!" I yelled up to her.

Then the real light came on, and I could see Biggie's lower half at the top of the stairs; I could also see well enough to remove the mousetrap.

"Bogus? What's going on?"

"Stepped in the damn mousetrap," I muttered.

Biggie sat down at the top of the stairs, allowing me to look up her skirt. She said, "But what were you doing down here, anyway?"

I had already surmised that it was going to get complicated. The answer prepared, I said, "I didn't want to frighten you with my feet. Thought I'd clean myself up a bit . . ."

She leaned forward, confused, and stared at me. From the bottom step, I tilted the sole of one foot up at her, a dramatic gesture; she squeaked. Then I held up the duck.

"See the duck, Big?" I said proudly. "I've been hunting, but it's hell on the feet."

Well, that threw her off—that, and the artful way I propelled myself up the stairs on my knees. In the hall, still kneeling, I handed her the duck, which she promptly dropped.

"Bringing home the dinner," I said winningly.

"It looks like someone's already eaten it."

"Well, we've got to wash it, Big. Clean it up a bit, then roast it in wine."

"Give it brandy," Biggie said. "Perhaps we can revive it."

Then Colm toddled down the hall and sat next to this oddly feathered surprise. *May he remember me as the father with fancy presents of all kinds.*

Colm protested when Biggie slung him over her hip and helped me down the hall to the bathroom.

"Easy, oh easy, my feet," I murmured.

Biggie examined me all over, searching for some specific explanation. In my ear? Under my mustache?

"You went hunting?" she began again.

"Yes . . . You know, I've never been interested in hunting before . . ."

"That's what I thought," she said, nodding. "But you went hunting and you shot a duck?"

"No, I don't have a gun, Big."

"That's what I thought," she said, pleased enough so far. "So someone else shot this duck and gave it to you?"

"Right!" I said. "But it was hell on the feet, Big. I was retrieving them in the marshes. Didn't want to get my boots wet, but I didn't know there'd be so much stuff on the bottom."

"What are boots for?" said Biggie as she started to draw a bath for me. I sat on the toilet, and remembered that I had to go. "Your pants didn't get wet, either," she remarked.

"Well, I took them off too. There were just those guys there, and I couldn't see getting all messed up."

Testing the water, Biggie pondered this. Colm crept to the bathroom door and peered down the length of the hall at the peculiar bird.

Then I had my fly open, and my feet painfully spread to straddle the hopper. I fumbled myself out and commenced to pee, while Biggie stared grimly at my pecker and watched me fill up the condom. Until the pressure and lack of noise was suddenly, awfully apparent to me, and I gazed down to see my growing balloon.

"And just who went on this little hunting party, Bogus?" Biggie yelled. "You and Ralph Packer and a pair he picked up?"

"Scissors!" I screamed. "For God's sake, Big. Please. This could make an awful mess . . ."

"You shit!" she screamed, and Colm fled down the hall to his friend the peaceful duck.

I feared Biggie would start stomping on my bleeding feet—as soon as she was logical again—so I struggled out of the bathroom, first on my heels, then more comfortably banging along on my knees, cradling the bulbous rubber in one hand. Colm clutched the duck, determined not to let his charging father take it away.

As I was only a few feet from the kitchen door, midhall, someone knocked on the front door at the hall's end and called, "Special Delivery! Special Handling!"

"Come in!" Biggie screamed from the bathroom.

The mailman entered, waving a letter. It happened so suddenly that he startled Colm, who shrieked back down the hall, dragging the duck after him. I waddled three more painful knee steps to the kitchen door, still clutching my balloon, and rolled out of sight into the kitchen.

"Special Delivery! Special Handling!" the mailman announced again flatly—not having been forewarned of the possibility that he might ever be in need of a more appropriate remark.

I peeked out of the kitchen. Obviously the mailman was pretending to be totally blind. Biggie, now at the end of the hall, appeared to have forgotten that she'd told anyone to enter, and was glowering at the mailman; in her mind, he was in some way connected with my hunting trip.

Bless his poor brains, the mailman shouted once more, "Special Delivery! Special Handling!" then dropped the letter in the hall and ran.

Skidding the duck along in front of him, Colm edged toward the letter. Another surprise! And Biggie, thinking that I too might have escaped, hollered, "Bogus!"

"Here, Big," I said, ducking back into the kitchen. "Oh, please just tell me where the scissors are."

"On a hook under the sink," she said mechanically, then added, "I hope you cut the whole thing off."

But I didn't. As I snipped in terror over the sink, I saw Colm crawl past the door, shoveling the duck and the letter down the hall.

"There's a letter, Big," I said weakly.

"Special Delivery, Special Handling," Biggie mumbled, the dullness heavy in her voice.

I flooded the nasty thing down the drain. In the hall Colm squawked as Biggie took his duck, or the letter. I looked at the bruised toes on one foot and thought, At least it wasn't your neck, Risky Mouse. Now Colm was garbling affectionately, talking to what must have been the duck. I heard Biggie ripping the letter. Without the slightest change in her flat voice, she said, "It's from your father, the prick . . ."

Oh, where have you gone, Harry Petz? After your splendid attempt, do they keep you in a nailed-down chair? Would you mind, Harry, if I borrowed your track-tested racing seat? Would you think me plagiaristic if I took a turn on your well-oiled casters and had a go at that fourth-floor window and that parking lot below?

19

Axelrulf Among the Greths

There is a moment in *Akthelt and Gunnel* when the subtle depths of a mother's priorities are probed. Akthelt wishes to take his young son Axelrulf along with him on his newest campaign against the warring Greths. The lad is only six at the time, and Gunnel is distraught that her husband could conceive of such heartlessness. *"Da blott pattebarn!"* she exclaims. "The mere baby!"

Patiently Akthelt asks her what, precisely, she is afraid of. That Axelrulf will be slain by the Greths? If so, she should remember that the Greths always lose. Or is it that the talk and habits of the soldiers are too coarse for the boy? Because she should at least respect her husband's taste; the boy will be well protected from such excesses. *"Dar ok ikke tu frygte!"* ("There is nothing to fear!"), Akthelt insists.

Shyly, Gunnel confesses what she fears. "Among the Greths," she tells him, not looking him in the eye, "you will take a woman."

This is true; Akthelt always takes a woman when he is off warring. But he still doesn't see what the matter is. *"Nettopp ub utuktig kvinna!"* he shouts. *"Nettopp tu utukt . . . sla nek ub moder zu slim."* ("Just a fucking woman. Just to fuck . . . she won't be a mother to him.")

The distinction is lost on Gunnel. She fears that young Axelrulf will associate the role of the Greth fucking-woman with his own mother's role —that Gunnel herself will be debased in her son's eyes, by association. With fucking.

"Utukt kvinnas!" ("Fuck women!"), Akthelt tells his old father Thak.

"Utukt kvinnas urt moders!" ("Fuck women *and* mothers!"), bellows old Thak.

But that's not the point. The point is that Akthelt left Axelrulf at home with his mother; he did it Gunnel's way, after all.

Hence, though not necessarily sympathetic to the Mother & Fucking Theory of the Greth Women, Bogus Trumper at least had some background reading to prepare him for Biggie's feelings about Colm—specifically, Biggie's feelings about Colm and that Greth whore, Tulpen.

Since it was difficult for Trumper to leave New York, and since visits to Biggie and Colm made everyone uncomfortable, especially Bogus, Biggie did allow Colm to make a rare trip to New York—on one condition: "That girl you live with—Bull Pen, is that her name?—in that apartment you're going to keep Colm in—well, I mean it, Bogus, I don't think you should be too familiar with her around him. After all, he remembers when you used to sleep with *me* . . ."

"Jesus, Big," Trumper told the phone, "he remembers when *I* used to sleep with you too, so what about Couth, Big? What about *him?*"

"I don't have to send Colm to New York, you know," Biggie said. "Please just understand what I mean. He lives with me, you know."

Trumper knew that.

The arrangements had been exhausting. The fretful synchronizing of watches; the repetition of the flight number; the willingness of the airline to allow an unescorted five-year-old on board (Biggie had to lie and say he was six) provided his pickup at the destination was certain, provided it was not an over-crowded flight, provided he was a calm child, not easily given to panic at twenty thousand feet. And did he get motion sickness?

Trumper stood nervously with Tulpen on the greasy observation deck at La Guardia. It was early spring weather—nice weather, really, and probably a nice day up where Colm was, twenty thousand feet above Manhattan. The air at La Guardia, however, was like a giant bottled fart.

"The poor kid is probably terrified," Trumper said. "All alone in an airplane, going around and around New York. He's never even been in a city before. Christ, he's never even been in an airplane before."

But Trumper was wrong. When Biggie and Colm left Iowa, they had flown away, and Colm had loved every minute of it.

However, airplanes did not agree with Trumper. "Look at them circling up there," he said to Tulpen. "Must be fifty of the fuckers stacked up and waiting for a free spot to land."

Though such stackups are imaginable, and even probable, there were none on this day; Trumper was watching a squadron of Navy jets.

Colm's plane landed ten minutes early. Fortunately Tulpen saw it come in while Trumper was still raving about the Navy jets; she also caught the number of the arrival gate over the loudspeaker.

Trumper was already mourning Colm as if the plane had crashed. "I should never have let him fly," he cried. "I should have borrowed a car and picked him up right at his back door!"

Leading the still-ranting Trumper off the observation deck, Tulpen got him to the gate in time. "I'll never forgive myself," he was babbling. "It was just pure selfishness. I didn't want to have to drive all that distance. And I didn't want to have to see Biggie, either."

Tulpen glanced through the gate at the passengers. There was only one child, and he held a stewardess by the hand. The top of his head came to her waist, and he was coolly sorting out the crowd; it looked as if the stewardess was holding his hand because she simply wanted to, or needed to; he simply tolerated her. He was a handsome boy, with lovely skin like his mother's but dark, blunt features like his father's. He wore a pair of lederhosen knickers, a rough pair of hiking boots and a fine tyrolean wool jacket over a new white shirt. The stewardess held a rucksack in her hand.

"Trumper?" Tulpen said, pointing out the boy. But Trumper was looking the wrong way. Then the boy spotted Bogus, dropped the stewardess's hand, asked for his rucksack and pointed out his father, who now was doing a mad pirouette, looking everywhere but the right place. Tulpen had to forcefully aim him in Colm's direction.

"Colm!" Bogus cried. After he had swooped down on the boy and picked him up, he realized that Colm had grown up a little and no longer liked being picked up, at least not in public. Of all things, Colm wanted to shake hands.

Trumper dropped him and shook hands. "Wow!" Trumper said, grinning like a fool.

"I got to ride with the pilot," Colm said.

"Wow," said Bogus, in a kind of hush. He was looking at Colm's Austrian costume, thinking of Biggie getting Colm all fancied up for the trip, dressing the poor kid like a showpiece for an Austrian travel agency. Bogus had forgotten that he had bought the whole outfit for Colm, including the rucksack.

"Mr. Trumper?" the stewardess asked him, being dutifully careful. "Is this your father?" she asked Colm. Bogus held his breath, wondering if Colm would admit it.

"Yup," said Colm.

"Yup, yup, yup," said Trumper all the way out of the terminal. Tulpen carried Colm's rucksack and watched the two of them, struck by Colm's inheritance of Bogus's peculiar way of ambling.

Bogus asked Colm what was in the pilot's cockpit.

"There was a lot of electricity," Colm told him.

In the taxi, Bogus bubbled about the number of cars. Had Colm ever seen so many? Had he ever smelled air this bad? Tulpen held the child's rucksack in her lap and bit her lip. She was about to cry; Bogus hadn't even introduced her to Colm.

That awkwardness took place at Tulpen's apartment. Colm was fascinated by the fish and turtles. What were their names? Who had found them? Then Bogus remembered Tulpen, and remembered, too, that she'd been just as nervous about Colm coming as he had. She wanted to know, What did five-year-olds eat, what did they like to do, how big were they, when did they go to sleep? Suddenly Bogus realized how important he was to her, and it chilled him. Almost as fiercely as he wanted Colm to like him she wanted Colm to like her.

"I'm sorry, I'm sorry," he whispered to her in the kitchen. She was preparing a snack for the turtles so that Colm could feed them.

"It's all right, it's all right," she said. "He's a beautiful child, Trumper. Isn't he beautiful?"

"Yes," Bogus whispered, and went back to watch Colm with the turtles.

"These live in fresh water, right?" said Colm.

Trumper didn't know.

"Right," said Tulpen. "Do you ever see any turtles in the ocean?"

"Yes, I have one," Colm said. "Couth caught him, a *big* one." He spread his arms—too wide, Trumper thought, for any turtle Couth could have caught around Georgetown, but a fair exaggeration for Colm. "We have to change his water every day. Sea water; that's salt water. He'd die in here," he said, peering into one of Tulpen's elaborate tanks. "And these turtles," he said, his voice bright with discovery, "they'd die in my tank at home, right?"

"Right," Tulpen said.

Colm turned his attention to the fish. "I had some minnows, but they all died. I don't have any fish." He watched their bright colors intently.

"Well," Tulpen told him, "you pick out your favorite one there, and when you go home you can take it with you. I've got a little bowl a fish can travel in."

"Really?"

"Sure," Tulpen said. "They eat special food, and I'll give you some of that too, and when you get it home, you'll have to get a tank for it, with a little hose thing which puts air in the water—" She was showing him the fixture, on one of her aquariums, when he cut her off.

"Couth can make one," Colm said. "He made one like that for my turtle."

"Well, good," Tulpen said. She watched Trumper slip off to the bathroom. "Then you'll have a fish to go with your turtle."

"Right," said Colm, nodding eagerly and smiling at her. "But not in the same water, right? The fish has to have fresh water, not salt water, right?" He was a very exact little boy.

"Right," Tulpen told him. She listened to Bogus, in the bathroom, flushing himself away.

They went to the Bronx Zoo: Colm and Bogus, Tulpen, Ralph Packer and Kent, along with about two thousand dollars' worth of movie equipment. Packer shot Bogus and Colm riding the subway out to the Bronx during that long ugly stretch when it is above ground.

Colm watched the laundry flapping from the grimy apartments in the grimy buildings alongside the tracks. "Boy, don't those clothes get dirty?" he asked.

"Yup," Bogus said. He wanted to throw Ralph Packer, Kent and the two-thousand-dollar movie equipment off the subway, preferably at high speed. But Tulpen was being very nice, and Colm obviously liked her. She was trying hard, of course, but there was more than enough that was natural about her to make Colm feel at home with her.

Colm had never liked Ralph, though. Even when he'd been a baby and Ralph had come to their place in Iowa, Colm didn't like him. When the camera ran on and on, Colm would stare into the lens until Ralph stopped, put down the camera and stared back. Then Colm would pretend he was bored and look away.

"Colm?" Bogus whispered. "Do you think Ralph would live in fresh water or sea water?" Colm giggled, then whispered to Tulpen and told her what Bogus had said. She smiled and told Colm something, which he passed back to Bogus. The camera was running again.

"Oil," Colm whispered.

"What?" said Bogus.

"Oil!" Colm said. Ralph would live in oil.

"Right!" said Trumper, flashing a grateful look at Tulpen.

"Right!" Colm shouted. Aware that the camera was running again and aimed at him, he proceeded to stare Ralph Packer down.

"The kid keeps looking at the camera," Kent told Ralph.

With exaggerated patience, Ralph leaned across the aisle and smiled at Colm. "Hey, Colm?" he said gently. "Don't look at the camera, okay?"

Colm looked at his father, seeking guidance on whether or not he had to obey Ralph.

"Oil," Bogus whispered.

"Oil," repeated Tulpen, like a chant. Then she started laughing, and Colm broke up too.

"Oil," Colm chanted.

Kent appeared typically baffled by the experience, but Ralph Packer, who was at least a keen observer of detail, put his camera down.

And after the zoo—the pregnant animals, the molting coats, the controlled little kingdom, from wart hog to cheetah—and after God knows how many feet of film, not of the animals but of the main character, Tulpen, Bogus and Colm ditched Ralph and Kent and the two thousand dollars' worth of movie equipment.

Ralph never really put the camera away. It hung in that heavy shoulder bag like a pistol in a holster, but you knew it was a pistol of large caliber, and you never forgot that it was loaded.

Tulpen and Bogus took Colm to a puppet show for kids in the Village. Tulpen knew all about such things: when museums put on films for kids, when there were dances and plays and operas and symphonies and puppet shows. She knew about them because she herself was more interested in seeing them than things for adults; most of *those* were awful.

Tulpen hit it right every time. After the puppet show they went to a place to eat called The Yellow Cowboy, which was full of old film posters from Western movies. Colm loved it and ate like a horse. Afterward, he fell asleep in the taxi. Bogus had insisted they take a cab, not wanting Colm to see any subway happenings at night. In the back seat, Trumper and Tulpen almost fought over whose lap Colm was going to lie in. Tulpen gave in and let Trumper hold him, but she kept her hand on Colm's foot.

"I just can't get over him," she whispered to Trumper. "I mean, you *made* him. He's part *you.*" Trumper looked embarrassed, but Tulpen went on anyway. "I didn't think I loved you this much," she told Bogus. She was crying a little.

"I love you too," he said hoarsely, but he wouldn't look at her.

"Let's have a baby, Trumper," she said. "Can we?"

"I have a baby," Trumper said sourly. Then he made a face, as if he couldn't stomach the self-pity he'd heard in his own voice.

She couldn't stomach it either. She squeezed Colm's sleeping foot. "You selfish bastard," she told Bogus.

"I know what you mean, but I do love you, I think," he said. "It's just such a fucking risk."

"Suit yourself, Jack," Tulpen said, and let go of Colm's foot.

Tulpen took Biggie's request that she and Trumper not be too familiar with each other more seriously than Trumper did. She arranged for Colm to sleep in her bed, facing the turtles and fish. Bogus was to sleep with him, if he could remember not to reach out and goose the child in the middle of the night. She slept on the couch.

Trumper listened to Colm's sweet breathing. How fragile children's faces are in sleep!

Colm woke up from a dream in the half-light before dawn, wailing and shaking, whining for a drink, demanding that the fish be quiet, claiming that a mad turtle had attacked him, then falling asleep again before Tulpen could bring him the water. She couldn't believe that a boy could be so worldly in the daytime and in such terror at night. Trumper told her that it was perfectly natural; some kids have rough nights. Colm had always been a wild sleeper, hardly ever passing two nights in a row without an outcry, mysterious and never explained.

"Understandable," he muttered to Tulpen. "Considering who the kid's lived with."

"I thought you said Biggie was good with him," Tulpen said, worried. "And Couth too, you said. You mean Couth?"

"I meant *me,*" Trumper said. "Fuck Couth," he mumbled. "He's a wonderful person . . ."

———

Tulpen was also struck by how totally children wake up in the morning. Looking out the window, Colm was a babble of talk, thinking what he wanted to do, prowling Tulpen's kitchen.

"What's in the yogurt?"

"Fruit."

"Oh, I thought it was lumps," Colm said, eating on.

"Lumps?"

"Like in cereal," said Colm. A-ha! Bogus thought, so Biggie is lousy with cereal. Or perhaps the overtalented Couth is responsible for the lumps?

But now Colm was talking about museums, wondering if there were any in Maine. Yes—for ships, Tulpen thought. Here in New York there were ones for paintings and sculpture and natural history . . .

They took him to one for machines. That's what he wanted. There was a giant contraption at the main entrance, a jumble of gears, levers, steam whistles and hammering rods as high as a three-story ceiling, as wide as a barn.

"What does it do?" Colm asked, standing transfixed by its terrible energy. The thing sounded as if it was constructing a building for itself.

"I don't know," said Trumper.

"I don't think it actually *does* anything," Tulpen said.

"It just sort of works, right?" said Colm.

"Yup," said Trumper.

There were hundreds of machines. Some were delicate, some were violent, some you could start and stop yourself, some were terribly noisy bashers and others appeared to be resting—like the great, potential animals in zoos who are always asleep.

In the big tunnel leading out of the building, Colm stopped and felt the wall with his hand, absorbing the vibration of all those machines. "Boy," he said. "You can feel them."

Trumper hated machines.

Another museum was showing W. C. Fields in *The Bank Dick,* so they took Colm to it. Both he and Trumper howled throughout the film, but Tulpen fell asleep. "I guess she doesn't like the movie," Bogus whispered to Colm.

"I think she's just tired," Colm whispered. After a pause, he added, "Why does she sleep on the couch?"

Deftly changing the subject, Trumper said, "Maybe she doesn't think the movie's so funny."

"But it is."

"Right," said Trumper.

"You know what?" Colm whispered thoughtfully. "Girls don't like funny things so much."

"They don't?"

"Nope. Mommy doesn't, and . . . what's her name?" he asked, poking Tulpen.

"Tulpen," Trumper whispered.

"Tulpen," said Colm. "She doesn't like funny things either."

"Well . . ."

"But you do, and I do," Colm said.

"Right," Trumper whispered. He could listen to the kid for days, he thought.

"Couth thinks things are funny, too," Colm went on, but Trumper lost him there. He watched W.C. Fields drive the terrified bank robber out to the end of the dock overhanging the lake. Fields said to the robber, "From here on, you'll have to take the *boat.*" Colm was doubled up, laughing so hard that he woke Tulpen, but Trumper couldn't even manage a convincing smile.

During Colm's last night in New York, Bogus Trumper had a nightmare about airplanes, and this time it was Trumper who woke up Colm and Tulpen with his howls.

Colm was wide-awake, popping questions and looking for turtles who might have attacked his father. But Tulpen told him that it was okay; his father had just had a bad dream. "I have those sometimes, too," Colm confessed, and he looked very sympathetically at Bogus.

Because of the dream, Bogus decided to borrow Kent's car and drive Colm back to Maine.

"That's silly," Biggie said on the phone.

"I'm a good driver," Trumper said.

"I know you are, but it will take so long. He can fly to Portland in an hour."

"Unless he crashes in the Atlantic," Bogus said. Biggie groaned. "All right," she said. "I'll drive to Portland and meet him, so you won't have to drive all the way to Georgetown."

A-ha! thought Trumper. What is there in Georgetown that I shouldn't see? "Why can't I come to Georgetown?" he asked.

"God," said Biggie. "You certainly can, if you want to. I didn't think you'd want to. I just thought, since I was going to drive to Portland, anyway, to meet the plane . . ."

"Well, have it your way."

"No, have it *yours,*" said Biggie. "Have you had a nice time?"

He did it Biggie's way. He borrowed Kent's awful car and drove to the Portland Airport. Tulpen packed them a lunch and bought a lovely little fishbowl for the fish Colm selected, a big purple fantail. Colm couldn't see that Tulpen was crying over his shoulder when she hugged him goodbye, and she snarled at Trumper on the sidewalk when he tried to hug her.

Before they were even out of New York State, Colm found a joint-roller in Kent's filthy glove compartment and four old marijuana cigarettes. In a panic about being busted—in front of his boy!—Bogus asked Colm to empty the contents of the glove compartment into a litter-bag, and the first moment they were alone on the road, Trumper threw the whole mess out the window.

Somewhere in Massachusetts Bogus realized that he'd thrown out all the registration papers for the car, and probably Kent's driver's license as well; all of the pot apparatus would be found with Kent's name and address. He decided to tell Kent that the glove compartment had been robbed.

Trumper relaxed driving through New Hampshire. He took the longer shore road along the Maine coast to stretch out his last moments with Colm. He had some thoughts about Biggie, and about Couth, and about what Biggie might have told Colm about his father, or even about his father's girl. But they were not dark thoughts; they were sometimes sad thoughts, but they were kind. Biggie was not poisonous.

"Do you like Maine?" he asked Colm.

"Oh, sure."

"Even in the winter?" asked Trumper. "What can you do near the ocean in the wintertime?"

"Walk on the beach in the snow," said Colm. "And watch the storms.

But we're going to put the boat back in the water when I get home . . ."

"Oh?" said Trumper. "You and Mommy?" He was asking for it, he was leading purposefully.

"No," said Colm. "Me and Couth. It's Couth's boat."

"You like Couth, don't you?"

"I sure do."

"Did you have a nice time in New York?" Trumper begged.

"I sure did."

"I like Couth and Mommy, too," said Bogus.

"So do I," Colm said. "And I like you," he said, "and . . . what's the girl's name?"

"Tulpen."

"Yup, Tulpen. I like her," said Colm, "and you, and Mommy, and Couth."

Well, that wraps it up, Trumper thought. He didn't know what he felt.

"Do you know Daniel Arbuthnot?" Colm asked.

"No, I don't."

"Well, I don't like *him* so much."

"Who is he?"

"He's a kid in my school," Colm said. "He's just a stupid kid."

At the Portland Airport, Biggie asked Trumper if he wanted to come to Georgetown; it was only another hour's drive and he could stay the night; Couth would like to see him. But Trumper felt that Biggie would really rather he didn't come, and he would rather not either.

"Tell Couth I'm sorry, but I have to get back to New York," he said. "Ralph's all hot to trot with a new film."

Biggie looked at the ground. "Who's the main character?" she asked, and when Bogus stared at her—a How Did You Know? stare—she said, "Ralph's been up. He flew up one weekend and talked to me and Couth." She shrugged. "I don't mind, Bogus," she said. "But I can't understand why you would have anything to do with a film about . . . about *what?*" she said angrily. "That's what I'd like to know."

"You know Ralph, Big. I don't think *he* knows what the movie's about."

"Do you know he tried to sleep with me?" she asked. "Again and again," she said, working herself into a rage. "Jesus, even when he came for the weekend, he even tried then, with Couth around and all."

Trumper just shuffled. "That girl," said Biggie, and Trumper looked up. "Tulpen?" Biggie asked.

"Right," said Colm. "Tulpen . . ."

They moved around to the other side of the car. Colm was absorbed in unwrapping the fishbowl, which was covered with tinfoil and tied with a ribbon.

"What about her?" Trumper asked.

"Well, Ralph says she's nice," Biggie said. "I mean, really nice."

"Yes, she really is."

"Well, he wants to sleep with her too," Biggie said. "You should know . . ."

Trumper wanted to tell Biggie that Ralph had already slept with Tulpen, and that he might still be sore that he couldn't any more, but that there really wasn't anything else to it, but he didn't say anything; he just looked as if he was going to try.

"Bogus," Biggie said. "Please don't say you're sorry. Just this once, don't say something like that. You always say it."

"But I *am* sorry, Big."

"Don't be," she told him. "I'm very happy, and so is Colm."

He believed her, but why did it make him so angry?

"Are you?" she asked.

"What?"

"Are you happy?"

He guessed he was, sort of, but he evaded an answer. "We had a nice time, Colm and I," he told her. "We went to the zoo and a puppet show . . ."

"And a museum!" said Colm. By now he had the fishbowl unwrapped and was holding it up to show Biggie. But the fish was floating on top of the water.

"Oh, it's lovely," Biggie said.

"It's dead," said Colm, but he didn't seem very surprised.

"We'll get you another one," Trumper said. "You can come down again," he added, not looking at Biggie. "Would you like that?"

"Sure."

"Or your father can come see us," Biggie said.

"Sure, and I could bring a fish with me," Bogus said.

"There was a yellow one and a red one, too," Colm told Biggie. "And all kinds of turtles. Maybe a turtle wouldn't have died so easy."

A small plane took off nearby, and Colm watched it. "I wish I could have taken the plane back," he complained. "It doesn't take so long on the plane, and maybe the fish wouldn't have died."

Fish-killer Trumper felt like saying, Maybe the great Couth can revive it. But he didn't really feel like saying that at all; in fact, he felt like a shit for even thinking it.

20

His Move

He left his wife and kid in Iowa,
and he bought a one-way ticket.

—Ralph Packer,
from the narration of *Fucking Up*

He stands on the dark sidewalk, shielded from the streetlight by a shrub, and pays his respects to Biggie's lighted window, and to Mr. Fitch, night watchman for his own and neighboring lawns. Fitch waves to him, and Bogus starts his tender-footed limp toward town, slow steps along the grassy strip between the sidewalk and the street; in the shadows between the lampposts he blunders into someone's pile of leaves.

"Got to get up early to get those ducks!" shouts Mr. Fitch, who is capable of believing anything.

"Right!" calls Bogus, and bleeds downtown to Benny's, where he finds Ralph Packer in a wallow of beer. Ralph, however, is sobered by Trumper's pained and spectacular appearance.

Packer is sensible enough to intervene when Bogus starts an assault on a harmless fat student in a white Ghandi robe who wears the sign of the Tao and electrocuted hair. Bogus is telling him, "If you say you love everyone, I'm going to disembowel you with a glass ashtray . . ." He picks one up and adds, *"This* glass ashtray."

Packer beerily ushers Bogus out onto Clinton Street and hobbles him along the curb to his racing bicycle. With the unfeeling stamina of the indestructibly drunk, Ralph pedals the two of them down to the river, across the bridge, and up the long, lung-killing hill to the university hospital. There Trumper is treated for festering foot wounds, chiefly punctures and lacerations, and is released.

All day Sunday Trumper kept prone, reclining on Ralph's couch, his throbbing feet stacked on a pile of pillows. Feverish visions in Ralph's nasty two-room apartment: smelling Ralph's mongrel, whom Trumper called Retch, and the odor of hair oil, which seeped upward through the floorboards from a Jefferson Street barbershop below Ralph's rooms.

Once the phone rang, on a table behind his head. After some groping

Bogus managed to answer it, and a strange angry lady informed him that he could go fuck himself. He didn't recognize the voice, but whether it was his fever or a clear-headed conviction, he didn't for a moment believe that the call was intended for Ralph.

By nightfall, Bogus had shaped several emotional impulses into what could vaguely be called a plan. Overturf, indulging his sense of drama, would have called it a scheme.

Trumper struggled to remember the brief letter from his father which had been torn up and hurled in tiny pieces to Risky Mouse:

Son:

I have had to think very seriously about everything, and I should at first say that I am most disapproving of the various ways you have conducted yourself, both in your personal life and in your career goals.

It is strongly against my better judgment that I have concluded to make you a loan. Understand: this is not a gift. The enclosed check for $5,000 should be ample to put you on your feet again. I will not be so inhuman as to set a specific interest rate on this figure, or to set a specific due date for its return. Suffice it to say that I hope you will consider yourself responsible to me for this money, and that you will accept this responsibility with a gravity quite lacking in your past behavior.

Dad

Bogus was capable of remembering that he had not torn up the check and hurled it into the basement too.

———

The next morning Trumper took slow, swollen steps to the bank. A day's transaction included the following: a deposit of five thousand dollars, which prompted the personal congratulations of Bank President Shumway; a twenty-minute wait in President Shumway's now-cordial office while the bank processed a new numbered checkbook for him (the old one was home with Biggie); a withdrawal of three hundred dollars in cash; and the theft of fourteen courtesy matchbooks from the little basket on the counter by the teller's window ("I intend to rob you," he whispered to the startled teller, then grabbed the matches).

Trumper limped to the post office and wrote out checks to the following:

> Humble Oil & Refining Co.
> Sinclair Refining Co.
> Iowa-Illinois Gas & Electric
> Krotz Plumbing
> Northwestern Bell Telephone Co.
> Milo Kubik (Peoples Market)
> Sears, Roebuck & Co.

Office of Financial Aid, State University of Iowa
Lone Tree Co-operative Credit Union
Shive & Hupp
Addison & Halsey
Cuthbert Bennett
The Jefferson International Travel Agency

Lacking was a check for the several thousand dollars owed National Defense Loans—government money for education, which he assumed must emanate from the U.S. Department of Health, Education and Welfare. Instead, he sent H.E.W. a note in which he declared himself "unwilling and unable to pay this debt, on the grounds of receiving an incomplete education." Then he went to Benny's, drank fourteen draughts and played a lot of violent pinball until Benny called Packer to come take him away.

At Ralph's, Bogus phoned a cable he wanted sent:

> HERR MERRILL OVERTURF
> SCHWINDGASSE 15/2
> VIENNA 4, AUSTRIA
>
> MERRILL
>   I AM COMING
>   BOGGLE.

"Who's Merrill?" said Ralph Packer. "Who's Boggle?"

Trumper hadn't heard a word from Overturf since the last time he'd been in Europe, with Biggie, more than four years before. If Ralph had known this, or known anything, for that matter, he might have tried to stop Trumper. Conversely, it later occurred to Bogus that Ralph might have some thoughts about Biggie being left alone.

———

The next morning, Trumper had a phone call at Ralph's apartment from Lufthansa Airlines. They had botched his reservation to Vienna and had him booked on a flight from Chicago to New York to Frankfurt. For some unexplained reason, this would cost him less, even if he took a businessman's flight from Frankfurt to Vienna. Especially if I hitchhike from Frankfurt, Trumper thought.

"Frankfurt?" said Ralph Packer. "Jesus, what's in Frankfurt?"

He told Ralph his "plan," sort of.

———

At four in the afternoon, Ralph phones Biggie and informs her that Bogus is "besotted at Benny's and about to get into a losing fight." Biggie hangs up.

Ralph calls back. He suggests Biggie bring Colm and the car right away, and that together they can safely stow Bogus in the trunk.

After Biggie hangs up again, Ralph encourages the three silent customers in Benny's to make a lot of background rumpus for the next attempt. That call rings unanswered for almost five minutes while Bogus, near to giving up hope, crouches behind a shrub on Mr. Fitch's well-kept lawn. Finally he sees Biggie and Colm leave.

Ralph stalls Biggie at Benny's door with grim tales of blood, beer, teeth, ambulances and policemen before Biggie suspects the hoax and walks boldly past Ralph into the bar. There is a drunk girl, all alone, playing pinball; there are two men in a booth by the door talking cheerfully. Biggie asks Benny if there's been a fight here.

"Yes, about two months ago . . ." Benny begins.

When Biggie darts outside, she finds that Ralph Packer has moved her car somewhere, and is strolling down the sidewalk with Colm. Packer won't reveal where he's parked the car until she threatens to call the police.

When she gets home, Bogus has been and gone.

He took his tape recorder and all the tapes; his passport; not his typewriter but all his thesis work on the translation of *Akthelt and Gunnel.* God knows why.

He cleaned out the refrigerator, putting all the food in the basement for Risky Mouse. He destroyed the trap.

By Colm's pillow he left a toy duck, with real feathers, made by Amish farmers. It cost $15.95, the most Trumper had ever spent for a toy.

By Biggie's pillow he left the new checkbook, with a remaining balance of $1,612.47, and a large French-uplift mauve bra. It was the right size too. In one of the big cups, he crumpled a handwritten note: Big, there was truly none finer.

This is all Biggie discovers of his trip home. She can't know, of course, about his other accomplishment. If Mr. Fitch ever cared to be nosy, he could describe for Biggie the sight of Bogus groping through the garbage cans outside his house and rescuing the abandoned duck, by now in an advanced state of decomposition. Fitch registered no surprise when Trumper wrapped up the duck in a plastic bag. Nor would Fitch ever describe Trumper's search for a sturdy box into which the bag containing the duck was crammed, along with a note reading, "Dear Sir: Please count your change."

The package was mailed to Bogus's father.

Watching Biggie's stormy return from behind Fitch's shrub, Bogus hung around just long enough to make sure that she didn't jump out any windows. At his see-through curtain with Mrs. Fitch, watching Bogus behind the shrub, Fitch had enough good sense to recognize secrecy when he saw it and didn't come out on his porch to make any inappropriate remarks. Once Bogus turned and saw the old couple observing him. He waved; they waved back. *Good old Fitch: he must have fussed for years with the Bureau of Statistics, but now he lets things ride. Excepting his lawn, the man knows how to retire.*

Later Bogus went to the library, to mull over his little-used alcove, not really expecting to find anything he'd want to take with him. Predictably, he didn't. His cubby-neighbor, M. E. Zanther, discovered him "doodling on an otherwise blank page," he later reported. Zanther remembered this well, because when Trumper left the library, Zanther slunk into Trumper's alcove to read the doodles. Actually, Bogus was hiding around the end of the row of cubbies. What Zanther saw was the crude beginnings of a poem about Harry Petz, a badly drawn obscene drawing, and, broadly printed with a Magic Marker across the surface of the desk blotter, HI, ZANTHER! ARE YOU RUNNING OUT OF THINGS TO READ?

"One thing I've noticed," said Dr. Wolfram Holster, Trumper's thesis chairman, "is that witless behavior can be a very calculated thing." But that was much later; at the time, he was thoroughly bamboozled.

Trumper called Dr. Holster and begged for a ride to the nearest Iowa airport with the quickest connection to Chicago. This would have been Cedar Rapids, about three-quarters of an hour from Iowa City, and Dr. Wolfram Holster was not in the habit of cultivating familiar relationships with his students. "Is this an emergency?" he asked.

"There's been a death in the family," Trumper told him.

They were almost at the airport, Trumper not speaking a word, when Holster asked, "Your father?"

"What?"

"Your *father*," Holster repeated. "The death in the family . . ."

"My own," said Trumper. *"I'm* the death in the family . . ."

Holster drove on, maintaining a polite pause. "Where are you going?" he asked after a while.

"I prefer to fall to pieces abroad," Trumper answered. Holster remembered that line; it was from Trumper's translation of *Akthelt and Gunnel*. On the battlefield at Plock, word comes to Akthelt that his wife, Gunnel, and his son Axelrulf have been foully molested and dismembered back home at the castle. Thak, Akthelt's father, suggests that they postpone their planned invasion of Finlandia. "I prefer to fall to pieces abroad," Akthelt tells his father.

So Dr. Holster suspected some melodramatics on the part of Trumper.

Actually, what Holster didn't suspect was more interesting. The whole passage—the battlefield at Plock, the business about Gunnel and Axelrulf being foully molested and dismembered, and Akthelt's comment—was bunk. Trumper had lost track of the plot, needed more work to show Holster, and had invented all of it. Later, he had thought of a way to revive Axelrulf and Gunnel: it was a case of mistaken identity.

So actually Trumper's line was original, after all.

"I prefer to fall to pieces abroad."

Holster's reaction must have shaken Trumper up a bit.

"Have a good time," Dr. Wolfram Holster told him.

The Lufthansa flight for Frankfurt was less than half full at the takeoff from Chicago. It picked up a few more passengers in New York, but it was still pretty empty. Even with all the seats available, a Lufthansa stewardess sat down beside Trumper. Perhaps I look like I'm going to throw up, he thought, and promptly felt sick.

The stewardess's English wasn't very good, but Bogus didn't feel up to speaking German yet. He'd be speaking it soon enough.

"Dis your furzt flighct?" the stewardess asked him in a sensuous guttural. Most people don't know what a lovely language German is, Trumper reflected.

"I haven't flown in a long time," he told the stewardess, wishing that his stomach wouldn't bank and circle with the plane.

Over the Atlantic they leveled off, climbed, then leveled off again. When the lighted sign saying PLEASE FASTEN SEAT BELTS went off, the nice stewardess unfastened hers. "Vell, here ve go," she said.

But before she could get up, Trumper tried to lunge past her into the aisle, forgetting that his own seat belt was still attached. He was jerked back against her, knocking her back in her seat. He vomited in her lap.

"Oh, I'm sorry," he gurgled, thinking how he'd lived for the last few days on beer.

The stewardess stood, holding her skirt up, making a tray of it, and smiled, or tried to. He said again, "Oh, I'm sorry."

She told him sweetly, "Pleeze, don't vorry about it."

But Bogus Trumper didn't hear her. He saw the blackness out his window and hoped it was only the sea. He said again, "Really, I *am* sorry . . ."

The stewardess was trying to get away from him to empty her skirt. But he caught her hand, not looking at her, and staring out the window fixedly, said again, "I really am sorry, really! Fuck it, anyway, damn it! But I *am!* So very fucking sorry . . ."

The stewardess knelt awkwardly in the aisle beside him, balancing her skirtful of slop. "Pleeze, you . . . hey, you!" she crooned. But he began to cry. "Pleeze don't even tink about it," she pleaded. She touched his face. "Look, pleeze," she coaxed. "You von't believe me, but dis happens all der time."

21

Home Movies

Kent ran the projector. It was a pretty beat-up print of the original which Tulpen had crudely spliced together so they could see how the concept was working.

Trumper ran the recorder. His tapes were as crudely cut as the film; they weren't always in sync, and he kept having to ask Kent to slow down the projector or speed it up or stop it altogether, and he was constantly fussing with the speed of the tape too. Altogether, it was about as amateurish an operation as Trumper had been privileged to see since he'd started working with Ralph. Most of the camera shots were hand-held, as jumpy as a TV newsreel, and most of the film was silent; the separately taped sound track would be laid over later. Ralph had practically given up on using sync sound. Even the film itself was substandard—high speed, grainy stuff—and Ralph, normally a wizard with light, had overexposed and underexposed half of the footage. Ralph was also a very patient genius in the darkroom, yet some of the footage looked as if the film had been handled with pliers and blotched with chemicals invented for the removal of rust rather than the development of film.

An excellent film craftsman, Ralph had done all this on purpose; in fact, some of the light holes in the film had been handmade with a jackknife. Since there wasn't a speck of dust in his darkroom, Ralph must have swept half of New York with the reels to achieve the mess he had. Perhaps when the film was distributed, if it ever was, Ralph would stipulate the use of a crushed plastic lens on the projector.

When Packer wanted to run through the whole crude beginning again, Trumper felt he'd had it.

"It's looking good," Ralph said. "It's looking *better.* "

"You want to know what it sounds like?" Trumper said, slamming the buttons on the recorder. "It sounds like it was taped in a tin-can factory. And you know what it looks like? It looks like your tripod got stolen and that you were so poor you had to pawn your light meter to be able to buy the cheapest film stock in Hong Kong."

Tulpen coughed.

"It looks," said Trumper, "like your darkroom was in a windowless building being sand-blasted."

Even Kent didn't say anything. He probably didn't like it either, but he had great faith in Ralph. If Ralph had asked him to load a camera with Saran Wrap, Kent would have tried it.

"It looks like home movies," Trumper said.

"It *is* a home movie, Thump-Thump," Ralph told him. "Can we run through the first reel just once more, please?"

"If this tape will even hold together," Trumper said. "I ought to copy it. It's got more splices than actual tape. It's about as stable as a pubic hair," he said.

"Once more, Thump-Thump?" Ralph asked.

"If I have to stop it just once," Trumper said, "the whole thing will fall apart."

"Then we'll run it straight through, okay, Kent?" Ralph said.

"The film might break too," Kent suggested.

"Let's just try it, shall we?" Ralph said patiently. "Just once more."

"I'll pray for you, Ralph," said Bogus. Tulpen coughed again. Nothing was meant by it; she simply had a cold. "Ready, Kent?" Trumper asked.

Kent advanced the film to the opening frame and Trumper located the sound he wanted. "Ready, Thump-Thump," Kent said.

The name was reserved for Ralph's use alone; Trumper didn't like being called Thump-Thump by fucking Kent. "What did you say, Kent?" he asked.

"Huh?" said Kent.

Ralph stood up, and Tulpen put her right hand in Trumper's lap, leaned across him and with her left hand flicked the tape to PLAY. "Go, Kent," she said.

———

The film opens with a medium shot of Trumper in a delicatessen in the Village. It is a big, crowded lunch-counter, and you can pick out sandwich makings as you move along, ending up with a whopper at the cash register. Trumper moves slowly, scrutinizing the pastrami, pickles and spiced ham, nodding or shaking his head to the men behind the counter. There is no sync sound.

The voice-over is Packer's, narrating from the tape. "He's very cautious now—like someone who's been stung has an eye open for bees, you know?" Trumper looks suspiciously at his sandwich. "It's natural, I guess, but he just won't get involved in anything."

Ralph's voice-over rattles on about Trumper's lack of involvement until we cut to another angle: Trumper standing by the condiment counter, applying mustard and relish. A pretty girl is looking self-consciously at the camera, then at Trumper to see if he might be someone famous. She also wants the mustard. Trumper slides it along the counter to her without looking at her, then carries his sandwich out of frame. The girl stares after him as Tulpen's voice-over says, "I think he's very careful with women. A good thing, too, by the way . . ."

Cut: Trumper and Tulpen are entering her apartment, both of them lugging groceries. There is no sync sound. Ralph, voice-over, says, "Well, naturally *you'd* think so. You live with him."

Tulpen and Bogus are putting groceries away in the kitchen; she is chattering in an apparently normal monologue; he is sullen, throwing an occasional irritated look at her, then at the camera. "I mean, he's just nice with me," Tulpen's voice-over says. "I think he's aware of the dangers, that's all . . ."

Walking straight into the camera's lens, Trumper makes an obscene gesture.

Cut: A series of stills, family photographs of Trumper, Biggie and Colm. Ralph's voice-over: "Well, he ought to be aware of the dangers, of course. He was married before . . ."

Tulpen: "He misses the child."

Ralph: "And the wife?"

Cut: Earphones on, Bogus is working on the tapes in Ralph's studio. There is no sync sound. The sound track is a montage of fragments we've already heard from the various voices-over: "It's natural, I guess . . ." "I think that's a good thing . . ." "You live with him . . ." "And the wife?"

Trumper appears to be switching these fragments on and off by his fingerwork at the tape recorder. Then Tulpen comes into frame, says something and points to something out of frame just beyond the two of them.

Another angle: With the bits from the voices-over still the only sound, Trumper and Tulpen are looking at a tangled mess of tape which has spun off a reel and is spilling into a great wormy pile on the floor. Trumper shuts something off: *clunk.* With this noise, the frame freezes to a still. There continues to be no sync sound. Ralph's voice-over says, "Stop it, right there! Now the title—hold it right there . . ." Then the titles for *Fucking Up* appear over the frozen image. "Music," says Ralph's voice-over, and in turn they appear over the frozen image: Bogus Trumper, in stop-action, is stooping to attempt to untangle a mess of spilled tape. Tulpen is looking on.

22

Slouching After Overturf

He was very lucky to hitch a ride from the Frankfurt Airport to Stuttgart with a German computer salesman who was proud of his company's Mercedes. Trumper wasn't sure whether it was the drone of the autobahn or the salesman's own peculiar drone that put him to sleep.

In Stuttgart he spent the night at the Hotel Fehls Zunder. Apparently, from the rows of photographs in the hotel lobby, Fehls Zunder had been a diver on the German Olympic Team of 1936; there was a photo of him in midair at the Berlin Games. The last photo showed him on the deck of a German U-boat, leaning on the port rail beside the *Fregattenkapitän*; FEHLS ZUNDER, FROGMAN, LOST AT SEA, read the caption.

There was also an unexplained photograph of dark, empty ocean, the shoreline—France? England?—in the distance. A white X had been painted on the crest of a heavy swell. The caption, ripe with irony, said: HIS LAST DIVE.

Trumper wondered where Fehls Zunder had learned to swim and dive in Stuttgart. From his fifth-floor window, Bogus contemplated a double-gainer which would have placed him precisely in the middle of a glistening puddle in the tram tracks below the hotel.

Bogus's longest dreams are about heroes. Accordingly, he dreams of Merrill Overturf sterilizing his hypodermic needle and syringe in a little saucepan, and boiling a test tube of Benedict's solution and pee to check his urine sugar. Merrill is being almost dainty in some impossibly large American kitchen; it's the kitchen at Great Boar's Head, where Bogus has never seen Merrill. Dr. Edmund Trumper is reading the newspaper and Bogus's mother is making coffee as Merrill squeezes a medicine dropper of pee into a test tube, plinking exactly eight drops into the Benedict's solution.

"What's for breakfast?" Trumper's father asks.

Merrill is watching the timer on the stove. When the little bell rings, Dr. Edmund Trumper's soft-boiled egg is done, simultaneously with Merrill's urine.

Merrill cools his pee in a fancy spice rack while Trumper's father fingers the steaming eggshell. Merrill shakes his test tube; Dr. Edmund strikes the egg a glancing blow with his butter knife. Merrill announces that his urine sugar is high. "At least two percent," he says, waving the opaque reddish mixture. "Clear blue would be negative . . ."

Something hisses. Actually, it's a large Mercedes bus below Trumper's Stuttgart window, but Bogus concludes that it's Merrill loading his syringe.

Then the three of them are sitting around the breakfast table. As Bogus's mother pours coffee, Merrill lifts his shirt and pinches up a small roll of his belly. Trumper smells alcohol and coffee as Merrill rubs his bit of fat with a cotton wad, then flicks the needle in like a dart and smoothly pushes the plunger.

Another hiss, louder than before, and Bogus rolls over and bumps into the wall of the Hotel Fehls Zunder; for a moment, the kitchen at Great Boar's Head tilts and slips off the bed. Hearing the crash, and another hiss, Trumper wakes up on the floor, with a fleeing vision of Merrill pumping himself full of air.

Now Merrill floats near the ceiling of Trumper's strange room at the Hotel Fehls Zunder, and somewhere, dimmed by the hiss of the bus doors opening and closing outside, Bogus hears his father say, "This is not a usual symptom of insulin reaction . . ."

"My urine sugar is too high!" shrieks Merrill, skidding like a helium balloon across the ceiling to the transom above the door, where Bogus sees the girlish face of a total stranger peering through one of the transom's tiny windowpanes. Actually, the glass is in splinters on the floor of Trumper's room, and the embarrassed hotel maid, on her hall stepladder, tells Trumper that she's sorry for the disturbance; she was just wiping the glass when a pane fell out.

Bogus smiles; he doesn't catch the German right away, so that the maid is forced to carry on. "It just fell right out when I was wiping it," she explains, then tells him she will come back with a broom.

Trumper dresses himself in the bedsheet; draped in it, he moves suspiciously to his window, trying to locate the real hiss. Whether the Mercedes bus looks so new and shiny and inviting, or whether he actually notes how much money he has, he splurges and takes such a bus to Munich—riding high and drowsily on the sightseeing deck through Bavaria; dreaming vaguely a sort of stepped-up cycle to Overturf's careless treatment of his diabetes. Merrill shooting the insulin, watching his urine sugar plummet; Merrill suffering an insulin reaction on a Vienna *Strassenbahn,* jangling the dog tags around his neck until the conductor, who's about to throw this weaving drunk off the tram, reads the bilingual messages printed on the tags:

> *Ich bin nicht betrunken!*
> I am not drunk!
>
> *Ich habe Zuckerkrankheit!*
> I have diabetes!

Was Sie sehen ist ein Insulinreaktion!
What you're seeing is an insulin reaction!

Füttern Sie mir Zucker, schnell!
Feed me sugar, quick!

Merrill gobbles sugar, Lifesavers, mints, orange juice and chocolate, raising his fallen sugar count so that he's out of insulin reaction and headed in the opposite direction, toward acidosis and coma. Which requires that he take more insulin. Which starts the cycle over again. Even in dreams, Trumper exaggerates.

Coming into Munich, Bogus tries to be objective; he unearths his tape recorder and on the bus records this statement: "Merrill Overturf and other irregular people are unsuited to conditions demanding careful routines. Diabetes, for example . . ." (Thinking, Marriage, for example . . .)

But before he can shut the recorder off, the man next to him asks in German what Trumper is doing, fearful, perhaps, of an interview. Feeling the tape is already botched, and sure that the man understands only German, Trumper keeps the tape running and replies in English, "Just what is it, sir, that you have to hide?"

"I speak English rather quite some well," the man replies, and they ride in deathly silence into Munich.

To make peace, at the bus terminal Bogus lightly asks the offended passenger who Fehls Zunder was. But the man expresses some distaste for the question; not answering, he hurries off, leaving Bogus to endure the stares of several nearby eavesdroppers, for whom the name Fehls Zunder seems to have rung an unpleasant bell.

Feeling foreign, Trumper wonders, with considerable surprise, What am I doing here? He bumps awkwardly along a strange Munich street, suddenly unable to translate the German shop signs and voices garbling around him, imagining all the terrors that could be taking place in America at this moment. A run-amok tornado lashing the Midwest lofts weighty Biggie forever out of Iowa. Colm is buried by a blizzard in Vermont. Cuthbert Bennett, drinking in his darkroom, accidentally swallows a highball glass of Microdol-X, retires to the seventeenth bathroom and flushes himself out to sea. While Trumper, isolated from these dreadful events, drains a heavy beer in the Munich Bahnhof, having decided to take the train from here to Vienna. He is aware that he's been waiting for the point in his trip when he'll be suddenly exhilarated, struck with the adventure of returning.

It's not until he arrives, still unfeeling, in Vienna that he considers the possibility that adventure is a time and not a place.

He wandered down the Mariahilferstrasse until the awkwardness and weight of his tape recorder and the other items in his duffel wearied him into waiting for a *Strassenbahn*.

He got off the tram at Esterhazy Park, near which, he remembered, there was a large secondhand shop; here he bought a secondhand typewriter with odd German symbols and umlaut keys. For his purchase, the shopkeeper agreed to give him a generous exchange of schillings for his German marks and U.S. dollars.

Trumper also bought an ankle-length overcoat; the epaulettes had been torn off the shoulders, and there was a neat, small bullet hole in the back, but otherwise it was in stunning shape. He proceeded to outfit himself as a sort of postwar spy, in a baggy, broad-shouldered suit, several yellow-white shirts and a six-foot purple scarf. The scarf could be arranged in various ways and made a tie unnecessary. Then he bought a suitcase with more straps and buckles and thongs than it had room. But it fitted with the rest of his attire. He looked like a traveling spy who had been a passenger on the Orient Express between Istanbul and Vienna since 1950. Finally, he purchased a hat like the one Orson Welles wore in *The Third Man.* He even mentioned the film to the shopkeeper, who said he must have missed that one.

Bogus sold the duffel for about two dollars, then lugged his recorder, extra shirts and the new typewriter in the spy's suitcase through Esterhazy Park, where he ducked into a large bush to pee. His rustling in the hedges alarmed a passing couple. Her look was anxious: A girl is being raped, or worse! His reaction was a sneer: A couple with no better place to do it. Trumper emerged from the hedge alone and with great dignity, lugging the suitcase in which a severed body could be stuffed. Or was he a parachutist who had just made a quick change out of uniform, his dismantled bomb safely hidden in the suitcase, now making his casual way to the Austrian Parliament?

The couple hurried away from his ominous costume, but Bogus Trumper felt just right. He felt the way he ought to look for an Overturf hunt through Vienna.

He took another *Strassenbahn* to the Inner City, riding around to the Opera Ring and leaving the tram at Kärntner Strasse, the city's biggest nighttime alley, smack downtown. If I were Merrill Overturf, *if I were still in Vienna,* where would I be on a Saturday night in December?

Trumper stalks quickly through the little streets off the Neuer Markt, looking for the Hawelka, the old Bolshevik *Kaffeehaus* still popular with assorted intellectuals, students and opera cashiers. The coffeehouse gives him the same cold shoulder he remembers—the same lean hairy men, the same big-boned sensual girls.

Nodding to an apparent prophet at the table by the door, Bogus thinks, Years ago there was one like you, dressed all in black, but his beard was red. And Overturf knew him, I think . . .

Trumper asks the fellow, "Merrill Overturf?"

The man's beard seems to freeze; his eyes dart as if his mind is remembering all the codes it ever learned.

"Do you know Merrill Overturf?" Bogus asks the girl who's sitting nearest the frozen beard. But she shrugs, as if to say that if she did, it hardly matters now.

Another girl, a table away, says, "*Ja,* he's in films, I think."

Merrill in films?

"Films?" says Bogus. "*Here,* you mean? In films here?"

"Do you see a camera running?" asks the fellow with the beard, and a waiter passing between them cringes at the word *Kamera.*

"No, here—in Vienna, I mean," Trumper says.

"I don't know," says the girl. "Just films, is all I heard."

"He used to drive an old Zorn-Witwer," Trumper says to no one in particular, searching for identifying marks.

"*Ja?* A Zorn-Witwer!" a man with thick glasses says. "A 'fifty-three? A 'fifty-four?"

"*Ja?* A 'fifty-four!" Bogus cries, turning to the man. "It had an old gearshift that slid in and out of the dash; it had holes in the floorboards— you could see the road moving. It had lumpy upholstery . . ."

He stops, seeing several Hawelka customers observing his excitement. "Well, where is he?" Trumper asks the man who knows Zorn-Witwers.

"I knew the *car,* was all I said," the man answers.

"But *you've* actually seen him . . ." Bogus turns back to the girl.

"*Ja,* but not in a while," she says, and the boy she's with gives Bogus an irritated stare.

"How long since you've seen him?" Bogus asks her.

"Look," the girl says, annoyed. "I don't know any more about him. I just remember him, is all . . ." Her tone silences those around her.

Trumper stares at her, disappointed; perhaps he begins to sway, or else his eyes roll, because a high-bosomed, thick-maned girl with neon-green eyeshadow catches his arm, pulling him down to her table.

She asks, "You have problems?" He tries to pull away, but she coaxes him more gently. "No, seriously, what is the problem?" When he doesn't respond, she tries him in English, even though he's spoken German all along. "You have troubles, do you?" She trills the word "troubles" in such a way that Bogus sees it floating, like a written word: Tttrrrubbles.

"You need help?" the girl asks, returning to German.

There's a waiter near them now, darting nervously. Trumper remembers that the waiters at the Hawelka always seemed fearful of tttrrrubbles.

"You sick?" the waiter asks. He takes Trumper's arm, causing him to strain against the girl's grip and drop his laden suitcase. It makes an unlikely *clank,* and the waiter backs off, awaiting the explosion. People nearby eye the suitcase as if it's stolen or lethal, or both.

"Please, just talk to me," says the neon-green girl. "You can tell me everything," she claims. "It's all right." But Bogus gathers up his suitcase, looking away from this fierce female . . . who would make a fine Den Mother for some Erotic Club.

Everyone stares while Trumper checks to see if his fly is closed. He distinctly remembers removing a condom . . .

Then he's out of there, not quite escaping the prophecy of the strange bearded fellow in black near the door. "It's around the corner," says the prophet with such conviction that Bogus shudders.

He turns out on the Graben, cutting toward Stephansplatz. It wasn't around *that* corner, he reassures himself, thinking that the prophet must have been speaking figuratively, which is the safe and sneaky way all prophets speak.

He means to look next for Merrill in the Twelve Apostles' Keller, but he loses his way and ends up in the Hohner Markt, all of whose wooden vegetable and fruit stands are tarpaulined for the night; he imagines the venders asleep under the canvas. The place looks like an outdoor morgue. The Twelve Apostles' Keller always was a bitch to find.

He asks a man for directions, but it's clearly the wrong person to ask; the man just gawks at him.

"Kribf?" he says, or something like that. Trumper doesn't understand. Then the man makes certain odd motions, as if reaching into his pockets for smuggled watches, fake meerschaum pipes, dirty pictures or a gun.

Bogus runs back to Stephansplatz and up the Graben. Finally, he stops under a streetlight to read his watch; it's past midnight, he's sure, but he can't remember how many time zones he's crossed since Iowa, or even if he's thought about this before and already corrected his watch. It says it's two-fifteen.

A well-dressed woman of uncertain age comes toward him on the sidewalk, and he asks her if she has the time.

"Sure," she says, and stops beside him. She is wearing a rich-looking fur coat, with her hands in a matching muff; and fur boots, with heels, which she shifts. She stares at Trumper, puzzled, then extends her elbow to him. "It's this way," she says, a little annoyed that he hasn't taken her arm.

"The time?" he says.

"Time?"

"I asked, 'Do you have the time?' "

She stares, shakes her head, then smiles. "Oh, the *time*—what time is it?" she says. "The *hour,* you mean?"

Then he realizes that she's a whore. He's on the Graben, and the first-district prostitutes cover the little streets off the Graben and the Kärntner Strasse at night.

"Uh," he says, "I'm sorry. I don't have the money. I just wondered, did you know what time it is?"

"I don't have a watch," the prostitute tells him, looking both ways along the street; she doesn't want to discourage a potential customer by being seen with Trumper. But no one's around except another prostitute.

"Is there a pension near here?" Bogus asks. "Not too expensive."

"Come on," she says, and walks off ahead of him to the corner of

Spiegelgasse. "Down there." She points to a blue neon light. "The Pension Taschy." Then she walks away, heading down the Graben toward the other prostitute.

"Thank you," Bogus calls after her, and she waves her muff over her shoulder, exposing for a second one ungloved, elegant, long-fingered hand with winking rings.

In the lobby of the Pension Taschy are two other prostitutes who have stepped in out of the cold and stand stamping their boots, slapping their pink calves together. In the light of the lobby, eyeing Trumper's long-traveled mustache and suitcase, they don't bother to smile.

―――――――

From the window of his room at the Taschy, Trumper can see one side of the mosiac roof of Saint Stephen's Cathedral, and also watch the whores clicking down his street to catch a late bite at the American Hamburger Spa a block up the Graben from Spiegelgasse.

At this apparently late hour the prostitutes are bringing few customers to the Taschy, where they're provided with a few dozen rooms on the second floor. But Trumper can hear them guiding men through the halls below him and see them escorting men down the Spiegelgasse sidewalk to the lobby.

One by one, the men depart alone, and Trumper hears the flushing of the second-floor bidets. It's this late-hour plumbing that makes him bold enough to ask Frau Taschy if he can take a bath. Reluctantly she draws him one, then waits outside the bathroom while he splashes about—*listening, to make sure I don't draw another drop.*

―――――――

Bogus was ashamed of the color of the bath water and hastily pulled the plug, but Frau Taschy heard the first thick gurgle and from the hall cried that she'd attend to the cleaning up. Embarrassed, he left her his ring to scrub, but couldn't help noticing the slight catch in her breath when she viewed it.

Frau Taschy had been pleasant enough when he'd registered, but as he stepped clean and chilled into his room, he noticed she'd done more than turn down his bed. His suitcase had been opened and the contents were neatly arranged on the broad window seat, as if the Frau had taken a careful inventory in preparation for an outstanding debt.

Though the room was unheated, he felt drawn to sit down for a moment at his new typewriter and try out all those funny umlauts. He wrote:

My room at the Taschy is three floors up, one block down Spiegelgasse from the Graben. The first-district whores use the place. They are first-class. I stay with nothing but the best.

Then Frau Taschy interrupted him, reminding him of the lateness of the hour and that his typing was noisy, but before he could ask her what late hour it was, she crept off. He heard her pause on the stair landing, and when she descended he resumed his typing:

Frau Taschy, an old hand at estimating a lodger's fate, can decipher pending doom from rings left in bathtubs.

Then he typed three lines of German diphthongs and attempted to write the typing-test sentence about the quick brown fox and the lazy dog, using only umlaut vowels. Or was it a lazy frög?

Listening for Frau Taschy, he heard another bidet flush and remembered the whores. He wrote:

In Vienna, prostitution isn't simply legal; it's both aided and controlled by law. Every whore is issued a sort of license to practice, renewable only with regular medical checkups. If you're not a registered prostitute, you can't legally be one.

Merrill Overturf used to say, "Don't ever buy until you see their safety stickers."

Just as officially, uncertain hotels and pensions in each district are licensed to handle the trade. Prices are supposedly fixed for both hotels and whores, and the first district has the youngest, prettiest and most expensive of them. As you move away from the Inner City, the whores in the outer districts grow older, uglier and more economical. Overturf was fond of remarking that he lived on a fifteenth-district budget.

Then Bogus got bored with writing and went to his window and watched the sidewalk. Below was the whore with the fur coat and matching muff. He tapped the double-pane window and she looked up. He turned his face back and forth in the window for her to see, trying to catch just enough light from his night table to show her who he was, thinking that from below he must resemble some embarrassed exhibitionist not quite daring to hold still.

But she recognized him and smiled up at him. Or she smiled out of habit, recognizing him only as someone simply male, summoning her inside. She pointed up to him and wagged her finger; again he saw the bright, bejeweled hand. When she started for the door, Trumper tapped fiercely on the glass: No, no! I'm not calling you inside. I was just saying hello . . . But she looked as if she took his wild tapping for excitement, and she actually skipped, tossing her face up to him. From a distance he couldn't see a trace of her make-up; she might have been a flirting cheerleader agreeing to a ride home after the game.

He thumped out into the hall, still wearing his towel; it rose over his navel when he straddled the stairwell and caught the draft of the closing lobby door below. He recognized the woman's hand on the banister, sliding up to the first landing. When he called down to her, her head jutted out of the stairwell and she looked right up his skirt, giggling like a fresh girl.

He shouted, "*Nein!*" But she moved up another landing, and he shouted, "*Halt!*" Again her face darted into the stairwell space and he pinched his towel together with his knees. "I'm sorry," he told her. "I didn't mean for you to come up." Her mouth turned down at one corner, causing sudden crow's feet to delta from her eyes; now she looked in her thirties, perhaps forties. But she kept coming.

Trumper stood like a statue, and she stopped a step below him, breathing in short, perfumed gasps, the outdoors cold still radiating off her clothes, her face nicely flushed. "I know," she said. "You only wanted to ask me the *time?*"

"No," he said. "I recognized you. I just tapped on the window to say hello."

"Hello," she said. Now she exaggerated her breathing, leaning on the banister, growing older in front of him, *just to make me feel especially bad.*

"I'm sorry," Bogus told her. "I don't have anything to give you."

She stared at his towel and touched the corners of her mouth. She really was quite lovely. In the first district, they often are. Not so whorish; more elegance than burlesque. Her coat was nice; her hair was simple and looked clean; her bones had taste.

"Really, I would like to," Bogus said.

Again she stared cruelly at his towel, and said—too sweetly, playing a mock mother to him—"Put some clothes on. Do you want to catch a cold?"

Then she left. He followed her nice hand along the banister all three flights down, then padded back to his typewriter; he was about to command his keys to be lyrical, to make some unembarrassed statement of self-pity, when he was interrupted by one more flushing bidet below, and by Frau Taschy scratching outside his door. "No more typing, please," she said. "People are trying to sleep."

People are trying to screw, she meant. His typing disturbed their rhythm or their consciences. But he didn't touch his funny foreign keys; they could prepare their lyrics overnight. Looking down on Spiegelgasse he observed the whore he'd twice misled arm in arm with another prostitute, headed for a coffee break. He thought about how the years must be for them, pacing young and glittering along the Kärntner Strasse and the Graben, then moving out, district by district, year by year, past the Prater amusement park and along the dirty Danube, getting mauled by factory workers and technical high school students for half the fare they had once charged. But it was at least as fair as the real world, perhaps fairer, because the district you ended up in wasn't always a predictable downfall, and in real life you couldn't always choose a glittering beginning.

Out the window, Bogus watched the ringed woman with her muff—once more the cared-for hand animated her talk with another whore; her hand snaked out in the cold, brushed something off the other woman's cheek. A speck of soot? A tear turned to ice? Some smudge made by her last mate's mouth?

With envy, Trumper regarded this careless, real affection.

Trumper went to bed, lying rigid until he had warmed a spot. He heard a bidet flush and decided he could never fall asleep to that lonely music. He danced nude across the room, retrieved his tape recorder from the window seat and scurried back to bed. Fumbling through a box of tapes, he found his 110-220 converter, plugged in the earphone jack, and clutched the earphones to his chest to warm them. "Come in, Biggie," he whispered.

REWIND.

PLAY . . .

23

Taking It Personally

(Fade in: A medium shot of the Pillsburys' boathouse, exterior, and the ramp leading down to the ocean. Cuthbert Bennett is scraping down an old rowboat like the ones whaling men used, and Colm is helping him. They're talking animatedly to each other—presumably Couth is explaining the algae, kelp, barnacle and crustacean world stuck to the boat's bottom, but there is no sync sound. The voices are Ralph Packer's and Couth's)

RALPH: Let me put it another way: I mean, you're living with his wife and child. Has that put a strain on your friendship with him?

COUTH: I think it must be very hard for him—but because of what he feels for her, that's all. It's hard for him to be around her and the boy now. It's got nothing to do with me; I'm sure he's still fond of me.

CUT.

(In the Packer studio, Bogus speaks [sync sound] into camera)

BOGUS: I couldn't be happier about who she's living with. Couth is an absolutely wonderful person . . .

CUT.

(The boathouse again, with Couth and Colm, voices-over)

COUTH: I know I'm very fond of him . . .

RALPH: Why didn't the marriage work?

COUTH: Well, look, you should ask her that, really.
RALPH: I just meant you must have an opinion . . .
COUTH: Ask her. Or him . . .

CUT BACK.
(In the studio, Bogus speaks [sync sound] into camera)

BOGUS: Shit—ask her!

CUT.
(On the deck in Maine, Biggie is reading a storybook to Colm. There is no sync sound; the voices-over are Biggie's and Ralph's)

BIGGIE: Did you ask him?
RALPH: He said to ask you.
BIGGIE: Well, I'm sure I don't know. I know that even if I knew why, it couldn't change anything, so what does it matter?
RALPH: Who left whom?
BIGGIE: What does it matter?
RALPH: Shit, Biggie . . .
BIGGIE: He left me.

CUT BACK.
(Bogus in the studio)

BOGUS: Well, she asked me to leave. No, actually, she *told* me to . . .

CUT.
(Biggie is sitting with Colm and Couth around an outdoor table under a large umbrella set up on the Pillsburys' dock. It is a deliberately formal, stilted scene, and the three of them look distrustfully at the camera. There is sync sound; Ralph [offstage] is interviewing them)

BIGGIE: I had no idea he was going to stay away, for so *long,* I mean . . .
COUTH: She had no idea where he was, even.
BIGGIE *(looking hard at camera, speaking to Ralph angrily)*: You knew more than anyone, you bastard. You knew where he was going—you even helped him! Don't think I don't remember . . .

CUT.
(Ralph Packer in the editing room of his studio, running film strips through a machine. Other strips clipped to rods overhead hang down all around him. There is no sync sound)

RALPH *(voice-over)*: That's true . . . I knew where he was going, all right, and I helped him to leave. But he *wanted* to leave!

(He pushes the heavy splice lever of the machine down emphatically)

CUT.

(The first in a series of still photographs. Bogus and Biggie in an Alpine village, leaning against a strange old car and smiling at the photographer. Biggie looks sexy in her stretch ski clothes)

RALPH *(v.o.)*: He went back to Europe, that's where he went. Maybe he was nostalgic . . .

(Another still: Biggie and Bogus clowning in a big rumpled bed, the covers pulled up to their chins)

RALPH *(v.o.)*: He never made it clear why he went to Europe, but he mentions this friend he had . . . a Merrill Overturf.

(Another still: A strange-looking fellow wearing a weird hat is sitting in an old Zorn-Witwer, '54, grinning at the camera out his rolled-down window)

BIGGIE *(v.o.)*: That's him, all right. That's Merrill Overturf.

CUT BACK.
(The table and umbrella on the dock. With sync sound, Biggie speaks into camera)

BIGGIE: Merrill Overturf was absolutely crazy, completely mad.

CUT BACK.
(Bogus in the studio [sync sound])

BOGUS: No! He wasn't; he wasn't crazy at all. She never really knew him like I did. He was about the most sane person I've ever known . . .

CUT BACK.
(In the editing room, Ralph raises the splice lever and looks through more film strips)

RALPH *(v.o.)*: It's very hard to get anything very concrete out of him. He takes it all so *personally.* He can really be uncooperative sometimes . . .

(He chomps the splice lever down again)

CUT.
(Sync sound. A dazzling series of stage lights are set up outside the closed bathroom door in Tulpen's apartment. Inside the bathroom a toilet flushes. Kent moves into frame, waiting in ambush at the bathroom door with a big microphone in his hand. Bogus opens the door, zips up his fly, looks up surprised into camera. He is angry; he bats Kent aside and glares at camera)

BOGUS *(yelling, his face distorted)*: Would you fuck off, Ralph!

24

How Far Can You Get
with an Arrow in Your Tit?

It warmed his heart to find Overturf still listed in the phone book at the same address, with the same number. But when he tried to call from the lobby of the Taschy, there was a strange whirring cry over the phone, some sort of signal. He asked Frau Taschy, who informed him that the noise meant that the number was no longer in service. Then he realized that the phone book was more than five years old, and that his own name was listed in it—at the same address, with the same number.

Trumper walked to Schwindgasse 15, apartment 2. A brass nameplate on the door said: A. PLOT.

Rather like Merrill, Bogus thought. Beating on the door, he heard scuffles, perhaps a growl. He pushed and the door opened, but only so far as the ball-and-chain device would let it. It was fortunate that it didn't open further, because the large German shepherd inside the apartment was only able to get the tip of his snarling muzzle in the crack of the door. Trumper jumped back unbitten, and a woman—blond, her hair in curlers, her eyes angry or frightened or both—asked him what in hell he meant by trying to sneak into her apartment.

"Merrill Overturf?" he said to her, standing well back on the landing in case she let her German shepherd out.

"You're not Merrill Overturf," she told him.

"No, of course, I'm not," he said, but she closed the door. "Wait!" he cried after her. "I just wanted to know where he was . . . ." But he heard her voice speaking low, presumably on the phone, and left quickly.

Out on the Schwindgasse, he looked up at what had once been Overturf's famous window box. Merrill had grown pot in it. But now the window box contained only some purplish dead plants poking out through a dusting of snow.

A child wheeled her tricycle up to the lobby door and got off to open it. Bogus helped her.

"Does Merrill Overturf live in this building?" he asked her. She either caught his accent or had been told never to speak to strangers, because she looked at him as if she had no intention of answering.

"Where do you think Herr Overturf went?" he asked her gently, helping

her get her trike inside. But the little girl just stared at him. "Herr Overturf?" he said to her slowly. "Do you remember? He had a funny car, he
wore funny hats . . ." The little girl didn't appear to know anything.
Upstairs the big dog barked. "What happened to Herr Overturf?" Bogus
tried once more.

The little girl was edging her tricycle away from him. "Dead?" she asked
him; it was a guess, he felt sure. Then she ran away, streaking towards the
stairs, leaving him with a chill equaled only by the one he felt when he heard
a door open above, heard the woman with the haircurlers yelling at the
child, heard the clatter of what had to be the big dog's toenails coming
downstairs.

Trumper fled. The little girl didn't know anything anyway; that was clear.
With some astonishment, he realized that the father of the child must be
named A. Plot.

With a bag of sidewalk-roasted chestnuts, Bogus slouches in the general
direction of the Michaelerplatz, where there's a grotesque statue he remembers. A Zeus-like giant of a man, or a god, is struggling with sea monsters,
snakes, birds of prey, lions and young nymphets; they are dragging him
down to the main spigot of a fountain that splashes his chest; his mouth
gapes in strain—or perhaps he is thirsty. The whole work is so overwrought
that it's hard to tell whether Zeus is in control, or whether the creatures
draped around him are wrestling him down or trying to lift him up.

Bogus recalls weaving through the Michaelerplatz one night, drunk with
Biggie. They had just swiped some huge white radishes as long as carrots
off a horsecart. Passing by this monstrous eternal struggle in the fountain,
Bogus boosted Biggie up and she placed a radish in the gaping god's mouth.
For energy, she said.

Thinking he'll feed the wrestler a chestnut, Trumper is surprised to find
the fountain shut off. Or the spigot has frozen; it spouts a thick, blunt
phallus, a rigid, wax-gobbed candle, and the Zeus figure's chest is layered
with ice. Somehow, though the pose is the same, the struggle appears to be
over. He's dead, thinks Bogus, and there's no point in feeding chestnuts to
the dead. He regrets the demise of the god, finally conquered by the snakes
and sea monsters, lions and nymphets. Trumper knows: It was the nymphets who finally got to him.

Surely Biggie would be miserable to hear the news. Surely she *is* miserable.

*Biggie, it may be hard for you to believe this, but . . . when you go duck
hunting, you wear a condom. It's an old sportsman's trick against the cold.
You see, all the duck hunters slip on a condom before they go retrieving fallen
birds from icy waters—when they don't have dogs, which we didn't. It works
on the same principle as a wet suit . . .*

Or—wandering now through the Habsburgs' courtyard, the Plaza of Heroes—*the reason I was wearing that unmentionable rubber, which I neglected to remove, was because of my new part-time job as a demonstration model for the Student Health Service's class for freshmen in Sex Education. I was too embarrassed to tell you about it. They hadn't told me there would be a session on contraception. Of course the class was surprised.*

But Bogus feels the cold eyes of the stony cupids on him; passing under these Baroque cherubs and the pigeons perched on the formidable palace buildings, he knows that Biggie is no sucker. *She is already too familiar with the improbability of me.*

He watches the *Strassenbahnen* tilting along the Burg Ring, their sharp bells gonging at the intersections. Inside, the streetcar passengers steam and smear the windows, and the men look like overcoats hung on a clothes rack with people in them. They jostle and sway with every lurch of the tram; their hands on the overhead rails are above the windows, and Bogus can see only that their arms are raised, like children in school, like soldiers at a rally.

Wanting to kill the afternoon, Trumper reads his way around a tattered kiosk. The afternoon, he feels, would die most painlessly at some Sunday matinée for kids, and miraculously he finds one, up Stadiongasse and behind the Parliament building.

There are many short subjects and an American Western. Trumper travels to Ireland, sees the happy peasants. In Java the travel guide tells the audience about the national pastime: boxing with your feet. But Bogus and the children are restless; they want the Western. And here it comes at last! Jimmy Stewart, speaking German, almost in time with the dubbed-in German voice. The Indians did not want the railroad. That was the plot.

Jimmy Stewart pumped a carbine from his hip, and it might have been a pre-ravaged Shelly Winters with an arrow sunk in her ample bosom. Whoever she was, she rolled off the caboose, down a gully, into a creek where she was trampled by wild horses—just passing by—and lecherously mauled by an Indian who was too chicken to attack the train. She was forced to endure all these things until she could locate the derringer stuffed in her bleeding cleavage, with which she blew a large hole through the Indian's throat. Not until then did she stand upright and sodden, all the creek- and blood-soaked parts of her garments clinging to her, and yell, *"Hilfe!"*—all this while wrenching away at the arrow stuck in her heaving tit.

Stopping for a greasy sausage and a glass of new wine, Trumper sat in the Augustiner Keller listening to an ancient string quartet and reflecting that Hollywood stunt women would be very interesting to meet, but that he hoped not all of them had hair in their cleavage.

As he walked back to the Taschy, the street lamps came on, but spastically, fading on and off, without a trace of the clockwork precision of Iowa City; as if Viennese electricity was a recent, unsure improvement over gas.

Outside a *Kaffeehaus* on Plankengasse, a man spoke to him. *"Grajak ok bretzet,"* he seemed to say, and Trumper paused, trying to place this queer language. *"Bretzet, jak?"* the man said, and Trumper thought, Czech? Hungarian? Serbo-Croatian? *"Gra! Nucemo paz!"* man shouted. He was angry about something and waved his fist at Trumper.

Bogus asked, *"Ut boethra rast, kelk?"* Old Low Norse never hurt a soul.

"Gra?" the man said suspiciously. *"Grajak ok,"* he added with more confidence. Then he shouted eagerly, *"Nucemo paz tzet!"*

Bogus was sorry he didn't understand, and began to say in Old Low Norse: *"Ijs kik—"*

"Kik?" the man interrupted, smiling at Bogus. *"Gra, gra, gra! Kik!"* he cried, trying to shake Trumper's hand.

"Gra, gra, gra!" replied Bogus, and shook hands with the man who weaved and mumbled, *"Gra, gra,"* nodding with greater conviction before he turned away and stumbled off the curb, veering across the street stooped over; like a blind man groping for the opposite sidewalk, he aimed his feet and protected his crotch with his hands.

Bogus thought that it had been like a conversation with Mr. Fitch. Then he glumly noted a crumpled scrap of newspaper on the sidewalk; it was unreadable, printed in what looked like the Cyrillic alphabet, the letters looking more like music than parts of words. He looked around for the little man, but there wasn't a trace of him. The article, torn from some paper in the queer language, looked important—phrases underlined with a ballpoint pen, comments scribbled emphatically in the margins in the same script— so he pocketed the strange scrap.

Trumper felt his mind floating. Back at the Taschy, he tried to focus on something familiar enough to bring it back home. He attempted to write a review of the Western movie, but his typewriter's umlaut keys distracted him, and he found that he'd forgotten the film's title. *How Far Can You Get with an Arrow in Your Tit?* Just then, as if by association, the bidets downstairs began their nightly flushing.

Bogus caught his own reflection in the ornate French window reaching nearly to the ceiling; he and his typewriter occupied only the bottom-corner pane. In an effort to rescue his small and sinking soul, he tore the review out of his typewriter and, avoiding umlauts, tried to write to his wife.

Pension Taschy
Spiegelgasse 29
Vienna 1, Austria

Dear Biggie:

Thinking of you, Colm, and you too, Biggie—the night your navel distended in East Gunnery, Vermont. You were in your eighth month, Big, when your bellybutton turned inside out.

We rode three hours from Great Boar's Head in Couth's old airy Volkswagen, with the sunroof missing. In Portsmouth it was cloudy; and in Manchester, Peterborough and Keene, it was cloudy too. And in each place, Couth said, "I hope it doesn't rain."

Three times I traded seats with you, Big. You were not comfortable. Three times you said, "Oh, God, I'm so *big!*"

"Like a full moon," Couth told you. "You're lovely."

But you bitched away, Biggie—still smarting, of course, over my father's crude manner of referring to our lewd and irresponsible mating.

"Think of it this way," Couth told you. "Think how happy the baby will be having parents so close to its own age."

"And think of the *genes,* Big," I told you. "What a masterful bunch of genes!"

But you said, "I'm tired of thinking about this baby."

"Well, you two will be together this way," Couth said. "Think of all the decisions you don't have to make now."

"There wouldn't have been *any* decisions," you told poor Couth, who was only trying to cheer you up. "Bogus would never be marrying me if I wasn't going to have this baby."

But all I said was, "Well, here we are in Vermont," looking up through the hole in the roof at the rusty girders of the bridge over the Connecticut.

You wouldn't let it drop, though, Biggie, even though we'd had this conversation several times before, and I wasn't about to be drawn into it again.

You said to me, "Bogus, you wouldn't have married me, ever. I know it."

And Couth, bless him, said, "Then *I'd* have married you, Biggie—at full moon, half moon or no moon at all. I'd have married you, and I still would, if Bogus wasn't going to. And think what that would have been like, now I ask you . . ." Then, hunched over the wheel, he turned his fabulous smile to you—showing you how he could manipulate with his tongue his front-four false teeth.

Which at least put a small smile on your face, Biggie. You were a little less pale when we got to East Gunnery.

But in the Pension Taschy, Bogus was distracted when he thought of East Gunnery. Reading over what he'd written, he decided he didn't like it. The tone seemed wrong to him, so he tried again, beginning after the line, ". . . when your bellybutton turned inside out."

We hid Couth and his Volkswagen in the lower field and walked up the long dirt driveway to your father's farm. Here comes the child bride, with a bundle in her belly! And I suspect I accused you of cowardice for not writing some word of this to your parents.

"I wrote them about you, Bogus," you told me. "Which is more than you ever warned your parents."

"Only not about your condition, Big," I remarked. "You said nothing about that."

"No, not about that," you said, tugging your tight raincoat away from yourself, trying to create the illusion that your coat was swollen only because you had your hands in your pockets.

I looked back at Couth, who waved a little fearfully, looming out of his sunroof like some hairy human periscope.

"Couth can come up to the house too," you said. "He doesn't have to hide in the field." But I told you that Couth was shy and felt better hiding in the field. I didn't mention that I thought we might appear more forgivable if we walked in alone, or that it would be nice to know that Couth and his car were safe in the pasture, in case I had to leave.

The most anxious time, I think, was when, passing by your father's jeep, you said, "Oh, my father's home too. God, Father, Mother, *everybody!*"

Then I reminded you that it was Sunday.

"Then Aunt Blackstone is here too," you said. "Aunt Blackstone is quite deaf."

They were eating dinner, and you kept your hands in your raincoat pockets, twirling your coke-bottle shape around the dining-room table, saying, "This is Bogus. You know, I *told* you! I *wrote* you!" Until your mother began to glide her eyes down your front, Biggie, and your deaf Aunt Blackstone said, "Hasn't Sue put on the old weight, though?" to your mother. Who stared rather stonily. And you said, "I'm pregnant." Adding, "But it's all right!"

"Yes! It's all right!" I cried out witlessly, watching your father's unmoving fork, dripping pot roast and an onion, poised an inch from his open mouth.

"It's all right," you said again, smiling at everyone.

"Of course it is," said Aunt Blackstone, who hadn't really heard.

"Yes, yes," I mumbled, nodding.

And your deaf Aunt Blackstone, nodding back to me, said, "Certainly *yes!* All that fat German food in her, putting the old weight on. Besides, the child hasn't skied all summer!" And looking at your dumbstruck mother, Aunt Blackstone said in her shrill, clear voice, "*Gracious,* Hilda, is that any way to greet your daughter? I can remember *you* always put the old weight on and off, anytime you pleased . . ."

While at the Taschy, two bidets flushed simultaneously, and Bogus Trumper lost the memory part of his mind. And perhaps other, closely related parts of his mind, as well.

25

Getting Ready for Ralph

In the fishy dark, the turtle murk of Tulpen's apartment, Trumper sat up in bed hopping mad and as rigid as a cigar-store Indian. Lately he'd developed a habit of furious fuming. He would concentrate fiercely on not moving at all, on simulating a brooding statue. It was a sort of isometric which eventually exhausted him. He was having trouble sleeping again.

"Oh, come on, Trumper," Tulpen whispered to him. She touched his wooden thigh.

Trumper concentrated on the fish. There was a new one who especially irked him, a beige sort of blowfish whose gross practice was to smear its translucent lips against the aquarium wall and belch little trapped bubbles against the glass. Unable to escape, the gas would bounce back into the fish, which would then swell up. As it grew larger, its eyes got smaller, until suddenly the air pressure inside it would propel it away from the glass, rather like a balloon someone has blown up and then released. In reverse, the beige blowfish would careen about the tank like a rotary motor broken loose. The other fish were terrified of it. Trumper wanted to prick it with a pin at the pinnacle of its swollen state. The fish always seemed to be facing Trumper when it began to bloat itself. It was a stupid way of antagonizing the enemy; the fish should have known better.

Actually, Trumper disliked *all* the fish, and his present irritation was enough to set him to imagining how he would dispose of them. Go out and buy a terrifying fish-eating fish, an omnivore which would scour the tank of every other swimming, crawling, gliding thing—and then eat all the shells, rocks, algae, and even the air hose. Then it would gnaw its way through the glass, let the water out and die for lack of oxygen. Even better: Flopping about on the dry aquarium floor, it would have the good sense to eat itself. What an admirable omnivore! Immediately he wanted one.

The phone rang again. Trumper didn't move, and the sidewise glance darted in Tulpen's direction convinced her that she'd better not answer it, either. A few minutes before, he had answered the phone, and that call had been partially responsible for his destructive impulses toward helpless fish and for his cigar-store-Indian imitation.

It had been Ralph Packer who had called. Though Bogus and Tulpen had just gone to bed, Ralph wanted to come over right away with Kent and several thousand dollars' worth of movie equipment. He wanted some footage of Tulpen and Bogus going to bed.

"Jesus, Ralph," Trumper said.

"No, no!" Ralph said. "Just going to bed, Thump-Thump. You know, domestic stuff—bathroom routine, teeth brushing, taking off clothes, little familiar affections, shit like that . . ."

"Good night, Ralph."

"Thump-Thump, it won't take half an hour!"

Trumper hung up and turned to Tulpen. "I don't understand," he shouted, "how you ever could have slept with him."

That set a lot of things off.

"He was interesting," Tulpen said. "I was interested in what he did."

"In bed?"

"Shove it, Trumper."

"No, really!" he yelled at her. "I want to know! Did you like sleeping with him?"

"I like sleeping with you much better," she said. "I did not sustain an interest in Ralph in that way."

Her voice had some ice in it, but Trumper didn't seem to care. "You realized it had been a mistake," he prodded.

"No," she said. "I just wasn't interested in doing it any more. It wasn't any mistake. I didn't know anybody else, then . . ."

"And then you met me?"

"I stopped sleeping with Ralph before I met you."

"Why did you stop?" he asked.

She rolled over in bed so that her back was to him. "My twat fell out," she said to the wall of aquariums.

Trumper didn't say anything; he began his trance then.

"Look," Tulpen said a few minutes later. "What is it? I just didn't feel much for Ralph that way. But I liked him, and I still like him, Trumper. Just not in that way . . ."

"Do you ever think about sleeping with him again?"

"No."

"Well, *he* thinks about sleeping with you again."

"How do you know?"

"Interested?" he asked. She swore to herself and turned away from him. He felt himself turning to stone.

"Trumper?" she asked him later; he'd been still a long while. "Why don't you like Ralph, Trumper? Is it the film?"

But it wasn't that, really. After all, he could have simply refused; he could have said that it touched him too deeply. But it didn't, and he had to admit that he had an interest in it. It was not a therapeutic interest, either; he knew he was basically a ham, and he liked seeing himself in a movie.

"It's not that I don't like Ralph, exactly," he answered. She rolled over, touched his wooden thigh, and said something he didn't hear. Then . . . he thought of killing the fish, and when the phone rang again, he would have killed the first person who touched it.

He had a cramp in his back from sitting up straight for so long, and Tulpen left him alone for a while before she tried again. "Trumper? You know, you don't make love to me enough. Not nearly enough."

He thought about that. Then he thought about his pending operation, about Dr. Vigneron and the water method. "It's my prick," he said at last. "I'm going to get it fixed up so I'll be good as new."

But he liked making love to Tulpen very much, and he was worried by what she said. He thought about making love to her right now, but he had to get up to pee.

In the bathroom he studied himself in the mirror and watched the fear come into his expression when he had to pinch himself open before he could go. It was getting worse. Vigneron had been right again; you sometimes *did* have to wait a few weeks for minor surgery.

It seemed essential to him that he make love to Tulpen right away, but then—perhaps because he recognized something in his expression in the mirror—he thought of Merrill Overturf and pissed so hard that tears came to his eyes.

He was in the bathroom a long time, until Tulpen, groggy, called to him from the bed. "What are you doing in there?" she called.

"Oh, nothing, Big," he said, then tried to swallow it back.

When he came back to bed, she was sitting up, the covers tight around her, crying. She'd heard him say it, all right.

"Tulpen," he said, and tried to kiss her.

She shoved him away; she was out to get him now. "I'll tell you one thing," she said. "Old Ralph Packer never called me anyone else's name."

Trumper moved away and sat at the foot of the bed.

"And you want to know what?" she yelled. "I think it's bullshit that you don't make love to me enough because of your old prick!"

Then the beige blowfish came up to the glass again, stared at Trumper and went through its gross routine once more.

What Tulpen said was true and he knew it. What pained him worse was that this conversation wasn't new. He'd had it all before—a number of times —with Biggie. So he sat at the foot of the bed, wished for catatonia and achieved it. When the phone rang a third time, he didn't care whether it was Ralph or not. If he could have moved, he would have answered it.

Tulpen probably felt just as lonely, because she answered it. "Sure," Bogus heard her say tiredly. "Sure, come on over and make your fucking movie."

But Trumper still sat there like a stone worrying about the next transition. To be in Ralph's movie required that he get out of the movie he was in now, didn't it?

Then Tulpen put her head in his lap, her face turned up to him. It was a gesture—she had many of them—as if to say, Okay, a bridge in our complex landscape is now at least defined, though not yet crossed. Maybe it can be.

They stayed in that position for a long time, as if that were as good a way as any to get ready for Ralph.

"Trumper?" Tulpen whispered finally. "When you *do* make love to me, I really like it."

"So do I," he said.

26

"Gra! Gra!"

Just how long his mind was lost he didn't know, or how fully he'd recovered it by the time he was aware of some more writing in the typewriter before him. He read it, wondering who had written it, poring over it like a letter he'd received, or even like someone else's letter to someone else. Then he saw the dark, crouching figure in the bottom corner of his French windows and startled himself by suddenly sitting upright and moaning, while simultaneously in the mirroring window, a terrifying gnomelike replica of himself reared up and bleared like a microscopic specimen.

It was when he recognized the moan as his own that he also heard the growing commotion downstairs in the Taschy lobby, or perhaps as close as the second floor. Not remembering where he was, he opened his door and screamed some hysterical gibberish at the faces peering from the open doorways up and down the hall. Matching him terror for terror, three faces screamed back at him, and Trumper tried to identify the other noise, which was rising like fire from the second floor.

Which tape is this? When was I in an asylum?

Cautiously he crept toward the stairwell; all along the hall no one ventured out a doorway—for fear, perhaps, that he'd scream at them again.

Up the stairwell, Frau Taschy's voice reached him. "Is he dead?" she asked, and Trumper heard himself whisper, "No, I am not." But they were talking about someone else.

He moved down to the half-landing and saw a crush of people milling in the hall below. One of the whores was saying, "I'm sure he's dead. No one ever passed out on me like that—never."

"You shouldn't have moved him," someone said.

"I had to get him off me, didn't I?" the whore said, and Frau Taschy looked scornfully down the hall at a man emerging from a room, zipping his fly, carrying his shoes under one arm. The whore emerging behind him said, "What is it? What's wrong?"

"Someone died on Jolanta," someone said, and they all laughed.

"You were too much for him," said another of the ladies, and Jolanta, who was wearing only her girdle and stockings, said, "Maybe he just had too much to drink."

Along the hall, dark and head-down men burst from rooms, carrying their clothes, as darting in their movements as startled birds.

"He's too young to be dead," Frau Taschy said, which seemed to make the scurrying men sidle past her even more fearfully. It was as if they'd never thought of it before: *Fucking can be dangerous. It can even kill the young!*

Such a notion hardly came as a surprise to Trumper, who moved confidently down from the half-landing into the sex-smelling hall, as if his mind had now adjusted and accepted the creature in the window as his own reflection, or as if he were asleep. In fact, he wasn't sure that he wasn't.

The whore said, "He went cold all over. I mean *cold.*"

But in the doorway of the stricken screwer's room, Frau Taschy said, "He moved! I swear he did!"

The gathering in the hall was almost equally divided between those who moved away from the doorway and those who moved closer in order to see.

"He moved again!" Frau Taschy reported.

"Touch him!" said the whore who'd been involved. "Just feel how cold he is."

"I'm not going to touch him, you can bet your life," the Frau said. "But you just *look* and tell me he's not moving."

Trumper moved closer; over a warm, perfumed shoulder he saw through the doorway a shocking flash of nude white rump aquiver on the rumpled bed; then the doorway filled and cut off his vision.

"*Polizei!*" someone yelled, and a man carrying all his clothes in a hasty wad bolted nude from a room down the hall, looked at the crowd and then hobbled back into his room. "*Polizei!*" someone repeated as three policemen came down the hall abreast, in step—the two flanking the broader one, solidly in the middle, flicking open any closed door along the way. The one in the middle stared straight ahead and brayed, "Don't anyone try to leave."

"Look, he's sitting up," Frau Taschy remarked to the doorway.

"Where's the trouble?" the middle policeman asked.

Jolanta said, "He blacked out. He went cold, right on top of me." But when she approached the middle policeman, one of the flankers cut her off.

"Move back," he said. "Everyone move back."

"What's happened here?" the middle policeman asked. The long gloves above his wrists were creased where his wrists cocked on his hips.

"Jesus, if you'll just let me," said the whore who'd been shoved off, "I can tell you all about it."

The same policeman who'd cut her off said, "Well, do it, then."

Then Frau Taschy cried, "He's getting up! He's not dead! He never was!" But by the ensuing crash and groan, Bogus knew that the revival had been momentary.

"Oh, dear," the Frau muttered.

Then the voice came up from the floor of the room, a voice just beginning to thaw out, slow and faint through all those chattering teeth. *"Ich bin nicht betrunken"* ("I am not drunk"), the voice said. *"Ich habe Zuckerkrankheit"* ("I have diabetes").

The middle policeman parted the mob at the doorway and swaggered roughly into the room, stepping on the outstretched hand of the pale creature curled on the threshold; the other hand weakly twitched at a tinny batch of tangled dog tags hung around the creature's neck.

"Was Sie sehen ist ein Insulinreaktion" ("What you're seeing is an insulin reaction"), the creature droned. It was like a recorded voice, an answering service.

"Füttern Sie mir Zucker, schnell!" ("Feed me sugar, quick!"), the voice cried.

"Oh, sure," the policeman said. "Oh, sugar. You bet." And he stopped to lift Merrill Overturf, as limp as an empty bathrobe, off the floor.

"Sugar, he says," the policeman quipped. "He wants sugar!"

"He's a diabetic," Trumper told a whore near him, and he reached out to touch Merrill's crumpled hand. "Hello, old Merrill," Bogus said, before one of the flanking policemen, apparently misinterpreting the gesture toward the draped Overturf, dropped an elbow in Trumper's solar plexus and sent him spinning into a soft, musky lady who fiercely bit this surprise attacker in the neck. Out of breath, Bogus flayed out, trying to make words with his hands, but the two policemen pinned him against the banister and bent his head back, upside down in the stairwell. Upside down, Bogus saw Merrill carried down the stairs to the lobby. Competing with the creaking of the opening lobby door, Merrill's voice sang out, brittle and frail, *"Ich bin nicht betrunken!"* Then the lobby door shut on his high, thin wail.

Trumper fought for breath to explain. But he had only managed to grunt, "He's not drunk. Let me go with him," before one of the policemen squeezed his lips tight together, kneading them like bread dough.

Bogus shut his eyes and heard a whore say, "He's a diabetic," while one of the policemen grumbled in Trumper's ear, "So you want to go with him, do you? What do you want to get your hands on him for?" When Trumper tried to shake his head and explain through his mushed mouth that he'd only reached out to touch Merrill because he was a friend, the whore said again, "He's a diabetic. He told me. Let him go."

"A diabetic?" said one policeman. Bogus felt his pulse throb behind his eyes. "A diabetic, eh?" the policeman repeated. Then they snapped Bogus upright and took their hands off his mouth. "Are you a diabetic?" one of the policemen asked him; they both stood warily, not touching him but ready to.

"No," Bogus said, feeling his stinging mouth, then said "No" again, sure that they hadn't heard him because his mouth was full of burrs. "No, I am not a diabetic," he said more distinctly.

So they grabbed him again. "I didn't think he was one," one policeman said to the other. As they bustled him through the lobby and outside into the first shock of cold, Bogus heard the faint, tired explanation of the whore behind them, calling, "No, no . . . Jesus. *He's* not the diabetic. Oh, Christ, I just meant he told me that the *other* one was . . ." Then the lobby door shut her off and left Bogus in motion on the sidewalk, flanked by the two policemen hustling him away.

"Where are we going?" Bogus asked them. "My passport's in my room. For Christ's sake, I don't have to be treated like this! I wasn't attacking that fellow—he's my fucking friend! And he's got diabetes. Take me where he is . . ." But they just stuffed him into a green *Polizei* Volkswagen, cracking his shins on the seat-belt fixture and bending him over double to fit him the way they wanted him in the back seat. They handcuffed him to a neat little metal loop fastened on the floor in back, so that he was forced to ride with his head between his knees. "You must be crazy," he told them. "You don't care what I say." He turned his head; through the peepsight between his calf and his bent knee he could spot the policeman riding with him in the back. "You're an anus," Trumper told him. "And so's the other one." He swung his head so that he bumped the back of the driver's seat and drew out a short oath from the driver.

The back-seat policeman said, "You take it easy, okay?"

"You gaping anal pore!" Trumper told him, but the policeman only leaned forward, almost politely inquisitive, as if he hadn't quite heard. "Your mind has syphilis," Trumper said, and the policeman shrugged.

The front-seat policeman asked, "Doesn't he speak any German? I know he was speaking some German; I heard him, I think. Tell him to speak German."

Bogus felt a chill jerk his spine upward and make his hands rattle the handcuffs. I could have sworn I was speaking German!

In German Trumper shouted, "You asshole!" Too late to move his head, he saw the black hard-rubber truncheon flick in the policeman's hand.

Then he heard the radio. A voice said: "A drunk . . ." And he heard his own voice murmur, *"Ich bin nicht betrunken . . ."* Then he regretted saying anything, seeing the truncheon lash out and hearing the *thwock!* against his ribs, not really feeling it until his next breath.

"A drunk," the radio reported. He tried not to breathe again.

"Breathe, please . . ." said the radio-announcing voice. He breathed, and went cold all over.

"He went cold all over," said a recorded whore.

"You mother," Trumper mumbled. "You recorded whore . . ." And the truncheon fell across his ribs, his wrists, his kidneys and his mind.

It took him a long time to swim out to the exact place in the Danube where he could see the underwater tank. Treading water and keeping a landsight on the light at the Gelhafts Keller's dock, he saw the tank's barrel swing up to where he thought he could almost touch it, or where it was perfectly aimed to blast him. Then the tank's top hatch opened, or seemed to, or at least fluttered in the water. Who is down the tank's hatch? Wouldn't somebody be interested to know they were there? But then he thought, I am in a Volkswagen, and if there's a hole in the roof, I am safe with Couth.

Then the bidets flushed and rinsed his mind.

Just how long his mind was lost he didn't know, or how fully he'd recovered it by the time he was aware of some more writing in the typewriter before him. He read it, wondering who had written it, poring over it like a letter he'd received, or even like someone else's letter to someone else. Then he saw the dark, crouching figure in the bottom corner of his French windows, and startled himself by suddenly sitting upright and moaning, while simultaneously in the mirroring window, a terrifying gnomelike replica of himself reared up and bleared like a microscopic specimen.

When he opened the door to the hall, he was met by a sea of faces— whores with their customers, Frau Taschy and a cop.

"What's the matter?" several of them said.

"What?"

"What's the trouble here?" the cop asked.

"What were you screaming about?" Frau Taschy asked.

"Drunk," a whore whispered.

Like a recording, Trumper said, *"Ich bin nicht betrunken."*

"You were screaming, though," Frau Taschy said. The cop stepped closer, peering behind Bogus into the room.

But the cop said only, "Been writing, eh?" Trumper looked for the cop's truncheon. "What are you looking at?" the cop asked him. He had no truncheon.

Bogus stepped softly back into his room and closed his door. He stuck his finger in his eye; it hurt. He felt his neck where the whore had bitten him; he felt no pain. His wrists and ribs where he'd been whacked by the truncheon weren't tender.

Listening to the murmur in the hall outside, he packed. *They are willing the door off its hinges.* But they weren't; they were only standing there when he came out. He felt that if he didn't take charge, they would take charge of him. So he said with great dignity, "I'm leaving. It's impossible to work here with all your noise." To Frau Taschy he held out what he figured to be more than enough money, but she made up some wild tale about his having been there for a couple of months. He felt confused; with the cop right there, he thought he'd better pay her what she asked for. His passport was peeking out of the pocket of his spy suit, and when the cop asked to see it, he nodded to the pocket, making the cop reach in gingerly for it.

Then Bogus made one last check, just to be sure. "Merrill Overturf?" he said. "He's a diabetic?" But no one seemed to respond; in fact, some of the crowd looked away from him, pretending not to hear, as if their embarrassment for him was so great that they feared that at any second he would take off his clothes.

Outside, the cop followed him for a block or two—waiting, no doubt, to see if he would leap in front of a car or dive through a store window. But Bogus set a brisk pace, walking as if he had in mind some place to go, and the cop fell back and disappeared. Trumper was alone, then, circling the Graben on safe little side streets; it took him a while to locate the Kaffeehaus Leopold Hawelka, and he hesitated before going in, as if he knew everyone who would be there, even as if his search for Merrill had never really progressed beyond his first inquiries here.

Inside, he saw the nervous waiter and smiled at him. He saw the young girl who'd known Merrill in some way at some other time. He saw the heavy girl with the neon-green eyeshadow, the Head Den Mother, who was briefing a table of disciples. What he wasn't quite prepared for was the great-bearded prophet who sat almost hidden behind the door—like the toughies who check ID's in America, or the wise-ass ticket-takers at dirty movies. When the prophet spoke, he bellowed, and Bogus wheeled around suddenly to see who was shouting.

"Merrill Overturf!" the prophet boomed. "Well, did you find him?" Whether it was the volume of the voice or the fact that it rendered Trumper motionless, frozen in an awkward pivot stance, almost all the Hawelka customers seemed to think the question was directed to them; they froze too, suspended over their coffees, mired in their rummed teas, beers and brandies; fastened, unchewing, to whatever they'd been gnawing.

"Well, *did* you?" the prophet asked impatiently. "Merrill Overturf, you said, wasn't it? Weren't you looking for him? Did you find him?"

All the Hawelka waited for an answer. Bogus balked; he felt as if he were a reel of film being rewound before he was finished.

"Well?" said the neon-green girl softly. "Did you find him?"

"I don't know," Trumper said.

"You don't know?" the prophet boomed.

With a sickening sympathy in her voice, the neon-green girl begged him, "Here, come and sit, you. You've got to get this off your mind, I think. I can tell . . ."

But he whirled himself and his bulky suitcase toward the door, hitting the waiter in the groin with it and causing that natty, agile man to fold— maintaining, for just a moment, a neat balancing feat with the sliding coffees and beers on his tray.

The prophet made a grab for Bogus at the door, but Bogus slipped by him, hearing the prophet announce, "He must be on something . . ." Just before the door closed, he heard the prophet call, "Ride it out. You'll come down . . ."

Outside the Hawelka, someone in the shadows touched his hand with something like affection.

"Merrill?" Bogus asked in a whimper.

"Gra! Gra!" the man said, turning like a quarterback and thrusting a parcel, *Whunk!,* in Trumper's stomach. When he straightened up, the man was gone.

Stepping to the curb, he held the parcel up to the light; it was a firm, white-papered package, tied up with white butcher's string. He undid it. It looked like chocolate in that neon light, smooth and dark, queerly sticky to the touch; it gave off a minted smell. A mentholated slab of fudge? Queer gift. Then he bent closely over it, sniffed it deeply and touched it with his tongue. It was pure hashish, a perfectly cut rectangle slightly larger than a brick.

A clamor rose in his head as he tried to imagine what it was worth.

In the fogged-up window of the Hawelka, he saw a hand rub a peepsight out to the street. A voice inside announced, "He's still there."

So then he quickly wasn't. He didn't intend to go back out on the broad Graben; it was just the direction he happened to jog in that brought him out onto this glittery whoreful street. He crammed the hashish brick into his suitcase.

He didn't intend to speak to anyone, either; it was just that when he saw the lady in the fur coat with the matching muff, he saw she'd changed her clothes. No more fur coat, no more muff; she wore a spring suit, as if it were warm.

He asked her if she had the time.

27

How Is Anything Related to Anything Else?

Ralph was attempting to explain the structure of his film by comparing it to a contemporary novel, Helmbart's *Vital Telegrams*.

"The structure is everything," he said. Then he quoted a blurb from the book jacket which said that Helmbart had achieved some kind of breakthrough. "The transitions—all the associations, in fact—are syntactical, rhetorical, *structural;* it is almost a story of sentence structure rather than of characters; Helmbart complicates variations on forms of sentences rather than plot," it read.

Kent nodded a lot, but Ralph was more anxious that Trumper and Tulpen understand him. The comparison to Helmbart's work was supposed to cast some needed light on Tulpen's editing and Trumper's sound tracking. "Do you see?" Ralph asked Tulpen.

"Did you like that book, Ralph?" Tulpen asked.

"Not the point, not the point, not the fucking point!" said Ralph. "I'm interested in it only as an example. Of course I didn't like it."

"I thought it was awful," Tulpen said.

"It was almost unreadable," said Trumper, marching off to the bathroom with the book under his arm. In fact, he hadn't even looked at it yet.

He sat in the bathroom surrounded by messages, due to the fact that the phone was in the bathroom. Ralph had moved it there when he became suspicious of the number of long-distance calls, which none of them would admit to making. He was sure that people were dropping in off Christopher Street to make long-distance calls. They sneaked in, according to his theory, when he and Bogus and Tulpen and Kent were busy in the other rooms of the studio. But someone dropping in like that wouldn't dream of looking for the phone in the bathroom.

"Suppose they drop in to use the bathroom?" Trumper had asked.

But the phone was installed there, anyway. The walls, the flush-box lid, the mirror and the shelves were dotted with reminders, phone numbers, urgent requests and Kent's garbled translations of messages.

Taking the phone off the hook, Trumper opened *Vital Telegrams*. Ralph had remarked that the success of the structure made it possible to open the book at random and understand everything immediately, no matter where you began. Trumper opened it in the middle and read Chapter 77 from beginning to end.

CHAPTER 77

From the moment he saw her, he knew. Still, he persisted.

We felt at once that the ball-joint system was all wrong for the blivethefter. Why, then, did we force it?

The very second the goat was slain, we saw we were in for it. Pretending otherwise was absurd. Yet Mary Beth lied.

There was no sense whatsoever to the socket wrench being put to such a use. But it just might have worked.

There was nothing in the least amusing about the vile disembowelment of Charles. Strange we weren't shocked when Holly laughed.

With his feet as they were, Eddy could not have had much hope. To have seen him, though, you would have thought he still had toes.

"Don't come near me!" Estella wailed, holding out her arms.

We knew that the thought of chickpeas with bagels defied the concept of spreading. Still, they were both brown.

There was, of course, no logic to the dwarf's fear of Harold's rather large cat. But if you've ever spent some time down on your knees, you're surely aware of how differently things appear from down there.

That was Chapter 77. Curious about the vile disembowelment of Charles, Trumper read it again. He liked the bit about chickpeas and bagels. He read the chapter a third time and was irked that he didn't know what was wrong with Eddy's feet. And who was Estella?

Ralph knocked on the bathroom door; he wanted to use the phone.

"I understand the dwarf's fear of Harold's rather large cat," Trumper told him through the closed door. Ralph went away, swearing.

What Trumper had some difficulty understanding was what relation Helmbart's work had to Ralph's film. Then he thought of one: perhaps neither of them meant anything. Somehow that made him feel better about the film. Relaxed, he approached the toilet. But he was too relaxed; he'd forgotten to pinch himself open. A hose with an obstructed nozzle is difficult to aim. He pissed in his shoe, jumped back and elbowed the phone into the sink. Wincing, he awkwardly peed his way back to the toilet. In his condition, although it hurt to go, it hurt worse to stop.

So much for relaxing, he thought. He was reminded of one of the many lessons to be learned from *Akthelt and Gunnel,* the forbidding story of Sprog.

Sprog was Akthelt's bodyguard, armor bearer, valet, knife sharpener, head huntsman, chief scout, favorite sparring partner and trusted whore fetcher. When they were visiting captured towns, Sprog tasted everything that Akthelt was served before Akthelt would eat it.

Old Thak had given Sprog to Akthelt for Akthelt's twenty-first birthday.

Akthelt was more pleased by Sprog than by any of his horses, dogs or other servants. For Sprog's birthday, Akthelt gave him a highly favored captured Greth woman named Fluvia. Akthelt had been quite taken by Fluvia himself, so you can see how much he thought of Sprog.

Sprog was not a Greth. There were no captured Greth men; only Greth women were captured. Greth men were forced to dig a large pit, then were stoned senseless, flung into it and burned.

One day Old Thak had been returning from a war along the coast of Schwud when his scouts rode up to him and reported that the beach ahead was blocked by a long rowboat, in front of which stood a man holding a huge driftwood log like a light mallet. Old Thak rode ahead with his scouts to see this phenomenon. The man was only about five feet tall, with curly blond hair, but his chest seemed to be about five feet around too. He was neckless, wristless and ankleless; he was simply a great chest with almost jointless limbs and a face as featureless as an anvil topped by blond curly hair. A driftwood log two feet thick rested lightly on his shoulder.

"Ride over him," Old Thak told one of his scouts, and the man charged this strange stumpy apparition who had blocked the beach with a rowboat. The giant dwarf swung the driftwood log like a fungo bat against the horse's chest, killing the animal instantly, then tore the scout out of the tangled stirrups and folded him up, breaking his back easily. Then he picked up his driftwood racket and stood in front of his rowboat again, staring down the beach to where Old Thak was watching with the other scout.

Trumper remembered thinking that the other scout must have been shitting his pants at that moment.

But Old Thak was not so wasteful as to sacrifice another scout. He recognized great bodyguard potential when he saw it, so he sent the scout hightailing it back to the legion. Thak wanted the thing alive.

About twenty men with nets and long gaffs eventually captured the super troll who blocked the shore of Schwud. It was a lieutenant of these men who first called the creature Sprog. *Da Sprog*—a rough translation would be the Devil's Toad—a kind of super toad who impersonated the Devil, or through whom the Devil hopped around on the earth, was a fixture of their religion.

But all that was nonsense. Sprog was as easy to train as a falcon, and he became as loyal to Old Thak as Thak's best dog, Rotz. So it was a demonstration of fatherly affection when Old Thak parted with Sprog and made a gift of him to his son Akthelt.

Trumper interrupted his memory of the tale to wonder if it had been at this point in life when Sprog had begun to relax and think that he had it made. Probably not, he reflected, because Sprog suffered some kind of inadequacy complex during his first few years with Akthelt. Old Thak had been less demanding, and Sprog had found the master-dog role comfortable. But Akthelt was Sprog's own age and tended to be more familiar with servants; in fact, Akthelt liked to drink with Sprog, and Sprog no longer knew what his place was. He was very loyal to Akthelt, of course, and would have done anything for him, but he was also treated just enough like Akthelt's friend to be confused. Equality is a rare and minor theme in *Akthelt and Gunnel*, though it emerges in its typically disruptive fashion here.

One night, Akthelt and Sprog got very drunk together in the tiny village of Thith, and then staggered home to the castle through an orchard, having contests to see who could uproot the biggest trees. Sprog won, of course, and perhaps that irritated Akthelt. Whatever the reason, they were crossing the moat arm in arm when Akthelt asked Sprog if he would be hurt if Akthelt slept with Sprog's new wife, Fluvia. After all, they were friends . . .

Perhaps the confusion was suddenly lifted from Sprog's life by this proposal. He must have realized that Akthelt could have simply taken Fluvia whenever he wanted to, and maybe he thought that by asking permission Akthelt was bestowing equality on Sprog.

Which apparently Sprog was not prepared for, because he not only gleefully told Akthelt to take his pleasure with Fluvia, but went barreling off to the royal quarters to take *his* pleasure with Akthelt's Gunnel. Akthelt had said nothing whatever about that. Obviously, Sprog had read the situation wrong.

Trumper could imagine poor Sprog rocketing down the labyrinthine corridors to the royal quarters like a five-foot bowling ball. *That* was when Sprog relaxed.

Ralph came and beat on the bathroom door again, and Trumper wondered what was on his mind. He looked at the book in his hands, somehow expecting it to be *Akthelt and Gunnel*, and was disappointed when he saw it was only Helmbart's *Vital Telegrams*. When he opened the door, Ralph followed the phone cord to the sink. He didn't seem surprised to find the phone there; he dialed it in the sink, listened to the busy signal in the sink and hung up in the sink.

Jesus, I should keep a diary, Trumper thought.

That night he tried. After he had made love to Tulpen, questions were raised. Analogies leaped to his mind. He thought of Akthelt stumbling in on the dark Fluvia, who was expecting her thick Sprog. Fluvia had been frightened at first because she thought it *was* Sprog. Fluvia and Sprog had an agreement never to make love when Sprog was drunk, because Fluvia was afraid he might break her spine. There was also an untranslatable word that had to do with how Sprog smelled when he drank a lot.

But Fluvia quickly guessed who was making love to her, perhaps because her spine wasn't breaking, or by his royal odor. "Oh, my Lord Akthelt," she whispered.

Again Trumper thought of poor, deceived Sprog barreling down to the royal quarters, lusting after Gunnel. Then he thought of babies and contraceptive devices and making love to Biggie as compared to making love to Tulpen. His diary was blank.

He remembered how Biggie always forgot to take her pill. Bogus would hang the little plastic dispenser from the light cord in the bathroom so that she would think of contraception every time she pulled the light on and off, but she hadn't liked the idea of the pills hanging out in public. Whenever Ralph was in the house, she got especially angry about it. "Take your pill today, Biggie?" Ralph would ask her, coming out of the bathroom.

Tulpen, on the other hand, had an intrauterine device. Biggie, of course, had *had* an ill-fated I.U.D. in Europe, but she left it there. Trumper had to admit that there was an added something about the I.U.D. You could feel it in there, like an extra part, a spare hand or tiny finger. Every so often it poked. He liked it. It moved around, too. With Tulpen, he never knew where he was going to come in contact with the string that felt like a finger. In fact, on this particular night he hadn't come in contact with it at all. It worried him, and remembering that Biggie lost or dissolved hers, he had asked Tulpen about it.

"Your device," he whispered.

"Which device?"

"The one with the string."

"Oh, how *was* my string tonight?"

"I never felt it."

"Subtle, huh?"

"No, really, are you sure it's okay?" He worried about it often.

Tulpen was quiet under him for a while; then she said, "Everything's fine, Trumper."

"But I couldn't feel the string," he insisted. "I nearly always feel it there." Which wasn't very true.

"Everything's fine," she repeated, curling up against him.

He waited for her to fall asleep before getting up to try his hand at beginning a diary. But he didn't even know what day it was; he couldn't have guessed the date within a week. And his head seemed so cluttered with *things.* There were a million images from the film on his mind, both real and imagined. Then Helmbart's puzzling passage about Eddy's feet returned to haunt him. And there was *Akthelt and Gunnel* to consider; he couldn't seem to get beyond the image of Sprog barreling through the castle, his hopes erect.

He did manage a sentence. It didn't seem to be a diary sort of sentence; in fact, it was a real cliff-hanger of an opening line. But he wrote it in spite of himself:

"Her gynecologist recommended him to me."

What a way to begin a diary! The question struck him: How is anything related to anything else? But he had to begin somewhere.

Take for example . . . Sprog.

He watched Tulpen curl into a tighter ball on the bed; she tugged his pillow to her, scissored it between her legs and then slept quietly again. *One thing at a time.* What happened to Sprog?

28

What Happened to the Hashish?

In East Gunnery, Biggie, your mother put us in separate rooms, even though that forced your mother to sleep with Aunt Blackstone and put your father on the hall sofa. And we forgot about poor Couth waiting for word in the lower field. He spent the night in his airy Volkswagen and woke up in the morning as stiff as a spring-back chair.

But there wasn't that much unpleasantness around the dinner table after the announcement—excepting, of course, the difficulty in making deaf Aunt Blackstone understand the conditions. *"Pregnant,"* you said. "Aunt Blackstone, I'm pregnant."

"Rent?" said Aunt Blackstone. "Rent what? Who's renting? What's to rent?"

So the incriminating news needed shouting, and when Aunt Blackstone finally got it, she couldn't see what all the fuss was about. "Oh, *pregnant,"* she said. "How nice. Isn't that something?" She fixed her gaze on you, Biggie, marveling at your metabolic wonder, glad to know the young were still fertile; at least there was one thing about the young that hadn't changed.

We were all quite understanding of your mother, tolerating her taking it for granted that we sleep in separate rooms; only your father was bold enough to imply that we must have slept together at least once before, so what was being saved? But he let it drop, seeing, with the rest of us, that your mother needed to be sustained by some formality. Perhaps she felt that though her daughter had been violated and stained beyond childhood, there was no reason why her daughter's *room* couldn't remain pure. Why tarnish the teddy bears on the headboard of the bed, or all the little trolls on skis, lined up so innocently along the dresser top? Something needed to be left intact. We could all see that, Biggie.

And in the morning, we met in the bathroom. I knocked Aunt Blackstone's teeth into the sink; they chattered noisily around and around the bowl, a mouth on the roam. This made you laugh while you clipped your toenails over the tub—my first taste of domesticity.

Outside the bathroom door, your mother was nervous. "There's another bathroom upstairs," she called twice, as if she feared you could get pregnant again, have twins or worse.

And you whispered to me, Biggie, as I sloshed water into my armpits, "Do you remember, Bogus, when you tried to wash in the bidet in Kaprun?" And my member shrunk from that icy memory.

In the morning, Trumper spoke into his dream, and into the soft hair nesting on his pillow. "Do you remember . . . ?" he began, but he failed to recognize the perfume and drew back from the figure on the bed beside him.

"Remem . . ." the whore said sleepily. She didn't understand English.

After she'd gone, all he could remember of the whore was her rings, and how she'd used them. It was a game she fancied: reflecting little facets of light, caught in the many-faced stones, all over her body and his. "Kiss this one here," she'd say, indicating a flickering spot of light. When she moved her hands, the little mirrored edges of light moved with them, racing bright squares and triangles over her deep-cut navel and down her taut thigh.

She had long, lovely hands and the sharpest, quickest wrists he'd ever seen. She played a fencing game with her rings too. "You try to stop me," she said, squatting opposite him on the teetering Taschy bed while she feinted, parried and thrust her flickering wrists at him, scratching him here and there with a ring's sharp edge, but never hard enough to break the skin.

When he was on top of her, she raced her rings over his back. Once he caught a glimpse of her eyes; she was watching her rings' prism patterns chase across the ceiling as she moved under him with slight and careless shrugs.

In the Josefsplatz he stopped walking around the fountain and wondered how he'd gotten there. He tried to remember how much he'd paid the whore, or even when he had. He couldn't remember the transaction at all and checked his empty wallet for some clue.

In his suitcase, the fine smell of mentholated chocolate laced with catnip made him swoon, and he remembered the hashish brick. He imagined paying for his lunch with a sliver of it—picking up a table knife, slicing off a wafer-thin strip and asking the waiter if that would do.

In the American Express office he found himself asking for Merrill Overturf at the information counter, behind which a man tilted his puzzled head, consulted a map in front of him, then a larger map behind him.

"Overturv?" the man asked. "Where is it? Do you know the nearest town to it?"

After this was straightened out, Trumper was directed to the mail desk. There a girl firmly shook her head; American Express had no permanent mailbox in Merrill's name.

Bogus wanted to leave a note anyway. "Well, we can hold it at the desk for him," the girl told him. "But just for a week or so. Then it's a dead letter."

A dead letter? Apparently even one's words could die.

On a bulletin board in the front lobby there were little notices about all sorts of matters:

ANNA, FOR GOD'S SAKE COME HOME!

SPECIAL TELETAPE REPLAY NFL GAME OF THE WEEK/
REG. SHOWING EV. SUN. @ P.M. 2 & 4/ ATOMIC
ENERGY COMM., KÄRNTNER RING 23, WIEN I/ U.S.
PASSPORT REQUIRED.

KARL, I'M BACK AT THE OLD PLACE.

PETCHA, CALL KLAGENFURT 09-03-79 BEFORE WEDS.,
ELSE RIDE WITH GERIG TO GRAZ, MEET HOFSTEINER
AFTER 11 THURS. EVE/ ERNST

To these, Trumper added:

MERRILL, LEAVE SOME WORD FOR ME/ BOGGLE

He was standing on the Kärntner Ring sidewalk, feeling the warm, springlike weather and wondering why December felt like this, when the man with apple cheeks and a bow tie first spoke to him. The man's mouth was so plump and round that his natty mustache was almost circular. Trumper wasn't a bit surprised to hear him speak English; he looked like a gas-station attendant Trumper had known in Iowa.

"Say, are you American too?" the man asked Bogus. He reached to shake Trumper's hand. "My name's Arnold Mulcahy," he said, shaking hands with a firm grip, a rapid pump. Bogus was trying to think of something polite to say when Arnold Mulcahy jerked him right off his feet with a perfectly executed falling arm-drag. For a cherub, he moved very fast; he was behind Bogus before Bogus could get off his hands and knees and had already torn the suitcase right out of Bogus's grasp. Then he slapped a double chicken-wing on Trumper and flattened him right down to the sidewalk.

Trumper was a little dizzy as a result of encountering the sidewalk with his forehead, but he wondered if perhaps Arnold Mulcahy was an old wrestling coach he'd known. He was trying to place the name when he saw the car pull up to the curb and two men get out quickly. Someone stuck his head into Trumper's suitcase and took a deep sniff. "It's in here, all right," he said.

The car doors were all open. I'm having this dream again, Trumper thought, but his shoulders really did feel as if they were popping out of their sockets and the two men helping Arnold Mulcahy throw Bogus into the back of their car felt very real.

In the back seat, they frisked him so fast and thoroughly that they could have told him the number of teeth on his pocket comb. Arnold Mulcahy sat up front reading Trumper's passport. Then he unwrapped the hashish brick, sniffed it, touched its sticky resin and licked it with his toady tongue. "It's pure stuff, Arnie," said one of the men in the back seat with Bogus. His English was pure Alabama.

"Yup," said Arnold Mulcahy, who wrapped the hashish back up, returned it to Trumper's suitcase, and then leaned over the front seat and smiled at Bogus. Arnold Mulcahy was about forty, twinkling and plump; among other things, Trumper was thinking that Mulcahy had just executed the best falling arm-drag and double chicken-wing that he had ever had the misfortune to experience in his entire wrestling career. He was also thinking that all the men in the car were about forty, and probably American. They were not all twinkling and plump, however.

"Don't you worry, my good boy," Arnold Mulcahy told Bogus, still smiling at him. His voice was a poor nasal imitation of W. C. Fields. "Everyone knows you're quite innocent. That is to say, almost innocent. What we mean is, we haven't noticed you trying to give the dope back." He winked at the men sitting on either side of Bogus. They released his arms, then, and let him rub his sore shoulders.

"Just one question, son," Mulcahy said. He held up a little scrap of paper; it was the note Bogus had left for Merrill on the bulletin board at American Express. "Who's Merrill?" Mulcahy asked, and when Trumper just stared at him, he went on. "Would this Merrill be a prospective buyer, son?" he asked, but Trumper was afraid to talk. He thought that whoever they were they knew more than he did, and he wanted to wait and see where the car was going. "My good boy," Mulcahy said, "we know you didn't mean to get the dope, but we can only guess what you were going to do with it." Trumper didn't say a word. The car rounded the Schwartzenburgplatz, circling behind the spot where they'd picked him up. Trumper realized he'd seen too many movies; there was an astonishing similarity between the cops and the crooks, and he didn't know for sure which these men were.

Arnold Mulcahy sighed. "You know," he said, "I personally think we may have saved you from an act of crime. Your only crime so far is one of omission, but if this Merrill character is someone you were planning to sell the stuff to—now, that's another sort of crime." He winked at Bogus and waited to see if Bogus was going to respond. Bogus held his breath.

"Come on," said Arnold Mulcahy. "Who's Merrill?"

"Who are *you?*" said Bogus.

"I'm Arnold Mulcahy," said Arnold Mulcahy, who held out his hand and winked. He wanted to shake hands again, but Bogus still remembered the falling arm-drag and double chicken-wing, and he hesitated before accepting Arnold Mulcahy's firm grasp.

"Got just one more question for you, Mr. Fred Trumper," Arnold Mulcahy said. He stopped shaking Trumper's hand and suddenly looked as serious as a plump, twinkling man could look. "Why did you leave your wife?" he asked.

29

What Happened to Sprog?

He was de-balled with a battle-ax. Then he was exiled to the coast of his native Schwud. To remind him of his castration, his lewd wife, Fluvia, was exiled with him. All this was the customary punishment for sexually assaulting a member of the royal family.

When I asked her why her gynecologist recommended that she have her intrauterine device removed, she does this infuriating thing with her hot-shit tit—flipping the big bosom of hers as if to tell me that her contraceptive device, or lack of one, is entirely her business.

"*When* did he take it out?" I ask, and she shrugs, as if she can't be bothered to remember. But I can remember that it's been several times now that I haven't felt its little string touching me in there.

"Why didn't you tell me, for God's sake? I could have been using a rubber."

She mumbles casually that her gynecologist would not have recommended a rubber, either.

"What!" I scream. "Why did he recommend that you have the thing pulled out in the first place?"

"For what I wanted," she hedges, "it was the first thing that was recommended."

I still don't get it; I suspect the poor girl doesn't understand reproduction. Then I realize I do not understand the girl.

"Tulpen?" I ask her slowly. "What is it you wanted for which removing your I.U.D. was recommended?" And of course she doesn't need to answer; making me phrase the question has been enough. She smiles at me and blushes.

"A *baby?*" I say. "You want a baby?" She nods, still smiling. "You might have told me," I say, "or even asked me."

"I've already tried that," she says smugly, about to flip her tit again, I can tell.

"Well, I ought to have something to say about this, dammit."

"It will be my baby, Trumper."

"Mine too!" I scream.

"Not necessarily, Trumper," she says, flitting across the room like one of her aloof fish.

"Who else have you slept with?" I ask her, dumb.

"No one," she says. "It's just that you don't have to have any more to do with the baby than you want to." When I look skeptical, she adds, "You won't have any more to do with it than I let you, either, you shit."

Then she waltzes into the bathroom with a newspaper and four magazines, waiting for me . . . to do what?! Fall asleep? Leave her alone? Pray for triplets?

"Tulpen," I tell the bathroom door. "You might already be pregnant."

"Move on if you want to," she says.

"Jesus Christ, Tulpen!"

"There's no need to feel trapped, Trumper. That's not what babies are for."

She's in there for an hour and I'm forced to pee in the kitchen sink. Thinking, It's just two days until I'm operated on—maybe they should sterilize the whole works while they're at it.

———

But when she came out of the bathroom, she looked less tough and more vulnerable, and almost instantly he found himself wanting very much to be what she wanted him to be. He was thrown off guard by her question, though. She asked it shyly and sweetly. "If you do have much to do with the baby," she said, "if you want it, that is, would you like a boy or a girl?"

Damn him, he hated himself for remembering the crude joke Ralph had once told him. There's this girl, see, and she's just been knocked up, and she says to her boyfriend, "You wanna girl or boy, George?" George thinks for a minute and then says, "A stillborn."

"Trumper?" Tulpen asked again. "A boy or a girl? Do you care which?"

"A girl," he said. She was excited, playful, drying her hair in a big towel, flouncing around the bed now.

"Why a girl?" she asked. She wanted to keep the ball rolling; she liked this talk.

"I don't know," he mumbled. He could lie, but elaborating on the lie was hard. She held his hands, sat down on the bed in front of him and let the towel fall off her hair.

"Come on," she said. "Because you've already had a boy? Is that it? Or do you really like girls better?"

"I don't know," he said irritably.

She dropped his hands. "You don't care, you mean," she said. "You don't really care, do you?"

That left him with no place to go. "I don't want any baby, Tulpen," he said.

She frisked through her hair with the towel, which made it hard to see her face. "Well, I do want one, Trumper," she said. She let the towel drop and looked straight at him, as hard as anyone, except Biggie, had ever looked at him. "So I'm going to have one, Trumper, whether you're interested or not. And it won't cost any more than it ever has," she said bitterly. "All you have to do is make love to me."

Right then, he wanted very much to make love to her; in fact, he knew he'd *better* make love to her, quick. But what mush his mind was! His brain was well trained at evasion. He was thinking of Sprog . . .

That old horse-basher, the uprooter of trees, thumping through the royal quarters, bowling over the guard of the royal bedchamber. Then into the lavish bed. No doubt a veiled and perfumed Gunnel lay there waiting for her Lord Akthelt. Enter the five-foot toad. Did he hop on her?

Whatever he did, he didn't do it fast enough. The text reports that Gunnel was "nearly humbled by him." Nearly.

Apparently Akthelt heard Gunnel screaming all the way down in the servants' quarters as he lay deep in the lush grip of Fluvia. It never occurred to him that his lady was being attacked by Sprog; he just recognized his lady's scream. He pulled out of Fluvia, flapped on his codpiece and hot-hoofed it up to the royal quarters. There he and seven castle guards netted the thrashing Sprog and pried him loose from the fainting Lady Gunnel with the aid of several fireplace tools.

According to custom, castrations always took place at night, and the very next evening poor Sprog's balls were lopped off with a battle-ax. Akthelt did not attend the event; neither did Old Thak.

Akthelt mourned for his friend. It was several days before he even asked Gunnel if Sprog had actually . . . well, got her, if she knew what he meant. She did; Sprog had not. Somehow that made Akthelt feel even worse, which made Gunnel rather angry. In fact, Akthelt and Old Thak had to persuade her from publicly demanding that Fluvia be thrown to the wild boars.

The wild boars were in the moat, for some reason Trumper had never been able to translate; it didn't make any sense. Moats were supposed to be full of water, but perhaps this one had a leak they couldn't fix, so they had wild boars charging around in there instead. It was just another example of what a ragged old ode *Akthelt and Gunnel* was. Old Low Norse was not known for its tight little epics.

For example, the matter of the legend of Sprog isn't even brought up until pages and pages after Sprog and Fluvia are exiled to the coast of Schwud. The legend says that one day a weary, ravaged traveler passes through the kingdom of Thak and begs for a night's rest at the castle. Akthelt asks the stranger what adventures he's had—Akthelt loves a good story—and the stranger tells this ghastly tale.

He was riding on the fine white sand of the beaches of Schwud with his handsome young brother when the two of them came upon a dusky lewd wench whom they took to be some wild fisherwoman, abandoned by her tribe and hungry for a man. Therefore the stranger's young brother fell upon her there on the beach, as she clearly indicated she wanted him to, and proceeded to satisfy himself. But this only partially slaked the thirst of the wench, so the stranger himself was about to mount the wild woman when he saw his brother swiftly seized by a round, blond, beastlike man "whose chest could inhale the sea." As the stranger watched with horror, his brother was bent, broken, snapped, crunched, folded and otherwise mangled by this terrible blond god "with a center of gravity like a ball."

The beach ball was Sprog, of course, and the woman on the sand who had laughed, moaned and implored the stranger to take her quick was Fluvia.

One way to look at it was that it was nice to know they were still together after all this time, still a team. But the stranger didn't look at it that way; he ran. He ran to where he and his brother had tethered their horses.

Both animals were dead, their chests staved in. They looked as if they'd been hit by a huge battering ram, and beside them lay a log which no man could have lifted. So the stranger had to keep running, because Sprog ran after him. Luckily the stranger had once been a messenger by profession, so he could run very fast and for a long time. He ran with great long easy strides, but whenever he looked back, there would be Sprog, who was so short that he ran like a woodchuck, thumping along on his little stunted legs. But he kept up.

The stranger ran a few miles, looked back, and there was Sprog. He had no style but he had a set of lungs like a whale.

The stranger ran all through the night, stumbling over rocks, falling, getting up, straggling along unable to see. But whenever he stopped, he could hear, not far behind and coming closer, the sound of Sprog thumping along like a five-foot elephant and breathing like a winded bear.

In the morning, the stranger crossed the border of Schwud and reeled into the town of Lesk in the kingdom of Thak. He stood gasping in the town square, his head bowed and his back to what he was sure would be thumping up behind him at any minute. He stood there for hours before the kind people of Lesk took him in and gave him breakfast and told the stranger that this was why none of the young men of Lesk ever went swimming off the shore of Schwud any more.

"Da Sprog," said a young widow, making the sign of the toad on her breast.

"Da kvinna *des Sprog"* ("The *woman* of Sprog"), said a young man with only one arm who had escaped. He rolled his eyes.

That was what had happened to Sprog.

And Bogus Trumper? What had happened to him? He had fallen asleep sitting up, his chin resting on the shelf by the turtle aquarium, his brain at last lulled by the gurgle of the air hose.

Tulpen had curled up beside him on the bed for an hour, waiting for him to wake up and make love to her. He didn't wake up, though, and she had stopped waiting. She'd waited quite long enough for him, she thought, so she lay back in the bed and watched him sleep. She smoked a cigarette, though she never smoked. Then she went into the bathroom and threw up. Then she ate yogurt. She was pretty upset.

When she returned to bed, Trumper was still there, sleeping next to the turtles. Before she went to sleep herself, she got the idea that if only she could find two of those big air-horns that diesel trucks have, she could blow one in each of his ears and scramble his brains so completely that it might wipe his memory clean. She thought that would help.

She probably wasn't far wrong. It would be hard for most people to sleep with their chins on a shelf, but Bogus was dreaming about Merrill Overturf.

$$30$$

What Happened
to Merrill Overturf?

Once Trumper had read a magazine article on espionage. He remembered that the U.S. Treasury Department controls the Federal Narcotics Bureau and the Secret Service, and that the C.I.A. coordinates all government intelligence activities. This seemed plausible; at least, he wasn't worried any more.

He was in a rear office of the American Consulate in Vienna, so he supposed he wasn't going to be murdered and dumped in the Danube—not yet, anyway. If he still had any doubts about where he was, they vanished when the vice-consul intruded on them nervously.

"I'm the vice-consul," he apologized to Arnold Mulcahy, who was apparently more important than a vice-consul. "I wish to inform you about your man out there, please . . ." Arnold Mulcahy went to see what the trouble was.

According to the vice-consul, one of Mulcahy's thugs, a big man with a livid burn scar, was frightening away people who were coming to take the U.S. immigration exam. In two minutes Mulcahy returned; the man with the burn scar had come to *take* the immigration exam, he told the vice-consul with some asperity. "Let him in," he advised. "Any man that mean-looking is good for something." Then he settled down to work on Bogus Trumper.

They had the goods on Trumper, and the bads too. Did he know he was a "missing person" back in America? Did he know that his wife was wondering where he'd gone?

"I haven't been gone so long," Trumper said.

Mulcahy suggested that his wife thought he'd been gone long enough. Trumper told him who Merrill Overturf was. He said that he'd had no plans to do anything with the hashish, though he probably would have sold it if someone had come along wanting to buy. He told him that a whore had taken all his money and that he was a little uncertain about things in general.

Mulcahy nodded; he knew all this already.

Then Bogus asked him to help him find Merrill Overturf, and it was then that Mulcahy made his deal. He would find Merrill Overturf, but first Bogus would have to do something for Arnold Mulcahy, for the U.S. government and for the innocent people of the world.

"I guess I don't mind," Bogus said. He really wanted to find Merrill.

"You *shouldn't* mind," said Mulcahy. "Also, you need plane fare home."

"I don't know if I'm going home."

"Well, *I* know," Mulcahy said.

"Merrill Overturf is in Vienna, I think," Trumper said. "I'm not going anywhere until I find him."

Mulcahy called in the vice-consul. "Locate this Overturf character," he ordered. "Then we can get on with it."

"It" was then explained to Bogus Trumper. It was pretty simple. Trumper would be given a few thousand dollars in U.S. hundred-dollar bills. Trumper was to hang around the Kaffeehaus Leopold Hawelka, wait for the man who said *"Gra! Gra!"* all the time and who'd given Trumper the parcel of hashish, and to give the man the money when he showed up. Then Trumper was to be taken to Schwecat Airport and be put on a plane to New York. He would take the hashish brick with him; his luggage would be searched at Kennedy Airport customs; the hashish brick would be discovered; he would be seized on the spot and driven away in a limousine. The limousine would take him anywhere he wanted to go in New York City, and then he would be free.

It all seemed pretty straightforward. The reasons for all this escaped Trumper, but it was obvious that no one was going to do any explaining.

Then he was introduced to a Herr Doktor Inspektor Wolfgang Denzel, who was apparently an agent at the Austrian end. Inspektor Denzel wanted as much of a description of the man who had said *"Gra! Gra!"* as Trumper could give. Trumper had seen Herr Doktor Inspektor Denzel before; he was the natty, agile waiter whose tray of coffee and beers Trumper had spilled.

The only part of the deal that Bogus didn't like was getting on a New York plane as soon as he had handed over the money. "Don't forget about Merrill Overturf," he reminded Mulcahy.

"My good boy," said Arnold Mulcahy. "I'll go with you in the cab to the airport, and this Overturf character will be sitting right there with us."

If Mulcahy wasn't quite the sort of man you'd actually trust, he was at least the sort whose efficiency you could have confidence in.

Bogus went to the Hawelka and sat around with his few thousand dollars for three nights running, but the *"Gra! Gra!"* man never showed up.

"He'll show," said Arnold Mulcahy. His overpowering confidence was chilling.

On the fifth night, the man came into the Hawelka. He didn't pay any attention to Bogus, though; he sat far away and never looked at him once. When he paid the waiter—who of course was actually Herr Doktor Inspektor Denzel—and then put on his coat and headed for the door, Bogus thought he should make his move. Walking right up to the man as if he'd suddenly recognized an old friend, he called, *"Gra! Gra!"* and grabbed the man's hand and pumped it. But the man looked petrified; he was trying so hard to get away from Bogus that he didn't even utter one little *"Gra!"*

Bogus went right after him out the door and down the sidewalk, where the man tried to break into a jog to get free. *"Gra!"* Bogus screamed at him again, and spinning the man around to face him, he took the envelope with all the money in it and crammed it into his trembling hand. But the man threw the envelope away and ran off as fast as he could.

Herr Doktor Inspektor Denzel came out of the Hawelka and picked the envelope up off the street. "You should have let him come to *you,*" he told Trumper. "I think you scared him off." Herr Doktor Inspektor Denzel was a genius at understatement.

In the cab to Schwecat Airport, Arnold Mulcahy said, "Suffering shit! Boy, did you ever blow it!"

Merrill Overturf was not in the cab.

"It's not *my* fault," Bogus told Mulcahy. "You never told me how I was supposed to give the money to him."

"Well, I didn't think you'd try to cram it down his throat."

"Where's Merrill Overturf?" Trumper asked. "You said he'd be here."

"He's not in Vienna any more," Mulcahy said.

"Where is he?" Trumper asked, but Mulcahy wouldn't tell him.

"I'll let you know in New York," he said.

They were late getting to New York; there'd been a delay on their Lufthansa flight. The runway in Frankfurt, their first stop, was stacked up, so they missed their first connection to New York, a TWA flight, and ended up on a big Pan Am 747. Their luggage, however, had gone through earlier on the TWA flight. No one could explain how this happened, and Mulcahy was nervous about it. "Where'd you put the stuff?" he asked Trumper.

"In my suitcase," Trumper said, "with everything else."

"When they find it in New York," Mulcahy said, "it would be good if you pretended to run away—you know. Not too far, of course; let them catch you. They won't hurt you or anything," he added.

Then Kennedy was stacked up, so they circled New York for an hour. It was late afternoon when they landed, and it took them an hour to locate their bags. Mulcahy left Bogus before he went through the customs declaration gate.

"Anything to declare?" the man said, winking at Bogus. He was a big, warm-faced Negro with hands like a black bear's feet, and he started pawing through Bogus's suitcase.

There was a pretty girl in line behind him and Trumper turned around and smiled at her. *Won't she be surprised when they arrest me?*

The customs man had taken out the typewriter, the recorder, all the tapes, and half of Trumper's clothes, but he hadn't found the hashish yet.

Bogus looked around nervously, the way he thought a potential smuggler would look around. By now the customs man had the suitcase completely emptied on the counter and was pawing back over all the stuff. He looked up at Bogus, worried, and whispered to him, "Where *is* it?"

Then Bogus started pawing through all the stuff with him; they went through it twice more, with the line behind them growing and grumbling, but they couldn't find the hashish.

"All right," the customs man said to him. "What did you do with it?"

"Nothing," Bogus said. "I packed it, I know I did, honest."

"Don't let him get away!" the customs man yelled suddenly, apparently figuring he'd better go ahead with the plan. Bogus did what Mulcahy had told him to and started to make a run for it. He ran out through the gate with the customs man yelling at him and pointing and setting off a horn that had a jarring shriek to it.

Trumper got all the way through the exit ramp and up to where the taxis were waiting before he realized that he'd probably escaped, so he ran back. As he neared the customs gate, a policeman caught up with him. "Christ, at last!" Trumper said to the cop, who looked puzzled and handed Bogus the envelope containing the few thousand dollars. Trumper hadn't given it back to Mulcahy, who hadn't asked for it; it must have fallen out of his pocket when he'd run through the terminal.

"Thank you," Bogus said. Then he ran back down the exit ramp, where he was finally captured by the Negro customs man who hadn't found the hashish.

"Now I've got you!" the man yelled, holding Bogus gently around the waist.

In a funny Formica-covered room, Arnold Mulcahy and five other men were hopping mad.

"Suffering shit!" Mulcahy yelled. "Someone must have picked it off in Frankfurt."

"The suitcase was in New York for six hours before you got here," one of the men told him. "Someone could have picked it off here."

"Trumper?" Mulcahy said. "Did you really pack the thing, boy?"

"Yes, sir."

They whisked him into another room, where a man who looked like a male nurse searched him all over and then left him alone. A long time later, he was brought some scrambled eggs, toast and coffee, and after another long wait Mulcahy reappeared.

"There's a limousine here for you," he told Bogus. "It will take you anywhere you want to go."

"I'm sorry, sir," Trumper said. Mulcahy just shook his head. "Suffering shit . . ." he said.

On the way to the car, Trumper said, "I hate to ask you this, but what about Merrill Overturf?"

Mulcahy was pretending not to hear. At the limousine he opened the door for Trumper and then shoved him inside quickly. "Take him anywhere he wants to go," he told the driver.

Bogus rolled his window down quickly and caught Mulcahy's sleeve as he was trying to turn away from the car.

"Hey, what about Merrill Overturf?" he said.

Mulcahy sighed. He opened the briefcase he was carrying and took out a photostated copy of an official-looking document with the raised seal of the American Consulate stamped on it. "I'm sorry," Mulcahy said, handing the photostat to Trumper. "Merrill Overturf is dead." Then he smacked the roof of the car, shouted to the driver, "Take him anywhere he wants to go!" and the car pulled away.

"Where to?" the driver asked Trumper, who sat in the back seat like an armrest or some other stationary part of the car itself. He was trying to read the document, which in officialese seemed to be called an Uncontested Obituary, and concerned one Overturf, Merrill, born Boston, Mass., Sept. 8, 1941. Father, Randolph W.; mother, Ellen Keefe.

Merrill had died nearly two full years before Bogus had returned to Vienna to find him. According to the document, he had bet an American girl named Polly Crenner—whom he had picked up at American Express—that he could find a tank on the bottom of the Danube. He had taken her to the Gelhafts Keller out on the Danube and Polly had stood on the dock and watched Merrill swim out in the Danube holding a flashlight over his head. When he located the tank, he was going to call to her; she had insisted that she wouldn't go in the water until he'd found it.

Miss Crenner had waited on the dock for about five minutes after she could no longer see the flashlight bobbing around; she thought that Merrill was kidding around. Then she'd run into the Gelhafts Keller and tried to get some help, but since she didn't speak any German, it took some time for her to make herself understood.

Overturf might have been drunk, Polly Crenner said later. Evidently she hadn't known he was a diabetic, and neither, apparently, did the consulate, for it wasn't mentioned. In any case, the cause of death was listed as drowning. The identification of Merrill's body had not been completely confirmed. That is, a body had been found three days later that was snagged on an oil barge bound for Budapest, but since it had gone through the propellers a few times, no one could be sure.

The story of the tank was never confirmed. Polly Crenner said that Merrill had started hollering about a minute before she lost sight of the flashlight that he'd found the tank, but she hadn't believed him.

"I would have believed you, Merrill," Bogus Trumper said aloud.

"Sir?" the driver said.

"What?"

"Where to, sir?" the driver said.

They were cruising past Shea Stadium. It was a warm, balmy night and the traffic was fierce. "This stretch is slow," the driver informed him unnecessarily. "It's the Mets and the Pirates."

Trumper sat baffled over that for a long time. It was December when he'd left and he couldn't have been gone more than a week or so. *They're playing baseball already?* He leaned forward and looked at himself in the rear-view mirror of the limousine. He had a lovely, flowing mustache and a full beard. His back-seat window was still rolled down and the steamy New York summer air rolled over him. "Jesus," he whispered. He felt frightened.

"Where to, sir?" the driver repeated. He was obviously getting a little nervous about his passenger.

But Trumper was wondering if Biggie was still in Iowa—if it was *summer* already. Jesus Christ! He couldn't believe he'd been gone so long. He looked for a newspaper or something with a date.

What he found was the envelope with a few thousand dollars in it. Arnold Mulcahy was a more generous man than he at first appeared.

"Where to?" the driver said.

"Maine," said Trumper. He had to see Couth; he had to clear his head.

"Maine?" the driver said. Then he got tough. "Look, buddy," he said, "I ain't taking you to Maine. This car don't go out of Manhattan."

Trumper opened the envelope and handed the driver a hundred-dollar bill. "Maine," Trumper said.

"Yes, sir," said the driver.

Trumper leaned back, smelled the wretched air and felt the heat. He didn't quite know it yet—or he couldn't make himself believe it—but he'd been away for almost six months.

31

A Pentothal Movie

(159: *Medium shot of Trumper putting down a small overnight suitcase in front of the reception desk at a hospital. He looks around anxiously; Tulpen, smiling next to him, takes his arm. Trumper asks the nurse behind the desk something and she gives him some forms to fill in. Tulpen is warmly attentive to him while he struggles with the papers*)

DR. VIGNERON *(voice-over)*: It's a very simple operation, really, though it does seem to frighten the patient a good deal. It is minor surgery, five stitches at the most . . .

(160: *Close-up of a medical drawing of the penis. A hand, presumably Vigneron's, draws with a black crayon on the penis*)

VIGNERON *(v.o.)*: The incision is made at the opening, here, to simply widen the passage. Then the sutures hold it open, here, so that it won't grow back the way it was. It will try to do that, anyway, by the way . . .

(161: *Long shot of a nurse leading Trumper and Tulpen down an aisle of the hospital. Trumper peers nervously into every room, bumping his suitcase against his knees as he walks*)

VIGNERON *(v.o.)*: There's just one night in the hospital to prepare you for surgery in the morning. Then rest the next day and perhaps stay that night too, if you're still . . . uncomfortable.

(162: *Medium shot of Trumper getting awkwardly into a hospital gown; Tulpen helps him tie the string in back. Trumper stares at the patient with whom he shares his room, an old man with tubes running in and out of him who lies motionless on the bed next to Trumper's. A nurse comes and deftly pulls the curtains around the bed, shutting off this view*)

VIGNERON *(v.o.)*: . . . to put it another way, it is forty-eight hours of pain. Now, that is not so very much pain, is it?

(163: *Sync sound. Medium shot of Ralph Packer interviewing Dr. Vigneron in Vigneron's office*)

PACKER: There is some psychological pain, I imagine . . . you know, a sort of penis fear?
VIGNERON: Well, I suppose some patients would feel— You mean like a castration complex?

(164: *A male nurse is shaving Trumper, who lies rigidly on his hospital bed watching the man's razor zip through his pubic hair*)

PACKER *(v.o.)*: Yeah, castration—Or, you know, afraid the whole thing will get cut off. By mistake, of course! *(He laughs)*

(165: *Same as 163, in Vigneron's office*)

VIGNERON *(laughing)*: Well, I assure you, I have never made a slip-up in that area!
PACKER *(laughing hysterically)*: Well, of course not . . . no, but I mean if you're the sort of patient who's at all paranoid about your prick . . .

(166: *Sync sound. Medium shot of Trumper lifting the sheets, peering under at himself, letting Tulpen peek too*)

TRUMPER: You see? Like a baby!
TULPEN *(staring hard)*: It's like you're going to *have* a baby . . .

(They look at each other, then look away)

(167: *Sync sound. Same as 163 and 165. In Vigneron's office, both Packer and Dr. Vigneron are laughing loudly and uncontrollably)*

(168: *Medium shot. Trumper, sitting up in bed, waves goodbye to Ralph and Tulpen, who waves back from the foot of his bed)*

VIGNERON *(v.o., as if leaving instructions with a nurse)*: No solid foods tonight, and nothing to drink after ten o'clock. Give him the first injections at eight tomorrow morning; he should be in the operating room by eight-thirty . . .

(Tulpen and Ralph walk out of frame together, escorted by a nurse. Trumper glowers after them darkly)
DISSOLVE

After which, you can bet your ass, I did not dissolve. I lay feeling my smooth-shaven parts—the lamb's neck fleeced for the slaughter!

I also listened to the gurgling man beside me, a man who was fed like

a carburetor; whose tubes, whose intake and output, whose simple functioning, seemed to rely on a mechanical sense of timing.

I was not worried about my operation, really; I had anticipated it to
death. What did worry me was the degree to which I had become predictable even to myself, as if the range of my reactions had been analyzed,
discussed and criticized to the point where I was as readable as a graph. I
wished I could shock them all, the fuckers.

It was nearly midnight when I convinced the nurse that I simply had to
call Tulpen. The phone rang and rang. When Ralph Packer answered, I
hung up.

(169: *Sync sound. Close-up from dissolve. At her bathroom mirror Tulpen
brushes her teeth; her shoulders are bare; presumably, so is the rest of her*)

PACKER *(offstage)*: Do you think the operation will change him? I don't
mean just physically . . .

TULPEN *(she spits, looks in the mirror, then talks over her shoulder)*: Change
him how, then?

RALPH *(o.s.)*: I mean psychologically . . .

TULPEN *(rinses, gargles, spits)*: He doesn't believe in psychology.

RALPH *(o.s.)*: Do you?

TULPEN: Not for him, I don't . . .

(170: *Sync sound. Medium shot of Tulpen in the bathtub, soaping her breasts
and underarms*)

TULPEN *(with occasional looks at camera)*: It's a very simplistic whitewash
to attempt to cover very deep and complicated people and things with
very easy generalizations, superficialities—you know. But I think it's just
as simplistic to assume that everyone is complex and deep. I mean, I think
Trumper really does operate on the surface . . . Maybe he *is* a surface,
just a surface . . .

(*She trails off, looks warily at camera, then at her soapy breasts, and self-
consciously slides down in the water*)

TULPEN *(looking at camera, as if Ralph were the camera)*: Come on, let's
call it a night.

(*The phone rings offstage and Tulpen starts to get out of the tub*)

RALPH *(o.s.)*: Shit! The phone . . . I'll get it!

TULPEN *(looking offstage after him)*: No, let me—it might be Trumper.

RALPH *(o.s., answering the phone; Tulpen, listening, freezes)*: Yeah, hello?
Hello? Hello, goddam you . . .

(*The camera is jerky; it tries to back up awkwardly as Tulpen steps out of
the tub. Clumsily embarrassed, she wraps herself in a towel as Ralph steps*

into frame with her. He wears a light meter around his neck and points it at her, then down at the tub)

RALPH *(irritably, he takes her arm and tries to steer her back to the tub)*: No, come on. We'll have to shoot this all over again . . . the goddam phone!

TULPEN *(pulling away from him)*: Was it Trumper? Who was on the phone?

RALPH: I don't know. They hung up. Now, come on, this won't take a minute . . .

(But she wraps herself tighter in the towel and moves away from the tub)

TULPEN *(angry)*: It's late. I want to get up early. I want to be there when he comes out of the anesthesia. We can do this tomorrow.

(She looks up, exasperated, at the camera. Suddenly, Ralph looks angrily at the camera himself, as if he just realized it was still running)

RALPH *(shouting at camera)*: Cut! Cut! Cut! Sweet Jesus, Kent! Stop wasting film, you royal fuck-up!

BLACK OUT

Early in the morning they came and emptied the pots, hoses and receptacles of all kinds belonging to the man beside me. But they did nothing for me; they wouldn't even feed me.

At eight o'clock a nurse took my temperature and gave me a numbing shot in both legs, high up on the thigh. When they came to wheel me down to the operating room, I couldn't walk very well. Two nurses supported me while they made me take a leak, but I still had *feeling* down there, and I was worried that the shots hadn't worked the way they were supposed to. I remarked on this to the nurse, but she didn't seem to understand me; in fact, my voice sounded strange even to me and I couldn't understand what I said either. I prayed I would be lucid in time to stop them from cutting.

In the operating room there was a stunning, full-bosomed woman in a green uniform like the kind all the surgery nurses wear, and she kept pinching my thighs and smiling at me. She was the one who stuck the needle leading to the dextrose jug into my vein; then she bent my arm in a special way, taped the needle to it, and then taped my arm to the table. The dextrose running down the yellowy hose was gurgling into me; I could follow it right down to my arm.

I had a thought about Merrill Overturf: If they had ever operated on him, they wouldn't be able to use dextrose, would they, since it's mostly sugar? What would they use?

With my free right hand, I reached over and pinched my penis. I could still feel everything, and this frightened me a lot. What was the sense of putting my thighs to sleep?

Then I heard Vigneron's voice, but I couldn't see him; instead, I saw a short, genial, spectacled old geezer who I guessed was the anesthetist. He came over and poked at the dextrose needle, then slid a jug of Pentothal alongside the dextrose jug and ran the hose from it right alongside the dextrose hose. Rather than stick the Pentothal needle in me, he stuck it into the dextrose hose, which I thought was very clever.

The hose to the Pentothal had a clamp on it, and I saw that the drug wasn't running into me yet. I watched it closely, you can bet your ass, and when the anesthetist asked me how I felt, I boomed in a great loud voice that I still had plenty of feeling in my prick and that I hoped they were all aware of it.

But they all just smiled as if they hadn't heard me—that anesthetist, the green nurse and Vigneron himself, now standing over me.

"Count to twelve," the anesthetist told me. He started the Pentothal running then, by unclamping the hose, and I watched the stuff trickle down until it mingled with the dextrose in the main rubber vein.

"One two three four five six seven," I said very fast. Only it took forever. The Pentothal changed the color of the dextrose running down toward my arm. I watched it run right up to the hub of the needle, and when it entered my arm, I cried, "Eight!"

Then a second passed, which took two hours, and I woke up in the postoperative room—the recovery room, whose ceiling looked so much like the ceiling in the operating room that I thought I was still in the same place. Hovering over me was the same stunning green nurse, smiling.

"Nine," I said to her, "ten, eleven, twelve . . ."

"We'd like you to try to urinate now," she said to me.

"I just went," I said. But she rolled me over on my side and slid a green pan under me.

"Please just try," she coaxed. She was awfully nice.

So I started to go, even though I was sure I had nothing to pee. When the pain came, it was like an awareness of someone else's pain in another room—or even more distant, in another hospital. It was quite a lot of pain; I felt sorry for the person enduring it; I was all through peeing before I realized that it was *my* pain, realized that the operation was over.

"Okay, okay, okay, now," the nurse said, smoothing back my hair and wiping the sudden, surprised tears off my face.

Of course, what they had spared me was the double pain of anticipating peeing that first time. But I couldn't see it that way. It was a betrayal; they had tricked me.

Then I went away again into dizzy sleep, and when I came back I was in my hospital room, Tulpen sitting there beside the bed, holding my hand. When I opened my eyes, she was smiling at me.

But I pretended that I was still drugged senseless. I stared right through her. There's more than one who can play the tricks and surprises, you can bet your ass . . .

32

Another Dante, a Different Hell

The driver had worked for the limousine service for about three years. Before that, he'd driven a cab. He liked the limousine service better; nobody tried to stick him up or maul him, it was more leisurely, and the cars were elegant. He'd had the Mercedes for the past year and he loved to drive it. Occasionally, he'd gotten out of the city—once as far as New Haven—and he loved the feel of the car on the open road. That was what he thought the "open road" was: driving to New Haven. It was as far as he'd ever been out of New York City. He had a family and three kids, and every summer he talked with his wife about taking his vacation out West, driving the whole family out there. But he didn't own a car himself; he was waiting until he could afford a Mercedes, or until the limousine service let an old one go cheap.

So when he contracted to drive Bogus to Maine, the driver undertook the journey as if someone had told him to drive to San Francisco. *Maine!* He thought of men who hunted whales, ate lobster for breakfast and wore rubber boots all year long.

He talked for two hours before he realized that his passenger was either asleep or in a trance; then he shut up. His name was Dante Calicchio, and he realized that this was the first time since he'd stopped driving a cab that he was spooked by a passenger. He thought that Bogus was crazy, and he put the hundred-dollar bill in his jockey shorts, right in the pouch where he could find it. Maybe he'll give me another one, he thought. Or try to take this one back.

Dante Calicchio was short and heavy, with a salad of black hair and a nose which had been broken so many times that it appeared to flap. He'd been a boxer; he liked to say of his style that he always led with his nose. He'd been a wrestler too, and had cauliflower ears from that. A lovely set, all folded and swollen and lumpy, like two unmatched wads of dough slapped on the sides of his face. He chewed gum loudly, a habit he'd developed years ago when he gave up cigarettes.

Dante Calicchio was an honest man who was curious about the way other people lived and what other places were like to live in, so he was not unhappy to be driving this nut to Maine. It was just that when they got north of Boston, and it was dark, and the traffic thinned out and almost disappeared, he got a little scared about driving off into this wilderness with a man who hadn't opened his mouth since they'd passed Shea Stadium.

The toll-booth attendant at the New Hampshire Turnpike looked at Dante's chauffeur uniform, stared into the plush back seat at Bogus in a trance, and then, since there were no other cars in sight, asked Dante where he was going.

"Maine," Dante whispered as if it was a holy word. "*Where* in Maine?" the attendant asked. Maine, in general, was only twenty minutes away from his daily life.

"I don't know where," Dante said, as the attendant handed him his change and waved him on. "Hey, sir?" he said, turning to Bogus. "Hey, where in Maine?"

Georgetown is an island, but in Trumper's mind it was even more of an island than it really is. It's the sort of island that might as well be a peninsula, because it's connected to the mainland by a bridge; there are none of the inconveniences of a real island. But Trumper was thinking of the lovely isolation Couth contributed to the place. But then Couth could probably give you a sense of isolation in Kennedy Airport.

Bogus wondered how he might best approach Biggie, realizing only now how much he missed her. She'd never stay in Iowa during the summer. At this moment she was probably in East Gunnery, helping her father and letting her mother help her with Colm. It was even conceivable that her abandonment had inspired an I-told-you-so sort of negative invitation from his own parents, but surely Biggie would have declined those helping hands.

In any case, she certainly would have written to Couth to ask if he knew where his friend Bogus was, and Couth would know where *she* was, and what her feelings were about her runaway husband. Perhaps Couth had even seen them and could tell him how Colm had changed.

"Hey, sir?" someone was asking him. It was the man in the front seat in the doorman's uniform. "Hey, where in Maine?" he asked.

Trumper looked out the window; they were coming through the deserted rotary by Portsmouth Harbor, crossing the bridge to Maine. "Georgetown," he said to the driver. "It's an island. You'd better stop and get a map."

And Dante Calicchio thought, *An island!* Sweet Jesus, how am I supposed to *drive* to an island, you frigging crazy bastard . . .

But Dante got a map and saw there was a bridge from the mainland at Bath, across a tidal inlet of the Kennebec River, to Georgetown Island. As he crossed the bridge sometime after midnight, Bogus rolled down the back windows and asked him if he could smell the sea.

What Dante smelled was too fresh to be the sea. The sea Dante knew smelled like the docks off New York and Newark. The salt marshes here smelled tangy clean, so he rolled down his window too. But he didn't like the driving any more. The road across the island had loose, sandy shoulders, was narrow and winding and didn't have a median stripe. Also, there weren't any houses, just dark black pine trees and stretches of high salt grass.

Also, the night was alive with sounds. Not horns and mechanisms, or tires squealing or unidentified human voices or sirens, but things—frogs and crickets and sea birds and foghorns out at sea.

The lonely road and the terrible sounds scared the shit out of Dante Calicchio, who kept sizing up Bogus in the rear-view mirror, thinking, If this nut tries anything, I can break his back in two places before his friends jump me . . .

Trumper was calculating how long he'd stay with Couth, and whether he'd phone Biggie or just go see her when the time seemed ripe.

When the road suddenly turned to dirt, Dante slammed on the brakes, locked the two front doors, and then the two back ones, never taking his eyes off Bogus for an instant.

"What the hell are you doing?" Trumper asked, but Dante Calicchio sat in the front seat with one eye on Trumper in the mirror and the other roaming the map.

"We must be lost, huh?" Dante said.

"No," Trumper said. "We've got about five miles to go."

"Where's the road?" said Dante.

"You're *on* it," Trumper said. "Drive on."

Dante checked the map, saw that this indeed was a road and drove on with trepidation; that is, he inched the car forward as the island narrowed down around him. A few unlighted houses appeared, solemn as moored ships, and he saw the horizon open on both sides of him; the sea was out there, the air felt colder, he could taste the salt.

Then a sign told him he was on a private road.

"Drive on," Trumper told him. Dante wished his tire chains were beside him on the seat, but he drove on.

A few hundred yards further on a sign said PILLSBURY, and the road dipped so close to the water that Dante thought the surf would break over them. Then he saw the magnificent old house with its barn-red wooden shingles, a high gabled house with a connecting garage, a boathouse and a tidy cove of the sea to itself.

Pillsbury—Dante thought he probably had one of them in the back seat. The only Pillsbury he knew was the competition for Betty Crocker. He peeked in the rear-view mirror, wondering if he was chauffeuring the crazy young heir to a cake-mix fortune.

"What month is it?" Trumper asked. He wanted to know if Couth was still alone in the place, or whether the Pillsburys would be here for the summer. They never came until the Fourth of July.

"It's the first of June, sir," said Dante Calicchio. He stopped the car where the driveway ended, and sat listening to the shrieking night—to what he imagined were whistling fish and great birds of prey, bears roaming the deep pines and an insect world of jungle ferocity.

When Trumper hustled up the flagstone walk, his eye on the one lit room in the house, the master bedroom upstairs, Dante hustled after him uninvited. He had grown up in a tough neighborhood and felt perfectly comfortable going out for a late-night six-pack when no one else would venture abroad in less than gang numbers, but the stillness of the island really threw him and he had no intention of facing the teeming animal potential singing and scuffling in those bushes and trees all by himself.

"What's your name?" Trumper asked.

"Dante."

"Dante?" Trumper said. A shot of light flickered down a hall of the house; a shaft stretched downstairs; a porch light went on.

"Couth!" Trumper yelled. "Heigh-ho!"

If there's just two of them, Dante thought, I can handle the mothers. He felt the hundred-dollar bill in his crotch for reassurance.

———————

I could recognize old Couth through the porch door, coming to let us in: that floppy bathrobe he wears which is cut from a patchwork quilt; the way he squinted through the screen at us. It must have given him a shock to see that hairy brute chauffeur in a doorman's uniform swatting at the mosquitoes as if they were carnivorous birds, but it must have been even more of a shock to see *me*.

I could tell as soon as you let us in, Couth, that you'd been dallying with a lady when we interrupted you. You wore her many perfumes like a bathrobe under the bathrobe you wore; and from the way you stepped back from the chill of the open door, I could tell you were coming from someplace warm.

But what's it matter among friends, Couth? I hugged you, picked you right up off your feet, you scrawny bugger! You sure smelled good, Couth.

———————

Trumper lugged Couth into the kitchen, waltzing him around until they collided with a shiny new vinyl kiddie raft moored by the sink. Bogus didn't remember the Pillsburys having any small children. He sat Couth down on the butcher's block, kissed him on the forehead and left him gawking while he boomed affectionately, "Couth, I can't tell you how glad I am to see you . . . Here you are saving my life again . . . You're the one fixed star in the heavens, Couth! Look—my beard's nearly as big as yours, Couth . . . How *are* you? I've been awful, Couth, you probably know . . ."

And Couth just kept staring at him, and then looking at Dante Calicchio, a squat monster in uniform trying to keep politely out of the way in a corner of the kitchen and holding his driver's cap in his big-knuckled hands. While Trumper skipped around the kitchen, opening the refrigerator door, peering into the dining room, poking into the laundry alcove—where, to his mischievous delight, he saw a wooden clothes rack with some lady's silky bras and panties hung up to dry.

Plucking up the nearest bra, he waved it with a leer at Couth.

"Who is she, you sly bugger?" he cackled, and once more he couldn't resist tickling his fingers playfully in the chin of Couth's long beard.

But all Couth said was, "Where have you *been,* Bogus? Where in hell have you been?"

Trumper was quick to catch the accusing tone and knew that Couth had heard from Biggie. "You've seen her, huh?" he asked. "How is she, Couth?" But Couth looked away from him, as if he were going to cry, and Trumper quickly added, quickly scared, "Couth, I've behaved rather badly, I know . . ."

He was twisting the bra in his hands and Couth took it away from him. Then, when he saw the bra in Couth's hands, Trumper suddenly thought, *That's a mauve bra,* and he remembered buying a bra so purple—a bra so big. He stopped talking; he watched Couth slip down from the butcher's block like some slow-moving meat which had been de-boned there; Couth went into the laundry alcove and put Biggie's bra back on the clothes rack.

"You were gone a long time, Bogus," Couth said.

"But I'm back now, Couth," Bogus said, which sounded pretty stupid. "Couth? I'm sorry, but I *am* back, Couth . . ."

Some bare feet were slap-slapping down the stairs and a voice said, "Please keep the noise down or you'll wake up Colm."

The feet came toward the kitchen. Crammed in the corner by the spice rack, Dante Calicchio was attempting the impossible by trying to make himself small and inconspicuous.

"Bogus, I'm sorry," Couth said gently, and touched his arm.

Then Biggie walked in, gave Dante a look as if he were a storm trooper who had arrived by U-boat and turned a remarkably unflinching and unsurprised stare on Bogus.

"It's Bogus," Couth whispered to her, as if she might not have recognized him with a beard. "It's Bogus," he repeated a little louder. "Home from the war . . ."

"I wouldn't say *home,*" Biggie said. "I wouldn't say that at all."

And I listened hard for the humor in your tone, Big; I was really straining to hear it. But I missed it, Big. It was absent. And the only thing I could think to say—because of the way both you and Couth seemed so nervous about the hulking wop in uniform crouched under the spices—the only thing I could do, Big, was introduce you both to my driver. There was nothing else I could begin with.

"Uh," Trumper said, as if backing away from a punch. "This is Dante. He's my driver."

Neither Biggie nor Couth could look at Dante; they kept right on staring alternately at Bogus and at the floor. And Bogus could only notice Biggie's robe, a new one—in orange, her favorite color; in velour, her favorite material. Her hair had grown out some, and she wore earrings, which she'd never done before; she looked sort of tousled and blowzy, a look he remembered her carrying well. You just wanted to rumple yourself up with her when she looked like that.

Then Dante Calicchio, under the strain of being introduced, tried to shoulder himself out of the corner where he'd crammed himself and hit the spice rack with his shoulder, propelling it with him into the center of the kitchen where he made a hopeless grab at it; Biggie and Couth and Bogus all rushed toward him and made things worse. Little spice jars shattered all over the kitchen, and Dante's last lurch for the empty rack splintered it against the unyielding refrigerator.

"Oh, God, I'm sorry," Dante said.

Biggie prodded a little spice jar with her foot and looked straight at Bogus. "A lot of people are sorry," she said.

Trumper heard Colm call out upstairs.

"Excuse me," Biggie said, and walked out of the kitchen.

Trumper followed her up the stairs. "Colm," he said. "That's Colm, isn't it?" He was right behind her when she stopped, turned and gave him a look he'd never had from her before—as if she were a strange woman he'd just goosed in some vile, surprising way.

"I'll be back in a minute," she said coolly, and he let her go on upstairs alone. He lingered on his way back to the kitchen, hearing her soft voice reassuring Colm about the crash of the spice rack; from the kitchen, he could hear Couth's equally reassuring tone to Dante Calicchio. Not all the spice jars had been broken, Couth was saying, and he could build a new rack in no time.

Dante Calicchio made some remark in Italian; to Trumper, it sounded like a prayer.

Then there was the business with the pool table. Couth got to feeling badly for Dante, who felt so miserably awkward hanging around in the house, afraid of the fierce outdoors, wondering if he should call his wife, and whether he should tell the limousine service about the delay or just drive back to New York quick.

"Sir?" he asked Trumper, who was waiting for Biggie to come downstairs. "Should I go?"

But Trumper didn't know what was what. "I don't know, Dante," he said. "Should you?"

Then Biggie came back down and gave a kind of brave smile to Couth and a hard nod to Trumper, who followed her outside and out onto the night-black dock.

Then Couth asked Dante if he shot pool. This brought Dante out of trauma for a while; he shot a lot of pool, in fact. He took eight straight games from Couth and then, after secretly devising a handicap system, won three of the next four. But they weren't playing for money. The way everyone in that house acted, Dante couldn't even think about money. Actually, though, whenever he bent over to address the cue ball, he felt the hundred-dollar bill in his underwear.

"That Mr. Pillsbury," he said to Couth, still thinking that Bogus was named Pillsbury. "What's he do for all his money?"

"He opens his mail once a month," Couth said, thinking that Dante meant *the* Mr. Pillsbury. Dante whistled, swore softly and sank the fiveball in the sidepocket, the cue ball gliding back to where he wanted it. Couth, who was wondering how Bogus could afford a chauffeur said, "That Mr. Trumper, Dante—what's *he* do for all his money?"

"Twelveball down in the right corner," Dante said. He never heard anything when he was planning a shot.

Couth was confused; he thought that perhaps Dante was being evasive. Looking out the picture window, he saw Biggie on the end of the dock, facing the ocean; by her moving hands he knew that she was talking. Ten feet away, leaning against the dock's mooring post, Bogus sat as still and silent as a barnacle—growing there, taking root.

Dante sent the cue ball whistling down the length of the table and socked the twelveball into the corner pocket, but Couth never turned from the window. Dante watched the cue ball nudge the ten away from the eight, then roll up cozily behind the fourteen, leaving him a perfect shot for the opposite corner. He was about to call it when Couth said something to the window.

"Tell him no," Couth said. It was almost a whisper.

Dante watched Couth standing there. Jesus, he thought, he opens his fucking mail once a month and they're all crazy here, the two of them nutty for that big broad. I'm not shutting my eyes tonight, baby, and I'm not letting the fuck go of this pool cue, either . . . But all Dante said was, "It's your shot."

"What?"

"It's your shot," Dante said. "I missed."

Lying was the handicap system which Dante Calicchio had devised for himself.

I threw a snail off the dock. It went *ploink!* in the water, and I thought of how long it would take that snail to get back to dry land.

And you went on and on, Biggie.

Among all the other things, you said, "Of course I can't stop caring for you. I care about you, Bogus. But Couth really cares about me."

I threw three snails rapid-fire: *Ploink! Ploink! Ploink!*

You went on, Big. You said, "You were gone such a long time! But after a while it wasn't the time you were gone that got to me, Bogus; it was the time when you were *with* me, as I remembered it, that I didn't like . . ."

I found a cluster of barnacles with the heel of my hand and ground my palm down on them, grating it against them as if it were a cheese.

I said, "I'll give you time, Big. All the time you want. If you want to stay here a while . . ."

"I'm here for good," you said, Big.

I *ploinked!* another snail. Then a fish slapped, a tern cried, an owl spoke, and, carried on that resonant air, across the bay a dog barked.

"You say," I said, "that Couth cares for you, and for Colm too. But what do you feel for Couth, Big?"

"It's hard to say," you said, and you turned away and faced the bay. I thought you meant it was hard because you didn't have much feeling for him, but then you said, "I care for him a lot."

"Sex?" I said.

"A lot," you said. "It's okay there, too."

Ploink! Ploink!

"Don't make me tell you how much I love him, Bogus," you said. "I don't feel like hurting you. It's been a long time, and I don't feel so angry now."

"Merrill's dead, Big," I said—I don't know why. And you came over and hugged me from behind, squeezing me so hard that I couldn't turn around and squeeze you back. In fact, when I wriggled free enough to reach you, you pushed me off.

"I wanted to hold you for Merrill, Bogus," you said. "Don't you try to hold me, please."

So I let you hold me your way. If you wanted to think you were hugging Merrill, I wasn't going to stop you.

I said, "What about Colm, Big?"

"Couth loves him," you said. "And he loves Couth."

"*Everybody* loves Couth," I said, and *ploink! ploink! ploink!*

"Couth is very fond of you, Bogus," you said. "And you can see Colm whenever you want to. Of course you're welcome to come here . . ."

"Thank you, Big."

Then you *ploinked* a snail of your own off the dock. "Bogus?" you asked. "What are you going to do?"

And I thought, *Ploink!* Then I spoke a handful: *Ploink! Ploink! Ploink! Ploink-ploink-ploink!* I watched you turn away from me and looked up at the two figures silhouetted at the picture window in the pool room; they stood side by side, pool cues on their shoulders like rifles during a parade. But they weren't marching; they were looking down at the dock, and neither of them moved until you started up the path to the house. Then the taller, thinner figure left the window, dissolving into the house to meet you; the shorter figure flexed his cue stick like a fencing foil, and then he too turned away.

Ploink! was what I thought as I heard the screen door slam.

From deep inland, beyond the salt marsh where Couth and I once swamped a boat in the salt-stunted pines, a loon said what was on his mind.

Dante took three straight games from Biggie before he began to miss shots on purpose just so he could see her arch her body over the table with all her bends and boulder-shapes hard under her soft, slinky robe. She held her lower lip in her teeth when she stroked the ball.

Down on the dock, her two lovers, he guessed, sat close together, their legs hanging off the end, striking a bargain with a handful of snails.

Jesus, Dante thought. Who's who here, is what I'd like to know.

You have always been kind, Couth, and that suits the way you look. As fair as I am dark, you're white with freckles, whereas I am linseed oil rubbed into coarse-grained wood. Your height conceals the fact that your hips are broader than your shoulders, but you don't look broad; those long, skinny legs and your pianist's fingers and your noble, unbroken nose make you look slender. You're the only strawberry blond I've ever liked. I know that you grew your beard to hide your freckles, but I never told anyone.

We're as different in the body as a seal and a giraffe. You must be a whole head taller than me, Couth, and I can't help remembering what Biggie used to think of people bigger than herself. Come to think of it, though, she must outweigh you.

I mean, your chest could fit in her cleavage, Couth.

Biggie used to like the idea that she couldn't get her arms all the way around my chest and keep her hands locked if I chose to fill my lungs. Well, she could collapse your lungs. And when she wraps her legs around your waist, beware of your back! In fact, it's a wonder she hasn't killed you. Yet clearly you've survived.

But all I said was, "You look well, Couth."

"Thank you, Bogus."

I said, "Well, you know, she wants to stay with you."

"I know."

I threw a snail as far as I could, and you threw one too. Yours went nowhere near as far as mine, though—not with that funny, twitchy way you have of throwing. You've got a lousy arm, Couth, and for all the time you've spent on boats, you row like a bird with a broken wing. And fancy you teaching Colm how to swim.

But all I said was, "You'll have to watch Colm around the water this summer. He's approaching a dangerous age."

"Don't worry about Colm, Bogus," you said. "He'll be fine, and I hope you'll come see him, whenever you want to. And us, too—come see us, you know."

"I know. Biggie told me."

Ploink!

But you threw your snail so badly that it didn't even reach the water; it went *fip!* in the mudflats.

"I'd appreciate lots of photographs, Couth," I said. "When you make some of . . . of Colm, you know, just make a print for me."

"I have some I can give you now," you said.

Ploink!

"Shit, I'm sorry, Bogus," you said. "Who could have known it would work out this way?"

"Me. I could have known, Couth . . ."

"She'd already left you when she came here, Bogus. She'd already made up her mind, you know . . ."

Ploink!

Fip!

"What about the Pillsburys?" I asked. "What are they going to think of you living here with this woman and a child?"

"That's why we got married," you said, and I thought that I must have become a snail—that I must have thrown myself in and swallowed too much water to be hearing you right, Couth.

"You mean you *want* to get married, Couth?" I said.

"No, I mean we *did* . . . sort of."

I brooded over this for about four *ploinks.* How was it possible? It didn't seem that it could be, so I asked, "How could that be, Couth? I thought *I* was married to her."

"Well, you *were,* of course, and this . . . thing hasn't legally gone through yet," you said, "but since you . . . deserted her, it was possible to get a kind of thing proceeding. I don't understand it myself, but one of the Pillsburys' lawyers has some things already drawn up . . ."

I thought, Well, you haven't just been sitting on your hands, have you, Couth?

"We had no way of knowing when or if you'd be back, Bogus," you said. Then you went on and on about how it was almost legally necessary to go through with this, because of the tax structure and the way dependents were regarded by law. *Thank you,* I thought, when you got to the part about there being no alimony this way.

"How much do I owe you?" I said.

"I don't care about that, Bogus," you said, but I already had the envelope out and was pressing nine hundred dollars out into your fine, thin hand.

"Jesus, Bogus. Where did you get this?"

"I've struck it rich, Couth," I told you, and tried to put the envelope back in my pocket as if it were a casual gesture—as if there were other envelopes stashed all over my body, and I wasn't exactly sure which pocket this one belonged in. Then, because I thought you were going to refuse it, I started to babble, beginning no place special.

"If I can't live with them, Couth, then I'm very glad it's you. You'll take better care of them than I have, I'm sure, and I won't ever worry about them with you. It's also a wonderful part of the country to grow up in, and you can teach Colm photography."

"Biggie is going to help this summer," you said. "You know, when the Pillsburys are here—shopping and doing some cooking and taking care of the house. It will give me more time to take pictures and work in the darkroom . . ." you trailed off. "I've got a part-time job at Bowdoin in the fall. It's only forty-five minutes away. You know, just one section of students—a sort of workshop in photography. They gave me a show this spring and the students even bought a few prints."

The weight of this small talk was crushing us.

"That's great, Couth."

"Bogus, what in hell are you going to do now?" you asked me after a long silence.

"Oh, I have to get back to New York," I lied. "But I'll be up again . . . when I get settled, you know."

"It's almost morning," you said. We watched an early orange sun rise out of the sea, its faint glow striking the shore. "Colm gets up early. He can show you his animals. I built a kind of zoo in the boathouse of things I caught for him."

But I didn't want to be around to see what he looked like and if he even liked me any more. Let the grave mound grow a little grass, I always say; then it's safe to look.

But all I said was, "I've got to talk to my driver now, Couth."

When I tried to get up, you caught me by the belt and said, "Your driver doesn't even know who you are, Bogus. What's going on with you?"

"I'm okay, Couth. I'll be all right."

You stood up with me, you frail angel bastard, and you took hold of my beard and shook my head gently, saying, "Oh, shit, oh, shit, if we could only both live with her, Bogus, *I* wouldn't mind—you know that, don't you? I even asked her that once, Bogus."

"You did?" I said. I was holding your beard tight; I half felt like kissing you, but also like snatching you bald. "What did she say to that?"

You said, "She said no, of course. But I wouldn't have minded it, Bogus —I think."

"I wouldn't have minded it, either, Couth," I said. Which was probably not true.

Like a buoy out on the water, all of the sun was showing itself now, bobbing on the surface of the sea, and suddenly there was too much light to see you by, Couth, so I said, "Get me those photographs, will you? I have to go now . . ."

We went up to the house together, taking the flagstone steps up to the boathouse path two at a time. I felt you slip the money I'd given you into my back pocket. And I remembered your bare ass one moonlight on these flagstones, where you lay singing on your belly, Couth, too drunk to stand. That girl with you—one of the two we picked up at the trailer park in West Bath—was putting on her bathing suit, fed up with trying to get you up to the house and the master bedroom. I was cozy with my half of those girls up in the boathouse loft.

I watched you strike out on the lawn, Couth, and I remember thinking to myself as I lay there smugly, not too drunk to screw, Poor Couth is never going to get a girl.

Well, Couth, I've been wrong before.

When they came into the kitchen, Biggie had just made a sandwich for Dante Calicchio. It was a large sandwich which Dante was gnawing off a serving platter shaped like a trough, and Biggie had poured him a beer which he was drinking out a stein the size of a flower vase.

Dante was wondering who was going to go off with whom next. If this is the part where I take the big blond broad down to the dock, I won't mind, he thought.

"Will you have something to eat, Bogus?" Biggie asked.

But Couth said, "He wants to go before Colm gets up."

Who? thought Dante Calicchio. Who in hell could be *sleeping* through a night like this?

"Well," Bogus said, "I'd like to see him, actually, but I don't want him to see *me* . . . if that's not too much to ask."

"He feeds his animals in the boathouse, the first thing when he gets up," Couth said.

"And he eats his breakfast on the dock," Biggie said.

Bogus thought, A routine. Colm has a routine. How kids love a good routine. Did *I* ever establish a routine with Colm?

But all he said was, "I could watch him from the pool room, couldn't I?"

"I've got some binoculars," Couth said.

"Jesus, Cuthbert," Biggie said. Couth looked embarrassed; she did, too. Bogus thought, *Cuthbert?* When was it anyone called you Cuthbert, Couth?

In a corner of the kitchen, wary of the spice-rack debris, Dante Calicchio wolfed his sandwich, quaffed his beer and wondered if the limousine service was worried, and if his wife had called the police. Or would it be the other way around?

"We'll be going pretty soon," Bogus said to Dante. "Why don't you take a walk, get some air . . ."

Dante's mouth was stuffed so he couldn't talk, but what he was thinking was, Oh, sweet shit, you mean I got to take you back with me? But he didn't say a word, and he pretended not to see Bogus slip a big wad of money— maybe as much as a thousand dollars—into the breadbox.

Dante sat below the high-water mark on the cool wet steps leading from the dock to the boat ramp and marveled at the miniature life he saw swarming in the tide pools on the mudflats, and in the teeming crevices of the bared rocks. It was the only mud he had ever seen that he wanted to stick his bare feet in, and he sat with his trousers rolled up to his knees and his blue-white city toes asquirm in the cleanest muck he'd ever felt. On the dock above him, his dusty black city shoes and thin black city socks looked so ominous and foreign that even the gulls were wary of them. The braver terns swooped low, then shrieked off in alarm at this strange deposit left by the tide.

Out at the mouth of the bay, a lobsterman was pulling in his traps, and Dante wondered what it would be like to work with his arms and his back again, and whether he'd get seasick.

He got up and walked gingerly out on the flats, feeling a shell prick his foot now and then, wary of the squiggling life all around him. An old lobster pot lay washed up against the far mooring post of the dock; Dante made his cautious way toward it, wondering what beasts would be inside. But it was staved in and its only contents were the bait, a fish head, picked clean. Then a clamworm scuttled across his foot and he yelped and ran painfully up the shoreline. When he looked up to see if anyone had observed his cowardice, he saw a dark handsome little boy watching him. The boy was in his pajamas and he was eating a banana. "It was just a clamworm," Colm said.

"Do they bite?" Dante asked.

"They pinch," said Colm, hopping off the low side of the dock and climbing barefoot over the sharp rocks as if his feet were soled with rope. "I'll catch one for you," he said. He handed Dante his banana and walked through the shells which, Dante was sure, had ribboned his own feet. Feeling sheepish, he resisted the temptation to examine himself for cuts and watched the boy prowl the mudflats, prodding with his fingers at terrible live-looking things Dante wouldn't have poked with a pole.

"They're kind of hard to catch sometimes," said Colm, squatting down and digging up a great glob of mud. His tiny hand shot into the hole and came up with a long greenish-reddish worm which wrapped itself around his hand. Colm had it pinched just behind the head and Dante could see the thing's black pincers groping blindly in the air.

Wise-ass kid, Dante Calicchio thought. You come near me with that thing and I'll drop your banana in the mud. But Dante held his ground and let Colm walk right up to him.

"See the pinchers?" Colm asked.

"Yeah," said Dante. He thought of giving Colm back his banana, but he feared the boy might think he was making an exchange. Also, Colm was covered with mud. "Now you're too dirty to eat your breakfast," Dante said.

"No," said Colm. "I can wash, you know." He led Dante to a tide pool trapped higher up in the rocks and they washed the mud away together.

"You want to see my animals?" Colm asked. Dante wasn't sure; he was wondering what Colm had done with that worm. "What's a chauffeur?" Colm asked him. "Like a taxi?"

"Uh-huh," Dante said. As alert as a rabbit, on the lookout for the animals lurking in there, he followed Colm to the boathouse.

There was a turtle with what looked like rocks growing all over its back, and a gull Colm told Dante not to get close to—it had a busted wing and liked to peck. There was a fiercely active little animal that looked like an elongated rat, which was a ferret, Colm said. There was a zinc washtub full of herring, half of which were dead and floating on the surface; Colm scooped these up with a net, as if these deaths were commonplace.

"Cat food?" Dante asked, meaning the dead herring.

"We don't have a cat," said Colm. "They kill more than they can eat."

When they came out of the boathouse, the sun was warm enough to flush Dante's face, and a sweet salt-smelling wind had picked up off the bay.

"You know what, kid?" said Dante. "You're pretty lucky to live here."

"I know," Colm said.

Then Dante glanced up at the house and saw Bogus Trumper at the pool-room window watching them through a big pair of binoculars. Dante knew that the boy wasn't supposed to know he was being watched, so Dante moved his bulky body between the boy and the house.

"Are you sometimes a soldier?" Colm asked, and Dante shook his head.

He let Colm try on his fancy driver's cap; the kid grinned and marched a few steps up the dock. Funny, Dante thought. Kids love uniforms, and most men hate them.

———————

Trumper watched Colm attempt a military salute. How tanned he was! And his legs seemed much longer than he remembered.

"He's going to have your length, Big," he mumbled. Biggie was exhausted; she lay sleeping on the couch in the pool room. Bogus was all alone at the binoculars, but Couth heard him. When he saw Couth looking at him, Bogus moved away from the binoculars.

"He looks fine, doesn't he?" said Couth.

"Yup, yup," said Trumper. He looked at Biggie. "I won't wake her up," he said. "You say goodbye for me." But he tiptoed up to where she lay; he seemed to be waiting for something.

Couth tried to be casual about looking out at the sea, but Trumper still didn't seem comfortable, so Couth ambled out of the pool room. Then Bogus bent over Biggie and kissed her fast and light on the forehead, but before he could straighten up, she reached a groggy hand into his hair, giving him a soft stroke and a sleepy groan.

"Couth?" she said. "Is he gone?"

———————

He was gone, all right. He had Dante stop at an Esso station in Bath and pack the tiny icebox in the back of the limousine full of ice. In Brunswick, he bought a fifth of Jack Daniel's, and in a Woolworth's across the street, one glass.

So he was gone by the time they crossed the Massachusetts line. He sat in the plush back seat with the glass divider shut tight, and drank until the tinted windows seemed a darker green, even though the day was getting brighter. In the soundless, air-conditioned Mercedes, he slumped like a dead king riding in his cushioned coffin back to New York.

Why New York? he thought. Then he remembered that it was because Dante was going there. He took out his envelope of money and counted up to a fuzzy fifteen hundred or eighteen hundred, give or take a hundred or so. It never came out the same twice, so after he'd counted it four times he put it back in his pocket and forgot about it.

But Dante noticed, and it was the first notion he had that the nut in back might not be so rich. If you took the time to count it, you didn't have enough.

By the time they got to New Haven, Trumper was so crocked that Dante didn't even have to ask if they could stop for a minute. Dante phoned New York and got a bawling out from the limousine service and a lot of tearful shouting from his wife.

When he returned to the car, Trumper was simply too stewed to understand what Dante wanted to tell him. Dante wanted to warn Trumper that "they" were waiting for him in New York. "You mean the cops?" Dante had asked the limousine service. "What do they want with him?"

"Bigger than ordinary cops," the limousine service told Dante.

"Oh, yeah? What'd he do?"

"They think he's nuts," the limousine service said.

"No shit," said Dante. "Is that a crime?"

Dante tapped on the glass divider and finally roused Bogus Trumper into some form of recognizable stare. Then Dante decided to let it go; he just waved to Trumper through the glass. Trumper smiled and he waved back.

But Dante was warming up to this nut now; he was moved by him. Even before they'd left Maine, he'd changed his mind about the guy. He'd asked Trumper if he could stop at a gift shop along the road; he wanted to get some souvenirs for his wife and kids.

Trumper had let him stop, and when Dante went inside to browse through plastic lobsters and seacoast watercolors painted on driftwood logs, Trumper looked at the photographs Couth had given him as he was leaving. There was a whole stack of pictures of Colm, big eight-by-tens: Colm on the mudflats, Colm in a boat, Colm on the beach in a snowstorm (so they had already moved in with Couth during the winter!), Colm formally posed in Biggie's lap. They were all lovely.

But the last photograph shocked Trumper. Perhaps Couth had put the photographs together too quickly and hadn't meant to include it, for it was obviously from a rather different series. It was a close-up of a nude, distorted by a wide-angle lens. The shot was focused on the woman's crotch, and she was lying in a field in such a position that the texture of the grass between her spread legs nearly matched the texture of her public hair; in fact, that was clearly the idea of the photograph. The wide-angle rounded the world above her, and her face was small and faraway and not in focus. But her twat was in focus, all right.

Mother Earth? Trumper thought. He didn't like the photograph, but he realized that if Couth had not included it by mistake—if Couth had meant to give it to him—that the gesture was generous and well-meaning, like Couth. And also like Couth, in surprisingly bad taste. The nude was Biggie.

Trumper looked up and saw Dante coming. He opened the door of the back seat because he wanted to show Trumper what he'd bought for his children: three inflatable beach balls and three sweatshirts with MAINE! across the chest; under the letters a large lobster cocked his claws.

"That's nice," Trumper said. "Very nice."

Then Dante saw the pictures of Colm, and before Trumper could stop him, Dante picked the stack up and started leafing through them. "I want to tell you, sir," he said, "that's a fine-looking boy you got."

Trumper looked away, and Dante, embarrassed, said, "I knew he was yours. He looks just like you."

Then Dante came to the crotch shot of Biggie, and though he tried to look away, he couldn't. Finally he forced himself to slip the photograph to the bottom of the stack and handed them all back to Trumper.

Trumper was trying to smile. "Very nice," Dante Calicchio said, his mouth a hard line, fighting a leer.

Then it was New York all around me, I could tell. And Jack Daniel's Old Time No. 7 Brand Quality Tennessee Sour Mash Whiskey, 90 proof, wallowing there in my brain, its good burnt taste so thick on my tongue that I could have chewed it.

I could see them out there, wanting to get at me. They rapped the window and fucked around with the door latch, and they shouted at my big brutish good-hearted driver, "Calicchio! Open up, Calicchio!"

Then they had my door open and I caught the first one smack on his forehead with that lovely squarish bottle Jack Daniel puts his whiskey in. Some others helped the man off the floor, and then they came at me again.

I was all right when they kept their distance, but when they moved in close, I'd lose the focus. I could make out Dante, though; that good man was begging them to go easy on me. He had a persuasive way of doing it; he would put his thick-fingered hands on their throats until they gargled a queer tune and danced gently away from me. "Here, here," he kept saying. "Just don't anybody hurt him, he hasn't done anything. I just want to give him something, a little present. Now, you let me do that, please." Then he'd add something in a slightly lower key, like, "You want to keep your teeth, or should I transplant them up your ass, faggot?"

They were tugging me one way and Dante was tugging me another. Then there was an awesome heave in one direction for a considerable distance, during which an unidentified man yelled out that he was being killed, and another stranger began bleating like a goat, and I was all alone and free for a minute. Then my guardian angel, Dante Calicchio, was reaching into his underwear—in his crotch, of all things—and from out of his crotch, of all places, he pulled a crinkled-up thing and stuffed it down my shirt front, saying breathlessly, "Here, here, here, for God's sake . . . I think you're going to need every bit of this you can hold on to . . . Now take off, if you're smart at all. *Run!*"

Then we were in rapid motion once more, and faraway from me I saw Dante Calicchio playing with two toy men. They must have weighed no more than ten pounds each, because Dante tossed one of them through the windshield of a parked car and shook the other one upside down like a rag-doll puppet until I could no longer see, because all the other people swarming around seemed to be trying to get into the game Dante was playing.

Then they had me again. They drove me around in a car with the window open, and they made me keep my head hanging out; I guess they thought

I needed air. But I was not so far gone that I couldn't recall the crinkled-up thing under my shirt front, and when they were riding me up in this elevator, I slipped it out and sneaked a peek at it. It was some kind of money —I couldn't read how much—and one of the men in the elevator took it away from me.

I *think* I was in an elevator; we were in a hotel, I think. But all I thought at the time was, What a funny thing to carry in your crotch!

ℬℬ
Welcome to the Order of the Golden Prick

Throughout Tulpen's hospital visit, I alternately dozed and stared, opening my eyes suddenly as if I'd been startled, gawking unfocused over my shoulder, acting a lolling stupor to perfection, though I had to pee something fierce.

Ralph came to visit later in the afternoon, pronounced me dead and asked Tulpen what my prick looked like. But she seemed genuinely worried and snapped at him. "I haven't seen it," she said. "He's all doped up. He doesn't know where he is."

Ralph circled the bed; he'd brought the mail, and under the pretense of looking for a place to put it, he peeked behind the drawn curtain at my roommate—the sloshing old gentleman with the erector set of intake and output tubes.

"Let's ask a nurse," Ralph said.

"Ask her what?" Tulpen said.

"To let us see it," Ralph said. "Maybe we could just lift his sheet?"

I rolled my eyes and mumbled a little German to impress them.

"He's in his Nazi period," Ralph announced, and I lay there as if lobotomized, waiting for them to say intimate things to each other or exchange touches. But they never did; in fact, they didn't appear to be getting along well at all, and I wondered if they'd seen through my pretense and were playing it cool.

When they finally left, I heard Tulpen ask the floor nurse when Vigneron would be coming around, and whether they planned to release me that night. But I didn't hear the nurse's answer; my roommate chose that moment to leak or ingest something loudly, and when he'd ceased his awful, liquid tremors, they had gone.

I had to get up and pee, but when I moved I caught one of my wiry stitches on the top sheet and let out such a piercing shriek that a covey of nurses burst into the room and the old gentleman gurgled in his dreams and hoses.

Two nurses walked me to the bathroom, and I held my hospital gown out in front like a jib so that it wouldn't brush against my wounded piece.

I made the foolish error of looking at myself before trying to pee. I could not see a hole; it was scabbed shut and a black tangle of stitches made me resemble the tied-off end of a blood sausage. I stalled by asking a nurse to bring me my mail.

There was a letter from my old thesis chairman, Dr. Wolfram Holster. He had enclosed an article from *The North Germanic Languages Bulletin,* written by that old comparative literature wizard from Princeton, Dr. Hagen von Troneg, which bemoaned the lack of studies in the ancestor tongues of the North Germanic chain. From von Troneg's point of view, ". . . any in-depth understanding of the religious pessimism in works from the Norwegian, Swedish, Danish, Icelandic and Faroese is impossible unless the task is undertaken to update the few translations we already have, and we undertake further to translate previously untranslated works from the Old West Norse, Old East Norse and Old Low Norse." Dr. Wolfram Holster's comment was that the time was certainly "ripe" for *Akthelt and Gunnel.*

In a p.s., Holster added his sympathies for what he'd learned of my "situation." He elaborated: "A thesis chairman rarely has the time to involve himself in the emotional problems of the doctoral candidate; however, in the light of such a timely and needed project, I feel a chairman must, to a more personal degree, be as constructively forgiving as he must be constructively critical." His conclusion: "Do let me know, Fred, how *Akthelt and Gunnel* is coming."

Which, in the toilet cubicle of the hospital, reduced me to laughter, then to tears. I put Holster's letter in the toilet, and this gave me the courage to piss on it.

In my wandering stupor in Europe, I had written to Holster twice. One was a long, lying letter wherein I described my research on the tragic Icelandic queen Brünnhilde and her possible relationship to the Queen of the Dark Sea in *Akthelt and Gunnel.* Of course there is no Queen of the Dark Sea in *Akthelt and Gunnel.*

My other communication with Holster was a postcard. It was a tiny detail from Breughel's great painting, "The Slaughter of the Holy Innocents." Children and babies are being ripped out of their mothers' arms; their fathers' arms, trying to grip them fast, are being hacked off. "Hi!" I'd written on the back of the postcard. "Wish you were here!"

After a while, one of the nurses came to the bathroom door to ask if I was all right. She walked me back to my bed, where I had to wait for Vigneron to come release me.

I looked at the rest of my mail. There was a large envelope from Couth full of documents about the divorce; I was supposed to sign them. A note from Couth advised me not to actually read them; they were worded in a "tasteless fashion," he warned me, so that the divorce would be taken seriously. I didn't know who had to take it this seriously, so I went against his advice and read a little. There was something about my "gross and depraved adulterous activity." Also mentioned was my "cruel and inhuman departure from all responsibility," and my "heartless abandonment, which bordered on the degenerate."

It seemed pretty cut and dried, so I signed everything. There's not much to signing things.

The rest of my mail wasn't mail at all. That is, it was wrapped up, but it was from Ralph and there wasn't any postage. A get-well gift? A joke? A vicious symbol?

It was a kind of diploma.

ORDER OF THE GOLDEN PRICK

Greetings! Be It Known By These Present
That
FRED BOGUS TRUMPER

Having Demonstrated Exceptional Bravery, Valor, Gallantry And Phallic Phortitude, Through Having Dauntlessly Endured The Surgical Correction Of His Membrum Virile, And Having Successfully Survived A Fearsome Urethrectomy With Not Less Than Five [5] Sutures, Is Hereby Recognized As A Full Knight

In The Brotherhood Of The Order Of The
Golden Prick
And Is Entitled To All Privileges And Braggartry
Pertaining
Thereto.

It was actually signed, too, by Jean Claude Vigneron, Attending Surgeon, and by Ralph Packer, Chief Scribe & Prick. But where, I wondered, was the signature of Tulpen, Chief Mistress of Interest?

Trumper was still batty and paranoid when Vigneron came to release him.

"Well, it went very well," Vigneron said. "And you don't have too much pain urinating?"

"I'm just fine," said Trumper.

"You should be careful not to catch the stitches on your underwear or bedclothes," Vigneron said. "In fact, you'll probably be most comfortable the next few days if you stay home and don't wear any clothes."

"Just as I thought," Trumper said.

"The stitches will fall out by themselves, but I'll want to see you in a week, just to make sure you're all right."

"Any reason to suspect I won't be all right?"

"Of course not," Vigneron said. "But it's customary, after surgery, to have a checkup."

"I may not be here," Trumper told him.

Vigneron seemed bothered by his aloofness. "Are you all right?" he asked. "I mean, do you feel okay?"

"Just fine," Trumper said. Conscious that he was making Vigneron uneasy, he tried to make amends. "I've never felt better," he lied. "I'm a new man. I'm not the old prick I was."

"Well," Vigneron said, "I'm not really in a position to vouch for that."

Vigneron was right, of course; Vigneron was *always* right. It was most uncomfortable to wear any clothes.

Trumper eased himself into his underwear, a greased gauze pad stuck to the end of his penis. This kept the stitches from tangling in the weave of his clothes; they tangled in the gauze pad instead. Walking was a gingerly accomplished feat. He plucked the crotch of his pants away from himself and ambled bow-legged, like a man with live coals in the pouch of his jockstrap. People stared at him.

He took his mail and the odd gift from Ralph. On the subway he stared at an austere and formal couple who looked as if they had meant to take a cab. Would you like to see my diploma? he thought.

But when he reached the Village, nobody paid any attention to him. People down there were always walking in strange ways, and he looked no more odd than half the people he saw.

As he fumbled for his key on the landing outside Tulpen's door, he heard the splashy squeegee-sounds of Tulpen in the bathtub. She was talking to someone, and he froze.

"It's a very simplistic whitewash," she was saying, "to attempt to cover very deep and complicated people and things with very easy generalizations, superficialities—you know. But I think it's just as simplistic to assume that everyone is complex and deep. I mean, I think Trumper really does operate on the surface . . . Maybe he *is* a surface, just a surface . . ." She trailed off, and Trumper heard her sliding in the bathtub and saying, "Come on, let's call it a night."

He turned away from her door, hobbled down the landing to the elevator, out and onto the moving street. *Let's call it a night,* he thought.

If he'd waited, he would have heard the scene cut and finished, heard Ralph bawling out Kent and Tulpen asking them to leave.

But I went straight to the Christopher Street studio and let myself in through Ralph's elaborate devices and sequence of locks. I knew what I was looking for; I had some things I wanted to say.

I found the cut strips of what Ralph called "fatty tissue." These were bits of overlong footage, or scenes considered weak in some way. Tulpen had them hanging in the dust closet of her editing room.

I didn't want to destroy anything valuable; I wanted to use footage I knew was second-rate. I looked through a lot of stuff. The parts with me and Colm and Tulpen on the subway were interesting. Also, there was a long shot of me, alone, coming out of a pet shop in the Village with a fishbowl sloshing under each arm—presents for Tulpen, one day when I was in the mood. The pet-shop proprietor, who comes to the doorway to wave goodbye to me, looks like a German shepherd in a Hawaiian sport shirt. He continues to wave long after I've left the frame.

I did a little rough splicing; I knew that I didn't have much time, and I wanted to do a good job of laying the sound strip over the footage.

My cock hurt so much that I took off my pants and underwear and walked around bare-ass, being careful to avoid the edges of tables and the backs of chairs. Then I took my shirt off, too, because it brushed against me, especially when I sat down. So then I was naked except for my socks. The floor was cold.

It was getting light out when I finished; I moved the projector into its place in the viewing room and dropped the screen down so that they'd know right away that something had been set up for them. Then I ran through the footage once, just to check.

It was a short reel. I marked the can with adhesive tape; THE END OF THE MOVIE, it said. Then I rethreaded the projector, advanced the film to just the right place, and adjusted the focal length; all they had to do was switch it on, and this is what they would see:

Bogus Trumper with his son, Colm, riding on a subway. The pretty girl with the nice breasts, the one who can make Colm laugh and Trumper touch her, is Tulpen. They are sharing a secret, but there's no sound. Then my voice-over says, "Tulpen, I am sorry. But I do not want a child."

CUT.

Bogus Trumper is leaving the pet shop, the fishbowls under his arms, and the German shepherd in a Hawaiian sport shirt waves goodbye to him. Trumper never looks back, but his voice-over says, "Goodbye, Ralph. I don't want to be in your movie any more."

It was a pretty short reel, and I remember thinking that they could probably stay awake through it.

I was looking around for my clothes when Kent let himself into the studio. A girl was with him; Kent was always bringing girls into the studio when he was sure we weren't going to be there. That way, he could show them around as if he owned the place, or was responsible for all that machinery in some grand way.

He was pretty surprised to see me, all right. He noticed I was wearing green socks. And I don't think Kent's girl ever knew that a person's pecker could look like mine. "Hello, Kent," I said. "Have you seen my clothes?"

———————

They discussed the operation while Kent tried to reassure his girl and Trumper agonizingly put on his gauze pad and underwear. Then Bogus told Kent that under no circumstances was he to preview the little reel that lay in wait on the projector; it was meant for Ralph and Tulpen to watch together, and would Kent be so kind, please, as not to touch *anything* until they were all there to watch it together.

Kent read the adhesive tape on the reel can. "The end of the movie?" he asked.

"You bet your ass, Kent," Trumper said. Then he walked out holding his crotch out in front of himself.

He might have waited. If he had, Kent might have told him about the bathtub scene they'd shot. If he'd waited longer, he might have noticed that Ralph and Tulpen didn't come to the studio together, or even from the same direction.

But he didn't wait. Later he thought about how he had this infuriating habit of leaving too soon. Later, after Tulpen had straightened him out about her nonrelationship with Ralph, he had been forced to confess that he'd never even had a good reason for leaving at all. In fact, Tulpen pointed out, he had simply made up his mind to go sometime before, and that anyone looking for excuses to leave can always find them. He didn't argue.

But now, with his raw new prick, he let a little of the morning pass, then went to Tulpen's apartment when he was sure that she'd be at the studio. There he picked up some of his things, and a few things that weren't his; he stole a cereal bowl and a bright orange fish for Colm.

It was a long bus ride to Maine. The pit-stops were endless, and in Massachusetts it was discovered that a man in the rear of the bus had died; a sort of quiet heart attack, the other passengers assumed. The man had meant to get off in Providence, Rhode Island.

Everyone seemed afraid to touch the dead man, so Bogus volunteered to lug him off the bus, though it nearly cost him his prick. Perhaps all the others were afraid of catching something, but Bogus was more appalled at the fact that the man was unknown to everyone around him. The driver looked in the man's wallet and discovered that he lived in Providence. The general reaction was that it was more bothersome to have missed your stop than to have died.

In New Hampshire Trumper felt compelled to introduce himself to some-one and struck up a conversation with a grandmother who was on her way home from a visit with her daughter and son-in-law. "I guess I just can't understand the way they live," she told Bogus. She didn't elaborate, and he told her not to worry.

He showed her the fish he was bringing to Colm. He'd refilled the cereal bowl with fresh water at every pit-stop along the way. At least the fish was going to make it. Then he fell asleep and the bus driver had to wake him up.

"We're in Bath," the driver told him, but Trumper knew he was in limbo. What's worse, he thought, I've been here before.

What had made this leaving different from the first leaving was not necessarily a sign of health. That is, it was easier this time, and yet he hadn't really wanted to go. All he knew was that he had never finished anything, and he felt a need, almost as basic as survival, to find something he could finish.

Which made him remember Dr. Wolfram Holster's letter, flushed down a hospital toilet with bloody pee, and that was when he decided to finish *Akthelt and Gunnel.*

Somehow the decision was uplifting, but he was aware that it was a queer thing to feel positive about. It was as if a man, whose family had for years assailed him about finding something to do, had sat down one night to read a book, only to be interrupted by a disturbance in the kitchen. It was just his family, laughing about something, but the man flung himself upon them, throwing chairs, punches and vile language until they all lay bruised and cringing under the kitchen table. Then the man turned to his horrified wife and said to her encouragingly, "I'm going to finish reading this book now."

One mauled member of his family might have dared to whisper, "Big deal."

Still, the decision was enough to give Trumper a sort of frail courage. He dared to call up Couth and Biggie and ask if one of them would pick him up at the bus station.

Colm answered the phone, and the pain when Trumper heard his voice seemed greater than if he'd tried to pass a peach pit through his sutured prick. But he was able to say, "I have something for you, Colm."

"Another fish?" Colm asked.

"A live one," Trumper said, and looked at it again to make sure. It was doing fine, it was probably seasick from the sloshing in the cereal bowl, and it certainly looked small and delicate, but it was still swimming around, by Christ.

"Colm?" Trumper said. "Let me speak to Couth or Mommy. Someone's got to come get me at the bus station."

"Did the lady come with you?" Colm asked. "What's her name?"

"Tulpen," Trumper said, passing another peach pit through his prick.

"Oh, yeah, *Tulpen!*" Colm said. He obviously liked her a lot.

"No, she didn't come with me," Trumper told him. "Not this time."

34

Into a Life of Art:
Prelude to a Tank on the
Bottom of the Danube

You asshole, Merrill! You were always hanging around American Express, waiting for lost little girls. I guess you found one, and she lost you, Merrill.

Arnold Mulcahy told me it happened in the fall. A restless time, eh, Merrill? That old feeling of needing to find someone to spend the winter with.

I know how it must have been; I was familiar with your American Express approach. I'll hand it to you, Merrill; you could cultivate a marvelous look. It was the former fighter-pilot look; the ex-Grand Prix racer who'd lost his nerve, and perhaps his wife too; the former novelist with a writer's block; the ex-painter, out of oil. I never knew what it was you *really* were. The unemployed actor? But you had a great look; you had the aura of an ex-hero, a former *somebody*. Biggie said it right: Women liked to think they could bring you back to life.

I remember the tour buses from Italy unloading in front of American Express, and the collection of sneering onlookers watching the clothes, imagining the money. A mixed group would leave the bus. Older ladies, unselfconsciously speaking English, expecting to be taken advantage of, wise enough not to mind looking foreign and perhaps stupid. Then a younger crowd—embarrassed even by being associated with such a crowd. They would try to set themselves apart and to look fluent in four languages. They wore a cool disdain for their fellow tourists, their cameras inconspicuous, their luggage not excessive. You would always pick the prettiest one of these, Merrill. This time her name was Polly Crenner.

I can visualize it. The girl at the information counter, perhaps with a copy of *Europe on $5 a Day,* reading through a furnished list of the pensions she can afford. You would come up to the counter briskly and speak a rapid German to the information man—some pointless question, like asking if anyone's left a message for you. But the German would impress Polly Crenner; she'd at least look at you, then turn away when you glanced at her and pretend to be reading something interesting.

Then, casually, you would say in *English*—the language making her aware that you and anybody else can tell she's American—"Try the Pension Dobler. A nice spot, on Plankengasse. Or the Weisses Huf, on Engelstrasse; the woman there speaks English. You can walk to them both. Do you have much luggage?"

Reading this as a pickup, she would only indicate her luggage with a nod; then she'd wait, ready to refuse your gentlemanly offer to carry her bags for her.

But you never offered, did you, Merrill? You'd have said, "Oh, that's not much to carry," and thanked the information man in your polished German when he returned to tell you there were no messages for you. *"Auf Wiedersehen,"* you'd say, and then walk out—if she'd let you get away. Polly Crenner must not have let you go, Merrill.

What then? Your usual comic tour of Old Vienna? "What's your interest, Polly? The Roman or the Nazi period?"

And some of your invented history, Merrill? "You see that window, the third one from the corner, fourth floor up?"

"Yes."

"Well, that's where he hid when they were all looking for him."

"Who?"

"The great Weber."

"Oh . . ."

"Every night he'd cross this square. Friends left food for him in this fountain."

And Polly Crenner would feel the old suspense and romance settle on her like dust from the Holy Land. *The great Weber!* Who was he?

"The assassin took a room in the opposite building—just there."

"The assassin?"

"Dietrich, the miserable bastard." And you'd glare at the assassin's window, Merrill, like a raging poet. "It cost just one bullet, and all Europe felt the loss."

Polly Crenner would stare at the fountain where food for the great Weber had been stashed. But *who* was the great Weber?

The dull old city glowing like a live coal all around her, Polly Crenner would ask, "What are you doing in Vienna?" And which mystery would you have used on her, Merrill?

"For the music, Polly. I used to play, before . . ."

Or, more enigmatically, "Well, Polly, I had to get away . . ."

Or, more daringly, "When my wife died, I wanted nothing more to do with the opera. But somehow I haven't been able to break completely clean . . ."

Then what, Merrill? Perhaps your Erotic Art Tour (E.A.T., Inc.)? And if the weather was nice, surely you would have taken Polly Crenner to the zoo. A heavy walk through the Schönbrunn Gardens. You used to tell me, Merrill, that the animals inspired sexual notions. A sip of wine on the terrace, watching the giraffes rub necks? Then into the tried-and-true patter: "Of course, this was all bombed . . ."

"The zoo?"

"In the war, yes . . ."

"How awful for the animals!"

"Oh, no. Most of them were eaten before the bombing."

"People ate them?"

"Hungry people, yes . . ." Here you would look worldly-sad as you reflectively extended a peanut to an elephant. "Well, it's natural, isn't it?" you'd ask Polly Crenner. "When we were hungry, we ate them. Now we feed them . . ." I imagine, Merrill, that you would have made that sound profound.

And then?

Maybe there was urgent mail you were waiting for, and would Polly mind stopping by your apartment for a minute so that you could check? Doubtless she didn't mind.

Somewhere along here there would be talk of swimming while the nights were still warm—which would prompt that nice awkwardness of having to go to your place so you could put on your bathing suit, and having to go to her place so she could slip into hers. Oh, you were smooth, Merrill.

But you blew it! You just had to bring up that one about the tank in the Danube, didn't you? True or not, you had to mention the story.

"*Die Blutige Donau,*" you would say. "*The Bloody Danube.* Have you read it?"

"It's a book?"

"Yes, by Goldschmied. But of course it hasn't been translated."

Then you would drive her out past the Prater.

"What do you call this car?"

"A Zorn-Witwer, 'fifty-four. Quite rare."

Crossing the old canal, you'd pour on the chilly mystique of Goldschmied's prolific river history. "How many men at the bottom of the Danube? How many spears and shields and horses, how much iron and steel and debris of thousands of years of war? 'Read the river!' writes Goldschmied. *'That's* your history! Read the river!' "

Who is Goldschmied? Polly would be wondering. Ah, pretty Polly, but who was the great Weber?

Then you'd say, "I know a piece of the river, a piece of that history." She would wait out your pregnant pause. "Remember the Ninth Panzer Division?" you'd say, and then go on, not waiting for her answer. "The Ninth Panzer sent two scout tanks into Floridsdorf on the night of New Year's Eve, 1939. The Nazis wanted to move a tank company into Czechoslovakia, and their armory was out along the Danube. The scout tanks were looking for trouble in Floridsdorf. There'd been some die-hard resistance out there, and the scouts wanted to divert any saboteurs' intentions on the big tank drive at the river. Well, the scout tanks got the diversion they were seeking.

One of them was blown to bits in front of a factory which made dry milk. The other tank panicked. It got lost in the warehouse monotony of Floridsdorf and ended way up on the Old Danube—the old canal that's blocked off. Did you see? We just drove over it."

"Yes, yes," Polly Crenner would answer, history crushing down on her.

Then you'd stop the Zorn-Witwer at Gelhafts Keller, Merrill. You'd open Polly Crenner's door for her, and she'd bubble, "Well, what happened?"

"To what?"

"The tank."

"Oh, the *tank* . . . Well, it was lost, see."

"Yes . . ."

"And it was New Year's Eve, remember. Very cold. And this wild bunch of resistance people, they were chasing it . . ."

"How do you chase a tank?"

"With a lot of nerve," you'd say. "They kept close to the buildings and tried to disable it with grenades. Of course, the tank gunner was doing some damage; he was blowing half of the suburbs in two. But the people kept after the bastard and finally cornered the tank down on the bank of the old canal. Blocked off, right? The water pretty still and pretty shallow—therefore frozen pretty solid. They forced the thing out on the ice; it was the tank's only chance to get away . . . Well, when the tank was right in the middle, they rolled some grenades out across the ice . . . It sank, of course."

"Wow," Polly Crenner would say, both to the story and to the great beer-steined walls of Gelhafts Keller, through which you would be strolling her, Merrill, right out onto the dock.

"There," you would tell her, pointing out into the Old Danube, where tiny boats with lanterns were paddling lovers and drunks about.

"What?" she would say.

"There! The tank—that's where it broke through the ice. That's where they sank her."

"Where?" Polly Crenner would ask, and you would gently pull her pretty head close to yours and make her sight along your outstretched arm at some black point way out on the water.

And you'd whisper, "There! Right out there she went down. And she's still there . . ."

"No!"

"Yes!"

Then, Merrill, she would ask what in hell you'd brought a flashlight for. You asshole, Merrill . . .

———————

That was, in fact, what Trumper said when the federal men, if that's who they were, steered him out of the elevator at the tenth floor of the Warwick Hotel in New York City.

A well-dressed couple who were waiting for the elevator observed the men guiding Trumper down the hall. One of the Feds said, "Good evening."

"Good evening," the couple mumbled warily.

"You asshole, Merrill," Trumper said.

They took him to room 1028, a two-room suite on the corner which looked up the Avenue of the Americas to the park. From the tenth floor, New York certainly looked like fun.

"You asshole," Trumper said to Arnold Mulcahy.

"Give him a shower, boys," Mulcahy told his men. "Make it very cold." They did. They brought Trumper back to the room wrapped in bath towels, his teeth chattering, and sank him like a sash weight into a voluptuous chair. One of the men even hung up Trumper's espionage suit, and another found the envelope with the hundred-dollar bills in it. That was handed to Mulcahy, who then asked all the men to leave.

Mulcahy had his wife with him, and they were both dressed up. Mulcahy was in a formal dinner shirt with black tie, and his wife, a motherly, fretful sort of person, wore an evening dress which looked like an old prom gown. She examined Trumper's suit as if it were the hide of a freshly skinned beast, then asked him sweetly if he'd like anything—a drink? a snack? But Trumper's teeth were still chattering too much for him to talk. He shook his head, but Mulcahy poured him some coffee anyway.

Then Arnold counted the diminished money in the envelope, whistling softly and shaking his head. "My boy," he said, "you certainly have a hard time adjusting to a new situation."

"That's only human, Arnold," Mulcahy's wife said. He silenced her with a businesslike look, but she didn't seem to mind being excluded from the conversation. She smiled at Bogus and told him, "I care as much for Arnold's boys as if they were *my* boys, too."

Trumper didn't say anything. He didn't think he was one of Arnold Mulcahy's "boys," but he wouldn't have put money on it.

"Well, Trumper," Arnold Mulcahy said, "I can't seem to get rid of you."

"I'm sorry, sir."

"I even gave you a head start," Mulcahy said. He recounted the money and shook his head. "I mean, I got you home again and gave you a little pocket liner—that wasn't even part of the deal, you know, boy?"

"Yes, sir."

"You went to see your wife," Mulcahy said.

"Yes, sir."

"Sorry about that," Mulcahy said. "Maybe I should have told you."

"You *knew?*" Trumper asked. "About Couth?"

"Yes, yes," Mulcahy said. "We had to find out who you were, didn't we?" He took a large manila folder off his dresser, sat down and thumbed through it. "You can't blame your wife, boy," he said.

"No, sir."

"So here you are!" said Mulcahy. "Embarrassing, really. I took some responsibility for you, you see. And you stole a chauffeur! And came back in no condition to be left alone . . ."

"I'm sorry, sir," Trumper said. He really was sorry. He sort of liked Arnold Mulcahy.

"You cost that poor chauffeur his job, boy," Mulcahy said. Trumper tried to remember Dante; dimly he recalled some strange heroics by him.

Mulcahy took about five hundred dollars out of the envelope, then handed the rest back to Trumper. "This is for the chauffeur," he said. "It's the least you can do."

"Yes, sir," Trumper said. Rudely, he counted his remaining money; there was eleven hundred dollars the first time he counted it, but the second time there was only nine.

"That will get you back to Iowa," said Mulcahy. "If that's where you're going . . ."

"I don't know . . . I don't know about Iowa."

"Well, I don't know much about the thesis business," said Mulcahy, "but I don't think there's much money in it."

"Arnold," Mrs. Mulcahy said; she was fastening an elaborate brooch. "We really will be late for the performance."

"Yes, yes," Mulcahy said. He got up and looked at his tuxedo jacket before putting it on; he didn't seem to know which way it went. "Ballet, you know," he said to Trumper. "I love a good ballet."

Mrs. Mulcahy touched Trumper's arm affectionately. "We never go out in Washington," she confided. "Only when Arnold's in New York."

"That's nice," Trumper said.

"Do you know the ballet?" Mulcahy asked him.

"No, sir."

"All those flitty people up on their toes," Mrs. Mulcahy chided.

Mulcahy grumbled as he fought himself into his tuxedo jacket; clearly, he must have been a ballet nut to put himself through this. Bogus had remembered him looking like an ambassador, but when he saw Mulcahy in evening dress, he knew that the man really didn't fit the role. Clothes didn't hang well on him; in fact, they appeared as if they'd been flung on him, wet, and when they dried, they chose to go their own peculiar and wrinkled way.

"What are you going to do now, boy?" Mulcahy asked.

"I don't know, sir."

"Well, dear," Mrs. Mulcahy told Bogus, "you should start with a new suit." She went over and plucked at it as if it might still be in danger of shedding.

"Well, we have to go," Mulcahy said, "and you've got to get out of those towels."

Bogus gathered up his clothes and moved delicately toward the bathroom; his head had something heavy and aching inside it, and his eyes felt so dried out that they felt fried; it hurt to blink.

When he came out, one of the federal men who'd brought him there was standing around with the Mulcahys. "Wilson," Mulcahy said to the man, "I want you to take Mr. Trumper wherever he wants to go—within the confines of Manhattan Island."

"Yes, sir," Wilson said. He looked like a hired killer.

"Where *will* you go, dear?" Mrs. Mulcahy asked.

"I don't know, ma'am," Trumper said. Mulcahy riffled through the manila folder again. Trumper caught a glimpse of a photo of himself and one of Biggie.

"Look, boy," Mulcahy said, "why don't you go see this Ralph Packer?" He pulled out a paper-clipped wad, with Ralph's hairy photo on top.

"He's in Iowa, sir," Trumper said. He couldn't imagine Ralph's history requiring as much authentication as Arnold Mulcahy seemed to hold in his hand.

"The hell he's in Iowa," said Arnold Mulcahy. "He's right here in New York, and doing rather well for himself, too, I might add." He handed Bogus a stack of newspaper clippings. "The missing persons people looked into your friend Packer quite extensively," Mulcahy said. "He was the only one who had an idea where you'd gone."

Bogus tried to visualize what missing persons people looked like. He saw them as invisible, materializing in the form of lampshades and subtle bathroom fixtures which asked you questions while you slept.

The clippings were reviews of Ralph's first movie, the National Student Film Festival winner, *The Group Thing,* whose sound track had been done by Bogus. The film had been shown in the art houses around New York; Ralph now had a studio in Greenwich Village and the distribution for two more of his films had already been contracted. One of the reviews of *The Group Thing* even mentioned how good the sound track was. "Bogus Trumper's infinite sound devices," it said, "are confident, ambitious techniques, extremely well crafted for such a low-budget film." Trumper was impressed.

"If you want my advice," said Mulcahy, "that's a better bet than that thesis business any day of the week."

"Yes, sir," Trumper said obediently, but he couldn't quite imagine Ralph actually getting money for what he did.

Mulcahy gave the hired killer named Wilson Packer's studio address, but the man, whose right eyebrow had just been shaved and stitched back together, seemed troubled about something.

"For heaven's sake, what's the matter with you, Wilson?" Mulcahy asked.

"That driver," Wilson mumbled.

"Dante Calicchio?" Mulcahy prompted.

"Yes, sir," Wilson said. "Well, the police want to know what they should do with him."

"I already told them to let him go," Mulcahy said.

"I know, sir," Wilson grumbled, "but I guess they'd like to have you confirm that personally, or something."

"Why, Wilson?"

"Well, sir," Wilson said, "the guy sure did a lot of damage, even though he didn't really know who we were, or anything. He was really pretty berserk."

"What happened?" Mulcahy asked.

"Well, some of our boys are in the hospital," Wilson said. "You know Cowles?"

"Yes, Wilson."

"Well, Cowles has a broken nose and a few ribs cracked. And you know Detweiller, sir?"

"What about Detweiller, Wilson?"

"Both collarbones busted, sir," Wilson said. "The guy was some kind of wrestler . . ."

Suddenly Mulcahy looked interested. "A wrestler, Wilson?"

"Yeah, and a boxer too, sir," Wilson said. "You know Leary?"

"Yes, of course," Mulcahy said eagerly. "What happened to Leary?"

"Had his cheekbone cracked, sir. The wop just cold-cocked him with a hook. He was mostly a body puncher, sir, but he was getting off those hooks pretty good . . ." Wilson gingerly touched his stitched eyebrow and smiled a little sheepishly. Arnold Mulcahy was smiling too. "And Cohen, sir. He threw Cohen through a windshield of a car. Cohen's got all kinds of lacerations and some water on the elbow."

"Really?" said Mulcahy. He seemed enormously pleased.

"So, sir," Wilson said, "the police thought you might want to reconsider and let them keep the guy awhile. I mean, that wop's sort of dangerous, sir."

"Wilson," Mulcahy said. "Get him out, *tonight,* and bring him here after the ballet."

"After the ballet, sir? Yes, sir," Wilson said. "You just want to bawl him out a little, huh?"

"No," said Mulcahy. "I think I'll offer him a job."

"Yes, sir," Wilson said, but he seemed pained. He looked at Trumper in a surly way. "You know, kid," he told Trumper, "it beats me why anybody'd want to fight over you."

"It beats me too," said Bogus. He shook Arnold Mulcahy's hand and smiled at Mrs. Mulcahy.

"Get a new suit," she whispered to him.

"Yes, ma'am."

"Forget your wife," Mulcahy whispered to him. "That's the best thing."

"Yes, sir."

The thug called Wilson was holding Trumper's well-traveled suitcase, less in friendliness than as a gesture of insult—as if Trumper wasn't capable of carrying it. He wasn't, either.

"Goodbye!" said Mrs. Mulcahy.

"Goodbye," Trumper said.

"God, I *hope* so," said Arnold Mulcahy.

Bogus followed Wilson out of the hotel and into a battered car. Wilson set the suitcase heavily in Bogus's lap.

Trumper rode in silence to Greenwich Village, but Wilson swore and gestured at every odd-looking, queerly dressed person he saw on the crowded sidewalks. "You're going to fit right in here, you fucking freak," he told Trumper. He swerved to avoid a tall black girl walking two handsome dogs and yelled out the window at her, "Eat me!"

Bogus tried to hang on just a little longer. A vision of Ralph Packer as savior; an odd role for Ralph, but then he saw Packer on a bicycle, crossing the Iowa River.

"Well, here we are, hair-pie," Wilson said.

One hundred nine Christopher Street was lit. There was still hope in the world. Bogus noted it was a quiet street with daytime shops, a luncheonette, a spice store, a tailor. But apparently it linked more night-traveled areas; lots of people were walking through it without stopping.

"You missing anything?" Wilson asked him. Bogus felt for the money envelope; yes, he had it, and he was holding his suitcase in his lap. But when he looked puzzled, he saw that Wilson was holding the crinkled-up thing that Dante Calicchio had taken out of his crotch. Bogus remembered then that it was a hundred-dollar bill.

"I guess you lost this in the old elevator, right?" Wilson said. Clearly he wasn't going to give it back.

Trumper knew he wasn't up to a fight; he'd never have been up to a fight with Wilson, anyway. But he felt sort of plucky; he was dancing light-headed on only the fringe of the real world. He said, "I'll tell Mulcahy."

"Mulcahy doesn't want to hear from you," Wilson said. "Just you try to find out who Mulcahy even *is.*" He put the crumpled-up bill in his pocket and kept on smiling.

Trumper didn't really have much interest, but Wilson angered him enough to make him think. He opened his door, slid the suitcase out on the curb and sitting half in, half out, he said, "I'll tell Dante Calicchio." He grinned at Wilson's puffy, freshly stitched eyebrow.

Wilson looked as if he was about to hit him. Trumper kept grinning but he thought, I really *am* crazy. This bohunk is going to beat me to death.

Then a kid wearing a knee-length Day-Glo orange bush-jacket came out on the sidewalk in front of RALPH PACKER FILMS, INC. It was Kent, but Bogus didn't know him yet. Kent approached the car, bent down and peered in the window. "There's no parking here," Kent said officiously.

Wilson was looking for some diversion, and he clearly didn't like Kent's looks. "Shove off, cunt-head," he snapped.

Kent shoved off; he went back inside the studio, perhaps to get a gun, Bogus thought.

"You shove off too," Wilson said to Bogus.

But Trumper had gone beyond sense; he wasn't being brave, just fatalistic; he thought he didn't care. "Dante Calicchio," Bogus said slowly, "can make of you, Wilson, something a dog wouldn't eat."

There was some faraway swearing in RALPH PACKER FILMS, INC. Wilson threw the crumpled-up hundred-dollar bill over Bogus's shoulder out onto the sidewalk, and Bogus barely had time to roll out the open door before the thug gunned the car ahead, the door handle catching Trumper's pants' pocket and spinning him down to the curb.

Trumper picked up the hundred-dollar bill before he picked himself up; he'd skinned his knees, and he sat on his suitcase with his pants pulled up, peering at his wounds. When he heard people coming out of the film studio, he fully expected a horde of Ralph's henchmen who, as surrogates for Wilson, would kick him to pieces in the street. But there were only two people: the kid in Day-Glo orange and the instantly recognizable shuffling gait of the hairy man beside him.

"Hello, Ralph," Trumper said. He thrust the hundred-dollar bill into Ralph's paw and got up off the suitcase. "Get my bag, would you, boy?" he said. "I understand you're in need of a sound tracker."

"Thump-Thump!" Ralph cried.

"It was the other one," Kent mumbled. "The guy who was driving the car . . ."

"Get the suitcase, Kent," Ralph said. He put his arm around Bogus, looked him over, noticed blood and worse. "Jesus, Thump-Thump," Ralph said, "you don't exactly look as if you've found the Holy Grail." He unwrapped the hundred-dollar bill, which Trumper snatched back.

"No Holy Grail to be found, Ralph," Bogus said, trying very hard not to wobble.

"You've been duck hunting again, Thump-Thump," Ralph said, steering him toward the studio door. Bogus managed a faint smile at this joke. "Jesus, Thump-Thump, I think the ducks won again."

At the steep step down to the viewing room, Bogus lost his balance and had to let Ralph carry him into the place. Here I go, he said witlessly to himself. Into a life of art. It didn't seem to be the life for him, but right now, he thought, any life would do.

"Who *is* he?" Kent asked. He hadn't liked what Bogus had said about sound tracking. Kent was the sound man now; he was appallingly bad at it, but he thought he was learning.

"Who is he?" Ralph laughed. "I don't know," he said, and leaned down to where Bogus sat slumped on the projector bench. "Who are you, really, Thump-Thump?" he teased.

But Trumper was giddy with relief, almost reduced to senseless giggles. It's amazing how you can drop your guard down among friends. "I'm the Great White Hunter," he said to Ralph. "The Great White Duck Hunter." But he couldn't even sustain the joke and his head lolled on Ralph's shoulder.

Ralph tried to guide him through the studio. "This is the editing room where we . . ." Bogus fought falling asleep on his feet. In the darkroom, the smell of chemicals was too much for him: the chemicals, the old bourbon, Mulcahy's coffee and the darkroom-reminder of Couth. His elbow slipped into a tub of stop bath, he slopped some fixer on his pants and threw up in a developer tank.

Ralph helped him out of his clothes, rinsed him off over the darkroom sink and searched through Trumper's suitcase for some clean clothes. He found none, but he had some old clothes of his own at the studio, and he dressed Trumper in them. A pair of yellow corduroy bellbottom pants; Trumper's feet stopped at the knees. A cream-colored blouse with ruffles and puffed sleeves; Trumper's hands stopped at the elbows. A pair of green cowboy boots; Trumper's toes reached to their arch. He felt like a dwarf clown of Robin Hood's Merrymen.

"Great White Duck Hunter not feeling so good?" Ralph asked.

"I'd like to sleep for about four days," Trumper admitted. "Then I want to make movies, Ralph. Lots of movies, lots of money. Buy some new clothes," he mumbled, stumbling in Ralph's yellow bell-bottoms. "And a sailboat for Colm."

"Poor Thump-Thump," Ralph said. "I know a good place for you to sleep." He rolled up the absurd bell-bottoms so that Trumper could more or less walk, then called a cab.

"So that's the great Thump-Thump," Kent said; he had heard stories. He sulked in a wing of the viewing room, holding a reel like a discus he would have liked to have thrown at Bogus. Kent saw his sound-tracking career being preempted by this clown called Thump-Thump who looked like an Elizabethan puppet in Ralph's big clothes.

"Get the suitcase, Kent," Ralph said.

"Where are you taking him?" Kent asked.

And Trumper thought, Yes, where am I going?

"Tulpen's," Ralph said.

It was German. Trumper knew the word; *Tulpen* means tulips in German. And Trumper thought, That certainly sounds like a nice place to sleep.

35

Old Thak Undone!
Biggie Puts on Weight!

Biggie and Couth were lovely to him. Without any talk about it, they made up the extra bed in Colm's room. Colm went to bed about eight, and Trumper would lie on the other bed, storytelling until Colm fell asleep.

The story he told was his own version of *Moby Dick,* which seemed appropriate for that sea-house. Colm thought whales were wonderful, so the story according to Trumper was the whale-as-hero, Moby Dick as unvanquished king.

"How big is he?" Colm asked.

"Well," Trumper said, "if you were floating in the water and his tail slapped you, you'd be worse off than an ordinary fly getting hit with a fly swatter." A long pause from Colm. In the fishbowl above his bed, he watched the fragile orange fish from New York, the bus-ride survivor.

"Go on," Colm said.

And Trumper went on and on. "Anyone with any sense would have known enough to leave Moby Dick alone," he said. "All the other whaling men just wanted to hunt the *other* whales. But not Captain Ahab."

"Right," said Colm.

"Some of the other men had been hurt or had lost their arms and legs hunting whales, but it didn't make them *hate* whales," Trumper said. "But . . ." and he paused . . .

"But not Captain Ahab!" Colm cried out.

"Right," said Trumper. The wrongness of Ahab grew clear.

"Tell me about all the things sticking into Moby Dick," Colm said.

"You mean the old harpoons?"

"Right."

"Well, there were old harpoons," Trumper said, "with ropes still hanging off them. Short harpoons and long harpoons, and some knives, and all the other kinds of things that men had tried to stick into him . . ."

"Like what?"

"Splinters?" Trumper wondered. "Sure, from all the boats he'd smashed, he picked up splinters. And barnacles, because he was so old; and seaweed all over him, and snails. He was like an old island, he'd picked up so much junk; he wasn't a clean white."

"And nothing could kill him, right?"

"Right!" said Trumper. "They should have left him alone."

"That's what *I'd* do," Colm said. "I wouldn't even try to *pat* him."

"Right," Trumper said. "Anybody who's smart would know that." And he waited for the refrain . . .

"But not Captain Ahab!" Colm said.

You should always tell stories, Trumper knew, in such a way that you make the audience feel good and wise, even a little ahead of you.

"Do the part about the crow's nest," Colm said.

"High up on the mainmast," Trumper orated dramatically, "he could see what looked like a couple of whales, way off . . ."

"Ishmael," Colm corrected him. "It was Ishmael, right?"

"Right," said Trumper. "Only it wasn't two whales, it was *one* whale . . ."

"A very big one."

"Right," said Trumper. "And when the whale spouted, Ishmael yelled . . ."

" *'Thar she blows!'* " yelled Colm, who did not appear very sleepy.

"Then Ishmael noticed there was something *funny* about this whale."

"It was white!" Colm said.

"Right," said Trumper. "And it had things stuck onto it everywhere . . ."

"Harpoons!"

"Barnacles and seaweed and birds!" said Trumper.

"Birds?" said Colm.

"Never mind," Trumper said. "It was the biggest damn whale Ishmael had ever seen, and it was white, so he knew who it was."

"Moby Dick!" Colm screamed.

"Ssshhh," said Trumper. They calmed down together; they could hear the ocean slapping the rocks outside, creaking the dock, flapping the boats on their moorings. "Listen," Trumper whispered. "Hear the ocean?"

"Yes," whispered Colm.

"Well, the whaling men hear it just like that, *slap, slap* against the ship. At night, when they sleep."

"Right," Colm whispered.

"And the whales come sniffing around the ships at night."

"They *do?*" said Colm.

"Sure," said Trumper. "And sometimes they brush against the ship a little, or bump it."

"Do the men know what it is?"

"The smart ones do," said Trumper.

"But not Captain Ahab," Colm said.

"I guess not," Bogus said. They lay quietly listening to the ocean, waiting for a whale to bump the house. Then the dock creaked and Bogus whispered, "There's one!"

"I know," said Colm in a hoarse voice.

"Whales won't hurt you," Trumper said, "if you leave them alone."

"I know," Colm said. "You should never *tease* a whale, right?"

"Right," Trumper said, and they both listened to the sea until Colm fell asleep. Then the only alert life in the room was the thin vermilion fish from New York, kept alive by constant care.

Trumper kissed his sleeping son goodnight. "I should have brought you a whale," he whispered.

It wasn't that Colm didn't like the fish; it was just that Trumper wished for something more durable. Colm liked the fish very much, in fact; with Biggie's help, he'd written a thank-you note to Tulpen, a most roundabout way for Trumper to apologize for the theft.

"Dear Tulpen," Biggie said. Then, letter by letter, she had to tell Colm how to spell. "D-E-A . . ." Biggie said. With fierce concentration, Colm carved the letters with his pencil clutched tight in his fist.

Bogus was shooting pool with Couth.

"Thank you for the little orange fish," Biggie dictated.

"Thank you *very much?*" Colm suggested.

"T-H-A . . ." Biggie said. Colm carved.

Bogus blew every shot he took. Couth was relaxed and played his usual lucky game.

"I hope sometime you'll come see me in Maine," Biggie dictated.

"Right," said Colm.

———————

But Biggie knew better. When Colm was asleep, she said to Bogus, "You left her, didn't you?"

"I think I'll be back with her, sometime," Bogus said.

"You always do think that," said Biggie.

"Why did you leave her?" Couth asked.

"I don't know."

"You never do," Biggie said.

But she was kind, and they talked easily about Colm. Couth was sympathetic to the idea of Bogus finishing his thesis, but Biggie didn't see it that way. "You hated it out there," she said, "and you weren't ever really interested."

Bogus couldn't think of an answer. His picture of himself returning to Iowa alone in no way resembled his memory of Iowa with Biggie and Colm. Biggie didn't pursue the point; perhaps she saw that too.

"Well, you ought to do something, I think," Couth said.

Everyone more or less agreed to that.

Bogus laughed. "It's important to have an image of yourself," he said. He'd gotten a little looped on Couth's apple brandy. "I think you have to start with a superficial image, like Graduate Student or Translator, something with an easy name. Then you hope you can broaden the image a little."

"I don't know what I started with," Couth said. "I just said, 'I'm living like I want to,' and that was a start. Later, I became a Photographer, but I still think of myself more as just a Living Man . . ."

"Well, but you're very different from Bogus," Biggie said. There was a silence in honor of her authority on that subject.

Bogus said, "Well, it just didn't work thinking of myself as a Film Maker, or even a Sound Tracker. I never really believed it." And he thought, or a Husband, either; I never really believed that. But a Father . . . Well, that was a clearer feeling.

There wasn't much else that was clear, though. Couth commented on the appropriate symbolism of the Maine fog around the house, and Bogus laughed. Biggie said that men were so queerly involved with themselves that simple things escaped them.

With the excuse of too much apple brandy, that was too deep a subject for either Couth or Bogus to pick up. They went to bed.

Bogus was still awake when Biggie and Couth made love in their room down the hall. They were quite discreet, but it was too familiar a silent tension for Bogus to mistake it. Surprised at himself, he realized that he was happy for them. It seemed the best thing in his life that they seemed so happy—that, and Colm.

Later, Biggie used the bathroom, then came quietly into Colm's room and checked his covers. She seemed about to check the covers on Bogus, too, until he whispered to her, "Goodnight, Biggie." She didn't come near him then; it was dark, but he thought she smiled. She whispered, "Goodnight, Bogus."

If she'd come near him, he'd have grabbed her, and Biggie never misread signals of that kind.

He couldn't sleep. After three nights with them, he was aware of himself as an imposition. He went down to the kitchen with *Akthelt and Gunnel;* time for a little worn Old Low Norse and a big glass of ice water. He liked the feeling of all of them asleep, and him their guardian, taking the night watch.

Affectionately he murmured some Old Low Norse and read over the part where Old Thak is killed. Betrayed in the fjord of Lopphavet! Slain by the foul Hrothrund and his cowardly band of archers! Old Thak is lured into the fjord by a false message: that from the vantage of the cliffs above Lopphavet, he can observe Akthelt's fleet returning from the great naval victory at Slint. Standing on the prow of his ship, Thak glides close under the cliffs, but just as he is ready to leap ashore, Hrothrund and his archers let fly at him from their ambush in the woods. Thak's man at the rudder, Grimstad, turns the ship out of range, but Old Thak is too riddled with arrows to even fall down; as prickled as a pincushion, he clings to the jib like a failed hedgehog.

"Find the fleet, Grimstad," Thak says, but he knows it will be too late. Faithful Grimstad tries to make him comfortable on the foredeck, but there is no flat surface on the old king's body; there's no way he can even lie down. "Let me lie in the sea," he says to Grimstad. "I am so full of wood that I shall float."

So Grimstad ties a line to Thak and lowers him overboard; he fastens the line to the gunwale of the ship and tows Old Thak out of the cold fjord of Lopphavet. Trailing behind his ship, Thak bobs in the sea like a buoy full of darts.

Grimstad sails out to meet Akthelt's fleet, returning all happy and gory from its great naval victory at Slint. Akthelt sails alongside his father's ship; "Hail, Grimstad!" he calls. But Grimstad can't bear to tell Akthelt about Old Thak. Akthelt's ship comes closer, and he spots the line tied to the gunwale; his eyes follow it to the curious sea anchor dragging behind, the feather ends of some arrows still above water. Thak is dead.

"Lo! Grimstad!" Akthelt calls, pointing to the line running from the gunwale. "What lies astern?"

"That is your father," Grimstad says. "Foul Hrothrund and his bastard archers betrayed us, my lord!" And while the great Akthelt beats his breast and the deck of his ship, he realizes what Hrothrund's plot must have been: to kill Thak and seize his ship; to sail out to meet the fleet flying Old Thak's flag; and to ambush Akthelt too, as the ships came together. Then, commanding the fleet, Hrothrund would return to claim the kingdom of Thak, would take Akthelt's castle and violate Akthelt's tender wife, Gunnel.

All this boils through Akthelt's mind while he tugs on the line with violent heaves, bringing the body of Thak aboard. He thinks of the long, sharp instruments Hrothrund had in mind for him, and of the thick, blunt instrument he has in mind for Gunnel!

Akthelt smears his body with the blood of his father, orders himself lashed to the mainmast and commands his men to whip him with the shafts of the fatal arrows until his own blood runs with his father's.

"Are you all right, my lord?" Grimstad asks.

"Soon we'll be back at the castle," Akthelt says oddly. But he has a curious thought; he wonders if Gunnel would have liked Hrothrund.

––––––––––

Early in the morning, Colm found Bogus sleeping on the kitchen table.

"If you come down to the dock," Colm said, "then I can come down to the dock too." So they went, Trumper having difficulty aiming his feet.

It was high tide; far out in the eddy the gulls were circling a large mass of seaweed and flotsam—from the look of it, what was left of a castaway rowboat. Trumper was thinking of Old Thak, but when he looked at his son he knew what Colm was thinking.

"Is Moby Dick still alive?" Colm asked.

Trumper thought, Well, why not? I can't provide the kid with God or a reliable father, and if there's something worth believing in, it ought to be as big as a whale.

"I guess he'd be pretty old," Colm said. "Very old, right?"

"He's alive," Trumper said. They looked out to sea together.

Trumper wished he could really produce Moby Dick for Colm. If he'd had a choice of any miracle he could perform, he would have chosen just that: to make the bay roll and swell, inspire a cacophony of gulls to circle overhead, raise the Great White Whale from the depths and make him leap like a giant trout, let them both be showered by the spray of his splashing fall as they stood in awe on the dock, have Moby Dick roll ponderously in the water—show them his scars, his old harpoons and things (but spare Colm the sight of the rotted Ahab lashed to the whale's great side); then watch the whale turn and steam out to sea, leaving them with the memory.

"He really is alive?" Colm asked.

"Yes, and everyone leaves him alone."

"I know," said Colm.

"But no one hardly ever sees him," Trumper said.

"I know."

But a wild part of Trumper's brain was chanting, *Show yourself, old Dick! Up out of that water, Moby!* Such a miracle, he knew, would have been as much a gift to himself as to Colm.

It was time to leave. At the car he even tried joking with Biggie and Couth, saying how nice it was to see them, but that he knew he was inhibiting them. He spoke German playfully to Biggie and had a mock boxing match with Couth. Then, to part on a note of lighthearted humor, he kissed Biggie goodbye and patted her ass. "You're putting on a little weight, Big," he chided.

She hesitated and looked at Couth. Couth nodded, and Biggie said, "That's because I'm pregnant."

"Pregnant!" Colm repeated gaily. "Yah! She's going to have a baby, so I'll have a brother or a sister . . ."

"Or maybe both," Couth said, and everyone smiled.

Bogus couldn't think of a thing to do with his hands, so he held out one to Couth. "Congratulations, old boy," he said, like a voice underwater.

Couth scuffed the ground and said he'd better see if the car would start. Trumper gave Colm another hug, and Biggie, her face turned away, but smiling, said, "Be careful." To Couth? To Bogus? To both of them?

"I love seeing you, always," Trumper said to everyone, and fled.

36

Akthelt Beset with Doubt!
Trumper Grinds to a Halt!

In Iowa his old stitches fell out. A great new hole was in his penis. He wondered if Vigneron had meant to make the opening so big. Compared with what he'd been used to, he now had a bathtub drain.

He went to see a doctor, just any old doctor; there was no provision for specialists in his Student Health Policy. He feared the diagnosis; some former veterinarian amazed at his prick?

"You say this was done in New York?"

But the doctor was a young South American; all the foreigners in the medical school appeared to be given the lowliest cases. The young doctor was very impressed.

"That's a beautiful meatoplasty," he told Bogus. "Really, I've never seen such a neat job."

"But it's so *big,*" Bogus said.

"Not at all. It's perfectly normal."

That shook him; it made him aware of how abnormal he must have been.

That doctor's visit constituted his sole entertainment in Iowa. He lived in his library alcove with *Akthelt and Gunnel* and slept in a spare room in Dr. Holster's basement. By his own choice he left and entered the basement through the cellar door; Holster would gladly have let him use the front door. Sunday dinners he ate with Holster and his married daughter and her family. The rest of his meals consisted of pizza, beer, sausage patties and coffee.

A girl in the adjoining library alcove was also doing a translation. It was from Flemish: "a religious novel, set in Bruges." Occasionally they'd look at each other's dictionaries, and once she asked him to dinner at her place. "I'm a good cook, believe it or not," she said.

"I believe it," he said. "But I've stopped eating."

He had no idea what the girl looked like, but in their library and dictionary way they remained friends. There was no other way for him to have friends. He didn't even drink his beers at Benny's because Benny was always trying to drum up conversation about some half-mythical "old gang."

Instead, he drank a few beers every night at a shiny bar frequented by the residue of the fraternity-sorority set. One night, one of the frat boys asked Bogus when he planned to take a bath.

"If you want to beat me up," Trumper said to him, "go ahead."

A week later, the same guy came up to him. "I want to beat you up now," he said. Trumper didn't remember him, and he executed a competent side leg-dive, picked up the guy's legs and ran him like a wheelbarrow into the jukebox. The frat boy's friends threw Trumper out of the bar. "Christ," Bogus said, bewildered. "He was a nut! He said he wanted to beat me up!" But there were two dozen other bars in Iowa City, and he didn't drink much anyway.

He worked on the translation with a dull, enduring sort of energy. He went all the way through it to the ending before he remembered that there were a lot of verses in the middle section that were made up, and others that were not even translated. Then he recalled that even some of his early footnotes were lies, and parts of the glossary of terms too.

In the back of his mind was a harsh echo he referred to frankly as Tulpen. She had always been one for facts. So he simply started over again and went through the whole translation straight. He looked up every word he didn't know, and conferred with Holster and the girl who knew Flemish about the ones he couldn't find. He wrote an honest footnote for every liberty, and a flat, direct introduction explaining why he had not tried to put the epic in verse but had elected to use simply prose. "The original verse is awful," he wrote. "And my verse is worse."

Holster was enormously impressed with him. Their only argument was over Holster's insistence that Trumper make some introductory remarks "placing" *Akthelt and Gunnel* in perspective in the broader picture of North Germanic literature.

"Who cares?" Trumper asked.

"*I* care!" Holster yelled.

So he did it, and he didn't lie, either. He mentioned all the other, related works he knew of, then admitted to knowing nothing about the writings in Faroese. "I don't have the slightest idea as to whether this work has any relation to Faroese literature in this period," he wrote.

Holster said, "Why don't you just say, 'I prefer to reserve judgment on the relationship of *Akthelt and Gunnel* to the Faroese hero-epics, as I have not researched Faroese literature extensively.' "

"Because I haven't researched it at all," Trumper said.

Ordinarily Holster might have insisted on his point, or claimed that Trumper *should* research Faroese writings, but Trumper's demonic work habits had so impressed Holster that the old thesis chairman let it go. In fact, he was rather a nice man. One Sunday dinner, he asked, "Fred, I would suppose that this work is a kind of therapy for you?"

"What work isn't?" Trumper said.

Holster tried to draw him out. He didn't mind Trumper living in his basement like a rarely seen mole, and occasionally he would call down into the basement and ask Bogus upstairs for a drink. "If *you're* having one," Trumper would say.

The only thing Bogus wrote that wasn't part of his thesis was an occasional letter to Couth and Biggie, and even more occasional letters to Tulpen. Couth wrote back and sent him pictures of Colm; Biggie sent him a package once a month with things like socks and underwear and Colm's finger paintings in it.

He didn't hear from Tulpen. What he wrote her was almost purely descriptive of how he was living: Trumper as monk. But at the end of every letter he would add hesitantly, "I want to see you, really."

Finally he did hear from her. She sent a postcard of the Bronx Zoo which said: "Words, words, words, words . . ." as many times as it took to nearly fill the postcard. At the bottom she left just enough room to add, "If you wanted to see me, you'd do it."

But he threw himself into the end of *Akthelt and Gunnel* instead. Only once—when he heard the girl who knew Flemish crying in her library alcove and didn't go ask her if he could help—did he stop long enough to consider that *Akthelt and Gunnel* might not be good for him.

Akthelt and Gunnel ends rather badly. It's all because of the foul temper Akthelt gets into while he's tied to the mainmast, smeared with his father's gore and being flagellated with the shafts of the father-murdering arrows. Moreover, when his fleet arrives back in the kingdom of Thak, Akthelt discovers that Hrothrund has come to Akthelt's castle, attempted to abduct the Lady Gunnel, failed (or changed his mind), and fled.

Akthelt searches the whole kingdom for the father-murdering, would-be rapist without success. Then he comes home to the castle, wondering why Hrothrund failed to abduct the Lady Gunnel (or changed his mind about it). Did he even try? And if so, how far did he get?

"I didn't even see him!" Gunnel protests. She'd been in the garden when Hrothrund had come to abduct her. Maybe he simply couldn't find her; it was a big castle, after all. Also, most of the people who had seen Hrothrund weren't yet aware of Thak's murder; therefore his appearance wasn't any big deal until the fleet returned and told the evil tale. *Then* people went around saying, "Why, that foul Hrothrund was just here!"

Akthelt is confused. Was Hrothrund the only one involved in the plot? Someone reminds him that it was just last Saint Odda's Fest when Gunnel was seen to dance with Hrothrund.

"But I always dance with lots of people on Saint Odda's!" Gunnel protests.

Akthelt behaves queerly. He demands a full search of the castle's laundry room and unearths one unclaimed pair of leather clogs, one unclaimed stained petticoat, and one unclaimed and boastfully large codpiece. Holding this grubby bundle at arm's length, he confronts Gunnel and attempts to make elaborate sense out of the evidence.

"*What* evidence?" she cries.

Hrothrund is not to be found anywhere in the kingdom of Thak. Reports trickle in from the coast that Hrothrund is at sea, is hiding in the northern fjords, is looting small and defenseless towns along the coast. A worthless pirate! Also, the reports imply, Hrothrund is less interested in looting for gold and food than he is in *sport*. (In Old Low Norse, *sport* means rape.)

Akthelt delves dangerously deeper into himself. "What is that mark there?" he asks Gunnel, fingering an old bruise on the back of her downy thigh.

"Why, from my horse, I think," Gunnel says sweetly—at which Akthelt bashes her in the face.

She cannot go on being wronged this way, so she begs her husband to allow her to try to capture foul Hrothrund by her wiles and prove her innocence before all. But Akthelt fears the trick will be on him, so he denies her request. But she persists. (All this stupid intrigue is the most trying point in the text, actually.)

Finally, after a lot of dithering for twenty-two stanzas, Gunnel loads a rich boat with wares, her maidservants and herself, intending to sail north up the coast, hoping to lure an attack from Hrothrund. But when Akthelt discovers her design, he believes the lure is really set for him; in a rage, he casts her rich ship, her maidservants and Gunnel herself adrift. With no man to sail them and no weapons to guard them, the defenseless ship full of hysterical, useless females sails north up the fjord toward Hrothrund, and despite the pleading from many in the kingdom of Thak, Akthelt refuses to follow.

The expected happens, of course; Hrothrund falls upon them. What a self-fulfilling prophecy to haunt Akthelt for all his remaining days! His wife was faithful, but by suspecting her, he casts her into infidelity. What else could Gunnel do when her maidservants are beset by a boatload of hairy archers, and she herself is faced with the ruthless swine Hrothrund?

Actually, what Gunnel does is pretty fucking shrewd. "Well met, Hrothrund!" she hails him. "For months, tales of your brave insolence have reached us. Make me your queen and our lord Akthelt will be undone!"

Hrothrund fell for it, too, but it cost her. For days and nights in his foul ship's cabin hung with animal skins, Gunnel gave up her body to his savage, slimy ways, until at last he fully trusted her. He would take her, unarmed, without his knife or broad-ax by his bedside, and rut like a contented beast, leaving her gasping. He was fool enough to think it was pleasure that made her gasp.

Then she had him. One day she told him about a safe cove he could sail into for the night; there, friends in favor of Akthelt's overthrow would meet them. So Hrothrund sailed right into the cove where the lookouts of Akthelt's fleet were always stationed. She led Hrothrund right into it. Then, in the long night, Gunnel gave herself to him so untiringly that she finally had him spread out, spent and groggy, beside her. Though barely able to move herself, she had cherished this moment for so long that her will was not to be denied. Groaning her way from his stinking bed, she took up his broad-ax and cut off his smug, ugly head.

Then, perfumed with the aroma of her sex, Gunnel sweetly asked the cabin guard to fetch her a bucket of fresh eels. "For his lord," she said, letting her robe bare her shoulder, and the dolt fetched her the eels quick.

In the morning, Akthelt's fleet fell upon Hrothrund's boats and massacred everyone above deck, including Gunnel's faithful maidservants, long since defiled and humbled by the filthy archers. Then did the bold, righteous and avenging Akthelt stride to Hrothrund's cabin door and cleave it with his two-edged sword, expecting to find his false lady in the arms of the cowardly father-murderer.

But Gunnel sat waiting for him in her best gown, and on the night table in front of her was the severed head of Hrothrund, stuffed with live eels. (In the kingdom of Thak, a legend claimed that this recipe would never let a man's brain rest.)

Akthelt dropped on his knees before her, whimpering his apologies and begging forgiveness for the burden he had forced her to bear. "I bear another burden," Gunnel said coldly. "Hrothrund's spawn is in my belly. You shall have to bear that for me too."

By this time Akthelt was ready to accept almost anything from her, so he agreed abjectly.

"Now," she said. "Take your true wife home."

Akthelt did so, and bore his burden well enough until the child of Hrothrund was born. But he could not fathom her affection for the child; to him, the spirit of the father-murderer, wife-raper lived within the babe, so he slew it and threw it to the wild boars in the moat. It would have been a girl.

"I could forgive you much," Gunnel told him, "but I will never forgive you this."

"You'll learn to," he said, but he wasn't so sure. He slept badly—and alone—while Gunnel roamed the castle every night like a streetwalker whose price was too high for any passer-by.

Then, one night, she came to his bed and made violent love to him, saying she at last felt reconciled to him. But in the morning, she asked the chamber girl for a bucket of fresh eels.

After that, the kingdom of Thak went the way of most kingdoms whose leadership is up for grabs. Gunnel was completely off her rocker, of course. She herself announced Akthelt's death at the morning session of the Council of Elders. She brought Akthelt's head, crammed with eels, to the meeting, placed it on a meat board and set it before the Elders, plunk in the middle of the great table. For years she had been in the habit of serving exotic dishes at these weekly meetings, so many of the Elders were caught off guard.

"Akthelt is dead," she announced, putting the dish down.

One of the Elders was so old that his eyesight was gone. He groped his hand toward the head on the table, which was his customary manner of identifying Gunnel's exotic dishes. "Live eel!" he exclaimed. The Elders were not sure what to do.

The obvious successor to the throne was young Axelrulf, Akthelt and Gunnel's only son, who was now in charge of the occupation of Flan. The Council of Elders sent a messenger to him, informing him of his father's murder at his mother's hand and pointing out that the kingdom of Thak was in danger of division without strong leadership. But Axelrulf was having an awfully good time among the Flans. They were a handsome, hedonistic and civilized people, the living was easy, and Axelrulf had never had political ambitions. At least, that was part of his reasoning. "Tell Mother I'm very sorry," he told the messenger.

In the meantime, some of the Elders were conspiring to appoint one of their own to the throne, and to murder Axelrulf should he come back to claim his birthright. That was the larger part of Axelrulf's reasoning for not being interested in the position. He was no fool.

What happened then was what *always* happens. When no strong leader emerged, the kingdom of Thak erupted in chaotic and ineffectual rebellion. At the castle, Gunnel became obsessed with a rash of lovers, and there were more buckets of fresh eels. Finally, of course, she took a lover who was not so spent and love-drugged as he looked, and he cut *her* head off. He didn't bother with the eels, though.

Finally, when the kingdom of Thak was hardly even a kingdom any more, but a disorganized land with hundreds of tiny, feuding fiefs, what happened then was what *always* happens too.

Young Axelrulf rode up from Flan. In fact, he liked the Flans so much that he brought an army of them into the kingdom of Thak and took over the whole mess very easily. He made peace in the kingdom by killing all the feuders who wanted war. So Thak became Flan, sort of, and Axelrulf married a nice Flan girl named Gronigen.

In the last stanza of *Akthelt and Gunnel,* the anonymous author slyly implies that the story of Axelrulf and Gronigen is probably not much different from the story of Akthelt and Gunnel. So why not stop it here?

Bogus Trumper was more than willing to agree. When he had finished all four hundred and twenty-one stanzas, it seemed a pretty empty accomplishment. In part this was because he had been so honest a translator that there was nothing of his own in the whole work. So he added something.

Remember the part where Gunnel cuts off Hrothrund's head? And then

Akthelt's head? Well, Trumper added an implication that she cut off more than heads. It fit, after all. It suited the story, it certainly suited Gunnel, and most of all, it suited Bogus. He really believed that Gunnel *would* have cut off more than their heads, but that for reasons of etiquette guiding the literature of the time, the author had been obliged to discreetly edit certain details. Anyway, it made Trumper feel better and gave him a small stake of his own in the translation.

Dr. Holster was very pleased with *Akthelt and Gunnel.* "Such a *rich* work!" he exclaimed. "Such a basic pessimism!" The old man moved his arms like a symphony conductor. "Such a crude story! Such a violent, barbaric people! Even sex is a blood sport!"

The notion was no surprise to Trumper. He was a little uneasy, however, that Holster had especially liked the implication he had added, and when the old man suggested a footnote to emphasize the boldness of such an act, Bogus declined by saying he didn't care to draw attention to it.

"And the part with the eels!" cried Holster. "Think of it! She cut off their pricks! How perfect—but I just couldn't imagine it!"

"I could," said Fred Bogus Trumper, B.A., M.A., Ph.D.

So finally he had finished something. He packed and reread his mail. With nothing to occupy him, he felt as if his pulse had slowed down, as if his blood was reptile-thick.

There hadn't been any more mail from Tulpen. His mother had written about his father's ulcer. Bogus felt a little guilty and tried to think of a gift. After some thought, he went to a fancy-food store and sent his father a prime boned Amish ham. Too late, he wondered if ham was good for an ulcer, and quickly sent a letter apologizing for the gift.

He heard again from Couth. Biggie had delivered an eight-pound baby girl, named Anna Bennett. Another Anna. Trying to imagine the baby, Trumper remembered that the ham he'd sent his father also weighed eight pounds. But he felt so happy for Couth and Biggie that he sent them a ham too.

And he heard from Ralph. Typically, a mysterious letter. It mentioned nothing about Trumper abandoning a film career or leaving Ralph Packer Films, Inc., in the lurch, but said simply that he thought Trumper should at least come see Tulpen. Surprisingly, Ralph spent most of the letter describing the girl he was living with now, someone called Matje, "like the herring, you know?" The girl was "not voluptuous, but a brimming person," and Ralph added that "even Tulpen likes her."

Trumper had no picture of what in hell was going on. He understood why Ralph had really written the letter, though; Ralph wanted Bogus's permission to release the film. *Fucking Up* was done, Trumper knew.

Bogus left the letter unanswered for a few weeks. Then one night after his thesis was finished and he was feeling especially aimless, he went to see a movie. It was a film about a homosexual airline pilot who is afraid of rain. By some slip-up, he sleeps with a sympathetic stewardess, who cures him of both his nasty homosexuality and his fear of the weather. Evidently he was afraid of rain *because* he was a homosexual. It was a sloppy and offensive movie in every way, Trumper thought, and afterward he sent a telegram to Ralph. "You have my permission," the telegram said, and it was signed, "Thump-Thump."

Two days later Trumper said his goodbyes to Dr. Holster. *"Gaf throgs!"* Holster hailed him cheerfully. *"Gaf throgs!"*

This was an inside joke from *Akthelt and Gunnel.* When people in the kingdom of Thak wanted to congratulate one another for a job well done, a war well fought or sex well made, they said, *"Gaf throgs!"* ("Give thanks!"). They even had a Thanksgiving Day devoted to such feelings; they called it Throgsgafen Day.

———

It was a perfect September football weekend when Trumper lugged his suitcase and his thesis bound copy of *Akthelt and Gunnel* to the Iowa City bus station. He had his Ph.D. and his memories of selling pennants and buttons and bells. He guessed he was going to look for a job. After all, what was a Ph.D. for? But it was a bad time of year to look for a teaching post; the academic year had just begun. He was too late for this year, and it was too early to find an opening for next year.

He felt like Maine, seeing the new baby and being with Colm. He knew he'd be welcome there for a while, but he couldn't live there. He felt like New York, too, and seeing Tulpen, but he didn't know how to introduce himself. He had an image of how he'd *like* to return—as someone triumphant, like a cured cancer patient. But he couldn't decide what disease he'd had when he left, so he hardly knew if he was cured.

He spent a long time looking at a Greyhound map of the United States before buying a ticket to Boston. He supposed there was much to recommend Boston, in the dim light of teaching jobs; furthermore, he had never seen the birthplace of Merrill Overturf.

Also, on the Greyhound map of the United States, Boston was roughly halfway between Maine and New York. And on a map of *me,* he thought, that's about where I am.

37

Audience Craze, Critical Acclaim and Rave Reviews for *Fucking Up*

Variety announced that "Ralph Packer's newest film is clearly the best thing to come out of the so-called underground this year. Of course this distinction could conceivably be awarded to any film with some content and style, but Packer's film is even subtle. He has at last expanded his documentary approach to a finely focused situation; he is dealing with characters at last, instead of groups, and technically, his work is as fine as ever. Admittedly, not many viewers will find much to interest them in Packer's rather self-centered and inert main character, but . . ."

The New York Times said, "If an era of commercially successful, low-budget films is truly upon us, we may at last give birth in this country to the vital documentary style which the Canadians have been producing with such excellence in recent years. And if small, independent film makers can ever achieve widespread and major theater-distribution, then the sleight-of-hand style—which Ralph Packer has at last found a home for, in his 'F——ing Up'—is going to be much imitated. I am not sure that it is a truly enriching or satisfying style, but Packer has sharpened his craft well. It is Packer's *subject* which eludes me. He doesn't develop a subject; he simply keeps bringing it up . . ."

Newsweek called the film "an elaborately polished, honed, slicked-over, bantering movie which disguises itself as a quest: to explore the psyche of its main character—through a choppy montage of pseudo-interviews with the character's former wife, present girlfriend, dubious friends, and with irritating interruptions from the main character himself, who plays a cute game of pretending he wants nothing to do with the movie. If that were true, he would indeed be wise. Not only does the film never get to the bottom of what makes the main character tick, but the film stops ticking long before its end."

Time, honoring a long tradition of disagreeing with *Newsweek,* trumpeted: "Ralph Packer's 'F——ing Up' is a beautifully compressed film—quiet and understated in every way. Bogus Trumper, credited with the film's innovative sound track, gives a fine acting performance in the role of an aloof, tight-lipped failure with one busted marriage in his past, one cool and shaky relationship in the present—an absolute paranoiac victimized by his own self-analysis. He is the unwilling subject of Packer's uncannily delicate scrutiny, which takes the form of a trim, point-blank documentary which pieces together and overlaps interviews and random comments with some exquisitely straight and deceptively simple shots of Trumper doing perfectly ordinary things. It is a film about making a film about someone involved in making a film, but Trumper emerges as a kind of hero when he rejects all his friends *and* the movie—Packer's subtle way of putting down a psyche-picking belief in the discovery of any true motives . . ."

Trumper read all these in his father's den at Great Boar's Head.

"Is that the *Time* review?" his mother asked him. "I like the *Time* review."

His mother had collected and saved all the reviews, and apparently the reason she liked the one from *Time* was that it mentioned Trumper by name. She hadn't seen the movie and didn't seem to realize that it was about her son's cruel, sad life. Neither did the reviewers.

His father said, "I don't suppose it will ever be shown up here."

"All the films we want to see never get up here," his mother said.

The film hadn't gotten out of New York yet, though it was scheduled to be shown in Boston, San Francisco and a few other big-city art cinemas. It might reach a few large campuses too, but it wasn't likely to turn up in Portsmouth, New Hampshire—thank God. He himself hadn't seen the film yet.

He'd been through a month of teacher interviews in and around Boston and had come home for a weekend now and then, to console his father's ulcer and to appear grateful—which he truly was—for the new Volkswagen his father had given him. A kind of graduation present, he supposed.

It looked more and more likely that he'd have to wait until spring to find a job; he had discovered that his new Ph.D. had about the same appeal and importance at an interview as having freshly shined shoes. About the only openings at this time of year were in the public high schools, and somehow a Ph.D. in comparative literature, with a thesis in Old Low Norse, did not seem suitable training for a class in world culture, from Caesar to Eisenhower, and English composition. Also, he didn't even know how to look at a sixteen-year-old.

His father fixed himself another milk and honey, and made Bogus another bourbon with an expression on his face that revealed how much he'd like to trade stomachs with his son.

Bogus read some more of his mother's collection of reviews.

The New Yorker said that it was "rare and refreshing to see an American film with enough self-confidence to trust in a light touch. What Packer manages with his crew of nonactors should make some of our superstars feel insecure—or at least angry with their screenwriters. Lead actor Bogus

Trumper (whose sound tracking is just a *bit* too clever) is remarkably effective in portraying the self-protective, shallow cool of a man who has failed to communicate with women beyond a self-satisfying level . . ."

"The women are beautiful!" proclaimed *The Village Voice.* "What's missing in Packer's film is any clue whatsoever as to why two such frankly open and stunningly complete women would have anything to do with such a weak, enigmatic, unfulfilled man . . ."

Playboy termed the film "hip and complex, with the sexual vitality of the characters just barely concealed, like the impression of a voluptuous body under silk . . ."

Though it enjoyed "the vivid pace of the film," *Esquire* found the ending "a cheap emotional device. The pregnancy scene is simply an old and overused gimmick for soliciting audience response."

What pregnancy scene? wondered Bogus.

The Saturday Review, on the other hand, found the ending "pure Packer at his understated best. The light casualness of the pregnancy brings all the airy intellectual speculations up against the hard fact that she loved him . . ."

Why? Trumper thought. Who loved him? Loved whom? Was Ralph wringing sentiment from Biggie's recent child by Couth? But how had he tied that in?

Life fumbled to articulate it. "The surfacy vignette approach almost demands a nonending sort of ending; a progression which fails to develop in depth, but instead elects to swivel a story—simply showing more facets on the surface—would be pretentious in choosing a dramatic ending centered on an inevitable event. 'F***ing Up' leads to no such inevitable event. Rather, in that last blunt image of pregnancy—brief and matter-of-fact— Packer achieves a definitive *non-*statement . . ."

A *what?* Bogus thought. He realized that he had to go see the fucking movie.

Part of the reason why he wanted to see it had nothing to do with the reviews. He wanted to see Tulpen again, but he couldn't quite bear the thought of her seeing *him.* Trumper as voyeur, and interested party, would go see *Fucking Up.*

He had a job interview at the Litchfield Community College of the Liberal Arts in Torrington, Connecticut, which was more or less on the way to New York. After his interview, he could sneak into the city and see the film.

It turned out that the job opening was for two sections of a survey of British literature and two sections of expository writing for freshmen. The chairman of the English department was impressed with Trumper's credentials, especially the Old Low Norse. "Gosh," the chairman said, "we don't even have a foreign-language requirement here."

His mind a simmering stew, Trumper got to the Village in time for the nine o'clock showing of *Fucking Up*. The sight of his name among the sound and acting credits impressed him, though he fought it. The finished version was a lot more fluid than he remembered it; he found himself looking at it expectantly, as at a photograph album full of old friends in funny clothes and ten pounds lighter. But it was all very predictable; he remembered everything, right up until the end, when he saw the scene he'd only overheard: Tulpen in the bathtub, telling Ralph and Kent that it was time for them to leave.

Then he saw the scenes he'd patched together of his own leaving. Ralph had reversed the order of their appearance. There was Trumper leaving the pet shop, saying, "Goodbye, Ralph. I don't want to be in your movie any more." There were Trumper and Tulpen and Colm on the subway to the Bronx Zoo, with Trumper's voice-over saying, "Tulpen, I am sorry. But I do not want a child."

Then came two new scenes.

Tulpen in exercise tights is performing the preparatory exercises for natural childbirth: deep-breathing, odd squat-thrusts, and the like. Ralph's voice-over says, "He left her."

Then a shot of Tulpen working in the editing room. The camera sees her from behind; she is sitting down, and only when she turns her head do we recognize her, in profile. Slowly, she acknowledges the camera's presence; she looks over her shoulder into the lens, then turns away. She couldn't care less about the camera. Offstage, Ralph asks, "Are you happy?"

Tulpen seems self-conscious. She gets up from her workbench with an odd gesture; from behind, her elbow lifts like the wing of a bird. But Trumper knows: she is lifting her lovely breast with the back of her hand.

When she turns in full-length profile to the camera, we see that she is pregnant.

"You're pregnant . . ." Ralph's voice nags.

Tulpen gives the camera a no-shit sort of look. Her hands are busy, tucking the shapeless folds of her maternity dress around her great abdomen.

"Whose baby is it?" Ralph says relentlessly.

There is no hesitation, only a casual shrug of her breasts, but she won't face the camera. "His," Tulpen says.

The image freezes to a still, over which the credits appear.

When the lights came on, there was a crush of Greenwich Village film addicts all around him. He sat as if anesthetized, until he realized that no one could get past his splayed knees; then he rose and walked up the aisle with the crowd.

In the lobby's miasma of sickly light and candy smells, kids were lighting cigarettes and milling around; trapped in the slow-moving crowd, Trumper overheard snatches of talk.

"What a perfect shit," a girl said.

"I don't know, I don't know," someone complained. "Packer gets more and more hung up on himself, you know?"

"Well, I liked it, but . . ." said a thoughtful voice.

"The acting was really okay, you know . . ."

"They weren't exactly actors . . ."

"Well, okay, the people, then . . ."

"Yeah, great."

"Good camera work too."

"Yeah, but he didn't *do* anything with it . . ."

"You know what I say when I see a film like this?" a voice asked. "I say, 'So what?' That's what I say, man."

"Give me the keys, motherfuck . . ."

"Another piece of shit is another piece of shit is . . ."

"But it's *relative* . . ."

"It's all the same."

"Excuse me . . ." Bogus thought of biting the slender neck of a tall girl in front of him, thought of turning and kneeing a covey of callow philosophers behind him who were calling the film "great nihilism."

Just before the door, he knew he'd been recognized. A girl with a drug complexion and dirty-saucer eyes stared at him, then plucked her companion's sleeve. They were a part of a group, and in a minute all of them turned to regard Trumper, wedged in a clutch of people by the door. It was a double door, but half of it was stuck closed. As someone snapped it open, a cheer went up, and for a second, Trumper actually imagined the applause was for *him*. Then a young man in a Union Army uniform, who had an elegant Smith Brothers' beard and yellow teeth, blocked his way.

"Excuse me," Trumper said.

"Hey, it's *you,*" the young man said, and turning to his friends, he called, "Hey, I told you—it's that *guy* . . ."

Instantly a dozen people were gawking at him in celebrity fashion.

"I thought he was taller," a girl said.

Some of the young ones—just kids, silly and laughing—followed him all the way to his car.

Another girl teased him. "Oh, come home and meet my mother!" she sang.

He got into his car and drove away.

"A new Volkswagen!" a boy said with mock awe. "Far out . . ."

Trumper drove around and got lost; he'd never driven in New York before. Finally, he paid a taxi to lead him to Tulpen's apartment. He still had his key to the place. It was after midnight, but he was thinking of *other* kinds of time. Like months, and how long he'd been gone; like how pregnant Tulpen had been when the film was finished; like how much time had passed before the film was released. Though he knew better, he had an image of Tulpen as he expected her to look *now*: only a little more swollen than in the film.

He tried to let himself in, but she had fastened the safety chain. He heard her sit up startled in bed, and he whispered, "It's me."

It was a long time before she would let him in. She was in a short bathrobe, cinched tight at her waist; her belly was as flat as before; she'd even lost some weight. In the kitchen, he collided with a box of paper diapers and crunched a baby's plastic pacifier under his foot. A perverted demon in his head kept telling bad jokes to his brain.

He tried to smile. "Boy or girl?" he asked.

"Boy," she said. Looking down, she pretended to rub the sleep in her eyes, but she was wide-awake.

"Why didn't you tell me?"

"You made yourself pretty clear. Anyway, it's *my* baby."

"Mine too," he said. "You even said so, in the film . . ."

"In Ralph's film," she said. "He wrote the script."

"But it *is* mine, isn't it?" he asked her. "I mean, *really* . . ."

"Biologically?" she said crisply. "Of course it is."

"Can I see him?" Trumper asked. She was very tense, but she faked a shrug and led him past her bed to a little nook made out of stacked bookcases and more fish.

The boy slept in a huge basket, with lots of toys around him. He looked the way Colm had looked at the age of a few weeks, and a lot like Biggie's new baby, who was probably only a month or so older.

Bogus stared at the baby because it was easier than looking at Tulpen; though there's not much to see in a child that age, Trumper appeared to be reading it.

Tulpen banged around in the background. From the linen cabinet, she took some sheets and some blankets and a pillow; it was clear she was making up the couch for Bogus to sleep on.

"Do you want me to go?" he asked.

"Why did you come?" she asked. "You just saw the movie, right?"

"I've been wanting to come before," he said. When she just went on making up the couch, he said stupidly: "I got my Ph.D." She stared at him, then went back to tucking in the blanket. "I've been looking for a job," he said.

"Have you found one?" She flounced the pillow.

"No."

She beckoned him away from the sleeping baby. In the kitchen, she opened a beer for him, pouring off some for herself. "For the breasts," she said, toasting him with her glass. "It makes the milk run."

"I know."

"Oh, right, you would," she said. She played with her bathrobe belt, then asked, "What do you want, Trumper?"

But he was too slow to answer.

"You just feeling guilty?" she asked. "Because I don't need that. You owe me nothing more than your straight, honest feelings, Trumper . . . If you *have* any," she added.

"How do you live?" he asked her. "You can't work," he began, then stopped, knowing that money wasn't the issue. His straight, honest feelings were a long way down in a bog he'd been skirting for so long that now it seemed impossible to dive in and grope.

"I *can* work," she said mechanically, "and I do. I mean, I will. When he gets a little older, I'll take him to Matje's while I work half-days. Matje wants to have a baby herself soon . . ."

"That's Ralph's new girl?" he asked.

"His wife," Tulpen said. "Ralph married her."

Trumper realized then that he knew absolutely nothing about anybody. "Ralph's *married?*" he said.

"He sent you an invitation," Tulpen said. "But you'd already left Iowa."

He was beginning to be aware of just how much he *had* left. But Tulpen was tired of his long interior monologues, and he guessed she didn't need any more of his silences, either. From the living room he watched her go to bed; she took her bathrobe off under the covers and threw it on the floor. "Since you remember babies, it won't surprise you that there's a two o'clock feeding," she said. "Goodnight."

He went into the bathroom and peed with the door open. He'd always left the bathroom door open; it was another of his foul habits which he only remembered in the midst of practicing them. When he came out, Tulpen said, "How's the new prick?"

What's this—*humor?* he wondered. He had no genuine instincts to rely on. "Perfectly normal," he said.

"Goodnight," she said, and as he tiptoed to his made-up couch he had an impulse to hurl his shoes against the wall and wake up the baby just to hear his piercing cries fill this empty place.

He lay listening to his own breathing, and Tulpen's, and the baby's. Only the baby was asleep.

"I love you, Tulpen," he said.

A turtle in the aquarium nearest him seemed to respond; it dove deeper.

"I came here because I want you," he said.

Not even a fish moved.

"I need you," he said. "I know that you don't need me, but *I* need you."

"Well, it's not quite like that," she said, so softly that he could hardly hear her.

He sat up on the couch. "Will you marry me, Tulpen?"

"No," she said. There was no hesitation.

"Please?" he said softly.

This time she waited, but then she said, "No, I won't."

He put on his shoes and got up. There was no other way to leave except by walking past the open alcove of aquariums around her bed, and when he reached the spot, she was sitting up, staring at him and looking furious.

"Jesus!" she said. "Are you walking out again?"

"What do you want me to do?"

"Jesus, you don't know?" she said. "I'll tell you, Trumper, if I have to. I won't marry you *yet,* but if you want to stay around a while, I could wait and *see!* If you want to stay, you should *stay,* Trumper!"

"Okay," he said. He wondered if he should take off his clothes.

"Jesus, take off your clothes," she told him. He did, and then crawled into bed beside her.

She lay turned away from him. "Jesus," she mumbled.

He lay without touching her until she rolled over suddenly, seized one of his hands and pulled it roughly to her breast. "I don't want to make love to you," she said, "but you can hold me . . . if you want to."

"I want to," he mumbled. "I love you, Tulpen."

"I guess so," she said.

"Do you love me?"

"Yes, Jesus, I guess so," she said angrily.

Slowly some instincts returned to him; he touched her gently all over. He felt where they'd shaved her; it was still stubbly. When the baby woke up for his two o'clock nipple, Trumper was out of bed ahead of her, brought the baby back to the bed and put him to her breast.

"No, the other one," she said. "Which one's harder?"

"That one."

"I get all confused . . ." she trailed off and cried softly while she nursed the child. Trumper had his memory in order; he held a diaper to her unused breast, knowing it would leak while the other was being sucked.

"Sometimes they really squirt," she told him.

"I know," he said. "They will, when you make love . . ."

"I don't want to make love," she reminded him.

"I *know.* I was just remarking on it . . ."

"You're going to have to be patient," she said. "I'm still going to say some things just because I want to hurt you."

"Sure, okay."

"You're just going to have to hang around until I don't want to hurt you any more."

"Sure, I *want* to hang around," he said.

"I don't think I'm going to want to hurt you much more," she said.

"I don't blame you," he said, which made her angry again.

"Well, it's none of your business," she said.

"Of course it isn't," he agreed.

Tenderly she said to him, "You just better not talk very much, Trumper, okay?"

"Okay."

When the baby went back to his basket, Tulpen came back to bed and snuggled up close to Trumper. "Don't you care what I've named him?" she asked.

"Oh, the baby!" he said. "Of course. What did you name him?"

"Merrill," she said, and she bore down hard with the heel of her hand on his spine. The back of his throat ached. "I must love you," she whispered. "I called him Merrill because I think you're very fond of that name."

"I am, yes," he whispered.

"I was thinking of you, see?"

He could feel her body getting angry with him again. "Yes, I know," he said.

"You hurt me like hell, Trumper, do you know that?" she said.

"Yes." He touched her stubble lightly.

"Okay," she said. "Just don't ever forget it."

He promised he never would, and then she held on to him and he dreamed his two most frequent nightmares. Variations on a water theme, he called them.

One was always Colm, in some imagined disaster which always involved deep water, the sea or cold mudflats. As always, it was too terrible to allow him to consciously remember the details.

The other was always about Merrill Overturf. He was in water too; he was opening the top hatch of a tank; it always took him too long.

At 6 A.M., baby Merrill's wailing woke him. Tulpen's breasts were drenching his chest and the bed had a sour-sweet smell of milk.

She covered herself with a diaper and he said, "Look at them leak. You must be aroused."

"It's because of the baby crying," she insisted, and he got out of bed to fetch the child for her. Trumper had a typical morning erection, which he did not hide.

"Have you seen my new prick?" he said, clowning. "It's still a virgin, you know."

"The baby's crying," she said, but she was smiling. "Get the baby."

"Merrill!" he said. How nice it felt to say that name out loud! "Merrill, Merrill, Merrill," he said, waltzing the baby to the bed. They had a nice debate about which breast to use; Trumper did a lot of excessive feeling around for the harder one.

Tulpen was still nursing when the phone rang. It was very early in the morning for a call, but she seemed unsurprised; watching Trumper closely, she nodded for him to answer it. He sensed he was being tested somehow, so he picked up the phone, but didn't speak.

"Good morning, young suckling mother!" said Ralph Packer. "How is the baby? How are your boobs?" Trumper swallowed while Tulpen smiled serenely. "Matje and me are on our way over," Ralph went on. "Do you need anything?"

"Yogurt," Tulpen whispered to Bogus.

"Yogurt," Trumper told the phone thickly.

"Thump-Thump!" Ralph cried.

"Hello, Ralph," Bogus said. "I saw your movie . . ."

"Terrible, isn't it?" Ralph said. "How *are* you, Thump-Thump?"

"I'm fine," Trumper said. Tulpen removed the diaper from her free tit and aimed her nipple at Trumper. "I got my Ph.D.," Trumper mumbled to the phone.

"How's the baby?" Ralph asked.

"Merrill's fine," Bogus said. Tulpen's free breast was squirting his leg. "I'm sorry I missed your marriage, Ralph. Congratulations."

"Congratulations to *you,*" Ralph said smartly.

"See you soon," said Trumper and hung up.

"You okay, Trumper?" Tulpen asked. There seemed to be one cool eye regarding him, and one warm.

"Just fine," he said, covering her leaking breast with his hand. "*You* okay?" he asked.

"I'm better."

He touched her stubble and looked at his hand lying there, the way one might look at an old friend with a new beard. They were both naked, except that he still wore his right sock. Baby Merrill nursed fiercely, but Tulpen wasn't looking at him. Her expression part smile, part frown, she was examining closely Trumper's new prick.

Bogus felt pleasantly embarrassed. Maybe they should get dressed, he suggested, since Ralph and what's-her-name, Matje, were coming over. Then he bent down quickly and kissed her lightly on her stubble. She seemed about to . . . but declined to follow up this timid beginning. She kissed his neck.

Okay, thought Bogus Trumper. Scar tissue takes a little getting used to, but I want to learn.

38

The Old Friends Assemble
for Throgsgafen Day

In the kingdom of Thak, they really knew how to throw a Throgsgafen Day. For weeks before the fest, wild boars lay about in marinades and great elk were hung to ripen on the trees; barrels of eels crowded the smokehouse; cauldrons of rabbits, rubbed with sea salt and apples, were simmered in the fat of a rendered bear; a caribou—of a now-extinct species—was stewed, whole, in a vat stirred with an oar. The fall fruits, particularly the blessed grape, were harvested, mashed, allowed to ferment, strained and sauced, and last year's long-aging brews were rolled out of the cellars, tapped and tasted, distilled and tasted again and again. (The common drink in the kingdom of Thak was a urine-sour, murky beer, a little like our own American beer when flat, mixed with cider vinegar. The special drink in Thak was a distilled brandy made from plums and root vegetables; it tasted like a mixture of slivowitz and anti-freeze.)

Of course, Throgsgafen Day actually took more than a day. There was the day before Throgsgafen when everyone had to sample everything, and the night before Throgsgafen when everyone had to prepare to make merry. On the morning of Throgsgafen, small parties were held to compare hangovers, and these flowed right into the main event itself—a continuous meal, lasting some six hours. Then vigorous physical exercise was recommended for the men, whose terrible athletic verve needed some release. This took the form of combative sports and sex. The women took part in the latter event; they also danced and made half-hearted attempts to de-gunk the castle.

On Throgsgafen night, all the lords and ladies carried great troughs of food and left-over debris through the villages, throwing out scraps to the wretched little peasant children. This was a sobering part of the evening, but the party returned to the castle at midnight to toast all the dead friends of Throgsgafens past; this went on until dawn, when a special court of the Council of Elders was traditionally held to determine penalties for all the murders, rapes and other petty crimes which had occurred in abundance over the exhausting holiday.

Our own tame dry-turkey version of Throgsgafen is indeed an embarrassing substitute, so Bogus Trumper and his old friends were determined to inject the spirit of *Akthelt and Gunnel* into the affair. A bold gathering was planned. Despite the unpredictable qualities of Maine in November, it was decided that Couth and Biggie had the only castle worthy of housing such a bash.

The presence of large dogs lent an original Throgsgafen flavor to the outing. One of the dogs was Ralph's. He'd bought it in celebration of Matje's growing pregnancy, and also for her protection on the New York streets. An uncategorizable beast named Loom, it made the trip to Maine from New York a bit trying. Trumper drove his Volkswagen with Tulpen beside him holding baby Merrill in her lap; in the crammed back seat, Ralph and his pregnant Matje fought with Loom. A burdened roof rack on top of the car held Merrill's crib, warm clothes, baskets of wine, booze, and such oddities as rare cheese and smoked meats which Biggie and Couth couldn't get in Maine. Biggie was handling the main dishes.

The other dog—Trumper's birthday present to Colm—was already in Maine. A Chesapeake Bay retriever with a thick, oily coat like a used doormat—Couth called it The Great Dog Gob.

Trumper and Tulpen didn't have a dog. "A baby, forty fish and ten turtles are enough," Bogus said.

"But you should get a dog, Thump-Thump," Ralph said. "You're just not a family without a dog."

"And you should get a car, Ralph," Trumper said, aiming his stuffed Volkswagen up the Maine Turnpike. "A great big car, Ralph," Trumper said. Loom, the back-seat beast, was salivating down his neck.

"Maybe even a bus, Ralph," said Tulpen.

By Boston there was no room left in the tiny glove compartment for any more of Merrill's awful diapers, and Matje had to stop to pee eight times because she was pregnant. Trumper drove furiously, his dull gaze riveted straight ahead; he ignored the wails of Merrill, Ralph's endless complaints about the leg room and the ominous breathing of Loom. What was I ever thinking of? Bogus wondered. It seemed to him a miracle when they finally arrived at the fog-shrouded sea-house glazed with falling sleet.

Gob and Loom hit it off right away; they romped themselves into a slaver of slush and mudflat muck, and Colm went wild trying to contain the brutes.

This day before Throgsgafen was an indoor day, and the menfolk organized pool games and bantered about who had brought what.

"Where is the bourbon?" Bogus asked.

"Where is the pot?" said Ralph.

"We're out of butter," Biggie told Couth.

"Where is the bathroom?" Matje asked.

Biggie and Tulpen had a discussion about the smallness of Matje's belly. She was a wrenlike creature whose degree of pregnancy, which was almost term, resembled a small cantaloupe.

"God, I was much bigger," Biggie said.

"Well, you *are* much bigger, Big," Bogus said.

"You were bigger too," Ralph told Tulpen. She looked at Bogus and saw that he might feel shitty about having no memory of his second wife's pregnancy with his second son. She went over and goosed him quietly.

Then all the men gathered around Matje and felt her tummy, under the pretense of assessing the child's sex. "I hate to tell you this, Ralph," Bogus said. "But I think Matje's going to have a grape."

The women arranged baby Anna and baby Merrill in a side-by-side display on the dining-room sideboard. Anna was older, but both of them were still in the phase where all that's required is to sleep them, slurp them and wash their bottoms.

Sightseeing in such foul weather was limited to the two nursing mothers' breasts and Matje's swelling grape, so there was much bad pool and good drinking. Ralph was the first one to feel the effect. "I must tell you," he said solemnly to Couth and Bogus. "I like *all* our ladies."

Outside, in the rolling fog and sleet flakes, The Great Dog Gob and the uncategorizable Loom wrestled in the slush.

Only Colm was in a rotten mood. For one thing, he was simply not used to so many guests; for another, the babies were placid, boring, unplayful creatures, and the dogs in their excited condition seemed dangerous. Also, usually when Colm saw his father, Bogus gave him undivided attention. Now there were just a lot of silly adults talking. It was foul out, but it was better out than in, so to demonstrate his boredom, Colm would track lots of slush into the house and schemingly allow the wild dogs in, almost urging them to break rare Pillsbury vases.

The grownups were finally sensitive to Colm's problem and took turns taking walks with him in the terrible outdoors. Colm would bring back one sodden grownup after another. *"Now* who wants to come with me?" he'd ask.

Finally it was time to do something in the way of preparing a minor warm-up feast for the evening—not to compare, of course, with tomorrow's major event.

Tulpen had brought some meat from New York.

"Ah, New York meat!" said Ralph, pinching Tulpen. Matje gouged Ralph with a corkscrew.

———————

After dinner, it was almost peaceful; the babies were in bed and the men were stuffed and woozy. But Colm was overtired, and irritable about having to go upstairs. Biggie tried to coax him, but he refused to budge from the table. Then Bogus offered to carry him upstairs, since he was so tired.

"I'm *not* tired," Colm said disagreeably.

"How about some *Moby Dick?*" Bogus asked him. "Come on."

"I want Couth to put me to bed," Colm said.

It was obvious that he was simply in a mood, so Couth lifted him up and started off upstairs with him. "I'll put you to bed if you want," he told Colm, "but I don't know *Moby Dick* and I can't tell stories the way Bogus can . . ." But Colm was already asleep.

Sitting at the table between Biggie and Tulpen, Bogus felt Biggie put her hand under the table and lay it on his knee; almost simultaneously Tulpen touched the other knee. They were both thinking he might feel hurt, so he said reassuringly, "Colm's just in a snit. It hasn't been such a hot day for him."

Across the strewn dinner table, Ralph sat with his hand on Matje's grape. "You know, Thump-Thump," he said. "We could do the movie right here in Maine. After all, this is sort of a castle . . ."

He was talking about his next film project: *Akthelt and Gunnel.* The movie was pretty well planned. They were going to Europe when Trumper finished the script; a production company in Munich was committed to backing it. They were going to take their wives and babies too, though Trumper had urged Ralph to consider leaving Loom behind. They had even thought of trying to include Couth in it as the cameraman. But Couth wasn't interested. "I'm a *still* photographer," he'd pointed out. "And I live in Maine."

In a passing, ungenerous moment, Trumper thought that the real reason Couth wasn't interested in the movie was because of Biggie. Bogus felt vaguely that Biggie still disapproved of him, but when he'd mentioned this once to Tulpen, he'd been confused by her response. "Frankly," Tulpen told him, "I'm glad Couth and Biggie won't be coming."

"You don't like Biggie?" Bogus asked.

"It's not that," Tulpen said. "Sure, I like Biggie."

Now this old confusion passed again over Bogus like a drunk's flush.

It was time to sleep. People groggily faced the unfamiliar upstairs of the great Pillsbury mansion, losing themselves in halls and stumbling into the wrong bedrooms.

"Where do I sleep?" Ralph kept asking. "Ah, God, take me there . . ."

"To think that it's only the day *before* Throgsgafen," Couth said plaintively.

Biggie was having a quiet pee in her bathroom when Bogus walked in on her. As usual, he left the door open.

"What in hell are you doing, Bogus?" she asked him, trying to cover herself.

"I think I'll just brush my teeth, Big," Bogus said. He didn't seem to realize he wasn't married to her any more.

Couth peered in the open doorway, mildly surprised. "What's he doing?" he asked his wife.

"He's brushing his teeth, I guess," Biggie said. "For God's sake, at least shut the door!"

Just when everyone seemed to be straightened out and settled in their proper rooms, Ralph Packer appeared naked in the hall. Through the open bedroom door behind him, Matje could be heard inquiring what he thought he was doing. "I am *not* going to pee out the window," he shouted. "There are bathrooms all over this bloody castle, and I intend to find one!"

Biggie sweetly led the nude Ralph to the right place.

"I'm sorry, Biggie," Matje said, hurrying after Ralph with his pants.

"Es ist mir Wurst," Biggie said, and touched Matje's tummy fondly. If Trumper had been there, he would have understood Biggie's Austrian dialect. "It doesn't matter" was what it meant, but the literal translation was, "It is sausage to me."

Trumper wasn't where he could have heard her. He was having delicious love made to him by Tulpen; he was too drunk to appreciate such loving, really, but it did have a startling aftereffect: he found himself wide-awake and sitting up very sober. Tulpen was deeply asleep beside him, but when he kissed her feet to thank her, she smiled.

He couldn't sleep, though. He kissed Tulpen all over, but she couldn't be aroused.

Wide, wide awake, Trumper got up and dressed himself warmly; he wished it were morning. Tiptoeing to Colm's room, he kissed the boy and tucked him in. He went to look at the babies, and then listened to the other adults sleeping, but it wasn't enough. He tiptoed into Biggie and Couth's room and watched them sleeping in a warm tangle. Couth woke up. "It's next door, down the hall," he said, thinking that Bogus was looking for the bathroom.

Wandering around, Trumper found Ralph and Matje's room and looked in on them too. Ralph lay splayed out on his stomach, his hands and feet dangling off the bed. Across his broad, hairy back, tiny Matje lay sleeping like a flower on a compost heap.

Downstairs, Bogus opened the French doors to the pool room and let in the air. It was very cold, and the fog was moving out of the bay. Trumper knew that there was a barren rock island in the center of the bay, and that this was what he saw, revealed and concealed by the shifting fog. But if he stared hard, the island actually seemed to roll, to rise and fall, and if he stared *very* hard, he could see a broad, flat tail arch up and smack the sea so hard that the dogs whined in their sleep. "Hello, Moby Dick," Trumper whispered. Gob growled and Loom staggered to his feet and then collapsed.

In the kitchen, Bogus found some paper and sat down and began writing. His first sentence was one he'd written before: "Her gynecologist recommended him to me." Others followed and formed a paragraph. "Ironic: the best urologist in New York is French. Dr. Jean Claude Vigneron: ONLY BY APPOINTMENT. So I made one."

What have I begun? he wondered. He didn't know. He put the paper with these crude beginnings in his pocket to save for a time when he had more to say.

He wished he understood what made him feel so restless. Then it occurred to him that he was actually at peace with himself for the first time in his life. He realized how much he'd been anticipating peace someday, but the feeling was not what he'd expected. He used to think that peace was a state he would achieve, but the peace he was feeling was like a force he'd submitted to. God, why should peace depress me? he thought. But he wasn't depressed, exactly. Nothing was exact.

He was chalking up his pool cue, thinking how he wanted the balls to break, when he became aware that he wasn't the only one who was up and awake in the sleeping house. "That you, Big?" he said quietly, without turning around. (Later, he would lose another night's sleep wondering how he knew it was her.)

Biggie was careful; she only skirted the borders of her subject—the phase Colm was going through, how he was at the age when boys turn more naturally to a father than to a mother. "I know it's going to be painful for you," she told Bogus, "but Colm's turning more and more to Couth. When you're here, I can tell the child is confused."

"I'm going to Europe soon," Trumper said bitterly. "Then I won't be around to confuse him for a good long time."

"I'm sorry," Biggie said. "I really like seeing you. I just don't like how it makes me feel, sometimes, when you're around."

Trumper felt a strange meanness come over him; he wanted to tell Biggie that she simply resented being confronted with how happy he was with Tulpen. But that was insane; he wanted to tell her no such thing. He didn't even believe it. "I get confused too," he told her, and she nodded, agreeing with such sudden vigor that he felt embarrassed. Then she left him alone again, fleeing upstairs so quickly that he thought she must be trying not to cry in front of him. Or not to laugh?

He was thinking that he actually agreed with how Biggie felt—that he liked to see her, but didn't like the way he felt around her—when he thought he heard her coming back downstairs.

But this time it was Tulpen, and Trumper saw at a glance that she'd been awake for a while herself and that she'd probably just passed Biggie in the upstairs hall.

"Oh, shit," he said. "It's so complicated sometimes." He went quickly over to her and hugged her; she seemed in need of some reassurance.

"I want to leave tomorrow," Tulpen said.

"But it's Throgsgafen."

"After the meal, then," she said. "I don't want to spend another night."

"Okay, okay," he told her. "I know, I know." His voice went on comforting her without much meaning to his words. He knew that back in New

York there'd be a week of trying to understand this, but it didn't pay to think too hard about what came after the holiday, about the often lonely business of living with someone. Surviving a relationship with any other human being sometimes seemed impossible to him. But so what? he thought.

"I love you," he whispered to Tulpen.

"I know," she said.

He took her back upstairs to bed, and just before she fell asleep, she asked him groggily, "Why can't you just fall asleep next to me after we make love? Why does it wake you up? It puts me to sleep, but it wakes you up. That's not fair, because I wake up later and the bed's empty and I find you staring at the fish or watching the baby sleep or playing pool with your old wife . . ."

He lay awake until dawn, trying to figure all that out. Tulpen was sleeping soundly and didn't wake up when Colm appeared at their bedside in layers of sweaters over his pajamas, wading boots and a wool hat. "I know, I know," Trumper whispered. "If *I* come down to the dock, you can go down too."

It was cold, but they were wearing lots of clothes; the slush had turned to ice and they slid on their bottoms down the steep flagstone path. The sun was hazy, but the air was clear inland and across the bay. Out to sea, a dense fog was slowly rolling in; it would take a while to reach them, though, and they had the clearest part of the coming day to themselves.

They shared an apple. They heard the babies waking up in the house above them: brief cries, then a renewed silence on receiving their respective breasts. Colm and Bogus agreed on the dullness of babies.

"I saw Moby Dick last night," Bogus decided to tell Colm, who looked a little suspicious. "It may have been just the old island," Trumper confessed, "but I heard a great *slap,* like his tail hitting the water."

"You're making that up," Colm said. "That's not real."

"Not *real?*" said Trumper. He'd never heard Colm use the word before.

"Right," said Colm, but the boy's attention was wandering—he was bored by his father—and Bogus wanted desperately for things to be lively between them.

"What kind of books do you like best?" he asked Colm. As soon as he spoke, he thought, God, I am reduced to making small talk with my son.

"Well, I still like *Moby Dick,*" Colm said. Was he just being kind? ("Be kind to your father," Bogus heard Couth telling Colm, shortly before they had all arrived.) "I mean, I like the story," Colm said. "But it's just a story."

On the dock beside his son, Trumper fought back sudden tears.

The great houseful of flesh above them would wake soon, almost like one giant person—perform its ablutions, feed itself, try to be helpful and kind. In this pleasant confusion a keen sense of things would be lost, but out on the dock, watching the sun slowly losing to the fog, Trumper felt bright and crisp. By now the fog covered the mouth of the bay and was bound to roll in on them; it was so thick that you couldn't tell what was behind it. But in his momentary piece of clear light, Trumper felt he could see through his brain.

Bogus and Colm heard a toilet flush, and then Ralph shouted from the house, "Oh, that goddamn dog!"

Upstairs, a window opened; Biggie was framed in it, Anna in her arms. "Good morning!" she called down to them.

"Happy Throgsgafen Day!" Bogus yelled, and Colm took up the cry.

Another window opened and Matje poked her head out like a parakeet from its cage. Downstairs, Tulpen opened the French doors of the pool room and held Merrill in the air above her head. Couth appeared in Biggie's window. Everyone was getting a last feel of the morning before the fog came in.

The kitchen door flew open, ejecting Gob, Loom and Ralph. He yelled, "Those goddamn dogs threw up in the laundry room!"

"It was *your* dog, Ralph!" Couth called from his window. "My dog never throws up!"

"It was *Trumper!*" Tulpen yelled from the pool room. "He was up all night! He was up to something! Trumper puked in the laundry room!"

Bogus protested his innocence, but everyone chanted his guilt. Colm seemed delighted by this weird adult performance. The dogs began the day's cavorting, falling heavily on the ice. Bogus took his son's hand and they made their careful, slippery way up to the house.

Heavy traffic conditions ruled the kitchen. The dogs fought furiously outside the door while Colm, seeking to increase the chaos, blew a shrill whistle. Ralph announced that Matje's grape had grown. The women demanded that all but the children fast instead of having breakfast; they were already at work on the midday feast. Biggie and Tulpen each flaunted a breast which lolled free, a nipple-glued child riding on each busy hip. Matje fixed breakfast for Colm and scolded Ralph for not cleaning up after the dogs.

Ralph and Couth and Bogus hung around, with their slightly off-putting morning smells and a certain prickliness of appearance. Matje and Biggie and Tulpen were blowzy, wearing not quite clothes: bathrobes and soft slept-in stuff—a warm rumpled sensuousness about them.

Bogus wondered what he could have thought he wanted. But the kitchen was far too flurried for thinking; bodies were everywhere. So what if dog puke still lurked unseen in the laundry room! In good company we can be brave.

Mindful of his scars, his old harpoons and things, Bogus Trumper smiled cautiously at all the good flesh around him.

The
158–Pound
Marriage

for

J M F

There were four of us then, not merely two, and in our quaternion the vintage sap flowed freely, flowed and bled and boiled as it may never again.

John Hawkes, *The Blood Oranges*

It was a most amazing business, and I think that it would have been better in the eyes of God if they had all attempted to gouge out each other's eyes with carving knives. But they were "good people."

Ford Madox Ford, *The Good Soldier*

1

The Angel Called
"The Smile of Reims"

My wife, Utchka (whose name I sometime ago shortened to Utch), could teach patience to a time bomb. With some luck, she has taught me a little. Utch learned patience under what we might call duress. She was born in Eichbüchl, Austria—a little village outside the proletarian town of Wiener Neustadt, which is an hour's drive from Vienna—in 1938, the year of the Anschluss. When she was three, her father was killed as a Bolshevik saboteur. It is unproven that he was a Bolshevik, but he was a saboteur. By the end of the war, Wiener Neustadt would become the largest landing field in Europe, and the unwilling site of the German Messerschmitt factory. Utch's father was killed in 1941 when he was caught in the act of blowing up Messerschmitts on the runway in Wiener Neustadt.

The local *SS Standarte* of Wiener Neustadt paid a visit to Utch's mother in Eichbüchl after Utch's father had been caught and killed. The SS men said they'd come to alert the village to the "seed of betrayal" which obviously ran thick in Utch's family. They told the villagers to watch Utch's mother very closely, to make sure she wasn't a Bolshevik like her late husband. Then they raped Utch's mother and stole from the house a wooden cuckoo clock which Utch's father had bought in Hungary. Eichbüchl is very close to the Hungarian border, and the Hungarian influence can be seen everywhere.

Utch's mother was raped again, several months after the SS left, by some of the village menfolk who, when questioned about their assault, claimed they were following the instructions of the SS: watching Utch's mother very closely, to make sure she wasn't a Bolshevik. They were not charged with a crime.

In 1943, when Utch was five, Utch's mother lost her job in the library of the monastery in nearby Katzelsdorf. It was suggested that she might be foisting degenerate books on the young. Actually, she was guilty of stealing books, but they never accused her of that, nor did they ever find out. The small stone house Utch was born in—on the bank of a stream that runs through Eichbüchl—connected to a chicken house, which Utch's mother maintained, and a cow barn, which Utch cleaned every day from the time she was five. The house was full of stolen books; it was actually a religious library, though Utch remembers it more as an art library. The books were huge poster-sized records of church and cathedral art—sculpture, architecture and stained glass—from sometime before Charlemagne through the late Rococo.

In the early evenings as it was getting dark, Utch would help her mother milk the cows and collect the eggs. The villagers would pay for the milk and eggs with sausage, blankets, cabbages, wood (rarely coal), wine and potatoes.

Fortunately, Eichbüchl was far enough away from the Messerschmitt plant and the landing field in Wiener Neustadt to escape most of the bombing. At the end of the war the Allied planes dumped more bombs on that factory and landing field than on any other target in Austria. Utch would lie in the stone house with her mother in the blacked-out night and hear the *crump! crump! crump!* of the bombs falling in Wiener Neustadt. Sometimes a crippled plane would fly low over the village, and once Haslinger's apple orchard was bombed in blossom time; the ground under the trees was littered with apple petals thicker than wedding confetti. This happened before the bees had fertilized the flowers, so the fall apple crop was ruined. Frau Haslinger was found hacking at herself with a pruning hook in the cider house, where she had to be restrained for several days—tied up in one of the large, cool apple bins until she came to her senses. During her confinement, she claimed, she was raped by some of the village menfolk, but this was considered a fantasy due to her derangement at the loss of the apple crop.

It was no fantasy when the Russians got to Austria in 1945, when Utch was seven. She was a pretty little girl. Her mother knew that the Russians were awful with women and kind to children, but she didn't know if they would consider Utch a woman or a child. The Russians came through Hungary and from the north, and they were especially fierce in Wiener Neustadt and its environs because of the Messerschmitt plant and all the high officers of the *Luftwaffe* they found around there.

Utch's mother took Utch to the cow barn. There were only eight cows left. Going over to the largest cow, whose head was locked in its milking hitch, she slit the cow's throat. When it was dead, she unfastened the head from the milking hitch and rolled the cow on her side. She cut open the belly of the cow, pulled out the intestines and carved out the anus, and then made Utch lie down in the cavity between the great cow's scooped-out ribs. She put as much of the innards back into the cow as would fit, and took the rest outside in the sun where it would draw flies. She closed the slit belly-flaps of the cow around Utch like a curtain; she told Utch she could breathe through the cow's carved-out anus. When the guts that had been left in the sun drew flies, Utch's mother brought them back inside the cow barn and arranged them over the head of the dead cow. With the flies swarming around her head, the cow looked as if she'd been dead a long time.

Then Utch's mother spoke to Utch through the asshole of the cow. "Don't you move or make a sound until someone finds you." Utch had a long, slim wine bottle filled with camomile tea and honey, and a straw. She was to sip it when she was thirsty.

"Don't you move or make a sound until someone finds you," said Utch's mother.

Utch lay in the belly of the cow for two days and two nights while the Russians wasted the village of Eichbüchl. They butchered all the other cows in the barn, and they brought some women to the barn too, and they butchered some men in there as well, but they wouldn't go near the dead cow with Utch inside her because they thought the cow had been dead a long time and her meat was spoiled. The Russians used the barn for a lot of atrocities, but Utch never made a sound or moved in the belly of the cow where her mother had placed her. Even when she ran out of camomile tea and the cow's intestines dried and hardened around her—and all the slick viscera clung to her—Utch did not move or make a sound. She heard voices; they were not her language and she did not respond. The voices sounded disgusted. The cow was prodded; the voices groaned. The cow was tugged and dragged; the voices grunted—some voices gagged. And when the cow was lifted—the voices *heaved!*—Utch slipped out in a sticky mass which landed in the arms of a man with a black-haired mustache and a red star on his gray-green cap. He was Russian. He dropped to his knees with Utch in his arms and appeared to pass out. Other Russians around him took off their caps; they appeared to pray. Someone brought water and washed Utch. Ironically, they were the sort of Russians who were kind to children and in no way thought Utch was a woman; at first, in fact, they thought she was a *calf.*

Piece by piece, what happened grew clear. Utch's mother had been raped. (Almost everyone's mother and daughter had been raped. Almost everyone's father and son had been killed.) Then one morning a Russian had decided to burn the barn down. Utch's mother had begged him not to, but she had little bargaining power; she had already been raped. So she had been forced to kill the Russian with a trenching spade, and another Russian had been forced to shoot her.

Piece by piece, the Russians put it together. This must be the child of that woman who didn't want the barn burned down, and it was because . . . The Russian who'd caught the slimy Utch in his arms as the putrid cow was thrown up on a truck figured it out. He was an officer, too, a Georgian Russian from the banks of the eely Black Sea; they have queer phrases and lots of slang there. One of them is *utch*—a cow. I have asked around, and the only explanation is that *utch*, to various offhanded Georgians, imitates the sound a cow makes when she is calving. And *utchka?* Why, that is a calf, of course, which is what the Georgian officer called the little girl who was delivered to him from the womb of the cow. And it is natural, now, that a woman in her thirties would no longer be an *Utchka*, so I call her Utch.

Her real name was Anna Agati Thalhammer, and the Georgian officer, upon hearing the history of Utch's family in the good village of Eichbüchl, took his Utchka with him to Vienna—a fine city for occupying, with music and painting and theater, and homes for orphans of the war.

When I think of how often I told Severin Winter this story, I could break my teeth! Over and over again, I told him he must understand that, above all, Utch is loyal. Patience is a form of loyalty, but he never understood that about her.

"Severin," I used to say, "she is vulnerable for the same reason that she is strong. Whatever she puts her love in, she will trust. She will wait you out, she will put up with you—forever—if she loves you."

―――――――

It was Utch who found the postcards. It was the summer we spent, ill advised, in Maine, ravaged by rain and biting insects, when Utch was bitten by the bug of antiques. I remember it as a summer littered with foul furniture, relics of Colonial America—a kick which Utch was soon off.

It was in Bath, Maine, that she found the postcards in some grimy warehouse advertising "Rare Antiques." It was near the shipyard; she could hear riveting. The owner of the antique shop tried to sell her a buggy whip. Utch implied there was a look in his old eyes that begged her to use it on him, but she's European, and I don't know if many Americans go that way. Perhaps they do in Maine. She declined the whip and kept herself near the door of the warehouse, browsing warily with the old man following behind her. When she saw the postcards in a dusty glass case, she immediately recognized Europe. She asked to see them. They were all of France after World War I. She asked the old man how he got them.

He had been an American soldier in World War I, a part of the army which celebrated the victory in France. The postcards were the only souvenirs he had left—old black-and-white photographs, some in sepia tones, poor quality. He told her that the photographs were more accurate in black and white. "I *remember* France in black and white," he told Utch. "I don't think France was in color then." She knew I'd like the photographs, so she bought them—over four hundred postcards for one dollar.

It took me weeks to go through them, and I still go through them today. There are ladies with long black dresses and gentlemen with black umbrellas, peasant children in the traditional *costumes bretons,* horse carriages, the early auto, the canvas-backed trucks of the French Army and soldiers strolling in the parks. There are scenes of Reims, Paris and Verdun—before and after the bombardments.

Utch was right; it's the kind of thing I can use. That summer in Maine I was still researching my third historical novel, set in the Tyrol in the time of Andreas Hofer, the peasant hero who turned back Napoleon. I had no use for World War I France at that time, but I knew that one day I would. A few years from now, perhaps, when the people in the postcards—even the children in *costumes bretons*—will be more than old enough to be dead, then I might take them up. I find it's no good writing historical novels about people who aren't dead; that's a maxim of mine. History takes time; I resist writing about people who are still alive.

For history you need a camera with two lenses—the telephoto and the kind of close-up with a fine, penetrating focus. You can forget the wide-angle lens; there is no angle wide enough.

But in Maine I was not pondering France. I was nursing infected fly bites and worrying with the peasant army of Andreas Hofer, the hero of the Tyrol. I was despairing over Utch's despair at the jagged Maine cliffs, the hazards of Maine water; our children were then in dangerous phases (when are they *not?*)—they were both nonswimmers. Utch felt they were safest in the car or in antique shops, and I would not encourage another bite from a black fly, a greenhead or a saltwater mosquito. A summer on the Maine coast, spent hiding indoors.

"Why did we *wont* to come here?" Utch would ask me.

"Why did we *want* to come here," I'd correct her.

"*Ja,* why did we *wont* to?" Utch would say.

"To get away?" I'd venture.

"From *vut?*"

It's ironic to think of it now, but before we met Edith and Severin Winter there was really nothing we needed to get away from. That summer in Maine we did not know Edith and Severin.

An example of the close-up lens occurs to me. I have several before-and-after photographs of the Cathedral of Reims. There are two close-ups, from the left doorway of the western porch, of the angel called "The Smile of Reims." Prior to the shelling of the cathedral, the angel was indeed smiling. Next to her, a forlorn Saint Nicaise held out his arm—his hand gone at the wrist. After the bombardment the angel called "The Smile of Reims" was headless. Her arm was gone at the elbow, and a chunk of stone was fleshed out of her leg from thigh to calf. The forlorn, forewarning Saint Nicaise lost another hand, one leg, his chin and his right cheek. After the blasting, his wrecked face described them both, much as her smile had once outshone his gloom. After the war, there was a saying in Reims that the *joie de vivre* in the angel's smile had actually attracted the bombs to her. More subtly, the wise people of Reims implied, it was her morose companion, that sour saint, who could not abide glowering alongside such ecstacy as hers; it was he who drew the bombs to them both.

It's commonly said in that part of France that the moral of "The Smile of Reims" is that when there's a war on, and you're in it, don't be happy; you insult both the enemy and your allies. But that moral of "The Smile of Reims" isn't very convincing. The good people of Reims haven't got eyes for detail like mine. When the angel has her smile and head intact, the saint beside her is in pain. When her smile and the rest of her head leave her, that saint—despite new wounds of his own—seems more content. The moral of "The Smile of Reims," according to *me,* is that an unhappy man cannot tolerate a happy woman. Saint Nicaise would have taken the angel's smile, if not her whole head, with or without the help of World War I.

And that goddamn Severin Winter would have done what he did to Edith, with or without me!

"Haf patience," Utch used to say, in the early rounds of her bout with English.

Okay, Utch. I see the close-ups of the shelling of Reims. The telephoto is still unclear. There's a long, broad view taken from the cathedral of the fired quarters of the city, but neither I nor the clever people of Reims have extracted a moral from it. As I advised, forget the wide-angle. I see Edith and Severin Winter only in close-ups, too. We historical novelists need time. Haf patience.

Severin Winter—that simple-minded ego, that stubborn Prussian!—even had some history in common with Utch, for all that it mattered. History occasionally lies. For example, the decapitation of the angel called "The Smile of Reims," and the rest of the damage done to the great Reims cathedral, is considered among the *human* atrocities of World War I. How flattering to an angel! How bizarre for sculpture! That the loss of art should be considered as similar to the rape, mutilation and murder of French and Belgian women by the Boche! The damage to a statue called "The Smile of Reims" doesn't quite compare to the shishkebabbing of children on bayonets. People regard art too highly, and history not enough.

I can still see Severin Winter—that schmaltz lover, that opera freak—standing in his plant-festooned living room like a dangerous animal roaming a botanical garden, listening to Beverly Sills singing Donizetti's *Lucia.*

"Severin," I said, "you don't understand her." I meant Utch.

But he was only hearing Lucia's madness. "I think Joan Sutherland carries this part better," he said.

"Severin! If those Russians had not tried to move the cow, Utch would have stayed inside her."

"She'd have gotten thirsty," Severin said. "Then she'd have climbed out."

"She was already thirsty," I said. "You don't know her. If that Russian had burned the barn down, she would have stayed."

"She'd have smelled the barn burning and made a break for it."

"She could have smelled the cow *cooking,* " I said, "and Utch would have stayed until *she* was done."

But Severin Winter did not believe me. What can you expect of a wrestling coach?

His mother was an actress, his father was a painter, his coach said he could have been great. More than ten years ago Severin Winter was runner-up in the 157-pound class at the Big Ten Championships at Michigan State University in East Lansing. He wrestled for the University of Iowa, and runner-up in the Big Ten was the closest he ever came to a major conference or national championship. The man who beat him in the finals of the Big Ten tournament was a lean, slick leg wrestler from Ohio State named Jefferson Jones; he was a black with a knuckle-hard head, bruise-blue palms and a pair of knees like mahogany doorknobs. Severin Winter said Jones put on a figure-four body scissors so hard that you were convinced his pelvis had that strange spread of two sharp bones like a woman's pelvis. When he rode you with a cross-body ride—your near leg scissored, your far arm hooked—Severin said Jones cut off your circulation somewhere near your spine. And even Jones wasn't good enough for a national championship; he never won one, though he was the Big Ten champion for two consecutive years.

Severin Winter never came close to a national title. The year he was runner-up in the Big Ten, he placed sixth in the national tournament. He was pinned in the semifinals by the defending national champion from Oklahoma State, and pinned again in the second round of the consolation matches by a future geologist from the Colorado School of Mines. And in the wrestle-off to decide fifth from sixth, he lost another convincing decision to Jefferson Jones of Ohio State.

I once spent some time trying to interview the wrestlers who had beaten Severin Winter; with one exception, none of them remembered who he was. "Well, you don't remember everyone you beat, but you remember everyone who beat you," Winter was fond of saying. But I discovered that Jefferson Jones, the wrestling coach at a Cleveland high school, remembered Severin Winter very well. Altogether, over a three-year period, Winter had wrestled Jefferson Jones five times; Jones had beaten him all five.

"That boy just couldn't get to me, you know," Jones told me. "But he was one of those who kept coming. He just kept coming at you, if you know what I mean. You'd break him down on his belly and he'd work like a stiff old dog to get back up to his hands and knees again. You'd just break him down on his belly again, and he'd get up again. He just kept coming, and I just kept taking the points."

"But was he, you know, any *good?*" I asked.

"Well, he won more than he lost," said Jones. "He just couldn't get to *me.*"

I sensed in Jefferson Jones an attitude I'd often felt radiating from Severin. A wrestler's ego seems to stay in shape long after he's out of his weight class. Perhaps their history of cutting weight makes them tend to exaggerate. For example, to hear Winter describe the exploits of his ancestors is to be misled.

His mother was the Viennese actress Katrina Marek. This much of his story is true. Katrina Marek's last performance in Vienna's Atelier was on Thursday evening, March 10, 1938. The papers claim she was an "astounding" Antigone, which seems a suitable role for her to have played at the time; she would have required loose garments for her costume, for she was eight months pregnant with Severin. The Friday performance was canceled due to her failure to show up. That would have been Black Friday, March 11, 1938, the day the Anschluss was decided, the day before the Germans marched into Austria. Katrina Marek knew the news early and got herself and her fetus out of the country in time.

She took a taxi. Apparently, even this much of Winter's story is true. She actually took a taxi—herself, her fetus and a portfolio of her husband's drawings and paintings. The paintings, oil on canvas, had been taken off their stretchers and rolled up.

Severin's father, the artist, didn't come. He gave Katrina the drawings and paintings and told her to take the taxi to the Swiss border, to take a train to Belgium or France, to take a boat to England, to go to London, to find the two or three painters in London who knew his work, to ask them to find a theater in London that would employ the Austrian actress Katrina Marek, and to show the drawings and the rolled-up canvases to anyone demanding proof of who she was. She was to say, "I am Katrina Marek, the actress. My husband is the Viennese painter Kurt Winter. I am Viennese too. You see, I am pregnant . . ." But clearly, even dressed as Antigone, anyone could see that.

"Don't drop that baby until you're in London," said Kurt to Katrina. "You won't have time to get it a passport." Then he kissed her goodbye and she drove out of Vienna on Black Friday, the day before the Germans drove in.

Incredibly, in Vienna alone, the first wave of Gestapo arrests took seventy-six thousand. (Katrina Marek and the unborn Severin Winter were boarding a train in St. Gallen, bound for Ostend.) And the father who stayed behind? To hear Severin tell it, his father stayed behind because he was devoted to the revolution, because there was still something a hero could do. Someone, for example, drove the daring, criminal editor Herr Lennhoff across the Hungarian border at Kittsee—after having been turned away by the Czechs. Another taxi was used. Kurt Winter could have been reading Lennhoff's editorial about the German *Putsch* as late as noon and still have gotten away with it; Hitler was in Linz only at noon. "That was cutting it close," Severin Winter has admitted. The first time he told the story, it sounded as if his father was the driver of the cab that drove Lennhoff to Hungary. Later this became confused. "Well, he *could* have been the driver," Winter said. "I mean, he needed a big reason to stay behind, right?"

And the business about the zoo. I checked the facts on that, and it's at least recorded. In 1945, just before the Russians got to Vienna, the entire zoo was *eaten*. Of course, as the people got hungrier, small raiding parties had escaped, mostly at night, with an antelope or a zebra here and there. When people are starving, it seems silly to be taking care of all that game. Yet the Army reserves were on guard duty, day and night, in the great sprawling zoo and botanical gardens on the grounds of the Schönbrunn Palace. Winter has implied that the reserves were rationing the animals to the poor people, one at a time—a kind of black-market zoo, according to him. But then the story gets cloudy. Late on the night of April Fool's Day, 1945, twelve days before the Soviets captured Vienna, some fool tried to let all the animals out.

"My father," Winter said once, "loved animals and was just the right sort of sport for the job, a devout antifascist. It must have been his last act for the underground . . ."

Because, of course, the poor fool who let those animals out was eaten right away. The animals were hungry too, after all. The freed animals roared so loud that the hungry children woke up. It was as good a time as any for butchering the last meat in Vienna; the Soviets were already in Budapest. Who in his right mind would leave a zoo full of food for the Russian Army?

"So the plan backfired," Winter has said. "Rather than set them free, he got them killed, and they ate him as a favor."

Well, if there ever was such a plan, and if Winter's father had any more to do with that zoo bust than with Lennhoff's escape. If he stayed behind, why not make heroics the reason?

Utch says she can sympathize with Severin's impulse. I'll bet she can! I once had a thought of my own about their similar ancestors. What if Utch's father, the saboteur of Messerschmitts in Wiener Neustadt, was something of a two-timer and led a double life? What if he knocked up this actress in Vienna, where he posed as a brash young artist, bought off a paternity suit with a bunch of drawings and paintings, blew up the Messerschmitts, got caught but not killed (he somehow escaped), had no inclinations to return to a raped wife in Eichbüchl, felt especially guilty on April Fool's Day, 1945, and tried to atone for his sins by liberating the zoo?

You see, we historical novelists have to be as interested in what might have happened as what did. My version would make Severin Winter and Utch related, which would explain parts of their later union which remain curious to me. But sometimes it calms me down to think that they just had their war stories in common. Two heavies from Central Europe with their bundle of shrugs! When she was cross, Utch was fond of reducing the world to an orgasm. Severin Winter rarely gave the world credit for much else. But when I think of it, they had more than a war in common.

For example, those rolled-up canvases and drawings that Kurt Winter gave to Katrina Marek are very revealing. All the way to England she never once looked at them, but at British customs she was obliged to open the portfolio. They were all nudes of Katrina Marek, and they were all erotic nudes. This surprised Katrina as much as it surprised the customs official, because Kurt Winter was not interested in nudes, or in any other form of erotic art. He was best known for rather spectral colorist work, and for some unsuccessful variations on Schiele and Klimt, two Austrian painters he followed and admired too much.

Katrina stood embarrassed at the British customs desk while an interested customs official looked carefully at every drawing and painting in her husband's portfolio. She was approaching a full-term pregnancy and probably looked very harassed, but the customs official who smiled at her and graciously let her into England (for the bribe of one of the drawings) probably saw her more as Kurt Winter had seen her—neither pregnant nor harried.

And the painters who were to help Katrina find theater work in London were never meant to feel obliged to perform this service out of their respect for the *art* of Kurt Winter. He did not send art to England; he sent an Austrian actress with poor English, pregnant, graceless and scared, into an English-speaking country without anyone to take care of her. What he gave her in the portfolio were advertisements for herself.

Painters and gallery directors and theater directors said to Katrina, "Uh, you're the *model* here, aren't you?"

"I'm the painter's wife," she would say. "I'm an actress."

And they would say, "Yes, but in these paintings and drawings, you're the *model*, right?"

"Yes."

And despite her nine-month growth, which was Severin Winter, they would look at her appreciatively. She was well taken care of.

Severin was born in London in a good hospital in April of 1938. I attended his thirty-fifth-birthday party and overheard him telling Utch, when he was quite drunk, "My father was a lousy painter, if you want to know the truth. But he was a genius in other ways. He also knew that my mother was a lousy actress, and he knew we'd all starve in London if we went there together. So he set up my mother in the best light he could imagine her in and removed himself from the overall picture. And it *was* her best light, too," he told Utch. He put the palm of his hand flat against Utch's belly, a little under her navel. He was as drunk as I've ever seen him. "And it's *all* our best lights, if you want to know the truth," he told her. At the time I was struck that Utch appeared to agree with him.

Severin's wife, Edith, would not have agreed with him. She had finer bones. She was the classiest woman I've ever known. There was so much natural good taste about her—and about what you imagined about her—that it was always a shock to see Severin beside her, looking like an awkward, maltrained bear beside a dancer. Edith was a relaxed, tall, graceful woman with a sensuous mouth and the most convincing, mature movements in her boyish hips and long-fingered hands; she had slim, silky legs and was as small- and high-breasted as a young girl, and as careless with her hair. She wore all her clothes so comfortably that you could imagine her asleep in them, except that you would rather not imagine her sleeping in any clothes. When I first met her, she was almost thirty—the eight-year wife of Severin Winter, a man who wore *his* clothes as if they were all hair shirts of the wrong size; a man whose shortness stunned you because of his width, or whose width stunned you because of his shortness. He was five feet eight inches tall and maybe twenty pounds over his old 157-pound class. The muscles in his back and chest seemed to be layered in slabs. His upper arms seemed thicker than Edith's lovely thighs. His neck was a strain on the best-made shirt in the world. He fought against a small, almost inconspicuous belly, which I liked to poke him in because he was so conscious of it. It was as taut and tough-skinned to the touch as a football. He had a massive, helmet-shaped head with a thick dark-brown rug of hair which sat on the top of his head like a skier's knit hat and spilled like a cropped mane just over his ears. One ear was cauliflowered, and he liked to hide it. He had a cocky boy's smile, a strong mouth of white teeth with one weird bottom tooth knocked askew—a V-shaped chip taken out of it, nearly as deep as the gum. His eyes were large and brown and far apart, and there was a knot on the bridge of his nose that was only noticeable when you sat to the left, and a crook where his nose had been broken another time that you saw only when you looked at him straight-on.

He not only looked like a wrestler, but wrestling was a constant metaphor to him—one he frequently mixed, being both romantic and practical. His gestures were those of a trained wild man; he was crude and chivalrous; he made much of dignity but often seemed foolishly out of place. At our faculty meetings he had a reputation for bilingual oratory, a belligerent belief that education was going to the dilettantes and "the Now-ist dogs," a principle that "knowledge of the wretched past" was essential and that at least three years of a foreign language should be a requirement for *any* college graduate. (He was an associate professor of German.) Needless to say, he was a baited man, but he was baited cautiously. He was too athletic a debater to be recklessly provoked; he had developed sarcasm to a point of fine pain, and he had the dubious ability to outlast anyone in a world (like the academic committee) where tediousness is a virtue. Also, despite his affiliation with the German Department, it was well known that he was the wrestling coach. In fact, he was stubborn about that, especially with strangers. When introduced, he would never admit that he taught in the German Department.

"Are you with the university?"

"Yes, I coach wrestling," Severin Winter would say. Once I saw Edith cringe.

But he was never a physical bully. At a party for new faculty members he had an argument with a sculptor who threw a substantial uppercut into Winter's misleading football of a belly. Though a head taller than Winter, and ten pounds heavier, the sculptor's punch caused his own arm to fly back like dead weight off a trampoline. Winter never budged. "No, no," he told the sculptor impatiently. "You've got to get your shoulder into a punch, get your weight off the back of your heels . . ." There was no hint of retaliation; he was playing the coach, a harmless role.

His insistence on the sporting life—to the boredom of more than a few friends—once led me to suspect that he'd never been a good wrestler at all, so when I was asked to lecture on the historical novel at the University of Iowa, I thought I might try to look up Winter's old coach. I had a sudden notion that Jefferson Jones of Ohio State might have *invented* an opponent he'd beaten five for five.

I had no trouble finding the coach, retired to some honorary job of fussing in the Athletic Department, and I asked him if he remembered a 157-pounder named Severin Winter.

"*Remember* him?" the coach said. "Oh, he could have been great. He had all the moves, and the desire, and he kept coming at you, if you know what I mean."

I said I did.

"But he blew the big ones," the coach told me. "He didn't psych himself out exactly. You wouldn't call it clutching up—not exactly. But he'd make a mistake. He only made *big* mistakes," the coach decided, "and not too many. In the big matches, though, one mistake's enough."

"I'm sure it is," I said. "But he *was* the runner-up one year, in the Big Ten, at 157 pounds?"

"Yup," the coach said. "But the weight classes have changed since then. That's actually the 158-pound class now. It used to be 123, 130, 137, 147, 157 and so on, but now it's 118, 126, 134, 142, 150, 158 and so on—you know."

I didn't, and I certainly didn't care. Everyone says the academic life is one long prayer to detail, but it's hard to match athletics for a life of endless, boring statistics.

Occasionally I would chide Winter about his great love. "As a former 157-pounder, it must be nice, Severin, to involve yourself in a field that's changed one pound in ten years."

"What about history?" he'd say. "How many pounds has civilization changed? I'd guess about four ounces since Jesus, about half an ounce since Marx."

Winter was an educated man, of course his German was perfect, and evidently he was a good teacher—though there is some evidence that native speakers of a foreign language don't always make the best teachers. He was a good wrestling coach, but the way he got the job was a fluke. He was hired to teach German, but he never missed a wrestling practice and rather quickly became an unofficial assistant to the head coach, a thunkish heavyweight from Minnesota who'd been both a Big Ten and national champion at the time Winter wrestled for Iowa. The ex-heavyweight shortly dropped dead of a heart attack while he was demonstrating a setup for the fireman's carry. (Winter said, "I thought he looked like he was setting it up all wrong.") Caught in midseason without a coach, the Athletic Department asked Winter to fill in. He told Edith it had been his secret ambition. His team finished the season so strongly that he was salaried as head coach for the next year, creating only a small, unuttered scandal among the more petty faculty who were envious of his double pay. It was only his enemies in the Division of Language and Literature who made any claim that Winter gave less than enough time to his German students because of his new work load. Naturally this disgruntlement was never expressed to his face. Enrollment in German actually soared, since Winter required every member of the wrestling team to take his language.

Winter claimed that wrestling helped him as a German teacher (but he would claim that it helped everything he did—indeed, he claimed it aloud and in various company, his hand on Edith's sleek bottom, shouldering her off-balance and jarring her drink: "It makes everything work a little better!").

Their affection for each other seemed real, if strange. The first night Utch and I had dinner with them we drove home very curious about them.

"God, I think he looks like a *troll*," I told Utch.

"I think you like how *she* looks," Utch said.

"He's almost grotesque," I said, "like a giant dwarf . . ."

"I know you," Utch said; she put her heavy hand on my thigh. "You go for her kind, the bones in the face—the breeding, you would say."

"He has almost no neck," I said.

"He's very handsome."

"You find him *attractive?*" I asked her.

"Oh *ja,* more dan dat."

"More than that," I corrected her.

"Ja," Utch said, "and you find *her* attractive, too?"

"Oh *ja,* more dan dat," I said. Her strong hand squeezed me; we laughed.

"You know what?" she said. "He does all the cooking."

I will say that Severin was no savage at preparing food—only at eating it. After dinner we sat in their living room; their sofa curved around a coffee table where we had brandy. Winter was still ravaging the fruit and cheese, popping grapes, slashing pears—gobs of Brie on bread and chunks of Gorgonzola. He continued with his dinner wine, to chase his brandy. Utch was sleepy. She put her bare foot on the coffee table and Winter seized it at the ankle, looking at her calf as if it were meat to be deboned.

"Look at that leg!" he cried. "Look at the width of that ankle, the spread of that foot!" He said something to Utch in German which made her laugh; she wasn't angry or embarrassed at all. "Look at that calf. This is peasant stuff," Winter said. "This is the foot of the fields! This is the leg that outran the armies!" He spoke more German; he clearly approved of Utch's sturdy body. She was shorter than he—only five feet six inches. She was rounded, full-hipped, full-breasted, with a curve at her belly and muscular legs. Utch had a rump a child could sit on when she was standing up, but she had no fat on her; she was hard. She had that broad face of Central Europe: high cheekbones, a heavy jaw and a wide mouth with thin lips.

Utch spoke some German to Severin; it was pleasant listening to their singsong Viennese dialect, though I wished I could understand them. When he let go of her leg, she left it on the table.

I picked up the candle and lit Edith's cigarette, then my own. Neither Utch nor Severin smoked. "I understand that you write," I said to Edith.

She smiled at me. Of course I knew, then, where her smile was from and where we all were going. I had seen only one smile as confident as Edith's before, and Edith's smile was even more heedless and alluring than the one on the postcard of the angel called "The Smile of Reims."

2

Scouting Reports: Edith (126 - Pound Class)

Edith Fuller left prep school in her senior year to go with her parents to Paris. They were the New York Fullers and there was no strife connected with the move; Edith was happy to leave, and her father said that she should not waste her time on education when she could live in Paris. She went to a good school there, and when her parents returned to New York, she chose to travel in Europe. When she returned to the States to go to college, her mother registered disappointment that Edith was "suppressing her natural beauty in an unnatural way, just to look like a writer." For two years at Sarah Lawrence, Edith looked like a writer—causing the only friction with her parents that ever existed. Actually, she really looked as if she was still traveling in Europe; being a writer had nothing to do with it. When her father died suddenly she left Sarah Lawrence and joined her mother in New York. Seeing no reason to upset her mother further, she took up the cause of caring for her "natural beauty" again, and found that she could still write.

Edith was instrumental in finding her mother a job—not that any of the New York Fullers ever needed a job, but her mother needed to have something to do. One of Edith's boyfriends directed the New Acquisitions Department at the Museum of Modern Art, and since both Edith and her mother had been would-be art history majors (neither of them ever finished college) and there was interesting volunteer work in the New Acquisitions Department, the matter was easily arranged.

All of Edith's boyfriends had interesting jobs of one kind or another. She had never dated a college boy when she was in college; she enjoyed and appealed to older men. The boyfriend at the Modern was thirty-four at the time; Edith was twenty-one.

She spent six months in New York keeping her mother company. One night she asked her to come see a movie with her, but her mother said, "Oh, I really couldn't, Edith. I have much too much to do." So Edith felt free to go back to Europe.

"Please don't feel you have to *look* like a writer, dear," her mother told her, but Edith was over that. There were friends in Paris from the Fullers' year there; she could have a room in someone's nice house; she could write;

and there would be interesting things to do at night. She was a serious young girl who had never worried anybody, she was leaving behind no serious boyfriend in America, and she wasn't rushing to Europe to meet one. She had never had a serious boyfriend, and though, as she later told me, she did think—in the back of her mind as she left New York—that this might be the time to "have the experience of really falling in love with someone," she wanted to finish a good piece of writing first. She admitted that she'd had no idea what that piece of writing was going to be, any more than she'd "bothered very hard to imagine what that first real lover would be like." She had slept with only two men before, one of them the man who was at the Modern. "I didn't do it to get Mommy the job," Edith told me. "She would have gotten the job all by herself." He was married, he had two children, and he told Edith he wanted to leave his wife for her. Edith stopped sleeping with him; she didn't want him to leave his wife.

It took her one day in Paris to be invited to use the sumptuous guest room and studio in the house of one of her parents' Paris friends for as long as she'd like to stay. Her first day out shopping she bought a fancy typewriter with a French-English keyboard. She didn't look like a writer, but at twenty-one that's how serious she was.

In the beginning she spent a lot of time answering her mother's letters. Her mother was excited about all the research projects she was given to do. She was in charge of "rounding out" what was called the Modern Movement Series. The Museum of Modern Art had most of the major representatives of every major and minor movement in the twentieth century, but they were still missing some minor painters, and Edith's mother was seeking available paintings by minor artists of more or less major schools. Edith had never heard of any of the painters her mother was so absorbed in. "But my own writing felt so minor," she told me, "that I had a pathetic sort of sympathy for all these unknowns."

We must have had similar parents. My mother began developing a keen interest in minor fiction simultaneously with the publication of my first historical novel. Most historical novels are pretty bad, of course, but my mother felt compelled to "keep up" with my field. I'd never read any historical novels before, but she began her habit of sending me her rare discoveries; it goes on to this day.

When I went home to see my parents shortly after my first book was published, my mother met me at the door in what was to become a ritual for all my publications. She had just finished my book, she told me, wringing my hands; she was surprised at how much it moved her, and (as we tiptoed through the hall) my father was just this minute finishing it. She thought he had liked what he'd read "so far." And we would creep through the old house, approaching my father in his den as one might sneak up on an unpredictable beast who was said to be "just finishing" his raw meat. It wouldn't do to arrive while he was still eating.

We would surround my father's sunken reading chair. Standing behind him, I could tell that he was asleep. He had a way of pinching his Scotch between his thighs when he fell asleep; somehow, he never relaxed his muscles and the drink never spilled. And all around him books would be splayed open, books he was "just finishing." There were usually at least two in his lap. One of them would be mine, but it was impossible to tell which book had put him to sleep. I never saw a *finished* book in his house. He told me once that the endings of all books left him overwhelmingly sad.

He was a historian; he had taught at Harvard for thirty-six years. When I was a student there I made the mistake of taking one of his courses. It was one of those Intellectual Problems courses, of which Harvard was very proud. The problem in this one was deciding whether or not Lenin was necessary to the Russian Revolution. Would it have happened anyway? Would it have happened *when* it happened? Was Lenin really important? Like most of the Intellectual Problems courses, you weren't really supposed to come up with the answer. About fifteen of us speculated on the question. My father speculated in his lectures, too. In the last class (I called him "sir"), I asked him if he would just state his own opinion, since he must have one: *Was* Lenin necessary?

"Of course not," he said, but he was angry that I had asked; he gave me a C. It was the only C I ever got anywhere. And when I asked him how he felt about my writing—I said I assumed that he thought the historical novel was bad for both history and literature, but in my particular case . . . "Quite," he said.

My first historical novel was about one year of the great plague as it was decimating France. I focused on one small village, and the book was a terrifyingly accurate, if clinical, account of how all the seventy-six inhabitants of the village eventually died of the Black Death. There were a lot of gibbet images. "I like it so far," my father said. "I haven't finished it yet, but I think you were wise to select a *small* village."

My mother was the fan. She sent me one bad historical novel after another, with a trail of notes saying, "I think your books are so much better!" And after each of my publications, the ritual would repeat itself. There I would be at the door on Brown Street, Cambridge, the only house I ever grew up in or went back to. At first I was alone, and then with Utch, and then with our children, and my mother would whisper us all inside, saying, "I just loved it so much, and your father's liking it a great deal. Better than the last, he says. In fact, I think he's just finishing it now . . ." And we would creep down the hall, approach the den, see my father sleeping with his Scotch held tight between his thighs. My book, along with all the others, lay culprit around him, possibly responsible for his stupor.

I never saw him finish a Scotch, either. It was my mother, like Edith's mother, who took her work—however minor—seriously.

I think that, as a rule, mothers are more serious than fathers. Once I sat down to dinner, patted Utch on her thigh and topped up my son's half-empty milk glass with wine. "Have you even looked at your children today?" Utch asked me. "Shut your eyes and tell me what they're wearing." But my theory breaks down with Severin Winter. *He* was the mother in their family.

Not more than a week after Utch had caught me mixing milk with wine, we were in Winter's active kitchen; everyone's children were everywhere, and Severin was making his bouillabaisse for us all. Edith and I were talking at the kitchen table; Utch was tying someone's shoe; and the younger Winter daughter was staring fixedly at her mother's earring. I hadn't heard the child say anything, either, but suddenly Severin turned at the stove and hollered, "Edith!" She jumped. "Edith," he said, "your daughter, who looks at you all day as if you were a mirror, has asked you the same question four times. Why don't you answer her?" Edith looked at her daughter, surprised to see her sitting there. But Utch knew; she, too, heard everything the children ever said.

Utch said, "No, Dorabella, it doesn't hurt very much." Edith still stared at her daughter as if she'd just learned that she'd had a part in the child's lovely flesh.

"Does it hurt to have your ears pierced, Mommy?" Severin boomed from the stove.

And Edith said, "Yes, a little, Fiordiligi." Right name, wrong daughter; we all knew; we waited for Edith to catch her own slip, but she didn't.

"That's *Dorabella,* Edith," Severin said; Dorabella laughed, and Edith stared at her. And Severin, as if to explain to Utch and me, said, "It's understandable. About four years ago Fiordiligi asked Edith the same question."

But suddenly it was very quiet in that energetic kitchen; only the bouillabaisse was speaking. Perhaps to break the tension we always felt when we recognized the peculiar alliances we felt toward each other, Severin said (but what a queer thing to say!), "Does it hurt to have your tongue nailed to a breadboard?"

We all laughed. Why? I thought about the four of us, but what I remembered was my father's reply to an interviewer from the *Times* who had asked him to say a few words about some new gesture in American foreign policy, "with some emphasis on the subtleties we laymen may have missed."

"It's about as subtle as the Russian revolution," my father said. No one knew what he meant.

My father's creepy wide-angle lens. I never agreed with him about Lenin. Lenin *was* necessary. People are necessary. ("How nice for you," Severin said to me once. "Edith's a romantic too.") And my mother's terrible books,

I sometimes think, were closer to the truth than my father ever came close enough to see. Edith and I were brought up unsure of ourselves as snobs —in love with our mothers' innocence.

In Paris, Edith went out and read everything she could find about all the minor painters mentioned in her mother's letters. There wasn't much to find out about some of them, but she tried. She didn't get much writing done, and just when she mastered enough research to respond knowledgeably to her mother's interests, she was proposed to by the father of the household in which she was a pampered guest. He was always very polite and fatherly to her, and she'd never suspected. One morning he struck his soft-boiled egg too hard; it catapulted out of its eggcup and landed on the Persian rug in the breakfast room. His wife ran to the kitchen to get a sponge. Edith stooped next to his chair and dabbed her napkin into the yolky mess on the rug. He put his hand into her hair and tilted her surprised face up to him. "I love you, Edith," he croaked. Then he burst into tears and left the table.

His wife returned with the sponge. "Oh, did he rush off?" she asked Edith. "He gets so upset when he makes a mess."

Edith went to her room and packed. She wondered if she should write ..er mother and try to explain. She was still wondering what to do when the maid brought the mail to her room. There was a new letter from her mother about minor painters. Could Edith tear herself away from her work in Paris just long enough for a business trip to Vienna? Her mother's boss was interested in rounding out one of the Modern Movement Series. Of course, they had something from the Vienna Secession; they had Gustav Klimt, who (Edith's mother said) did not really belong to Vienna's Late Art Nouveau, since he was really a forerunner to the Expressionists. For Viennese Expressionists, they had Egon Schiele and Kokoschka, and even a Richard Gerstl (a *who?* Edith thought). "We do have a dreadful Fritz Wotruba," Edith's mother wrote, "but what we want is someone from the thirties whose work is random and imitative and transitional enough to represent it *all.*"

The painter on whom this dubious distinction was about to fall had been a student of Herbert Boeckl's at the Academy. He had appeared to be "peaking" at about the time the Nazis marched into Austria in 1938. He was twenty-eight at the time he disappeared. "All his paintings are still in Vienna," wrote Edith's mother. "There are four on loan to the Belvedere, but most of them are in private homes. They are all owned by his only son, who apparently wants to sell as many of them as he can. We only want one —two, at the most. You'll have to get slides made, and you're not to promise anything in the way of a price."

"Leaving today for Vienna," Edith wired her mother. "Delighted to take a break. Perfect timing."

She flew from Orly to Schwechart. She'd been in Vienna in December three years ago; she'd hated it. It was the most Central European city she'd ever seen, and the cold slush in the streets seemed to belong with the city's squat Baroque heaviness. The buildings, like the men, had seemed to her to have an unhealthy color and ill-cut, elaborate clothes. It was not as friendly as a village, but it had none of the elegance she associated with a city. She felt that the war was just barely over. Throughout the city she kept seeing signs indicating the few kilometers to Budapest; she had not realized she was almost in Hungary. She spent only three days and saw only one opera, *Der Rosenkavalier*; it bored her, though she thought it shouldn't have, and at intermission a man made a vulgar pass at her.

But now when her Paris flight landed in Vienna, it was a different season: early spring weather, wet-smelling with a sunny wind and a hard-blue Bellini sky. The buildings, which had all seemed so gray before, now shone in such rich and subtle shades; the fat putti and the statuary everywhere seemed like a stone welcoming party hanging off the buildings. People were out walking; the population seemed to have doubled. Something in the atmosphere was changed, felt chiefly by the sight of baby carriages; the Viennese were feeling fit to reproduce again.

The taxi driver was a woman who knew the English word "dear." "Say to me where you want to be gone, dear," she said. Edith showed her the addresses in her mother's letter. She wanted a hotel which was near the Belvedere; more important, she wanted to know where the painter's son lived. The son had graduated from an American university a few years ago and had gone back to Vienna because his mother was dying; afterwards he inherited all the father's paintings. He was staying in Vienna just long enough to complete a degree at the university, and he wanted to sell as many of the paintings as he could. He had written a very literate and witty letter to the Museum of Modern Art. He had begun by saying that the people at the Modern had probably never heard of his father, which was forgivable because he wasn't a very important painter and they shouldn't feel they had missed anything. The son was twenty-seven, five years older than Edith. She found out that his address was a two-block walk from the Belvedere.

Her driver took her to a hotel on the Schwarzenberg Platz. Outside the hotel waiters were setting up big red-white-and-blue Cinzano umbrellas for the café. It was still too brisk to sit outside for long; the sun was weak, but Edith had the feeling that she was arriving early to a party still in the preparation phase. She thanked the cabdriver, who said, "Okay, dear."

Edith had one more thing to ask; she didn't know how to pronounce the son's first name. "How do you say this?" she asked the driver, holding out her mother's letter. She had the name underlined: *Severin* Winter.

"*Say*-vah-rin," the cabdriver crooned.

Edith was surprised how she liked to say that name. "*Say*-vah-rin," she sang in her hotel room as she took a bath and changed her clothes. There was still sunlight on the west faces of the buildings on the Schwarzenberg Platz. Behind the spuming fountain was the Russian War Memorial. It no longer felt like the afternoon of the same day a man had put his hand in her hair, said, "I love you" and then burst into tears. She would send them both one of those Dresden pieces of great delicacy; she caught herself smiling at the idea that it might arrive smashed.

She put on a sleek, black, clingy blouse and a soft, gun-gray cashmere suit. She wrapped a bright-green scarf twice around one wrist and knotted it; she did things like that and got away with it. "*Say*-vah-rin *Vin*-ter?" she said to the mirror, holding out her hand, the bright scarf like a favor.

She hated the telephone, so she would not call; she would just take a walk and drop in. She tried to picture the son of a minor artist. She had no idea whether he would buy her a drink, invite her to dinner, suggest the opera, make a phone call to have the Belvedere opened at night—or whether he would be poor and awkward and she should really offer to take him to dinner. She did not know whether to be smart and businesslike and say she had come to Vienna representing the Museum of Modern Art, who in response to Herr Winter's letter about his father's paintings . . . or whether she should confess just how unofficial her visit really was.

She'd been so glad to leave Paris that she hadn't thought about what she was doing here, and now she even began to have doubts about what she was wearing. She put on knee-high, glossy-green boots and decided to leave it at that. Few enough people in Paris dressed the way Edith did, and she assumed that no one in Vienna did. Severin Winter had been in America, after all. Edith always thought of New York when she thought of America. She didn't know that Severin Winter had spent most of his time in *Iowa,* dividing his time between wearing headphones in a language lab and ear-guards on a wrestling mat (for these reasons and reasons in his genes, his ears lay flat against his head).

"*Say*-vah-rin," she said again, as if she were tasting soup. She pictured a thin, bearded man who looked more in his thirties than twenty-seven. She had not looked twice at a single graduate student in America, and she could not imagine a Viennese graduate student at all. A degree in what? A doctorate in minor painting?

The sun now struck only the top row of cupids on the old buildings along the Opernring. She would need to wear a coat. She felt like buying one, but she remembered Austrian clothes as being either leather or thick, scratchy loden, so she put on her black Paris cape. It was a little dressy; when she saw herself in it, she decided she *was* representing the Museum of Modern Art in New York—just flown in from Paris. What was the harm?

After a short walk she was standing outside the Schwindgasse address, just around the corner from the Belvedere. Somehow, it was already dark. The street was small and cobblestoned; the apartment building was opposite the Bulgarian embassy and next-door to something called the Polish Reading Room; there was a dim coffeehouse of faded elegance a half-block down the street. She read the brass nameplates in the lobby of the Schwindgasse apartment house, then walked up a marble flight of stairs and rang a bell on the first landing. "*Say*-vah-rin," she whispered to herself. She poised her chin, expecting to look up when he opened the door; she had decided he would be thin, bearded and tall. To her surprise, she had to look down a little. The boy in the doorway was clean-shaven, and wore sneakers, jeans and a T-shirt; he looked like the rawest of American tourists in Europe. He wore a blatant college letter-jacket, black with leather sleeves and a thick, oversized gold "I" on the breast. American Baroque, Edith thought. Obviously he was a young friend from Severin Winter's college days.

"Does Severin Winter live here?" Edith asked, not at all sure.

"I sure do," said Severin; he bounced backward in the doorway, more like a boxer teasing an opponent to come after him than like a man inviting anyone in. But his smile caught her completely off-guard. It was boyish, but it wasn't, and she noticed the one askew tooth with the V-chip sliced deep to the gum. In the light behind him, she saw that his dark hair was thick and fluffy and clean. It's a baby bear, she thought, stepping inside.

"My name is Edith Fuller," she said, and was surprised at how self-conscious she felt with him. "I'm here to look at your father's paintings. You wrote a letter to the Museum of Modern Art?"

"Yes, yes." He smiled. "But I never thought they'd actually *want* one."

"Well, I'm here to look," she said, and embarrassed herself by sounding cool.

"At night? Don't they look at paintings in daylight in New York?" he asked. She felt flustered; then she saw he was teasing her; he was all fun, this bear, and she laughed. She stepped into a living room with so many paintings everywhere that she didn't see one of them. It was a room with at least four doorways, leading off everywhere, and it was crammed with books, photographs and objects of a most peculiar taste. She suspected that the living room was only the tip of an iceberg—one hill of a continent. There was so much stuff in the room that she didn't notice the people, and when she realized that he was introducing her, she gave a little leap. There was a woman who could have been forty-nine or sixty-two; she wore a blowzy off-the-shoulder dress which was gathered and belted and slit in a way Edith couldn't fathom—as if it had been hastily made from an Art Nouveau bedsheet. This was Frau Reiner. "A friend of my mother's," said Severin Winter. "She was a model too." Frau Reiner's deeply lined face, her huge mouth and dusky skin were all that Edith could evaluate in terms of what Frau Reiner had to model; her body was lost in the art of her dress.

Then came two almost twin men whose names were as baffling as their appearance. Their names were something on a menu you wouldn't dare to order without advice. They were in their sixties and looked like spies, or gangsters, or retired prizefighters who'd lost more than they'd won. Edith didn't know then that they were like loving uncles to Severin Winter. They were Zivan Knezevich and Vaso Trivanovich, old Chetnik freedom fighters who'd fled Tito and the Partisans at the end of the Yugoslav civil war; like a lot of others, they'd found that Vienna was close to the East. They'd had as much to do with Severin Winter's upbringing as Katrina Marek. They'd taught him how to wrestle; they'd told him to go wrestle in America and one day beat the Russians. They were former members of the Yugoslav freestyle wrestling team. Vaso Trivanovich had won a bronze medal in the Berlin Olympics in 1936; Zivan Knezevich had been almost as good.

Like two old knights out of armor, Vaso and Zivan each kissed Edith's hand. But Frau Reiner held her hand up; Edith dimly realized she was supposed to kiss it and did so. The hand was a jewel box of rings; the perfume, Edith realized with a shock, was the same as her own. One of her tastes must be suspect.

And around a heavy hardwood table with a large tile chessboard in its center, Severin Winter restlessly moved with the grace and the spring of a bizarrely muscled deer. "Will you have some Kremser Schmitt?" he asked Edith. "Or a beer?"

She did not like beer, and Kremser Schmitt sounded like a kind of sausage to her, but she dared it and was relieved to find out that it was a nicely chilled and decent white wine.

The old Chetniks babbled at each other in Serbo-Croatian. Even Edith could tell that their German was halting; one of them was slightly deaf and needed to be shouted to. Frau Reiner smiled hugely at Edith, as if she were an hors d'oeuvre. She felt most comfortable looking at Severin, who in relation to his friends was changing radically in her eyes. He seemed like their Darling Prince; she had never seen anyone less self-conscious. Mozart was playing on a terrible phonograph, and Severin could not sit still. He swayed in his chair; he tossed his head. Why does he wear that awful jacket, Edith thought, imagining scars on his arms.

Frau Reiner asked Severin one question after another, which he translated to Edith. "Frau Reiner thinks you never got that cape in Vienna," he said.

"I got it in Paris," Edith told him, and Frau Reiner nodded.

"And your boots could only be from New York?" Right again.

None of the colleges Edith could think of began with a garish yellow "I".

Somehow, they all went out together. Edith thought they must look like a circus act. The two old wrestlers in their dark spy-suits and the kind of trench coats for concealing weapons; like the old locker-room boys they still were, they jostled and shoved and batted each other as they walked. Frau Reiner took Severin's arm on his right, and Edith found herself naturally holding his left. He walked them along bilingually. He would say to Edith, "Schiele liked to eat lunch here, on occasion," and Frau Reiner would pick up on the word "Schiele" and hum her rich German into his ear.

"She says," Severin told Edith, "that she was a child model for Schiele in the last year of his life."

"He died when he was only twenty-eight," Edith offered, then felt like a fool because he looked at her as if she'd just said, "When it rains, things get wet."

"But I don't believe it and neither should you," Severin said.

"What? He wasn't twenty-eight? He didn't die?"

"I don't believe Frau Reiner was ever a child model for him. No painting or drawing of her exists among Schiele's workbooks and unfinished canvases, and everything he painted in that last year has been looked over. Unless it was something so bad that he destroyed it, which was not his habit. Frau Reiner has modeled for a lot of people—though not so many as my mother modeled for—but she has always regretted that she could only be a child model when Schiele and Klimt were alive."

Frau Reiner said something and Severin said, "She's admitting she never modeled for Klimt."

Frau Reiner said something else.

"But she claims he spoke to her once," Severin whispered to Edith. "This could be true, but she would hardly have been old enough to remember it."

Edith was struck by how close he moved toward her when he talked. He couldn't talk without touching, squeezing and coming very close, but she felt there was nothing sly or sexual about it. She noticed that he also touched the old Chetniks when he talked to them.

This is true: Severin could never keep his hands off anyone he spoke to. Later it irritated me how he would be all over Utch—I mean in public, at large parties. He would be mauling her in conversation. Of course, Edith and I were more discreet. But I confess Severin mauled *me* in conversation too. There was always an arm around you, or he would seize your wrist in his hand and squeeze it between sentences. Sometimes he pinched; I even remember that he used to touch my beard. But it was just a way he had, a part of his restless movement. I don't think I agree with Edith that he was unselfconscious—whether he really was, or whether he might have been so self-conscious that you assumed no one could be *that* self-conscious and decided he was completely natural.

Anyway, he struck Edith as a friendly animal. When he talked he seemed much older, and when he smiled she found herself liking his boyishness.

I think, when we meet people, we can like them right away if we see how much their friends like them. Most of all, Edith said, she was aware of how much Frau Reiner and the two Chetniks adored Severin.

"But I'd have loved him anyway," Edith told me, "because he was the first man who treated me lightly. I mean, he was comic. He wasn't the sort of awful comic who tries to make everything funny, either. He was a *pure* comic. He simply found the comic ingredient in most things—even in me, and I took myself very seriously, of course."

Well, I won't split hairs. I think that what really got to Edith is what can get to any of us: she discovered jealousy.

They went to a Serbian restaurant where the whole crowd knew that Vaso and Zivan were heroes and clapped their backs and threw celery stalks at them, and where Edith and Severin and Frau Reiner were treated as partial heroes themselves. There was torturous string music and too much spice in everything, and too much of everything, but Edith had a wonderful time.

Severin Winter told her stories about his mother and father (I'm sure the zoo fantasy must have been a part of it); he told her stories of Zivan's and Vaso's escape from Yugoslavia; he told her stories about Frau Reiner when she was the hottest model in the city (Edith was beginning to believe it). "She learned everything she knew from my mother," said Severin. And he told her that the "I" on his jacket was for Iowa, and that the closest he'd ever come to winning a major conference or national championship was when he was runner-up in the Big Ten at 157 pounds.

"What do you weigh now?" Edith asked. He looked so much bigger, though he was lean in those days.

"One fifty-eight," he said. She wasn't sure if this was a joke. With him you never knew.

Then he leaned across the table and said, "In the morning, then? We'll see the Belvedere, I'll take you around to a few apartments—old friends of my parents have some of the best ones. I don't believe my father ever *sold* a damn thing; at least, he didn't make any money. I can't tell you how glad I am that you came here." Edith looked at his eyes, his hair, that one weird tooth. "I'm dying to leave Europe," he told her. "Everything and everyone is dying here. I want to go back to America very much, but I've got to unload some of these paintings first. This is a break for me, I must tell you." And it suddenly struck Edith that he was talking about *money*; he was talking to the representative from the Museum of Modern Art in New York, just flown in from Paris to give old Kurt Winter a second look. She realized she had no idea how much money the Modern would pay, but she didn't think it would be much. God, maybe they would only consider a Kurt Winter as a *gift!* Wasn't that the way it usually happened? And only one —two at the most—her mother had said.

For some reason, she touched his hand; his damn physical habits were catching. But before she could say anything, Frau Reiner leaned against Severin; she bit his ear, took his chin in her hand, turned his head toward her and kissed him lushly on the mouth. Edith could see where Frau Reiner's tongue went. Severin didn't seem surprised, only interrupted, but Frau Reiner gave Edith a very clear look which Edith wilted under. She felt like a very young girl. *His mother's friend,* indeed. So she blurted, "I've been looking at your dress all night and I still can't figure out how it works." Frau Reiner was surprised that Edith spoke to her; she couldn't understand, of course. But Edith was saying all this for Severin. "I wonder if Gustav Klimt designed that dress for you," she said; Frau Reiner stiffened at the word "Klimt" while Edith went on, "I mean, it looks like a Klimt: the shiny gold gilt, the little squares, the Egyptian eye forms. But the way you've got it wrapped around you, it doesn't seem to show itself quite right." She stopped, embarrassed; she couldn't remember ever showing off before.

And Severin replied in his boy's face but with the same irritating fatherliness she was used to from other men. "I don't think you want me to translate for you," he said. But he was smiling; he showed her his teasing tooth. "I *will* translate, though, if you wish."

"Please don't," she said. And in a burst of candor, "I think she's too old for you." That got to him; he looked self-conscious for the first time. But she felt uneasy that she had said it; Why do I care? she almost said aloud.

They all rode home in the same cab. Frau Reiner sat on Severin's lap; twice, she licked his ear. Edith was crammed between them and either Zivan or Vaso—she still couldn't tell them apart—the other one rode up front.

They dropped Edith off at her Schwarzenberg Platz hotel. "Ah, *Geld,*" said Frau Reiner, regarding the hotel. Edith knew enough German to know that meant *money.*

"Well, you know the Museum of Modern Art," Severin said in English. It was to Edith—not to Frau Reiner—that he spoke, and Edith knew that he knew *she* had a lot of money. Possibly the Museum of Modern Art was just another thing he found funny.

She felt terrible. But as she was slipping out of the cab—one old Chetnik wrestler holding the door for her, like a bodyguard—Severin picked Frau Reiner up off his lap, put her down in the back seat, came around the cab and said to Edith, "I agree with you. And I'll meet you at the Belvedere at ten." He shook her hand so quickly that she did not have time to firm her grasp before he bounced back into the cab. The old wrestlers shouted something to her in a chorus, and she was inside the hotel lobby, seeing herself in twenty gold-edged mirrors, before she realized that she wasn't sure what Severin Winter agreed with her about. Frau Reiner's Gustav Klimt dress? Or that Frau Reiner was too old for him?

Edith went to her room and took another bath. She was angry at herself. She decided that she had felt so much out of her element that she had performed. She decided they were all very odd people, dwellers in a city, as her mother had written, that "never took the twentieth century seriously." The remark is quite true. Once I asked Severin if he regarded the new so-called Sexual Freedom as a fad. "I regard the twentieth century as a fad," he said. But there was his tooth winking at you. He never told the truth!

Before Edith went to bed she went through all her clothes trying to decide what to wear to the Belvedere. Then she got angry at herself about that too; she had never been self-conscious about what she wore. In bed she watched the city lights struggle through the high windows and the rich cream-colored drapes. Why do I wear black so much? she brooded. Before she fell asleep, she wished that Severin Winter would not wear that awful letter-jacket to the Belvedere.

I saw that letter-jacket only once. By the time Utch and I met him, he had outgrown it—physically, I mean. I assumed that it was thrown out or packed away. Then one day Utch and I were sitting on the steps of our house when Edith came along the sidewalk alone and sat down between us. Severin was upset about "the whole thing," she told us. Utch and I had just been talking about that. This was at a time when Edith had already expressed her fears to me that she doubted whether "the whole thing" could work. We all knew Severin was unhappy, but our relationship was very new and Severin had never made it clear what he was unhappy about. "I thought we all ought to talk," Edith told us. "I mean, all four of us—together." We sat on the steps waiting for Severin. He was driving his daughters to some friend's house to play. Our children were out. It was early spring, and in the sun's warm hours, it was barely possible to sit on the steps.

"Does Severin want to talk?" Utch asked Edith. "I mean, all together."

"Well, I thought we should," Edith said. We sat there.

Severin parked his car in front of us, then sat in the car after he shut the motor off and looked at the three of us together on the steps. He was grinning. I realized I was holding Utch's and Edith's hands. He sat in his car like a smiling camera, and when he got out and started toward us, I felt Edith's grip spasm in my hand. Then I saw that he was wearing that goddamn letter-jacket. The sleeves stopped halfway down his forearms and the jacket's waist barely reached below his chest. The T-shirt and jeans and sneakers were familiar, almost a uniform, but though I'd never seen it, I knew about that jacket. Even the fucking weather that day must have been like it had been in Vienna!

He never reached the steps. Edith jumped up and ran to him while he was still on the sidewalk. "Where did you find that?" she cried; she seized him by the jacket. She had her face toward him, away from us, so that we couldn't see whether she was angry or happy. She shook the jacket, then hugged him. It was imperceptible, but I think he steered her to the car—or maybe she turned toward the car herself and he simply supported her. She sat in the passenger seat in severe profile, so I couldn't read her face. Severin bounced into the driver's seat and waved to us hurriedly; I don't think he actually looked at us. "Later!" he called. Edith never moved as he drove off.

"Severin will not easily relinquish the driver's seat," Edith told me later.

"How do you feel about that?" I asked.

And Edith said, "I always felt, from the first, that he was a pretty good driver."

A firm believer in the past, Severin Winter dug up his old letter-jacket and stole our scene before we could have it.

3

Scouting Reports:
Utch (134 - Pound Class)

On July 9, 1945, the Allies quartered the city of Vienna for occupation. The Americans and British grabbed up the best residential sections, the French took over the markets and the major shopping areas, and the Russians (who had long-term, realistic plans) settled in the worker-industrial districts and within the Inner City, nearest to the embassies and the government buildings. During the carving of the great game bird, the dinner guests revealed their special tastes.

Everyone knows that the Soviets could not quite work in Vienna what they had worked in Berlin; perhaps not everyone knows how hard they tried. Sixteen out of twenty-one districts had Communist chiefs of police, a kind of Russian magic. During the ten-year occupation, as many as a third of the anti-Soviets in Vienna ended up missing; perhaps they never understood whose zone of occupation was whose and got lost. Whatever, Chancellor Figl was prompted to confess: "We have had to write down against a very long list of names simply the word 'disappeared.'" More magic.

Unless you were a Communist, or were untroubled by rape and machine-gunning, you would not have chosen to live in the Soviet zone of occupation. Utch, of course, had no choice. Only seven years old, she had good reason to be a Communist; if her guardian Captain Kudashvili was not a hero to many of the good women of Eichbüchl, he was at least her savior. If not her father, he was at least the available midwife who'd delivered her from the cow where she'd been kept so safe.

Captain Kudashvili, of course, moved into a district in the Russian zone, the fourth. It is fortunate for Utch that he was an idealist. He had never seen a postwar orphanage before. Utch had never seen Vienna. The day that Captain Kudashvili walked up Argentinierstrasse (the orphanage was near the Südbahnhof) was the first day she could remember being outside a barracks or a barn. I imagine that if you've spent two days inside a cow, being outside anywhere is uplifting. And the buildings along the Argentinierstrasse were so ornamental that they reminded her of her mother's stolen books.

Utch had her birth certificate pinned to the lapel of her coat. Kudashvili had given her a dead soldier's scarf; it wrapped around her neck four times and still dragged on the sidewalk. When they got to the orphanage, Utch somehow knew she'd been brought here to stay. Kudashvili had been telling her, of course, but she didn't understand Russian yet.

Inside the building they were holding a demonstration of a generation gap —the gap being the generation that was missing. There were grandparents galore, giving children away; it was the parents' generation that had lost (and been lost in) the war. Utch remembers that Kudashvili was the only member of his generation there; everyone stared at him. One old woman came up to him and spat on his chest, but that was because of the Russian uniform. One grandmother was trying to free herself from five or six children. An orphanage attendant was restraining one child, and another attendant was handling two, but there were always two or three the grandmother couldn't get free of. Just as she'd get to the door, one of them would get to her and cling. All her grandchildren were screaming, but it wasn't the screaming ones who impressed Utch, it was the children who'd already been left. They were not crying; they were not even moving. They were mute voyeurs, and Utch somehow inferred that they would never have any expressions on their faces again.

Kudashvili was trying to sign something, but Utch grabbed his writing hand. She wouldn't let go, she bit him, and she tried to tie him up in the long scarf he'd given her. Kudashvili did not protest; it's possible he never had his heart set on the idea of an orphanage anyway. He picked her up and carried her out of there. To this day, she claims that she shouted, *"Auf Wiedersehen!"* to everyone.

As they walked back down the Argentinierstrasse into the fourth district, Kudashvili unpinned Utch's birth certificate from her coat lapel and put it in his leather folder with his own papers. On his chest, under his medals, the old woman's spittle shone like a gob of cold chicken fat. Kudashvili cleaned himself with a handkerchief. He removed one of his medals and pinned it on Utch's coat lapel. She has it to this day: a Medal of Excellence, signifying—as nearly as anyone has been able to tell me—Captain Kudashvili's valorous participation in the defense of the great city of Kiev, the capital of the Ukraine. But perhaps that's only a symbol.

So Utch went back into the fourth district with her guardian, Captain Kudashvili, and for the ten years that the Allies occupied the city of Vienna she shared the captain's quarters with an occasional housekeeper, babysitter and laundress named Drexa Neff. Frau Neff didn't care for the Russians any more than most of the Viennese, but she did care for Captain Kudashvili. She was a sarcastic old woman whose husband had left her before the war and who'd had some fun when a young Austrian boy who was too sickly to be a soldier had paid her twenty schillings a week, when he picked up his mother's laundry, for doing something extra to him in the steam room.

Drexa Neff scolded and teased Utch, but she took care of her. Kudashvili protectively walked Utch to school every day, and Drexa Neff was at school to meet her and walk her home. When the other kids would bully her, Drexa Neff would tell her to say to them: "Captain Kudashvili is a moral man, even though he is a Russian, and a moral man is more than some of you can call your fathers, if you have a father left . . ." Which, of course, Utch never said.

It was Drexa Neff who prepared Utch for becoming a Russian. Drexa thought school was a waste for Utch. "*Ja,* but did they teach you how to do it in *Russian* today?" she'd ask after school. "Because that's where he'll take you, *Liebchen,* if he doesn't leave you here—and *der* Kudashvili is too moral a man to leave you just anywhere, you should already know." So Utch paid attention to her guardian and learned the Russian language from him, as well as a game called *Telephon.* She learned never to go outside without first phoning 06-036-27. In those days there was no direct dialing; Utch would have to tell the operator the number. She learned it by heart: *"Null sechs, null sechsunddreizig, siebenundzwanzig."* It was Captain Kudashvili's office number; she never knew where it was, and the captain never answered the phone himself. She would call and then wait in the apartment or the laundry where Drexa Neff steamed and talked.

Usually, two men came for her. They were never other Russians; they were never in uniform. But they were working for the Russians. Utch remembers that they were very watchful. Sometimes they would follow her at a short distance instead of walking beside her, and whenever someone spoke to her, the two men would come up very suddenly and whoever had spoken to Utch would say that he was very sorry.

It was much later, of course, when she realized who the men were and why she needed to be protected. Most people in the Russian sector needed protection, but Utchka was "that Russian captain's daughter, or something," and needed to be protected from the anti-Soviets. The men who were her bodyguards were members of the most notorious criminal gang in Vienna: the Benno Blum Gang, a cigarette-smuggling ring and black marketeers of the precious nylon stocking, to mention only their lighter trades. What they were really responsible for was the "disappearance" of that famous one-third of the anti-Soviets in Vienna. They were allowed to flourish in their petty crimes, protected from the police in the Russian zone for the services they rendered the Russians in return. They killed people. It is likely Captain Kudashvili was in partial charge of them, and of course it's likely that people in Utch's neighborhood knew this. Any Viennese knowing her story would not wish her harm, but she was a link to Kudashvili and they certainly wished him considerable harm. The Benno Blum Gang smuggled more than cigarettes and nylon stockings; they transported people—forever. Utch may have been the best-guarded child in the fourth district.

Severin Winter, who has never enjoyed being a runner-up, has said that Utch was not the best-guarded child in the fourth district; he claimed that *he* was. Of course, he was being protected from the Russians, not by them; his situation was more typical. His mother had brought him back from London at the end of the war; she still had many of Kurt Winter's paintings left, and many had been left in Vienna. She came looking for Kurt Winter, on the slight chance that she'd really find him, and insisted on reoccupying her old apartment on the Schwindgasse, even though her friends told her that it was in the Russian district. She insisted. Where else would her husband look for her?

Katrina Marek had not been an actress in London during the war, and she never returned to the stage again. She had been an artist's model in London, and she took that up in Vienna in 1945. She was quite well known by the time Severin was marched off each morning to a boy's academy. She did not want her son to forget his English. "It's your ticket out of this old horse stable, this greasy *Küche,*" she told her son, and she insisted that he be marched each day out of the Russian sector, into an American sector and the American school, and then back home to the Russian zone. It was a feat of beating red tape few could have pulled off, but Severin had escorts who knew the ropes. Friends of his mother, Severin's escorts were the two most sought-after male models of any in Vienna. Severin claims they were nearly as popular as his mother in Guetersloh's classes at the Vienna Academy. Katrina had met them when a painter had asked her to model with them at a joint session. They were, of course, Zivan Knezevich and Vaso Trivanovich, the wrestlers from the '36 Berlin Games. In the years of the occupation of Vienna, Vaso and Zivan were still young and strong. They were also former Chetnik guerrillas, and their abiding contempt for the Russians made their daily sorties in and out of the Russian zone very satisfying to them.

But Severin Winter is full of shit if he wants me to believe that two ex-wrestlers would ever have been a match for the Benno Blum Gang. It is fortunate for him that their paths did not cross. Those former athletes would have been found bloated in the Danube, nylon stockings over their faces and twisted round their necks—a Blum Gang specialty.

It's a wonder, though, that their paths did not cross—Utch off to school each morning with the captain, or out to shop with Benno Blum's hired murderers carrying her chocolate; it's a wonder that she didn't once pass on the street that short, dark, athletic boy in the company of his wrestlers. Perhaps they simply don't remember it. It's likely they saw each other at least once, because for ten years Utch lived in a second-floor apartment next to the Bulgarian embassy, directly across the Schwindgasse from the Marek second-floor apartment. They could have looked in each other's windows.

And they used the same laundress. At least once, while Utch sat listening to Drexa Neff or helped her stack the clean clothes, surely Severin must have walked into the steam, flanked by his wrestlers, and asked if his mother's laundry was ready.

"She didn't have much laundry," Winter said. "Her dress was quite informal."

Such understatement. Katrina Marek went out modeling each morning in her calf-length brown coat of muskrat fur, the gift of an American painter she had modeled for in London. It had a collar that rolled up above the top of her head, and beneath the coat peeked the bottoms of her thigh-high orange stockings. They were the same stockings—that is, the same orange, if not the same pair—that the model wore in Schiele's *Vally with Red Blouse* (1913) and *Woman with Purple Boa* (1915). Katrina Marek had several pairs. Her workday laundry was characteristically light. Central heating was rare in Vienna; when she wasn't modeling, she kept her muskrat coat on. Under the coat, she wore orange stockings and nothing else.

"Mother would dress when she came home," Winter said. "Or if it was late, she might not bother."

Utch remembers hearing about Katrina Marek, but she can't remember ever seeing her. "Was she tall?" she asked Severin. "A blonde, yes! I remember her. She had a very thin face—"

"She was short and dark," Winter said, "and her face was as broad as yours."

But he couldn't visualize Captain Kudashvili either, although he swears he heard the name every day. "*Ja,* of course, *der* Kudashvili. He was the sergeant of the block, the general of the Schwindgasse. 'You watch out, you mind your manners,' the mothers would tell you, 'or *der* Kudashvili is taking you away.' Oh *ja,* he was blonder than a German's German, he was as fat as a Russian's bear. He wore elevator shoes."

"He never did," said Utch. "He was tall and lean, with a long sad face and a mustache like black wool. His eyes were gray-blue, like a revolver."

"Oh, *that* one!" Severin Winter cried. "Of course I remember him." But he didn't; it was just his clever tooth talking again.

But why couldn't they remember? Children were scarce. Out of rarity, alone, all the children must have looked at one another. Children stare at one another—even now, when there are so many.

"There was a lot of forgetting going on," Utch told me.

Yes, and much of it was hers. She must have been uncomfortable about her guardian captain's job. Drexa did not make things easier for him. At supper, Kudashvili allowed her to eat with Utch and himself, despite Drexa's babble.

"Well, Captain, you must have heard," Drexa would say. "Old Gortz is gone—the machine-parts store up Argentinierstrasse? He owned it for years."

"Gortz?" Kudashvili would say; his German was better than he let on.

"Just disappeared," Drexa would say. "Overnight. His wife woke up and the bed was empty. She woke because suddenly she felt cold."

"Men are poor, weak creatures, Drexa," Kudashvili would say. "You have to marry a good one if you don't want him to run away." And to Utch he'd say, "You're going to be lucky. You won't ever have to marry anybody until you want to."

"*Ja,* Utchka will marry a czar!" old Drexa would cackle. She knew that was old Russia, but she liked it when the captain raised his black eyebrows at her.

"The czars are gone, Drexa."

"*Ja, mein Hauptmann,* and so is Gortz."

"You must have known what was going on," Severin said once to Utch.

"I knew what was going on before too," Utch answered.

"So what's the difference between one Gestapo and another?" Winter asked.

"Kudashvili took good care of me," she said.

We were sitting in our living room late one evening after dinner. It was often awkward when all four of us tried to have a conversation; by then, it was Edith and I who talked to each other, and Utch and Severin. Still, if such things are ever going to work, it must be thought of as a relationship between four people, not two couples. The whole point was not to be clandestine, but it was Severin who would never give the four of us a chance. He would either be sullen and say nothing, or he would get into these long family-history harangues with Utch and expect Edith and me to listen. He was uncomfortable, so he tried to make us uncomfortable too. Sometimes, at their house, he'd appear holding Utch's coat out to her immediately after supper, in the middle of a fairly relaxed conversation. He'd say suddenly to her, "Come on, we're keeping them from talking about their writing." That was a habit at his insistence too: somehow he always took Utch home, or stayed with her in our house, and I would end up with Edith in their house. He made a Prussian routine out of our relationship, and then made fun of it for being a routine! "Exasperating," he said one night when the three of us were very much aware that he hadn't said a word all evening. "We're just biding time before we go to bed. Why not forget the dinner part and save a little money?"

So we tried it a few times, and he seemed to enjoy the coldness of it. I'd arrive at their house after dinner and he'd slip out the back door as I came in the front. Or when he came to our house first, he sat around with his coat on, mumbling "Yes" and "No" until I left to see Edith. Then he would take his coat off, Utch told me.

But it didn't have to be that way, or like other times when he'd consciously set out to bore us all, engendering a monologue at dinner which he'd carry to the living room afterwards with every intention of making us all fall asleep. One night he talked so long that Edith finally said, "Severin, I think we're all tired."

"Oh," he said. "Well, let's call it a night, then. Let's go to bed, then," he said to *Edith!* He kissed Utch goodnight and shook my hand. "Another time, then. We've got lots of time, right?"

I remember the endless evening which began with his saying to Utch, "Do you remember the riot at the Greek embassy in 'fifty-two?"

"I was only fourteen," Utch said.

"So was I, but I recall it very clearly," Severin said. "A horde of rioting Communists attacking the Greek embassy; they were protesting the execution of Beloyannis."

"I don't remember any Beloyannis," Utch said.

"Well, he was a Greek Communist," Severin said, "but I'm talking about the attack on the Greek embassy in Vienna. The Soviets wouldn't let the police send an armed force to break up the riot. The funny thing was that the rioters were *brought* to the embassy in Soviet Army trucks. Remember now?"

"No."

"And even funnier is that the Soviets disarmed all the police—in our sector, anyway. They even took away their rubber truncheons. I always wondered if that was Kudashvili's idea."

"I forget a lot," Utch said.

"So does Severin," Edith said.

"Like what?" Winter asked her.

"Your mother," said Edith. Utch and I chewed our food quietly while Winter sat looking as if he was remembering.

"What about my mother?" he asked Edith.

"Her modeling," said Edith lightly, "and the fact that she was naked nearly all the time."

"Of course I remember that!" he hollered.

"Tell the story about her coat and the guard," said Edith. "That's an interesting story." But Severin went back to eating.

I know the story Edith meant. On weekends when Katrina would go modeling, Severin was out of school and had to come along. He sat in various artists' studios painting, drawing and pasting while the real artist attempted to render his mother. One of the studios was in the Russian sector, and the building had a guard. It was normal to tip the guard when he admitted you to the foyer, but Katrina, who had been coming there almost every Saturday for years, would never tip anyone. With little Severin beside her, she would approach the guard. He would put his truncheon down and smile, and just as she was abreast of him, she would fling open her brown muskrat coat for just a few steps, until she was past him. *"Heil* Stalin!" she'd say.

"Guten Tag, Frau Winter!" the guard would say. *"Guten Tag,* Sevi!" But Severin would never answer him.

I think Severin thought about his mother too much. The first time I saw those erotic drawings and paintings Kurt Winter did of her, I'll admit I was startled. It was the first time I slept with Edith. She took me upstairs in their house; I had never seen the upstairs before. All of us had agreed to be very careful about the children, so Edith and I tiptoed and she peeked into their rooms. I saw the laundry in the upstairs hall. I went to look at the tooth-brushes in the bathroom. Edith's nightgown hung on the back of the bath-room door; I brushed my beard against it, nuzzling it. I saw an open box of hemorrhoid suppositories (those would be Severin's, surely).

Edith's and Severin's bedroom was dark and neat. She lit a candle; the bed was turned back. For some days all four of us had projected this. Severin had quietly taken Utch home, and Edith and I had suddenly real-ized we were not just alone in the living room; we were alone in the whole house. Later, it surprised me that Utch claimed it never began that way. In her version she and Severin had been talking in the kitchen, and when they returned to the living room to join us they discovered we had gone upstairs, so it was *then* that Severin took Utch home.

What's it matter? I looked at everything in their bedroom. I wanted to see clothes lying about, but there wasn't anything. There were books (Utch and I never read in bed), and evidence that candles were frequently burned —a few hardened puddles of dull, colored wax on the window ledge. I was surprised that Edith was playful when I undressed her; it seemed so unlike her, and I had the feeling that with Severin she roughhoused a bit in bed. I did not roughhouse. It was not until I lay beside her on Severin's high Baroque bed that I saw the goddamn paintings and drawings all over the walls—the erotic dowry Kurt Winter had given his wife for her journey to London. Even as new and exciting as Edith was to me, I had to look at those damn paintings; nobody could have stopped looking at them. At that time I didn't know the full story of Kurt Winter; Edith and I had done most of our talking about ourselves. "What the hell!" I said. "Whose . . ." I meant who had painted them, but Edith assumed I meant the model.

"That's Severin's mother," she said. I thought it was a joke and tried to laugh, but Edith covered my face with her light body and blew out the candle so that I wouldn't see his mother any more that evening.

We historical novelists are somewhat hung up on *what if*'s of this world. What if Utch and Severin had met in those early years? What if her guardian had met Katrina Marek? (One night on the Schwindgasse, past the curfew hour, when Severin's mother was walking arm in arm with one of her admiring painters, who was always enough of a gentleman to walk her home when he'd kept painting her long after dark. Under the light by the Bulgarian embassy, Captain Kudashvili would have stopped them with his sad, official face. "Your papers, please?" he might have asked. "You must have special papers if you're out after the curfew." And the painter would have groped for canvas strips, wet brushes, other signs of identifica-tion. And Kudashvili—politely, from all I've heard of him—would have asked Katrina to open her brown muskrat fur coat. Who knows how history could have been altered?)

But Utch and Severin did not meet in those years. "That's a frumped-up idea of yours, anyway," Utch told me once. "I mean, if we had met, we probably wouldn't have liked each other. You assume too much." Maybe.

It's clear they led different lives. In March of 1953, for example, Utch attended a funeral. Severin was not there. It was a memorial funeral; the body was not in Vienna. She remembers the hearty mournfulness of the Soviet Army chorus and Kudashvili weeping; lots of Russians wept, but Utch thinks to this day that Kudashvili wept more for whatever the Soviet Army chorus evoked in him than for the deceased. She herself didn't weep a drop. She was fifteen and already had the beginnings of the bosom that would later stun so many. She thought that memorial funerals were a rather nice way to die, considering the other kinds of dying she had known.

Severin was fifteen too; he was out with his mother and the former Olympic warriors from Yugoslavia, and they were drinking themselves sodden and hollering themselves hoarse with happiness. There was little chance of crossing paths with Utch that day. Though it was a public and crowded beer hall, Katrina left her coat open a little during the celebration. It was the first time Severin got drunk enough to throw up. I'm told that the Russian radio station played Chopin all day.

The death that had provoked both celebration and mourning was, of course, the death of Iosif Dzhugashvili—a Georgian, better known as Joseph Stalin—who, speaking of *what if*'s, was himself a figure surrounded by a horde of *what if*'s.

What if, for example, Utch had gone to Russia? And if the world were flat, as the poet says, people would be falling off all the time. The poet knows that people fall off all the time as it is, and Captain Kudashvili was one. It surely was his intention to adopt Utch legally and take her with him to the Soviet Union. But we historical novelists are aware of how carelessly good intentions are regarded.

Kudashvili and the occupying force of the Soviet Army left Vienna in 1955. The day they left is called Flag Day in Austria now; very few Viennese were sorry to see them go. Utch was seventeen; her Russian was excellent; her German was native; she was even making progress with her English, at Kudashvili's suggestion. He was making arrangements for her to become a Russian. He thought she should be a translator, and though German was useful, English was more popular. He wrote her from Russia, closing his letters with: "How goes Utchka's English?" They would live in the great city of Tbilisi and she could go to a university.

Utch had moved out of the Schwindgasse apartment, but she still brought her laundry—considerably out of her way—to old Drexa Neff. In the new *Studentenheim* on Krügerstrasse, Utch was happy, because for the first time people didn't know her as *der* Kudashvili's "something" or a Russian spy.

It took her about three months after the Russians left to realize that she was attractive to other people. She realized that it was enviable to have breasts like hers, but that she had to learn what to do with them, and that her legs were the most peasant part of her and she had to learn how to hide them. That she liked the opera and the museums is to Kudashvili's credit; that her clothes were strange is probably his fault. She was the top-rated student at the language school, which was then a part of the Diplomatic Academy, but at times, between letters from Kudashvili, she wished that her second language was English or French instead of Russian. Most of all, she liked walking alone in Vienna; she realized that her view of how the city really looked had been colored by the fact that she'd always seen it in the company of the Benno Blum Gang. She did not miss them, especially her last escort among them, a short bald man with a hole in his cheek. It looked like an impossibly large bullet hole, except that if it had been a bullet, something would have had to come out the other side. It was a crater about the size of a ping-pong ball, like an extra eye socket below one of the man's real eyes. It was gray-black-pink on the edges, and deep enough so that you could not, so to speak, see the bottom. *Der* Kudashvili had told her that the man had been tortured during the war with an electric drill, and that the hole in his cheek was only one slow wound among several.

Since her new liberty, Utch read more than the Communist-supported newspaper. There was something every week about Benno Blum's Gang; every week they captured another old-timer. Benno's boys had a popularity second only to the unearthed executioners and experimenters from the death camps. She did not harbor any great nostalgia for her old protectors.

She felt guilty that she did not miss Kudashvili as much as she thought she would, and she made her weekly trips to the Soviet embassy with a little uneasiness, though she signed all the necessary immigration forms and many times gave the oath that she was a member of the Communist Party. She supposed she was, but it occurred to her that she was going to Russia for Kudashvili's sake, not her own. That's the point about Utch: she never once thought about *not* going. Kudashvili had loved her and made himself responsible for her. He had not left her in Eichbüchl; he had not left her among those blank-faced children in the orphanage; she owed him.

I don't think that Severin ever realized what was rare about Utch. She thought that doing something because of a debt was perfectly natural. It was unthinkable that you wouldn't do it; it was unwarranted to complain. And that thought has a complicated sister: when you don't owe anybody anything, you're free. Seventeen years old, Utch wasn't free; what's more, she didn't think it cause for self-pity. She was falling in love with Vienna, but when Kudashvili was ready she would go to Russia.

It was the good people of Budapest who freed her. On October 25, 1956, a lot of people's good intentions were upset. The Hungarians did not feel that because Russia had liberated them from the Nazis they owed the

Russians anything as unreasonably large as their country. The Hungarian revolution must have been something of a wonder to Utch; from her peculiar point of view, the notion of "dying for one's own freedom" must have seemed like a terrible self-indulgence. It must have confused her; the refugees streaming across the border seemed almost like another war. Into Vienna, unstuck on barbed wire and unexploded by the former minefields, came a hundred and seventy thousand Hungarians. They were still trickling across two days later when Vienna celebrated its first Flag Day. It was the first anniversary of the official end to the occupation. Kudashvili had been back in Russia for a year.

The week after Flag Day, Utch went to the Russian embassy and discovered that all her immigration papers had been returned—rejected. She asked why, but no one would tell her anything. She went back to the *Studentenheim* and wrote Kudashvili. She had not heard from him when, less than a week later, she received a message from the Russian embassy that a M. Maisky wished to see her.

M. Maisky took her to lunch at a Russian club near the Graben. After the fish course, he told her the news. Captain Kudashvili had been sent to lend his assistance at the disturbance in Budapest, and during a nighttime investigation of a university building, he had been shot and killed by an eighteen-year-old sniper. Utch cried with remarkable control through the main course and dessert. M. Maisky produced a photograph of Kudashvili. "This is for you, my dear," he said. He also produced the slight portion of Kudashvili's leftover wages, which the captain had designated were to go to Utch in the event of his death. It amounted to four thousand Austrian schillings, or one hundred and sixty American dollars. Maisky thumbed through a thick file, which was Utch's life story up to 1956. He said her life had been a model of suffering under fascism, which made Captain Kudashvili's rescue of her all the more meaningful—and his death all the more tragic. But he wanted Utch to know that she still had the Communist Party, and sometime in the future she could go to Russia if she wanted to. She shook her head; she was confused at the number of uses the word "fascism" could be put to. The Russian embassy, Maisky was promising, would help her in any way they could. Utch's translation ability, for example: when there were Russians in Vienna who were in need of an interpreter, he would try to break Utch into that circuit, "though they're a very jealous and competitive group," he warned her.

"Keep up with your English," M. Maisky told her. "That's what *he* would have wanted you to do." Utch knew they had read all her letters, but she also knew that a little Russian money for translating would be helpful. She thanked M. Maisky for lunch and went back to the *Studentenheim*, where she lived—almost alone—until 1963.

In those seven years her English got better, her Russian got practice, and her native German was spoken almost exclusively to two boyfriends who were both in love with her and were roommates down the hall. It took almost three years of knowing them before she decided to have sex with one of them, and when she saw how this affected the other, she had sex with him too. Then she stopped having sex with both of them because it seemed to hurt them, but they continued to court her, perhaps waiting for her to make another decision and start the cycle again. They remained roommates. But Utch decided that it was impossible for her—at least at that age—to make love to more than one person at a time, and she found a third young man, altogether outside the old friendship (he was an understudy for a great tenor in the Vienna Opera Company), and made love to him for a while. When her two old boyfriends discovered her new affair, they waylaid the tenor-understudy one evening in the maze of scaffolding supporting St. Stephen's Cathedral and told him they'd tear out his vocal chords if he saw any more of her without proposing marriage to her. This may seem quaint, but Utch didn't find fault with her old boyfriends' adolescent behavior. They were hurt, and they were going to hurt the tenor-understudy if he didn't pay for something. Utch always felt that there was no reason for any kind of hurting that anyone could stop, so she told the tenor-understudy that he'd better propose to her if he wanted to see her again. He changed opera companies instead, which she thought was a perfectly decent way of not hurting anybody, and she warmly declined the renewed, invigorated courtship from her old boyfriends. "No, Willy, *nein,* Heinrich," she told them. "Someone would get hurt."

Severin, whose perceptions often ran parallel to Utch's, surprised us one evening when we were all trying to talk about what our relationship meant to us. At least Edith and I were trying; Utch rarely said much about it and Severin had just been listening in his irritating, bilingual way. Edith and I said that it wasn't the *sex* so much that made our mutual agreement so exciting; it was the newness of meeting someone—that old romance was eight years old, more or less, for all of us—that was so enhancing.

"No, I think it's sex," Severin said suddenly. "It's *just* sex, and that's all it can be in a thing like this. There's nothing very romantic about hurting anybody."

"But who's getting hurt this way?" Edith asked him. He looked at her as if there were some information between them that was too special for Utch and me to hear, but he'd said nothing to Edith before about "hurting." We'd all agreed that if any of us suffered for any reason from our quaternion, the relationship would end. We'd all agreed that our marriages and children had priorities. And here was Severin (feigning martyrdom?) casting his ambiguities among us as carelessly as gerbil food. We'd all agreed that the relationship was good only if it was good for *all* of us—if it enhanced our marriages, or at least took nothing away.

And we'd all nodded our heads—of course, of course—when, in the beginning, Severin seemed to think it was necessary to say, "Sexual equality between two people is a difficult thing, and among *four* . . . Well, nothing's really equal, but it has to feel pretty equal or it can't go on. I mean, if three of us are having a good time and one of us is having a bad time, then the whole thing is bad, right? And the one person who blows it all shouldn't be made to feel that it's his or her fault, right?" Yes, we had nodded.

"If you're unhappy, we should stop it," Utch told him.

"It's not that, exactly," he said. "Everyone else seems so happy with it."

"Well, it's *supposed* to make people happy," Edith said.

"Yes, *sex* is," Severin said.

"You call it what you want to; I'll call it what I want to," Edith said. He always seemed uncomfortable about her independence of him.

"*Ja,* I think it's just sex too," Utch said. I was surprised at her, but then I thought that she was just trying to help him out. He was always so insistent on setting himself apart from the rest of us.

"Look, Severin, if you're unhappy, we'll stop the whole thing right now," I said. That was *his* loose phrase: "the whole thing." I asked him, "Are you unhappy, Severin?"

But if Severin had ever been questioned by God, he'd have found a way to evade *Him.* "It's not that simple," he said. "I just don't want any of us getting in over our heads." I know that Edith was insulted by that. She'd already told him how much in control of herself she was.

"I think we're all pretty stable, Severin," I said. "Nobody's going to leave anybody, or run off with somebody else."

"Oh, I know that," he said. "I don't mean anything like that."

"Well, what *do* you mean?" Edith asked him; he was exasperating to her.

He shrugged her off. "I guess I feel that I have to do the worrying for all of us," he said, "because no one else seems worried about anything. But let's give it time; everything takes time." I felt angry. He seemed so insensitive—to Utch, for example. His way of reducing our relationship to "just sex" must have hurt her feelings a little. And since he clearly behaved as if he were unhappy, I know that Utch must have had thoughts that it was *her* he was unhappy with.

Edith laughed. "Well, we certainly don't have to worry," she said. "You're doing enough worrying for everyone." I laughed; Severin smiled, but his smile was nothing I'd care to wake up to. Utch said later that she'd been angry with Edith for using a tone toward Severin that you might use toward a child, but I felt he'd deserved it. As if Severin were out of the room, Edith told us that we mustn't worry if Severin appeared unhappy sometimes. "He's more unhappy than us, anyway," Edith said lightly, "and it's a mistake to think that he's unhappy *because* of anything. I think we're all just happier people than Severin," she said, and looked at him—for confirmation? He'd said the same thing about himself once, but now he seemed sullen when Edith said it—as if, typically, he never took anything he said seriously, but had to believe Edith.

It was an awkward moment, and suddenly Utch had her coat on and was standing between Severin's chair and where I sat on the sofa with Edith. *"Vitch* one of you is taking me home?" she asked. "Who gets me tonight?"

Well, we all had to laugh. And I stood up, and bowed, and said to Severin, "Please, the honor is all yours," and he stood up and bowed and *hesitated* —and I thought that he might be on the verge of saying, "Take your goddamn wife home yourself and let me have mine!"

But with a look to Edith which was mostly in fun, he said, "Allow me to do you such a favor sometime." And he picked Utch up in his arms, easily resting her over his shoulder, and left with her worrisome laughter dying away outdoors.

In the way Edith and I then smiled at each other, I sensed that *time* was not what Severin Winter needed. I think we felt conscious of him as the driver (any one of us could have asserted ourselves, too, but we didn't seem to have the need for it)—and we knew that he might choose to stop it. (Any one of us could have done that, but we felt that if anyone would stop it, it would be Severin.)

Usually Edith and I talked a long time after we were alone—about each other and about writing. I would read her some of my new work; occasionally I gave her latest things a good critique. It was often two o'clock in the morning when we'd realize the time and know that Severin would be home in an hour or so, and then we would go upstairs and always be careful not to be still making love when he returned. Usually we were asleep; he'd knock once on the bedroom door to wake us, and I'd get dressed and go home to Utch.

But that night we went to bed almost as soon as Severin took Utch home. I suppose we may have felt some anxiety that it was going to end. When I told Utch about it, she said, "Don't try to tell me it's not sex."

"Edith and I mean it's not *just* sex," I said. "At least not for *us.*" But I think that such distinctions—like self-pity and dying for freedom—were dubious to Utch. She had been brought up, better than any of us, to know the difference between what you are willing to do for someone else and what you do for yourself.

4

Scouting Reports:
Severin (158-Pound Class)

The new gym included an indoor hockey rink, three basketball courts, a swimming pool, various exercise rooms, men's and women's locker rooms, and an awful hall displaying trophies and photographs of all the old heroes. From the outside, it had the tomblike appearance characteristic of public skating arenas and modern libraries. There was considerable murmuring among the old guard that the place should have at least been made to resemble the old campus—bricks and ivy—but it was clear that ivy could never be encouraged to cling to all that slick concrete and glass. Severin Winter loved the building.

What was left of the old gym was a vast underground labyrinth of squash and handball courts, and the old locker rooms, now used by visiting teams —perhaps to depress them. This maze was connected to the new underground of shiny steel lockers and ingenious shower nozzles by a long tunnel to what was called "the old cage."

The cage was an ominous humped dome of brick; it looked like a crematorium for athletes. It was laced with ivy as thick as a girl's wrist; the roof was a beehive of glass, skylight windows so old and dull that they'd lost their glint. A huge circular space with a hard-packed mud and cinder floor, it was used primarily for indoor track and field events; it smelled like a greenhouse, except that plants don't sweat. ("Everything sweats," said Winter.) To prevent discuses from breaking the skylights during track meets, they'd drop nets all over the inside of the dome, like a see-through shroud. Indoor tennis was played there, too.

Around the inside rim of the cage was an elevated board track so that runners could operate on two levels; the ones below used spikes in the mud and cinders; on the board track, you ran in rubber soles. The track was banked at the curves; it assumed you ran with some speed; if you were just walking around it, you drifted toward the rail. People claimed that if you ran too many laps on that track, one leg would become longer than the other. ("Not if you occasionally reverse your direction," said You-know-who.)

When the cage was busy, it was a noisy place. The track thundered and shook; starting guns sounded for the trackmen on the mud and cinder floor below; the wind and snow made the old skylight windows hum and creak.

The only modern addition to the cage was a long rectangular room partitioned off to one side of the board track, up in the rafters under the skylights; it was also glaringly lit with long fluorescent bulbs and had two roaring blow-heaters and its own thermostat. Its walls were padded in crimson matting, and from wall to wall it was carpeted with crimson and white wrestling mats.

Winter claimed that the wrestling room was perfectly situated for "psychological reasons." Prior to a match, the team would assemble in their little wing off the abandoned cage and watch the gym gang take away the mats. They were carried to one of the dazzling basketball courts in the new gym and properly spread out and taped together. There would be a few mats left in the wrestling room, and the wrestlers would warm up on these.

When it was time, Severin would lead them out of the wrestling room and around the creaking board track; he would turn lights off as he went, so the great gloomy cage would grow darker as they left it. (Winter scheduled all his home matches at night.) He would take his wrestlers through the long connecting tunnel to the new gym. To each side of the clammy tunnel, bright slots of light winked at the wrestlers from the squash and handball courts, where, like prisoners in strange cells, a few solitary athletes played those lonely games. Everything echoed in the tunnel. Winter would kill the lights as he went. An occasional squash player would holler, "Hey, what the fuck!?" and open his cell. The effect of the wrestlers in single file, solemn in their robes and hoods (Winter's choice), was quieting. Timidly, the squash and handball players often came out of their cells and followed the procession. It was a rite. The wrestlers had the longest, quietest, darkest walk imaginable; they had a weird way of concentrating. When they came to the light at the end of the tunnel, Winter always paused at the door. He looked them all up and down, as if he could see in the darkness. *"Wie gehts?"* he'd ask them; in the tunnel, his voice boomed. The squash and handball players hung back in the shadows, not wanting to disturb the ritual. *"Wie gehts?"* Severin Winter would holler. They were all his German students, you see.

And in unison the wrestlers would bellow in that tunnel, *"Gut!"*

Then Winter would fling open the door, and like moles emerging into daylight, his wrestlers would blindly follow him into the new gym and startling light and yelling crowd and out onto that shining crimson and white wrestling mat. To the spectators they always looked as if they had been brainwashed in a dungeon and sent out on some grim task into the real world. They *had*.

The Viennese are old hands at psychology. Severin didn't get the best material in the country, and he frankly admitted that he was not the best coach, either. The university wasn't what you'd call a wrestling power, but Winter's teams never lost a match at home. Of course he was clever at scheduling.

The lure of the university's old Eastern academic prestige was more responsible for bringing Winter the few good wrestlers he had than anything he was able to muster in the way of recruiting. He did his duty and made himself remembered by a few big high school coaches in the serious parts of the real wrestling country, but though he was remembered by a few coaches of his generation as a former contender, he was not known by the younger wrestlers, who remembered only the champions. And though he did get a few good wrestlers, they were drawn to the university because they were flattered as students; if they'd really wanted to wrestle, they wouldn't have come to New England. In short, he got athletes but not fanatics. "I don't get the ones with the real killer instincts," Severin complained. "I get guys who think. If you think, you realize you can lose—and you're right."

But I pointed out that the effect he got out of his famous tunnel-walk would probably be lost on wrestlers who didn't think. "Why do you think I do it?" he asked me. "All the great wrestlers have tunnels of their own —long, dark, empty walks through their long, dark, empty heads. I'm just creating a little illusion for my intellectuals. I'm just playing Plato."

He didn't pick an easy schedule; he just fostered his illusions at the home matches. He'd take his team on the road at least twice a season, and they'd wrestle three or four matches with the Big Ten and Big Eight schools. He'd always lose out there, of course, but he'd lose respectably. Usually he'd win one or two weight classes, and not many of his losing wrestlers would get pinned. This class of competition was necessary so that his team could win at home. There wasn't another school in New England that could beat him; he routed the Ivy League, and he'd usually schedule one home match a year with one of the big Eastern powers. He was very clever at anticipating the weakest of those powers in a given year, and he'd stage one great upset for his tunnel-walkers every season. Once it was Army or Navy; once he edged Penn State. He'd always lose to those schools when he took his team on the road, of course, and in the Eastern championships he had to struggle to have place winners in a couple of the weight classes.

He'd pick out his best wrestler each year and take him on the lonely and humiliating trip to the national tournament. The boy would get knocked off in the early rounds, but Winter never expected better, and he was kind to these boys and never misled them. He took only one wrestler each year— there was always one who qualified—just so he could write off a trip to the nationals as a school expense. "He has a dark-horse chance," Winter would tell the Athletic Department. It was an inoffensive lie.

Winter knew that he could not bring the old, dark cage and his long tunnel out to Stillwater, Oklahoma, or Ames, Iowa. "Out there," he said, "they have their own tunnels." And he'd tap his shaggy skull. "Very private tunnels, very tough to crack."

I used to wonder about *his* tunnel—how circuitous was it, and how long?

But it was Edith who invited us to dinner that first time. Her reasons were straightforward: she wanted to talk to me about writing. At thirty, she had still not engaged the novel, but her stories—mostly of small, closely observed relationships—had been published, most of them in little magazines, but one of them in either *Harper*'s or *The Atlantic*. She was in the habit of taking a creative writing course every year, though she was not interested in completing a degree, or she would work independently with the university's writer-in-residence. That was not me; I was hired by the History Department, and I told her that I'd never taught a creative writing course and never wanted to. She talked so well about her work, though, that I agreed to look at it. For the last two years, the writer-in-residence had been the famous Helmbart, and Edith confessed that she liked neither his work nor him. I was, I admit, pleased to hear this; Helmbart's sort of haughty kingship over what was called "the new novel" was nauseating to me. Edith and I agreed that when the subject of fiction became how to write fiction, we lost interest; we were interested in prose, surely, but not when the subject of the prose became prose itself.

We had a good talk. I was flattered to know that she had read at least one of my books—the third one, about Andreas Hofer. She questioned my insistence on the term "historical novel," which for her had bad associations. But I insisted on the history, I said, because I felt that novels which did not convey real time conveyed nothing. We kicked that one around; I didn't convince her of anything. Severin, she said, had read all my books. I was surprised. I looked at him, awaiting his comment, but he was speaking German with Utch. "Of course, Severin reads everything," Edith said. I didn't know quite how to take that; she could have meant he was not a discriminating reader, a kind of book glutton, or that she admired his reading very much. Edith fixed her eyes on you when she talked to you, and she was animated with her hands—perhaps a habit acquired from Severin.

Helmbart, she said, had spent his time analyzing her "hang-ups"; he'd never talk about her writing or characters at all. She said he told her once that she couldn't begin to write until she could "describe a table and show its soul and its sex." It's this kind of shit that makes him king of "the new novel," I guess.

In discussing my Andreas Hofer book, Edith was wise and, well—kind. I told her that occasionally it angered me that my work was so disregarded. Even the university, when it listed faculty publications, failed to list my books. There would be Helmbart's fiction, and a raft of the usual scholarly articles—a piece, for example, on "the furniture symbols of Henry James." I'd always felt that there was a greater similarity between these articles and Helmbart's tiny fictions than the respective authors would admit.

Edith said she admired the energy of someone like myself—virtually unrecognized, but prolific.

"Yes," Severin said suddenly; I hadn't known he was paying attention. "You really crank them out." I wondered about that, and he said, "It's very hard to find your books, you know. They're all out of print." Sadly, this was true.

"How did you find them?" I asked him. I had never met anyone other than my mother and my editor who had read all my books. (I suspected Utch of having my father's habit with endings.)

"The library here buys everything," Severin said. "You just have to know how to dig them out." And suddenly I pictured my books as some archeological discovery. Severin Winter gave me the feeling that he considered the feat of finding them more significant than that of writing them. He didn't say anything further to me about them then, but I learned later that he liked to categorize books by wrestling weight classes. Such as: "That's a pretty fair 134-pound novel."

He came by our house the next day on his bicycle. Utch was out with the children, and though I suspected he might have come to see her, since he found me alone, I thought that he might mention my novels. He didn't. He'd brought me some of Edith's stories. "She's really very excited to be working with you," he told me. "Helmbart didn't work out."

"Yes, she told me," I said. "I'm really very happy to know another writer here. She'll certainly be a relief from students and colleagues."

"She's very serious about her work," Severin said. "Helmbart gave her a hard time. He told her he felt he could get closer to what was wrong with her writing if she slept with him." Edith hadn't told me that. "I think he thought she was just another faculty wife out to get laid by a new mentor," Severin said.

I suspected his reasons for telling me this, but I laughed. "I thought, right away," I said, "that she was interested in *writing.*" He laughed too.

He rode that ten-speed bicycle every day in good weather, pumping up and down for miles in a tank-top style of wrestling uniform—what they call a singlet. He was sweating; he was tanned. "When Helmbart got to the point when he couldn't see Edith without pinching her, she gave it up," he said. We laughed again.

"That was a fine evening we had with you," I told him. "You're an excellent cook."

"Well, I love to eat," he said. "And I enjoyed talking with your wife."

"You have a lot in common," I told him, but he looked puzzled.

"No, not much," he said seriously, but then he laughed again—nervously, I thought—and back-pedaled his bicycle, jamming something in his complicated gears, so that he had to get off to tinker with it. We both agreed to see each other again soon.

It was later that I learned the rest of the story about Helmbart's pinching. From the start, Edith had told Severin about the man's advances. "Next time knee him in the balls," Severin had told her. But that was hardly Edith's style. She kept thinking she must be able to get something valuable from Helmbart. She asked Severin if he would speak to Helmbart for her, but he told her that this would make the fool so self-conscious that everything he'd say to her would be a lie. I think this was wise. So Edith went on trying, fending off the pinches and squeezes.

Then there was a large party, mainly of English and Art Department people. Because of her writing, Edith was usually invited to such things, and Severin always went along; he enjoyed teasing those people. At this party Helmbart again pinched Edith. She gave him a look, she told me, which was "truly annoyed," then went over and told Severin that she was really fed up. "It's the only time I've really wanted Severin to do anything physically to anyone for me," she said. "I was ashamed at how angry I was, because Severin is rarely that way with people. I don't remember what I told him, but I wanted him to make an ass out of Helmbart. I suppose I expected him to *wrestle* the bastard. It was very unfair of me. Severin had always given me a great deal of confidence in myself by letting me know that he believed I could take care of myself—and here I wasn't able to."

Severin patted her hand and went bobbing off into the party crowd looking for Helmbart. Edith followed him, fascinated. Severin moved up behind Helmbart, who was telling a story to four or five other people. He is a tall man; Severin comes up to about his shoulder. Standing behind him on tiptoe, Severin must have looked like a dangerous elf. He quickly pinched Helmbart hard on the ass and *kissed* him loudly and wetly on the ear. Helmbart dropped an hors d'oeuvre in his drink, gave a little leap, blushed rosy. When he saw it was Severin, he handed the drink to the man standing next to him; the drink got dropped. Helmbart got pale; he thought he was in a fight with the wrestling coach.

And Severin, winking lewdly, said, "How's the writing coming, Helmbart?" Edith was there, hanging on Severin's arm, trying to restrain her laughter. But when he saw the man's face, Severin burst out laughing himself, and Edith let herself go before they were out the door together— laughing, actually baying like hounds. "It gave me such enormous confidence," Edith told me, "that I tossed my head back and took one last look at poor horny Helmbart. He wasn't laughing; he looked absolutely *gelded!* Severin and I kept laughing. It was late afternoon; the children were home with a baby-sitter, getting ready for supper. We drove around. I put my head in Severin's lap; I unzipped him and took him in my mouth. He talked nonstop, driving very fast, all the way home. I don't know what he said, but it was hilarious; even with him in my mouth, I couldn't stop laughing. We ran in the back door, through the kitchen where the children and the sitter were, upstairs and into the bedroom. I locked the door; he turned on the shower in the bathroom, so that the sound would drown out *our* sound —also, I guess, so that the children would think we had rushed home to *wash.* We knew we wouldn't fool the baby-sitter. My God, we went at each other like leopards. I remember lying on the bed, after God knows how many times I'd come, and I saw the steam from the shower rolling out the bathroom door. We took a shower together and soaped each other until we were slick, and then Severin pulled the bathmat into the shower and laid it down on the floor of the tub, and we had it all over again with the soap in a great lather and the water beating down like a storm and the soggy bathmat soaking up all of it and *sucking* underneath me like a giant sponge.

"When we finally went downstairs, the children told us the sitter had run home. I think it was Fiordiligi who said, 'What a long shower you had!' And Severin said, 'Well, your mother and I were very dirty.' And we started laughing all over again; even Fiordiligi, who never laughs, started laughing with us, and Dorabella, who laughs at everything. We all laughed until we ached.

"I remember that next morning I hurt all over, everywhere; I couldn't even move. Severin said, 'That's how it feels after a match.' I realized that I was about to start laughing again, and that if I did, we would be doing it *again.* I felt so sore that I tried to hold it back, but Severin saw that, and he got fantastically gentle; he came into me very slowly and we did it again. That was nice, too, but it was completely *different.*"

Poor Helmbart, I thought. He never knew what he was up against.

So Severin was clearly not the usual paranoid about his wife, was he? She gave him no cause to be. She married him and lived with him for eight years without having even a quick lover; she was faithful, and only rare fools like Helmbart couldn't tell this when they met her. But I can appreciate why he tried.

Severin Winter was too vain to be jealous. He struck me as very much a man's man; aggressive and egocentric, he took you on his terms. But neither Utch nor Edith really agreed with me. Utch claimed he was the only man she'd ever known who actually treated women as if they were equal to men; I agree that he was equally aggressive and egocentric with both sexes. Edith said that Severin's kind of equality could be very insulting to a woman. He seemed to make no distinctions between men and women— treating both with a kind of maleness which made women feel they were just one of the boys. For the sake of equality, few women really care to have men go that far. Even with his physicality—his hands all over you when he talked—women felt relaxed at once by his touch, but also a little put out. There was no mistaking his touch for a cheap feel; his touches had such an absence of sexuality that women felt he didn't notice them as women at all.

Severin had been married nearly eight years before he'd had time or cause to consider that there might be pleasanter mornings to wake up to, livelier beds to lie in, other lives to lead. The thought upset him. You can see how naïve he was. And when he first had the courage to mention his new thinking to his wife, he was all the more upset to hear that his dangerous daydream was already familiar to her.

"You mean there have been other men?"

"Oh, no. Not yet."

"Not yet? But you mean you've thought about other men?"

"Well, of course—other situations, yes."

"Oh."

"I don't mean that I think of it very *much*, Sevi."

"Oh."

It was not the first time he found actual equality difficult to bear. He was someone who was always embarrassed to discover his own innocence. I think that a feeling of superiority came naturally to him. With all their chatter about equality, Edith and Utch miss one point about Severin: he thought of himself as protecting Edith from his own complicated feelings. What a shock for him to learn that *she* was complicated too.

But if he wasn't essentially a jealous man, he was demanding in other ways. He needed to make himself the source of the important feelings in Edith's life. If he had no need to make her more *his* than she already demonstrably was, he needed her *work* to be his too—and I know this troubled her. Though he was fond of saying that it was sex, when things were bad—or when things were good, for that matter—I'm sure that much of his uneasiness about Edith's and my relationship was the intimacy we shared through our writing. He was not a writer, though Edith claimed that he was her best reader. I doubt it; his categories—his notion of weight classes—were irritating. I never knew when it was our sex that was troubling him, or when it was his notion that I had replaced him as a source of Edith's ideas. I always thought it important to know, but I doubt that he usually knew the difference. "It's the whole thing," he would say—his heavyweight aesthetics crushing us all.

"I'll indulge you all the writers, colleagues and mentors that you want," he told Edith once in a rage, "but presumably you won't need to *sleep* with all of them!" Obviously he was obsessed with his bizarre sensitivity to a kind of double infidelity. That Edith and I could talk together was more painful to him than our sleeping together. But what did he expect? Everything can't be equal! Would he have felt better if Utch had been a wrestling coach?

At least she was a fan. It grieved Winter that Edith wasn't. He'd beg her to come to the matches, he'd bore her with stories of his boys until finally she'd have to tell him that she just didn't care for it. She could see why he liked it, and that was fine, but it had nothing to do with her. "Everything that has to do with you has to do with me," he told her. She didn't think it ought to be that way. "I read everything you write, I read lots of stuff you don't write—and lots of stuff you don't read. We always talk about it!" he'd say.

"But you *like* to read," Edith pointed out.

"So much of that has to do with you," he told her. "What makes you think that I like it so much?"

I understood perfectly what Edith didn't like about the wrestling. She was attracted by an aspect of Severin that could also weary her; she liked his cocky sureness, his explosiveness; she wasn't that way, but she liked it in him, except when it seemed too strong, threatening to suck her up in it. And that aspect was strongest when he was involved with his wrestlers. How crazily committed all Severin's wrestlers looked to her! They seemed hypnotized by themselves, drugged in ego, which unleashed the moment their physical frenzy was peaking. It was too loud, too serious, too intense. It was also more struggle than grace; though Severin insisted it was more like a dance than a fight, to her it was a fight. To me, too. Also, more to the point, it was boring. So few of the matches were really close; often you just watched someone maul someone else—the only issue in doubt being whether or not the obvious winner would finally pin his victim or have to be content with just rubbing him all over the mat. Of course, I was never an athlete; I don't care for sports. I don't mind a walk now and then, but I do it to help me think. Edith was no jock either. She liked wrestlers' *bodies,* she said, "from the lightweights through the middleweights," but big men were repulsive to her. Though she was tall, she liked Severin's shortness. She liked wrestlers' thickness, the queer proportions of their weight that was mostly in their upper bodies. She liked men "with no asses, with small legs." Severin was like that.

"Why do you like me?" I asked her once. I am tall and thin; even my beard is narrow.

"Well, you're such a change," she said. "You're so different that it's nice. Maybe it's your beard; you have an older look that I like."

"Well, I *am* older," I told her. Four years older than Utch and Severin; eight years older than Edith.

Utch's tastes were mysterious to me. She claimed she liked most bodies. She said she liked the older part of me, too, but mainly she liked how much I obviously liked women. "Though I knew it would be troublesome, I never met anyone who was so attentive to women," Utch told me. She implied that I was a woman's man; in fact, she often used the word "womanize." Well, I am more of a womanizer than Severin Winter, but so is the Pope.

"Don't you think I'm *nice* to women, though?" I asked Utch.

"Oh *ja,* I guess so. You encourage a woman to indulge herself in being a woman," she said; then she frowned. "In being a *kind* of woman," she added. Then she said, "Maybe women are your friends easily because they see that you're not so nice to men. Because they see that you don't have men for friends, perhaps they trust you."

"And Severin?" I asked her. "How is he nice to women?" I was just teasing; I didn't feel I had to know.

"Well, he's different," she would say and look away. She did not like to talk about him.

She would talk about his wrestlers, though. She knew them by their weight classes, by their styles, by everything Winter had told her about them—and he told her everything. Before the home matches, he'd often give her the rundown of the match—picking points, estimating who was going to win or lose. And Utch would sit through the match, taking notes of her impressions for him—how the 142-pound match differed from his prediction, and why. I'd have thought that he would have loved her companion-ship in this; Edith and I both thought that it would take some of the burden off her. But no, he made us all come to his home matches. Utch would tell us what to watch for in each match. I felt manipulated; it was as if he needed us all there to watch *him*—and he did seem to like looking up in the stands and seeing all three of us.

Utch's favorite wrestler on the team was a 134-pound black from Lock Haven, Pennsylvania, named Tyrone Williams. He was a languid-looking wrestler, sleepy but explosively quick, and it delighted her that he weighed exactly as much as she did. "If he needs someone to work out with," she would kid Severin, "just send him to me." In practice, Tyrone Williams was a good mover, always alert, but he tightened up against outside competition. He had stunning speed, and a slow-motion movement between his bursts that often lulled his opponents out of pace. But he seemed to psych himself out of every match. He was given to trances, sudden lapses in everything which made him appear to have heard a secret final-period bell in his head. He seemed to be already dreaming his way to the showers while still moving stiffly on the mat, groping on his back, gazing up at the high ceiling and the glaring lights. Usually he was pinned, and then he seemed to wake up —jumping to his feet, hollering, holding his ringing ears and staring at his opponent as if he'd been beaten by a ghost.

Patiently Severin would show him the match films later. "Now here it comes, Tyrone. Here's where you go to sleep—you see your head loll back there, your left arm just hanging at your side? Do you see what sort of . . . comes over you?"

"Mother," Tyrone Williams would say reverently. "Incredible, mother-ing incredible . . ." and he'd go off into a trance right there, in disbelief at his whole performance.

"You see?" Winter would go on. "You let his ankle go and you hooked over his arm; you wanted to hook *under* that arm, Tyrone—you know that. Tyrone? Ty-*rone!*"

Utch loved Tyrone for his lamentable trances. "It's so human," she said.

"Utch could break him of that habit," I said, kidding Severin. "Why don't you let Utch work on his trances."

"Tyrone Williams could have a trance right on top of Utch," Severin Winter said.

I thought this a bit crude, but Utch just laughed. "There's little evidence of anyone suffering trances on top of me," she said, arching her back for Severin and me. Edith laughed; she wasn't at all jealous. We all seemed very close and good-humored in those days.

"Why do you like him?" Edith asked her; she meant Tyrone Williams.

"He's just my size," said Utch, "and I think he's a wonderful color. It's like caramels."

"Yummy," Edith said, but she didn't mean it. She had no favorites among those wrestlers; to her, they were all perfectly nice and boring boys, and as a result they behaved awkwardly around her. Winter had them all to dinner every month; Edith said that they hulked and bumped through the house, knocking paintings askew on the walls. "Somehow they break all the ashtrays—and they don't even smoke. It's as if they need the softness of mats and the space of an arena in order to be agile."

At least once a week, one of them would come to their house to be tutored in German. Reading, listening to music or taking a long bath, Edith would hear Severin crooning to "some bulky boy."

"Wir müssen nur auf Deutsch sprechen," he'd say gently.

"Wir müssen nur auf . . . auf what?" the wrestler would ask.

"Deutsch."

"Oh yeah. Oh God, Coach, I feel so stupid."

"Nein, nein, du bist nicht . . ."

Severin liked Williams, but there was a limit to how much he could like a loser, no matter how interestingly they lost. He liked winners better, and the winningest wrestler on his team was a 158-pound stranger from Waterloo, Iowa, named George James Bender. He'd been the state high school champion of Iowa for three consecutive years and had been recruited by the home-state powerhouse, Iowa State. This was before freshmen were eligible for competition, and Bender had spent a year entering only open tournaments. He'd won them all; he'd never lost. As a sophomore, he was expected to go all the way through the nationals, but he tore up his knee in the Big Eight championships. He'd always been a strange, serious student; he'd won some kind of science prize his junior year in high school. He was a straight-A student at Iowa State; his major was pre-med, but he really wanted to be a geneticist.

On crutches at the national tournament he couldn't wrestle in, Bender introduced himself to Severin. "Professor Winter?" he said; Severin was a professor, of course, but he wasn't used to being called one. "I understand you have one of the few undergraduate majors in genetics in the country, and you have the top geneticist in the world in your department."

"In *my* department?" Winter said. He was thinking of German or wrestling, I guess. He looked at George James Bender on his crutches and suddenly realized that the boy was talking about transferring and wrestling for *him*. Winter had heard of Bender, of course; every coach and wrestler in the country had.

But Bender's knee was slow to heal. He couldn't wrestle for the university the first year following his transfer, anyway, and Severin was shaken in the middle of the boy's ineligible year when Bender had to have a second operation on his knee. He'd been working out lightly with the team—whipping them all, though Winter refused to let him play with the heavyweights. Bender could have whipped them too, but anyone can make a mistake, and Severin didn't want "one of those clumsy football players" to fall on the boy and hurt the precious knee. He didn't re-injure the knee wrestling; he hurt it leg-lifting too much weight on the weight machine.

Winter also wondered if Bender hadn't become too much of "a goddamn geneticist, of all things," to be a real wrestler anymore. He awaited Bender's senior year with more expectations than he'd ever allowed himself to have for any of his other wrestlers. Bender spent the summer at home in Iowa working out every day with a few of those zealots from his old Iowa State team. But when he came back East in August to work privately with our geneticist, the great Showalter, Winter fretted because there was no one on our summer campus for Bender to wrestle with.

Bender walked around campus in his long white lab coat. He was nearly as pale as the coat—a short-haired reddish blond with a beard that grew six or seven scattered hairs like corn silk on his face; he shaved them once a week and always managed to cut himself while removing one of those six or seven hairs. He had faded blue eyes and wore black heavy-framed glasses with thick lenses. He looked like a powerful farm boy from decades ago, and he may have been a superior genetics student—the great Showalter certainly liked him as a disciple—but he was the dullest young man I've ever met.

Severin decided he'd have to wrestle with George James Bender himself. He still worked out with his wrestlers, and he'd kept himself in good shape, but he never wrestled a full workout with any of them. Still, he had been good enough so that even now he was in a class slightly above most of them. He'd have had to cut off his head to make weight in his old 158-pound class, but he ran or rode his racing bicycle every day, and he lifted weights. Nevertheless, he was no match for Bender; he knew that he wouldn't ever have been a match for Bender—even as a trim competitor more than ten years ago. But in August no one else was around, and even when his other wrestlers came back to school in September, they wouldn't be up to Bender's conditioning, much less his class.

The only time the wrestling room was tolerable in August was in the early morning before the sun through the skylights had broiled the mats and turned the room into a sauna. But Bender's lab experiments in genetics required his early-morning attention, and he wasn't through with Showalter until almost noon.

Severin Winter was insane. By late morning, the wrestling room was over 100 degrees, even though they left the door open. The mat was hot to the touch. "But they're liquid," Winter said. "A kind of liquid plastic. When it's hot, they're very soft."

Every day he would meet Bender and try to last long enough to give the boy a workout. When Severin needed to rest, Bender would run laps, furiously fast, on the old board track, while Winter lay on the soft, warm mats, staring at the sun, listening to his own heart pounding in unison with Bender pounding his way around the wood. Then they'd go at it again until

Severin had to stop. He'd move out of the cage and sit in the shade, cooling off, while Bender returned to his mad running. The heat blew out of the big open cage doors in those waves like mirror distortions you can see rising off a summer highway. A constant sprinkler system kept the mud and cinder floor from turning to dust.

"In this weather," I asked Severin, "why doesn't that fool Bender run outdoors?" It was a shady campus; the footpaths were empty of students; there was always a cool breeze along the river.

"He likes to sweat," Winter said. "You'll never understand."

I'd been walking with my children down to the playing fields beyond the old cage when I saw Severin sitting outside the cage door, collapsed against a survivor elm. "Listen to him," Severin gasped at me; he could hardly talk; his normal breath was still a few minutes away. "Take a peek."

I forced myself to step inside that steaming, dank place. The air choked you. A pounding as rhythmic as a machine's crude function was echoing steadily around the track. George James Bender would be visible for a half-moon turn; then he'd disappear over my head. He was wearing a sweatsuit over one of those rubber costumes, elasticized at the neck, ankles and wrists; the sweat had soaked him and made his shoes squeak like a sailor's.

Winter tapped his dripping head. *"There's* a tunnel," he said admiringly. "You know what you have to have on your mind to do that?"

I watched Bender for a while. He ran cloddishly, but he looked as determined as the tide—like the ancient messenger who would die on arrival, but never before. "I can't imagine that you could have *anything* on your mind," I said.

"Yes, that's exactly it," Winter said. "But try it sometime. Try to have pure nothing on your mind. That's what people don't understand. It takes considerable mental energy *not* to think about what you're doing."

On those hot days in August, I used to go watch Severin get mauled by Bender. Sometimes he'd get so tired that it would be Bender who'd tell him when to stop. "I'm going to run a few," he would say, getting up off Winter, who would lie just as Bender had left him, recovering his arms and legs, rediscovering breathing. When he saw me, he'd wave a finger, and in a few minutes, he'd try speech. "Come to watch me . . . get slammed . . . around?"

He grinned. There was a fine froth of blood against his teeth; some hard part of Bender had split his lip. He flopped on his back. Through my socks, the mat felt like a warm, wet sponge. Winter made all visitors leave their shoes at the door.

"Severin," I said while he was still too limp to complete a sentence, "it's a strange way for a thirty-five-year-old man to have fun."

"He's going to be a national champion," Severin managed to say.

"And you'll be runner-up," I told him. But though he joked about his runner-up history, he didn't like me to talk about it, so I changed the subject. No, I told him a bad allegory which I thought he'd think funny.

I told him about the World War I French ace Jean Marie Navarre, who swore he hated to kill. Navarre claimed he was an entertainer; when he couldn't locate any German planes, he put on air shows of his acrobatics for the troops in the trenches. He had more than two hundred and fifty dogfights over Verdun, and by May of 1916 he had shot down twelve German planes. But he was wounded shortly after that and spent the rest of the war in and out of hospitals. His temper was bad; his brother died; he took frequent "convalescent leaves"—a dashing dandy, he wore a lady's silk stocking as a cap. In Paris, he is reported to have chased a gendarme along a sidewalk in his car. Somehow he survived the war, but he was killed in a peacetime stunt, less than a year later, attempting to fly a plane through the Arc de Triomphe.

When I saw how the story touched him, I was embarrassed for Severin. "I don't think there's anything funny about that story," he said. Of course he wouldn't; even humor had to be on his terms.

Like the subject of trances: no one agreed. Utch was fond of speculating on how Tyrone Williams might gain control of his famous lapses, but her suggestions were not really coaching methods which Severin Winter could employ. And Edith liked to tease Severin about George James Bender, to whom she felt he gave too much of his time.

"George James Bender is in the greatest trance of all," Edith said. "I think his *mind* constantly takes showers."

"Don't be a snob," Severin answered. "That's a kind of concentration. It's different from the concentration you need to write, but it's similar in the energy it takes." (You can see how seriously he took wrestling.) "Sure, Bender is an unsophisticated kid, and very naïve. He's shy, and not very attractive—at least, not to women. Of course, he must be a virgin—"

"A virgin?" Edith said. "Sevi, I don't believe that boy has ever had a *hard-on!*"

But she seemed to regret her joke as soon as she said it, though Severin laughed a little. Severin didn't appear bothered, but Utch and I noticed how anxious Edith was with him the rest of the evening, as if she was making up to him; she touched and rubbed him even more than usual, and *she* was the one who said she was tired and would really prefer to make it an early evening. Utch and I went home together, and she stayed with Severin. No one felt really disappointed; we got to see a lot of each other, and everyone had to be generous.

But in the car I said to Utch, "What do you make of that?" I had the feeling that lately there might have been a lot of talk about hard-ons.

"Hm," said Utch, a woman fond of single syllables.

We went to bed; she, too, said she was tired. I lay awake on my side of our bed, not really wanting to pursue the subject, but when I thought Utch might be asleep, I asked, "Severin doesn't have any trouble, does he? I mean, you know, with you?"

No answer. I assumed she was asleep.

I was almost asleep myself when Utch said, "No."

I thought about it; I was awake again, and I could feel her awake, too. I thought of some things I really didn't want to ask, but it was as if she heard me asking them to myself. "Of course," she said, "it's my impression that Severin *always* has a hard-on."

That broke a slight tension which occupied, like an electrical field, that small area of the bed between us. I laughed. "Well, I suspect that between times it really does go down, Utch, or get a little soft, and you just haven't noticed."

I'd meant to be funny, but she said, "No."

Then I was awake. I said, "If it never goes down, then he doesn't come, for Christ's sake. Utch? He must not *come.*"

"And you say Severin asks too much," Utch said. "You say he asks Edith too much." True, I knew, you shouldn't ask too much.

But I persisted. "Utch, does he come?"

She was quiet a long time. Finally she said, "Yes."

For some reason I had to add, "With *you,* anyway."

Utch reached over and held me in her hand. In the context of this conversation, I felt embarrassed about not being particularly hard myself at that moment. She held me awhile, then let go; it was the way she said goodnight. And together we achieved that practical silence, a kind of wisdom, which you can learn only after a number of years of a good marriage. We both pretended to be asleep until we were.

5

Preliminary Positions

At first, the thought of Severin with Utch was exciting. It rekindled an old lust which had not been entirely absent but which had been perhaps too occasional. Edith said she responded very much the same; that is, the thought of him with Utch re-excited her feelings too. Well, you whet one appetite, you whet them all. Maybe. Utch said she felt that way toward me sometimes; at other times she admitted the effect was not so good. What effect it had on *him* is typically baffling.

Severin was too short to make love to Edith standing up. Not that she particularly liked making love standing up, Edith was quick to add, but I confess I took an interest in learning that he had any physical shortcomings. Edith and I liked to make love in the shower standing up; this would be before we went to bed, where we often made love again. It was an innocent enough beginning; the next thing we knew, we had a ritual. ("The first, next and last thing we always know," said Severin, "is a ritual.")

Edith put her arms over my shoulders and let me soap her breasts. She worked up a thick lather on the back of my neck and ran gobs of it down my back, all over my body. I worked up a lather as stiff as egg whites and dabbed her with it. Then we would wet ourselves under the shower and let ourselves foam together; we had the ideal height-proportions for it (Severin, I suppose, just couldn't reach). She slipped under my arms and hugged herself tight to my chest, and I pushed her against the cool, wet tiles until I could feel her reaching behind me for the towel rod, which was something hard for her to hold on to and yank herself against me.

We went to bed clean and soap-smelling and whispering, touching and looking at each other in the candlelight, smoking cigarettes, sipping a little chilled white wine until we felt like it again. But I never quite felt the same about it in bed with her. She'd told me that "prone," Severin was just the right size for her ("top or bottom or side by side"). In the shower, I knew I was nice and new.

I never heard him knock; it was always Edith who woke me. He would give one sharp rap, and Edith would say, "Just a minute, love," and wake me up. I loved that sleepy, slept-in smell—as if sex were cellular and our aroma of spice and fermentation was the old sloughed-off cells. Sometimes I wanted to make love to her quickly then, before I dressed and left, but she never let me. She said Severin didn't like waiting for me to leave; it was a hard time for him, apparently. I often offered to be the one to leave first. I told him I wouldn't mind waking up him and Utch; I said I wouldn't mind waiting. But he had to be the one. Only once, when he agreed to let me come to them, did he and Utch stay together until I arrived home. And then I was late—as if it mattered! I'd said three or four o'clock, but Edith and I had overslept; I came home closer to five and found him pacing the sidewalk in front of our house, not even staying with Utch, fuming and shivering in the cold. He got into his car and drove home before I had a chance to speak with him.

When you get out of bed at three or four in the morning, it's always cold. I stumbled downstairs after kissing Edith goodbye—her breath a little sour from the cigarettes and wine and sleep, but it had a ripe smell, like the bed, and it always aroused me. Downstairs, Severin emptied ashtrays, rinsed glasses and loaded the dishwasher. He never wanted to talk; he'd nod goodnight. Once, when I could tell by his restless bustle around the dishwasher that I'd taken too long getting dressed, he offered me a cold can of beer to drive home with. "It helps to cut the phlegm," he said.

And I went home to Utch, whose breath was fruity and sweetly sickish; our bed lay strewn with her clothing, the mattress half sliding to the floor. And then *I* would trot about the house—not emptying ashtrays but disposing of the apple cores and spines of pears, cheese rinds, salami skins, grape stems and empty beer bottles. He knew how food in the bedroom revolted me! "And you know how he hates Edith's smoking," Utch said. "He says you leave ashtrays smoldering like fireplaces all over the house." A slight exaggeration. He was a maniac for the care of his phonograph records, too, and apparently raved at how I treated them. He would always use those inner envelopes; he turned them sideways so that you had to take a record out and put it back twice. "He thinks you abuse his record collection intentionally," Utch said.

"It's like the damn ice trays," I told her. "He bawls out Edith for not refilling the ice trays, for Christ's sake. We're filling a bucket to chill the wine, and he wants all the ice trays refilled the second they're empty."

"And you're in too much of a hurry?" Utch asked.

"Jesus!" I cried.

When I saw Utch in those pre-dawn hours, sprawled out, randy and ravished, I was attracted to her and to the passion I imagined he had evoked in her. I always went to her, amazed that my desire was up again for the third or fourth time that evening. And sometimes she'd respond, as if her appetite were endless too—as if Edith's smell on me drew her out again and made the foreignness of our familiar bodies especially alluring. But often Utch groaned and said, "Oh God, I couldn't, please, I can't do it *again*. Would you get me a glass of water?" And she'd lie still, as if wounded internally and fearful of silent hemorrhage, and sometimes her eyes were frightened and she squeezed my hand against her breast until she fell asleep.

Edith said that, like me, she felt the same aroused responsiveness when Severin would finally come to bed; she'd keep warm the spot I'd left in their bed for him, and her imagination of him with Utch excited her and kept her awake—though he often fussed and puttered around the downstairs of the house for a long time after I'd gone. When he came to bed, she'd hum and whisper at him; she liked to smell him. We were all in that rich phase where sweet scents turn to decay. "Sex sniffers," Severin called us once.

But Severin Winter would climb into bed like a soldier seeking comfort in a wet foxhole; it was necessary for him to first rid the room of wine glasses, ice bucket, another ashtray, the burnt candle—all of which, Edith said, he touched as if they were tainted. Then he would lie chastely on his far edge of the bed; when she touched him, he seemed to cringe. She'd rub against him, but it was as if he were choking down a gag at her smell. Self-conscious, hurt, she'd roll away from him and ask, "Did you have a bad evening?"

"Did you have a good one?"

"I want to know how it was for you."

"No you don't. That doesn't matter to you."

Whew. Of course, he wasn't always so obviously dark, but he could pervert the most frankly innocent, erotic things. ("You smell rich," Edith told him once, nibbling his ear. "You *reek,*" he said to her.)

I know there must have been times for him when the pure sensuousness of our belonging to each other must have excited him and stopped his adolescent brooding, but these times were so rare that I remember them most vividly. For example, once we spent a weekend on the Cape at Edith's mother's place. There were just the four of us—no children; we'd successfully farmed them out. It was late September, and the great Cape house was sunny and cool. Like Edith's mother, most of the summer people had already migrated back to Boston and New York.

We started out in Severin's car so early that we were there before lunch. Edith and Severin were familiar with the place, of course, but it was Utch who first acknowledged our isolation and privacy; she was the first to undress down on the blowy and abandoned beach. I noticed how Edith looked at her. Back in the house, both women looked at each other naked, while Severin prepared an enormous paella and I opened raw oysters for a first course. There was a lot of liberal touching, and everyone was very loud. Severin went for Utch's ass with a lobster claw. In his white cook's apron, with nothing on underneath or behind, he stood with one hand on Edith's long thigh and the other on Utch's round one. As his hands moved up he said to me, "The New York loin is a leaner cut than the Central European variety, but a good cook can bring out the flavor of both."

"Different flavors, surely," I said.

"Long live the difference!" said Edith, who reached under Severin's apron for something and touched hands with Utch there.

I fed Edith an oyster; I fed Utch an oyster. I was wearing my shorts and Edith unzipped them; Utch pulled them down and said to her, "Why are these men hiding themselves?"

"I'm the cook," Severin said. "Don't want to burn anything."

"I'm opening oysters," I said. "One slip of the hand . . ."

Edith hugged Utch, suddenly, around her hips. "You're so solid, Utch, I can't get over it!" she cried, and Utch hugged her back. "It must seem like quite a handful after *me,*" Edith said to Severin.

He spattered and hissed at the stove; he flipped up his apron and fanned himself. Utch ran her square, broad hand down Edith's sloped stomach. "You're so *long,*" she said admiringly; Edith laughed and drew Utch to her; the top of her head fitted against Edith's throat. Utch picked Edith up quickly, with astonishing strength. "And you don't weigh anything at all!" she cried.

"Utch can pick me up, too," I said. Edith looked suddenly alarmed as Utch picked me up with a low grunt.

"Heavens, Utch," Edith said. Severin had taken off his apron and had wrapped himself in sausage links. He pressed himself against Edith, who squealed and jumped away from him, feeling the cool, slick sausage against her. "My God, Severin—"

"Got a whole string of pricks for you, my dear," he said as his paella fumed and conspired behind him.

When Severin and Utch went for another swim, Edith and I made love on the long corduroy L-shaped couch in the living room. We were lying there drowsily, after the act, when Severin and Utch came back cold-skinned and salt-tasting from the ocean; they were shivering. They made me feel like swimming too, but Edith wasn't interested. I leaped up from the couch and ran naked across the pale-green lawn just as it was getting dark and onto the sand which was still warm from the sun. The water stung; I hollered as loud as I could, but there were only gulls and sandpipers to hear me. I sprinted back to the house where so much flesh awaited me.

When I came in through the French doors to the sunroom, I could hear that no one had actually missed me while I was gone. I could not see them in the living room, and I discreetly went into the kitchen and warmed myself over Severin's steaming paella until the three of them were finished. The three of them! Utch told me later that she and Severin, chilly and shaking, had curled up with Edith on the couch because she had opened her arms to their shivering, or they were attracted to how warm and sticky she was. She covered Utch and kissed her, and Severin touched and rubbed them both, and suddenly Utch was pinned under them, with Severin kissing her mouth and Edith kissing her deeply, until Utch felt herself coming and wanted Severin inside her. Edith didn't mind and Severin came into her; Edith held Utch's head against Severin's shoulder; she was mouth-to-mouth with Edith, their tongues exchanging recipes, when Severin made her come. Utch said that Edith almost came then too. Then it was Edith's turn, because Severin had been holding out, and she held Edith's head while Severin came inside her; he came quickly and rolled away. But Edith had still not come, Utch knew, so Utch helped her. Edith was so light that Utch could easily manipulate her; she picked up Edith at the hips and drove her shoulders against Edith's slim buttocks and very lightly touched her tongue to Edith where she was wetter and saltier than the sea. When Edith screamed, Severin covered her mouth with his own. I heard just a short cry before the orchestra of the paella captured my attention again.

Then Severin was beside me in the kitchen, smelling more distinctly than shellfish. He shoved me in the direction of the living room. "Go on," he said, "you don't know anything about paella. Let me. Go keep the ladies . . .

happy," he said, and gave me a bewildered roll of his eyes (the most honest, worried and intimate confession I believe he ever made to me). "Go on, man," he said, shoving me again. He dug a wooden spoon deep into the paella, brought up that unlikely and delicious mixture—chicken, pork, sausage, lobster, mussels and clams—and slid the steaming spoon into his mouth. A bright red tongue of pimento hung down his chin, and I found my way to the couch where Utch and Edith were drawn tight together, curled against each other; they were touching each other's breasts and hair, but when I came up they parted and let me fit snugly between them. I did not object to how they used me.

Then we felt like a swim and ran, all three, across the lawn, green-black now, and saw the lights on the channel buoys blinking out in the water. And we all three entered the sea and saw that startling figure alone against the lights from the sunroom's open doors. He sprinted down the lawn toward us and cleared the first long dune like a broadjumper. At a glance you would have picked him for a winner in a rare pentathlon—cooking, eating, drinking, wrestling and fucking. "Here I come, you lovers!" he shouted. A wave rocked us and tilted the horizon, so that Severin momentarily disappeared, and then he burst through it and hugged the three of us; we were chest-deep in the ocean. "The paella's ready, team," he said, "if we can stop screwing long enough to eat it." A vulgar man.

But we stopped until after dinner, when I think we'd all had a long enough time to engage in the normal, relatively civilized process of eating, which we'd done together many times before, so that our awareness of how we'd behaved that afternoon had sunk in and left us all happy but shy.

Severin reviewed his paella, suspected the tenderness of the pork, cast aspersions on the age of the chicken, suggested shortcuts in the making of the Italian sweet sausage, allowed that clams were, usually, clams, that mussels were better than clams anyway, and that the lobster was the undefeated George James Bender of the sea.

"Don't make me lose my appetite," Edith said. "Show some restraint in your images."

"This is a vacation from restraint," Severin said. "I don't see anyone else showing any restraint." He flipped a lobster claw in my lap; I flipped it back; he laughed.

"This is no vacation," I said. "This is a beginning." It was a toast. Edith stood up and drank down her wine the way I was used to seeing Utch drink hers.

But Severin said, "No, it's just a holiday. It's like calling time out."

Utch wasn't saying anything; I could tell she was a little drunk. Edith announced that she wanted to change her brand of cigarettes. "I want non-filters," she said, crumpling a full pack of mine; she'd been out of her own for hours. "If this is just a time out," she said, "I'm going to enjoy myself."

Severin said he'd go get her cigarettes. "What's the worst cigarette? What's the strongest, vilest, most throat-rending, lung-gunking cigarette on sale? Because I'll get you a carton of them," he told Edith, "and we'll force-feed them to you all weekend. You can chain-smoke until they're all gone. Maybe that will cure you."

"Go with him," Edith said to me. "He'll probably buy me a box of cigars."

"You shouldn't smoke," Utch said to Edith. "You know it upsets him." She had a fixed smile on her face, and I knew she wouldn't remember anything she said tomorrow. Her left hand lay in the salad as if it were comfortable there. Edith smiled at her and took her hand out of the salad. Utch winked at her and blew her a kiss.

In the car Severin said, "Christ, we better hurry back or those women will go to bed without us."

"Does it bother you?" I asked. "It seems natural to me that they should have those feelings for each other. I don't know why, but it doesn't bother me."

"I don't know what's natural," Severin said, "but, no, it doesn't bother me, either. I just don't want to get back and find us locked out of the bedrooms. I mean, I didn't come all this way to spend a weekend with *you.*" But he was joking; he wasn't really angry.

We had an argument about whether to buy Edith Lucky Strikes, Camels or Pall Malls. Severin insisted on the Pall Malls because they were longer and he thought they would burn her throat more. Riding back, I wanted to tell him how good I felt—how I couldn't believe that he'd suddenly relaxed here, and how optimistic I was about all of us. I wanted to say that I thought our future looked fine, but he said suddenly, "We should be careful no one gets too excited." It was like his saying that we were all on a holiday, and I didn't know what to make of it. "Why does Utch drink so much?" he asked me. "Why do you let her get so plastered?"

I said, "You know, one kind of excitement leads to another."

"I've noticed that in four-year-olds," he said.

"Come on," I said. "I mean, it really excites me when I know Utch has been with you. And being with Edith—well, that also makes Utch very arousing to me."

"Polymorphous perverse," said Severin. "Something like that. It's normally a phase of childhood sexuality."

"Come on," I said. "Doesn't it excite you? Don't you find that generally you're more sexually aroused?"

"There have always been certain moments in the day when I think I could fuck a she-goat," Severin said.

I was angry at him. "I hope you don't mean Utch."

"I hope I didn't mean *Edith,*" he said.

"You know, Severin, I'm just trying to get to know you."

"That's a little difficult," he said. "It's a little late. I mean, it's not as if we were friends first and things just naturally led to this. Things began with this, and now you're Edith's friend, first and last."

"I've never had too many men friends, anyway," I told him. "I know you have. We're just different."

"I have a few old friends," he said, "but no one around me now. I don't really have any more friends than you. I just used to have them."

"And women friends?" I asked. "I mean, since Edith and before Utch?"

"Not as many as you," he said. But he was assuming; he didn't know anything.

"How many is 'not so many'?"

"Counting she-goats?" he asked, but there was that slashed tooth, that mischief-making tooth, that storytelling tooth. "If you want to know, ask Edith," he said.

"You mean she knows?" I asked.

"Everything. We don't have any secrets."

"Some people would rather not know everything," I said. "Utch and I agree—not that we're that frequently unfaithful, or whatever you want to call it—that if one of us has someone, some light occasion only, we don't want to know. Just so it doesn't show, just so it doesn't affect us together. And if it's a little nothing, why *should* we know? We might get upset when there's no reason to."

"I couldn't have 'a little nothing,' " Severin said. "What's the point of having nothing? If I were having a relationship with someone and it *didn't* show—and Edith couldn't see it and feel it—then I couldn't be having much of a relationship. I mean, if you have one good relationship, why would you be interested in having a little nothing of a relationship? If you have a good relationship, that's all the more reason to want to have *another* good one. Which is what the trouble is," he added.

I asked Edith once, "Do you tell him everything about us?"

"If he asks," she said. "That's how he wants it." Then she smiled. "*Almost* everything," she said. "But if he always knew what to ask, I'd always tell."

In the car, I asked him, "Don't you think that's an invasion of privacy? Don't you think it violates someone else's independence?"

"*What* independence?" he asked me. "I honestly admit the degree of independence that I *don't* have if I live with someone," he said, "and I expect whoever's living with me to do the same." (Later I remember him yelling: "There's a precious amount of having-one's-cake-and-eating-it-too shit going on around here!")

The Cape house was darker than we'd left it. "I'll bet they're in there lapping each other right up, so to speak," Severin said. But I knew how drunk Utch had been when we left, and I wasn't surprised to see her flopped on the couch—passed out from the wine, I was sure, not love-drugged by a bout with Edith. Edith sat braiding Utch's hair while she snored. Braids were not flattering to Utch.

"Brunhilde's been felled by the mead, or the lords of the hall, or both," said Edith. She'd washed her hair; it was done up in a big mint-green towel that came from the bathroom adjoining the Green Room. Like some grand English country home, the house had named bedrooms: the Green Room, the Cove Room, the Master Red, the Lady Yellow. I had never met Edith's mother, but Severin mimicked her perfectly, Edith said, and he had re-named all the rooms for us when he'd shown us the house on arrival. There was the Wet Dream Room—it had a single bed—and the Hot & Cold Flashes Room (Edith's mother's room; she complained of such symptoms), and the Come If You Can Room, so named for being next to Edith's mother's room (and a trial in the early days of their marriage, Severin claimed; Edith laughed), and the Great Green Wrenching Orgasm Room —the most private of the upstairs rooms, most separate from the others and, when the house was full, most coveted. "It has the best orgasm record," Severin claimed. "Daughters have trouble having orgasms in their mothers' houses." It had a brass bed which was notorious for falling apart. From the gleaming foot-rail, tied on a satin cord, hung a wrench for emergency repairs.

By her choice of the mint-green towel, Edith had indicated that the Great Green Wrenching Orgasm Room was to be ours. "Love?" she said, touching Severin nicely, "you take Come If You Can, okay? I mean, when Mother's not here, the room doesn't deserve its name, does it?"

But Edith told me later that when I went off to pee, Severin said to her, with a nasty jerk of his head toward the snoring Utch, "You mean Come If *She* Can, don't you? What's the going price for baby-sitting? Why should he get it free?"

I could tell there was something between them when I came back, so I offered to put Utch to bed; Severin waved me off. "She usually just sleeps it off," I told him.

"Any special instructions?" he asked. I thought he was kidding; I saw his tooth. But Edith left us and went to bed. *Whose* bed, I wondered? "She's in the Green Room," Severin told me. "I'll look after Utch; don't worry about a thing."

I went up to the Great Green Wrenching Orgasm Room, where Edith was sitting up, smoking in bed and fuming about Severin. "He's not going to spoil this weekend for me," she said. "Or for any of us, though he's certainly trying." I reminded her of what had happened between us all in the afternoon; we had enjoyed ourselves, after all, and it had been surpris-ing. She smiled; I suspected that she sulked with him when he upset her, but she had never done that with me.

"Go on," she said tiredly. "Just talk to me." But then she wanted to tiptoe down the hall and say goodnight to Severin. I didn't know what her motive was, but I let her go. I surveyed the green walls, the green drapes, the notorious brass bed, the wrench dangling from the foot-rail. I listened to Edith in the hall as she knocked on the door of the Come If You Can Room. "Sleep tight!" she cried out to Severin brightly. "Come if you can!"

When she came back, I got angry with her; I told her that the quickest way to end our relationship was to use our being together as a kind of provocation of Severin. Then she sulked with me. I very much wanted to make love to Edith at that moment because I knew that Utch and Severin *couldn't,* but I saw that her anger with him had made her angry with everything, and that making love to her was unlikely.

When I thought she was asleep, she whispered, "It's got nothing to do with you sometimes. It's just between us. Don't worry. You see, he doesn't know what he wants; it's himself he's upset with most of the time." A few minutes later she mumbled, "He only thinks of himself."

We were both asleep when Severin woke us with his knocking on the door. "Goodnight!" he called. "Be careful what you use that wrench for! It's only meant to fix the *bed!* Goodnight, goodnight . . ."

But Edith started to huff and moan and pant and thrash around, gripping the head-rails of the old brass bed and thumping up and down—sounding like she never sounded when she was actually doing what she pretended to be doing now for his benefit. "Ooooh!" she cried out; the bed heaved. "Uuuuh!" she grunted, and the casters moved us across the green room like some boat on choppy water. "God!" she cried out, her long thin arms as rigid as those brass rails. When the bed collapsed under us, Severin was probably on his way back to Utch, but he heard it. Edith sat laughing on the floor; at least I think she was laughing—it was strange laughter. The bed, detached entirely from the head-rails and clinging still to the right foot-post, had pitched the mattress and us across the scatter rug and sent the night table spinning into the chaise longue.

"Are you all right?" Severin asked at the door. Edith laughed.

"Yes, thank you," I said. Then I wondered how to fix it. I had no idea what one was supposed to do with the damn wrench.

Edith curled up on the chaise with a wild look at me and said, "If you can fix it, I really will fuck you." I'd never heard her talk so crudely. But the bed was hopeless; mechanically, I have never known what goes where. I was going to suggest that we move to another room when we heard Utch being sick down the hall.

"It's okay," Severin was saying soothingly. "Let it all come and you'll feel better." We listened to Utch's terrible retching. I had to go to her, of course; Edith kissed me hurriedly and I went down the hall.

Severin was holding her head over the toilet in the bathroom adjacent to the Come If You Can Room. "I'm sorry," Utch said weakly to him, then threw up again.

"I'm here, Utch," I said.

"I don't care," she said. She heaved some more, and then Severin left us alone together. We inherited the Come If You Can Room and I heard him move with Edith into the Hot & Cold Flashes Room. Evidently Severin didn't feel like fixing the brass bed at such a late hour, though he had fixed it many times before, I knew.

Utch and I hugged each other in the Come If You Can Room while Severin and Edith had no apparent difficulty coming next door. Hot & Cold Flashes, indeed. I listened to Edith sound the way I knew she really sounded. Utch's strong hand bore down on the base of my spine. We each knew what the other was thinking: we'd all spoken of this weekend as being an opportunity to break the 3 A.M. arrival-and-departure schedule. We'd thought it would be nice to be real lovers, who occasionally got to wake up in the morning together.

But I woke up with Utch, her breath echoing vomit. Edith made jokes about it at breakfast, but Severin said, "Oh, I don't know, it was still a novelty for *us,* Edith. I've always wanted to nail you in your mother's room."

"Poor Mommy," Edith said.

The day cheered up; Utch took off her jersey at noon. Severin, making sandwiches, put a dab of his homemade mayonnaise on one of her available nipples, but no one offered to lick it off and Utch had to use a napkin. Edith kept her blouse on. Severin announced he was taking a swim, and Utch went with him. Edith and I talked about Djuna Barnes. We agreed there was a kind of bloodless immorality to *Nightwood;* it was art, but wasn't it clinical? Edith said suddenly, "I suppose they're doing it down on the beach. I wonder if they ever *talk* about anything."

"Why do you mind if they're doing it?" I asked.

"I don't, really," she said. "It's just that it's Severin's idea that we all keep the times even, or something, and the thought's contaminating. And he knows that you and I didn't, last night."

"I think Utch thinks we *did,* " I said. "I think she feels she missed out."

"You didn't tell her what happened?"

"No," I said. She thought it over, then shrugged.

When they came back, Edith asked lightly, "Well, what have you two been doing?" She thrust her hand down Severin's bathing suit and squeezed. Utch had put her jersey back on.

Severin winced; his eyes watered; Edith let him go. "Well," he said, "we've been enjoying our holiday." That word again!

"What's it a holiday *from?*" Edith asked.

"Children and reality," he said. "But mostly children." At that time I didn't know how much he implied by "children." Over his head, above the knife rack, was a wretched painting of decapitated fish with scales resembling Gustav Klimt's little squares of color-forms. It was an original Kurt Winter, of course; the Museum of Modern Art hadn't wanted it. Edith's

mother had been stuck with a lot of minor paintings over the years. She felt
no sense of responsibility for the estate of Van Gogh, but when they rejected
a Haringa, a Bodler or a Kurt Winter, *then* she was touched. She ended
up buying a lot of paintings the Modern turned down.

"She's such a sweet person," Edith said. "She's especially moved by bad
paintings because she feels such embarrassment for the painter, even if he's
dead." It's true. There wasn't a decent painting in the bunch of Kurt
Winters; she had bought his very worst.

Edith hardly did better. In Vienna, she had met Severin on the twentieth-
century floor of the Belvedere, as planned. Though he wore his letter-jacket,
confirming her worst fears, they still made a kind of art history together.
Pausing by the great square canvas by Gustav Klimt—"Avenue Leading
Up to Castle Kammer on the Attersee," c. 1912—Severin said, "See that
green? My father just didn't have it. With my father, trees were trees and
green was green."

"I want you to know that I'm not officially employed—" Edith started
to say.

"This is Klimt's 'Judith with the Head of Holofernes,' 1901," Severin said.
"His brother, Georg, made the frame with the inscription."

"The Museum of Modern Art has not committed itself to a price," Edith
went on doggedly. "In fact, they might only want one painting. But how
much money do you need? Will you go straight to America? Would you
consider traveling about first?"

"Schiele's 'Sunflowers,' 1911," Severin said. "Not what you'd expect of
Schiele."

"My mother and I might be able to buy one or two paintings ourselves,
but what will you do with the money, exactly? I mean, will you work at
some job? You're getting a doctorate? In what?"

"Do you like 'The Kiss'?" Severin asked.

"What?"

" 'The Kiss,' 1908. It's one of my favorite Klimts."

"Oh, mine too," Edith said. They looked at it for a while, but it was
"Judith with the Head of Holofernes" which prompted Edith to ask, "Do
you think Klimt liked women?"

"No," said Severin. "But I think he desired women, was tantalized by
them, intrigued by them, attracted to them." They regarded Judith's strong
jaw, her open mouth, her wet teeth, her startling dark hair. Her flesh was
gauzy, perhaps in decay, and her long fingers were in Holofernes' hair; she
held his severed head matter-of-factly against her stomach, her shadowy
navel almost in line with his shut eye. Her breasts were high, upstanding,
girlish but soft. One was naked, the other covered by a filmy blouse; the gold
gilt was carefully placed so as not to obscure the nipple. Fruits, vegetation,
a possible forest and garden, grew over Judith's shoulder and framed her
cold, elegant face. But the dead head of Holofernes was casually cropped

out of the painting; his one shut eye and part of a cheek was all of him that was in the picture.

"Tell me what it means to you," Edith said to Severin.

"She's a woman by whom you would not mind being beheaded. She wouldn't mind doing it, either."

" 'Doing it'? You mean the beheading?"

"Both."

They laughed. Edith felt astonishingly wicked. "She had him make love to her before she beheaded him," Edith said. "You can tell by her smile." But there was something lewd about the painting which suggested more, or worse, and she felt like shocking Severin Winter. "Or maybe she tried to after she beheaded him," she said. Severin just stared at the painting, and she asked him, "Which do you think she preferred?"

But it was Severin who shocked her when he said, "During."

He took her next to the Museum of the Twentieth Century. They did not discuss Kurt Winter's paintings there, either.

"Is Frau Reiner going to America with you?" Edith asked.

"What are old friends for?" said Severin. "Old friends don't travel with you. Old friends stay when you leave."

"So you're traveling alone?"

"Well, I might have to take sixty or seventy Kurt Winters along."

"My mother's position isn't very official," Edith said. (She had never realized how sneakers make a man appear to bounce.) "Does Frau Reiner live with you?" she asked.

They were looking at Gerstl's "The Schoenberg Family," c. 1908. "A minor painter who made it," Severin said. "Of course he had to die first. Not one of his paintings was exhibited during his lifetime. My father, of course, didn't get the chance to develop very much after 1938 . . ."

"Will you hold on to your mother's apartment, perhaps for vacations?" Edith asked.

"Vacations?" echoed Severin. "If you're living the way you want to, the concept of holidays becomes obsolete. Once Mother and I took a trip to Greece. We were packing up when Zivan or Vaso asked her if she was going to do any modeling there. 'Of course,' Mother said. 'If someone wants to paint, I want to pose.' We were just going to Greece, you see, but my mother liked what she did; she wasn't taking a vacation *from* anything."

"And what do you like?" Edith asked.

"Languages," he said. "I wish everyone spoke two or three languages and used them—all together. There are only so many ways to say things in one language. If we could only talk even more, make more description, add more confusion—but it wouldn't be confusion, finally; it would just be wonderfully complicated. I love complexity," he said. "Take food, for example. I'd like to be a great cook. I want to learn how to cook things better and better—subtle things, overpowering things, delicate and rich things, *all* things! I love to eat."

"Would you like to run your own restaurant?"

"What?" he said. "God, no. I want to cook for myself, and, of course, close friends."

"But how do you want to make a living?" Edith asked.

"The easiest way possible. I can teach German. I'd rather teach cooking, but there's not much money in it. And I'd love to coach wrestling, but I don't have a doctorate in wrestling. Anyway," he said, "how I live matters more than what I do. I have ambitions for the *quality* of how I live; I have no ambitions for making money. Ideally I'd marry a rich woman and cook for her! I'd exercise every day—for the benefit of us both, of course—and I'd have time to read enough to be a constant source of information, ideas and language. Ah, *Sprache!* I'd be free to devote myself to the basics. I would prefer to have my income provided, and in turn I would provide quality talk, quality food and quality sex! Oh, forgive me . . ."

"Go on," Edith said. She wanted to be a writer, and what she did mattered more to her than how she lived, she thought. She never wanted to cook anything, but she loved to eat. This man was saying to her that his ambition was to be a *wife!* "Please go on," she told him.

"I'm afraid you've seen all of my father that's here," Severin said. "The rest is all privately owned. We could have lunch first."

"I love to eat," Edith said.

"We could have lunch at my place," Severin said. "I just happen to have cooked up a *Gulaschsuppe,* and I'm trying a new vinaigrette for asparagus."

"And there's more Kurt Winter to see at your place," Edith said helpfully.

"But some of those are not for sale," Severin said.

"I thought everything was for sale."

"Just the art," said Severin. "All the art is for sale."

The pornographic drawings and paintings of Katrina Marek were not art, of course; they were his mother and his history; they were his *basics*—which perhaps Edith understood about him from the first. The ones of Katrina Marek were in the bedroom; art was in the living room.

"Look around," Severin said as he heated the *Gulaschsuppe*. She found the real thing in his bedroom, of course: a circus of positions and erotic poses surrounded his neatly made bed. She might have been troubled if she hadn't known the model was his mother. But when she thought about it, she wondered if this shouldn't be more troubling. I think that Edith must have seen Katrina Marek as competition. She sat down on the bed. At its foot was a set of barbells which appeared as immovable as her memory of Frau Reiner's use of her tongue.

When he came into the bedroom to tell her the *Gulaschsuppe* was hot, he'd finally taken off his letter-jacket, and Edith knew, with alarm, that if he touched her, she would let him. He opened a window on the far side of the bed. Very enhancing, Edith thought. And now he'll—

"Perfect," he said; from the window box outside he picked up a wooden salad bowl containing the asparagus. "Keeps it cool," he explained; "I never have enough room in the refrigerator." He dangled a limp asparagus spear in front of her; it glistened with vinegar and oil. "Taste?" he asked. She opened her mouth and shut her eyes; he cupped her chin, tipped back her head and fed her the asparagus spear. It was delicious. When she opened her eyes, he was banging around back in the kitchen, calling, "Wine or beer?"

Edith did not want to get up. In some of the poses Katrina Marek appeared to be masturbating; Edith realized she had never touched herself in some of the ways suggested by Severin's mother.

"Wine or beer?" Severin called again. She lay back on the bed, and when she heard him coming, she shut her eyes.

"Are you all right?" he asked.

"I've lied to you," she told him. She waited for his weight on the bed beside her, but he remained standing. She kept her eyes shut. "I have no official authority to buy any of your father's paintings, and even my mother is just about the most unofficial person at the Museum of Modern Art. I really don't know a single thing about the museum, except that no one there actually likes your father's painting. And *these*," she said, her eyes still closed, waving her arm at the bedroom walls, "my God, these are *appalling*."

She felt him sit down beside her on the bed, but she kept her eyes closed. "These aren't for sale," he said quietly.

"They should never leave your bedroom," she said.

"They never *will* leave my bedroom," Severin said.

Edith opened her eyes. "Aren't you angry with me?" she asked him. "I'm sorry about the Modern."

"I never believed it anyway," he said, which made her a little angry. He just sat there, in profile to her, very properly not looking down at a woman lying on her back. "But there's you and your mother," he said. "You said you might buy some."

Edith sat up. She was convinced he would never touch her, even if she undressed. "What would you do if you got a lot of money, anyway?" she asked.

"I don't want a lot," he said. "I just want enough to be able to take the paintings I can't sell with me." He looked around and smiled; she loved his smile. "That's a lot," he said. "And I want enough money to look around for a job in America without having to take a bad one. And," he grinned, "I'd like enough to be able to go to Greece before I do any of that. I'd like to leave right now," he said, and he lay back on the bed and shut his eyes.

"I want to stay in clean little hotels; I want to be on the ocean. It's warm there now, but it's not the tourist season. Nothing lavish, but deny nothing! Eat well, drink well, take some good books along, read in the sun, swim. And when the tourists started coming, I'd come back here, pack up and go to America . . ."

"Say goodbye to Frau Reiner?" Edith asked.

"And to Vaso and Zivan," Severin said. "Tell them I'll be back soon, which will mean," he said, opening his eyes, "that I'll be back before they die. But I probably won't." He shut his eyes again. "Greece is the first thing," he said. "That's where I want to go."

"And how many paintings does someone have to buy so that you can go to Greece?" Edith asked. He opened his eyes. Edith liked his eyes when they were open, but she liked being able to stare at his mouth when his eyes were closed. "Close your eyes and answer me," said Edith. "How many paintings?" He appeared to be thinking, and she slipped off the edge of the bed, went into the kitchen and turned off the flame under the *Gulaschsuppe*. She brought the wine and two glasses back to the bedroom with her. His eyes were still closed, and she slipped off her shoes; she poured them both some wine and edged back on the bed beside him. She wanted to smoke, but he seemed too white in the teeth and too broad in the chest to possibly approve. He was so narrow in the hips, so small in the thighs.

"Maybe five of the big canvases," he said. "But of the five I'm thinking of, you haven't seen two."

"I'll take your word for it," she said, "but I want my pick, for my mother and me." He opened his eyes and she handed him some wine; he sipped; she took the glass from him and motioned him to lie back and shut his eyes again. He did as he was told. "Two conditions," she said when he was lying very still; he opened one eye but she brushed it shut with her hand. She almost kept her hand over his eyes but she thought better of it and rested her hand on the bed close to his face. She knew he could smell the perfume at her wrist; she could feel his slow breathing against her fingers. "First condition," she said, and paused, "is that one of the five paintings be one of *these*—you don't need to look, you know what I mean. I promise it will never be a public painting; I will never sell it or loan it to any museum. Frankly, I want it for my bedroom."

"Which one?" he asked.

Edith looked at the one she wanted. "She's on her back, with one leg lying flat and the other bent at the knee. She's touching herself, very lightly, I think, but her face is turned toward us and she's touching the fingertips of her other hand to her lips—as if she's kissing her fingers goodbye to us, or maybe just hushing herself so she won't cry out."

"She's *tasting* herself," said Severin. Suddenly Edith saw the painting. "She's got one orange stocking on?" he asked. "The stocking's half off her right foot? Her eyes are closed? You mean that one?"

"Yes," said Edith, almost whispering. "That's my favorite one."

"Well, you can't have it," he told her. "It's my favorite, too." He didn't open his eyes to negotiate. Edith was surprised, but she charged ahead as if her feelings were unshaken. I am completely lost, she thought; I don't know myself.

"Second condition," she said, "is that you must answer one question, either yes or no. Either one satisfies the condition. You mustn't feel obliged —just be honest: say yes or no."

"Yes," Severin said. When she looked at him, his eyes were open. She tried to put her hand over them, but he caught it and held it lightly against his chest. "Yes," he said again.

"But I haven't asked the question," she said, looking away from him. He would not close his eyes or let go of her hand.

"Yes, anyway," he said. He already knows the question, she thought, and felt humiliated. She pulled her hand away and decided to ask him nothing more. He was cruel; he didn't know when to stop teasing.

But he said, "Now I have one condition." She looked at him. "You have to come to Greece with me." That had been her question: Did he want her to come with him?

She shrugged. "Why would I want to do that?" she said. "I don't have the time, anyway." She got up from the bed, found her purse and lit a cigarette. "Is the *Gulaschsuppe* hot?" she asked.

"If you didn't turn the heat off," he said, and rolled away and lay on the bed face-down.

Edith went to the kitchen, turned the heat on under the *Gulaschsuppe* and banged a few pots around, but Severin didn't appear. She looked at a photograph of his mother with Frau Reiner and the two Yugoslav wrestlers. They were clowning for the photographer, who, Edith dimly thought, might have been Severin. The three survivors were all much younger. She could tell that Frau Reiner had at least once had a body, for everyone in the photograph was naked. They stood in front of an elegantly prepared dinner spread out on a table in several courses; they all had knives and forks in their hands. Vaso or Zivan wore a napkin on his head, and between Frau Reiner's ample breasts, a full glass of wine tilted dangerously. Looking older and more dignified than the rest, Severin's mother stood smiling shyly at the camera, her hands folded demurely over her crotch. She was nothing like the Katrina Marek in the bedroom; though naked, she looked fully clothed.

"Did you take this photograph?" Edith called into the bedroom. And he was supposed to say, "What photograph?" and she would say, "This one," and he would have to get up off that dangerous bed and come out. But he didn't answer. "Soup's hot!" she called. When she heard nothing, she went back; he hadn't moved since she'd left the room.

"You don't have to buy any of the paintings if you don't really want to," he said, talking into the mattress. "And if you really want that one"—his hand waved at the wall—"you can have it."

"I want to come with you to Greece," Edith admitted. He still didn't move.

"I want *you,*" he said. Edith decided, All right, he's said enough. She dropped her skirt at her feet and stepped out of it, then pulled her blouse off over her head so that her hair crackled. She wore a bra in those days, and she unhooked it and looped it over the back of a chair. Then she tossed her panties at Severin, who still lay across the bed like a felled steer. ("The panties fluttered over one of his ears and rested there like a downed parachute," she wrote in one of her more forced pieces.) She was preparing to look at him directly when he sat up and stared at her; he came up off the bed very suddenly, awkwardly handing the panties back to her and dashing from the room. She thought that her shame would kill her, but he called, "Jesus Christ, the *Gulaschsuppe*—don't you smell it?" Boiled over and burnt, she supposed. "My God, what have I gotten myself into?" she whispered to herself. When she got under the covers, she recognized her perfume—that is, Frau Reiner's perfume—already on his pillows. He didn't even look at me, she thought.

But he didn't leave her alone long; he returned shedding clothes. She had not known enough men to know that athletes, like women, are used to changing clothes and therefore are smooth and careless undressers. He stood naked beside the bed and let her look at him; she had thought that only women did that, and she pulled back the covers for him so that he would look at her. He looked her over a little too quickly for her feelings, but he touched her just perfectly and was under the covers with her very gracefully. Well, she thought, nakedness is almost a family tradition with him; maybe he will look longer later. Before he kissed her and didn't stop, she barely had time to say, "I think I'm going to like you." She was right, of course.

They left for Greece five days later; they'd have gone earlier, but it took that long for Edith to make and send slides of Kurt Winter's best work to her mother. "Mother," she wrote, "I hope the Modern will buy one or two of these. You and I have already bought numbers one through four, and a fifth not enclosed. I am going to Greece; I must get back to my writing."

The morning they were to leave, Frau Reiner and the Yugoslav wrestlers gave them a ritual goodbye. Edith and Severin were in bed, which was where they could have been found regularly in those five days, when Edith heard Frau Reiner and the Chetniks whispering and tromping about in the living room just as she and Severin were waking up. "Frau Reiner still has an apartment key," Severin told Edith, who scowled. "Mother gave it to her," Severin whispered. "And anyway, over the years Vaso and Zivan probably have collected about four keys apiece." What were they up to out there, Edith asked. Severin listened. The sounds they were making were apparently familiar to him; he rolled his eyes. "It's a kind of family joke," he told her.

"What is?" she whispered.

"You'll see," he said; he looked worried. "It's really almost a tradition. You must take it as a sign of great respect." Outside the bedroom door she heard thumping and giggles. "It goes way back," he said nervously; he put his arm around her and smiled toward the bedroom door. It opened, and into the room blew Frau Reiner, as flushed and beefy and naked as a Rubens. Vaso and Zivan were carrying her, with some difficulty, and they were naked, too. At the foot of the bed they quickly assembled in a group pose which Edith recognized as the one from the old photograph. Only Severin's mother was missing; a space for her separated Vaso from Zivan. They all held knives and forks in their hands, and Vaso or Zivan had a napkin on his head. But Frau Reiner was missing the wine glass; her breasts could no longer have clamped it tight in her cleavage. It must have been sad for Severin to see so much sagging flesh. *"Gute Reise!"* Frau Reiner croaked, and the old wrestlers burst into tears.

"They wish us a good trip," Severin told Edith. Later she learned that the photograph had also been taken at a goodbye party for Severin when he was leaving for Iowa and a future perhaps bright in wrestling.

Then they were all standing around the bed, weeping and patting and kissing everyone. Edith realized that the covers were peeled back and that she was as naked as they. The old wrestlers seemed hardly to notice her— a professional numbness, perhaps—but she saw that Frau Reiner's close survey of her young body reflected both the sincerity of her affection and the agony of her envy. Suddenly Frau Reiner hugged her with a frightening passion; for a grip on her real life, Edith held onto Severin's thigh while he was being buffeted and cuffed by the bawling old Olympians.

Crushed against Frau Reiner's bosom, a playground of history, Edith remembered her mother's letter, which said, "He has no surviving family." Frau Reiner pinned her to the bed; her tears—her sweat?—wet Edith's face; she was at least two weight classes superior to Severin. Edith tightened her grip on Severin's thigh, which, for all the confusion around the bed, might have been Vaso's or Zivan's, and hoped Frau Reiner would not suffocate her. He has no family? Her mother was quite wrong. Edith knew that Severin Winter's sense of family was more ferocious than most. We should all have been warned.

I admit that my own sense of family suffered from our foursome. I remember the children least of all, and this bothers me. Of course, we all had other friends, too, and our own lives with our children. But I forget where the children were. Once when I was with Edith, Dorabella knocked weakly on the bedroom door. I flinched; I thought it was Severin coming home early, though I couldn't imagine him knocking so softly. There was a hasty confusion of knees and other limbs, and I know Edith was worrying that Severin had heard her.

"Mommy?" Dorabella said. I got down under the covers and Edith let her into the room.

There had been a dream; the child described it in flat, unbroken tones, her hand nervously plucking and patting the lump beside her mother which was me. "Ssshhh," said Edith gently, "don't wake up Daddy."

The child poked me. "Why is Daddy sleeping like that?" She started to lift the covers, but Edith stopped her.

"Because he's cold," Edith said.

In the child's dream there were howling dogs and a pig squealing under a car whose wheels "had folded under itself," she said, "like the wheels on an airplane." The pig was crushed, but not dead; the dogs were howling because the pig's squeals hurt their ears. Dorabella ran around and around the car, but there was nothing she could do for the pig. "And then it was *me* who was under the car," the child said, her voice trembling with the injustice of it. "And it was *my* sound that I heard and was making the dogs howl." She was punching my rump like dough, her little fists rolling her knuckles over me.

"Poor Fiordiligi," Edith said.

"It's Dorabella, Mommy!" the child cried.

Edith turned on the light. "Oh, Dorabella," she said. "What a terrible dream."

"That's not Daddy's shirt, is it?" Dorabella asked, and I knew whose clothes she was staring at.

"Well, Daddy traded something for it," Edith said. She was very quick; there wasn't a pause.

"What did he trade?" Dorabella asked, and I remember the silence.

Fiordiligi and Dorabella were the Winters' children, of course. My own children I hardly remember at all, and I used to know them quite well.

"What did he trade?" Dorabella asked again. I forget the children, but I remember that silence.

Who's on Top?
Where's the Bottom?

Once, when all of us were together, I looked at my boys and announced, "Look at that Jack" (my older one, lean and lithe, with a face even prettier than Edith's). "Look at his back; see the graceful bend to it? That isn't what they call 'sway-backed,' is it? He looks like a Renaissance print I once saw of an archer; he was bent like his bow. Jack is the delicate one. He likes music. I hope he'll be a painter."

And Severin answered, "If he ever develops any strength in his arms, he might be a 142-pounder." Severin liked Bart, my younger boy. He was brick-shaped, and all he inherited from Utch was her breadth of cheek and her shortness. In fact, if we had known the Winters back then, I might have suspected Severin of engendering Bart because the boy's body was nearer to Severin's than to mine. And as to the source of Bart's genes which gave him a turtle's pain threshold, I could only guess. "From Utch, of course," said Severin. "She had a pain threshold like a planarian's." How did he know? What did he mean?

Jack was the older but the last one in the water; he was bigger, but in close combat Bart would sink his teeth into him and hold on. When Bart ran at a door, he ran at it as if the door would open for him. I winced to see the child move; a potential collision seemed to precede him like a prow. Neat, graceful Jack was curious, careful and shy. He woke up slowly. He said to me, "Sometimes are you ever sad and feel like crying even when nothing bad has happened to you?" Yes, of course! He was my son; I knew him well. He could spend an hour brushing his teeth because of the mirror —looking at himself as if it would help him figure out a way to be.

But Bart was born a bludgeon, with the ankles and wrists and insensitive cheerfulness of the good peasants in the orchards of Eichbüchl. He woke up breathing deeply, bleating for his breakfast.

When we took the children to the city, Jack looked up, scanned rooftops, hunted for gargoyles, girls waving out windows, spirits in the sky. Bart scuffed along, looked in the gutters for what got dropped there.

Severin's girls dressed up for Jack, wrote him bawdy notes and said, "Sit down, Jack, and let's play 'What Can We Get You?' " They wrestled with Bart, playing with him as they would with a pet. Dorabella told Edith that she was going to marry Jack; Fiordiligi laughed and said, "Then I'll be his mistress!"

"His mistress?" Edith said. "You don't know what a mistress is."

"Yes, I do," said Fiordiligi. "You get the presents."

Severin said, "That Bart, he's my boy. He's going to be a great cook; he'll eat anything."

"He's built like a bookend," I said, "but not like a writer."

"He's going to be at least a 177-pounder," said Severin. "Would you look at the chest on that kid!"

"He's got the sweetest temper," Utch said. Bart was a boy only a mother and a wrestler could love.

"That Jack," said Edith. "He's going to kill more women than the plague." I hoped he would be a good son and show some of them to me. His eyelashes were longer than Utch's and Edith's together.

"Why did you give your children such American names?" Edith asked Utch.

"They're simpler," said Utch, "and the boys like them. What kid in America wants a name like Helmut or Florian?"

"I love Italian names," said Edith. "After I called my first one Fiordiligi I *had* to call the second one Dorabella."

"It was going to be Dante if it was a boy," said Severin. "But I'm glad they're girls. Boys are such selfish shits." He was always trying to make the girls read. "You've got to be smart," he'd tell them, "and you've got to be kind. But if you're kind without being smart, other people are going to make you miserable."

"I love everything Italian," said Edith.

"You've never been there," Severin reminded her. And to us, "Edith is most attracted to things that are unfamiliar to her."

"Not true!" Edith said. "And when I'm familiar with something, do I throw it away?"

"Wait and see," said Severin. Of course, he was looking at me, but I kept my eyes on Jack and Bart. I was impressed that two people I loved so much could be so different.

"That's not surprising," Edith said.

"No," Utch disagreed. "There is one that you always love more."

"Here we all are again," said Severin Winter, "stumbling toward profundity."

Well, he could be funny. But at whose expense?

"He is *not* cruel," Edith said once; she was angry. "You should just stop trying to understand him. I stopped trying, and now I enjoy him much more. I hate it that men feel they have to understand everything." She was depressed, she said, that Severin and I would never be friends.

Also, her writing was taking a turn. An *off*-turn, I thought, but she defended herself with surprising calm. In the beginning she had responded to my criticism; now she seemed to be going off on her own, and I felt it was due to his brainwashing—his 118-pound theorizing, his disparaging remarks about so-called historical novels.

I often heard Severin tell his wrestlers, "If you can't get off the bottom, you can't win." But that's another story.

I remember once when the four of us stayed overnight at the Winters' —all the children, too. We hauled mattresses into the TV room and parked the children there to be mesmerized by various *Late Show* horrors; they ate potato chips all night. In the morning, we couldn't find Severin. I was alone in one of the children's rooms; I'd crawled off from someone's bed to sleep by myself.

We looked and looked. Finally Edith discovered Severin in the TV room, all four children sleeping huddled round him, wedged against him, sprawled on top of him. He had appeared there in the early dawn hours when some *Late Show* ghoul had convinced my youngest son of another reality, and his howls had convinced the other children. Severin had staggered away from one of the warm women, grabbing the nearest garment handy, and had fallen among them and promised not to leave until daylight. The garment was Edith's mauve dressing gown, a sheer, flowered, ankle-length thing. Edith called us all to come see. The groggy children were slowly waking; they curled and snuggled against him as if he were a large pillow or friendly dog—and Severin Winter lay among them in Edith's gown, looking like a transvestite weight lifter dropped through the roof of an elementary school like a benign bomb.

We drove our sons home, Utch wearing Edith's long wrap-around skirt because she'd been unable to find her own.

"I'm sure it'll turn up," I said.

"I remember where I took it off," Utch said, "but it's not there."

I drove with my hand on Utch's leg, on Edith's skirt. Everywhere, comparisons pleased me! But that was another time.

We returned from Cape Cod in a flood of headlights of other weekenders bathing our faces. Edith and I were in the rear seat; under my shirt, her fingers were cool against my stomach. There was a comfortable noise, tire-hum and engine-drone, so that I could speak to her in a normal voice without Utch and Severin hearing. Not that there was anything I wanted to say which wouldn't have been suitable for them to hear; the point is, it was intimate, riding at night that way. The impersonal quality of the flickering headlights illuminating us and leaving us in darkness made me feel isolated, overlooked, special. In the front seat, Utch and Severin sat chastely apart—more due to the design of his car than by choice, I was sure; it had bucket seats. Also, Severin insisted that everyone wear seat belts. In back, Edith and I had slipped ours off so that we could sit closer together; he must have known. I could hear the singsong tones of his voice, occasionally rising above the engine, the tires, and my own voice, but when I strained to listen to him, I realized he was speaking German. A story? Another tale of Old Vienna? What did they talk about?

"Nothing," Utch told me once. I thought she sounded bitter. "Whatever Severin and I have in common is your idea. If you met another American when you were living, say, in Vienna, and the other American was from Cambridge, Massachusetts, would you assume you'd have much more in common than the English language and some regional characteristics?" Whew. Ask a simple question, receive a speech.

But I saw our bedroom after he left it; I saw my wife after he left her. I have seen their communication in the twin apple cores, empty bottles, bitten hunks of cheese and bread, the stems stripped of grapes, the sheets knotted like a great balled fist which I imagine pounding the mattress askew! I have found pillows in distant corners of the room, and once I found the frail chair I usually throw my pants on stuffed upside down in the laundry hamper. On each of the chair legs dangled a shoe (my shoes), so that it resembled a four-legged creature with human feet, perhaps murdered violently and inverted to bleed among our dirty clothes.

"It looks like you two have some rapport," I said to Utch.

She laughed. "I think," she said, giving me a soft poke on the nose, "that you should think what you want to think"—interrupted by a gentle punch on the arm—"because you *will* anyway." She had never indulged in those damn locker-room physicalities, those chin-chucks and rib-pokes and ear-cuffs, until she met him.

Past Boston the traffic thinned out, and we were driving for the most part in darkness. I stopped talking. Severin's German was music. I could tell we were both listening, though Edith never understood the language any better than I did. Utch wasn't answering; he was just going on and on. I couldn't remember when he had turned the radio off (to listen to what I was saying to Edith? to make us listen to him?), but Edith asked him to turn it back on. She had to lean forward to make him hear, and she kissed the back of his neck.

"Put your seat belt on," he told her.

"Can we have some music back here?" Edith asked, ignoring him.

"No," he said. "Not unless you put your seat belt on."

Utch did not turn in her seat.

After a while, Severin turned the radio on; Edith had waited as if she knew he would, but she didn't settle back against me until the music was playing. She didn't put her seat belt on. Severin stopped talking at last. I touched Edith's breasts very softly, I pinched her nipples; I was trying to make her laugh, but she sat stiffly against me as if she were still waiting for the radio. The music was terrible and the station wasn't coming in well. Finally Utch fixed it. She had to take her seat belt off to fiddle with the dials, and when she started to put it back on, Severin spoke a little German to her. She answered and he argued with her; she left her seat belt off, and he took his off, too. Edith squeezed my hand; she was rigid. Severin spoke again to Utch. *"Nein,"* she said.

We were driving faster. I looked between their shoulders at the lengthening red tongue on the speedometer. When he dimmed the dashboard lights, I felt Edith tense against me and heard Utch quietly say something in German. I found myself thinking of Severin Winter's psychological coaching method, his tunnel-walk in the imposed darkness. I felt we were moving at great speed and at any moment would burst into harsh public light and the roar of a crowd. Utch repeated whatever she'd said in German. I felt Edith was about to reach forward—and do what? Tap his shoulder, kiss his neck, fasten Utch's seat belt?

When Severin Winter spoke again, this time Utch didn't say *"Nein."* She lay across the front bucket seats and put her head in his lap. I saw her soft green sweater flow past the space between the seats like water. The dashboard was black. The speed felt the same. Edith pulled away from me, found her seat belt and clamped it shut around her waist; the metallic joining seemed exaggerated. Did Utch have him in her mouth? She wouldn't! Not with Edith and me right there. But did Severin want us to think that she did?

I couldn't let it go on. But I know the value of obliqueness. I said, "How do you think the children are doing?" Edith smiled; I knew I had him. "Does it bother you to leave them overnight, to be so far away from them? It gets easier as they get older, but don't you worry even so?" The questions were for Severin; Edith, of course, didn't answer me. Utch glided back to her bucket seat and sat up. (Later she said, "I should have rolled down the window and *spat* right after I sat up. That would have fixed you. That's what was on your mind, wasn't it? If that's what you were thinking, I should have let you *really* think it."

I yelled, "Then why'd he ask you to do it?"

"He just asked me to put my head in his lap."

"So what did he want us to think?"

"Think what you want to think," she said.)

Jesus! It serves him right—the way he threw up the children so often to Edith, as if they were sacred objects she didn't adequately worship. His idea of love was always tangled with his idea of guilt.

In the car, he said stonily, "I think the children are all right. But of course I worry about them, I always worry about them." The dashboard glowed again; the red tongue of the speedometer shrank.

"I just asked because I knew that at first you hadn't wanted to go on this weekend—you didn't want to leave the children," I said. "And I wondered, provided they're okay—and I'm sure they are—if you'd feel better about doing this kind of thing more often now? I mean, I think it's good to get away. It's been a great weekend, don't you think?" Edith and Utch didn't say a word, and Severin must have already known about the new laws—

or his new version of the same old laws that he would lay down to Edith as soon as they were alone. He must have been already rehearsing it. That he didn't want her spending time with me unless he was spending equal time with Utch simultaneously. And that we would always arrange ahead of time —so that he could be "prepared" for it (he didn't like surprises). And that being away from the children for such an extended time wasn't an experience he cared to repeat. Without the children we lacked a certain perspective, as he liked to call it. But what was he afraid of? Oh, I know: the children. But what *else?*

He drove Edith from Vienna to Greece in a 1954 Zorn-Witwer, crossing the Yugoslavian border at Jerzersko because, he told her, the name of the place appealed to him and he wanted to see it. No other reason; I've looked at a map, and Jerzersko certainly isn't the best place to cross if you're en route to Greece. The point is, he didn't always need to plan out everything in advance. When they went to Greece, they just went.

I have tried to visualize them as young lovers, and, of course, Edith has told me a lot about their romance, but Winter's car eludes me. A 1954 Zorn-Witwer? Edith said the gearshift slid in and out of the dashboard like a plumber's helper. I've never heard of such a thing. There were places where the floor was rusted away and you could see the road running beneath you. It was some sort of primitive convertible; it had a roll-back canvas roof which leaked. The last year the car was ever made was 1954. Severin has told me that Zorn was a military manufacturing company which turned to farm and road construction machinery after the war. Witwer, he claims, was a failed motorcycle firm. They made unicycles on the side, no doubt. Can anyone believe anyone else? Who the hell ever heard of a Zorn-Witwer? Edith knew nothing about cars. Severin Winter went too far; they drove to Greece in some mythical car.

The weather grew warmer. Winter had a nose for water; he knew where to turn off the main road and find a lake. He found villages the instant they were hungry. When they got to talking about folk art, he would find them a room with an engraved wardrobe and a great feather bed—one with farm animals embroidered on the quilts and pillowcases. In a tiny pension in Thrace, he showed Edith a rare folk toilet: the flush handle was a perfectly carved penis.

They discovered sex in the cradle of democracy. They kept track of the different beds. For a while, Edith favored the bed in Ljubljana, but Severin liked the one in Piraeus—it was so warm there, and they were in sight and sound of the harbor; all night they heard the boats flapping on the water "like thighs slapping together," Severin told Utch. In the morning a fish market opened below their window. Edith lay in bed and heard the fish knives hacking and slitting, the bartering tongues. The suction sound of removing the innards seemed magnified; the garrulous haggle rose and fell. She knew the fishmongers liked to behead a fish at the exact moment they were making a point about the price. *Thok!* for emphasis. After that, who could argue?

They made love in the morning, sometimes twice, before getting up. They went to bed soon after the evening meal, and if making love made them too wide-awake, which it often did, they would get up, go out again and eat another supper. Then they'd make love again. In the country, they'd often "find some water" in the middle of the day. Apparently that was a euphemism they liked.

Edith's first short story was a thinly disguised version of leaving Piraeus for a drive in the country. (This was before they went island-hopping.)

The story begins with the fish market in Piraeus.

I knew when I first heard them cutting the fish that they'd be sold out and gone by the time I'd see the cobblestones. I made love in the morning and got up late. The fishmongers had packed up, but the hotel's man with the hose hadn't rinsed the cobblestones, which were wet with fish-blood and slime, phosphorescent with scales, flecked blue with intestines. It wouldn't do, our head waiter told us, to leave the mess until evening when potential guests might be alarmed at the gore and think that this slop was the remains of some unfortunate suicide from the fourth floor, or the ritual slaying of a wronged lover caught and ripped apart at the scene of his indiscretion.

I was discreet myself and made him drive me into the country, because though our stone room was cool in the daytime, the hotel maids would listen outside our door. At night and in the morning it was fine to use the room, but by midday we were on the road. It was apparently an underpowered car. We were often stuck behind a slow-moving vehicle—even horse-drawn carts—because it didn't have the necessary kick. The roads were curvy, his arms and the back of his neck were very brown. We were driving toward the ferry crossing at Patras. Where there was a ferry, we knew there was water, and we were looking for water. Though I read somewhere that a girl was rushed to the hospital with severe cramps from making love underwater—an air bubble in one of her Fallopian tubes. Is that even possible? I didn't believe it.

It seemed that wherever we drove in Greece, we drove into the sun. He had his shirt off, I had unbuttoned my blouse and rolled it up under my breasts and tied it in a knot. My breasts were small but they stayed up; my stomach was very brown. It was an old-fashioned, unslanted, glass windshield, which magnified everything a little. In the back, on the floor behind my seat where there was some shade, we kept a watermelon cool in a bucket of water which had been icy cold when we'd filled it; it was turning tepid now. I would slice pieces of watermelon in my lap; the melon was cool and wet and felt lovely against my stomach. I sprinkled water on his shoulders as if I were baptizing him. It was watermelon country; in the villages and on the roadside stands, melons and eggplants competed. He said the watermelons were the winning size, but the eggplants won the color prize.

In an unappealing, dry-looking landscape with short hills spiked with olive trees, we discussed how far away the sea was, and whether we would smell it before we saw it, when we came up on a large, swaying truck full of watermelons. We had to slow down fast. In the back of the truck a teenage Greek boy sat on a mound of melons with a grin on his face which suggested that his mental age was four. From his vantage point, my breasts and bare belly must have looked wonderful to him, and when we pulled out to pass, he didn't want to lose his view. He leaped up and poised an enormous melon over his head; if our wretched car tried to pass, the boy's demented grin implied we would regret it.

For thirty-four kilometers, until the ferry at Patras, that boy on the pile of watermelons sat displaying himself to me. There was nothing we could do. Except for his disturbed face, he was interesting to look at. I sliced more watermelon. We talked about stopping and letting the truck pull ahead, but I confessed that I wanted to see what the boy would do.

Just before the road widened to four lanes to handle the ferry traffic, the boy fell moaning on his back on the watermelon pile and lay writhing among the green globes until he ejaculated into the air. His stuff struck our rigid windshield like bird-dribble, a thick *whap!* against the glass on the passenger side. My head snapped back as if I'd been slapped.

Then the road widened, the road ahead was free, and we pulled out to pass. The boy didn't even try to threaten us; he slumped sulkishly on his pile of melons and didn't even bother to watch us pass. I had expected him at least to spit. I turned my head and saw the truck's driver: an old man with the same shocking face as the boy's, grinning obscenely at me, twisting in the driver's seat, trying to raise his lap to window level to show me *his!*

"Like father, like son," I said, but *my* driver's arms were hard-flexed, his fingers white around the steering wheel, his face withdrawn, as if he'd suddenly seen such an appalling hunger in the world that he felt ashamed to reflect it.

He didn't feel like swimming. For something to do, we took the ferry back and forth across the Gulf of Corinth, standing on deck together, leaning over the rail, imagining history and civilization. I told him it excited me, but he said he felt as alone at that moment as he felt whenever *he* masturbated. I have never understood why men have such trouble with that.

For the first time in my life, I was shocked at myself. I knew I could make love *anywhere*. We glided back and forth across the Gulf of Corinth. My desire was excruciating; I touched him as much as he would let me and whispered that when we got back to the hotel, I would make him come before he was inside me.

Eventually, of course, he snapped out of it. He came around.

I'll bet! He always did. He used to sulk when the four of us were together, trying to make Edith and me feel guilty, trying to provoke Utch into calling a halt to the whole thing. Utch would beg him to tell her what he wanted. All right, she'd tell him sometimes, we'll stop if that's what you want, but you have to *say* something. But he'd be a stone and she knew what she'd have to do to bring him out of it. Of course; that's what he *wanted* her to do! Why didn't she see? I don't know how he managed to make self-pity so alluring.

"When he's in one of his moods," Utch said, "the only thing I can do is fuck him out of it."

I complained to Edith, but she said, "What's wrong with that? You can't worry about what's right until you know what works." But sex is only a temporary cure.

We were an hour from home, both of the women asleep, when Severin stopped because he had to pee. Utch woke up when he got out and dashed into the short dark trees clumped along the roadside like soldiers. We were alone on the road now; it was as if no one else was returning from a weekend, as if around here they didn't take weekends off. I don't know exactly where we were.

When Utch woke up, I asked her to move in back with Edith; I wanted to talk with Severin. I sat quietly beside him until I was sure both Edith and Utch were asleep. Every town had a church, every church a lighted steeple. Finally I said, "I think you're calling all the shots. I think everything's on your terms. But there are four of us."

"Oh, is that *you* there?" he said. "I thought Utch's voice had changed."

Ha-ha. "We see each other as if we're registered for courses—same time, same place. That's *your* idea. If that's how you want it, that's fine for you, but a little of it should be on our terms, too, don't you think?"

"I have a recurring dream," he said. "You want to hear it?"

Oh, suffering shit, I thought, but I said, "Sure, Severin, go ahead." I know that in sexual matters it is difficult to say things directly.

"It's about my children," he said. I had heard him talk about them a hundred times, almost always in wrestling terms; he called them his weakness, his imbalance, his blind side, his loophole, the flaw in his footwork, the mistakes he would always repeat and repeat, his one faulty move. Yet he could not imagine not having children. He said they were his substitute for an adventurous, explorative life. With children his life would always be dangerous; he was grateful for that, the perverse bastard! He said his love for Edith was almost rational (a matter of definition, I suppose), but that there was nothing reasonable about the way he loved his children. He said that people who didn't have children were naïve about the control they had over their lives. They always thought they were in control, or that they could be.

I complained about how much "control" meant to him; I argued that people without children simply found other things to lose control over. "In fact," I said, "I think human beings find that control is more often a burden than not. If you can give up your control to someone or something, you're better off."

I have seen how his wrestlers look at their opponents with a cold, analytical scrutiny, a dead eye. Severin Winter gave me such a look. Though he couldn't have been oblivious to the ridiculousness of his controlled behavior, he cherished the ideal.

"God save us from idealists, from all true believers," Edith said once.

God save us from Severin Winter! I thought.

His dream, as he called it, was not entirely fiction. Over and over again, he was stuck behind the watermelon truck, unable to pass, his life controlled and manipulated by the willful, masturbating Greek on the melon pile— threatening him, forever holding him at bay, squirting his vile seed and more and more of his kind into the air, on his windshield, everywhere— until the mindless depravity of it forced Severin in his dream to pull out to pass. But the watermelons the boy held over the passing car would suddenly become Severin's children, and—too late to meekly fall back in the lane behind the truck—Severin Winter would see his children hurled down on him and splattered against the windshield.

"How's that for a dream?" he asked.

How's that for a loophole? I thought. How's that for a flaw in the footwork? How's that for a faulty move?

"God save us all," I muttered. He had turned off the dashboard lights again, but I knew he was laughing. What I wanted to say was, Spare me the allegory, just stick to the facts. Who's controlling *this?* All of us or just you?

The car stopped; we were home.

"I'd give you your choice of whom you'd like to remove from the back seat," Severin said, "but there's the awkwardness with the baby-sitter, and I'm anxious to see the children."

"We've really got to sit down and talk sometime," I said.

"Sure, anytime," he told me.

I crawled in back to shake Utch, but she was awake. I saw at once that she'd been awake for all our talk; she looked frightened. I nudged Edith gently as I backed out of the seat and kissed her hair above her ear, but she slept soundly.

When Utch went up to Severin, he shook her hand—his idea of understatement? Utch wanted to be kissed. He said, "Get a good night's sleep. We can sort out all the stuff later."

I knew that our belongings intermingling—Edith's clothes in my suitcase, Utch leaving her gloves at their house—really pissed him off. One morning, Edith told me, he opened his drawer and pulled out a pair of my underpants. "These aren't mine," he said indignantly.

"I just pick up what I find lying around," Edith said cheerfully.

"They're *his!*" he roared. "Can't he keep track of his own fucking underpants? Does he have to leave his goddamn laundry around?"

He stretched my underpants, snapping the waistband out wide enough to contain us both, then wadded them into a ball and kicked them into a corner. "They like to leave their things behind so that they'll have an excuse to come back. She does it too," he muttered.

To Edith, he simply wasn't making any sense. She brought back the underpants—to Utch—that morning. She and Utch thought it was very funny.

It wasn't long afterward that I pulled on what must have been the same pair. Something was wrong; the crotch had been slit through with a razor, so that it was like wearing an absurdly short skirt. One was left free to flap, so to speak.

"Utch?" I said. "What happened to my pants?" She told me that they were the ones Edith had brought back. Later, I asked Edith if she had cut them—perhaps as a joke? But she hadn't, of course. It was no joke; it was *him*. He was not one to be subtle with his symbols.

"Damn him!" I yelled to Utch. "What's he want? If he wants to stop it, why doesn't he say so? If he's suffering so goddamn much, why does he go on with it? Does he like being a martyr?"

"Please," Utch said softly. "If anyone's going to stop it, we know it's going to be him."

"He's teasing us," I said. "And he's testing Edith and me—that's it. He's so jealous that he assumes that we *can't* stop it, so he's trying to see how much we'll take. Maybe if Edith and I call it off, he'll see that nobody's going to hurt anybody else. Then he'll feel better about it and want it again."

But Utch shook her head. "No, please don't do anything," she said. "Just leave him alone, just let him have things his way."

"His way!" I screamed. "You don't like his way either—I know you don't."

"That's true," she said. "But it's better than no way at all."

"I wonder," I said. "I think Edith and I should say that we'll stop it right now, and maybe that will convince him."

"Please," Utch said. She was about to cry. "Then he *might* stop it," she said and burst into tears.

I was frightened for her. I hugged her and stroked her hair, but she went on sobbing. "Utch?" I asked. I didn't recognize my own voice. "Utch, don't you think you could stop it, if you had to? Don't you?"

She squeezed me; she pressed her face against my stomach and wriggled in my lap. "No," she whispered. "I don't think I can. I don't think I could stand it if it were over."

"Well, if we *had* to," I said, "of course you could, Utch." But she said nothing and went on crying; I held her until she fell asleep. All along I'd thought that it was Edith and I who had the relationship which threatened Severin, though not Utch. All along I'd felt that Severin was disgruntled because he felt everything was unequal, that Edith and I shared too much—the implication being that he and Utch had too little. So what was this?

Weeks before, at a large and public party, I could sense that Severin was angered by the attention Utch was giving him, and by the attention Edith and I were giving each other—though we were always far more discreet than they were. Utch, a little drunk, was hanging on Severin, asking him to dance and making him uncomfortable. Much later that evening, when he came home and woke up Edith and me, he said as I was leaving, "Take

care of your wife." I was irritated by the imperious tone in his voice and
went home without saying a word. I thought he meant that I shouldn't let
her drink so much, or that she'd confided in him about some act of neglect.
But when I confronted Utch with it, she shook her head and said, "I can't
imagine what he's talking about."

Now I wondered. Was he warning me of the depth of Utch's feelings for
him? His vanity knew no bounds!

It was late at night when I carried Utch to bed and left her to sleep in
her clothes; I knew I'd wake her if I undressed her. I called Edith. I didn't
do it often, but we had a signal. I dialed, then hung up after only half a ring,
waited and dialed again. If she was awake and heard the first ring, she'd
be waiting to snatch the phone up immediately the next time. If the ringing
persisted even for a whole tone, I'd know she was asleep or couldn't talk,
and would hang up. Severin always slept through it.

When she answered now, she said, "What is it?" She sounded cross.

"I was just thinking of you."

"Well, I'm tired," she said. Had they been arguing?

"I'm worried," I confessed.

"We'll talk later," Edith said.

"Is he awake?"

"No. What is it?"

"If he wants to stop the whole thing," I said, "why doesn't he?"

There was no answer. "Edith?" I said.

"Yes?" she said, but she wasn't going to answer my question.

"Does he want to stop?" I asked. "And if he does—and, Jesus, he *acts*
as if he does—then why doesn't he?"

"I've offered to stop," she told me. I knew this was true, but it always
hurt me a little to hear it.

"But he doesn't take you up on the offer," I said.

"No."

"Why?"

"He must like it," she said, but even without her face in front of me, I
knew when she was lying.

"He has a strange way of liking things," I said.

"He thinks I have leverage on him," she said.

"Leverage?"

"He thinks he owes me something."

"You never told me," I said. I didn't like the sound of leverage, of debts
owed, at all. It seemed an important omission, and I had always believed
Edith told me everything important for lovers to know.

"No, I never have told you," she admitted. By her tone, she wasn't about
to begin, either.

"Don't you think I should know about this?" I asked.

"There are lots of things you believe in not telling," she said, "and I've always thought that an attractive philosophy. Severin believes you tell wives and lovers everything, but you don't believe that, so why should I?"

"I tell important things," I said.

"Do you?"

"Edith—"

"Ask Utch," Edith said.

"Utch?" I said. "What does Utch know about it?"

"Severin tells everything," Edith said.

"I love you."

"Don't worry," she said. "Whatever happens, everything will be all right."

This wasn't what I wanted to hear. She seemed resigned to something I didn't know anything about.

"Goodnight," I said. She hung up.

I tried to wake Utch, but she lay in bed as hard and round and heavy as a watermelon. I felt like biting her. I kissed her all over, but she just smiled. Leverage? Another wrestling term. I didn't like its application to couples.

In the morning I asked Utch what Edith had on Severin, or what he *thought* she had on him.

"If Edith felt good about it," Utch said, "she'd have told you herself."

"But you know. I want to know too."

"It hasn't been any help to me," Utch said. "Severin wanted me to know; if he'd wanted you to know, he'd have told you. And if Edith wanted you to know, she'd tell you."

"If she didn't want me to know," I argued, "she wouldn't have told me I could find out from you."

"Well, you *can't,*" Utch said. "I promised Severin I'd never tell. Go work on Edith for her version." She rolled away; I knew her position—knees drawn up, elbows in, hair hiding her face. "Look," she said; I knew what was coming. "We're playing by your rules. You're the one who says, 'If you see someone else, I don't want to know. If I see someone else, you don't have to know.' Right?"

"Right," I said. I pushed my face into her hair. "And I think I know that in all these years there hasn't been anyone else for you, right?"

"Don't ask," she said. She was bluffing, I was sure. "And I think I know that there have been a few for you," she added.

"Right," I said.

"I wasn't asking."

"Well, I *am* asking, Utch."

"You're changing the rules," she said. "I think you ought to give a little advance notice when you change the rules." She backed her hips into me and drew my hand between her thighs. "One rule is, Take it when it's offered."

She was already wet; she rubbed herself against my hand. "Which one of us are you thinking of?" I asked her. Was that cruel?

But she said, "All of you," and laughed. "Two and three and four at a time," she said. I was in her mouth very quickly and she covered my ears with her thighs. Utch tasted like nutmeg, like vanilla, like an avocado; she was careful with her teeth. Was it only with me that Edith lacked control in this position? Did Severin really say to her, "You've both got quite the setup. Utch and I are supposed to keep each other occupied while you have a perfect guiltless affair. It wouldn't do to have Utch and me feeling useless and pathetic, would it?" How could he regard Utch that way? She tasted sweeter than roast lamb, like the pan juices; she had a mouth large enough for illusions.

I asked her, "Do you feel manipulated? Is *that* what Severin feels? And I *know* you never had another lover before Severin, right?"

She pushed herself firmer against me. "I never asked you about Sally Frotsch," she said, "though you never changed your mind overnight about a baby-sitter before." I was in and out of her mouth so her sentences were short. I was amazed at what she knew. "Or that Gretchen What's-her-name? An independent study in *what?*" I couldn't believe it. "And that poor divorced Mrs. Stewart. I never knew you were so talented fixing hot-water heaters." She put me neatly back in her mouth and kept me there.

Did she know about the others? Not that there were many, and they were never serious. I couldn't think of a time when it seemed likely that she'd had a lover; there'd never been a man I was suspicious of. But who could be sure? At least I knew that until me, Edith had never been involved. I reached into Utch's mouth to ask her, but she rang my ears with her thighs. What her thighs said was, "Better go ask Edith again." I resisted, but her rhythm made it hard to hold back. And Severin? Surely that moral absolutist could never have had a dalliance before he and Utch went to the mat together.

"Ask Utch," Edith had said. I was trying. When I came, her mouth turned as soft as a flower with the petals pushed back. But though I'd felt her on the edge at least twice, I knew that she hadn't come herself. "It's all right," she whispered. "I'll get mine later." From him or me? I wondered. I went to the bathroom and drank three glasses of water.

When I came back to the bedroom, she was helping herself to get there. Occasionally she got overstimulated and could only finish by herself. It was delicate because sometimes I could help her, but other times I got in the way. It was a matter of not getting too involved. I lay down beside her but didn't touch her. I watched her touching herself, her eyes shut tightly, her concentration a marvel. Sometimes if I touched her then, it would be just what she needed; other times, it would destroy it. I recognized her rhythm; I knew she was close. Her breathing skipped, then picked up; her lips made a familiar circular motion. Sometimes a word would push her over; any word would do; it was the sound of my voice which mattered. But when I looked at her squint-shut eyes and her clenched face, I suddenly knew that I had no idea which one of us she was seeing—or if it was either of us! I wanted to shout at her, "Is it him or me?" but I knew that would distract her. And then she was coming, her voice starting in her throat and reaching deeper, her whole diaphragm moving like a lion's way of roaring. She slowed her rhythm, as if drawing out each note of a groan. She was coming and nothing would stop it; I could do anything—scream, bite, even slide into her. It was downhill now, but I did nothing. I watched her face for some clue. I listened for his name—or mine, or someone else's.

But what she said wasn't even in English. *"Noch eins!"* she cried. Twisting, grinding into the bed. *"Noch eins!"*

Even I could understand it; I'd been in enough bars to know it. It's what you say when your beer's finished and you want another. *"Noch eins!"* you holler, and the waiter brings you "one more."

Utch lay relaxed with one hand still touching herself and the other to her lips. She was tasting herself, I knew; she liked herself, she had told me. In that pose she looked like Kurt Winter's drawing of Katrina Marek.

We historical novelists are frequently struck by meaningless coincidences, but I wondered if I knew Utch at all—and whether the four of us were wise to want to find out more about each other than we already knew.

I lay beside my wife who wanted one more. She looked content to me.

7

___

Carnival's Quarrel with Lent

Then one night Severin took Utch to the wrestling room. Throughout dinner we had all noticed that he was not as morose as usual—not as caustic, not as consciously trying to make us feel guilty for his great unnamed *Schmerz*. When he helped Utch into her coat, he winked at Edith. I could see she was surprised. She was used to getting a martyred look from him—that son-of-a-bitch, as if he were saying, "Well, here I go, off to do my duty." He made it appear that sex with Utch was just another good husband's task, as if he were doing us all a favor.

But on this night he touched Utch a lot at dinner and spoke German quietly to her. Both Edith and I were struck by how attentive he was; I noticed Edith watched them more than usual. Was he trying to make her jealous? She'd told him repeatedly that she wasn't in the least jealous. "Of course you're not," he said. "It's a perfect setup. You've got yourself a lover of your choice, and you've placated me with a poor cowlike creature whom you've no need to be jealous of—and you know it." But Utch wasn't a "poor cowlike creature." That swinish, snobbish, self-important *cuntsman!* I've seen my bedroom after he left it; there was little evidence of condescension there.

So—one night—he was cordial, devilish, comically lewd. He goosed Edith goodnight, and when he was helping her into her coat, he cupped Utch's breasts.

"I think he's coming around," I told Edith after they'd left. She watched their headlights run across the ceiling of the living room, but said nothing. "Don't you see what he's doing?" I persisted. "He's trying to make you jealous. He's trying to induce *his* reaction in you."

She shook her head. "He's not acting naturally," she said. "He hasn't been like himself since the whole thing began."

I tried to reassure her. "I think he's adjusting to it. He's letting himself relax more with Utch." Edith shut her eyes; she didn't believe me, but she wouldn't elaborate. "Well, anything's better than having him mooning around," I said, "waiting for one of us to ask him 'What's wrong?' so that he can say 'Nothing.' " Edith did not look convinced.

We took our love shower and went to bed, but she was restless. She wanted to call my house and ask Severin something, but she wouldn't tell me what. I argued against it. We might catch them in the middle of something, and he might think the phone call was intentionally timed—

"Bunk," Edith said; she was cross with me.

Severin came back later than usual. I'd gotten out of bed to pee and when I came back I found that he'd taken my place. He was giggling, lying in bed next to Edith with all his clothes on. I had the feeling he'd been waiting outside the door for me to get up, just so he could pull this stunt. He undressed under the covers, churning up the bed, disturbing Edith, who woke up, startled, stared at us both, shook her head and rolled over.

"Well, you're in high spirits," I said; it was awkward getting dressed in front of him, but he obviously enjoyed it.

"Take the old ashtray when you go, okay?" he asked.

I decided to keep his game going; I said, "I've been meaning to speak to you about the apple cores, Severin. I don't mind the crumbs in bed, really, but the apple cores and cheese rinds are a bit much."

He laughed. "Well, you won't find a mess tonight," he said. "We've been as neat as a pin." His teeth, I swear, glowed in the dark. I wanted to kiss Edith goodnight. Was she asleep? Was she angry? I blew out the candle on the dresser.

"Blah-*urf!*" Edith said, as if he'd touched her suddenly.

"Goodnight, Edith," I said in the dark. His hand reached out and caught my wrist as I passed their bed. His grip frightened me; it didn't hurt, but I knew that it could hold on all day. Maybe it was just an affectionate goodnight grasp. "Goodnight, Severin," I said. He laughed and let me go.

I was chilled in the car. I had a momentary vision, terrible and clear, of coming home and finding Utch murdered in our bed, her limbs twisted and tied into some elaborate wrestler's knot; the rest of the house would be "neat as a pin."

I shouldered open the door and found her sitting at the kitchen table, fully dressed, drinking tea and picking at the remains of an impressive-looking breakfast. It was almost dawn. She smiled when I came in; she looked sleepy but happy. "What's the matter?" she asked.

"I thought something might be the matter with *you.*"

She laughed. They certainly had a bounty of giggles and chuckles tonight, I thought.

"What have you been doing?" I asked, surprised to see her dressed. When I opened the bedroom door, the bed was cleanly made, as tucked-in as at noontime, the pillows undented.

"We went to the wrestling room," Utch said. She burst out laughing and blushed. Then she told me.

Severin had parked the car at the rear of the new gym and blinked the headlights on and off, on and off. When a watchman came out of the maintenance entrance, Severin called out, "It's me, Harvey. I'm going up to the room tonight."

"Okay, Coach," the watchman said. Utch realized that this was not the first time he'd done this.

It was midnight when he led her through the dark corridors; he knew every turn. They undressed in the locker room. Only Utch shivered. They dressed in clean wrestling robes, the crimson and white ones with the ominous hood. Like monks engaged in some midnight rite, they walked through the fabulous tunnel; he kissed her; he felt her under her robe.

In the blackness of the tunnel, Severin never even brushed a wall. Utch felt his arm reach out for the door just as they reached it. Moonlight glazed the mud and cinder floor of the old cage and the skylight dome was etched with dark vines of ivy. The old board track shrieked when they walked around it. The pigeons under the eaves were disturbed and fretted like grandmothers. Somewhere a high-jump bar clanged; she froze, but he kept walking smoothly, in rhythm. Severin Winter was familiar with that place at night.

Inside the wrestling room, the moonlight made the mats ripple like a blood-colored pond. Utch said she was excited, but a little frightened. He took off her robe; the mats were a perfect body temperature against her skin. They "rolled around," she said; they "loosened up." She tried some yoga positions; he showed her some stretching exercises. The thermostat kept the room warm constantly, and soon they were both sweating. Utch said she never felt so limber. Then Severin moved to the ghostly white rim of the starting circle on the center mat, his bare toes lined up behind the line. He waited for her; he was not smiling. Utch said she felt uncertain, but she trusted him. She stood across the circle from him and breathed deeply; she let her head loll, stretching her neck. His hands were restless against his moonlit thighs. She shimmied her fingers the way Tyrone Williams did before the whistle.

"Wie geht's?" asked Severin in his tunnel voice.

"Gut," Utch said—huskily but loudly.

Now Severin heard some whistle in his head, and he started across the circle toward her—not rushing, not coming at her directly. Again she felt a little fear, but when his hand shot out and cupped the back of her neck, she came alive; she dove in under his chest and hit him at the knees, driving hard. He glided away, then floated toward her again; she swiped at his head —a mistake, she knew—and he had her. He dropped in so deeply under her that she was surprised; he hit her hard but cleanly; nothing hurt. He had her so snugly that nothing moved. The round weight of his shoulder was in her crotch, his arm snaked through her legs, the palm of his hand lay flat against her spine. She reached back to break her fall and discovered she was already down on the mat; she squirmed off her back (he let her) and bucked back into him, got up to her knees and tried to stand. He rode her closer than a coat. He was the opposite of rough; he made her feel that she had two bodies which moved in time with each other. There was no strain, but his weight wore her down. Her arms grew heavy lifting his arms; her back dipped under the weight of his chest. She let her head droop and felt his mouth on her neck. She sank back onto the mat. Their bodies glistened —even seemed phosphorescent—in the moonlight. The mat gave off heat. Their bodies slid. Bending was never easier. Slickness was everywhere, but her heels found a way to grip the mat. Over his snug shoulder she saw the moon sailing through a maze of vines. Either the pigeons were talking excitedly or she was failing to recognize her own voice; she swore she felt their wingbeat lifting her lightly off the mat. She was coming, she came, she was waiting for him; when he came, she expected the hand of an invisible referee to smack the mat hard and flat, indicating a fall. Instead there was a crushing weight, a foreign silence; the great fans for the blow-heaters whirred on, a sound too constant to be called a noise. They rolled apart, but their fingers touched. She doesn't remember who started laughing first when he got a towel and wiped up what they'd spilled on the mat. He flipped the towel back into the corner, where Utch said she imagined it reproducing towels all night. The next day, a great stack of towels would be towering there to greet the shocked wrestlers.

Their laughter caromed around the old board track; it echoed in the caverns under the swimming pool. They swam; they took a sauna; they swam again. I imagine them conquering new territory, leaving prints and spores behind like dogs.

"Christ, did you *talk?*" I asked. Utch smiled. I couldn't imagine how many eggs they'd eaten; the sink seemed full of shells.

"*Ja,* we talked a little."

"What about?"

"He kept asking me how I was: '*Wie geht's? Wie geht's?*' And I kept telling him: '*Gut! Gut!*' "

How good? I wanted to ask, as sarcastic as a stone, but Utch's placidity among the toast crusts and yolk stains made me mute.

Over our kitchen table is a print of Pieter Bruegel's *The Fight Between Carnival and Lent;* I lost myself in an image from years before. I imposed myself on Bruegel's painting. I walked into his cosmos; I shrank, put on wooden clogs, browsed through the old Netherlandish town.

"Are you all right?" Utch asked, but it was 1559; I smelled the waffles baking (it was almost Ash Wednesday; Shrovetide customs were everywhere). I wriggled in my leggings. My codpiece itched.

In the great painting, I nudge against droves of the subservient masses, dark and cloaked. They are milling about the church, but their devotion is dull. Women are selling fish. Lent and her followers prepare for a joust— a gaunt woman drawn into battle by a nun and a monk. Astraddle a barrel, probably sour from ale, a fat representative of Carnival thrusts forward a suckling pig on a skewer; his masked revelers surround him, comic and lewd with their instruments. Everywhere, children tease or ignore them; everywhere, cripples are ignored. The inn is busier than the church. I watch a performance of the comedy "The Dirty Bride." I imagine I am touched— tweaked under my breechclout—but nearly every woman's smile is randy. I push on, I am beseeched, I have difficulty not stepping on the maimed and deformed—the beggars, the blind, the dwarfed, humped, bent and bizarre. Bodies take up every available space. A woman with a pilgrim's emblem on her hat pleads to me: "Kind sir, regard this legless, stump-armed thing before me." Its upturned mouth is a hole.

From the twentieth century, Utch calls to me: "Are you coming to bed?"

How should I know? I'm just playing my life by ear. But in the painting fantasy I always recognize myself: I am the well-dressed one. A well-to-do burgher? Possibly a patrician? I have never identified my station exactly. I am in a black tunic, fur-lined, expensive; my hair is cut like a scholar's; a rich purse hangs at my chest, a richly bound prayer book protrudes from my pocket; my cap is soft leather. I pass a blind man, but he is more than blind; appallingly, he is without eyes! His face is unfinished—the cruel intention of the painter: where the sockets should be, pale, translucent scar tissue stretches over slight indentations. Without looking at him, I give him a coin. A numbing smile, by nuns in unison, follows me. Am I a big tipper?

Do they desire something from me? I am pursued, or perhaps simply followed, by a boy or a dwarf carrying what appears to be either an easel or a piano stool. For *me?* Am I a painter? Will I sit down somewhere to play? Actually, I'm the only one in the painting who clearly isn't a peasant, the only one who has a servant. The item my servant carries looks like one of those golf seats, but it is probably my church stool. Others—peasants lugging crude country furniture—are also bringing their own seats to church; only I have a servant to carry mine. I think I must be a lawyer, or maybe the mayor.

I have never bothered to find out. I am more pleased guessing at my identity and purpose. I am moving from the church toward the inn; this seems wise. Once I made up a story of my day in the old Netherlandish square. It was to be my second historical novel, but I never followed through. I went little further than to approach my father for a loan. That was in 1963. I had finished with my higher education and was a young, available Ph.D. who did not want to be available just yet. I wanted to go to Vienna, see the original Bruegel, discover my main character's role and choose my supporting cast from among that Shrovetide crowd. The book, based on Bruegel's painting, would have been called *Carnival's Quarrel with Lent.* At one point in the novel, my characters would all come together and be doing just what they're doing in the painting. I had already selected the well-to-do man with the prayer book in his pocket to be me, to be the narrator of the book.

"I don't know how you come up with such academic and pretentious ideas," my father said.

"I'll look for a teaching job next year," I said. "I'd just like this year off, to get a good start on the book."

"Why don't you forget the book? Wasn't the first one enough?" he asked. "I'd rather finance a vacation—something good for you." I maintained silence; I knew what he thought of historical novels. "Why don't you find out everything about the painting *before* you go all the way to Vienna to see it?" he asked. "You might find out that your leading character is the town tax collector or a Flemish fop! There's available iconography of every painting Pieter Bruegel ever made. Why don't you be *professional,* for Christ's sake, and find out what you're doing before you start doing it?"

He didn't understand; he thought that everything was a thesis project to be accepted or rejected. I'd told him a hundred times that I didn't really care about the history behind everything as much as I cared for what it provoked in me. But he was hopeless, a diehard *factualist* to the end.

He gave me the money; in the end, he always did. "Apparently it's all I have to give you that you'll take," he said. "My God, Vienna!" he added with disgust. "Why not Paris or London or Rome? Take my advice and have a good time before you start taking yourself so seriously. Next thing, you'll get married. Oh God, I can see it: some countess, in name only.

Penniless, but used to the finer things. Her entire family of raving hemophiliacs wants to move from Vienna to New York but can't bear to leave the horses behind.

"Take my advice," my father said from his easy chair. "If you have to knock up anybody, knock up a peasant. They make good wives; they're the cream of womanhood." Books, magazines, notecards, slid about in his lap; my mother stood surprised beside him. I thought of Bruegel's painting and of my father as he might appear in it: scrolls in both hands, sitting legless, as amputated as a beggar, his goblet of bad wine pinched between his stumps.

"You want to make a novel from a sixteenth-century painting!" my father cried. "An education clearly wasted—at least, run amok. Why don't you try the Orient? They make excellent wives."

Shellshocked, I left for Europe. I said goodbye to my mother at the airport (my father refused to drive). "Thank God you have enough money to do what you want to do," she said to me.

"Yes, I do."

"I pray you'll remember your father in happier moods."

"Yes, yes." I tried to remember some.

"Thank God for your education, despite what your father says."

"I do."

"He's not himself lately," my mother said.

"God?" I said, but I knew she meant my father.

"Be serious."

"Yes, yes."

"He reads too much. It depresses him."

"I'll send you pictures of Vienna," I promised. "The prettiest postcards I can find."

"Just tell us the good news," my mother said. "And don't try to write anything on the backs of the postcards. There's never enough room."

"Yes, yes," I said, remembering another thing that depressed my father: people who write on the backs of postcards. "Do they think they're saying anything?" he used to yell.

He gave me a note when I shook hands goodbye with him. I didn't look at it until the plane was descending on Schwechart Airport. Suddenly, in the midst of our downward pitch and roll, the stewardesses played an old recording of Strauss's "Blue Danube." The eerie, gooey music blaring from nowhere startled nearly everyone, and the stewardesses smiled at their little trick. A man beside me went into a rage. *"Aaach!"* he cried to me; he knew I was an American. "I am Viennese," he told me, "and I love Vienna, but I get so *embarrassed* when they play that wretched Strauss. Why don't you break that awful record?" he hollered at the stewardesses, who went on smiling.

The man reminded me of my father, and I remembered the note. As the plane touched down, I read it.

Say hello to Schmaltz for me.
Give my regards to Kitsch City.
Love, Dear Old Dad

And the rest is history. Edith Fuller and I came to Vienna and fell in love with our tour guides. In her case, Severin elected to be her guide, but in mine Utch was more literally employed.

I met her when I went to see the Bruegels in the Kunsthistorisches Museum. I asked for the standard tour in English. I said I was especially interested in the Bruegel rooms, and that I wouldn't mind skipping the Rubens and all that. It was November, stone-gray and Baroque-cold. The tourist season was over; Vienna was turning indoors. A tour guide would be available in a moment; I was told I could have a special Bruegel tour. ("He's one of the favorites.") I felt as if I were waiting in a delicatessen for one of the more popular meats. Everything felt cheap. I remembered what my father had said and wished I had come prepared and could stride through the Bruegel rooms as an authority on the Northern Renaissance. I wondered if I had conceived of an historical novel from the point of view of a tourist. When my guide was introduced, I was struck by her Russian name—and also by the tilt of her nametag perched on her high breast.

"Fräulein Kudashvili?" I said. "Isn't that Russian?"

"Georgian," she said, "but I am an Austrian. I was adopted after the war."

"What's your first name?"

"My name is Utchka," she said. "I am not familiar with Americans."

"Utchka?"

"*Ja,* it's slang. You won't find it in the dictionary."

Nor are there words, I'm sure, for all the things Utch and I did in Vienna those first few weeks of November 1963. Are there words, for example, for the faces of Utch's ex-roommates in her *Studentenheim* on Krügerstrasse? Over a line-up of gleaming sinks, we three shaved each morning in the *Herrenzimmer.* Willy had a goatee which he avoided like his jugular; Heinrich had a mustache no thicker than the artery at his wrist. I watched their razors and whistled. After the third night I spent with Utch, Willy shaved off his goatee, tears in his eyes. After the fourth night, Heinrich emasculated his mustache. Then Willy emptied a can of shaving cream into his curly blond hair and leered over my shoulder as my own razor shakily skimmed my throat. After the first week with Utch, I asked, "These fellows down the hall, the ones I meet in the men's room each morning—you know them?"

"*Ja.* "

"Uh, what were they to you?" I asked.

And Utch would go on and on about her guardian Captain Kudashvili, about Frau Drexa Neff's steam room, about attending the memorial service for Stalin. And every morning while I shaved, Willy and Heinrich took off more hair. It was my second week in the *Studentenheim* when Willy shaved the furry ridge off his stomach and made strong strokes through the blond clump hiding his navel.

"Their demonstrations are getting worse," I told Utch. "I don't think they like me."

So Utch told me about the Benno Blum Gang—especially the man with the hole in his cheek, her last bodyguard. The next morning Heinrich loomed over my shoulder in my mirror, and shaved a quick swath through the dark forest on his chest, slashing a hidden nipple in the process. His blood turned the shaving lather pink; he dabbed it on his eyebrows and grimaced at me.

"I think I'll grow a beard," I said to Utch. "Do you like beards?"

We went to the opera and the zoo; like the opera fans, the animals kept to themselves. She showed me the little streets, the famous Prater, the parks with their neighborhood orchestras, the gardens, Kudashvili's old apartment house, the Soviet embassy. But it was November; it was more fun indoors. Her room at the *Studentenheim* was almost anti-girlish; she was twenty-five, after all, and had inherited no mementos from her mother. She had grown up with a Soviet Army officer and, more recently, with dictionaries and art history. She had grown up a little with Willy and Heinrich too, though I wouldn't know this until later. She had a narrow single bed, nearly as firm and compact as Utch herself, but she allowed me to rest my head between her breasts.

"Are you comfortable?" I kept asking her. "Are you all right?"

"Of course!" she said. "Aren't Americans ever comfortable?"

In the mornings, I still had to brush my teeth; I could not avoid the *Herrenzimmer* altogether. As my beard grew, Willy and Heinrich grew balder, and I said to Utch, "It's as if they're trying to suggest symbolically that my presence has deprived them of something."

I heard more about the man with the hole in his cheek, another symbol. Utch had compressed him into all her bodyguards, into all her years of growing up in the occupation. The man had become Benno Blum; she dreamed of him; she swore to me that even now she occasionally fantasized him; he would appear in the windows of passing cabs or in the aisles of swaying *Strassenbahns,* no doubt lurking behind a raised newspaper. Once she saw him when she was conducting a tour in the Kunsthistorisches. He appeared like a fallen angel in the bottom corner of a huge Titian, as if he'd dropped out of the painting and, wholly out of grace, was waiting to be discovered.

For two weeks Utch kept her job and I had to trail behind her tours. But it was November; the tourists were going south or home; guides were being laid off. She said she liked the job because it was nonpolitical. In winter, she was often in the service of the Soviet embassy's M. Maisky. She had been the interpreter for a ballet troop, a string ensemble, a mystic, a colonel out of uniform and several "diplomats" with an undisclosed rank and purpose.

Most of them had made Russian propositions to her. She had always thought of her future as narrow. "I can either be a Communist in Vienna," she told me, "or I can be a Communist in the Soviet Union."

"Or you can come to America with me," I said.

"I don't think America's a very good place to be a Communist," Utch said.

"But why are you a Communist?"

"Why not?" she said. "Who else took care of me?"

"I'll take care of you."

"But I don't know any other Americans," she said.

Her room was full of plants; she liked the color green. We could talk and breathe hard in there all day and night and always have fresh oxygen. But it was November; some of the plants were slowly dying, too.

In the *Herrenzimmer* one morning Heinrich shaved his head. My beard had grown almost a half-inch. Heinrich's skull glinted at me. "I think Utchka and I are going to live in America," I told him. He didn't appear to understand English; he stared at me, filled his mouth with shaving cream and spat in the sink. His opinion was pretty clear. I turned back to my sink; I'd been getting ready to brush my teeth when Heinrich's shining dome distracted me. When I picked up my toothbrush, all the bristles were shaved off; Willy had done the deed while I'd been talking to Heinrich. I looked at Willy, standing at the sink next to mine; he was grinning at me, changing razor blades. He didn't appear to understand English either.

"That's funny," Utch said. "Willy and Heinrich have had about seven years of English in school. Sometimes they speak it to me."

"Fancy that," I said.

"Was ist 'fancy'?"

So we went to the gold-edged, red-brocaded office of M. Maisky in the Soviet embassy. M. Maisky looked loose-skinned and old; he gazed at Utch the way a sickly uncle lavishes fondness and bitterness on a robust niece.

"Oh Utchka, Utchka," he said. He went on and on in Russian, but she asked him to speak English so that I could understand him, too. He regarded me sadly. "You want to take her away from us, dear boy?" he asked. "Oh Utchka, Utchka, what would poor Kudashvili say? America! Unashamedly he weep would!" Maisky cried.

"He would weep unashamedly," Utch corrected.

"Yes," Maisky said, his old gray eyes aswim. "Oh Utchka, Utchka, to think of all the years you grow that I have watched! And now this . . ."

"I'm in love," Utch said.

"Yes," I said stupidly. "So am I."

"How could this happen?" Maisky wondered. His suit was a loud gray, if that's even possible; his tie, a shiny sort of cardboard, was gray too, and so were his hair, his once-white shirt, the tinted lenses of his glasses and even the color in his cheeks.

"Sir," I said, "I think it will be necessary for Utchka to say she's not a Communist anymore—or even that she never really was—so that my country won't delay her immigration. But we hope you know that this isn't personal. She has told me how you've helped her."

"Renounce us, you mean?" Maisky cried. "Oh Utchka, Utchka . . ."

"I hoped you'd understand," Utch said, unmoved by poor old Maisky. I was quite touched by him, actually.

"Utchka!" Maisky shouted. "If you go to America, there can be no God!"

"There is no God anyway," Utch said, but Maisky gazed heavenward as if he were going to summon Him. Perhaps he will call upon the Workers of the World, I thought, but he just shook his head.

Outside it was all November; Maisky regarded the weather. "I am by everything so discouraged," he said. "This weather, the price of things, East-West relations—and now this." He sighed. "By the deteriorating quality of life everywhere I am discouraged, though perhaps where you're going it will be exciting because everything deteriorates a little faster over there." He arched his stiff back and gave out a gray groan. "By the values I see young people abandoning I am discouraged. The sexual liberties taken, the terrible self-righteousness of children, the probability of more wars, the extravagance of having so many babies. I suppose you want to have babies too?"

I felt guilty for all the things discouraging Maisky, but Utch said, "Of course we'll have babies. You've just gotten old." I winced. Who was this callous young woman I wanted to take home with me? She was not sentimental; I saw her inspiring blank shock in my mother. But perhaps she would flatter my father's pessimism.

Later Utch said, "Some things about America *do* bother me."

"What?"

"The terrible poverty, the automobile accidents, the racial violence, the sexual crimes . . ."

"What?"

"Does everyone cook in—what you call it?—a barbecue pit?" she asked. I tried to imagine her vision of America: a country of one vast smoldering cookout—with rapes and police skirmishes, car crashes and starving black children on the side.

We acquired the necessary papers for Utch at the American consulate. The man we talked to was discouraged by many of the same things which were discouraging to M. Maisky, but Utch and I remained cheerful. We returned to the *Studentenheim* on Krügerstrasse, where Utch practiced her renunciation speech. When I went to the *Herrenzimmer,* Willy was shaving his eyebrows. "At this moment," I told him, "Utchka is practicing her entry into the United States."

"Go practice your own entry," he said.

Heinrich came into the *Herrenzimmer* bare-chested, stood at the mirror and aimed the shaving-cream can at himself as if it were an underarm deodorant; he filled both armpits with a lathery foam, turned away from the mirror and flapped his arms against his sides like some violent, awkward bird. Lather squirted on the walls, oozed over his ribs, dappled his shoes. "I think you better marry her before you take her anywhere," Heinrich said.

"*Ja,* " said Willy, eyebrowless, as startling as a newborn owl. "That's the only decent thing to do."

I went back to Utch's room to ask her if she agreed. We compared our philosophies on marriage. We spoke of fidelity as the only way. We considered conventional "affairs" as double deceptions, degrading to everyone involved. We regarded "arrangements" as callous—the kind of premeditation that is the opposite of genuine passion. How people could conceive of such things was beyond us. We speculated on the wisdom of couples "swapping"; it hardly seemed wise. In fact, it seemed an admission of an unforgivable boredom, utterly decadent and grossly wasteful of the erotic impulse. (Philosophy is a pretty simple-minded subject when you've just fallen in love with someone.)

There were further permissions needed from and granted by the American consulate before we could get married. Since Austria is a Catholic country and I wasn't Catholic and Utch was long lapsed, the easiest thing was to be married in a nondenominational church. The American consul told us that this church was preferred by most Americans who got married in Vienna. It was called the American Church of Christ and was in a modern building; the minister was an American from Sandusky, Ohio, who said he'd been raised a Unitarian. "But it doesn't matter," he told us; he smiled a lot. He said to Utch, "They're going to love your accent in the States, honey."

The church itself was on the fourth floor and we took an elevator to it. "Some young people like to use the stairs," the minister told us. "It gives them more time to think about it. Last year one couple changed their minds on the stairs, but no one's ever changed his mind in the elevator."

"What's 'change your mind' mean?" Utch asked.

"Isn't she charming?" the minister said. "She's going to knock them over back home, you know."

The form for the American consulate required the signature of a witness —in our case, the church janitor, a Greek named Golfo who had not yet learned to write his last name. He signed the form "Golfo X."

"You should tip him," the minister told me; I gave Golfo twenty schillings. "He wants to give you a present," the minister said. "Golfo witnesses lots of our weddings and he always gives a present." Golfo gave us a spoon. It was not a silver spoon, but it had a tiny colored picture of St. Stephen's Cathedral engraved on the handle. Perhaps we were to pretend that we had been married there.

The minister walked us around the block. "You should expect that you'll have your little differences," he told us. "You can even expect some pretty good unhappiness," he said. We nodded. "But I'm married myself and it's just great. She's a Viennese girl, too," he whispered to me. "I think they make the best wives in the world." I nodded. We all came to a halt suddenly because the minister stopped walking. "I can't walk around that corner," he told us. "You'll have to go on by yourselves. You're on your own now!"

"What's around the corner?" I asked him. I assumed he'd been speaking metaphorically, but he meant the actual corner of Rennweg and Metternichgasse.

"There's a pastry shop there," he said. "I'm on a diet, but I can't resist the *Haselnusstorte* if I see it in the window."

"I want a *Mokkacremetorte,*" Utch decided; she tugged me along.

"There's too much *Torte* in this city," the minister confessed, "but do you know what I miss the most?"

"What's that?"

"Hamburger," he said. "It's just not the same as back home."

"Hamburger is cooked in the barbecue pits, right?" Utch asked.

"Oh, listen to her!" our minister cried. "Oh, you have a winner there!" he told me.

On our way back to the *Studentenheim* Utch drew her breath in, dug her nails into my wrist and screamed—but the vision she thought she'd seen had disappeared down the escalator that underpasses the Opernring. She thought she'd seen the man with the hole in his cheek. We historical novelists know that the past can be vivid; it can even seem real. "But it is *so* real," Utch told me. "He actually seems to age between the times I see him; I mean, he now appears like I think he would look if he were ten years older than when the Russians left. He's grayer, he's bent a little bit over— you know."

"And the hole itself?" I asked. "Does it ever change?"

"The hole's a hole," Utch said. "It's an awful thing. You think at first it's a shadow, but it doesn't move. You think it's some kind of dirt, but it goes *in*—like a door that's open. And the eye is pulled a little toward the hole, and the cheekbone is funny on that side of his face."

"A nightmare," I said.

We discussed the frequency and occasions of the vision. Did he appear at times, such as now, when she was breaking away from her past—when, say, she was freeing herself from her history—as if the vision were the psychological part of herself that was reluctant to abandon her past?

No, not necessarily; she didn't believe there was any pattern to it. She shrugged; she did not try hard to figure such things out. I suggested the man was a father-replacement. After all, he had been provided by Kudashvili for her protection; since she couldn't ignore that Kudashvili was dead, she had replaced him with the most vivid protection-symbol in her life. For years she had followed the arrests of the Blum Gang in the papers, and I told her that if she had ever seen a photograph of the man with the hole in his cheek —captured at last, or killed—she would probably have felt a great loss.

"Not me," Utch said. (Years later, she would say, "Psychology is better suited for plants.")

She did exercises like a man—sit-ups and push-ups and others. Captain Kudashvili had done them, of course. I certainly liked watching her do them.

"How do you say 'We're married' in German?" I asked.

"Wir sind verheiratet," she said.

I went down the hall to the *Herrenzimmer,* but Heinrich and Willy weren't at their sinks; it was not the shaving hour. One of them had left a can of shaving cream on the glass ledge. I shook up the contents, imagining writing with lather the full length of the mirror: *WIR SIND VERHEIRA-TET!,* but there didn't seem to be enough left. When the man with the hole in his cheek stepped out of the crapper stall behind me, the shaving cream can went off in my hand.

He was quite old, and the hole was just as Utch had described it. I couldn't tell if it was black because it was bottomless, or because his flesh had somehow stayed scorched. That terrible raw hole drew your eyes, but you couldn't stand looking at it.

"Wir sind verheiratet," I told him, because that's what I'd been prepared to say.

"Yes, yes, I know," he said tiredly, impatient with me. He moved slowly to the row of sinks and leaned on one, staring at himself in the mirror. "So," he said after a pause, "she tells you about me—I know by how you stare."

"Yes," I said, "but she thinks you're a fantasy. So did I."

"Good, good," he said. "Just as well. The job is over. You are going to take her away, and I am too old and too poor to follow her anymore. America!" he cried out suddenly, as if something hurt him. "I wish someone is taking *me* to America!"

He looked at me. He didn't look like a gangster or hired killer or body-guard or spy anymore; he looked like a seedy jeweler who spent nothing on his health or clothes, but only on expensive rings and necklaces for women who always left him. He would better have spent his money on an elaborate brooch to hide the hole; what he needed was a kind of cheek pin. Of course, it would be complicated to attach. I did not think he wore a gun.

"What do you think of my English?" he asked.

"Pretty good," I said.

"Ja, it is," he said. "She learns it, so I learn it. She walk around that old museum, I walk around it too. She go out for *Strassenbahn* rides at the worst times, I try to go after her. Most of the time she never see me, but a few times I am careless. I get old," he said. "That is what happens."

"Why do you follow her?" I asked him. "Are you still working for the Russians?"

He spat in the sink and shook his head. "Russians and Americans are the same," he said. "I promise Kudashvili. I tell him I look after her until she goes to live with him. How do I know Kudashvili is going to be killed? I make a promise: I look after his Utchka. But no more. Who is thinking she takes twenty-five years to get married?"

"My God," I said. "You should have told her."

"She hates me," he said. "It's unfair, of course. So once I work for Benno Blum, so what? So then I work for Kudashvili. Does she think *him* an angel?"

"Come tell her now," I said. "Come let her see that you're real. But you better let me say something first, or—"

"Is you crazy?" he asked me. "It's all finished. She never see me again, why let her see me now? She thinks I'm a dream. You tell her she's not going to dream me anymore. That is the truth. You marry her, now you look after her."

"Oh, I will, I will," I told him. He seemed even more sincere than our minister. My pledge to him seemed more charged than my marriage vows. But suddenly he sagged against the sink, took a short, sick look at himself in the mirror, turned away sobbing and slumped against the row of crapper stalls, weeping softly.

"I am lying to you," he said. "All these years I hope she sees me just once without screaming and shaking like she see a monster. When she is younger, she look at my face as if it doesn't really bother her—just that she is sorry for me, that such a thing happen to me. She is a sweet little girl, I must tell you."

"What did you lie about?"

"I watch her get into that mess with those two boys. I think one time I am going to kill them both! I think another time I am going to kill *you*," he said, "but you are so *hit* by her—I can see. I am hit by her like that, too."

"You're in love with her?"

"*Ja!*" he choked, "but it's over, finished! And you better not ever say a word to her about this or I am hunting you down wherever you go to live. Even if it's Oklahoma," he said, "I am finding you and cutting your eyeballs out."

"Oklahoma?"

"Never mind!" he wept. "I take care of her. Kudashvili himself never do it any better! He say to me once that he is going to watch her every minute until she marries the right sort of man, and I say, 'What are you going to do if she falls in love with the *wrong* sort of man?' And he say, 'Kill him, of course.' Now there is a love that is pretty strong, I must tell you."

"Love?" I said.

"*Ja!*" he shouted furiously. "What do you know about it? All you care about is fucking!"

He pulled himself together, smoothed his suit and tucked his shirt in tight. I had been wrong; I saw the gun when he straightened his tie. It had a horn handgrip, bluntly protruding from a high chest-and-shoulder holster of green leather.

"If you ever tell her about me," he said, "I am hearing it across the world. If you do not take care of her good, I am feeling my pistol cock, I am feeling it in my lungs. The way I feel," he said, "I can dream that you die and make it so."

I believed him; I think I still believe him. As he walked past me to the door, the long overhead light tried vainly to penetrate his ghastly hole.

"Goodbye," I said. "And thank you for looking after her."

I must have looked untrustworthy, because suddenly he seemed to need to convince me. He walked down the row of sinks, turning all the faucets on full, then up the row of stalls, flushing all the toilets. He flushed the long urinal too, and the *Herrenzimmer* roared with the rush of water. When he drew his gun, I thought I was about to join Benno Blum's awesome statistics.

"Put down that shaving-cream can," he ordered. I set it on the sink beside me; he took quick aim and blew it, spinning, down the line of sinks; it landed in the last one, bobbing in the filling bowl, a hole drilled neatly in its middle. What was left of the shaving cream spurted and then flowed and then dribbled from the hole. One by one, the toilets stopped flushing; one by one, he shut off the faucets in the sinks while the shaving-cream can bled on.

"*Auf Wiedersehen,*" he said. He shut the door behind him. When I peeked out in the long hall, he was gone. No Heinrich, no Willy, no Utch to see him go.

Back in Utch's room, I hugged her, told her I would never hurt her, told her she would always be safe with me. "I'm going to live with you, yes," she said, "But I'm not going to be guarded by you." I didn't elaborate.

There remained only one last thing to do. We rented a car and I drove Utch to Eichbüchl, the town she'd been born in—twice, so to speak. She had not been there since Kudashvili had taken her away.

On the outskirts of Wiener Neustadt, where Utch's father had been caught sabotaging Messerschmitts, we drove past the vast, untouched ruin of the Messerschmitt factory. Barbed wire circled it. Messing around in that debris was *verboten* because so many bombs had been dropped there, and not all of them had gone off. Two or three times a year one of them exploded; probably cats and squirrels and prowling dogs set them off. It was feared that if the place was not enclosed, children would play there and blow themselves up. Leveling the ruins was slow and risky work; it was not a job for bulldozers. The great shell sat by the roadside as lifeless as a gutted ship. On the far side of town the long, pocked runway lay unused—the largest landing area in Europe even now, bigger than Orly or Heathrow. It would be a simple matter to repair the runway surface, but the people of Wiener

Neustadt were against it; they had heard enough planes overhead.

We found the village of Eichbüchl past the monastery at Katzelsdorf where Utch's mother had borrowed books. There were lots of new houses in Eichbüchl—weekend places, belonging to doctors and lawyers from Vienna. The peasants were still there, but like peasants everywhere throughout history, they were a part of the landscape—the background of the place. You had to look carefully to see what it was that they actually did. In Eichbüchl they grew apples, raised bees, butchered a frequent pig, an occasional calf. They made their own sausage; they grew their own vegetables; they hunted pheasant, rabbit, deer and wild boar. Everyone had a potato cellar with apples in it, and potatoes and cabbages and beets; everyone had a vineyard plot and made his own wine; everyone kept a few chickens and ate his own eggs; two people had their own cows and everyone got milk and cream from them. There was just one *Gasthof,* one place to drink, one place to eat the one dish a day on the menu. The day we stopped there, it was Serbian bean soup, black bread and wine or beer. It was midafternoon. There was what looked like a barn a little way up the one-street village road, but Utch did not want to look at it; nor did she want to ask anyone about Frau Thalhammer's little girl who'd impressed a Russian officer.

The old lady who ran the *Gasthof* did not appear to recognize her or her resemblance to her mother. She was only mildly interested that I was an American; another American had been there about eight years ago; I was not her first. In the *Gasthof,* some old men were playing cards and drinking wine. Utch looked at them quietly; I knew she was thinking about the stalwart village menfolk who had raped her mother, and I said, "Go on, introduce yourself. See what they say. Isn't that why you wanted to come?" But she said she simply didn't have any feelings anymore. The men were so old that they were not the men in her mind. Everyone who looked like the men in her mind was her own age now, and innocent then; everyone who would have been the right age then was too old and innocent now.

She picked at her soup and added, "Everyone except *that* one." She fixed her eyes on one of the cardplayers—old like all of them, yes, but rougher and stronger-looking. He was not a pitiable old man; his arms were thick and muscled, his shoulders and neck were not stringy. He had a tough, aggressive jaw and his eyes moved quickly, like a young man's. Also, from time to time, he looked with interest at Utch. I wanted to leave, but Utch had to watch the man; she thought she might work up the nerve to speak to him.

The man seemed to be discomforted by the way Utch looked at him; he fidgeted in his chair as if Utch made him itchy or his legs were cramped. When he stood up I realized that the crutches hooked on the back of the long bench were his; he had no legs. When he lurched out from behind the table of cardplayers, I understood why his arms and neck and shoulders were so young. He swung his way toward our table, a stumped puppet, an amputated acrobat. He balanced on his crutches in front of us, swaying slightly, sometimes inching the tip of one crutch forward or backward to keep himself steady. The handgrips of the crutches were worn smooth, the armpit pads sewn from old bed quilts. Initials, names, etchings of faces and animals were engraved on the dark, oiled crutches—as complex and historical as the archways of some cathedrals. He smiled down at Utch.

She told me later that he asked her if he was supposed to know her; was she back for a visit? "Everyone grows up so fast," was the way he put it. She told him no, she was visiting for the first time. Oh, he had misunderstood, he said. When he left, Utch asked the lady who ran the place how he had lost his legs. The war; that was all the old lady would say. The Russians? Utch asked. The old lady admitted that it might have been on the Russian front; that was a popular place to have lost limbs.

But when we were outside the *Gasthof,* one of the old cardplayers came up to us. "Don't listen to her," he told Utch. "He lost his legs right here in the village. The Russians did it. They tortured him because he wouldn't tell them where his wife and daughters were hidden. They did it to him on a cider press. He never told them, but they found them anyway, of course."

Why such an old man would want to tell strangers such a story is beyond me, but Utch claims her translation of the dialect was accurate. We drove out of Eichbüchl before it was dark, Utch crying softly in the seat beside me. I stopped the car near the river, just to hold her and try to comfort her. The river was called the Leitha, a clear, shallow stream with a pebbled bottom—very beautiful. Utch cried for a while, until, of all things, we found ourselves staring at a cow. It had lazed away from the herd down by the river, and grazed up to the roadside. It looked at us curiously. "Oh my God," Utch sobbed.

"It's okay," I said. "It's just a cow."

The cow stared at us blandly, stupidly; all history looks pretty much the same to cows.

Finally Utch laughed out loud—I suppose because she *had* to. "Goodbye, Mother," she said to the cow. Then I drove us across the wooden-plank bridge, over the Leitha, where all the other cows looked up at us as we rattled the bridge. "Goodbye, Mother!" Utch yelled as I drove faster. November was everywhere. The vineyards were plucked clean; the root vegetables were stacked inside the cellars; the cider was surely pressed.

Utch cried most of the night in her room full of plants at the *Studentenheim* and I made love to her whenever she wanted me to. For a couple of hours she was out of the room, and for a while I thought that she was taking a hot bath down the hall. But when she came back about dawn, she told me she'd been saying goodbye to Heinrich and Willy. Well, goodbyes were clearly in the wind; we were leaving the next day.

In the *Herrenzimmer* I said goodbye to Willy and Heinrich. They were polite, quiet, up to no mischief. I said I was sorry about what had happened to their shaving-cream can, but they refused to accept apologies of any kind. "You've got a good beard going," Willy told me. "Why do you want to shave?"

Then we were in the cab, heading for Schwechart Airport. A cold gray day for flying, a poor ceiling. At the airport I bought an international *Herald Tribune*, but it was a day old. It was November 22, 1963. We were waiting for an evening plane. The loudspeaker at the airport made announcements in German, French, Italian, Russian and English, but I didn't listen. In the airport bar I recognized lots of other Americans. Many of them were crying. I had seen strange things in the last two days, and I had no reason to expect that the strange things would cease. Like everyone else, I watched the television. It was a video-tape replay. The reception was lousy, the narration in German. I watched a big American convertible with a woman climbing out of the back seat and onto the trunk behind to help a man hop up over the rear bumper and climb into the car. It didn't make much sense.

"Where is Dallas?" Utch asked me.

"Texas," I said. "What happened in Dallas?"

"The President is dead," Utch said.

"What president?" I asked. I thought she meant the president of Dallas.

"Your President," Utch said. "You know, Herr Kennedy?"

"*John* Kennedy?"

"*Ja,* him," Utch said. "Herr Kennedy is dead. He got shot."

"In Dallas?" I asked. Somehow I couldn't believe that my President would ever even go to Dallas. I stared at Utch, who wasn't even familiar with Kennedy's name. What must she think of this place she is going to? I wondered. In Europe, of course, they kill their aristocracy all the time, but not in America.

In front of me a large, befurred woman bawled her head off. She said she was a Republican from Colorado but she had always liked Kennedy, even so. I asked her husband who had done it, and he said it was probably some dirty little bastard who didn't have a decent job. I saw that Utch was bewildered and tried to tell her how extraordinary this was, but she seemed more concerned for me.

When we changed planes later that night in Frankfurt, we found out that whoever they thought had shot Kennedy had himself just been shot by someone else—in a police station! We saw that on television too. Utch never blinked, but most of the Americans went on crying, outraged and scared. For Utch, I suppose, it was not at all unusual; it was the way they would settle scores in Eichbüchl. Nobody had taught her to expect any other part of the world to behave differently.

When we landed in New York, some magazine had already printed the picture of Mrs. Kennedy which was to be around for months. It was a big color photograph—it was better in color because the blood really looked like blood; it showed her stunned and grieving and oblivious of her own appearance. She had always been so concerned about her looks that I think the public liked seeing her this way. It was the closest thing to seeing her naked; we were voyeurs. She wore that blood-spattered suit; her stockings were matted with the blood of the President; her face was vacant. Utch thought the photograph disgusting; it made her cry all the way to Boston. The people around us probably thought she was crying for Kennedy and the country, but she wasn't; she was reacting to the face in the photograph, that grief, that look of being so totally had that you just don't care anymore. I think that Utch was crying for Kudashvili, and for her mother, and for that terrible village she came from, which was just like any other village. I think she empathized with the vacancy on the face of the President's widow.

We took the subway to Cambridge. "It's sort of like an underground *Strassenbahn*," I explained, but Utch wasn't interested in the subway. She sat tensely, the wrinkled picture of Mrs. Kennedy in her lap. She had thrown away the magazine.

In Harvard Square we walked past a lot of Kennedy mourners. Utch stared at everything, but she saw nothing. I talked about my mother and father. If the suitcases hadn't been so heavy, we would have walked the long way home to Brown Street; as it was, we took a cab. I talked on and on, but Utch said, "You shouldn't make jokes about your mother."

Mother was at the door, holding the same damn picture of Mrs. Kennedy that Utch had. It may have been one of those false sororities of identifying yourself with another person; it works out all right because you never find out that you meant wholly different things by whatever it was that united you.

"Oh, you've really gone and done it!" my mother cried to me and opened her arms to Utch.

Utch ran right to her and cried against her. My mother was surprised; it had been years since anyone had cried all over her like that. "Go see your father," Mother told me. Utch's crying appeared inconsolable. "What's her name?" Mother whispered, rocking Utch in her arms.

"Utchka," I said.

"Oh, that's a nice name," Mother crooned, rolling her eyes. "Utchka?" she said, as if she were humoring a baby. "Utchka, Utchka."

I didn't see my wife again for hours; my mother kept her hidden from my father and me. Occasionally she would appear to offer pronouncements, such as, "When I think of what happened to that poor child's mother . . ." or, "She's a remarkable young woman, and I don't know what you've done to deserve her."

I sat with my father, who explained to me everything that would happen to the country in the next ten years because of Kennedy's assassination, and everything that was going to happen regardless of the assassination. The distinction confused me.

Utch was restored to me at dinner; whatever had accumulated to unbalance her appeared to be in control. She was relaxed, alluring and mischievous with my father, who said to me, "I think you got a good one. Jesus, when your mother was running in and out earlier I had the impression that you'd brought home some war waif, some woman of catastrophe." When the old bore finally stopped muttering, the house was asleep.

I looked out on the dark sidewalk. I think I must have been looking for the man with the hole in his cheek, to see if he was checking up on me. But history takes time; my marriage was new. I would not see him for a while.

The next morning my father asked, "How's that stupid Bruegel book coming?"

"Well, it never got off the ground," I admitted.

"Good for it," he said.

"I've been thinking of another one," I said. "It's about peasants." Unknown to us both at the time, this idea would become my third historical novel, my book about Andreas Hofer, the hero of the Tyrol.

"Please don't tell me about it," my father said. "I feel like flattering you; your taste in women is admirable. I think it exceeds your literary taste. *The Fight Between Carnival and Lent,* indeed!" he scoffed. "Well, it looks like Lent lost. That girl is Carnival through and through! If I ever saw a less Lenten figure, I do not recall it. Bravo, Carnival!" he cheered. The old lecher.

But he was right. Utch was a Carnival character all the way.

For example, how she slept. She did not curl tight and protect herself; she sprawled. If you wanted to cuddle against her, she didn't mind, but she herself was not one to cuddle. Edith slept like a cat—contained, a fortress, snug against you. Utch spread herself out as if she were trying to dry in the sun. When she lay on her back, she didn't seem to notice where the covers were, and she lay on her stomach like a swimmer frozen at the instant of the breaststroke kick. On her side she lay like the profile of a hurdler. In the middle of the night she would often lash an arm out and swat the bedside lamp off the night table or bash the alarm clock across the room.

I attempted to have humorous conversations with Severin about Utch's flamboyant shapes asleep. "It's obviously a kind of violent reaction," I surmised, "no doubt a rejection of being cramped inside the cow."

"I sleep that way myself," he said seriously, and that was that.

Edith and I were the snugglers; we tucked ourselves up against each other, neat and small. We often joked about Severin's and Utch's loose sprawls, trying to imagine them fitting on a bed.

"That's obviously why they went to the wrestling room," I said to Edith. "It's the biggest bed in town."

Edith sat up suddenly and turned on the light. I blinked. "What did you say?" she asked. Her voice was oddly dead. I had never seen her face look ugly before; perhaps it was the sudden, harsh light.

"He took her to the wrestling room," I said. "Last week, when we thought they were acting so strange? They went to the wrestling room." Edith shivered and hugged herself; she looked as if she was going to be sick. "I thought Severin told you everything," I said. "What's wrong? Doesn't it suit them? Can't you just see them rolling around on the mats?"

Edith swung her legs off the bed, stood up and lit a cigarette. She clutched her fists against her thighs; I had never noticed how thin she was; the veins at her wrists and on the backs of her hands stood out. "Edith?" I said. "What's wrong with them going to the wrestling room?"

"*He* knows what's wrong!" she wailed awfully; she seemed so unaware of her own body that I felt ashamed to be looking at her. She paced back and forth beside the bed. "How could he *do* that!" she cried. "He must have known how he'd hurt me." I didn't understand; I got out of bed and went to her, but she made a startled, awkward move back to the bed and drew up the bedcovers to hide herself.

"Go home, please," she whispered. "Just go home. I want to be alone."

"Edith, you have to talk to me," I said. "I don't know what's wrong."

"It's where he used to take Audrey Cannon!" she screamed.

"Who? What?"

"Ask *him!*" she yelled at me. "Go on! Please get out, go home. *Please!*"

I stumbled out in the hall, dressed on the stairs, found my car keys and drove home. I heard her lock the bedroom door behind me. There is nothing so confusing as finding out that you don't know someone you thought you knew.

Severin's car was parked in my driveway. At least they weren't at the wrestling room again. As I crossed the sidewalk, I heard Utch's German song. It was her coming song, but it was going on longer than usual. Through the walls of my house, through the shut windows, I heard my wife coming. What a voyeur's treat our sidewalk was. Something was knocked over, and Severin snorted like a certain hooved species. Utch was a soprano, though I'd never known it; I had not heard her sing quite that way.

I looked down the dark street, imagining the crude conversation I could have with a sudden passer-by. "Boy, someone's really getting it in there," he'd say.

"Sure is," I'd say, and we'd listen.

"Boy! She goes on and on!" he'd say.

"Sure does."

"Some guy sure has a lively one," he'd say, the envy showing on his streetlit face. "That guy must have some wang on him."

And I'd say, "Oh, that's a lot of bullshit, an old myth. It's got nothing to do with your *wang.*"

And he'd listen to Utch's highest aria and say, "Oh yeah? If it's not a wang making that happen, there's somebody who knows something I don't."

Finally Utch came. I heard her broken voice and saw a faint light flicker in our bedroom. No doubt their breathing had blown the candle out. I thought of the children and how scared they'd be if they ever woke up to that sound. I thought of what a long time it had been since I *had* thought of the children. And down the dark street I looked for my accuser, the man with the hole in his cheek. "I am hearing that," he'd say. How had he put it? *I am feeling my pistol cock, I am feeling it in my lungs.* It seemed like a good time for him to come save Utch. I would have hung my head if I'd seen him; I felt I had let her get into trouble, though I didn't exactly know what kind.

I closed the door of my house loudly, opened the closet and rattled the coat hangers, though I had no coat to hang up. Severin surprised me; he sprang into the living room naked, ready to maul the housebreaker. "It's just me, for Christ's sake," I said. His wang, I was relieved to see, looked more or less like anyone else's. Utch came up behind him and handed him his pants; she'd already slipped into her robe. I guess they could tell something was wrong by the way I looked.

"Edith's upset," I said. "It's probably my fault. I told her that you two had gone to the wrestling room." Severin shut his eyes; Utch touched his shoulder. "Well, no one told me *not* to tell her," I said. They just stood there, Severin with his eyes shut and Utch looking at him. It was clear that they both knew what Edith was upset about. I was angry that I was the only one in the dark. "Who's Audrey Cannon?" I asked angrily. Utch took her hand from Severin's shoulder and sat down on the couch. "Come on, Severin," I said. "You used to take *her* to the wrestling room, too." I may have sounded bold but when I looked at Utch, I got scared. She was looking at me with the kind of pity which could only be knowledge. She was telling me that I didn't really want to know, but I asked anyway: "Who is Audrey Cannon?"

8

The Wrestling-Room Lover

In September the wrestlers who didn't play football or soccer ran laps at the stadium track or plodded through the leaves on the cross-country course. Later they would have plenty of laps to run on the board track in the old cage; as long as the weather stayed warm, they ran outdoors. They were not all cut in the curious mold of George James Bender.

They played basketball together—funny, stumpy-looking figures bungling the ball, missing the basket cleanly, jarring the backboard. Two of them took up handball until one of them ran into the wall. Other sports appeared to frustrate and bore them, but by October they took on many restless sports, built their wind and lost some weight—and when they'd finished exercising they'd make for the wrestling room, turn up the thermostat and "roll around."

Unless they'd been wrestling through the summer months—and only the Benders of the world did so—Severin did not allow them to actually wrestle. It was too early, he said; they weren't in shape. They cooperated, putting each other through moves and holds at half-speed. Occasionally they got playful and brief flurries of real combat would erupt, but for the most part, they just drilled. They also sat on the soft mats with their backs against the padded walls, letting the temperature rise to eighty-five, ninety, ninety-five, moving around just enough to keep loose.

Anyone seeing them in the wrestling room would have thought they were a parody team miming wrestlers, moving with an exaggerated gentleness antithetical to their purpose. They lumbered and rolled and carried each other around in an almost elderly fashion. Some of them, tired from running in the woods or straining against the weight-lifting contraptions, actually slept. They came to this hothouse wearing double layers of sweatsuits with towels around their heads, and even as they slept they kept a sweat running. Tight against the wall and in the corners of the room where they would not accidentally be rolled on, they lay in mounds like bears.

Severin Winter, their coach and German professor, came by the wrestling room just to look in on them—like a father observing his children in some incubator phase. He did not really believe that these hibernating metabolisms represented life as he knew it; not yet. He appeared almost embarrassed for his wrestlers, as if, in the shape they were in, there was nothing he could offer them but hope and a few words to enhance their German vocabularies.

(At this time of year, he *did* hold occasional German classes in the wrestling room.)

But in the pre-season before Bender was on his team—the same pre-season before he and Edith knew us—Severin was low on hope. "I knew he was low on hope," Edith told me, "because he talked a lot about going back to live in Vienna. That's a low-on-hope sign with him."

"No, no," Severin disagreed. "First it was the insomnia. It all started with the insomnia."

I could have told him that insomnia after eight years of marriage is very little trouble. If I'd known him then, I could have recommended some remedies less drastic than the one he chose. (When my typist, the History Department's secretary, was typing the manuscript of my third historical novel, I couldn't sleep and knew I wouldn't until it was done. I found that the only place I could sleep was in her tiny apartment while listening to her typing new pages. Her name was Miss Ronquist. I told Utch I was using the department's big office typewriter to type the manuscript myself, and that the only time I could use the typewriter was at night, when the office was closed. It was impossible to reach me by phone because the university switchboard shut off all calls after midnight. It took a long time to type that manuscript. Miss Ronquist was tired all the time and could manage only about five pages a night. Slow for a typist, but she found other ways to help me sleep. And when the book was finished, I went home and slept very well with Utch. Nothing was amiss; no one was upset.)

But Severin was inexperienced with insomnia, and his reaction was typically unreasonable. You can tell a lot about someone by how he deals with insomnia. My reaction—to insomnia and to life in general—is to give in. My best-trained senses are passive; my favorite word is *yield*. But Severin Winter would not yield to anything, and when he had insomnia, he fought it.

It began one night when he was lying awake beside Edith after they'd made love. She was drowsy, but he lay there like an overcharging battery. "I have nothing to do," he announced and got out of bed.

"Where are you going?" Edith asked.

"I can't sleep."

"Well, read something," Edith said. "The light doesn't bother me."

"There's nothing I want to read right now."

"Well, write something and then read *that.*"

"You're the writer," he said. "One's enough."

"Why don't you wait until I fall asleep," Edith said, "and then very gently see if you can make love to me again without waking me up."

"I tried that last night."

"You *did?*" said Edith. "What happened?"

"You didn't wake up," he said. He put on his running shorts and track shoes, then stood there as if he didn't know what to do next. "I'm going to ride the bicycle around," he decided. "That will make me tired."

"It's after midnight," said Edith, "and you don't have a light on the bike."

"I can see the cars coming. Or I can hear them if they're sneaking around with their lights off."

"Why would they be doing that?" Edith asked.

"I don't know!" he shouted. "Why am I doing *this?*"

"I don't know," Edith confessed. *I'm* the writer, she thought. I should have his energy, I should be as crazy.

But I don't think either of them really understood it. When I told Severin that I sympathized with his insomnia, he told me that I understood nothing. "I'm not like you," he said. "I was simply unable to sleep. I went out to ride my bike. That's how it started."

It was a warm early fall night. He rode through the sleeping suburbs, his racing bicycle going *tzik-tzik* past all the people safely in bed. He passed only a few lighted windows and these he pedaled by slowly, but he was rarely able to see anything. He was glad he didn't have a light; it made his journey more secretive. In town he held to the sidewalks; in the country, he could hear and see the occasional cars coming and simply get off the road. That first night he rode for miles—all around the campus, out of town and back in. It was almost dawn when he unlocked the gym and carried his bike into the locker room. He slipped into a wrestling robe, went up to the wrestling room, lay down on the great warm mat and slept until the sun through the skylight woke him. He took a sauna, swam and rode home in time to bring Edith her breakfast in bed.

"It was marvelous!" he told her. "Just what I needed."

But that didn't take care of it. A few nights later he was up pacing the house again. Outside, lurking near the garden shed, his white racing bicycle glowed in the moonlight like a ghostly thin dog. "It's waiting for me," he told Edith. Soon he was out riding three or four nights a week. At first, like a lot of things with Severin, he turned his habit into an endurance feat. He tested himself for distance, striking out for the farthest towns and making it back before first light. Then he timed himself for forty-mile jaunts. But always, before dawn, he would catch an hour's deep sleep in the wrestling room.

Edith didn't object. He made love to her before setting out and was back in the house before she was awake; fresh from a sauna and a swim, he'd often wake her nicely by making love to her again. One night a week his loss of sleep would crash down on him and he'd fall into a stupor after supper and drowse about the house until the middle of the next day. But that was merely his body knowing what it needed.

To hear him tell it, nothing was wrong until the first night he rode past the old cage, after midnight, and saw the light on in the wrestling room. At first he thought it was the watchman's error, even though he saw an unfamiliar car. Severin Winter was on his way to another county and thought he'd see about the light when he visited the wrestling room later for his dawn nap. But he hadn't ridden much further when the light began to bother him and he turned back. Whoever was in the wrestling room after midnight would certainly be up to something nonathletic. He imagined the fun of catching a judo couple copulating on the mat, their stupid pajamalike costumes wildly abandoned.

He was going to go straight to the room, but then he thought he might have more authority if he dressed for the part he was about to play, so he suited up in full wrestling gear. As he made his stealthy way to the tunnel, he reminded himself to give the watchman a piece of his mind. Not even faculty had permission to be in the gym after 10 P.M., and since Severin was the only person in the Athletic Department who ever used the facilities at such odd hours, he probably felt his monopoly was threatened.

He stalked around the old board track like a predator, and at the closed door to the wrestling room, his suspicions seemed to be confirmed: music was playing in there. Severin was a Viennese with an education; he recognized Schumann's "Papillons." At least the invaders had taste, he thought. He could not conceive what lewd karate act awaited him, what weird rite was in progress within! Silently he slipped the key in the lock. Suddenly anxious, he wondered what anyone could be doing to the accompaniment of Schumann.

All alone, a small, dark woman was dancing in sleek black leotards. She was tiny, sinewy, tense; her movements as graceful and nervous as an antelope's. She did not notice him slip in and slide the door closed behind him. She was working very hard to an insistent, staccato passage. Sweat drenched her elastic body; her breathing was hard but deep. A portable tape recorder was responsible for the Schumann; it sat neatly out of the way on a stack of towels in the corner as she ranged the room in an athletic interpretation that was close to gymnastics. Severin leaned against the padded wall of the wrestling room as if his spine were sensitive to Schumann.

He knew who she was, but something wasn't right; he also knew she was *crippled.* Her name was Audrey Cannon; she was an assistant professor of Dance and Theater Arts, and something of a metaphor for everything that was ironic and unlikely. She was a former dancer who taught dance, but she was a tragically graceless, even awkward person whose career had been ruined by some mysterious accident which was never discussed. She limped —in fact, she *clomped* her way around campus. The way she was used as a metaphor was cruel; of a ridiculous plan, say, someone might joke, "That makes about as much sense as Audrey Cannon teaching me how to dance."

She was a single woman, pretty and small but so shy and self-conscious and seemingly scarred that no one knew much about her. She declined invitations to parties and went to the city every weekend; she was thought to have a lover there. Edith claimed that the best story about Audrey Cannon had been invented by Severin. It was not malicious; it was pure speculation. Severin used to say that the woman's past "shone on her face like a fresh sin"; that her accident was no doubt a wound of love; that in her mid-thirties she had lived more than any of them; that the accident probably happened on stage as she was dancing with her leading lover, and that a jealous woman in the audience (who had been taking rifle lessons for months, for just this occasion) precisely shot off her left foot so that she would never be graceful again. She was still a beautiful woman, Severin claimed, but her awkwardness made her feel ugly. "Dancers are concerned with grace," Severin said. That he thought her beautiful was a surprise to almost everyone; no one else thought she was even very attractive (Edith described her as "neurasthenic"). But Severin claimed that her beauty was in her grace, which was in her past. He claimed that he could love a person's past. We historical novelists are rarely as sentimental.

When Severin Winter saw Audrey Cannon dancing, he must have imagined that some hypnotic power had possessed her. It was no cripple who was dancing on his wrestling mats. But when the tape recording ended, he was treated to another shock: she collapsed into a neat bundle in the center of the mat, breathing hard and deep, and when she'd recovered herself enough to stand, she *limped* toward the recorder in the corner like the crippled woman she'd previously been.

She was a very private woman in the midst of a very private moment, and when she saw Severin frozen against the padded wall she screamed. But Severin bounced out on the mat, calling, "It's all right, it's all right, it's just *me*—Severin Winter. Miss Cannon? Miss Cannon?" as she huddled, cringing on the mat, wondering, no doubt, what her dance had inspired.

They talked a long time. He'd caught her with all her defenses down and she had to tell him about her whole life; she felt as if he'd *seen* her whole life. He would never tell Edith or me what that "whole life" was. He remained faithful to that intimacy. "I think when a private person tells you everything, you're bound to each other in a way no one really planned," he said. But Edith reminded him bitterly that he'd always thought Audrey Cannon was beautiful; he'd had feelings for her even before their dramatic meeting. I never heard him deny it.

Audrey Cannon could dance on wrestling mats because they were soft; they gave under her slight weight and didn't distort her balance the way a normal surface would. It was an illusion, of course. I think she was able to dance on wrestling mats because of the trance she put herself in; it's my opinion that Severin Winter's wrestling room inspired trances. She said she had relearned dancing there. Harvey, the watchman, had made an exception for her.

"But we just *talked!*" Severin insisted. "That first night she just talked to me. We talked all night." No sauna, no swimming? "No! Just talk—"

"Which is the worst kind of infidelity," Edith said. Of course; it's what bothered Severin the most about Edith's relationship with me.

That first night, then, there was nothing more intimate than storytelling —except that she showed Severin her crippled foot, the muscular, highly arched remnant missing the ball of the foot and the three biggest toes. Jesus, what a sick story! A dancer with a maimed foot!

And he told her the history he'd imagined about her. And did he tell her he'd always thought she was beautiful? "No!" he cried. "It wasn't like that. I was just available . . . to listen." Well, it was no jealous woman who shot off her toes. Audrey Cannon had squared off her left foot years ago when mowing her lawn in a pair of sandals; she pulled a rotary-blade power mower over her own foot. It cut the first three toes off clean, chewed the next-to-last one and took all but a bit of the ball of her foot. There was so much blood she didn't know anything was missing. When they told her in the hospital she was convinced that some over-eager doctor had amputated everything too hastily.

I think I know the part of the story which must have touched Severin to his curious core. When she came home from the hospital, there was her lawnmower out in the yard where she'd left it, with a severed sandal-thong nearby. And when she looked under the lawnmower, there were her toes and the ball of her foot, looking like a halved peach. "Her old toes!" Severin said. "And do you know what? They were covered with ants."

My God, what a love story.

"But if you just talked, that first night," I said, "why didn't you tell Edith when you went home? You never said a word."

It discomforts Severin Winter to believe in his own premeditation. But he must have known that later there would be more than talk. I think he knew back when he knew nothing about her, except that to him she was beautiful.

We always know.

Still, he likes to stress the fact that he went back to riding his bicycle after that first meeting. Knowing she was in his wrestling room, riding by and seeing the light, he would ride on, reaching ever more faraway towns, pedaling furiously and not allowing himself to reach the wrestling room until his customary pre-dawn hour when Audrey Cannon would have long since limped home. No harm, was there, in his habit of looking for traces of her? Small, warm dents in the mat. Her dark hair in the sauna. A ripple not yet vanished from the surface of the swimming pool.

In the morning, bicycling home to Edith, he'd take the route by Audrey Cannon's small apartment. Just to see if her car was legally parked? To see if her window shade was properly down?

What a fool. I am familiar with the ways we talk ourselves into things. One way is by pretending we are talking ourselves out of them. Severin can tell me all day that he's not like me. ("I was falling in love with her!" he has cried. "I wasn't out to grab a quick piece and get my rocks off any old way like *you* do!") But a part of him knew what he was getting into. He can use any euphemism he likes.

The fact remains that one night he rode by the gym and couldn't keep the pedals going. He felt faint of heart at the notion of yet another faraway town. He circled the old cage, he stood in the dark trees, he crouched by the softly blowing rows of tennis nets, he scuffed up dirt on the baseball diamond, but he kept ending up back where he began. Suddenly he was tired of bicycling, of course; also—pure coincidence, of course—he had not made love to Edith before starting out that night.

And did he shower in the locker room before he slipped into a clean robe? I'll bet he did. And was it simply neglect which made him dress lightly under the robe? When he slid the door closed behind him, he saw that Audrey Cannon wasn't dancing. Schumann was playing, but she was resting. Or meditating? Or waiting for Severin Winter to make up his mind? And did he say, "Ah, um, I came to ask you if I could watch you dance?" And did Audrey Cannon stumble up to her foot and a half?

Clearly, there were positions in which her lost toes were no loss.

So much for bicycling; so much for Severin's fabled endurance. When he came home to Edith now, he wasn't up to making love to her. He had pedaled to too-faraway towns, established new time records. When he came home now, he slept until noon. How long did he think Edith would put up with it?

I don't think he saw anything clearly. Outside the wrestling room, out in the real world, he had no vision. He saw and thought and acted clearly under the moonlit dome, within the clear circles inscribed on the wrestling mats, but he left his mind behind whenever he hung up his clothes in his locker.

Severin's feelings and worries were always as obvious as boils; he could conceal nothing. ("I'm not good at lying, if that's what you mean," he told me. "I don't have your gift.") He must have known that Edith would find out. How long did he think she'd believe that he was bicycling all night in the rain? And after Thanksgiving, it snowed. For a while she thought that Severin was just indulging his masochism—the last struggles of an over-the-hill wrestler, one more feat of foolish stamina.

What else could she have wondered when he bought the Air Force survival suit, the bright orange one-piece zippered sack designed to float in the ocean or withstand sub-zero weather? The pretty white bike came back bent, rusted, its vital parts scraping. Daytimes, Severin would repair and oil it. He put up a map in the kitchen—supposedly of all the roads he'd traveled. That he was too tired to make love when he returned was understandable; that he was often too excited to make love before he left was slightly harder for Edith to bear. And what was that music he whistled around the house?

Though all his wrestlers were supposed to keep their nails cut, some of them were sloppy, so Edith was used to an occasional scratch on his back or shoulders. But not on his ass; those were *her* scratches or they were nobody's. And gradually she was sure that they weren't hers.

Twice she actually said to him tentatively, jokingly, in real but concealed fear: "Sometimes it's as if you have a lover."

I don't know what his reply was, but I can't imagine him responding naturally.

What finally convinced her was the way he was with the children. He took too long putting them to bed, told them extra stories, and often she found him standing in their room after they'd fallen asleep, just staring at them. Once he was crying. "Aren't they beautiful?" he said. She recognized the look in his eyes: he was saying goodbye to them, but at the same time he couldn't.

The night of the great December blizzard, Edith woke up with the shutters flapping, the storm door slamming, the wind howling under the eaves like mating cats. The trees appeared to be bent double. She doubted that a bicycle could even be held upright in such weather. It was 3 A.M. when she managed to get the car unstuck in the driveway and slithered her way down the snowy streets. She had always believed the part about the wrestling room and gym and sauna and swimming; she could smell the chlorine in his hair while she was sniffing him for other odors. She saw the light on in the wrestling room. She also recognized the parked car; on the dashboard was a pair of ballet slippers. The slippers weren't the same size as each other, but neither were Audrey Cannon's feet.

Edith sat in her car with the windshield icing over and the dark hulk of the new gym squatting over her. Ironically, she thought of how angry Severin would be with her for leaving the children alone at this hour on a night like this. She drove home. She smoked in the living room and played a record; she smoked in the bedroom, where she found Severin's ring of extra keys. There was the extra car key, the extra house key, the extra gym key, the extra wrestling room key . . .

She did not want to go there. At the same time, she imagined confronting them. She did not want to slide open the door to the wrestling room and catch them at it; on the other hand, she imagined various shocks she might give them. They would be walking around the old board track—did she always limp? would they be wearing anything?—and Edith would start toward them around the track, headed for a confrontation.

No. She lit another cigarette.

She imagined catching them in the tunnel. Surely he would lead his maimed dancer through the tunnel; he was always showing off. At mid-tunnel, by the light switch to one of the squash courts, Edith would brace herself and wait for him to walk into her. His startled hands would grope and find her face; she was sure he would recognize her bones. He might scream; then Audrey Cannon would scream, and Edith would scream too. All three of them yelling in that echoing tunnel! Then Edith would flick on the squash court light and show herself to them—blind them with herself.

Somehow her distress had woken Fiordiligi. "Where are you going?" the child asked; Edith had not realized that she looked as if she was going anywhere, but her coat was still on, and when her daughter asked, she realized she *was* going. She told Fiordiligi that she'd be back before breakfast.

All the slithery way back to the gym, Edith thought of the smell of chlorine in Severin's hair. When she saw that the light was still on in the wrestling room, she let herself into the gym and groped her way through it with her cigarette lighter. Once her lighter went out and couldn't be relit and she cried for a few, controlled minutes in what turned out to be the men's showers; they opened into the swimming pool. She found the underwater lights, flicked them on and then off again, climbed the stairs and sat in a corner of the first row of the balcony. She wondered if they swam in the dark or turned on the underwater lights.

It seemed to her that she'd been there for a long time before she heard their voices; they were coming through the showers from the sauna. She saw their silhouettes—a short, thick one and one which limped. They dove separately into the pool; there were moans from each when they surfaced, and they met near the middle of the pool. Edith was surprised that they had turned on the lights; she'd expected that Severin would prefer the dark, but she didn't know *this* Severin. They were as graceful and playful as seals. She thought with particular pain that Severin must love Audrey Cannon's smallness; how strong he must feel with her; he was a strong man anyway, but with her he was also big. For a moment she wished she could hide in the balcony; she felt so ashamed that she wanted to disappear.

Then Audrey Cannon saw her sitting in the first row of the lower balcony, and her voice pierced them all; in the sound-bouncing swimming pool it came at them in stereo. She said, "It's Edith, it must be Edith." Edith was surprised to find that she was already on her feet and coming down the stairs toward them; in a moment she was standing at the side of the pool. Lit up, bobbing in the aqua-green glowing pool, Audrey Cannon and Severin were suddenly as vulnerable as creatures in an aquarium. Edith said that she wished she had secretly assembled an audience—that she had filled the entire balcony, perhaps with the wrestling team, certainly the German Department, and of course his children. "Later I wished I'd had the courage to be waiting there for them with just Fiordiligi and Dorabella," she said. "Just the three of us, perhaps with all of us in our pajamas."

"He really *was* thinking of you," Audrey Cannon told her, but Edith roamed the rim of the pool as if she were looking for hands to stamp on, as if she were a cat intent on eating every fish in the bowl. When Severin tried to get out, she shoved him back in. She was crying and shouting at him, though she doesn't remember what she said. He said nothing; he treaded water. While he held Edith's attention, Audrey Cannon slipped out of the far side of the pool and limped toward the showers. It was the last Edith ever saw of her: her narrow, bony back, her lean sprinter's legs, her small pointy breasts, her hair as dark and rich as wet chocolate. Her painful, grotesque limp jarred her sharp hips but failed to even jiggle her high, hard ass, as small as a twelve-year-old boy's.

"I could catch you, you cripple!" Edith screamed after her. "I could run you down and snap your fucking bones!" But Severin hauled himself out of the pool and offered her a larger, unmoving target. She began to beat him with her fists, kick him, scratch him; she bit his shoulder and would have sunk her teeth into his throat had he not pried open her mouth with his strong fingers and held her at arm's length. She bit deeply into his thumbs; he used his thighs to shield himself from her knees, but she remembers the spurts of blood. She was wearing the Tyrolean boots he had given her, and she mashed his toes with them. She kicked and bit and hit as hard as she could until she was too tired to swing her arms anymore. She tasted the blood from his thumbs in her mouth. She looked at the tears streaming down his face—or was it simply water from the pool? She realized that she was doing what he probably most wanted from her, and that if she shoved him back in the pool, he would probably gratefully drown. She could not bear what he had done to her, but his obvious guilt sickened her even more.

On their silent way home, she told him that she would never let him see the children again, that he would have to beg her to even see a photograph of them. He sobbed. She realized how helpless he was, and the terrible power she had over him made her feel ugly; it made her be cruel, but it also made her feel that she needed to love him. "You've confused me terribly," she told him.

"I've confused *myself* terribly," he said, which enraged her. She scratched him slowly and deeply down one cheek; she drew blood; he never moved his face. She was horrified that she could do this, and even more horrified that he would let her. "The whole thing gave me an awful responsibility," she told me.

For weeks she thought of leaving him, reconsidered, tried to hurt him, tried to forgive him—and he took it all. "He was un-Severined," she said. He was completely at her mercy except when she wanted to strike back at Audrey Cannon. Then he said dumbly, "I loved her. I loved you at the same time."

What melodrama.

One night Edith said she was going to call Audrey Cannon. When she picked up the phone, Severin pushed the buttons down; Edith whacked him on the fingers with the receiver over and over, bloodied his nose and wrapped the phone cord around his neck. But you couldn't strangle Severin Winter, not that thick neck. He made no move to protect himself, but he wouldn't let her make the call.

"What were you going to do?" I asked him. "If Edith hadn't caught you, where would it have ended?" Edith had saved him and he knew it. He must have wanted her to catch him all along. How strange it must have felt to him to be in a situation where he was completely passive.

Audrey Cannon moved to the city and commuted to school for her classes; she announced that she would keep her position at the university only as long as it took her to find something else. Though I'm told she occasionally appears in town, no one has ever pointed her out to me. Both Edith and Severin say they have never seen her.

A long time after Audrey Cannon last swam naked in the university pool and a short time before they met us, Edith and Severin made love together again. She beat him all over his back and pulled his hair and drummed him with her hard heels, but she loved him again. Afterward she lay crying and told him that she could never forgive him for all the time alone, lying awake, she had suffered, imagining the strength of the passion for this crippled dancer that had driven an honest man to lie.

It was after they made love again that Edith told him she was going to pay him back. "I'm going to get a lover," she said, "and I'm going to let you know about it. I want you to be embarrassed when you make love to me—wondering if I'm bored, if *he* does it better. I want you to imagine what I say that I can't say to you, and what *he* has to say that you don't know."

"Did you just think of this?" he asked.

"No," she said. "I was waiting for you to really want me again. I was waiting to see if you'd ever enjoy making love to me again."

"Of course I do."

"Yes, I could tell," she said. "But now I've got this leverage on you. I can feel it, and you can too. And I don't like having it any better than you do, so I'm going to use it and then it will be gone and I won't have it anymore."

"Everything isn't equal," Severin said.

"Listen to who's talking," she answered. Later in the night she woke up; the bed was empty. Severin Winter was crying in the kitchen. "No, I won't ever do that," she told him gently. "Come back to bed. It's all over." She hugged him. "Don't worry, I love you," she said. But later she whispered, "But I *should* do that. But I won't." Later still she said, *"Maybe* I won't. You always say you like to know what I'm thinking."

She felt they both wore fresh scar tissue which each could see on the other. "It made us self-conscious with each other," Edith told me.

And Severin told me, "So, you see, you and Utch were inevitable. We'd talked about foursomes before, and I think we were each interested in the *idea,* but we each had our doubts. I think we both thought it was better than the clandestine affair, but that it could be terrible if you didn't find the right people. Well, I never felt that you and Utch were the right people for us —not for me, at least. But since there were other motives for Edith . . . do you see?"

"What are you trying to say?" I asked. Utch had gone to bed. He couldn't have said all this to her, I thought. "If you're trying to tell me that Edith is having this relationship just to pay you back, I don't believe it."

He shrugged. "Well, it's not *just* to pay me back. There are always other reasons . . . for everything."

"Edith and I are genuinely attracted to each other," I said.

"You and Edith wouldn't ever have gotten together at all," he said evenly, "if there hadn't been this other thing. I just didn't quite have the right to ask her not to."

"And what about Utch?" I asked.

"I'm fond of Utch," Severin said, "and I would never hurt her." Fond of her! That ass! Such fondness I have rarely seen.

"Do you mean that you don't have any reasons of your own to keep our relationship going?" I asked. "Do you expect me to believe that you're just doing Edith a favor?"

"I don't care what you believe," he said. "I'm simply telling you why the whole thing *began*. Things were not equal between Edith and me, do you see?"

"I see that you're jealous," I said. "Never mind how anything began. I see how you are *now*." But Severin just shook his head and said goodnight. I wondered if Edith would let him in.

He persisted in this line about equality with Edith too. He made us feel as if we had nothing to do with it! He reduced us; he implied that the responsibility was all his.

"It wasn't all *your* decision!" Edith screamed at him.

"It was all my *in*decision," he said. "And I'm never going to be less than equal to you again. It's all right now," he told us all lightly. "I feel I'm back to being even now."

"*You* do," Edith said scornfully. "It's always *you*. And I suppose you'll never sleep with someone else again?"

"No, never," he said. He was enough of a fanatic so that you could believe him—or at least believe that he believed himself.

"I don't want to talk to you about this anymore," Edith said coolly. "I refuse to listen to you."

"Don't treat him like a child," Utch said to her.

"He *is* a child," Edith said.

"Look," I said. "There are four of us, and there are four versions of all of us, and there probably always will be. It's silly for us to try to make each other agree. All of us can't be expected to see what's happened in the same way."

"There are probably five or six versions," said Edith, "or eight or nine." But Severin could not keep quiet.

"No," he said. "I see it better than any of you because I've never really been involved in it." I could have killed him for saying that with Utch right there. He *was* a child. "If I'm a child," he said, "that's okay with me."

"With you, yes!" said Edith harshly. "It's always what's okay with you —*you, you, you!*"

But this was later. That night she *did* let him in. They came by our house the next morning, after all the kids were in school. Edith would not look at me; she held Utch's hand and smiled at her. When I saw that Edith had a bruise on her face, I grabbed Severin's wrist and said, "If you were pissed off last night, you could have hit me before you left. I'm not any match for you either, but I could have offered more resistance than Edith." He looked at me as if he doubted this. A mark the color of a plum stretched Edith's skin tight over one cheek and tugged one eye half-closed; her bruise was the size of a good novel.

"It was an accident," Edith said. "We were arguing, but I was just trying to get away from him. I twisted loose and ran into something."

"A wall," Severin muttered.

"Coffee?" Utch asked everyone.

"I don't want to stay that long," Edith said to Severin, but she sat down at the kitchen table. "We want to stop it," she told the sugar bowl.

"Well, *I* want to stop it," Severin said. "It's not good for Edith and me." Utch and I said nothing. "I'm sorry," Severin said, "but it just isn't working out. I told you I've felt—well, *pressured*—to keep going on with it. It's not a pressure that Edith or either of you has put on me; it's all my own doing. I simply felt compelled to make something work which I never felt quite good about. I felt I owed it to Edith. But she really didn't make me feel that."

"Yes, she did," Utch said. I was surprised. Edith sat, her lips together.

"No, she really didn't," Severin said quietly. "It was just me. I thought it would seem more natural as it went on, but it hasn't. I thought that things between Edith and me would get better, but they haven't."

"What things?" I asked. "What things were wrong before this started?"

"This whole business made things between us worse," Severin said. Edith still said nothing. "It made me feel badly with Edith—it made me feel badly *about* her. I got to thinking that the only times I was behaving well were when I was with Utch. I haven't behaved very well with Edith, and I don't like to behave as I have. I'm very embarrassed about it."

"Nothing's your fault," Utch told him. "Nothing is anybody's fault."

"I *did* hit Edith," Severin said, "and I've never done that before. I feel terrible about that. Before this whole thing began, I would never have lost that much control."

"That's my fault, too," Edith said. "He *had* to hit me."

"But I shouldn't have."

"Maybe you should have," Utch said. What in hell was she saying, anyway!

"Anyway," Severin said, "it's over. That's the best thing."

"Just like that?" I said.

"Yes, just like that," Edith said, looking directly at me. "That *is* the best thing."

"May I talk to Edith alone?" I asked Severin.

"Ask Edith."

"Later," Edith told me. And again I felt that the more we knew each other, the less we actually knew. "I want to talk to Utch now," Edith said.

"*Ja,* get out," Utch said to us. "Go sit outside, go take a trip around the block."

"Go to a movie," Edith suggested. "A double feature," she added. Severin stared at his hands.

Then Utch screamed some German at Severin; he mumbled, *"Es tut mir leid."* But Utch went on and on. I took Severin's arm and made him stand up while Edith steered Utch toward our bedroom. After a while, we heard both of them crying in there. The language they were speaking was stranger than English or German.

Severin went and stood outside our bedroom door. "Utch?" he called. "It's better not to see each other for a while. Then it gets a lot easier."

It was Edith who opened the door. "Forget what you're thinking," she snapped at him. "I wish you'd stop trying to make this like the Ullmans. It's not the same." She slammed the door.

"Who are the Ullmans?" I asked Severin, but he pushed past me and went outside.

"I have to go to the wrestling room," he told me. "I don't suppose you want to come along." It didn't sound like an invitation. I was struck that at least Edith and Utch could talk to each other.

"Who were the fucking Ullmans?" I yelled at him.

"The fucking who?" he asked.

"Severin," I said. "Suppose what's wrong between you and Edith doesn't stop; suppose it's not us who are making things bad, but just you—or something else. Then what?"

"Nothing's wrong between Edith and me," he said, walking away; he was leaving the car for Edith.

"I can't stay here," I said. "They want to be alone. I'll come with you."

"Suit yourself."

For a short-legged, stumplike man, he walked fast. I was winded halfway to the gym; I thought of his lungs sucking up more than his share of air —air that other people could use.

"What did you hit her with?" I asked. The mauve mark on Edith's face was almost a rectangle, too big to be covered by a fist. I didn't think that Severin Winter would slap anyone with his open hand.

"It was just something lying around the bedroom," he said.

"What?"

"A book," he said. Of course; leave it to him to hit a writer with what hurts.

"*What* book?" I asked.

"Any old book," he said. "I just used it. I didn't stop to read it."

We were near the gym; I had no intention of actually going in there. Coming toward us were two of Severin's wrestlers. I recognized their hipless, assless, bowlegged walk, and their shoulders crouched awkwardly alongside their ears like yokes on oxen.

"Did the Ullmans come before or after Audrey Cannon?" I asked.

"You have no right to anything that's not freely offered," he said to me.

"For God's sake, Severin. This is going to upset Edith and Utch terribly!"

"If we keep on with it, it could upset them more," he said.

The wrestlers merged with us. One of them—that dolt Bender—gave Severin Winter an apish blow on the back, a clout with his cat-quick paw. The grinning one with the baboon arms was Iacovelli. He was in my Introduction to European History course, and I'd once had to tell him that the Dordogne was a river in France; Iacovelli had thought it was the name of a king. Dordogne the First, I suppose.

"Hi, Coach," Iacovelli said. "Hello, Doctor." He was one of those who thought a Ph.D. was rarer than admiralty, but it's odd that he didn't seem to know that Severin Winter had one too.

"I'll call you," I told Severin.

"*Ja,*" he said. Watching him heading for the gym, flanked by his wrestlers, I couldn't resist yelling, "I know whose book it was. It was *mine!*" I had just given Edith a copy of my first historical novel, the one about the French village being wiped out by plague; it was long out of print and the only one of mine that Edith hadn't read. We'd spoken of our early styles, and I'd wanted her to see my first effort. What a book to hit someone with! Over four hundred pages, a heavy weapon. (Later he would say to Edith, "The presumptuousness of that bastard to think that it was *his* book. As if a 118-pound novel could leave any marks on a person at all, not to mention a bruise." But it *was* my book; it *must* have been! No doubt they had been arguing about me when it happened, and what better symbol could he have found for his frustration?)

But Severin ignored me. He never turned or broke his bearish gait. Only Bender looked back at me, as if he thought I might have been calling to him. His machine-steady gaze was as lifeless as the building he was entering: gray, concrete, steel and glass—its insides of chlorinated water, disinfected mats, ice frozen by cooling pipes, ointments and powders which dealt harshly with fungi of the feet and crotch, and countless bouncing balls pumped full of air. That was Severin Winter's world, and I knew I did not belong in it.

So then it was over. Severin retreated to his wrestling room. I went to the library and waited until I thought Edith and Utch had talked all they needed to. But it was hard to imagine them talking at all.

When I went home, the kids were playing in the kitchen and Utch was cooking. She was making a complicated meal, though I doubted she felt like celebrating.

"Get out of here and find something to do," I told the kids. "Don't get in your mother's way." But Utch said she wanted them around; she liked the feeling that she was in a busy place. I sliced radishes, and Jack read to us from an old edition of *Europe on Five Dollars a Day*. He read all the parts about what to do with children in various cities, then told us which city he wanted to visit. Bart ate radishes as fast as I could cut them up; occasionally, he spat one at Jack.

All through dinner, Utch chattered with Jack and Bart pushed his uneaten food in my direction. I remembered that it had been a long time since we'd eaten with the children. After dinner, while Jack was promising to fix Bart a bath without pushing his head under, Utch said, "When the children go to bed, I think I'm going to die. We've got to keep them with us. Can't we all go to a movie?"

I took a bath with Bart and Jack; their small bodies were as sleek as wet puppies. Afterward the first pair of underpants I tried to put on was the pair Severin had redesigned with a razor. As I threw them away I wondered why Utch had kept them. Now she was splashing in the tub with Bart and Jack; it seemed she would never stop talking to them. The second pair of underpants I tried on also had the crotch slit through, and so did the third and the fourth. *All* my underpants were uncrotched with a single slash.

I slipped on my old corduroys without underwear and we went to the movies. It was one of those films without sex and full of simple violence, and therefore all right to take your children to. Someone named Robert is a kind of rookie in the wilderness; he meets various savages, white, Indian and animal, all of whom teach him how to survive. The film is about survival, I guess. Robert learns how to make mittens out of skinned squirrels; he wears rabbits on his feet; he keeps his head warm with an Indian's head of hair. He meets lots of weaker people who are crazy or cowardly or about to become one or the other; they haven't learned all of Mother Nature's harsh little tricks as well as he has. Robert enters the wilderness blond, clean-shaven, boyish and wearing clothes that fit him. He emerges bearded, wrinkled and bundled in animal hides, looking like the animal which grew the hides and somehow shrank inside its own skin. He learns not to be afraid and not to feel anything. Apparently a part of survival is getting over things. By the end of the movie, Robert has adapted to the wilderness and is very good at getting over, for example, the rape, mutilation and murder of his wife and children.

The film was absolutely humorless about this crap, which the audience took very seriously—all except Utch. She knew a little bit about survival, and she started laughing at the very first scene of meaningful slaughter.

Jack whispered, "Why is that funny?"

"Because it's not truthful," Utch told him.

Pretty soon Jack started laughing every time his mother did, and Bart, who was used to cartoons, laughed with them. I felt badly, but I laughed more than any of them. We were at odds with the audience; a certain hostility came through to us, particularly during the film's funniest scene. I had to take Bart to the bathroom and so missed some of it but in the part I saw, Robert is about to open a door to an old woodshed. This takes a long time so that the audience can absorb the increasing tension. We know that behind the woodshed door is a crazed mother who's been hiding there for days with her dead children all stashed around her like groceries. There's been an Indian massacre and the mother hides in the woodshed and kills everyone who peeks in the door, then drags the bodies inside with her to wait for more Indians. It's unclear whether she or the Indians have massacred her children. Robert is about to open that terrible door, and we're supposed to hope that by this time he has learned enough from Mother Nature to be smart about it. Of course, it would be smartest not to open the door at all, but it appears he is going to.

Some rows in front of us several young girls in the theater tried to warn Robert. He puts his squirrel-skinned hand on the latch. "No, no," the young girls moaned. But from some other part of the house, another voice hollered, "Go on! Open it, you simple son-of-a-bitch!" Utch and the kids burst out laughing, and so did I, though I recognized that crazy voice. It was Severin Winter, of course.

When the movie was over, I hurried Utch and the kids to the car. It was not that I felt we had to avoid the Winters at that moment; it was just that it was raining. "Stop pulling me," Utch said. "I like the rain." But we were in our car and driving away when they came out with their children.

"I see Fiordiligi!" Jack said. "And Dorabella!" Bart shrieked.

"Open it!" Utch shouted, but her laughter chilled me.

When the kids were in bed, Utch said, "I'm not going to break down."

"Damn them, anyway," I said. "They've always called all the shots."

"Oh, now it's 'them,' is it?" Utch asked. Then she took my hand and said, "No, we'll all still be friends, won't we?"

"After a while," I said. "Sure."

"I know it's going to be bad at first," she said, "but it will be comfortable to see each other again without the sex, won't it?"

"I hope so," I said. "We can just go back to being friends."

"You simple son-of-a-bitch," she said; then she shook her head and cried for a while. I held her. "We never *were* friends," she said. "We were just lovers, so there's nothing to go back to being." I thought of shaggy Robert opening doors around the world, tromping around in the bodies of dead creatures, his face gradually simplifying into an expression of stupid endurance. And this pointless, gory journey of always one more unwanted discovery was called survival and thought to be heroic.

"I don't even know if we were lovers," Utch bawled.

"Of course you were," I told her.

"I think we were just *fuckers!*" she cried.

"No, no. Give it time. Time is what matters."

"You think history actually means something," Utch said to me bitterly. I wondered who had told her that it didn't. "Don't touch me," she said. Then she softened. "I mean, not for a while."

I undressed. "I need some new underwear," I said, but she was silent. "Why did you do it?" I asked her gently; I wasn't forcing her.

"How could you have let this happen to me?" Utch said; her face was frightened, hurt, accusing. "You weren't looking out for me!" she cried. "You weren't even thinking about me!"

I wondered if Edith and Severin were shouting tonight.

"You're even thinking of her right now," Utch said. (The poor, dangerous woman in the woodshed with her murdered children strewn around her had grinned at Robert and told him, "It's a good thing I'm so smart. I knew just where to hide the children so that no one would hurt them.") Utch grinned at me with an unsettling expression and snatched the razored underpants from my hand. "I did it," she said, and she put them on her head like a hat.

"I know you did," I said; I was trying to be comforting, but she kept shaking her head at me as if I didn't understand. Then I understood that she had done that *first* pair, too—the pair I thought Severin had slashed. She saw the change in my face and nodded vigorously. "Yes, yes," she said brightly. "That's right, it was *me!*" She seemed delighted by this revelation until she started to cry again. "I love him," she sobbed. "Don't you see what terrible trouble we're in?"

"It'll be all right," I said. She laughed for a while, then cried herself to sleep.

Then Jack had a nightmare and woke up whimpering. He was remembering a dirty trick from the movie. A lot of tough old savages are reminiscing about the meanest things they've ever seen, and one of them tells the story of how he saw someone's belly slit open just a little bit—enough to pull out a part of the intestines and wave this offal in front of a dog who tried to bolt it down whole, then ran off with it, unraveling the person's insides in a nasty fashion. But I told my delicate boy that the world wasn't like this at all. He wouldn't have that nightmare again, I said. "It'll be all right," I said. Ah, the lies we fall asleep to.

Bart slept through Jack's dream like a turtle in its shell. Utch was asleep too. I waited for Jack to go back to sleep; I waited until I knew Severin would be asleep too. I was wide-awake and I was sure that Edith was too. I smoked about my quiet house; I could see Edith smoking from room to room. I had to speak to her, to hear her voice. When I thought I had waited long enough, I tried our signal of letting the phone ring half a tone, then hanging up. I waited. I could see her moving to the phone, lighting a fresh cigarette; she would curl a long strand of hair behind her ear. I could feel the way her hand would lie on the receiver, waiting for my second call. Her wrist was so thin, so angular. I dialed again. As usual, the phone didn't even ring once all the way through before the receiver was snatched up.

"Edith is asleep," said Severin Winter.

⑨

The Runner-Up Syndrome

When it was over and before all of it had sunk in, feelings were raw in the supermarket, distant in parking lots, awkward whenever the four of us encountered each other. Because, of course, such meetings were out of context with what we'd once been together. And the children still wanted to play with each other. We could manage as much as a week without encounters; then, when we did meet, the shock of how we'd grown apart made the occasion more unsettling.

In a brief exchange with Edith—absurdly, we were in line at different tellers' windows—I said, "Utch and I hope we can see you again soon. I know it's going to be hard at first."

"Not for me," she said brightly.

"Oh."

"Forget it," said Edith. "That's what I'm doing."

But she didn't mean it. She was clearly insulating herself from her real feelings for me; she had to, no doubt, because of Severin's nonstop, needling ways.

Utch's silence bore into me like a wound. She said that when she ran into Severin, he would not look her in the eye. "I disgust him," she said, and when I tried to hold her, she pulled away.

At first her insomnia only made her go to bed later and later. She slept in her underwear. Then she began getting up in the night to take walks.

"Since when were you ever a walker?" I asked, but she just shrugged; she didn't want to tell me where she went. I knew insomnia had to be handled delicately.

Months earlier we had planned to make the weekend of the national wrestling championships a lovers' interlude. Edith and I would stay with all the children while Utch followed George James Bender and Severin to his vicarious victory in Stillwater, Oklahoma. We all agreed that Bender would be so far gone in his tunnel trance that he wouldn't notice the strange but familiar woman who was one door down the motel hall from Severin's room. Edith and I were frequently seen together, but with the children around us all day, we would not be, as Severin continually feared, linked together in an overtly public manner. He had finally agreed: Utch would be his fan while he nursed Bender, match by match, through the nationals, and while Bender slept the dead sleep of gladiators, Severin and Utch could shock the motel's bed-vibrator.

Ah, Stillwater, Oklahoma—a Paris looming in Utch's future. But it never came off.

"It was a Paris in your future too," Utch said. "You were looking forward to all that time here with Edith, waking up with her in the morning, sneaking feels all day, resting up for another night. Don't say it was just me who was looking forward to it."

"Of course not," I said. "We were *all* looking forward to it."

"*He* wasn't," Utch said. "I think Severin was dreading it."

I tried to comfort her, but she would just go out walking again. The whole time Severin was with Bender in Stillwater, she walked. And one evening while he was away she walked to the Winters' house to see Edith. I can't imagine why. She found the Winters' house full of the wrestling team and Coke and cheeseburgers and potato chips. Iacovelli and Tyrone Williams and all of Severin's other nonchampion wrestlers were baby-sitting; Edith had gone to Stillwater with Severin and George James Bender.

Edith in Stillwater? A swan in the cornfield!

I have never been in Stillwater, Oklahoma, the home of the Oklahoma State Cowboys, a traditional wrestling power. What could it be like? A flat land, trampled by cattle, cowboys and wrestlers, and seeping oil? Even its name sends a shudder through me: *Stillwater.* I see an oasis, a swampish lagoon, a string of air-conditioned motels, thirsty wrestlers on horseback malingering around the one saloon. The big drink of the town is *Tang.* Poor Edith!

"Why did she go, if she didn't want to?" Utch asked.

"Because he didn't dare leave her alone here. He didn't trust her," I said.

"You don't know that," Utch said.

"He's never trusted her," I said. "Throughout this whole thing."

We could only follow what was going on in the papers, and wrestling is not popular with *The New York Times.* On Thursday there was only this:

Iowa State Favored for Team Mat Title

STILLWATER, Okla. (AP)—Host Oklahoma State, third-ranked, hopes to upset defending national champion Iowa State in the national collegiate wrestling tournament beginning here today. Oregon State's second-ranked Beavers and the fourth-ranked University of Oklahoma Sooners are also contenders. Iowa State has three returning individual champions, but one of them— 158-pounder Willard Buzzard (23–0–1)—is not picked to repeat. Though the defending champion, Buzzard is seeded second behind Eastern collegiate champion George James Bender (20–0–0)—the only wrestler east of the Mississippi favored to win a championship title. Bender, voted outstanding wrestler in the Eastern tournament at Annapolis two weeks ago, has pinned eighteen out of his last twenty opponents . . .

No information on what brought Edith to Stillwater. No itinerary of her day. Did she attend the Historical Museum of the City of Stillwater? Did she see the prize portrait of the largest Hereford ever slaughtered in Oklahoma?

On Friday *The New York Times* offered more bare statistics. In the 158-pound class, Willard Buzzard of Iowa State advanced through his preliminary matches with a fall over a Yale boy in 0:55 of the first period and a decision over Colorado State, 15–7. Lehigh's Mike Warnick, runner-up to Bender in the Easterns, advanced by upsetting the Big Ten champion from Minnesota (4–4, 5–4 in overtime) and by pinning the cadet from Army in 1:36 of the second period. Oregon State's Hiroshi Matsumoto flattened Wyoming's Curt Strode in 1:12 of the first and mauled an imported Iranian from UCLA, 11–1. And George James Bender—treading water—advanced with two falls, pinning Portland State's Akira Shinjo in 1:13 of the third, and Les McCurtain, the hope of Oklahoma, in 1:09 of the first. These four also passed untouched through the quarterfinals.

Et cetera. It's a wonder to me that they all weren't *bored* into a pinning position. I could just see Severin whispering over his fruit cup to Bender —the table strewn with match results, brackets of the possible outcomes, notes about what Matsumoto is looking for when he sets up. And Bender, a mat burn raw on his chin and one eye weeping from a poke by Portland State, would gobble his shrimp cocktail, the tiny fork foreign to his stubby fingers, his knuckles swollen and taped. "Watch how much of that crap you eat," Severin would be saying. Between them, Edith would pick at her lobster bisque. "You should know better than to order lobster in Oklahoma, Edith," Severin would tell her.

What could be going on? Utch went to see how the wrestlers were doing with the Winters' children. I knew she was hurt that we had not been asked to look after them.

"The children seem happy," she reported when she returned. "They're certainly eating a lot of hamburg." Probably raw, I thought, but Utch went on: "The team says that if Bender beats the Japanese in the semis, he'll go all the way. They say he used to beat Buzzard every day in practice back at Iowa State."

"Do you think I care?" I asked her. She sulked; I knew she was wishing she was there. "He should have taken you anyway," I said to her. "You could have kept to your separate rooms, after all. But he's so paranoid that he can't believe a thing is over even when he's called it off himself. My God, did he think I'd be sneaking down to his house to rape his wife every night he was gone?"

"If I was there," Utch said, "I'd sneak into his motel room and rape *him.*" I was shocked; I couldn't say anything. She took another walk. I pictured Edith out walking in Stillwater—the cowboys drunk, the cattle staring at her, the coyotes ululant.

In Saturday's *New York Times* the 158-pound class had narrowed down predictably. Iowa State's Willard Buzzard had a hard time with Lehigh's Mike Warnick, but survived the semifinal round to beat Warnick by two points, 12–10. (Bender had pinned Warnick in their Eastern final match; by comparative scores, Buzzard appeared to be in trouble.) Bender, coasting 9–0 in the third period of his semifinal with Oregon State's Hiroshi Matsumoto, separated Matsumoto's shoulder and advanced to the finals by forfeit—as good as a fall. "Well, that's that," Utch said. "The Jap was supposed to be the only one who could give him any trouble. He's got it wrapped up."

"'Wrapped up!'" I said. I hated that goddamn language. "I hope he gets stuck in an elevator and misses the match. I hope he eats a diseased steer and throws the whole thing. I hope he's seduced by a cowgirl and wilts under pressure. I'm going to set up a shrine to Willard Buzzard and pray to it all night. I hope Bender loses himself in a genetics problem—preferably his own. I hope Severin is so humiliated that he never dares to coach anyone again!"

"Stop it," Utch said. "Please stop it. Do we have to hate them now? Do we?"

On Sunday *The New York Times* said nothing. The finals took place after 8 P.M., Oklahoma time, and the results would be in Monday's paper.

"I could call the boys over at the Winters'," Utch said. "I'm sure they'd know."

"Jesus, 'the boys,'" I said. "Go ahead, if you must."

"Well, I can wait, of course," Utch said, and she did.

I ran out of cigarettes a little after midnight and had to go to Mama Paduzzi's Pizza Parlour. It was the only place in town open after midnight and was always full of students, or worse. I met Edith at the cigarette machine. Severin hated smoking so violently that he now refused to buy them for her if she ran out. Edith disliked the pizza place so much that she actually looked pleased to see me. Two seedy youths were hanging around the machine, eyeing her.

"You're back," I said.

"It's not that far."

"I thought it was another country," I said.

"Oh, it *is.*" We laughed, and then she seemed to remember when we had last laughed together and looked away. "I left my headlights on," she said. Outside, she got into the car, turned the lights out and sat staring at the wheel. "I can't see you at all, under any circumstances," she said. "It just doesn't work out very well."

"If Severin would just *talk* to Utch sometime," I said. "She's pretty bad, she is really, well . . . *taken* with him, you know."

"I know that," she said, exasperated. "Didn't *you* know that? Severin *can't* talk to her. I don't think he can stand her. He doesn't want to hurt her any more than he already has."

"He doesn't have any right to hate us," I said.

"It's me he hates," she said. I touched her arm, but she pulled away. "Go look after Utch," she said. "I'm all right, I'm not suffering. I'm not in love with you."

"You didn't have to say that," I said.

She started the car; I saw that she was crying. But for whom?

When I got home, Utch had left a note; she had gone to see Edith. But I knew she hadn't found Edith at home. At 4 A.M. I went to the Winters' house to get her. She was curled up on their living room couch and wouldn't come home with me. Severin had gone to bed.

"He went to bed hours ago," Edith told me, "and I'm about to go to bed myself." She said Utch could stay on the couch if she wanted to, and she did. I left her after about an hour; it was clear she wasn't going to talk to me.

It was the university paper that I saw on Monday; I never did see how *The New York Times* wrote it up. But the school paper had more local information.

Bender Upset in Finals; Winter to Resign

An interesting headline, I thought, and it wouldn't have made *The New York Times*. I couldn't believe it. I doubted that Iowa State's Willard Buzzard could, either. Bender was quoted as saying, "I just didn't get up for it." Willard Buzzard—a former teammate of Bender's at Iowa State—said he sensed that Bender wasn't ready for him from the very first take-down; Bender looked listless. Remembering their old practices together,

Buzzard said, "George used to push me around pretty good, and I never forgot it. I owed him this one." Buzzard wrestled a very physical, aggressive match. "I just never rose to the occasion," said George James Bender. Coach Severin Winter agreed. "George wasn't himself. I think he shot his wad the night before." Winter was referring to Bender's semifinal victory over Oregon State's Hiroshi Matsumoto. Coach Winter announced to the reporters in Stillwater his plans to retire. Back on campus, he denied that Bender's loss in the finals had any influence on his decision. "I've been thinking about stepping down for some time. I'd like to spend more time with my wife and children, and continue my studies for the German Department." Asked if he would stay with the team until a new coach could be found, Winter said he would. "I hope to still get up to the wrestling room from time to time," Winter said, "just to roll around." Bender had nothing but praise for Severin Winter's coaching. "He was instrumental in getting me to the finals," Bender said. "He got me there, and it was up to me to take it from there. I'm sorry I let him down." Coach Winter shook his head and smiled when asked if he thought Bender had let him down. "We only let ourselves down," Winter said. "We should try to minimize all this responsibility we feel we owe other people."

A curious remark to find in a sports column.

"Incredible!" I said to Utch. "What was the score? The stupid paper doesn't even give the score."

"Buzzard was leading twelve to five in the last period when he pinned Bender."

"A slaughter," I said. "I don't believe it. Bender must have been sick."

I could see the look of bored superiority that Utch suddenly showed before she turned her face away. She was afraid I had seen it, and I had. "What is it?" I asked her. "What happened out there?"

"Bender didn't get up for it," Utch said, her back still turned to me. "Just what the paper says—he shot his wad the night before."

" 'Shot his wad!' " That disgusting sports talk!

" 'I just never rose to the occasion,' " Utch said, quoting Bender, but suddenly she burst out laughing. I did not like the tone of her laughter; harsh and derisive, it was not her tone.

"You talked with Edith," I said. "What happened?"

"You'd have liked to talk with her, wouldn't you?" Utch said.

"Never mind," I said. "What did she say?"

There's nothing vengeful in Utch, and I was surprised to see her face so suddenly determined to pay me back. For what? "Edith was angry that Severin made her come along," she said.

"See?" I said. "What did I tell you?"

"Shut up," she said; her temper was quicker than I'd ever seen it. "If you want to hear the story, shut up."

"Okay."

"You're going to love this story," Utch said; there was a meanness in her voice I'd never heard. "It's just your kind of story."

"Just tell it, Utch."

"Edith was angry that he didn't trust her, angry that he wouldn't leave her here for three nights and three days because of you. He said he trusted Edith but not you; that's why he wanted her to go."

"What's the difference?" I said. "If he *really* trusted her, it wouldn't matter whether he trusted me or not, right?"

"Shut up," Utch said. She was wound up and seemed on the verge of hysteria. "Edith resented what Severin had made of her independence— or so she said," Utch went on. " 'I wanted to teach him that he couldn't cram his life down my throat and not leave me free to live mine,' was the way she put it. 'Within reason, of course; I'd always accepted the limits that he set up,' she told me. 'Therefore, when he said the whole thing had to stop, we all stopped.' That's what she went on and on about," Utch said.

"Go on."

"Well, he wouldn't even let her do what she wanted when they got to Stillwater," Utch said. "She wanted to fly to Denver for a day and a night; she'd never been to Denver. But Severin made her stay. Finally, she just wanted to amuse herself in her own way in Stillwater, instead of going to the wrestling every day."

"And he wouldn't let her?"

"Edith says he wouldn't."

"Jesus."

"So," Utch said, "she decided to show him that if he wouldn't trust her, she wouldn't be trustworthy. She hit him close to home."

" 'Close to home!' " I yelled. "Would you stop that language, those horrible sportscaster phrases!"

"Bender was exhausted after Friday's semifinal," Utch said. "Severin told Edith to drive Bender back to the motel; Severin said he'd meet her there after the rest of the semis were over. They had a rented car, and Bender doesn't know how to drive."

"He doesn't know how to drive?"

"He doesn't know how to do a lot, apparently," Utch said.

I stared at her. "Oh no," I said. "Oh no you don't. You're lying."

"I haven't told you yet," she said.

"You're lying anyway!"

"Then Edith was lying," Utch said. "She took Bender back to the motel."

"No."

"And she put him to bed."

"No, no . . ."

"Apparently," Utch said, her voice—mocking—imitating Edith's voice, " 'he couldn't get up for it, he never rose to the occasion.' "

"*I* don't believe any of this," I said. "Edith *seduced* Bender? It couldn't have happened!"

"Maybe she told him it was the coach's orders," Utch said. "Maybe she said it would relax him. Anyway, she told me he was unable to."

"She's lying," I said.

"Maybe she is," Utch said. "I don't know."

"Yes, you do," I said. "Go on."

"So Severin came back to the motel and found them together."

"I don't believe—"

"And Bender was very hangdog about the whole thing."

" 'Hangdog!' " I cried. "Good Christ . . ."

"I mean, he'd been unable to do it with Edith, and he'd let his coach down . . . I suppose that's what he thought."

"Bullshit!" I screamed.

"And the next night just before the match, Severin told Bender, 'I hope you get your ass knocked off.' And Severin sat in the coach's chair and watched the match in an absolutely emotionless way. So Bender lost, of course."

"And I suppose Edith sat in the balcony and waved a pennant and cheered her heart out!" I hollered. "Oh, come on!"

"Do you know what Edith said to Severin?" Utch asked. "She said, '*Now* we're even, if you still think being even matters.' "

"And I suppose Severin decided that he'd had enough of wrestling and resigned?"

"Right."

"Wrong," I said. "Edith's a lousy storyteller, or *you* are."

"Edith thinks you're a lousy writer," Utch said. "She doesn't believe you can teach her a thing."

"Did she say that?" I asked. But Utch just put her head down and sighed, and I knew that was all I was going to hear.

"Severin told you that," I said. "Edith wouldn't say that about me." But when Utch lifted her face, she was crying.

"Don't you see?" she asked. "It just gets uglier. We've stopped it, but we *can't* stop it. It just goes on and on. You shouldn't let it."

"Utch, come here," I said. I went toward her but she ran from me.

"You haven't even noticed what's wrong!" she screamed.

"What?"

"I can't come," she cried. I stared at her. "I can't *come!*"

"Well, you don't have to shout about it," I said. She ran out the door into the yard yelling, "I can't come! I can't come! I can't come!" Then she went into our bedroom and sprawled on our bed and cried. I left her alone.

I called Severin and said, "Look, how are you two getting along? Utch told me."

"Told you what?"

"Edith told Utch what happened out there," I said.

"Oh *ja,*" he said. "Bender really blew it."

"Be honest with me, Severin," I said. Then I told him the story I'd heard. He denied it, but of course he *would* deny it.

A little later Edith called Utch and said that Utch had betrayed her. Apparently Edith had told her not to breathe a word to me—knowing Utch would breathe right away, of course. Utch answered that Edith had betrayed Severin's confidence by telling the story in the first place. Then I called Edith and told her I knew it was a lie.

"Of course it is," she said. But she meant that Utch had lied.

"No, *you* lied," I said.

"Fuck you," Edith said.

We didn't see the Winters for weeks, and when they invited us to dinner, we weren't sure what the dinner was for.

"They're going to poison us," I said, but Utch didn't smile. "Severin likes to make everything official," I said. "He needs to hold a banquet to announce that everything is indeed over between us."

"Maybe they want to apologize."

"For what?" I said. "For using us? I'm sure they're not sorry."

"Shut up," Utch said. "Maybe they want to try the whole thing again."

"Fat chance."

"And if they wanted to try it again," Utch said, "you'd jump at the chance."

"Like hell I would."

"Ha!"

"Shut up."

When Severin greeted us at the door, he said, "Edith's given up cigarettes, so we're not going to have a very long cocktail hour. That's when she feels most like smoking." He kissed Utch on the cheek the way I'd seen him kiss his children and shook my hand. For a wrestler, Severin had a very weak handshake, as if he were trying to impress you with how gentle he was.

Edith was eating a carrot stick in the living room; she turned her cheek and let me kiss her while both her hands clutched her carrot. I remembered the first evening we had eaten with them; they were both much freer with themselves.

"We're having squid," Severin said.

"Severin spent the whole day cooking," Edith said.

"Actually, it's cleaning them that's the most time-consuming," he said. "First you have to strip the skin off. It's sort of like a film—a membrane —very slimy. Then you have to take the insides out."

"Squid are like prophylactics," Edith said. "It's like turning a rubber inside out."

"Edith helped me do it," Severin said. "I think she gets her rocks off turning squid inside out." Edith laughed, and Utch snapped a carrot between her teeth like the neckbone of a small animal.

"How's the work coming?" I asked Edith.

"I've just finished something," Edith said. She was eating one carrot after another. I wanted to smoke but there were no ashtrays.

"Have you put on weight since you stopped smoking?" Utch asked.

"I only stopped a week ago," Edith said. I couldn't tell about her weight; she wore a shapeless peasant dress, the kind of thing she never wore. I felt that Severin had dressed her for the occasion, making certain that the outline of her taut body was not visible to me.

"Time to eat!" Severin said.

The squid was on a large platter in white ringlets and grayish clumps of tentacles in a red sauce; it resembled little snippets and chunks of fingers and toes. Upstairs we could hear Fiordiligi and Dorabella taking a bath together; splashes, the tub filling, their girlish voices, Fiordiligi teasing, Dorabella complaining.

"I haven't seen the girls in a long time," Utch said.

"They're taking a bath," Edith said. Stupidly, we all listened to them taking their bath.

I would have been grateful for the interruption of our awkward silence by the great shattering crash, except that I knew exactly what it was. There was a sound like the machine-gunning of several upstairs windows, followed in a split second by the shrieking of both children. The stem of Edith's wineglass snapped in her hand and she screamed terribly. Utch's hand jerked the serving spoon across the platter and sent the squid splattering on the white tablecloth. Severin and I were moving upstairs, Severin ahead of me, moaning as he ran, "Oh God no, no, no—I'm coming!"

I knew what had happened because I knew that bathroom, bathtub and shower as well as Severin; I knew my wet love nest. The crash had been the sliding glass door on the bathtub rim; many nights, Edith and I had precariously opened and closed it. Old-fashioned heavy glass, loose in its rusting metal frame, the door slid in a blackened groove, slimy with old soap slivers and tiny parts from children's bathtub toys. Twice the door had eased out of the groove and Edith and I had clutched it and kept it from falling as we guided it back in its proper track. I'd said to Edith, "Better have Severin fix that. We could get hurt in here." Time and time again, Severin had told *her* to get it fixed. "Call a bathroom man," he said absurdly.

I had always known that if the door fell on Edith and me, Severin would at least delight in whatever injury it gave me. And if something were to be cut by the falling door, I never doubted what it would be.

"I'm coming!" screamed Severin witlessly. I knew there would be blood, but I was unprepared for how much. The bathroom looked like the scene of a gangland slaying. The old door had pitched into the tub and broken over the naked girls, the glass exploding from the frame, sending shards and fragments flying everywhere; it crunched under Severin's shoes as he plunged his arms into the tub. The tub was pink, the water bloody; you could not tell who was cut where. Out the faucet the water still poured, the tub a churning sea of glass and bleeding children. Severin lifted Dorabella out to me; she was quivering, conscious but no longer screaming; she looked nervously all over her body to see where she was wounded. I pulled the shower handle and doused us all so that I could see where her deepest cuts were. Hunting for severed arteries, Severin lifted the bent door frame over Fiordiligi's lovely head and held her under the shower while she howled and wriggled and he examined her body for cuts. Both of them had a multitude of flack-like wounds, boil-sized punctures and swellings on their arms and shoulders. I found one deep cut on Dorabella, in her sodden hair above one ear—a gash that had parted her hair and scalp, nearly as long as my finger but not quite as deep as her skull. It bled richly but slowly; there were no arteries there. Severin tied a towel around Fiordiligi's leg above her knee and twisted it into a fair tourniquet. A wedge of glass, like the head of a broad chisel, protruded from Fiordiligi's kneecap and the blood welled and flowed but never spurted. Both children were perhaps in shock and were in for a tedious and messy glass-picking session at the hospital. It would be long and painful, and there would be stitches, but they would be all right.

I knew that Severin had feared one or both of them would bleed to death in his arms, or be already drowned and bled dry by the time he reached them. "They're all right!" I yelled downstairs, where Utch was holding Edith, who would not move from her chair, sitting as if frozen, Utch said, waiting for the news. "I'll call the hospital," I said, "and tell them you're coming."

Severin took Dorabella from me and carried both nude children down to Edith; white-faced and shaking, she reviewed each wound on each daughter with wonder and pain, as if she had caused them herself.

"Please help yourselves to supper." Edith said vacantly. She did not care. She was only aware of the priority of her children.

Severin suddenly blurted, "It could have happened to you." Clearly he meant, to her and me; he meant *should* have.

With a shock, I realized that I didn't care what they thought. I realized that my Jack and my Bart had taken baths in that hazardous tub; I was thinking only that it could have happened to them, and that it could have been much worse.

We threw their coats around the children and Utch opened the car door for them. Edith never waved or said thank you as she sat with both her slashed daughters against her and let Severin drive them to the hospital, where they were to be picked clean and sewn back together, nearly as good as new. As the car backed out, I was glad to see that Edith was smoking.

Utch insisted that we clean up the bathroom. We agreed that they shouldn't have to see all that blood when they came home. Together we lugged the heavy door frame and few large pieces of glass to the trash pickup; together we vacuumed fragments from every crevice. I found a piece of glass lying across the bristles of a toothbrush; danger was everywhere. We scrubbed that bathroom spotless, drained the blood-filled tub, scrubbed the blood stains on the stairs, put all the stained towels in the washer and started it. With a screwdriver I gouged little slivers of glass out of the vile groove of the glass door. I remembered that Edith had once braced her heels against that door. I knew where the fresh linen was kept (You *would,* said Utch) and we put fresh towels on the racks. I hoped to myself that there might be a slice of glass left behind on the tub floor for Severin to sit on.

When we were done, we weren't hungry. Severin's cold squid was not appealing; it lay dead on the tablecloth, where Utch had slopped it; Edith's spilled wine had bled into it. The dish looked like the terrible debris from an operation.

I hardly said a word as we drove home. Utch broke the silence once: "Your children are more important to you than anything," she said. I didn't answer, but it wasn't because I disagreed.

That night I woke up alone in the damp bed. A window was open and it was raining. I looked everywhere, but Utch was out walking. Where can she go in this weather? I wondered. I checked the children's windows and closed them against the rain. Bart lay sunk in his pillow like a hammer, his fingers bunching the sheet in his sleep. Slim Jack lay in his bed as perfectly as the dream of a dancer. But there was no sleep coming to me, I realized. I checked the children's breathing, regular and deep. I found the umbrella. Utch did not need it where she was. I knew that she had not returned her keys to the gym and wrestling room to Severin.

I thought, if Utch is going to take up walking, I can too. Outside in the rain I greeted insomnia like a peevish mistress neglected for too long.

10

Back to Vienna

"I just go there to be alone," Utch told me. "It's a good place to think—to just rest."

"And you just might run into him up there one night," I said.

"Severin doesn't go there anymore," Utch said. "He's retired, remember?"

"I doubt that he's retired from that."

"Come with me next time," she said. "I know what you think of that whole building, but please come with me and see."

"I wouldn't set foot in there at night," I said. "It's just a place full of old jock-itch germs running around in the dark."

"Please. It's special for me, and I want you to see."

"Yes, I'll bet it's special for you," I said.

"It's almost the last place I had an orgasm," Utch said. She was certainly not shy about it. "I thought maybe we might try."

"Oh no," I said. "I don't go that way. That's not my style."

"Please just try," Utch said. "For me."

I hated Severin Winter for making my wife pathetic in my eyes. But what could I do? I took her to the gym.

In the darkness the great cage hulked like an abandoned beehive, its dangerous sleepers fled from their cells. In the new gym my shin struck an open locker door, and a tin *whang!* echoed among the sweat-stiff socks hung up to dry, the hockey sticks leaning in corners, the kneepads and bandages at rest. Utch said, *"Ssshhh!* Don't let Harvey hear us."

"Harvey?" I thought of a watchdog prowling in the dripping showers.

"The watchman."

"Well, surely he knows *you,*" I said, colliding with a low bench and greeting the cool cement floor with my cheek. There was a film of powder on the floor, a sort of deodorant designed for whole buildings. "For Christ's sake, Utch," I whispered, "hold my hand!"

She led me to the tunnel. Passing the little cave doors, I thought of the squash courts harboring bats. The air was stale. When we emerged into the moonlit cage, the pigeons stirred. Around the groaning board track, I lurched after Utch. "I think I lost the keys," I said.

"*I* have the keys," she said.

When she slid open the wrestling-room door, the rubbery blast from the heaters hit us. I shut the door and she turned on the lights. I knew that from outside one cell of the beehive was brightly lit, like the eye of a domed prehistoric animal.

"Isn't the moonlight enough to see by?" I asked.

She was undressing. "It's not the same," she said. I looked at her strong, round body; she was a ripe, firm woman, but she still moved like a young girl. I felt a fresh want for her, like what Severin would have felt if he could only have forgotten himself and let himself go. Maybe he did, I thought. I looked at a stranger watching me undress.

Utch tackled me! By mistake my elbow caught her in the mouth and made her bite her lip; she said, "Not so rough. Be easy, be smooth."

Don't *coach* me, I thought, but I wriggled against her. I touched her; she was already wet, and I knew in that instant that there were men—or ideas of men—who could make her come with no effort at all. She slipped me into herself so quickly that I hadn't yet reacted to the mat; it itched; it smelled like a foreigner's refrigerator. She was sliding us across the white-lined inner circle toward a padded wall, and I steered her back to the center, as so often I'd heard Severin holler to his wrestlers, "Don't let him get off the mat!"

Utch was beginning to thrash, to actually bridge under me. She was coming—so quickly—and then I was aware of her keening, a high humming like a bee gone berserk in the hive. I thought of the pigeons in panic, and of Harvey, the watchman, crooning quietly in the darkness, masturbating on the soft dirt floor under the wrestling room. My God, I thought, so it was like *this* for them; Severin Winter knew all this.

We seemed to be jammed into a far corner of the room; we had slid across two mats and were out of bounds, but Utch was still coming. I felt myself grow smaller inside her, and when she was done I had shriveled and completely lost contact.

"I came," Utch said.

"You certainly did," I said, but there was no concealing the jealousy in my voice and she knew that I had shrunk from her.

"You can spoil anything you've made up your mind to," she said. She got up, grabbed a towel from a stack in the corner and covered herself.

"Is it time for a few light calisthenics?" I asked. "Or should we run a few laps?"

She had swept up her clothes and was moving out the sliding door. "Turn off the lights when you leave," she said.

I went after her, around the sloping track. I picked up a splinter in my heel. By the time she reached the tunnel I had caught up; I followed her with my hand on her spine. "Got a splinter," I said. "Damn track."

She sat in the corner of the sauna away from me, her knees drawn up, her head between them, the towel under her. I said nothing. When she went into the pool, I waited for her in the shallow end, but she swam a few solitary laps.

I was following her to the showers when she turned and threw something back into the pool. "What was that?" I asked.

"The keys," she said. "I'm not coming here again."

In the green underwater light I saw the key ring settle on the bottom of the pool. I didn't want to leave them there. I would rather have had them sent to Severin for Christmas, packed tightly in a tidy box full of turds. I don't know why I wanted them, frankly, but I dove into the pool and brought them up after Utch had gone into the showers.

Which was how I came to have the keys, and they were in my pocket the night I went walking alone and saw Severin's car parked in the shadow of the gym. The light from the wrestling room shone like the pinhole-opening for a telescope in some mysterious observatory.

So he doesn't go there anymore? I thought. And he hadn't come here alone, I was sure. I looked for cast-off, unmatched shoes, but there were no

signs. Who was it this time? I wondered. I thought of going to get Edith
—to show her how much her vengeance had accomplished. Then I thought
of Utch at home, still so convinced of Severin's great suffering. She forgave
him, but she had not forgiven Edith or me.

All right, Utch, I thought; I'll show you what sort of suffering Severin's
up to. As I ran down the footpath past the library, suddenly it was clear
to me: Severin had been seeing Audrey Cannon all the while; he had never
stopped seeing her. Did Edith know?

"Utch is *going* to know!" I cried aloud as I panted past the new science
building—wherein, no doubt, George James Bender was breeding fruit flies
and pondering the predictable results.

Utch was lying languidly in the bathtub. "Get out," I said. "Put on
anything—we'll take the car. Would you like to meet Audrey Cannon?" I
held up the keys to the gym and wrestling room and waved them in her face
like a gun. "Come on," I said. "I'll show you who's retired."

"Whatever you're doing, stop it," she said. "Please don't be crazy."

"You think he's suffered so much," I said. "Well, come see him suffer.
Come see what his whole problem is." I yanked her out of the tub.

"I don't like leaving the children without even telling Jack where we've
gone."

"Stop stalling, Utch!" I yelled at her. "Severin is getting laid in the
wrestling room! Don't you want to see who he's fucking now?"

"No!" she screamed at me. "I don't want to see him at all."

I snatched up her blouse and handed her my writing pants; they always
hung on the bathroom door. "Get dressed," I said; it didn't matter what
she wore. I found my jacket with the leather elbow patches and made her
put that on. She was barefoot but it wasn't cold outside, and we weren't
going to be outside for long. She stopped resisting me, and at the car she
slammed the door after herself and sat staring straight ahead while I slipped
in beside her. I said, "This is for your own good. When you see what a super
bastard he is, you'll feel better about all of this."

"Shut up and drive," she said.

The light was still on in the wrestling room—they were having a long
session—and I insisted that we wait for them at the pool. "It might make
him remember something," I said. "Caught twice at the same act! How
stupid can he be!"

"I'll look at whatever you want to show me," Utch said, "but just stop
talking to me."

I couldn't find my way out of the locker room and through the showers,
but Utch knew the way. We went up to the first balcony above the swimming pool and sat where I imagined Edith had once waited. I said, "I should
go get Edith too."

"It can't be Audrey Cannon," Utch said. "He's simply incapable of
seeing her again."

"Then it's *another* Audrey Cannon," I said. "Don't you see? There's going to be one Audrey Cannon after another for him, because that's how he is. It's probably some volleyball player who's missing four fingers. It's Audrey Cannon again and again, with him. I know."

"You know *you*," said Utch. "That's all you know."

She huddled on the hard bench in her wet blouse, in my jacket with the elbow patches hanging at her wrists, in my pants with the crotch sagging to her knees. She looked like a clown whose house had burned down in the night and had only managed to get dressed in whatever was handy. I put my arms around her, but she struck at me, grabbed my hand and bit it hard so that I had to pull away from her.

"Just wait and see," I said.

"I'm waiting."

We waited a long time.

When I heard Severin singing in German in the shower, I realized that of course Utch would know the song, and that maybe this hadn't been such a good idea. Then the underwater lights flicked on and two naked bodies sprinted, laughing, across the tiles and into the water. Nobody had limped. The short, powerful, seal-like body that broke water at midpool and snorted like a walrus was Severin, of course, and the slim, graceful woman who glided through the green light and slid against him, her hand fondly cupping his balls, was Edith.

"It's Edith," I whispered.

"Of course it is," said Utch.

They saw us as soon as we spoke. Edith swam to the far edge of the pool and hugged the curb. Severin, like a buffalo in his wallow, treaded water in the deep end and stared at us. No one spoke. I took Utch's arm, but she freed herself and walked down the balcony stairs. It took us forever to reach the shower door. My only thought was that our misunderstanding was now complete, because I was sure the Winters thought that Utch and I had just finished a ritual of our own.

My last look at Edith was not returned. Her slim back was to me, her wet hair lay on her shoulders, her body was pressed against the side of the pool. Severin still bobbed out in the water, his round face puzzled, apparently finding the coincidence quite funny because he was grinning—or was he just straining to keep afloat? Who knows? Who knows what he ever thought?

At the shower door I turned and flung the key ring at the tempting target of his head. He ducked and I missed.

When we got home, Jack was awake, his narrow body like a knife in the shadow at the top of the stairs. "Why are you wearing Daddy's pants?" he asked Utch. She slipped out of them right there on the stairs and kicked them away.

"I'm not anymore," she said. She led Jack back to his bed, his hand on her naked hip, though I've told her a hundred times that he's getting too old for her to be naked in front of him.

"I didn't know where you were," Jack complained. "What if Bart had woken up? What if he'd had an earache or a bad dream?"

"Well, we're home now," Utch told him.

"I wasn't really worried," he said.

"Have a good dream," Utch said. "We're going to take a trip. Dream about that."

"Who's going to take a trip?"

"You and Bart and me," said Utch.

"Not Daddy?" Jack asked.

"No, not Daddy," Utch said.

"Whatever you're thinking," I said to her later, "there's no need to involve the children, is there? If you want to get away from me, leave the children here. Go off by yourself for a while, if that's what you want."

"You don't understand," she said. "I'm going to leave you."

"Go ahead," I said. "But Jack and Bart stay here."

It had been a wet spring, and a cool beginning to the summer, but the kids were happy to be out of school. When I took them to the University Club pool, I realized that the girl who followed after Jack, teasing him and allowing herself to be shoved in the pool, was Fiordiligi Winter. The scar that marred the knee of one lovely leg was the shape of a chicken's beak and the curious color of a trout's gills. I saw that Dorabella wore a bathing cap; probably her hair had not grown back. I didn't see whether Severin or Edith had brought them; I had a book with me, and I read it.

It was my fifth historical novel, just out, and I was angry at how it was being distributed—as children's literature! My publisher insisted it was not really children's literature and that I had nothing to be upset about; he told me it was being suggested for pre-teens and older. How they could have made such a blunder was beyond me. The book was called *Joya de Nicaragua,* and it was about refugee Cuban cigar growers, after Castro, nurturing Havana seeds on plantations in Nicaragua. The book was concerned only with the Cubans who had died in Nicaragua. *Joya de Nicaragua* is the brand name of a quality Nicaraguan cigar. My editor admitted to me that they weren't actually "pushing" the book very hard; my other four historical novels hadn't sold very well; not one of them had been seriously reviewed. A self-fulfilling prophecy if I have ever heard one! And my department chairman had once again failed to list my book among the members' new publications. In fact, my chairman had confided to me that he considered my only publication to be a small article published years ago, a chapter excerpted from my Ph.D. thesis. The thesis was unpublished; it was called "The Application of Bergsonian Time to Clerical Fascism in Austria." *Joya de Nicaragua* is a much better book.

When I brought the kids home from the pool, Utch had finished packing.

712 - The 158-Pound Marriage

"See you in a quick while!" Bart said to me at the airport.

Jack, feeling grown up, wanted to shake hands.

After I'd come home and searched the house for signs of them which Utch might have left me, I discovered Utch had taken my passport with her. That would make it difficult for me to follow her right away.

I found her note pinned to the pillow that night. It was long and entirely in German. She knew very well that I wouldn't be able to read it. I picked over what few isolated words made some kind of sense, but it was clear that I needed a translator. One of the phrases was "*zurück nach Wien*"; I knew that meant "back to Vienna." Another word was "Severin." Who else had she meant for me to use as a translator? Of course she knew I couldn't ask just anybody who spoke the language; the note's contents might be embarrassing. Her intent was obvious.

In the morning I took the note to him. A summer morning. Severin and his daughters were in the kitchen, where he was packing a lunch for them to take to the beach with friends. There was a strange car in the driveway; the car was full of children and the woman driver, whom I didn't recognize, looked like the sort of idiot who could actually have fun in a car full of children. She seemed to think it was uproarious that Severin was packing the lunch and getting the girls off, though everyone who knew the Winters was aware that Edith never did that kind of thing.

"Furthermore," Severin grumbled to me as the car backed, honking, out of the driveway, "it's a better lunch than she's made for her own kids. Drive carefully!" he bellowed suddenly; it sounded like a threat.

"Edith is writing," he told me in the kitchen.

"I came to see you," I said. "I need a little help." I handed him the note. Still reading it, he said, "I'm sorry. I didn't think she'd leave."

"What's she say?" I asked.

"She's gone to Vienna."

"I know that."

"She'd like you to leave her alone for a while. She'll write you first. She says she's perfectly responsible, and that you shouldn't worry about the children."

It was a longer note than that. "Is that all she says?" I asked.

"That's all she says to you," he said.

There was a long, thin knife spangled with fish scales on the cutting board; it shone in the sunlight through the kitchen windows. He must have been preparing fish for supper. Severin was so singular a sort that he could hack open raw fish in the morning. While I was staring at it he picked up the knife and plunged it into the soapy water in the sink.

"Just give her a little time," he said. "Everything will straighten out."

"There's something in the note about *chickens,*" I said. "What is it?"

"That's just a phrase," he said, laughing. "It doesn't have anything to do with the word in English."

"What's it mean?"

"It's just a phrase," Severin said. "It means, 'It's time to move, time to go,' something like that."

I picked up the slimy cutting board and swung it around as if it were a tennis racquet. "What *exactly* is the phrase?" I asked him. "I want a literal translation." I couldn't seem to stop trembling.

" 'Saddle the chickens,' " he said. " 'We're riding out.' "

Staring at him, I kept waving the fish-smeared cutting board. " 'Saddle the chickens, we're riding out'?"

"An old Viennese joke," Severin said.

"Some sense of humor you Viennese have," I said. He held his hand out and I gave him the cutting board.

"If it helps you to know," he said, "Utch hates me."

"Not likely."

"Look," he said, "she just needs to get her pride back. I know, because I have to get my pride back, too. It's really very simple. She knows I didn't really want the whole thing, and she knows you were thinking more about yourself than about her. We were all thinking more about ourselves than about Utch. And you were all thinking more about yourselves than about me. Now you just have to be patient and continue to do as you're doing— only a little less aggressively. Help her to hate me, but do it easy."

"Help her to hate you?"

"Yes," he said. "Edith will hate you too after a while; she'll be sorry about the whole thing. And I'll help her to be sorry. It's already beginning."

"All this hatred isn't necessary," I said.

"Don't be stupid," Severin said. "You're doing it yourself. You're trying to make Utch hate me, and you'll succeed," he said cheerfully. "Just be patient." Severin Winter was at his most obnoxious when he thought he was doing you a favor.

"Where is Edith?" I asked.

"Writing. I told you," he said, but he could see I didn't believe him. He shrugged and led me to the foot of the stairs, where he gestured that I remove my shoes. Silently we crept upstairs, through their tousled, strewn bedroom—the melted candle gave me a strong twinge—to the door of Edith's study. Music was playing. She could never have heard our voices down in the kitchen. Severin pointed to the keyhole and I looked in. She was sitting very still at her desk. Suddenly she typed rapidly three or four lines. Then her movement was again arrested and she seemed to hang above the machine with the perfect concentration of a seagull suspended over water—over its food, its whole life source.

Severin motioned me away and we tiptoed back to the kitchen. "She just sold her novel," he said. He might as well have slapped me with the cutting board, stunned me like a fish and slit me open.

"Her novel?" I said. "*What* novel? I never knew she was working on a novel."

"She didn't show you everything," Severin said.

That night I tried to take up sleeping again. I found an old slip of Utch's in the laundry basket and dressed a pillow in it and slept against it, smelling her smell. But after a few nights it smelled more like me—more like the whole bed and the whole house—and after I washed it, it simply smelled like soap. The slip became stretched and tore a shoulder strap, but I took to wearing it myself in the mornings because it was nearest me when I woke up. I also found Bart's striped T-shirt with a smiling frog face on it and a silver cowboy jacket that Jack had outgrown. In the mornings while I ate breakfast I hung Bart's T-shirt over the back of one chair and Jack's cowboy jacket over another, and sat down to eat with them in Utch's old torn slip. I was sitting that way the morning Edith rushed in and told me they were all going to Vienna, and did I have any message for Utch?

Vaso Trivanovich and Zivan Knezevich, those diehard Chetnik Olympians, had died within two days of each other. Frau Reiner had cabled. Severin was the executor of their will, which included more awful paintings by Kurt Winter.

"Isn't it ironic?" Edith asked. "Schiele's wife died of the Spanish flu in the 1918 epidemic, and Schiele died just two days later. It's just like Vaso and Zivan. And Schiele's wife's name was Edith, too."

I realized she wasn't making any sense because of *me*. She was staring at the kitchen chairs dressed like children and at Utch's old slip, and I knew that she was embarrassed and couldn't wait to get away from me; that whatever Severin had failed to convince her of about me I was demonstrating for her now.

"No message," I said. I had heard twice from Utch; she'd said the children missed me and that she was doing nothing to make me ashamed of her. In her second letter she had sent me back my passport, but with no invitation.

"I decided to go with Severin because it's summer, after all, and the kids have never seen where their father's really from, and it might be fun to go back," Edith babbled. "No message?" she asked. "Really?" She was scatterbrained. I realized that she could see through Utch's slip, so I remained sitting down. I was embarrassed too, and wanted her to leave. I had to keep myself from asking her about her novel; I wanted to know who was publishing it, and when it would be out, but I didn't want her to know that I wanted to know. She hadn't said a word to me about *Joya de Nicaragua;* I knew she hated it—if she had even read it. She was looking at me as if she thought I was pathetic and there was nothing to say.

"Saddle the chickens," I said. "We're riding out." Which must have convinced her of my lunacy, because she turned and left as quickly as she'd come.

I went into the bedroom, threw Utch's slip in a corner, lay down naked on the bed and thought of Edith until I came in my hand. It would be the last time, I knew, that I could come with Edith on my mind.

A little later Severin called. I was sure Edith had told him that I was completely crackers and that he ought to check up on me. "Give us Utch's address," he said. "Maybe we can talk to her and tell her you two ought to be together." I didn't hesitate to give him the wrong address. It was the address of the American Church of Christ, where Utch and I had been married. Later, I thought that the trick I had played on Severin was the kind he would play, and that it would somehow please him.

I wrote Utch that they were coming, and why. "If you see a couple carrying an ugly painting down the street, arguing about what to do with it, stay out of their way," I wrote.

Then the dreams started and I couldn't sleep. They were about my children, and Severin Winter would have understood them. There was one in which Jack is riding on the *Strassenbahn.* He argues with Utch to let him stand on the open platform, and she gives in. The tram comes to a whiplash bend, and when Utch looks back, Jack's gone. Then there's one about Bart, unused to city people. Utch is getting some bread to feed the pigeons in a park, and Bart is standing where he's been told to wait. The car, which looks like an old Mercedes taxi and reeks of diesel fuel, is not a taxi; it pulls to the curb, motor spluttering, and the driver says, "Little boy?" Because it's a dream the driver speaks English, even in Vienna, and Bart walks over to see what this terrible man wants.

I had to go somewhere; I had to get away. If I was going to Vienna, I needed to borrow a little money from the old source. Oddly, I was even thinking about the Bruegel painting again—about my unidentified character, the lost burgher and that abandoned book. And I owed my parents a repeat of the old ritual. It was better than staying at home.

My mother met me at the Brown Street door. She gushed, "I never knew so many Cubans went to live in Nicaragua, and I never knew what was so special about Havana cigars before. I'm glad you used the foreign title—how do you say *Joya de Nicaragua?*—because it seems, well . . . different. I'm just not sure it's at all suitable for children, but I suppose publishers know who's reading what these days, don't they? Your father, I think, is still finishing it. He seems to be finding it very funny; at least he laughs a lot when he's reading, and I think that's what he's reading. I didn't find it all that funny myself—in fact, it seemed perhaps your bleakest book—but I'm sure he's found something I missed. Where are Utch and the children?"

"On vacation," I said. "Everything's fine."

"It is not, you look simply awful," she said and burst into tears. "Don't try to tell me," she said as she led me down the hall, crying in front of me. "Don't talk. Let's see your father. Then we'll talk."

In the den, the familiar late-afternoon sunlight dappled the open pages spread around my father and in his lap. His head was familiarly bent, his hands typically slack, but when I looked for the glass of Scotch pinched between his knees, I knew immediately. My father's knees were splayed apart and the spilled Scotch puddled the rug at his feet, which were twisted uncomfortably—that is, uncomfortably for anyone who could still feel. My mother was already screaming, and I knew even before I touched his cold cheek that my father had finally finished something, and that once more the particular book responsible for putting him to sleep was not knowable. But it might have been mine.

After the funeral, I was touched that my mother's recovery seemed slowed by her worries about Utch and me. "The best thing you could do for me right now," she told me, "is to get yourself to Vienna immediately and clean up the trouble you're having with Utch." My mother was always a great one for cleaning up everything, and, after all, it's rare when there's something we can do for ourselves which also pleases someone else.

"Remember the good times, can't you?" my mother said to me. "I thought you writers were supposed to have such good memories, but I guess you don't write that sort of thing, do you? Anyway, remember the good times; that's what I'm doing. I think you'll find that once you start the process of remembering, you'll just go on and on."

So. I remember—I will always remember—Severin Winter in his infernal wrestling room on a day we three were supposed to pick him up there. We were all going to the city for an overnight—a movie and a hotel. (Our first hotel and our last.) Severin said he'd wait to shower and change when we reached the hotel.

"God, then he'll sweat all the way in the car," I complained to Utch.

"It's his car," she said.

Edith picked us up. "I'm late," she said. "Severin hates me to be late."

Near the gym I saw Anthony Iacovelli trudging through the snow. He recognized Severin's car and waved.

"An ape loose in a winter resort," said Edith.

We waited, but Severin did not appear. "Thank God, he's probably taking a shower," I said.

Then Tyrone Williams came out of the gym, his black face like a coal moon floating above the snow; he came over and told us that Severin was still up there, wrestling with Bender.

"God, we'll have to carry him to the car," I muttered.

"Let's go up and get him," Edith said. I knew she was thinking that he wouldn't be so angry if we all appeared.

Down on the dark mud floor of the cage a lone shotputter was heaving his ball. It whapped the mud like a body dropped unseen from the board track. An irregular thudding came from the wrestling room. Edith pulled on the door, then pushed it.

"It slides," said Utch, opening it. Inside, the incredible damp heat blew against us. Several wrestlers sagged against the walls, sodden with sweat, watching Severin and George James Bender. Earlier, it might have been a match, but Severin was tired now. He grunted on his elbows and thighs, straining to lift his stomach off the mat; whenever he'd struggle to his hands and knees, Bender would run him forward like a wheelbarrow until Severin's arms buckled and he pitched down on his chest. When Edith said, "Sorry we're late, love," Severin looked too tired to get up again. He raised his head off the mat and looked at us, but Bender pushed it back down; Bender hadn't heard anybody—I doubt if he ever did. Severin fought up to his hands and knees again and Bender drove him forward. Then Severin began to move. He sat sharply under Bender and pivoted so fast that Bender had to scramble to keep behind him. Then he shrugged Bender's weight off his back long enough to stand and grabbed a fistful of the boy's fingers around his waist, peeling them apart and suddenly sprinting across the mat like a halfback breaking a tackle. Bender dove for his ankles but Severin kicked free; his breathing was fierce, great, sucking breaths drawn from some old reservoir of energy, and he crouched, bent double, hands on knees.

Then Bender saw us, and he and the other wrestlers filed from the room as serious as Druids. Edith touched Severin's heaving back, but quickly wiped his sweat off her hand on her coat. Utch gave Severin's drenched chest a hearty smack.

Later I said to Utch that I thought Bender had let him go, but she said I didn't know anything about it. Severin had broken free, she could tell. Whatever, his extra burst had been a special performance for us, so I said, "I didn't know you had it in you, old boy."

He could barely talk; his throat seemed pinched, and the sweat ran in an unbroken rivulet off his bent nose, but he winked at me and gasped, loud enough for the women to hear, "Second wind of the cuckold."

Our first and last night in a hotel, and Severin Winter, as always, provided us with a topic for conversation. His vulgar one-liner kept Edith and me up all night.

"And what did *you* talk about?" I asked Utch in the morning.

"We didn't talk," she said.

––––––

Early one morning I took a goodbye walk. I was on hand to see the maintenance men unlock the new gym, unbolt the old cage and air out all the ghosts and germs in there. Behind the tennis courts a young girl was hitting a ball against the backboard; her soft blows made the only sound I could hear. No one was running on the board track. I stood on the dusty floor of the cage, which was beginning its slow summer bake, and in the loose system of nets that keep the baseballs from breaking the skylights. I sensed someone standing, as still as I was standing, at the door of the wrestling room. There was a shadow near his cheek—or was it a hole? I suppose I gasped, because of course I was sure it was Utch's old bodyguard come to America to perform a promised slaying: mine. Then the figure seemed discomforted by my stare and moved out from behind the concealing nets. He was too young; there was no hole in his cheek, I realized, merely a black eye.

It was George James Bender; he recognized me and waved. He hadn't been exercising; he was dressed in ordinary clothes. He'd only been standing in the old cage, remembering, like me. I hadn't seen him since his upsetting loss, and suddenly I wanted to ask him if it was true, if he'd slept with Edith, if any of that impossible tale was true.

"Good morning, Professor," he said. "What are you doing here?"

"It's a good place to think," I said.

"Yes, it is," said Bender.

"I was thinking about Severin Winter," I said. "And Edith. I miss them." I watched him closely, but there were no revelations in his dead-gray eyes.

"Where are they?" he asked; he didn't seem interested.

"Vienna."

"It must be very nice there," he said.

"Just between you and me," I said, "I'll bet Edith Winter is the best-looking piece of ass in all of Vienna."

His reptile calm was untouched; his face showed only the faintest trace of life as we know it. He looked at me as if he were seriously considering my opinion. Finally he said, "She's kind of skinny, isn't she?" I realized, with revulsion, that George James Bender was actually smiling, but there was nothing about his smile that was any more accessible than his blank eyes. I knew once again that I knew nothing.

So I am going to Vienna, and I'm going to try the Bruegel book again. But of course there are other contributing factors. ("There are always contributing factors," Severin used to say.) It's a way to be near the children, and I admit that I want to assure Utch of my availability. We historical novelists know things take a little time. And Vienna has a fabulous history of treaties; the truces made there over the years run long and deep.

And I'd like to run into Edith and Severin sometime. I'd like to see them in a restaurant, perhaps dining out with another couple. I would know everything about that other couple at a glance. Utch and I would be alone, and I would ask the waiter to send a note from us to that couple. "Watch out," it would say. And the husband would show the note to his wife, and then to Edith and Severin, who would suddenly scan the restaurant and see us. Utch and I would nod, and by then I hope I would be able to smile.

Some other time, there's a question I would like to ask Severin Winter. When it rains or snows, when the heat is unrelenting or the cold profound —whenever the weather strikes him as an adversary—does he think of Audrey Cannon? I'll bet he does.

Yesterday Utch wrote that she saw Edith sitting in Demel's eating a pastry. I hope she gets fat.

So. Today I bought a plane ticket. My mother gave me the money. If cuckolds catch a second wind, I am eagerly waiting for mine.

About the Author

John Irving was born in Exeter, New Hampshire, in 1942. He is the author of eight novels, among them *The Hotel New Hampshire, The Cider House Rules, A Prayer for Owen Meany,* and *A Son of the Circus.* His fourth novel, *The World According to Garp,* was nominated for the National Book Critics' Circle Award, the Pulitzer Prize, and the National Book Award. Mr. Irving is married and has three sons; he currently lives in Vermont and in Toronto.